'The narrative of *Sunday at the Cross Bones* is as lively and ambiguous as its main character ... Pacy and entertaining, elegantly written, funny yet ultimately tragic, *Sunday at the Cross Bones* is full of hypocrisies and moral ambiguities'

TLS

'John Walsh propels his narrative forward with irresistible vigour and delineates a host of entertaining characters'

Literary Review

'An engaging and sympathetic portrait of a misguided man [and] of a city eaten away by the gangrene of exploitation'

Irish Times

'Like Peter Ackroyd, Walsh demonstrates an intimate knowledge of London and the unique spirit of place that permeates different nooks and crannies of the city ... Walsh captures dialect brilliantly from the cockney 'innit'-speak of the rector's protégées to the patronising but ever-so-polished tone of his Mayfair benefactress. Though we know how the story ends, there is a dreadful fascination in following it to the end of the journey'

Sunday Business Post

By the same author

The Falling Angels
Are You Talking to Me?

JOHN WALSH

SUNDAY AT THE CROSS BONES

A NOVEL

HARPER PERENNIAL

London, New York, Toronto, Sydney and New Delhi

Harper Perennial
An imprint of HarperCollins*Publishers*
77–85 Fulham Palace Road, Hammersmith, London W6 8JB
www.harperperennial.co.uk

Visit our authors' blog at www.fifthestate.co.uk

This edition published by Harper Perennial 2008

1

First published in Great Britain by Fourth Estate in 2007

A catalogue record for this book is available from the British Library

ISBN 978-0-00-713933-0

Set in Bembo & Didot by Palimpset Book Production Limited,
Grangemouth, Stirlingshire

Printed and bound in Great Britain by Clays Ltd, St Ives plc

Mixed Sources

Product group from well-managed
forests and other controlled sources
www.fsc.org   Cert no. SW-COC-1806
© 1996 Forest Stewardship Council

FSC is a non-profit international organisation established to promote the
responsible management of the world's forests. Products carrying the FSC
label are independently certified to assure consumers that they come
from forests that are managed to meet the social, economic and
ecological needs of present and future generations.

Find out more about HarperCollins and the environment at
www.harpercollins.co.uk/green

To my darling Sophie –
an inspiration, always

For years I have been known as the Prostitutes' Padre – to me the proudest title that a true priest of Christ can hold. I believe with all my soul that if He were born again in London in the present day, He would be found constantly walking in Piccadilly.

– Reverend Harold Davidson

'The Working Girl's Life'

Monday in the nursery ward,
Tuesday in the schoolyard,
Wednesday painting lipstick on,
Thursday going with George and John,
Friday at the Crown with Billy,
Saturday weeping down the 'Dilly,
Where will she rest from her tears and moans?
Sunday at the Cross Bones

– Old rhyme, *c.*1880

Well go ahead and call the cops –
You don't meet nice girls in coffee shops

– Tom Waits

AUTHOR'S NOTE

This is a work of fiction, based on true events.

My damaged hero, the real-life Reverend Harold Davidson (1875–1937), spent many years in London in the 1920s and early 1930s, improving the lot of unfortunate boys and fallen women. We know little of what he did from day to day, nor what thoughts might have filled his head as he went about the business of salvation. I have taken several liberties with time and place in imagining his version of the life he lived in 1930–32. I have invented characters, events, conversations, letters and relationships. This is a chronicle, not of what happened, but of what might have happened.

CHAPTER 1

Journals of Harold Davidson
Central Beach, Blackpool
6 September 1932

Some child of Satan has deposited a quantity of candyfloss in my hair. I suspect it may have been the gormless boy in the Edwardian sailor suit, four or five at most, whose mother lifted him up in her meaty arms to be kissed by the famous rector. A sulky, unbiddable young man with a face that Raphael himself would have found it a burden to render adorable, he performed his task with reluctance, turning his putty cheek away so that my lips found only his ear, and leaving me the inestimable gift of sticky spun sugar clamped to my snow-white locks. By the time I realised the damage that was done, she and he were long gone. I must have greeted a dozen visitors looking like a Lancashire barmaid permed and pink-rinsed for a night on the tiles.

Cramped legs; sticky hair; kissing babies; enduring the sniggers of the ungodly. These are hardly the ideal circumstances of the modern clergyman, no matter how nationwide his renown. But then neither is this barrel in which I sit for the second morning of my ten-day-long stint. I do not say it is uncomfortable. Mr Gannon has kindly provided me with a cushion upon the narrow seat where I perch like a maiden aunt. The structure of the barrel has been cut away to allow me a kind of counter upon which to rest my arms, or to write in this journal, or to sign autographs – that puzzling new phenomenon, as though the inscription of one's name on an envelope or ticket stub forged a connection of sorts with a complete stranger, who will display it later as proof of his having met me, as though a lion in Chessington Zoo might have volunteered to him a paw-print of brotherhood.

Above my head, raised on a metal stalk, a wooden roof houses a small electric fan to circulate the late-summer air and disperse the cigar fumes. 'We generally disapprove of the exhibits having a smoke, Padre,' said Mr Gannon with his habitual air of a man supervising an event of vast importance, 'but we'll make an exception for you.'

On my left is Mr Gavin Tweedy's World-Famous Flea Circus, a ludicrous entertainment constructed from a plywood door laid across two steel drums, upon which tiny insects are encouraged to jump over obstacles, walk through hoops, pull tiny carts and dance together to a tinny foxtrot. If Jonathan Swift were to walk by this bonsai extravaganza, what a metaphor he would find for human endeavour: the vanity of display, the pointlessness of striving, the folly of courtship, the puniness of ambition! On my right, a Miss Barbara Cockayne sits in a barrel similar to mine. Her beard is remarkable, an elaborate, flourishing beaver similar to that of Lord Rosebery, or St Jerome as imagined by Rubens. She has a limited repertoire of conversation, contenting herself with growls and oaths and lavatorial remarks; I suppose it must be hard for her to find subjects of chatty inconsequence to share with those who have paid twopence merely to come and gawp at her hairy chin.

I suppose I should be grateful that twopence is also the tariff they pay to come and inspect me, in my snug, brandy-scented wooden casket. It would be a little *too* cruel if I were paid less than the bearded lady and the waltzing fleas. As to the fee structure enjoyed by my other neighbours here on the strand – the Dog-Faced Man and the Three-Legged Boy of Italy – I am in the dark.

The soft crash of the incoming tide from the Irish Sea can occasionally be heard when the music – that endless, jaunty, soul-deadening jingle-jangle of popular tunes further down the promenade, played apparently on a broken pipe organ – comes to a blissful halt for a moment or two. It fills my heart with sadness, for it reminds me of the waves on the Norfolk strand at Wells-next-the-Sea, where Mimi and I would take the children for Sunday picnics in happier days, the breeze from the salt marshes stinging our nostrils, the gulls flapping and barking over our heads. Those lines from Milton's 'Lycidas' come unbidden into my head:

> . . . the stormy Hebrides
> Where thou perhaps under the whelming tide
> Visit'st the bottom of the monstrous world.

For there is no doubt that I have found the bottom of the monstrous world here, in Blackpool. I, who have devoted my life to the betterment of others, sit now like Diogenes the philosopher, a man who gave up the luxuries of the material world to find enlightenment, to end his days in a barrel in the Athenian market-place. Have I found enlightenment? No. Instead, I wrestle with the events of the last two years, picking over the past, looking for the reasons why I find myself here, gazing across a multitude of day trippers, sunburned holidaymakers, squalling children, ignor-ant matrons perusing their puzzle magazines, scrofulous bank clerks surreptitiously kissing their new girlfriends on the lips as if amazed at their daring. They have come to see me, a line of several hundred scorched and moronic spectators, some way down the devotional scale from my kindly, God-fearing flock at Stiffkey. There, in the pulpit at St John's, I would survey the expectant faces and know that I was called by the Lord for a purpose. But my purpose here? It is inscrutable. They pay their twopence. They shuffle past. They offer their compliments. (Some, even, their abuse; and one, a generous gout of his saliva.) I thank them, utter some words about the trial, call on their support in my appeal against the bishop, and bless them on their way with a raised hand. What have I, or we, achieved except a hollow exchange between an adventitious 'celebrity' (me) and a curious, sympathetic but morally indifferent public?

Mr Gannon will soon, I hope, regale me with tea and biscuits, and, when twenty or thirty of them have gathered round, I may deliver my little speech of self-exculpation and warning about the conduct of the Church of England. But let me put down this journal and think for a moment of the road that led me to the Palace of Amusements. To this place where I no longer enjoy a small congregation. I have only a huge audience.

Two years earlier . . .

Notebooks of Charlie Norton, *Evening Standard*
London
1 July 1930

I'd just popped into the Old Coal House on the Strand for a few sharpeners after the final edition had been put to bed, and I was nursing a whisky and water with Benny from the *Gazette* when this guy comes in. Little short-arse he was, five foot two or so, but with an air about him. Bustle, bustle, Hi there, girls, little wave to the barmaids, and he sits down in the snug like he owns the place, and looks about him. He gestures to Bella, the fat lass from Scarborough, with a raised clump of fingers signalling a glass of beer in anyone's language. Only, when it came, it looked like a pint of orange squash with a foaming head an inch thick.

Orange squash? In the Coal House?

I had him down as a masher of the old school, the kind of gutter swell you'd have seen ten years ago, smarming down the Haymarket with a carnation in his buttonhole and two iffy tarts hanging on his elbows, but this fellow was a masher down on his luck. His greatcoat was too long, it skimmed the pub's scabby floor. His shirt cuffs were frayed, his collar was open, revealing a turkey neck, lined and wattled, and his corduroy breeches had seen better days. And his shoes! I'm not one to offer advice to geezers about what they choose to adorn their plates of meat, but this was bordering on the offensive. These were brogues that could've been through the trenches – shabby, flappy, held together with some kind of surgical tape.

'Who's he?' I asked Benny.

'Oh, him,' said Benny, with that annoying, I-know-everything tone of his. 'Surely you've seen the rector.'

The little chap in the snug was a reverend father? No dog collar, no black suit, no prayer book? What kind of clergyman was this?

'He's always in here,' said Benny. 'Right character he is. He sets up house at the same table every Tuesday, drinks dandelion and burdock, sarsaparilla, you know, kids' drinks, and buys lemonade for kids that come in. Kids and brasses.'

4

Brasses, eh? I looked round the pub. The Coal House wasn't the most respectable dive in Christendom, but you wouldn't come in here to try your luck with Fanny Hill, if you know what I mean. It wasn't that kind of billet. Old guys in the corner yarning about the war, young shavers from the City talking about the money they'd rescued from the Crash by investing in South African diamond mines, ash-lapelled lawyers talking in whispers about dodgy wills, I was used to that level of clientele. But this was the wrong milieu, pardon my French, for chaps out for a spot of how's-your-father with ladies of the night. Or kids. That's just disgusting. We're not keen on that stuff down here. In Fleet Street and the Strand, we don't hold with that Oscar Wilde rigmarole.

Anyway, me and Benny got talking about other things. Benny's chasing a story about a racehorse owner down at Goodwood whose wife has been dancing the blanket hornpipe with some junior political at the Treasury. He's been heard swearing and cursing to his pals about how he'll have him put away if it doesn't stop. There's a stable lad Benny knows who'll sing like a canary about terrible things that've been said, or hinted at, by the horsey grandee at point-to-point meetings and stockbreeder dinners, about the shocking state of morals in public office, that kind of thing.

Benny's very funny about it, though he's never met the cove in question. 'How can this government,' he rants, taking off the guy's high rhetorical style, 'seek to impose yet more swingeing taxes on the innocent, hard-working men of this country, when they themselves are mired in corruption, one hand in the Treasury till and the other down the undergarments of their malodorous doxies?'

'But where can you go with it, Ben?' I asked, laughing, 'I mean, where's the story? You can't get the chap to admit what's really buzzing in his breeches, can you?'

'No, and there's the problem,' said Benny. 'Of course, we can't write a line about the adultery side because we are, you know, the *Gazette*, and we don't do fuck stories.' He poured a little water into his cloudy glass, reducing the amber fluid to the shade of afternoon wee. 'But there may be some mileage in the Treasury chappie.'

'How so?'

'Constituency politics, old boy. *Cherchez les politiques locale*. He's

MP for Beckenham, wife and four kids, supposed to be a solid citizen, loving family man, et cetera. His father-in-law's Lord Silchester, the peer with the bee in his bonnet about family life. Makes speeches all over Kent and Surrey about the importance of the family hearth and the awfulness of the modern world. If we can hint to the old martinet that his own son-in-law is having it away with a lady that's not his wife, and furthermore that she's connected to a leading light of the turfing demi-monde, well, I could predict some fireworks.'

'I can't see it, Ben,' I observed. 'These are powerful people.'

I took our glasses to the bar for refreshment. Up beside me comes the parson geezer, still in his long coat despite the warmish fug in the place. He only comes up to my shoulder, but he signals to Bella with a show of impatience, as if he's seven foot tall.

'Two large Johnnie Walkers, please,' I say, since it's my shout. 'Ice in the glass and water on the side.'

He looks at me as if I'd just spat in his eye.

'Bella,' he says, his voice commanding and surprisingly deep for such a small man, 'has Dolores been in tonight?'

His voice was like chocolate, smooth, low, melting, oddly caressing.

'Dolores?' says Bella, yanking the Bass pump so the maternal bosom inside her drawstring blouse wobbled like a milk pudding. 'Haven't seen her for three days.'

'She should be here by now,' he says, his fleshy lips working themselves into an extravagant pout. 'I specifically asked her to join me here by seven o'clock.'

'Sorry, Reverend,' says Bella, 'but brasses don't keep strict working hours.' Her lips were pursed like a cat's arse.

'She is a troubled young woman,' says the parson with a hint of asperity, 'and is worthy of your respect, if not your sympathy. Will you let me know if Miss Knight comes by this evening? I may be occupied in the snug.'

'Mm-hmm,' says Bella, disapprovingly. 'If she comes swannin' in here, I'll make sure you hear about it.'

I picked up the glasses. I wanted to say something, but he'd gone by the time I turned his way. Back to the little cubicle where he stayed, hunched and preoccupied, for an hour over little bits of paper spread before him. I took the drinks back to Benny, and we shot the breeze about the stable boys, the politician and the errant wife.

'How's tricks at home?' said I, changing the subject. 'Married life going well?'

'Oh, that's all fine,' said Ben, leaning back and stretching expansively. 'Me and Clare are snug as moles in a hole. She goes to ballet Tuesdays and Thursdays, night class in fine art on Wednesdays, we stay in and play French horn together Friday evenings, and most Saturdays we head for the Dog in Dulwich and have a few laughs and bit of a sing with her sister and brother-in-law. Every marriage should have, you know, a structure.'

'French horn?' I asked. 'What's that, some kind of polite term for it?'

'What? Oh, I see. No no no.' Benny was laughing now, a bit pissed. 'You silly sod, no, I don't mean *that*. We first met playing actual French horns together in the Vintage Musick Ensemble in Whitechapel. You *knew* that.' He chuckled, man to man. 'No, believe me, we don't have to make a special evening of the old how's your father. Christ, we've only been married six months. She's still keen as mustard, she is.'

'Benny,' I said, waving a hand, 'spare me the details, old son.'

'Oh yes,' he said, 'she's always on for a touch. Sometimes, in the mornings, it's all I can do to pull her off the old –'

Nice chap, Benny, but I really didn't want to have to visualise his larks in the morning. Seeking a distraction, I looked around the pub.

The vicar was still in the snug, his pint of squash dangerously low. He wasn't alone any longer. There was a boy beside him, about ten, with a dozen evening papers under his arm. He was a last-edition runner, the kind employed for tuppence ha'penny an hour to take the final round of the *Standard* to pubs and railway stations around town when the street vendors have packed up for the night and gone home to their lady wives. I assumed the kid was trying to flog the news to the old geezers, but there was something about his pinched demeanour which made me think he was waiting for something more.

I know these runners. They're little more than urchins and strays, most of them, trying to make a few bob before heading home to their alky dads and their vicious mothers and their yowling siblings wandering around eating dripping sandwiches at nine o'clock at night. They should be in bed, after a day when they should be in school, but aren't because they're hanging around Smithfield Market, hosing down the stalls for a tanner or pinching offcuts of scraggy veal for their supper. Those that have homes, I mean.

I don't have a social conscience, most of the time. I just report on things. But sometimes I get a bit hacked off about kids that age selling newsprint, with their dirty little faces and their weirdly deep voices, like they've been smoking Players since they were two.

Benny was still on about married bliss. He felt I should know that his wife sometimes cooks him lamb chops standing in the kitchen wearing an apron and nothing else. Now I've met Clare, just once. A nice girl and a whizz on the French horn, no doubt, but she wouldn't start a riot at the peepshow. I tried to shake the vision of her aproned rear out of my head.

'We should go out in a four some time,' I said, not really meaning it. 'You and Clare, me and Sal. One Friday, we could meet in town and have a bit of a carouse.'

'Ooh. I see the rector's making friends.'

I looked. The clergyman and the boy had been joined by an older man, a churchy greybeard in a black suit, side whiskers and droopy eyebags. Man of the cloth or manager of a chapel of rest, there was a whiff of the mortality business about him. The kid stood between them, as awkward as a bullock in a fishmonger's.

'What they up to, Benny, you reckon?'

'Couldn't say, old son. The kid's flogging newspapers, but our friend hasn't bought one. The old cove looks like a headmaster, so maybe the kid's been bunking off school and the rector's rounded him up. Either that or he's selling him into white slavery.'

'Be serious, Ben, this is interesting.'

'Go and find out if you're so keen. Go on. I'll still be here. I got my paper.' He tapped my arm. 'But don't get bogged down. Half an hour of bollocks about the Undeserving Poor and Homeless, you'll wish you never started.'

So I went to the bar again, but this time I passed by the snug and hovered until the men stopped their chat and turned to me.

'Can I help you?' said the vicar.

'I've had a bit of a windfall,' I said, using an ancient ploy, 'and I'm standing everyone in the pub a drink. Would you gentlemen care for a tipple on me?'

They looked at each other.

'No *thank* you,' said the whiskered loon, 'I don't care to be bought drinks by strangers.'

Well, excuse *me*, I thought. I looked at the kid, who just stood there, the fingers of his right hand the colour of beetroot because of the weight of the newspapers he carried. His head was bowed, poor chap, because it would never have occurred to him that he might be included in a round.

'Yourself, sir?' I nearly called him 'Reverend'.

'Come now, Mr Forsyth,' the vicar said, turning to his surly chum, 'surely every impulse of philanthropy should be encouraged, no matter how random its provenance.' He talked like a Victorian gent, though he couldn't have been all *that* old, and he smiled at me, his piercing eyes suddenly fixing on mine. 'Thank you, my friend. I will take another orange cordial with a slice of lemon and plenty of water.' He was so fastidious in his order – like a man demanding Angostura bitters in his gin Martini.

I came back with the drinks into an awkward silence.

'Can I just ask you a question or two?' I asked him.

'My time is limited,' he said. 'I have many affairs to transact. What would you like to know?'

'I won't pretend with you, Vicar –' I began.

'– Rector, if you don't mind.'

'Rector. I'm a reporter on the *Evening Standard*. I've been hearing about your work among the less fortunate members of society. I wondered if maybe –'

'Gerald.' He cut across me, addressing the spotty youth with the newspapers. 'Do *not* stand there so passive and round-shouldered like some professional mute. Mr Forsyth is your new benefactor. He will be your friend and employer. He can furnish you with a livelihood which will, with the Lord's help, keep your family solvent and your poor mother able to furnish your table with meat and greens until Christmas. And if – mind me now – *if* you prove to be a good and biddable boy, and do as you are told, and fetch messages to and from the turf accountants, your work will stretch well into the new year.'

Gerald stood blinking pathetically, as if longing to get away. Who could blame him? He was a child still, as uninterested in the prospect of work as a pit pony being apprised of a favourable pension scheme.

'I gotta –' he ventured.

'I want you now,' said the rector, turning his remarkable eyes upon the raggedy kid's, 'to shake Mr Forsyth's hand and promise to come to his office on Monday in your best jacket and shorts, and conduct yourself like the admirable young man I take you to be.' He smiled at the spotty boy. 'Remember St John's Gospel. "He that followeth me shall not walk in darkness." You have followed me this far. Mr Forsyth will guide your steps henceforth.'

The boy nodded. The rector touched the boy's pustular cheek softly, like a duchess fingering an ermine tippet.

'I gotta go,' said the boy unhappily. 'Gotta be in the King's Arms.' And he was gone.

Mr Forsyth – revealed, for all his grave demeanour, to be only a common bookie – swallowed some beer and, avoiding my gaze, addressed the clergyman.

'I'll do my best, of course, Harold. But I cannot . . .' He sighed. 'I cannot guarantee he won't disappear out the door on day three like the last delinquents you sent me.' He swigged more pale ale. 'You cannot keep passing these runaways on to me, to transform into citizens. I am a businessman –'

'A man of honour,' said the rector, 'a man of moral rectitude, whose indulgent interventions in the lives of these unfortunates have, as I've said many times –'

'Harold, there is no need for this –'

'Let me finish. Whose kindly impulses –'

'Harold, really –'

'– not only do you credit in the public arena, but rack up untold credits in the balance sheet of Heaven. I speak to you in the language of the businessman, but my admiration is that of a minister of a higher power.'

'Ahem,' I said. I'd been standing witnessing these interchanges like a gooseberry.

'My dear fellow,' said the rector, 'I'd forgotten you were there. Forgive me. There were urgent matters at hand.'

'You mean finding news runners jobs as bookies' runners?' I said, perhaps unkindly.

He regarded me coldly. 'You evidently know nothing of my work. Yet you said you were acquainted with it. Explain yourself.'

'I'm a news reporter on the *Standard*. I'm doing an article about poverty in London, how much it's worsened in the last couple of years, who's doing anything about it, private individuals, I mean. I want to ask about your experiences.'

He seemed hesitant.

'Sorry about just now,' I went on. 'I got a bit of a short fuse where these newspaper kids are concerned. I hope you didn't –'

'Have you indeed? In that case, my dear fellow, we shall get on very well.'

Giving a rather curt wave to the grumpy sod from the bookie's, he indicated I should get out notebook and pen. But just at that moment, the pub door opened and these two young dames strode in.

Very dramatic they were, one tall, one short, both dead swishy in their long rustling skirts, tight bodices and fancy hats. You'd have thought they'd have come straight from the Windmill Theatre, though whether part of the audience or part of the stage ensemble, it was hard to judge. Modern girls, you see, the kind we write about in the 'Trends' pages – a little shocking, a little too damn pleased with themselves. They were no strangers to the Coal House.

'Ah, Dolly,' said the vicar, 'I was beginning to worry.' He seized the hand of the smaller one – the one with the huge brown eyes under the rakishly tilted cloche hat – and kissed her on the cheek.

The eyes of the pub followed him. He was short, as I've said, and his hair was snow white and he had terrible rabbity teeth, but here he was talking to a brace of posh young flappers like they were at a cocktail party in Henley.

'And this is . . . ?' he says, indicating her friend, a plump piece of work in a French hat with a torn veil covered in spots, possibly to match her complexion.

'This, Harold, is Jezzie,' says the bird in the cloche. 'She started out as Jessie, changed it to Eleanora, then Zuleika, then Maudie for a while, then some horrible swell called her Jezebel in a pub one night, and made her cry, so we told her, Use it, darling, don't let him put one over on you, and she's been Jezzie ever since.' She paused and looked around the snug. 'Flip me, what's a girl got to do to get a drink around 'ere?'

The reverend ignored her. He was too busy gazing at Jezebel (well named, what with her crimson petticoat peeping out from under her long crackling skirt) and trying to see the face through the spotty veil.

'You have the look,' he said, or rather breathed in her ear, or would've done if she hadn't stood a good six inches taller than him, 'of Miss Greta Garbo. You must surely have seen *Flesh and the Devil*?'

Jezzie regarded him with a mild stare, the way girls do when they can't believe you're taking liberties exactly ten seconds after meeting them.

'What, Greta Garbo? Me?' she said and went off into a spasm of titters.

I took the only initiative I could, and said, 'Would you ladies care for a drink?'

Why yes, they'd love a drink, though they'd have been better off at night class in needlework than hanging round in the Strand. They both fancied Brandy Alexanders.

I went to the bar for the fourth time that night. Benny tried to stick around and ingratiate himself with the dames, but he didn't have the lingo to handle two young *poules de luxe*. They could probably sniff him as an off-limits married man right from the word go.

'I'm going home,' he said. 'You got your hands full here.'

'See you next week, Ben. Give Clare one for me, all right?'

In the snug, the girls sat together on the cracked-leather divan, leaning together in a sisterly fashion, sometimes swaying a bit to right and left as if in a chorus line. The rector leaned forward a lot, his long face inches away from the girls' cheeks, turning his shining eyes first to Dolores, then to Jezzie. He did 90 per cent of the talking. For minutes they smiled vacantly, like little girls listening to an elderly grandpa grinding on about the war, hoping that they might get a chocolate biscuit. Reckoning I'd bought myself an introduction, I took the stool beside him, and listened in.

'. . . and Mrs Lake will, I'm afraid, no longer countenance your irregular hours and gentlemen callers, Dolores,' he was saying. 'I spoke with her on Tuesday. She has developed a singular aversion, I'm afraid, to your Maltese gentlemen friends, whom she describes, with a singular lack of racial accuracy, as Hottentots.' His face essayed a brief, high-table smile. 'She does not want, she says, "them swarthy chancers" dropping in and out of her establishment at all hours. So we will have to find you some new haven. I have asked about your secretarial studies at Mrs Moody's and I fear – no, do not interrupt – you have failed to honour your commitment. I hear your morning session last week saw Mrs Moody cooling her heels for an hour with no sign of your –'

'I can't go studying squiggles in the middle of the bloody night,' said Dolores, grumpily.

'Nine o'clock in the morning is hardly the small hours. I told Mrs Moody of your circumstances, and she agreed to take you on at a very reasonable rate. It hardly repays me, or her, for our considerate impulses if you choose to spend every morning lying in bed reading rubbishy magazines and drinking chocolate.'

'I didn't come here for a lecture,' said Dolores, an astonishingly self-confident young thing for her age. 'I thought you was going to introduce me to Ivor Novello, so I could tell him about my singing.'

Jezzie giggled (again). 'Ivor Novello?' she said, sneeringly. 'Ivor pain in my rear end, more like.'

The rector looked hurt. 'You underestimate my contacts in the world of what the Americans call show business. Though I have never met the delightful Mr Novello, I have friends who've had the pleasure of meeting him backstage. They say he is charming to strangers, polite to ladies and friendly to young persons starting out on the musical scene.'

Jezzie unfurled herself from the banquette and took herself off to the Ladies. We all watched her go. Her sizeable young rump, tightly encased in the crackling shiny material, had a distinct wiggle.

'Charming,' said the rector with the fond appreciation of an uncle, 'though unfortunate to bear such a name, whatever the eccentricity of its genesis. Have you known her long?'

'Couple of weeks,' said Dolores. 'We met at the Hippodrome,

hanging round the stage door for Jack Buchanan. Bloody freezing it was, and when he came out he just whisked past us and got in a cab. Not as big as you'd have expected neither.'

'Where does she live?'

'Oh —' she waved a vague hand — 'here and there.'

'You can be a little more precise,' said the rector.

Dolores, or Dolly, regarded him steadily. 'I dunno what you're thinking, right this minute, Harold, but you're not to *start* with her.' She brazenly took out a cigarette case, extracted a Virginia and lit it. 'All right? Just don't start in on her, the minute my back's turned.'

The rector looked around, with a faint whinny of disavowal. 'My dear girl —'

'And who's this geezer, anyhow?' demanded the young harpy. 'What the hell does he want?' She leaned forward, her dark eyes lit up with suspicion.

'This is a gentleman from the press, who seeks information about my pastoral work.'

'Oh great,' said Dolores, rising to her feet. 'Bloody reporter, that's all I need. Informer, more like.'

'There is no reason to fear —'

'I'm going to see what's happened to Jezzie,' she said, and flung herself away from our table, leaving a hefty waft of Woolworths scent and brass's armpit.

That left us together.

'I'm afraid I've upset your young friends, Padre,' I said, as airily as I could. 'All I was after was a few facts about your crusading work. Perhaps I should leave you to it.'

He put his hand on my arm, a gentle and insinuating gesture. 'Stand your ground, my boy,' he said, opening his greatcoat and taking out a huge cigar from a pocket within. 'They will be back. These young girls regard me as their only hope in this vale of sin. They cleave to me instinctively, as though to an oak in a torrent.'

He crinkled the cigar — it was huge, *I* couldn't afford a cigar like that — then picked up Dolly's box of Swan vestas and lit it. Clouds of expensive blue smoke briefly enveloped his head in a foggy halo. He appeared to devour the enormous tube, running it two inches inside his distended lips, then sucked at it with hungry kisses — mpuh!

mpuh! mpuh! – until the tip glowed wide like an orange sun, and the smoke poured from his nose and mouth like some kind of sulphurous ectoplasm.

'Perhaps I should go,' I said. 'They obviously don't like newspaper men.'

He studied the end of his Havanan torpedo. 'No, no, I have always been convinced of the power of the press to do good rather than mischief. Without the help of journalists, we shall never reveal to the world the troubles of the homeless, the young strays and runaways, the army of fallen women.'

'Perhaps,' I ventured, all innocent-like, 'we should concentrate on the work of one man. Readers don't like being told depressing tales about kids dying in poverty and girls on the game. But a story about One Man's Quest to take care of, you know, tarts who don't want to be . . .'

He looked at me coldly. '*Nobody*, my young friend, *wishes* to be a prostitute. Any girl who finds herself in such employment has not sought it volitionally. It is not a matter of *choice*. They are driven into lives of degeneracy by the circumscription of choice. Young girls in their natural state are the innocent lambs of Creation. Without worldly knowledge, they would have no will to sin.'

'And how can you help them?' I asked, puzzled.

He sucked on his cigar again. 'By showing them a route back to righteousness. By befriending them, and revealing there is a finer life, a life of the mind and of the soul, in which they may find redemption, a career in the arts or the drama.'

At that moment, the girls came back. Such a transformation! Dolores was all smiles. Jezzie carried her hat, with its spotty veil, in her hand, her face now revealed in all its seventeen-year-old wonder: her fat cheeks aglow, her hair blonde and fine as a pedigree Saluki's, her eyes shining. You'd think they'd just won some money, these lambs of Creation.

'We made some new friends,' said Dolores, 'in the public bar. They was very nice, weren't they, Jez?'

'He was lovely,' breathed the other one. 'They're taking us to a party in a while, to meet some people who are going to put on a show at the Palladium.'

'What an amazing stroke of luck,' I said. 'Don't tell me they happen to be looking for two young actresses of no previous experience to appear in the chorus?'

'Yeah, as a matter of fact —' Her young face hardened. 'How'd you know that?'

'Oh, journalist's instinct.'

'Don't listen to him, Jez,' said Dolores. 'He's taking the mick. They're all the same, fucking news hounds.'

I wondered if the rector had heard the obscenity, or if he had learned to ignore the startling rudeness of his young charges.

He turned to Jezzie. 'Where did you say you lived?'

'Mmm?' said Jezzie, still dreamy from her recent brush with the arrow of Eros. 'Oh, Spitalfields. I got this horrible landlady, she cooks greasy breakfasts, and ticks you off for using too much toilet roll. And no pets and no men in your room after 10 p.m., and if you want to have a bath —'

'But your address?'

'Oh right, 16 Fournier Street. What, you going to *write* to me?'

The rector, with an operatic flourish, opened his big coat wide, and ferreted about in the lining. He buried his head under his armpit, like a swan having a kip. He appeared to search in one aperture, then another, a third — Jesus, how many pockets did he *have* in there? — and pulled out a red ledger, the kind a fellow might keep a note of his expenses in, and gravely inscribed the name of young Jezzie's fragrant domicile. Then he pressed a business card into the girl's hand. 'And here is my address. I gather you are but recently arrived in the metropolis. I hope you will ring me on this number, Vauxhall 9137, if you are assailed by feelings of loneliness or desperation or feel in need of conversation.'

Jezzie tucked the card away in her blouse. Dolores regarded her cigar-puffing benefactor with a look of warning.

'Harold,' she said, evenly, 'we've got to talk.'

The rector snapped the ledger shut, returned it to its home in the gaberdine folds, glanced at Jezzie's newly enlivened presence — her mountainous blonde hair, her even more mountainous bosom — and smiled at his young protégée like a fond uncle at a family reunion.

'We are among friends, my dear, and can talk freely about your future employment –'

'It's not about the bloody *job*, Harold,' she hissed. 'It's about Max. What you done with him?'

He suddenly looked a little nervous. 'Max?' he asked. 'Was that the man I met you with outside the National Gallery?'

'You know perfectly well. And you put the law on him,' said Dolores. 'How could you? The bloody *peelers*.'

My ears were out on stalks, if that's the phrase. I seemed to have stumbled into an interesting little row. The vicar, the tart, the villain, the mystery disappearance, the constabulary . . . All my antennas were quivering.

They were quivering a little too obviously. The vicar and the girls were suddenly all looking at me, none too friendly. Dolores's enormous gob had lost its pouty allure and was thin as a Gillette blade. The rector's cigarry animation had evaporated, leaving him with a look on his face like a man just kneed in the nadgers. In this pub snug, there was suddenly an Arctic chill. Even the birdbrain Jezzie could feel it.

'I think,' said the rector, and I was relieved to hear anyone saying *anything* to break the silence, 'we must not keep you any longer from your friends. If you wish to interview me about my work, you must make an appointment by telephone. I keep irregular hours. It has been pleasant to make your acquaintance.' And with that, he turned his whole chair, away from me so I was looking at his back, as he leaned into the girls again.

'I was just going, Reverend,' I said, rising sheepishly. 'Unless you fancy one more drink, on me, I mean, and we could . . .'

He ignored me. Dolores, the little bitch, turned a look of pure contempt my way. 'You still 'ere?' she said. 'Thought you were goin'. And takin' your big flappin' ears with you.'

And that was that. I gathered my dignity, my jacket and briefcase and left. At the door, I looked back. The reverend and the two girls were the best of friends again, laughing and yarning away. It was after eight. The pub was now as smoky as Hades, crushed as a Calcutta omnibus, the young lawyers and Friday-night *demoiselles* getting noisily hammered, the guy at the piano singing 'Paper Moon', and

I was sorry to leave. I'd just met the oddest geezer I've come across in years. I rather envied him his funny entourage, and I itched to find out more about their set-up. So I'll ring him tomorrow on Vauxhall 9137 and see if there's a story in it. His old-fashioned way of talking, it ran through my head on the way home. And his coat with all the special pockets. And the girl with the torn veil who'd said, 'What, you going to *write* to me?' like nobody'd ever written her a letter in her life.

Journals of Harold Davidson
London
1 July 1930

The newspapers are full of Iraq. It seems that Britain has agreed to the recognition of Iraqi independence, and the dismantling of our protectorate, set up during the war by the Sykes–Picot Agreement. I am far from convinced that this is a beneficial move. The presence of Europeans in the Ottoman territories is, of course, seen as an outrage by the Muslim hordes. They may admire our scientific advances and our armaments in war, but they resent our occupation of their land – and they bridle when they see our distaste for their corrupt and primitive ways. Most of them would wish Mr Sykes and M. Picot at the bottom of the Tigris and the Euphrates, picked clean by sharia fish. And yet, is it not imperative that we bring modern European ideas to this benighted territory? Could any Iraqi look at the clockwork precision of London life, the fruits of the Enlightenment in our libraries, the technical advances in our roads and in the air, the literacy of our common folk, and not wish the same for his own community?

Perhaps I should preach about this on Sunday. Through conversations at St Ethelreda's with Henry, an Arabist of many years' study, I know how passionately some enlightened Muslims wish to replace the religious tyranny of their lands with a liberal constitution, a monarchy of restricted powers and a parliamentary representation of the people's will. It was Henry who lent me *Admonition to the Nation*, a striking work of far-sighted intelligence by Sheikh Mohammed

Husein Naini, one of the leading intellectuals of Najaf, who draws connections between the tenets of the Qur'an and the secular policies of British governance. He argues that to curb the tyranny of rulers is an act worthy of the Shia, and to establish a government bound by a constitution may be interpreted as the return of the 'Hidden Imam' – the twelfth imam in the succession from the Prophet, who disappeared from view (i.e. died, in Western terms) or has been miraculously concealed by God since 934, and who, some believe, will return one day to usher in an era of perfect justice and perfect government.

It is just one of their myriad madcap beliefs – so bizarre, so capricious and fanciful, when set beside our own happy certainty of the Second Coming of Christ and the promise of eternal bliss in His sight.

An admirable subject for high-table debate, though perhaps a little too sensational for a sermon in Stiffkey. We must see if Iraq subsides into the Ottoman murk where she lay stagnant for so long, or if she embraces the modern light of the West.

Humph. How metaphorically unhelpful that the West is where the light *declines*, while the East is where it *increases* and is constantly reborn. *Most* inconvenient.

A pleasant evening in the Old Coal House with Dolores Knight, despite her continued aversion to any kind of hard work, study or kindly counsel. I told her of Mrs Lake's objections to the gentlemen callers and Mrs Moody's exasperation over the secretarial course. Dolly laughs them away. Now I have rescued her from the sordid company of St Katherine's Dock, Wapping, found her accommodation in Whitechapel, brought a doctor who would treat her unfortunate condition ('Mat' low's Clap' they call it, rather brutally, in dock regions) and paid her regular visits to discuss her future, I ask myself: What more can I do? The great Schweitzer himself, in the jungles of wherever-it-was, could not work harder at the sharp end of salvation than I, without expectation of reward, but in the hope of seeing results. In the case of Miss Knight, my labours have produced only a bored, disaffected girl, unwilling to embrace the opportunities offered by a virtuous life. Instead, she complained last evening – in front of complete strangers — that I had caused her unpleasant gentleman friend Max to be taken into custody. I may have hinted to the constabulary that he appears to own a great quantity of French brandy, which he retails in small barrels from a back room in the George Inn, London Bridge. I did not say he was a smuggler; that was their interpretation. But he was no good for Dolores — I am quite sure he was a former client, returning to his prey — and she is better off without him. She is bitter, though, and will take some placating.

She brought with her a delightful young friend, comically named Jezebel (!), a thickset, giggling, foolish, boy-loving ninny of a girl in a torn veil. She may well be in danger (from the company of Dolores, as much as from any man). I gave her my card and may call on her tomorrow. Around 1 a.m.

Met a journalist, from the *Evening Standard*, who wishes to know more about my work and publish feature. Excellent. Seemed nice enough chap, but with tendency to linger and eavesdrop. Ah well, that is the nature of the beast. I have little time for scandal sheets and penny dreadfuls. They deal in such foolish, trivial stuff. I represent something deeper and more serious, at the coalface of modern urban life where the battle every day is between the largest armies of all: sin; damnation; virtue; redemption. But I will grant him an interview if he calls.

Feature article, *Evening Standard*
5 July 1930

AT HOME AMONG THE HOMELESS
*How an unusual clergyman is working for
the betterment of London's poor*

By Charles Norton

Sam Gillespie was six years old when his parents were drowned in a boating accident. Orphaned, bereaved and shocked, he was taken in by an aunt who lived in Wapping, then sent to nearby Tower Hamlets School. Unable to stomach the cruel taunts of fellow pupils about his parentless state, he regularly played truant. His aunt could not feed him from her limited

stipend. Finding it hard to gain work because of his extreme youth, he turned to crime, stealing bicycles. Now fifteen, he has been in prison twice. It is hard for him to secure a job with legitimate enterprises. He is in danger of having to look for a livelihood among the criminal fraternity. What is a boy such as Sam to do?

Step forward, the Reverend Harold Davidson, 54, one of the most remarkable clergymen in England, a man who has brought life and hope to hundreds of misfortunate men, women and children. Davidson is the founder of a number of charities for homeless men, destitute boys and women forced into a life of vice. His work takes him to all corners of London, looking for young people in danger of falling into bad company. 'It is fortunate that I seldom sleep,' laughs Davidson, 'for I find myself summoned to my ministry from morning to night. London is bursting with runaways, who have come here in search of jobs and excitement, and found nowhere to live. For 10 years, the public parks have been their only refuge in snow and rain. Every day they risk arrest for vagrancy; the girls risk fines and imprisonment for soliciting, quite unjustly. Their crime is not prostitution but *destitution*. Something must be done.'

Davidson's crusade is the more remarkable because he is not based in London. He is rector of the Norfolk parish of Stiffkey and Morston where he lives with his Irish wife, Moyra, and their five children, Sheilagh, Nugent, Patricia, Arnold and Pamela. He teaches religious instruction at the local school, recites poetry and presides over amateur dramatic productions. 'I used to do a bit of acting, in my student days and after,' he recalls with a smile, 'and I fear there's still a bit of the ham about me!' He is a frequent visitor to the theatres of London's West End. While barely past his school examinations, Davidson set up an organisation to help child newspaper sellers – always a prey to bullying and exploitation – acquire a basic education. After gaining a degree at Oxford University, he helped to found the Young Lads' Apprenticeship Fund, looking to provide an artisanal career for otherwise unemployable youths. 'It is the most worthwhile work imaginable,' he told me, 'attaching these lost boys to employers and helping them become future plumbers, bookbinders and carpenters ...'

He is also the founder of the Runaway Boys' Retreat, where street urchins, on the run from difficult domestic circumstances, are fed and tended by older boys and given a basic education. Davidson has also become known to

Londoners for his work with streetwalkers, finding them work and decent dwellings, 'helping them', as he puts it, 'emerge from the crepuscular alleys of sins, the dim corridors of corruption and return to the stony but sure pathway to the Light. These women are often scarcely more than children, young girls preyed upon by men no better than the slave owners of yore. It is my gift sometimes to discover them before they have strayed, and to divert the course of their lives from Perdition. To the fallen, I can offer help and succour. I will go on doing so while there is breath in my body, and friends able to assist in this most necessary and demanding work. I owe it to the girls.'

When we parted company, he was on his way to the Kardomah restaurant in Holborn, to meet another prospective employer of the poor unfortunates to whom he represents a kind of earthly Saviour. Motivated by simple Christian goodheartedness, Harold Davidson is too modest of his achievements to accept such an appellation; but it is deserved nonetheless.

CHAPTER 2

Journals of Harold Davidson
London
7 July 1930

As I was passing the Lyons Corner House tea room in the Strand today I saw, through the window, a remarkable sight. A young girl, evidently a waitress, wearing a thin raincoat and no hat, was sitting on a chair the wrong way round. Her knees were spread wide around the chair's backrest, her arms folded along the top. In this posture, she was talking to the lady by the till, who seemed to find nothing unusual in her friend's wanton arrangement of limbs.

I walked in. My usual table to the rear of the tea room was occupied, and I was forced to sit by the window. I dug into my Stationery and Publications Pockets, and set to work making notes on the findings of the Bishops' Conference in Liverpool, until I saw the young girl on the chair cease her conversation, and I felt able to intervene.

'Good evening, my dear,' I said, giving a grave bow. 'Am in the presence of Miss Marlene Dietrich?'

'You what?' said the girl, blankly. 'Who's that? Who're you?'

'I see I am mistaken,' (I smote my brow theatrically), 'but surely you must be aware of Miss Dietrich, the German actress. Why, you resemble her so closely, I could have sworn it was she sitting on this chair.'

'You mean I look like her?'

'It is not just the look, my dear. It is the pose. You must have seen Miss Dietrich's new film, *The Blue Angel*, in which she plays a nightclub entertainer, who sits, upon the stage, in precisely the same attitude in which you are sitting now?'

'No I haven't. I can't afford to go to the flicks.'

'Dear girl, are you destitute? Have you no work to bring you a living wage?'

'I work here,' she said, coolly. 'Only, I've just come off duty and now I'm going home.'

'How fortunate. And do you find the work in this tea room congenial?'

'What you mean, congealing?'

'Congenial, my dear, do you find the work pleasant?'

'Yeah, it's all right. It's nice when everyone's friendly. But we get some right tough characters. The other day, this bloke, he comes in throwing his weight around, he looks at me and goes, "Oi, you! Get me some hot chocolate!" like he's ordering some squaddie around.'

'And did you retaliate?'

'We're not supposed to say nothing, in case they turn nasty. So I just got his drink and brought it over. Yvonne, my friend, she reckoned I should have upended it into his lap.' She beamed wickedly at the prospect.

'I hope you are not abused by gentlemen on a regular basis?'

'What? No chance. Miss Tewkesbury here, she doesn't take no cheek from people who're rude.'

She was a sweet-faced young thing, not a beauty but a healthy, clean-skinned innocent girl, nervous of men. Yet, given a moment's rest from her labours, she falls into the wayward, legs-apart posture of Lola in *The Blue Angel*, like the most shameless *poule de luxe*! Something must be working upon her; some malign influence has her in its grip. I have an antenna for when a girl is going to the bad – or, if not yet going, then disposed in time to slide towards corruption.

Her parents were in Evershot, she said, a village near Yeovil, in Dorset. They had (thoughtlessly, I feel) allowed her to leave school and travel to London with her older sister, to seek employment. The girls live in Camberwell, off the Dog Kennel Hill, and the sister, Delia, has a 'young man' who takes her cycling at weekends. She herself (Sandra) has no young man, she says, though she is all of seventeen. Some of the gentlemen who came in for tea made rough jokes about taking her 'up the town' one night, but they never (she says) mean it and she wouldn't wish to. I asked how she spent her evenings. At the Camberwell room, it seems, reading and listening to the radio, although sometimes she and Delia go to the nearby park and drink cider with her gentleman friend and his associates. 'It reminds us,' she said, 'of home.' My godfathers. I know a girl in imminent trouble when I hear one. But one small light gleamed out from her blank revelation of a blank life. Every so often she goes to the Quakers Hall on Camberwell Church Road, to watch girls from the local school rehearsing their end-of-term drama.

The dear child. So bleakly comforted by so little! Impetuously, I leaned forward.

'Would you do me the honour of accompanying me to the theatre?' I asked. 'I am fortunate to have two tickets to *The Young Idea* by Mr Coward at the Hippodrome this Friday, and I would like you to come.'

'Well, I dunno,' she said, untwining her legs from the back-to-front chair, 'I don't know you. You might be a murderer for all I know, mightn't you?'

I gave a light laugh. 'I am a clergyman, my dear, and I assure you that murder is the last thing on my mind. To speak plainly, I feel you may have a considerable future as an actress. Please do not smile. I am perfectly serious. Before I took to the cloth, I was a professional actor in London, in Kent, Surrey and Hampshire, and I know talent when I see it. You have no business waiting at tables where boorish men speak to you roughly. There is a world out there of achievement, of glamour and fame, where a girl like you will not have to fetch and carry for a pittance. Perhaps on Friday you will let me introduce it to you?'

She stood before me in her mackintosh, her mouth open (to reveal charmingly white but crooked teeth) in surprise.

'Call in tomorrow, and ask me again,' she said, 'and I'll see.'

'I appreciate your caution,' I said, delighted. 'And I'm glad to say that you are about to enter, come Friday, a world of sublime happiness.'

When I left she was smiling. A splendid evening's work. I must look in at the Hippodrome later, to acquire some free tickets from dear Ivy, whom I rescued from a life of vice only last spring.

London
9 July 1930

Things to do:

1. Elsie Teenan to Mrs Teasdale, 15 The Close, Bermondsey. Rent 3/9 wk. No dogs. Persuade E to part with Biscuit. Poss work at Vincent's seamstress factory? Must ask.
2. Check employment roster at Labour Exchange, Stratford Road, Battersea. Maids, cooks, etc. in good houses. Lily Beane, Sally Anstruther, Joanna Dee still unplaced.
3. Boots pharmacy. Fresh supplies of rash salve, shingles ointment, gingivitis balm, surgical spirit, bathroom tissue, etc. Wrights Coal Tar soap for Elsie. Special offer beauty soap/shampoo still avlbl? Box set to Marina Carter – bthday 28 July. Mauve ribbons for Patricia. Soft toy for Pamela.
4. Lunch, Monsignor Coveney, Mount St, Weds. We need cash for Christian Rehabilitation of Immoral Youth fund or will surely go under.
5. Visit Fenella Royston-Smith, Ch X Hotel. NB bring Dream of Gerontius for her. Urge her to join Virtue Reclamation League and enlist Kenya friends.
6. Sandra from Strand T-rooms to The Young Idea, Friday, Hippodrome. Tickets from Ivy Bareham.
7. While at it, tkts to see Journey's End at Her Majesty's. Cheap dress-circle seats to 1 Sept.
8. 6 p.m., meeting with Eddie Bones & Howard Shiner, Runaway Boys' Retreat.
9. New girl, Jezebel (!) friend of Dolores Kt. In danger. 16 Fournier St, Whitechapel.
10. Ring Mimi. There must be emergency boilerman somewhere in Norfolk.
11. Sermon – St Augustine? 'Salus extra ecclesiam non est'.

Delightful evening with Sandra Hunt, the young waitress I befriended in the Strand on Monday. I popped in on Tuesday to renew my invitation to the theatre and found she had all but forgotten about it! How thoughtless are the young about things that should most demand their attention. Said she thought I had been 'throwing her a line' in inviting her to the West End. Reassured her I desired only her company in Hippodrome stalls, mentioning that I was a widower who enjoyed the thrill of live drama. She finally accepted. Angry glances from the dragon-lady in charge of tea room, who kept telling the put-upon girl to return to work.

She was waiting for me on Wellington Street, wearing the same blue raincoat as when we met, silky blonde hair quite straight, except for one charming kink where it falls over her right ear. Caught my breath as I realised how much her face reminded me of –

Enough. She had never been to theatre before! Not just in the West End – she had never been in *any* theatre, not even a school play, nor even mummers calling in her Hardyesque home village. She loved the stalls, the proscenium arch, the programme, the ladies in their finery nodding at us (doubtless counting us as father and daughter), the velvet curtain. 'Is there a big screen behind the drapes?' she asked, in her artless way. She loved the play, its clipped and brittle rallies corresponding to many young girls' notions of sophistication. She even essayed a twirly little dance on the cobbles of Covent Garden Market. Delightful. Bought her sausages and chips at the Brigham Café, and learned more of her family. She has not, after all, been abandoned. Parents sent her and her sister on rail journey to the metropolis with cash subvention, and are coming to London next month to check their progress. So Sandra has no immediate need of guardian and protector against baser instincts. Excellent.

Sandra asked me about our first conversation in the café. Which film star had I taken her for? I explained about Miss Dietrich and *The Blue Angel*.

'She plays a performer,' I said. 'A kind of exotic dancer in a club, wearing only underwear and a top hat, and sitting astride a chair.'

'Is it good?' said Sandra. 'I mean, would I like it?'

'I know nothing of your taste in such things, but it is a remarkable study in moral corruption, one that may hold lessons for a young person, about the power of sensual gratification.'

'So there's dancing and singing, and this woman in a hat?' she said. 'Isn't there a story? I like a nice story.'

'Indeed there is,' I said, 'a story about a respectable man, a professor, who falls in love with a femme fatale, gives up everything for her and ends his life as little more than a clown.'

'Ooh,' said Sandra, 'I think I'll go and see that. It sounds great.'

Even as I described the plot, I felt a tintinnabulation of alarm. It occured to me that, though it served as a conversational topic, *The Blue Angel* is perhaps *not* a film impressionable young girls should be encouraged to see.

I got the bill. We caught a cab and I dropped this sweet-faced young girl outside her cramped lodgings in Camberwell Green.

London
15 July 1930

Yesterday my fifty-fifth birthday, a day for sober self-examination, yet I rose in excellent spirits, like one – thank God! – perpetually reborn to the fray. Surveyed my ageing flesh in the silvered bathroom mirror. A touch of rheum about the eyes, a deal of sag about the neck, and the brow-lines now feature a cross-hatched complexity like a Piranesi drawing; but on the whole, no need to send for the mortician yet! In a sudden impulse of vanity, I sought out the nail scissors and snipped at the profusion of hairs extruding from my auricular cavities. The eyebrows too have a new tendency to bolt and straggle, and with them too I dealt severely.

Mrs Parker cooked a celebratory breakfast of kippers and scrambled eggs with too much milk in the beaten eggs (*comme d'habitude*, alas!), and we clinked teacups in a domestic parody of a banqueting toast. The feast day of St Alice of Ravenna, that sweet young flower of sixteenth-century martyrdom. Too few Renaissance paintings commemorate her uncomplaining death, crushed between millstones by Moorish brigands in the Saharan wastes. She will remain, I fear, a dim footnote in the history of North African missions unless I single-handedly rescue her from obscurity.

There was no time to regret my lack of anniversary cards from the children. M, I fear, is preoccupied with our houseful of lame dogs, and the state of the boiler. I should have telephoned. By 10 a.m., I was patrolling Fleet Street – the sunlight blazing off the noble frontage of the law courts, a divine birthday gift.

In Somerset House, I endeavoured to find Elsie Teenan's birth certificate, in the hope of locating her errant mama, but only an unmannerly crew of Teahans, Teemans and Teamonts appeared beneath my flicking fingers. Most frustrating.

I will not give up on poor Elsie. I will not have her spend one more night outside Waterloo Station among the taxis, flagging for custom in her grey Tipperary shawl. There is no sight in London more pathetic than a young harlot who has found no clients by 3 a.m. I wish she would cease her doomed attempts to sell her body (or to 'find some young feller to go home with' in her clue-lessly romantic turn of phrase) and embrace a more virtuous life as, say, a maidservant, until she finds a passing Dublin construc-tion worker who will recognise her potential, embrace her spindle-framed loveliness, sing to her from Moore's *Irish Melodies*, stop her complaining mouth with appreciative kisses and bear her away to a fulfilled life of twins and St Patrick's Day shamrock in the new suburban Eden of Tooting Common. I have seen it work. One *can* build a Jerusalem, of sorts, in London's green and burgeoning suburbs.

At noon, I popped into St Paul's where a funeral was in full swing. Nobody I knew, but I derived a cold comfort from the digni-fied obsequies, the profusion of flowers, the fume of expensive cathe-dral incense. I was cheered at this sad event by the sight of the dead man's family. The widow was a handsome woman in her fifties, 'piss-elegant Mayfair' as Rose would have said. The lady's dignified bearing softened by the swell of her bosom in a well-cut black crape gown, she extended an eloquent arm around the waist of her eldest daughter as the Bishop flapped the fuming censer around an expensive mahogany coffin. The daughter laid her head on her mother's shoulder in a gesture both needy and sweetly supportive. I gazed at this charming tableau of womanhood, admiring their mutual support. I longed to go up and interpose my body between them, to extend caring arms about their waists and tell them they had nothing to fear, since the Life Eternal had embraced their husband and father – yet something stopped my impetuous impulse. So I remained at the end of the pew, singing the climactic hymn, 'As We Walk the Paths of Sorrow to the Shores of Galilee', remarking inwardly how similar is the tune to the chorus of 'The Man Who Broke the Bank at Monte Carlo', a great favourite of mine.

I popped into the offices of the *Church Times* in Fleet Street, hoping to interest Mr Humphrey Goodman in the progress of our charitable work at the Runaway Boys' Retreat in Whitechapel. I brought along a score of the new leaflets (a piteous tableau of a woman clutching her luckless infant, driven from her father's door into a snowy field populated by expiring robins, above the legend 'More To Be Pitied Than Scorned!' – surely an image to melt the sternest heart) hoping to persuade him that one might be reproduced on the front page with a suitably affecting editorial. But Mr G, despite his Bunyanesque name, was 'engaged', they told me, 'in writing up the Bishops' Conference' and could not spare ten minutes.

Luncheon at the Jolly Farmers with Vincent Doughty, whose clothing manufactory goes, he tells me, from strength to strength. He has started to take snuff! Every fifteen minutes, he punctuates our discussion by flourishing a tin box, extracting from it a 'pinch' of the brown powder in his sausagey fingers, and ramming it up his nose. 'Fancy a go?' he asked me several times. He is an oaf, a boor and a man of few spiritual leanings, yet he has undoubtedly been of assistance to the girls. They almost always leave his workplace for more elevated positions, sometimes for a dress shop in the provinces, sometimes for a career in catering. I have little opportunity to ask them about this gratifying advancement. Usually, I am brought the news of their departure by a third party. I am convinced that Vincent gives them a little 'pep talk' about their future prospects, and directs them towards more congenial employment.

'That Erica,' he said, as we smoked cigars after the veal-pie crumbs had been cleared away, 'the young one from Swansea, *she* was a lively piece of work. A demon at pressing she were, pressing and folding, pressing and folding, like she was born to it. Lovely young thing. Had a bit of sass to her as well, talked back to the lads on the pressing machines, gave as good as she got. I got to hand it to you, Rector, you can pick 'em. Sad she had to go.' He took another elaborate pinch of snuff, shedding much of it on his serge trousers. 'She wasn't open to all the opportunities on offer.'

'And where exactly did she go?' I enquired.

'Oh, Beckenham way, I believe.' He seemed suddenly vague. 'Got an aunt there, runs a flower shop or some such. Lovely girl, though. If you got any more like that, I hope you'll send 'em over. There's always room for more of your lively young folk, 'Arold. Always raises the morale in the factory, a bit of new blood.'

Heartened by this endorsement, I told him about Elsie Teenan and her efforts to find work. 'A naive girl,' I confided, 'but strong and healthy, charmingly grateful to all who try to help her.'

'That so?' said Vincent. 'Sounds ideal. Send her over for a little chat with me, soon as you like.' What a good, solicitous fellow he is!

Evening. It is years since I celebrated my birthday with a dinner party, or any communal meal, unless in Stiffkey on the day itself, consuming mutton chops with Mimi. Settled instead on a visit to Maddox Street, to see Emily Murray and Nellie Churchill in their charming 'bed-sitting room'. Nobody could accuse me of having favourites, but the presence of Miss Murray is always a delight.

'Oh, Harold, how *lovely*,' she breathed as she opened the door. 'I've been longing for you to come by, so I could show you my new friends.'

She led me by the hand into a room in which the fume of cheap scent battled for the upper hand with the odour of fish and stale nicotine.

'Close your eyes!' she cried. 'I must make them presentable to such a noble guest.' I complied, and was led across an unappealingly sticky carpet to her bed. 'You mustn't look, Harold, or it will be too naughty of you. Dickens and Jones are all tumbled and listless, and I must smarten them up. Sit up, you bad boys. All right, Harold, you may open your eyes.'

I did, and saw upon the coverlet the familiar profusion of soft toys, lolling drunkenly over half its area. There must have been close on forty wool bears and rag dolls. In pride of place were her new acquisitions, a flop-eared rabbit and a cross-eyed giraffe, humorously arrayed so that one of the giraffe's soft legs encircled the rabbit in fond camaraderie.

'You see what friends they are!' cried Emily. 'I found them in Bermondsey Market, and adopted them and took them in, and now they have such larks together, I can scarcely bear to leave them to go to beastly work. Don't you love them too, Harold?'

'Delightful, Emily,' I said. 'Quite the nicest-looking fauna I have encountered outside Chessington Zoo.'

It was the wrong thing to say. 'Oh, Harold, how can you? I couldn't bear to think of my darling Dickens and Jones in a horrid zoo. The keepers might be cruel to them, they might be hungry and cold in the night.' She made a show of pulling the counterpane over the wool creatures, as if to warm them. 'No harm is going to come to them here, not if I must stay home and starve.'

'Is Nellie not home this evening?' I asked, keen to change the subject.

'No, my dear, Nellie is off with one of her gentlemen friends,' said Emily with a sweet smile. 'One of the newer kind, which means she will be home later, rather than staying out all night. I fear she is grumpy with me, Harold. We never have a conversation when she returns home, as we used to.'

How delicately she spoke of her previous life of rampant prostitution. She behaves as a child but is twenty-three. When I met her, just four months ago – in Soho, outside a pub in Rupert Street – I remarked then on the sweet passivity of her nature, her simple acquiescence towards one whom she felt she could trust.

'Hello, sir – Do you want me?' were her opening words. They could have been the assistant in a hat shop saying, 'Can I help you?'

I have learned that you must attend to what Emily says, however foolish, because her utterances come studded with information in code. So I asked, 'Nellie is grumpy with you? In what way grumpy?'

'She says she is too tired to speak, or to heed what I am saying, or kiss me goodnight. She sleeps until 3 p.m. on a Sunday, and scratches her arms until they are quite bleeding and welcomes gentlemen who come to the door with little messages contained in tiny envelopes.'

I glanced across the room to the other bed, in the dark corner. It was brutally utilitarian. Beside it, the wall was covered with notes and scraps of paper, addresses, times of appointments. Nothing gave a hint of character, or smacked of comfort or adornment.

'I hoped you might be free tonight, Emily,' I said. 'I have two tickets to see *Mister Cinders* at the Adelphi. It is light as a soufflé, but full of appealing tunes that will lift your spirits.'

She impetuously kissed my cheek. 'Harold! You know how I adore the theatre. Give me five minutes to get ready in my going-out frock and I – oh but wait. Perhaps I shouldn't.'

For a moment, I feared that I might have to reassure her that Dickens and Jones would not object to being left alone. But no.

'Tomorrow I start work, thanks to you, my dear friend, at the Café Royal. Perhaps it would be better if I had an early night. I should not wish to disappoint my new employers by arriving late.'

It is very satisfying to me that she should respond so willingly to my placing her in a job at the kitchens of the distinguished Regent Street restaurant, away from her life of sin. I was moved to find how seriously she was taking it.

'Your worries do you credit, Emily, but I was not planning on a late night. Decide what to wear tomorrow and put the clothes upon a chair. Set your alarm clock for 7 a.m. We shall go to the play, eat a light supper at Brown's, I shall see you home and you will be tucked up in bed with, ah, Marshall and Snelgrove –'

'Dickens and *Jones*, Harold. How *can* you tease me like this?'

' – with your charming menagerie by eleven o'clock, and will awake refreshed to start your new employment and your new life.'

'Oh, Harold –' she clutched my arm – 'I'll get changed.' I made a gesture towards the door. 'There's no need to go out into the horrid cold wind. You might look away, though, while a lady is dressing.'

I sat on Nellie's unyielding bed, talking inconsequentially and listening to the noises behind me of rustle and snap, the tiny lady-like grunt that accompanied the fastening of hooks and eyes, the sigh of a lady's arm sliding into a silken sleeve, all the sonic paraphernalia of a woman at her toilette. Some men might find the scene eroti-cally promising, but I am inured to such things. Ten years of dealing with the sisterhood of vice have left me overfamiliar with the female boudoir. Odd to think I have been in hundreds of bedrooms over the last decade, but none has been that of a woman of decent moral address. Not one. What a curious state of affairs.

The door opened and Nellie came in. It was, frankly, awkward timing.

'Oh,' she said, seeing me first. 'What are *you* doing here?' I rose and glanced to Emily for guidance – to find her seated on a wooden chair, attaching the top of a silver stocking to the rubber flange of some item of corsetry. Her left leg – rather a beautiful sight! – was fully exposed.

'Am I interrupting?' In the doorway Nellie glanced from Emily's leg to me, where I had half risen from the bed. 'Shall I go?'

'No, you silly thing,' said Emily with a girlish laugh, 'I was changing. Harold's taking me to a play. You know lovely Harold, don't you?'

'We've met,' she said shortly. 'When was the last time? The Windmill Theatre, or the Carter woman's cathouse in Drury Lane?'

'I cannot recall,' I said. 'Perhaps the latter. How is life treating you, Miss Churchill?'

She didn't reply, but crossed the room to her bed and began rooting around underneath it. Miss Churchill does not like me. Her presence casts a pall on every occasion. She seems to regard me with a suspicion I find frankly offensive. Of course, her experience of men is limited almost entirely to clients, clubland swells and prosti-tutes' bullies. Show her a man intent only on the welfare of sinners, and she is puzzled, discomfited and keen to infer the worst.

'I don't know what you two are up to, but could you finish it and leave me in peace?' she said. Her long face was blank with hostility. 'There's some things I need to do, and I could live without spectators, if that's all right with you.'

Emily raised to me an enquiring eyebrow. How could I have communicated, in dumbshow, that her friend was looking for her supply of narcotics, her syringe, etc., without which she could not venture to Oxford Circus for an evening of drugged soliciting in alleys and cheap hotels?

'Of course, Nellie,' I said lightly. 'Emily and I are just off to see *Mister Cinders*. I shall have her back here in bed early, because tomorrow she starts her exciting job at the Café Royal.'

Nellie's face set in a sneer. 'Oh yeah,' she said. 'She told me. Washin' up for toffs. Hands in the sink from morning to night. *Very* exciting.'

'It won't be like that, Nellie, you beast,' said Emily, in a hurt, schoolgirl voice. 'I'll probably be waiting on Ramsay MacDonald himself in the restaurant by Christmas. That's what Harold says, anyway.'

'It won't be long,' said Nellie, 'before you're dying to be back on the street. Or dying of boredom. Or dead on your feet. Go on and do it, but don't say I didn't warn you.'

If I were a young woman, I would sooner share living quarters with Cassandra, or Medea, or Lady Macbeth and all three witches, than Nellie Churchill. It took all my powers of persuasion to convince Emily that her life would soon change for the better.

She loved the play, however, and left the theatre, humming and chattering about the loveliness of the costumes.

Over a Spanish omelette, I assured her about the dignity of service, especially in so elevated a venue as the Café R, and promised to visit her in a couple of weeks. Home in Maddox Street, I instructed her to brush her teeth and say her prayers.

'I'm *so* glad you took me, Harold,' she breathed. 'All them men who promised to care for me. Only *you* ever did. I'm ever so grateful.'

She pulled me towards her. I laughingly desisted and told her to get some sleep, for it was already 11.05 p.m.

'Ain't you going to tuck me up,' she said, 'and give me a little kiss?'

I would have helped her to bed, and bestowed a chaste kiss on her brow. But the image of Nellie seemed to loom from the dark bed in the corner. Before I left, I taught Emily to say, in bed every night, the words:

> Matthew, Mark, Luke and John,
> Bless the bed that I lay on,
> Ever this night be at my side,
> To light and guard, to rule and guide. Amen.

'I had a friend once called Mark,' she said dreamily, 'and one called Luke. And lots called John, or so they said. No Matthews, though. They all promised to take care of me, but they were all pretty rude in the end, all of them.'

I hastened away, to let her sleep, and wake in the arms of the Lord. It has been a most happy birthday.

Stiffkey
20 July 1930

Church attendance low this morning, fifty-five in all, but my sermon well received. Inspired by Mr Charles Sheldon's fascinating book, *Our Exemplar* (1898), I took the simple proposition, 'What Would Jesus Do?' and enjoined the congregation, each and every one, to act on it in their daily lives.

Tired of modern sermons that offer mere exegeses of Bible texts, or dilate on abstractions (I have seldom heard a sermon on the Mystery of the Holy Trinity that conveyed any sense of their being more than a family vaudeville act – a conjuror impersonating simultaneously the Father, the Son and the Ghostly Dove), the congregation was gratifyingly, audibly, startled by my bold innovation.

Asking them to make a habit of rethinking their daily actions in the light of Christ's teachings is, if I may immodestly call it so, a masterstroke. It sends them back to the Gospels and the Acts of the Apostles, searching for clues to correct behaviour. I smile to imagine Mrs Redwood, say, and her charming daughters perusing the Gospel of St John the Beloved in the same spirit that sends my young metropolitan friends, Madge and Agnes, to the advice pages of *Peg's Paper* and *Women's Illustrated* for counsel about the correct deployment of a hatpin in the fashionable bonnet.

How would it be if every question about modern life could be answered in relation to the teachings of Jesus? If every mystification were clarified by reference to what Jesus said and did, his actions and sermons, his attitude to the woman caught in adultery, the moneylenders in the Temple, the thieves on the Cross . . . The mind reels at the prospect.

Some of them slunk away from the porch without catching my eye, and headed home as if I had been trying to enlist them in some branch of the armed forces. The majority, Lord be thanked, crowded round me to ask how they might begin this wondrous, emulatory adventure. 'I have seldom felt more inspired, Rector,' said Mrs Russ, 'and I want to start right away. But apart from cooking lunch for Mr Russ and his sister, my day holds little prospect of moral drama. So how exactly . . . ?'

'My dear Margaret.' I smiled at her willingness to enter the fray of the Church Militant while roasting parsnips. 'I do not mean you must seek out occasions of Christlike activity while performing everyday chores. It is only in time that you will discover the moral crossroads which will make demands on your conscience. And only in your own conscience that you will find the answer to the question I have adumbrated today.'

'But what kind of thing will it be, Rector?' she asked. 'I mean, where will the question . . . *turn up*?'

Sometimes I feel a Sunday-school teacher in the local mixed-infants class would be of more use than I, when dealing with Mrs Russ.

'Well – imagine a starving beggar came to your front door, looking for, say, cold cuts of meat, or a drink of buttermilk, or a bed for the night. Will you turn him away, or will you say, "Enter, poor misfortunate traveller, and eat with me, and drink with me, and sleep with me, if that is what your wretched condition requires . . ."?'

Mrs Russ pursed her mouth into an unbecoming moue.

'. . . Or if a young woman, recently abandoned by her family, should meet you in the street and say, "I'm cold and lonely and pregnant, and need to be taken in and found a doctor," will you ask yourself –'

But Mrs Russ's look of benign imbecility had changed to one of outrage.

'Indeed. Good day to you, Rector.'

Fortunately, my other parishioners were more relaxed about applying my radical tenet to their lives. I spent a happy forty-five minutes discussing the practical applications of my plan. I asked them to give me, in a week's time, tales of how they put into practice what I preached.

The only fly in the ointment, so to speak, was the major. He has sat and brooded in the front pew, these last few weeks, like a wounded old soldier – which of course is what he is, having served his country in the Boer War. He bears the legacy of that elderly conflict in the extraordinary succession of physical jerks and twitches he displays, both at rest on the wooden seat (he rarely kneels to pray) and before the altar. I have allowed him, for a whole year now, the luxury of reading the lesson, in his sonorous militiaman tones. But there is, I fear, evidence these last weeks that he is in the grip of some mental convulsion. Not just in the bizarre spasms of arms and elbows with which he punctuates his readings, but in his odd vocal technique.

In today's lesson, for example, a beautiful passage from the Book of Proverbs, the major swayed before the lectern like a rating before a force-niner, and intoned the words: 'There be three things which are too wonderful to me, yea, four which I know not: The way of an eagle in the air; the way of a serpent upon a rock; the way of a ship in the midst of the sea; and the way of a man with a maid.'

A simple enough text, yet the major, a man lately too preoccupied with his local ambitions, and too enthralled by the lure of his wine cellar, delivered these lines in a roaring theatrical style. To evoke the eagle, his voice rose to a high falsetto, swooping down to the serpent in a low, basso profundity; then the ship – he drew himself up to a high Admiralty bellow, as if he had spent years of barnacled hardship before the mast, rather than bullying his men out of their trenches and into the firing line; before finally mangling the climactic revelation of 'the way of a man with a maid' (what a charming wistfulness lies in that circumlocutory 'the way of . . .') in a disgusted mutter, completely spoiling the beauty of the image. I love that passage – in which the thought of making love to a woman is 'too wonderful' to be borne, like the prospect of flying. Such an eloquent rapture from the beating heart of the celibate! And the words were thrown away by a broken-veined, harrumphing, venal boor of a military charlatan. I stood watching him read, and my heart darkened. I felt a wave of anger. I could have struck him!

Forgive me, Jesus, for what I have said. I have given way to thoughts of violence on thy Sabbath. But he infuriates me so. I shall not allow him to desecrate future services in St John's. I shall confront the major, no matter what the cost.

CHAPTER 3

Letter from Miss Joan Tewkesbury, Proprietor, Lyons Corner House, The Strand, to Mrs Elvira Samuel, Head of Personnel, Lyons Ltd
30 July 1930

Dear Mrs Samuel,

I have had ocasion to write to you before on the matter of the underseribales who to offen frekwent the premisses of our Corner Houses. You have always been kind enoght to advise me as to the correck proceedor and I want your help regarding one spechial case.

He is not your ushal rodwy. He is not a drunk nor a tramp, in fact he come on like a perfeck gent, he does not try and nick anything, he is not one to start a sing song in his cupps, fact is he dont drink annything but tea, he is not one of the yellers or screemers after the pubs shut. And that is the truble. Nothing he dose is ever bad enoufh to mean we got to call the constabbulary. But I feer he is a bad influence on the young wimmin we employ.

He comes by every other night, 9pm reglar as clockwork, he comes sidling in wearing the same gastly long coat, he orders tea and a bun. He sits in the same placc, table 5, hes always there fiddling in his pokets and scriblign things down in his horible purpel writing, looking arond him, talkign to peeple on the tables rite and left, chat chat, natter natter, how are you wot splendid wether were having, like evryones his pal. And then it happens. A yong Nippy take Sandra, only come on the staff last month – he clocks she's a new girl and calls her over. As you knoe, we try and teach new girls, be frendly to the customers, you taut me that your-self when I started Mrs Samuel, but inside five seckons, he starts on em. 'O hello, my, youre beoutiful, my word youre the dead spit of Binnie Hale, she's lovly like you, you should be on stage sumwhere. What lovly hair etcetera. Do you like Noel Coward, O shurely youve seen his work, a classy girl like you. Ive met him menny times, only the other nigth I was out with him and CB Cockrain, shurely you must know the great impressario. You *must* be a singer, far too good to be working in a clapped out teashop like this, the bloody nerve of it, clapped out indeed, anyway he says, would you care to ackompany me to a play in the West End on Teusday, it will be my pleshure.

I tell the Nippies, first rule of waitressing, be friendly but dont get involved with male customers. Theyre lonly men, or they wodnt be in here at 9 o clock of a Saturday night loking for sympathy. If they was respectable, theyd be at home with there wives and sproggs. But some of these girls, they gets taken in so cruel – like they think, O blimey, a real show, the Qwality go and see them, maybe if I go then I'll be qwality too, poor delooded saps. And next thing you know, theyve had the big nigth out and theyre all diffrent in the morning, tired and droopy and wistful, you cant make them do any washing up for starters and theyre offhand with the customers, they drop plates and canot reckoin bills and go off for a weep in the Toilets. Then the bliter comes in two days later and treets them like old mates, hell stand with an arm round em, talking and talking and skweezing their waste, need, need like its a wodge of doe, and their eyes ull shine all angelic like they seen a vishion but before you know it theyll be in the Ladies agen having another big weepin seshon. I know that within a week theyll be gone and I dont know where but it aint to anywhere thats good for them.

Ive said to him, now look here, Ive lost six or seven good girls, nice girls who was happy at there work before you started in on them, so Id be obliged if you take your custom elsewhere. Well thats no good because he just starts puffin on his big old cigar and qwoting the Bibel at me and giving out about the fall of man and such like until Im reddy to screem and brane him with a spatuler.

So what am I to do Mrs Samuel? I cant call in the law becoss he aint done nothing wrong. Can I tell him to buger off and bar him like from a pub when he comes back? Pleese advise. We cant go on like this. Sandras just come back from the ladies (for the third time) and handed in her notice. She says she wants to be in modern dramer for which she has a Magicall Talent. Her exack words, the birdbrain.

Yours in dessperation,

Joan Tewkesbury (Mrs)

Journals of Harold Davidson
London
6 August 1930

I have met the most extraordinary young girl. In my long experience of dealing with the fallen, she stands out (already) as a case that will require all my ingenuity and moral strength to bring into the Fold.

I met her at lunchtime outside the travel-luggage shop beside Marble Arch. I was standing, becalmed in thought, wondering if a turn in Hyde Park might be productive, when she passed by my side. She was an attractive young thing, by no means yct grown to womanhood but sturdy and strong, with rich ropes of curly brown hair, always an index of health in a young girl, and strong (if shockingly discoloured) teeth, disclosed in a charming smile as she walked past, perhaps amused to see a gentleman (I wore no dog collar that day) standing still in the bustle of Oxford Street, apparently lost in the blinding sunlight.

I caught and held her glance of appraisal – her eyes were enormous dark marbles, full of intelligence – but could not quite read her expression.

Summoning up all my Christian charisma, I gained her side in an instant and said, 'Can I possibly be the first, my dear, to remark on your extraordinary resemblance to the American actress Mary Bryan?'

She scrutinised me coolly.

'Well, that's a new one,' she said. 'I get Miriam Hopkins some-times, I get Esther Ralston from the really blind boys, but never Mary Bryan before.'

'I assure you, the resemblance is uncanny. You could be sisters.'

'Go on, you old charmer. You say that to all the girls, don'cha?'

'Well,' I conceded, 'only the exceptionally pretty ones.'

'How long you been standing there in your big coat,' she asked. 'Poor old duck, you look like you're going to melt.'

'I am a little warm. Do you happen to know where one can find a water ice? I am enfeebled with dehydration. I fear I may soon expire in this parching heat.'

'Come with me *this instant*,' she said, 'I don't want to 'ave your death on my hands.' She linked my arm in a forthright manner, as impetuous modern girls will, and led me up Edgware Road, as if we were adventuring friends. 'I'm saving your life,' she said, looking at me as though I were some sort of domesticated pet. 'You and me're going for a little stroll and I'll find you a cool billet out of the sun's rays, and you'll buy us both a lovely ice-cream sundae. OK with you?' I could hardly refuse this comely girl's kind offer, couched though it was in the tones of a young gold-digger looking for a victim. But we conversed amiably enough en route to the Alhambra tea rooms.

'Nice,' she said, looking around her, unbuttoning her linen jacket. Beneath it she wore a white cotton blouse with charming blue, heart-shaped buttons. It was evidently a garment purchased some time ago. The buttons, when she leaned forward, strained against her newly maturing figure. A heady whiff of scent enfumed the café air.

I summoned the waitress, a bored-looking slattern in an unflat-tering ochre tunic. 'Bring me a long glass of iced tea, my dear, as deliciously cold as your facilities will allow. And for my young guest' – I waved my hand in choose-anything-you-like largesse – 'perhaps an ice-cream sundae . . .'

'Nah,' she said, suddenly businesslike. 'You got any lamb chops? I'm starving. Two, no, make it three lamb chops, and spuds and some veg, and plenty of gravy if you don't mind. Bread and butter on the side. And a glass of milk, no, make that a beer, you need something more thirst-quenching in this blinking heat, don't you?'

'That all?' said the waitress, scribbling with a stub of HB pencil.

'Don't fancy a few dumplings an' lardy cake as well, do you?' Her tone was indefinably hostile. Perhaps she wasn't used to receiving such commands from a customer young enough to be her granddaughter.

'If anything else takes my fancy,' said my new friend coolly, 'I'll be sure to let you know.'

The waitress raised her eyes heavenwards and left.

'This place,' said the girl, 'used to be all right. They'd let you come in an' have a little sit-down with tea and a penny bun for an hour, when you was tired. Now they fire you out of here if you're not spending a whole quid.' She shook her head – such nostalgia from a mere child of –

'How old are you, exactly, my dear?'

Her upper lip curled. 'I'm old enough,' she said. 'I'm sixteen.'

'And what is it that brings you strolling in Oxford Street in your best frock at two o'clock in the afternoon?' I asked, as neutrally as possible.

She picked up the à la carte menu, a redundant gesture since her sizeable repast had already been ordered. 'Same as you, I expect. Looking for a bit of company to while the hours away.'

'Mmmm,' I said, unsure of my ground. It was inconceivable that this lively, shining-eyed young woman could be a professional sinner. Yet she had clearly outgrown any institutions of learning. The confidence of her bearing suggested employment at some thriving business. Had I learned that she presided over a superior hat shop in Bond Street, I would not have been surprised.

'What kind of company do you seek out in your lunch hour?' I asked. 'Have you a passion for the conversation of strangers?'

She sat back and made a lattice of her fingers. Blue nail polish made lapis lazuli jewels of their extremities. 'I can talk to anyone,' she said, with a hint of pride. 'I'm very . . . flexible. My old dad used to say it's the most underrated virtue, flexibility.'

'Indeed so. I admire your father's wise counsel. "If you can talk with crowds and keep your virtue, / Or walk with Kings – nor lose the common touch . . ."'

'Come again?'

'Kipling,' I said. 'Surely a well-educated lady like you must know "If"?'

'Oh yeah. Course. A bloke asked me about him one day in the park. "Do you like Kipling?" he says. "I dunno," I says right back. "I don't believe I ever Kippled."' She laughed. 'I didn't make it up, though. I got it off a seaside postcard down Southend.'

The waitress returned, sulkily, with the food and drink. My cold beverage was a far cry from the Long Island Iced Tea I have enjoyed on occasion at the Savoy. Tea, undoubtedly. Cold, up to a point. An enterprising soul in the kitchen had added two spoonfuls of sugar, as if for a workman, and a slice of lemon floated like a shipwreck victim in its caramel depths.

When I looked up, two of the three lamb chops had been stripped to the bone and the girl was wolfing down mashed potato in sweeping forkfuls.

'You seem to be enjoying that,' I said indulgently. 'God bless your appetite.' I forbore to confide that I always found a hearty appetite an attractive trait in a young woman. A hunger to devour . . . strange that it should make the gentle sex more appealing than alarming.

Three minutes of silence passed. I have seen stevedores at Tilbury Docks, onshore after months at sea, demolish their meagre ration of Cornish pasty and greens with more decorum. I watched as a hunk of crusty bread was ushered back and forth through the lees of gravy and the detritus of lamb fibre and popped between her fleshy, pouted lips.

'I trust it was to your liking,' I said. 'Can I interest you in pudding?'

She wiped her greasy mouth with a paper napkin and, still masticating the last of her lunch, delivered herself of this remarkable speech.

'For afters, I have it in mind that we could get better acquainted. I got a room only a cab ride away in Camden Town. Ten minutes from now, you can come up the stairs behind me, looking at my fleshy arse in my tight skirt, and when we get to my room you can lift it up and look at my black stockings and these really nice white knickers I got on today, with little teeny pink roses on the front, and you can undo these blue heart buttons on my chest that you been staring at for the past half an hour and suck my big tits, only not too hard 'cause they're real sensitive, and you can lay me down on the divan in my sunny blue room and fuck me hard as you like until you're done. It's two quid for an hour, 'cause after that I'll have to kick you out. And if you're real sweet beforehand and bung me ten bob extra, I could give you a chew before we get down to business, only I don't take it down the throat because I'm a nice girl, and anyway you really want to finish up buried to the bollocks in my furry quim, don't you, that's what you gentlemen want, isn't that right?'

Well, well. A harlot, after all. In ten years of dealing with ladies of the night, I have met the gamut — every age, every colour, every disposition, every temperament (even every class!) and I am no longer shocked to discover the base occupation of seemingly decent girls. But in this case I felt a distinct disappointment. My initial suspicion, that she was a lady of uncertain moral direction, was proved correct. But the suspicion had been eclipsed by a growing appreciation of her strength of character, her forthrightness. It is easy to grow close to prostitutes as friends, to feel fond of them as substitute children who have strayed from the Path. One never, however, feels admiration. Knowing the moral dereliction that is their daily choice precludes any possibility of such private approbation. Yet I had begun to admire this young woman, in our brief acquaintance — and to feel that, because I admired her, she could not be one of the sisterhood.

'What is your name?' I asked, a little sadly.

'They call me lots of things round 'ere,' she said. 'But you can call me Barbara.' She stretched out a hand. 'Barbara Harris.' Her cotton sleeve trailed across the table, soaking up tea spill and gravy puddle. 'Pleased to meet you.'

'Barbara,' I said sternly, 'as you can see, or should be able to surmise, I am not a man given to dallying with ladies of the street —'

'All I can see,' she retorted, 'is, you're a man, no different from any other, for all your long words.'

'— and I wish only to befriend you. I would not dream of honouring your outrageous suggestion.'

Barbara took a swig from her beer glass. 'You familiar with the music hall?'

'Indeed I am,' I said. 'I used to perform on the public stage in my youth.'

'You sound like one of them burlesque routines. D'you know the one I mean? The bloke's tellin' his pals — "She offered her honour.

I honoured her offer. And all night long, I was on'er and off'er."
D'you get it?' She chuckled, a noise like perfumed bathwater escaping.
'That's all you really want, isn't it?'

The grim waitress was back. 'We're closing,' she said. 'You want
anything else?'

'We're just leaving,' said Barbara, looking round for her jacket.
Her self-assurance startled me. I could see in the fish-eyed glance of
the slattern, how we must have looked. One well-fed lady of business and one middle-aged client, about to depart to consummate
their lunch transaction. Her face was a mask of contempt.

'Lamb chops three-an'-nine, veg platter sixpence, beer and tea
one-an'-six, that's five-an'-ninepence, ta,' said the waitress. 'Sure I
can't get you anythin' more?' She rolled her eyes to heaven.

I paid the bill. Outside, the Edgware Road was bathed in strong
sunlight. Motor cars puttered by with frightening celerity, myriad
walkers bustled past, a man pathetically encased in a 'sandwich board'
announced a sale of haberdashery at Selfridges, as we stood awkwardly
on the pavement.

'Well?' she said.

'Miss Harris,' I announced, as plainly as I could, 'I am sorry our
first meeting has ended in this awkward fashion. I would enjoy
making your acquaintance, but in a less, ah, businesslike context. I
would like, if you allow me, to take you under my wing and find
you a more congenial occupation than your current one.'

'Oh yes?' She raised an eyebrow. 'So you want to be my pal. And
what would be the point of that? What would be in it for you?'

'I see in you a young woman who deserves a better life than you
currently inhabit. A girl whose impulses towards decency have been
fatally compromised by circumstance.'

'What are you, some kind of sky pilot?'

'I will tell you in due course. All you need know for now is that
I wish you well, and will endeavour to improve your lot. I shall not
accompany you home but, if you give me your address, I will call
on you during the week to discuss your future.'

'Number 14, Queen Street, Camden,' she said. 'Ground-floor flat.
There's lots of bells. Call any time. It's pretty rare for me to entertain gentlemen callers after midnight, but you never know your luck.'

'My luck?' Once again, I was shocked almost beyond words. 'I hope you do not imagine for one second that I –'

'And while I'm partial to a little discussion, no praying, all right? Any suggestion we kneel down together, an' I'll kick you out. Got that?' She smiled. 'You can 'ave *me* kneel down in front of *you*, but that's your lot.'

Mystified by her meaning, I made to search in my Stationery Pocket for pen and notebook, with which to inscribe her address. But the press of passers-by was so busy – and their looks so disapproving – that I stayed my hand. Anyone seeing this vivid strumpet by my side could only have their suspicions confirmed, were I to be seen taking down her address *in the street*. I committed it to memory, and we shook hands. A passing motor cab rattled dangerously close to the pavement, and I ushered her aside with a touch of my hand on her waist – a simple, Samaritan gesture that she greeted with a laugh, as though I were guiding her into a dance. Her lace-gloved hand came lightly down on my shoulder.

'What you tryin' to do?' she asked. 'Sweep me off my feet?'

'I was merely trying to protect you from –'

'OI, CAB!' she cried, in the tone of a fishwife. The vehicle stopped dead, five yards away. 'Got to go. Bye now,' she said, looking at me with curiosity. 'I get the feeling we'll meet again soon, one way or the other.'

By the time I had divined her meaning, she had gathered her skirts into the motor cab and was gone.

London
9 August 1930

THINGS TO DO:

1. *Visit Arthur Trench, Holborn, about Ladies' Academy, ask re Esther and Matilda as poss. vocational students?*
2. *Boots pharmacy: talcum powder for Madge P, bunion cream for Sally A, sal volatile for Joanna D, deodorant for Bridget C.*
3. *Runaway Boys' Retreat – talk to Eddie and Howard re funding.*

4. *Previews of Coward's* Private Lives *at the Phoenix start soon. Cheap tickets on sale, Friday a.m.*
5. *Call on Emily M, Café Royal. Lunch at Bradley's?*
6. *Sermon: Galatians 5:22 – 'But the fruit of the Spirit is love, joy, peace, longsuffering, gentleness, goodness, faith, meekness, temperance . . .'*
7. *Lady Fenella R-Smith. Time for action re her rich Africa friends?*
8. *Somerset House for records of Lily Beane's parents?*
9. *Sandra (Lyons C House) – speak to Marina re possible stage work?*
10. *Barbara Harris. 14 Queen Street, Camden.*

Stiffkey
10 August 1930

Summer has filled the meadows with vivid primary colours, bright yellow marigolds, light green corn waving in abundance, red poppies, heady smell of jasmine. It is blissful to be out in the fresh air. Rose early and drove bike v fast to Sheringham in high spirits. Made 65mph around Weybourne. How speed invigorates a mind stupefied by London.

I have been looking at motor-bicycle catalogues, gazing with frank covetousness at the Brough Superior SS100, a wonderful machine with elegantly serpentine exhaust pipes curling sinuously all its length and doubling back. Its headlamps are a joy to behold. It is the Rolls-Royce of motorbikes. It is also £170, which I cannot afford. I shall go on riding my beloved 500cc Ariel Squarefour until something turns up!

Sermon well received. 'Nice to find you in such a jolly, positive frame of mind,' said Briony Jones. 'It must be the weather.'

Mrs Willoughby hung back after 11 a.m. service to say how pleased she is to put into practice my 'What Would Jesus Do?' advice. When approached last Thursday by young pedlar from Gt Yarmouth on doorstep, selling dusters, tea cloths, kitchen paraphernalia, instead of sending him about his business with flea in ear, she invited him into kitchen, fed him tea and scones and enquired about his life. Discovered that he was student of philosophy, trying to raise enough cash to fund college studies for new term at Oxford. She bought frankly ill-advised number of clothes pegs, gave him £10 and kissed him goodbye on Welcome mat. Unfortunately, seen by troublesome neighbour, and soon her largesse was talk of village. Had he been a plausible crook, not Oxford chap at all? Husband not impressed, particularly by loss of £10, supposed to be put towards summer vacation to Hunstanton.

What could I say? Assured her she was on right track re spiritual impulses. 4.53 p.m., received telephone call from Emily Murray, in tearful state. Job at Café R not working out. 'Horrible, *horrible*' working conditions was all she would impart. Must visit her, get back on straight and narrow. Perhaps Friday? All she needs is a little fortitude.

London
15 August 1930

In Regent Street, looked in at the Café Royal to see what has become of Emily; she did not last long in the kitchens. I should have predicted this. I never liked the maître d' here, a stern-faced bully who today looked at me with cold, jellied-eel eyes when I stated my business, listened with infinite ennui as I enquired after the poor girl, as though it could be no interest to him, then dismissed me with the words, 'If there are no other *relevant* questions, I'm afraid you must excuse me.' *Relevant*? As if the whereabouts of a suddenly penniless girl in London are of no moment when weighed against the vital importance of feeding Sir Ambrose This and Lord Benjamin That.

Asked in the kitchens, when MD's back turned. Head shakes all round. No, we don't know where she's gone. She left on Wednesday, there were raised voices in the Hot Beverages area, a flung teapot, tears and shouts, a dented silver sugar bowl and a slammed door. No payment, sadly, because she was taken on as probationary. No forwarding address. I am aghast at the level of neglect in this once respectable establishment.

I decided to call on her, at her shared rooms in Maddox Street, where I saw her so recently – my birthday! – with Nellie Churchill. Found Emily gone and Miss Churchill abed with fever.

'Oh, it's you, Reverend,' she said. 'I'm not well. Caught a chill from hanging about Vauxhall Gardens, and it went straight to my lungs. If it weren't for the neighbours upstairs, I don't know what I'da done.' She coughed violently.

'Where is Emily?'

'Emily? She's gone. Somewhere up on the north side, she said she was headed. Maybe to her sister Flo, who's got a little place she rents, I think it's in one of those Guinness Estate blocks.'

'Why is she no longer here?' I had to fight internally, to keep dislike and suspicion of this human icicle out of my voice.

'Why'd you think?,' said Nellie with a sneer. 'She wasn't enjoying it. They were nasty to her at the café, like I told her they would be, she done a bunk, came back here crying about having no future, and next thing I know, she's gone.'

'Would it be the case,' I asked, 'that you sent her away by crowing, in your unpleasant way, over her inability to keep a legitimate job? Would that be it? I can hear it in your voice. I can imagine how you would have jeered at her, and told her of her folly in – Oh!'

I startled myself with a horrible thought.

'Oh what?' asked Nellie, coolly.

'She has not gone back to a life on the street, has she, Nellie?' I was becoming very severe, and she knew it. 'Tell me that she has not returned to the embrace of prostitution, spurred on by your jeers and scorn?'

'No she *ain't*,' said Nellie, with a flounce. 'Whatever's happened to her, it's not my fault. If it's anyone's it's yours.'

'Mine?' I almost shouted. 'How can it be *my* fault? All my energies are spent in *saving* girls like Emily from vicious ways.'

'If you wanna see vicious ways, Reverend,' said Nellie grimly, 'you shoulda seen the way they treated her in the sinkroom at the Café. She was miserable as sin. She tried to come the kid, doing all that little-girly wide-eyed routine, and it went down bad, Rector. It might work with a gentleman client, but not with the bitch skivvies. Someone must've blabbed about her past, for they started calling her Skittles, after that royal mistress, and the boys would slip their hands round her waist and fiddle with her chest as she stood with her arms in the sink, and instead of giving them a sound wallop, she'd just weep, which made them worse. So it wasn't much of a favour what you done her.'

'It was work, Nellie, honest work for an honest wage. Better by far than taking money for intimate liaisons forbidden by the state and by God.'

'If I remember,' replied the foolish girl, 'the only intimate liaison that's forbidden in the Commandments is adultery. Everything else that's forbidden was added on afterwards by people like you. No screwing, no kissing, no dressing nice for gentlemen, it all came under the heading of adultery, didn't it? It doesn't make sense.'

'Nellie, you are a simpleton when it comes to scripture. I fear the delirium of fever may have rendered you more argumentative than you might wish.'

She seemed chastened. 'You got anything for a bloody horrible cough? It keeps me awake all night.'

'You must visit the physician in Glasshouse Street,' I said. 'He is called Dr Ledger and will help you. For your present needs, however, if you tell me where Emily has gone and where I can find her, I may have something here . . .'

I delved in my Pharmacy Pocket and from a mass of ampoules, pill packets and ointment tins extracted a tiny phial of tinct. Laudanum.

'Boil a kettle, Miss Churchill, dissolve this in five parts water, and sip the result over thirty minutes. You will find it promotes refreshing sleep and interesting, sometimes inspiring, dreams.'

She looked pleased. 'Well, thanks, Reverend. Good luck finding Emmy, if you can. And all right then, it's true we had words and I regret what I said, about her being a hopeless tart and then a hopeless washer-upper, that was a bit mean and I didn't expect her to flounce out, but Christ, she's so *stupid* sometimes. Anyway, she's somewhere in Islington or Highbury, I got an address somewhere, could hardly read her writing, something like Herbert Street, number 140 or 142. She said she'd be staying with friends of her sister Flo, and beyond that I don't know nothing, OK? And now I'm a bit tired and I think you should go.'

'Does this Florence work?' I asked, cautiously, ambiguously. When asking pros about other pros, one has to be wary of giving offence. That word 'work' is itself capable of a dozen interpretations.

'She's a chanteuse in a Palace of Varieties,' said Nellie, closing her eyes. 'It's not what you're thinking, either. She makes proper money from her voice, and she's given up the other, I mean the alternative employment.'

'That is most encouraging,' I said. 'Perhaps you might yourself benefit from her example.'

'I just don't care, to tell you the truth, Harold,' said Nellie. 'I really couldn't care less about anything any more.'

I left her to her thoughtless life and her laudanum dreams. My thoughts were for poor Emily, ensconced in squalid surroundings in north London, her apartment abandoned, her job aborted, her morale dismally low, her soft animals unlooked-after, her flatmate comatose with narcotics. How has it come to this, when all was so promising, barely a month ago?

Should I write a stern letter to the Café Royal, demanding to learn the details of her foreshortened employment? Should I have shaken Nellie, and told her to go and find her former pal and fetch her back? Should I give the whole thing up as a failure? But then I applied to myself the words, 'What would Jesus do?' and my course was clear. I will set out to find Emily Murray, and bring her safely home.

CHAPTER 4

Letter from Mrs Moyra Davidson
Stiffkey Rectory
15 August 1930

My dearest Oona,

Sometimes I think I'm going off my head here. I spent the morning searching for a screwdriver, because the lock on the bathroom door is half off and Mrs Maitland is coming to tea today to discuss the Home Management classes and there is nobody in the *world* more dainty than Mrs M when she puts a mind to it. I simply cannot have her sitting in there terrified someone's going to come in and catch her with her best bloomers round her ankles. I asked the colonel if he'd perchance have an implement of that nature in his box of tricks, and he said, 'My dear Mimi, you will recall I arrived here one day with a suitcase and two boys, and one day I will depart with a suitcase and, God willing, the same two boys, but at no time did I ever acquire a toolbox, I would be a strange house guest if I were to begin kitting myself out with a saw, a chisel and a set of nails, for you might reasonably wonder what could possibly be my intentions.' (This is the way he goes on.) I asked Nugent, who was writing letters in the parlour, to run down to the shop and find me a screwdriver, so I may reattach the lock on the bathroom door, and he did as I asked after only, ooh, an hour or two because he's writing to apply for a job in the Civil Service, very swagger I'm sure, he has the confidence of the devil, but then sure he's only just out of the college and why wouldn't he be bursting with energy and ambition after being pumped with learning for three whole years like a Strasbourg goose? I wish young Sheilagh would find proper employment for a young intelligent girl instead of (rainy days) floating round the house all day reading books or (fine days) riding Joshua Judges at point-to-point meetings in Holt and Wells. I keep urging her to go into nursing like her mother did, but she wrinkles her nose and tosses her hair and complains about having to manhandle the sick and dying all day, that she'd rather hang on for something on the stage. She's had her hair ringletted like Helen Twelvetrees, that actress in the films who's always weeping, but I can't really see my darling S as an actress, she's too earnest, she doesn't have a fluent technique. I tell her nursing is a fine career for a girl looking to make a difference in the world, but she says well, why, in that case, Mother dear, did you yourself abandon nursing to go on the stage? And I haven't an answer for that, except to say I was following a dream buried deep within me.

Anyway, Nugent came back after God knows how long and reported that he couldn't find a hammer to buy anywhere, I could have boxed his ears, it was a screwdriver I wanted.

I'm tired of this stupid story. What's really bothering me is the major. Did I tell you about the galloping Major Hammond? He was one of the *nouveau* grandees who came along twenty years back, when the land around these parts was sold at auction by the Townshends who used to own it and a yelping battalion of new squireens moved into the neighbourhood, ex-army types who fancied themselves as landowners because they'd bought the deeds to a few acres for a song. You could hear them in the Townshend Arms telling their mess pals, with their civvy suits and their suburban wives, 'Oh yairs, I own all the fields around here as far as you can see to yonder copse.' Jesus, yonder copse forsooth, they wouldn't know a copse from a hole in the wall, but they give themselves such airs, it makes me sick – me who's been here since King Edward was on the throne.

Anyway, the good major, ever since he bought the old hall at Morston, he's been dropping hints left, right and centre about wanting the churchwarden's job.

My friend Cathy Dineen is on the JP bench at Holkham, hearing cases of trespass and poaching and aggravated affray at

Cromer on bank holiday weekends. She cannot stand the way the major runs the bench and tells everyone how to think. Take poor young Edward Fenny, a simple-minded lad who's been caught fecking ripe pears from the orchard beside Blakeney Church, and selling them by the side of the road. Not a trace of compassion for the poor lad will you find in the major. 'Speaking as the local magistrate,' he says, making it sound like it's Speaking As Your Commanding Officer, 'I feel we must apply the full force of the law to this unwashed miscreant. There can be no pleas in mitigation. We must press for a conviction.'

Cathy says, 'Just a minute, Your Honour,' and he won't even look at her, like he's heard some tiny sound in the courtroom but he can't identify where it's coming from. 'All that's been stolen here are a few dozen piece of ripe fruit that nobody's breaking their necks to pick off the trees, and nobody's livelihood is threatened by a bit of schoolboy scrumping. Why are we discussing this, and conspiring to send to jail a young simpleton who is only trying to make, what, three or four shillings to buy himself a pair of shoes?'

'He Is A Thief,' says the major with that awful slow politician voice he puts on in public, 'a furtive trespasser on Church lands, a stealer of Church property. Would you, Mrs Dillon, be equally sanguine about his crime if he were to break into the church and abscond with the silver Communion chalice and the gold platter? Would you find that no matter for judicial inquiry? I rest my case.'

Well, it's Mrs *Dineen*, as a matter of fact, not Dillon, and it's not a chalice either, it's called a *ciborium*, you dish out the communion wafers from it, and the plate for the breaking of bread, that's a paten for God's sake – *platter* indeed, he's spent too much time in roadside hostelries being asked if he'd like the seafood platter, if they can interrupt his drinking, you know he drinks like a bloody fish. Poor Cathy, she's sitting there like a fish herself, opening and closing her gob with amazement that anyone could be so unfair, but she says, nonetheless, 'The pears are not holy objects. The fruit on the trees are not consecrated to God. Simony is not the issue here. Young Edward Fenny may have stolen the fruit, but it would have rotted on the branch. Rather than send him to rot in prison like one of the pears, we should applaud his enterprising spirit and encourage him to direct it into more legal and lucrative arenas.'

It was no good. The major directed the bench to find him guilty of theft and he was sentenced to three months banging metal panels in Norwich Prison. But while giving his summing-up, the major made a point of saying the purloining of property from Church premises must be discouraged in the parishes and he himself was the man to do it. Listen to him: 'We need a tighter deployment of manpower to ensure no recrudescence of such casual felonies. If the church warden at Blakeney were doing his job, this unfortunate youth would not now be losing his liberty. The work of a churchwarden must not be undertaken lightly. I shall be looking into the current arrangements in all the outlying parishes of north Norfolk, and recommending changes.' Which was pretty well saying, 'ME! Me, *I'll* be churchwarden around here. Just you try and stop me.'

What Mr Reynolds, our churchwarden these twenty-three years, will make of it, I cannot imagine. He and Mrs R have been our neighbours and best friends as long as we've been in the village. Mr Reynolds is a dear, good man, a devout churchgoer and helpful handyman. He is not equipped to fight the likes of the major, with his fearsome eye and the broken veins in his cross old face, and his blustering ambitions and his running the bench like some American lawman.

There will be a fight, mark my words. As I told you, there's no love lost between him and H and I'm fearful of the outcome. In fact, Oona dear, I think I'll go round to the Reynoldses right this minute, so had better close. Write and tell me all the news from Dublin. God, I miss the place something awful, these days, I get so lonesome with H away so much. But maybe at least Mr R will have a screwdriver to save Mrs Maitland's blushes.

Your loving friend,
Mimi

Journals of Harold Davidson
London
19 August 1930

Set out this morning to find poor Emily. Took the omnibus from Waterloo Station north to Islington Green. Had only sketchy information from Nellie Churchill, whom I left slumbering. I asked many strangers for Herbert Street and was rewarded with directions to all four points of the compass.

New shops are springing up all along Upper Street – furniture and brass appliances, dresses and hats and bolts of silk and cotton, pie and sweetmeat emporia, ironware, stationery, wine and cigars. A gratifying sign of prosperity in these doldrum times. We may not be suffering a Depression as badly as has befallen our friends in the United States, but we are far from enjoying an Elation. A new world of things, though, an outbreak of colours, can be relied upon to raise the spirits. Who would have thought the eye could be so thrilled by the sunlight gleaming on a mass of brand-new copper piping in Balcombe's Yard, or the heart so lifted by the sight of a paint lorry unloading vats of pigment, their lids leaking creamy half-moons of crimson, yellow and aquamarine?

Speaking of our transatlantic cousins, a potent image of their current state of mind has appeared in the window of the Gilbert Gallery, on Essex Road. It is a new painting called *American Gothic* by Mr Grant Wood and depicts a poor farmer, presumably from one of the 'Dustbowl' states, standing in front of his run-down homestead with his helpmeet by his side. They are clearly a long-married couple but there is something severe and unyielding about the man's looks – an unappeasable steel in his eyes, a cruelty of aspect symbolised by the pitchfork he holds – that is matched by the indomitable graceless-ness of his lady wife. One extends Christian sympathy for their resilience in the face of poverty, yet one also feels sympathy for anyone dependent on their assistance, or indeed their hospitality, for five minutes.

But the title, *American Gothic*? I know only a Gothic style of church architecture, popularised by Mr Pugin and characterised by spires and spikes, whether on arches, windows, doorways or ceilings.

What application can the word have to this portrait, unless to suggest that the Church in America is in the hands of these unsmiling (and incontrovertibly spiky) rustics?

And the Church of England? What arrangement of features, what painted, unsmiling visage would sum up the Church today? Why, surely a portrait of my old friend Cosmo Lang, once the greatest duffer that ever tried to construe Catullus in front of a teacher, more recently famous as the holder of the highest religious seat in the country. In this notional picture, he would be seated on a throne, noble as St Peter, arrogant as Saul and all-conquering as Neptune, fingering the purple satin of his archepiscopal glory, luxuriating in his triumph, wholly unable to see how the vast majority of his co-religionists live, on the long flat shore between need and comfort.

Cosmo Lang, well, well. I simply *cannot* understand his elevation to the See of Canterbury, and his pre-eminence over all of us. I am reminded of what F. E. Smith, the Earl of Birkenhead, as a young advocate, said to a judge one day, when he had inadvertently begun to instruct the jury on their duty. 'What do you suppose, Mr Smith,' said the judge, 'I am doing here on this bench?' 'It is not for me, Your Honour,' Smith replied, 'to attempt to fathom the inscrutable workings of Providence.' Quite so.

Half a mile down the Essex Road, I found a Herbert Street, but no number 140 or 142. Instead, a dismal terrace of small stucco houses petered out into a ghost estate of shuttered and condemned hovels. I had been directed to the wrong street. Tsk. I uttered a silent prayer for Emily, and set off again. Seven streets later, a friendly publican cashed a cheque for me and, on hearing my enquiry, said there was a Halberd Street not half a mile away. My satisfaction at the news was tempered by the wretched environs through which I passed on the way. The hovels of Herbert Street were like the Taj Mahal, compared to the sights which now met my eyes.

The cramped rows of two-storey brick houses – acres of them, winding into the distance like a hope fading into the future – were bad enough. So were the stinking courtyards I passed, pieces of wasteland randomly flooded with pools of stagnant water and, here and there, the backwash from the sewage. So were the horrid cellars I glimpsed from the pavement as I passed – dreadful, Miltonic catacombs, seen but peripherally, before one's eye recoiled in horror from the upturned faces below, the dim lights in the gloom of noonday, the white limbs seen through the gratings, the grim sense that perhaps a dozen human souls must live and have their being down in these shabby dungeons. I nearly turned back in despair and headed for the cheerful daylight of Essex Road. But I prayed to St Jude, patron saint of lost causes, to steady my resolve.

The worst was soon upon me. Round the corner of Halberd Street, looming over it like a beetling grey cliff, a huge tenement building, six storeys high, reared up from the pavement. There was no front door in this cliff of masonry – or rather, there were several doors but none that would admit a caller from the street. Instead, the vile construction spread tentacular concrete legs, each entwined by a mass of spiral stairwell, over half an acre of land. Through pillars, archways and walkways, one could catch glimpses of the dwellers in this morale-sapping prison. I went in as far as I could bear, and found a dozen grubby children, no more than three or two years old, playing on the stone stairs, their jerseys streaked with what I hoped was mud, their ears assaulted with the hiss and whine of the gas jets that lit their greasy faces like Caravaggio beggars.

They had no sky to look out upon, no sun or moon to tell them it was day or night, no sight of grass or river, nothing of the outside world to meet their eye, only more concrete roofs and angles, walls and stairs, gas jets and hellish courtyards. Wherever they looked, blankness looked back at them.

I felt a surge of indignation, such as I have seldom experienced, that children should have to live like this. For thirty years, I have campaigned ceaselessly to find homes for homeless boys and girls. But when I look at the homes in which the poorest are expected now to live, I could cordially wish them an early death and a roomy grave. God forgive me, it is not a Christian thought. Give me strength, dear Jesus, as thou wert strong in the garden of Gethsemane when faced with the knowledge of thy imminent suffering and death, although at least thou didst not have to put up with the foul stench that came from the great metal bins ranged along the far-left wall. I took just one step in their direction, then froze to see a score of furry bodies writhing and tumbling over each other

in a frenzy to consume some vestigial fragments of pie on a card-
board tray.

I found number 142 on the fourth floor, a vertiginous climb. The
door opened the thinnest of cracks. 'I am looking for Emily Murray,'
I told a single eye, a thin nose and a twisted mouth, through the
crack. 'I am her friend, Mr Davidson. They tell me she has moved
here. It is imperative I speak with her.'

'What's she done?' said the twisted mouth.

'She has done nothing wrong,' I said. 'She is not in any trouble.
I wish to speak to her and satisfy myself that she is well.'

'Who're you?'

'I told you. I am a clergyman. Mr Davidson is my name. Miss
Murray is a protégée of mine. I have been directing her steps and
finding her work and it is vital —'

'We don't need no sermons here,' said the face, expressionlessly.
'It's about the last thing we need.'

'*Will* you let me see Miss Murray?' I practically shouted. The face
betrayed no emotion and I could see it was about to close the door
for good. I changed tack. 'Let me in, and I will pay you ten shillings
as — as an entrance fee.'

A hand appeared at chest level, or at least some very thin fingers,
cupped together in a beggar's cringe. 'Let's have it then,' said the
face.

'Five now, and five when I have had satisfaction,' I said.

'Satis—Well, why didn't you *say* that's what you was after?' She
opened the door and I was admitted into a room perhaps the size
of Mrs Parker's kitchen in Vauxhall. The only light was a dim
electric bulb, poking down from the low ceiling. One bed and
two mattresses on the floor took up most of the space, although
a table and two chairs appeared, half hidden behind the figures.
For in the room, apart from myself and the lady doorkeeper, there
were five women.

Foolishly, seeing an older lady in their midst, I took them to be
a mother and her many daughters, a family in straitened circumstances. But a second look quickly disabused me. The women were
of many ages ranging from a barely pubertal thirteen to a prema-
turely lined two-and-thirty. Their clothes shone with the kind of

greasy patina that comes of much hand-wiping and no washing, and a rank odour of overhung lamb and citric perfume pervaded the room. The youngest girl was round-faced and ringletted, and looked up expectantly from her vantage point on one of the mattresses, like a little girl playing with her dog in a Pears soap advertisement; but she was dolled up in skirts and high-heeled shoes, quite unsuitably. The eldest, whom I had momentarily taken for the mother, sat at the table, still as a Maltese madonna, a shawl around her shoulders. Her dark eyes reflected the light from a single half-curtained window, but she would not look in my direction. The thin-faced woman who had opened the door stepped back into the shadows, gripping my five shillings in a fist. On the bed, a dark-haired girl in a dirty green blouse and a Negress in a white lace garment that accentuated her powerful amplitude, lay side by side against a bolster talking with an absorption from which no stranger's arrival could distract them.

'What's he doing here?' said a voice. 'What you let him in for?' and the sixth woman came up beside me. She had a pronounced nose, but a handsome enough face with a generous mouth, which opened to reveal surprisingly fine teeth. Her hair appeared red but may have been dyed with henna in the gypsy style.

'He's looking for Emily Murray,' said the thin-faced one, 'and then he said he was after satisfaction. So I thought –' She glanced around the packed and fetid room, as if identifying several places where sexual activity might be conducted in comfort and privacy.

'No, no, no!' I said. The stupid girl. I repeated my quest and looked around the room with a sudden wild suspicion. Could one of these defeated slatterns be my dear Emily, whom I saved from the travails of sin at the hands of a procurer in Soho? Could Fate have so changed her features that I now did not recognise her?

'. . . and so I am here,' I concluded. 'Can you help me?' I drew closer. 'Can it be that –' I faltered – 'that one of you ladies knows of her whereabouts?'

There was a silence apart from the chatterers on the bed ('Well, 'e fuckin' never dunit ter *me*,' one was remarking to the other).

'In fact,' I asked, 'is one of you called . . . Flo?'

'That's me,' said the red-haired termagant. 'What's it to you? An' what's a protterjay when it's at home?'

'But this is marvellous,' I cried. 'I am getting somewhere at last. You are a singer in the local Palace of Varieties, I believe?'

'You what? Girls, did you 'ear that?' She gazed around the room, taking in her venal sisterhood in a glance. 'I'm a well-known singer down the Palais according to his lordship here.'

There was raucous laughter. 'Yeah,' said one, 'me too. An' I *always* sing much better with me knickers off.'

'Does your sister come to see you perform?' I persisted. 'Emily, I mean?'

'Sister? She's not my sister. I ain't got no sister. I know her, she lives here, on and off, but that's it. She's not, like, *family*. Someone's been telling porky pies, mister.'

'She lives *here*?' I waved a hand that took in the squalor, the smell and the defeatedness that hung in the room like a miserable fog. I meant to imply, 'How could anyone else fit in here?' It came out as 'How could anyone *at all* live here?'

'She lives here when there's room,' said the thin woman from the shadows. 'Been turning up and going again for three weeks. Stayed here last weekend when Katrin was off working, but she came back and Em had to go. Any more'n six, and the landlords complain the privy'll break down and they threaten to boot us all out, even though the rent's paid regular.'

'But where would she have gone when there was no room for her?' I cried.

The thin woman pursed her lips and blew a little puff of air between them. The henna-haired one, Flo, said, 'Where'd you think? She went on the street. Probably met a fancy gent with one of them new Bentleys, who took her back to his place and fed her sherry and cake and tucked her up nice with a little story.'

The others laughed again. Flo seemed to be the humorist in this sorry sorority.

'And if she met no fancy gent?' I asked with some asperity. 'What would have befallen her?'

The thin woman puffed her cheeks out again. 'She'll take her chances. We all take our chances.' She raised her fist and jingled the five shillings within. 'You going now? Some of us have to get on. If she calls, we'll say you was asking for her.'

I could not wait to depart from that Calcuttan hole. 'Please take this note and make sure she receives it,' I said, writing my address and the Vauxhall telephone number. 'It is vitally important that I speak with her soon. Here is five shillings more for you – and there will be a substantial cash reward if you bring us together. Do you understand?'

'Oh, we understand, sir,' laughed Flo, the non-chanteuse. 'You can be sure you'll 'ear from us the minute she comes back from Park Lane.'

I hurried away. The smell of decay, of month-worn bloomers and stale semen, of leaking gas and bletted fruit, of lies and tidal sewage, of traded flesh and cascading rubbish bins, of twining and scrambling and greed-frenzied rats, seemed to stick to me as if it would hang around me and cling to my coat for ever. I strode through Islington like a swimmer coming up from the depths, rising up gasping, lung-burstingly, towards the light.

Letter from Mrs Moyra Davidson
Stiffkey Rectory
19 August 1930

My dear Oona,

Lovely to get your letter with all your exciting news. I am so glad Finbar's violin lessons have paid off, it is a marvellous thing to be able to fill the house with music, I mean real music played on instruments, not just having the radio on all the time like Sheilagh and Nugent. I thought all this flapper nonsense was over and done with, but not at all. Here I am in the rectory study, trying to collect my poor thoughts and in the next room the wireless is playing Jack Hylton and his Orchestra and he's singing 'If I Had a Talking Picture of You'. Such nonsense. I get distracted by thinking, well, if I *did* have a talking picture of H, it'd be a step up from what I have now, which is a silent picture of him in the living room, a framed photograph of him sitting in a chair holding one of his big cigars and looking – well, rather more crafty than sacred, truth to tell, and sometimes when it gets too quiet around here, I wish I could make it talk to me. I've got used to not seeing him all week, I mean, literally all week except for Sundays. Sometimes I feel lucky if he turns up for the Sabbath itself. Sometimes it's so late on Saturday night, I can't be bothered waiting up for him, and I go off to bed and read lovely Charlotte Yonge instead. The first I know of the presence of the Lord is when he's eating a boiled egg in his study on Sunday morning and trying to cobble a sermon together from a dozen scraps of paper and the Bible. And then God help me if I interrupt to tell him about the dead seagull in the chimney, or the liberties that the Du Dumaine children have been taking, using my writing paper for crayon likenesses. He'll only shush me and wave a hand as if to say, 'Not now, don't bother me with this trivial nonsense.'

'Harold,' I say, 'this is a home. I know it is a haven for the sick and misfortunate, a confessional for the sinful and the desperate, a place of succour and retreat for the spiritually confused. But it is first and foremost, Harold, a home, where your children live and I live, and Cook and Mrs Henryson and Enid and Polly and the dogs and, while I'm at it, Colonel Du Dumaine and his sons. It's a home where people live whom you love or at least are supposed to love when you get five minutes to devote to them in between showing your love for your fellow man in every fiddly backstreet in London, and it's no use your sitting there with your breakfast egg and your sermon text playing the great Shepherd with his Flock if you cannot even spend five minutes with your own domestic flock where they need you most, namely here in the home.'

He's surprised by this unaccustomed outburst. 'I am shocked, my dear Mimi, shocked,' he says, wiping crumbs from his lips, 'by this imputation of neglect. That I, who spend the lion's share of every day the Lord sends in working for the betterment of my fellow creatures, should be so cruelly accused of failing in my duty . . .' He shakes his head, like he's trying to get my words out of his ears. 'Would you like to suggest, in the few minutes that remain before I go to address the village congregation on matters of Heaven and Hell, where my sin of omission lies?'

All I can think to say is, 'You're never here,' and 'You never talk to me, not properly any more, and you never take me out the way people take their wives out, not even to see the pierrots at the Hunstanton Empire.' But it sounds so foolish and trivial and clingy. I know exactly what he's going to say, because he always brings up St Matthew: 'Need I remind you of the ocean of want that surges all around us? It is laid down in the Gospel of St Matthew: "For I was an hungred and ye gave me meat: I was thirsty and ye gave me drink: I was a stranger and ye took me in . . ."' I try to stop him around this part, because his voice takes on a bleating quality, and I know how it is going to end, but he is unstoppable: '"Naked, and ye clothed me; I was sick and ye visited me; I was in prison and ye came unto me." Now my dear,' (this is how he goes on, it drives me crazy) 'nowhere in St Matthew, to the best of my recollection, can be found the words, "I was a touch bored at home and ye came and took me to a dinner dance in Holt." You may search the Gospels for a month without finding the words, "I was restless and bored from spending all day gossiping with Mrs Reynolds, and ye took me to see Mr Coward in *Private Lives* at the Phoenix Theatre." I must be at my work, my darling, among the genuinely conflicted and truly wretched. But that is not to say I cannot listen to your aches and woes with a sympathetic ear. Perhaps after lunch we might discuss what is troubling you.'

You see the real trouble, Oona? I have to make an appointment to see my own husband. And that casual mention of the theatre, he knows how it cuts me to the quick. It reminds me what a stage-struck pair we were when young, him on the boards with the comic monologues, me with the lovely singing voice. I was a mezzo of course.

Did I ever tell you of the first day we met, at the Oxford Playhouse? I was part of Miss Horniman's company of Abbey Singers, and we were visiting the students from the University Drama Society. Some of us were invited to tea with the president, Sir Reginald Kennedy-Cox, and there to welcome the Irish songbirds was Harold. He stood out, not because he was tall or handsome, but because he was older than the rest of the students, properly grown-up at twenty-three or twenty-four, and he'd seen life and was a proper actor. He'd performed at the Wigmore Hall and had lived off his stage earnings to pay for his time at college. People spoke of him with respect, they called him the 'Holy Actor' as though it was amazing to find a theology student able to stand up onstage and declaim comic monologues about young boys being eaten by lions at the zoo. I liked him because all the evenings spent onstage had given him a very easy manner. His voice was low, never harsh nor quarrelsome, quite deep and musical, it sort of flowed along but slowly, a river of chocolate. Of course he was 'theatrical', but not in the way people use the word to say someone's false and untrue, he was theatrical as a way of putting a point across. He'd fix you with his intense brown eyes, and tell you about the poor boys in the East End of London he was trying to help by setting up a club where they could get warm food and play games at nights instead of fighting. He argued the case for giving every street child a proper education and start in life and training and an apprenticeship so they wouldn't need handouts from grand ladies such as myself, and he argued with such passionate eloquence, I was won over to the cause, to him and to his big brown eyes. As he got to the climax of his speech, I looked down and found his hand had been gripping my forearm for so long, I'd lost any feeling in it. You could have jabbed a pin into me and it wouldn't have hurt. 'Why, Mr Davidson,' I said, 'you have become quite carried away.' Harold clutched my little white hand in his and impetuously kissed it, with the ardour of a desert sheikh. 'I am sorry to have spoken with such heat,' he said, 'and sorry to feel your hand so cold. But perhaps something of what I have said has penetrated into your heart, my dear Miss Saurin.' And of course it had, for I never knew anybody could so arouse an audience as Harold, with that voice reverberating like the throb of an Underground train. I began to fall for him at that moment, Oona, though of course there was no question of anything happening, with him being so poor and my father expecting great things for me and the Cartwright boy in Castle Lambert. But it started then all right.

Dear me, Oona, how I've rattled on again. No time for proper news, except to say the major has been up to even worse tricks. Apart from his public attempts to wrest the churchwardenship from poor Mr Reynolds, he's taken to drinking in the middle of the day and making a scene in the church. On Wednesday, he shambled in and made a scene at the war memorial in the porch, complaining about the presence in the list of someone he hadn't liked or who was unworthy, and someone else whose name should have been there but wasn't. Mostly I just walk away from any such dispute, but this time I caught such a waft of whisky off the major's breath I had to ask him to leave. He swayed about and glared at me with such desperate eyes, I was scared for my life. That man is capable of anything. But, please God, Harold will deal with him, should he ever get home from ministering to the hungred, thirsty, naked, ill and imprisoned.

My love to you,
Mimi xx

Journals of Harold Davidson
London
21 August 1930

Emily Murray's breasts are a miracle of nature. Though she is lying on her back, they do not loll towards her armpits but poke upwards like proud hills, like Sheba's mountains in *King Solomon's Mines*, and draw the hand to them as if the first impulse of mankind were not shelter, food, drink or conquest but the impulse to stroke and caress this firm softness, these astounding hills.

Her skin is white as milk, save on her forearms and the V of her throat, which have been burnished by sunlight. I believe it is called a Farmer's Tan, the product, not of Côte d'Azur beaches, but of working in the open air under the summer's rays with sleeves rolled up and top shirt-button undone. The tanned flesh of a working girl, as she was when I found her, and as I persuaded her not to be for a moment longer; a working girl when she resumed the calling merely two weeks ago despite all my efforts, and a working girl as she remained until yesterday.

Her eyes are closed, but her lips are set in a charming pout, the face of a young woman sure of getting her way. Her teeth were always a joy to behold, so tiny and regular but for the two in front, which stuck out in a small, enchanting overbite, to rest on the soft cushion of her lower lip. Below her ribcage, the skin is taut as a sand tarpaulin, a soft down of hair making a golden meadow of her abdomen. The pudenda are neatly hidden behind a tangle of dark curls, surprisingly black and springy when her hair was always so fair and smooth. I gaze at this secret jungle, musing on Shakespeare's lines on his mistress's body – 'If snow be white, why then, her breasts are dun; / If hairs be wires, black wires grow on her head' – and thinking, Why, these *are* genuine wires – the electrical circuits of Emily's secret self, masked by her street finery, her hair dye and the stews of north London where her dismal journey took her. Here, in this jungle of wires lies the truth. Maybe the wires could be likened to a telephone exchange, a seemingly incoherent Gordian knot of flex and string which nonetheless connects disparate parts of the self, the conscience to the hand, the brain to the soul . . .

It's no good. All sermons have deserted me. To wring metaphors from every corner of experience is second nature to me; yet even I cannot elaborate a seam of instruction from the dark pubic hairs of a dead blonde woman.

My poor Emily. Only four days after my encounter with the dismal sisterhood in Islington, I am here, called upon by the authorities, to identify her body. The ladies of Halberd Street, those oily-faced wretches, gave my name as her next of kin, in order to save them-selves from implication in a police inquiry.

I asked the mortuary sergeant the reason for her death. He hummed and hawed and muttered about Exposure and how she was found sleeping on a park bench in Highbury Fields. I pointed out that it was August, and the weather not unseasonably cold. He countered by saying that, while living in an overcrowded tenement building, she had been bitten during the night by the dreadful bug known as the *Cimex lectularius*, which brought her arm up in pustules and turned her blood septic. A night or two in the open, far from airing the wound, only worsened it and when she returned to the crowded apartment, she was turned away by the sextet of b*tches and directed to go off and find a hospital that would treat her gangrenous limb.

'And consider as well,' said the sergeant, his plausible manner not quite making up for the vagueness of his words, 'what she's been up to lately. It's not just the sleeping in the parks, is it? It's doing the business with strangers behind bushes and against trees, isn't it? No telling what extra diseases they pick up in the middle of the night, is there?'

'I am surprised to hear a supposed medical orderly speak such nonsense,' I said in a voice like iron, 'but one thing is clear. Despite the evidence of insect bites, exposure, neglect and sexual abandon, she did not die from any of them.' I paused, in the vain hope that he might take in my words. 'She died of poverty.'

This was no Disraelian flourish. Being poor, being a woman and being in London did for her as surely as a knife stabbed in her back. I have seen it happen again and again until I am wearied in contemplating the scale of the problem. The last four years have seized the festering sores of poverty and prostitution, and made them infinitely worse, blown them into cancerous lumps on the metropolitan body. Since the General Strike, that brave, doomed public uprising, the working class has lost its energy, its indomitable spirit. Jobs are being shed by the score every week. The roads are filling up with unemployed carters and dockhands, farm labourers and lathe operators, colliers and shipmen. For a woman of the working class, what work is there but domestic service, or drawing beer in a saloon, or seeking a position exhibiting herself to artists or the public in a coarse revue? And when she has learned that the secret of success in each of these workplaces is to find more inventive ways of pleasing men and doing their bidding, why, what is to stop her proceeding down the final half-mile to whoredom and moral decay?

Poor Emily. She is – was – no more than twenty-three. When I met her, just six months ago, outside a pub in Rupert Street, I noticed the passivity of her nature. I took her to a café in Dean Street where I learned little of her recent circumstances but much of her younger days, her brothers and sisters, her pets, her attic bedroom, the trees in the yard in whose branches she used to hide from her indulgent, tree-climbing papa. It was like talking to a child of a mildly emetic sweetness. She seemed a girl stuck firmly in her infant world, who clapped her hands together with delight if you bought her a pastry, who laughed with the angelic tinkle of Christmas chimes if you told her stories of parishioners' follies, and who probably responded to the brutal business of sexual penetration by cries to the perpetrator to cease tickling her.

It was all a pretence. The childhood was an invention, drawn from a dozen storybooks of nursery, bathtime and barnyard adventures, of a loving mother and father, of exciting discoveries in the secret woodland. It was all make-believe. So was her breathless, ingénue surprise at everything. It was as though she had never been taken out to a beef supper before ('Is this where lords and ladies dine?'), nor to a cathedral ('But how could the painters have done them lovely pictures up so high?'); nor even for an innocent walk in Green Park in the moonlight: 'Why have you brought me here?' she would say in a breathy mumble, one hand over her mouth. 'You are not going to – *use* me, are you?'

She was an actress who seldom left off playing a virgin – a woman in her early twenties playing an urchin child in ragged skirts and off-white pants. It was a pose that, she confided to me, 'many gentlemen like'. Presumably it appealed to the kind of feeble-minded City clerk who felt himself to be a gentleman because a feathery young strumpet discerns him to be one. I cannot bear to think of the poor girl suffering in her last extremities. Nor suffering the torments of employment at the Café Royal, a position I found her, specifically to rescue her from being nightly brutalised in Soho, as she explained about her pet lamb into the ears of her straining and pounding clients. But must I blame myself? My wish was only to help her, to protect her – very well then, to save her, as one would save a robin with a crushed wing on one's front doorstep.

I am assailed with doubts. Should I have left her alone, with her babyish fantasies? Did I make her life worse or better by taking her from gutter to decency, from Soho to Regent Street? Now she lies before me on this slab, her beauty fled, her childish patter dead as carbon.

She seems to accuse me. I cannot stand to hear her say it again, for her body to breathe the words at me, through her breasts and her ringlets and her pale skin:

'Why have you brought me here? Harold? Why have you brought me here?'

CHAPTER 5

Journals of Harold Davidson
London
1 September 1930

Rather an exhausting day. The 8.05 from Wells ran thirty-five minutes late, and I suffered the ennui of sharing a carriage with Mr Hagerty, the Blakeney surveyor, all the way to Piccadilly. A dull man in a dull employment to which he is admirably suited, presiding over the placement of new traffic lights and pedestrian walkways, he seldom leaves the vicinity of Norfolk, and I had to suffer his foolish blatherings for the best part of two hours about the great Adventure of visiting the metropolis. He has been there on two occasions in the last eight years, and every detail is imprinted on his bovine, provincial memory. I learned more than I could endure of his sister's delightful home in Peckham Rye, the wonders of its indoor plumbing and drawing-room gramophone, her husband's fulfilling hobby of visiting racetracks – not horses, mind, but Bugatti automobiles – and returning home with printed catalogues of motor cars over which he pores for hours of acquisitive greed. I learned of Hagerty's forays into music halls and cinemas, which he finds racily modern, his encounters with London policemen with whom he likes to converse regarding their experiences of riots and affray in the General Strike, his plodding notations of London fashions – 'I saw a man wearing shoe-spats in Regent Street, and it were only *lunchtime*,' he said wonderingly – and his prurient fascination with urban vice. Like English tourists returning from Paris forty years ago, he dilates upon the 'sinfulness' of London with that mix of condemnation and shivery excitement that marks the furtive voyeur. If only he knew the grubby truth about the poor girls whose lives I seek to better! Perhaps he feels on safe ground employing the word 'sin' with me, anent the moral shortcomings of city behaviour. He expects some answering repertoire of clucking disapproval about the frightful times we live in, and hopes for salty anecdotes about my colourful female charges. If so, he was disappointed. I avoided any yellow-paper revelations of sordid liaisons, and recommended he visit the lovely side chapels of Southwark Cathedral for inspiration. We were both, I think, glad to see the back of each other when we parted at Piccadilly Station and he shambled off carrying his theoloditic paraphernalia, like one of Hardy's overambitious sons of toil stumbling into the heady glare of Christminster.

I was met with a show of hostility from Mrs Parker at the lodging house. Dolores and Jezzie had both called to see me on Sunday night, at midnight, then again at 1 a.m., to seek moral guidance and, discovering I was away, voiced their disapproval to my landlady, as she stood (I can imagine the ghastly sight all too clearly) in her mildewed shift and berated them for calling at an hour when, she said, 'good Christian folk should be slumbering'. She has a charmingly Victorian turn of phrase. I tried to make her see that the impulse towards confession, the redemptive nature of simple talk, knows no time or formal appointment. But Mrs P was adamant. 'I would not admit a gentleman caller at such an hour,' she stated flatly, 'and nor would I let the likes of them wake up the household with their big voices and their brassy boots when everyone's in bed. I've told you six times before, Rector,' she bleated, 'I don't know what ministry they're expecting at such an hour, but it's got to stop.'

No matter. Monday is my day for Holborn. I cut some sandwiches (hard-boiled egg and tomato, ham and lettuce), packed them into my pilgrim's scrip with two apples, distributed supplies of salve, ointment, surgical spirit, tissues, soap, shampoo, etc., in my Pharmacy Pockets, included Bible pamphlets 103, 112 and 149, *Dream of Gerontius* plus theatre tickets in my Literature Pockets, updated files on Elsie, Marina, Bridie, Lily, Sandra, Esther and Matilda in the Needy Cases Pocket, and set off.

Unusual crowds around the British Museum, summer tourists, idle road-builders work-shy in the morning sunshine, a brace of school parties, forty or fifty young scholars milling about in their uniforms. Fell into conversation with a crowd of youngsters headed for Tutankhamun exhibits who benefited, I felt, from my extemporised dilations on the Egyptian cult of worship and burial. Charming young teacher, no more than twenty-four, auburn curls, fetching dimple, was puzzled at first by my interest in her brood but responded to my little sermon on the misguided heathen fixation on Golden Sepulchres vs the Life Eternal.

One girl, charming blue eyes, shining teeth, asked about mummies and the binding of bodies – were they so apparelled, she asked, in order to meet their Maker in robes of white rather than black funeral shrouds? At a loss, momentarily, I explained they were so bound as to keep the late lamented from putrefaction while journeying home-ward to Heaven's door. Why, she asked, did not Christian burial 'think also of wrapping up the dead so they'll look their best'? I told her of the Four Last Things and the certain hope of resurrection, body intact, at the Day of Judgement. 'But what will my body be like by *then*?' she wailed. Her teacher, the dimpled one, took me aside and said that the poor child recently lost her uncle and should not be encouraged to brood on such things. I desisted, only telling her, as she was led away, that we will all meet again, reconstituted in body and soul, looking as we did *at our best* in this life.

Passed down Museum Street, wondering if my explanation was theologically sound. When we meet again, all these Christian souls now disporting themselves in these sunlit thoroughfares, shall we all look as we look now? The teacher will never appear better than in her current incarnation. Nor the blue-eyed scholar, with her finely enamelled incisors. I myself will return on that awful day looking, I presume, as I do now, in my fifty-five-year-old prime. But others? It remains a puzzle. One for the Stiffkey pulpit, perhaps. Made note in Notebook 6 from Stationery Pocket.

Looked in at Museum Tea Rooms, but nothing. Glanced through windows of George's Café in Coptic Street, received insipid wave from poor, defeated-looking Catherine, but I was not disposed to enter. Too awkward. One tries to provide pastoral aftercare, but I cannot stand bleatings about 'lack of custom/why am I here/my life is slops and insult/O woe is me that I am not on the Hippodrome stage/you promised me this, you told me that' etc. There is no fathoming the mystifying ingratitude of the Saved.

Walked to Southampton Row, looked in at Gerry's Fishmonger's and spoke with Sally Anstruther. 'It's a living, Harold,' she said, 'if you can stand gutting a sinkful of pollock at eight in the morning, but it's not what I had in mind. There's tea and biscuits at eleven. I'm not saying I'm not grateful. I just wish I didn't always go home reeking of salt cod. Nothing will shake it off. They make fun o' me in the Princess Louise.'

I pressed some Wrights Coal Tar soap into her hand and told her to pray for strength. 'A present?' she said. 'I haven't had nobody buy me soap since my mum died.' Her buxom young frame seemed to heave with emotion. I have always been moved by the rural-milk-maid type, especially when seen in disarray, with a ringlet of sweaty blonde hair falling over one eye. Small, yet bursting with goodwill, her generous hips suggesting a natural disposition to child-rearing, Sally will do well when she finds a husband among the fish-loving customers of Bloomsbury, one who will not mind her daily delving in piscine entrails, when he is guaranteed each night the God-given delights of her unsheathed bosom.

I told her of my enquiries at the labour exchange for a position as lady's maid in Chelsea, and she perked up appreciably. Gerald, the boorish owner, interrupted our sweet embraces and told her to get back to filleting the haddock or whatever duties she had to endure that morning, and I went away rejoicing. A delightful, almost-fulfilled woman with, at nineteen, a real future ahead of her.

Turned into Theobald's Road, where motor carriages and omnibuses are more plentiful than I have ever seen them. Will everyone soon own a motor car? In Doughty Street, I paused at number 48, Chas Dickens's house in 1837, the place where he wrote the latter part of *Pickwick Papers*, all of *Oliver Twist* and *Nicholas Nickleby* and the beginning of *Barnaby Rudge*, and all in two and a half years. It opened to the public five years ago, and is a place of wonder to me. Such concentration and energy! I look at his first-floor study, the writing table, the lock of his hair, the 'Dingly Dell Kitchen' with its pewter plates and warming pans, the reading desk he valued so much it accompanied him on his travels to America when he was nearing the end of his labours. One naturally imagines him alone, writing day and night to produce such prodigious masterpieces of imagination, busily inflamed with social concern, as if that were all his occupation in this tiny cell. But here was also the birthing scene of his daughters Mamie and Kate, and all the chaos and swaddling and cloacal atmospherics of tiny babies.

I know well how one is torn between fond indulgence at such familial sights and smells, and the guilty licence one gives oneself to depart from them at any pretext, and plunge oneself into the less claustrophobic arena of other people's problems.

I remember the winter day (was it 1907? '08?) when Sheilagh was yet a baby, and I arrived home from an exhausting week in London to discover she had been left for the afternoon at old Nanny Sedgwick's, two miles from home in the hamlet of Binham, while Mimi was visiting her sister, over from Dublin and staying in Norwich. Snow had been falling all day across East Anglia, and the journey home from Wells in the pony and trap was a slow progress through drifts of white powder, waist-high. Mimi was home a half-hour before me, weeping that the roads to Binham were impassable, and the tiny infant must remain overnight with her aged companion.

'Mrs Sedgwick is a mother three times over, and will know how to cope,' I reasoned. 'It is nine o'clock and the child will sleep till dawn, whereupon Sam can be dispatched to bring her home.' Mollified, she poked the fire, we talked for a while and she readied herself for bed. Then – I have never forgotten this extraordinary event – she emerged from the bathroom in disarray, crying 'Harold! Harold!' I rushed to her side. She stood in the bathroom doorway, clad in her long cotton nightdress from the Liberty department store.

'What is it?'

'Sheilagh has woken up, and you must go and fetch her home,' she said in a tone of voice that brooked no demur.

'How can you possibly know?' I asked. 'Are you a mind-reader?'

In answer, she gestured to the front of her night attire, where two damp patches made clammy circles over her nipple region. The mysteries of the female anatomy were never more mysterious to me than at that instant.

'Are you sure?' I said.

'Must I draw you a diagram?' she cried. 'Go and fetch her this minute!'

Understanding little of this mother–child collusion across the miles, I sought my bicycle, rejected it as no use in ferrying an infant, and telephoned Mr Phillips who plies a taxi service in the village. Twenty minutes later, we were stuck in an impassable snowdrift. Mr P handed me a shovel and together we dug the icy mounds from around the tyres and manoeuvred our craft – oh so slowly! – through the falling white Communion flakes.

Mrs Sedgwick greeted us like knights come to rescue a tiny Rapunzel from a castle. I took Sheilagh in my arms, swaddled in white blankets with young Anthony's tweed cap protecting her membranous fontanelle, walked her through the icy path, treacherously frozen, and gained the taxi only after minutes of dangerous manoeuvre, skidding now this way now that, my free arm clinging to gatepost, fence and bramble hedge. My hands were frozen. I twice sank heavily to the icy cobbles, clutching my precious burden, trying to rise by the strength of my right arm alone, torn again and again on the thorns of the hedgerow. The brief distance to the taxi was, may God forgive the comparison, like the road to Calvary.

Mr Phillips rotated the starting handle, I bundled the baby into the back seat and we set off for home. The frozen engine began to roar, its note an angry crescendo of cold fury becoming hot passion in these frozen wastes. Exhilarated by the success of our rescue mission, I gazed at my firstborn and watched her sweet face as she woke, emerging from that unguessable foreign land of an infant's dream. Her tulip mouth formed into a petulant moue and blew small, sucky kisses at the air. She was hungry. Mimi had been right, the secret evidence of her milky secretions confirmed. To distract the babe, I lifted her blanketed form in my arms – the lightest burden I ever carried! – and removed her cap so she could see through the windows.

'My darling girl,' said I, 'this is snow. These white precipitations are flakes from Heaven, sent to settle upon the fields and hills, the houses and trees and streets of your village, and upon the people too, on Mr Phillips, our deliverer tonight, the gentleman whose back you see before you, and upon your mother, who is now standing on the Rectory porch wondering what has become of you, and upon your hapless father's snow-white head, and upon you too. It is a boon of nature, for all its cold and sodden malignancy, for it settles on all things like divine grace covering the land and its inhabitants, binding us all, the virtuous and the unjust, in an eternal present, reminding us of the kindly folds of Redemption that will wrap us all, one day, in the bosom of the Lord, if we give up our sins and follow His precepts.'

My tiny daughter understood not one word of my elegant homily, but something happened that will never leave my memory. Her eyes gazed through the window at the falling snow, as incurious as if I had shown her one of those glass toys in which, when shaken, a snowstorm riots over a miniature hamlet. But then her eyes flicked into mine a look of steady interrogation, as though pondering these elevated sentiments, then flicked back to the window and the descending flakes, and she made, as if calling up a bitter-sweet memory, a secret smile. I held my breath – I had never seen her smile before – and thanked God for this small epiphany, and thanked Him also for the snow and ice that had occasioned it, no matter that we had to freeze and suffer for its arrival.

At home, Mimi seized the child, protested that never again would she let her stray from her loving arms et cetera, and fed her from both bursting breasts for full half an hour, while I plied Mr Phillips with hot brandy and water to thaw his frozen extremities. I built up the fire, procured some fruit cake from the larder and we ate it together like huddled refugees, and to this day I can recall no moment more redolent of family love, for all the strange upsets that befell us half a dozen years later, when I went away to war, and Mimi had a baby without my –

But these father's tales are idle nostalgia. I left Dickens's house, regained Theobald's Road, went down Gray's Inn Road and I lunched on a park bench set back from the road for the convenience of fatigued travellers, and fell into conversation with a young nanny who parked her black perambulator by the wooden seat. A comely girl of limited social graces, she met my enquiries as to her employment, her address and her current state of mind with a guarded hostility that one finds too often in young women nowadays. My genial enquiry as to which music-hall performer she would like to meet fell on stony ground. I turned the conversation to the Stimulation of the Infant Mind, and the folly of too early an exposure to language-learning, and we were away for half an hour, as she complained about her employers, their insistence on her holding up cards for the infant, showing the words 'CAT' and 'APPLE' and 'BONNET' and even 'POLICEMAN'. I agreed vigorously about the importance of giving children the freedom to wander in the wild wood of fairy tales and nursery rhymes. She listened with interest to my tales of Sheilagh and Nugent in the nursery, their screams and laughter as we enacted together the tale of Hansel and Gretel and the crone in the Gingerbread House. But I went too far. Emboldened by our brief acquaintance, I acted the part of the Witch and, while demonstrating the scene in which she prods Hansel in the rib to determine if he was fattened enough to eat, the young lady took fright. Such a fuss, when I merely poked her playfully in the chest and said (in character, of course), 'There needs to be more meat on this girl before she is ready.' She shrank away, gathered the remains of her luncheon, her hat and the perambulator, and fled down Fetter Lane.

I watched her flight (women run so oddly, do they not?), tinged with concern that she may have misinterpreted my little performance as an attempt at seduction. How could she know that for years I acted on stages from Oxford to Bayswater, in student and amateur theatricals? I can, when occasion demands, impersonate a fearsome predator, as easily as I can a saintly family doctor. The stage has always been my second calling. I cannot help it if the suspicious-minded see the performance, rather than the kindly Samaritan behind it.

The afternoon passed agreeably in the Public Records Office, as I sought the documented provenance of Lily Beane. A splendid girl, full of vim and zest but with no discernible ambition, she channels all her energies to whatever is immediately in front of her: laundering (Oh! her rhythmic drubbing of a washboard), selling fruit from a stall at Greenwich Market, buttering rolls in licensed premises on the Strand, talking to men sixteen to the dozen – such undisciplined enthusiasm! How does Browning put it in 'My Last Duchess'?

                                              'She had
A heart – how shall I say? – too soon made glad,
Too easily impressed; she liked whate'er
She looked on, and her looks went everywhere.'

I arrived in her life just in time to stay her from sliding into exploitation. I have an instinct for these things. I knew it would be only a
matter of weeks before some foul opportunist enlisted her good-
natured *joie de vivre* for venal purposes. I saw the way they looked at
her in the Jolly Gardeners in Putney – the leery gang of off-duty
lawyers' clerks and fly-by-night office boys who beguile the female
bar staff with lies about their status, and lure them to casual indecency
in omnibus shelters. I know how these convivial evenings of conversation and piano-centred hilarity can conclude with invitations to less
innocent revels elsewhere. 'Parties' – that simple word that covers a
multitude of vices, the social obsession of the last decade, along with
the multicoloured folly of 'cocktails' – have come to represent all the
headlong sinfulness of the modern age. I am no wet blanket when it
comes to social gatherings. Many are the times I have entertained the
Rectory company with recitals – sometimes a little near the edge of
propriety! – from the music hall and the dramatic stage. But the parties
to which young Lily was invited, Friday after Friday, left me sitting
in the snug chewing my fingernails with concern for the fate of the
poor girl in the company of such reprobates.

As soon as I could, I engaged her in conversation at the bar, talked
with fervour about the danger she faced from plausible youths with
too much drink in them, how they would lead her astray with promises of love. She laughed at me. She *laughed* at me!

'You don't know much about the boys round here, mate,' she said.
'They're a long way off talking about love. What century're you livin'
in?' She yanked the beer tap until a pronounced blue vein stood out
on her cottoned forearm.

'I assume a young woman of your disposition will not suffer local
louts to paw you like a piece of veal when you are so evidently –'

'I don't let anyone take advantage of *me*, matey, thank you very
much,' she remonstrated – her bright brown eyes like button mush-
rooms agleam in a stew – 'and I don't so much as kiss a boy unless

he's told me about his folks. Once they tell you about their folks, you know they're not wrong 'uns. And even then, it'll take more than a bit of chat to make me go home with nobody, because I got to be up for work, dead early.' She paused, handed over two foaming pints to a pink-cheeked, high-collared young City type, no more than eighteen, took his money with the words, 'Thank you, 'andsome.' You could almost hear the dereliction of her morals in the immediate future, crashing down in a matter of weeks.

'You have a friendly disposition, Lily,' I said. 'It's what makes you so popular. You are generous, good-natured, and wish to see the best in people. But do you not realise it is this idealistic nature that renders you a prey to ignorant men who misconstrue your warmth as – as an invitation to come closer?'

'You don't have to worry about me,' she said with a brassy laugh. 'I'm a good girl. I don't go anywhere I shouldn't with boys. Well, not unless they're goin' to treat me like a lady, and buy me a nice roast supper at the Stockpot.'

There, in one sentence, is the reason for my presence among these young victims! Poor creature, she could not see that she had already entered the sloping path that leads, with increasing celerity, to the shanty towns of Hades. Part of my mission is to educate foolish youth about the economic underpinning of impurity. Male behaviour which they would not countenance on sober first acquaintance, they will accept as due reward for being bought dinner and port wine at a squalid men's chophouse in Panton Street. The first impulses towards prostitution, I have often said, arrive with the appearance of the à la carte menu. Sexual abandon that results from misconceived notions of love I can understand, as I have had to understand them in my own family. But sexual abandon that results from gratitude for soup and pork loin with gravy – that is an index of the corruption that threatens to engulf us.

I have worked at the cause of Lily Beane for months, removing her from the public taverns, finding her work as a life-class model in a respectable art establishment in Shaftesbury Avenue, where her sturdy physical architecture and winning smile have proved immensely popular.

I am glad to see Lily safe for the present. But there is no end in sight for my work among the fallen. At times I despair of my chosen occupation. An image comes to me in a dream, some nights, in which I am standing in a great corn meadow through which girls in white shifts are running – so many girls, spread out across such a wide region the eye can hardly take them all in – and I alone know that they are running towards a cliff, an unseen, mighty precipice over which they will surely tumble to their doom. I endeavour, in the dream, to catch them up in my arms, to break their headlong rush, to save them from perdition and put them down in a place of safety, but as they hurtle towards and past me, I see that only a handful can be saved, and a swoon of hopelessness comes over me, and my feet drag as though through treacle, and more and more of the wild children in their fluttering nightshirts appear over the horizon until I am tormented with frustration as to where to run first, trying to save the ones nearest, as they approach, speeding past my outstretched arms . . .

I ended the day in Drury Lane, with Marina Carter and her company of girls, professionally occupied in sin. We talked about Elsie Teenan, and about Joanna and Lily, and where they have gone to better their employment in this wicked town. Madge and Sara came by and we opened some bottles of sherry wine and elderflower cordial, and one of the girls procured a modest fruit cake with three candles to represent Mrs Carter's three decades on earth. There were toasts, and Sara played show tunes on the pianoforte and I was prevailed upon to sing 'She was Only an Engineer's Daughter', a favourite of mine for all its bawdy sentiments, and was rewarded by Blanche, the Jamaican mulatto, sitting on my knee and giving me girlish kisses with her enormous juicy lips. The evening wound down with the arrival of some off-duty constables who were disposed to fuss but were ushered upstairs to 'inspect the facilities' as Mrs Carter charmingly put it. She was pleased with my modest gift of beauty preparations, and promises to divert some of her profits towards my Virtue Reclamation League. Another reason to celebrate this long day.

Called in on Jezzie at midnight, offering to take her for coffee at the Up All Night in Spitalfields, but she was slumbering. Called to rouse Dolores in Aldgate at 1 a.m., to reiterate the importance of her rising early for shorthand lessons; she remains grumbly and ill-tempered about the fate of Max, her fancy man, now awaiting trial, and sent me away (aided by her unpleasantly suspicious landlady). Home at 3 a.m., to find a note from Mrs P pushed under my door, saying a Miss Harris had been calling at the house, and that she, Mrs P, didn't think she could stand 'no more of this kind of thing'. I slumbered in my chair, dreaming of nannies, fish, gingerbread houses, birdcages and an urchin girl asking, 'Why have you brought me here?'

Woke at 6 a.m., resolving to visit Barbara H as soon as possible.

CHAPTER 6

Journals of Harold Davidson
London
8 September 1930

To the Windmill Theatre with Joanna Dee, my aspirant ballerina, saved since June from patrolling the streets of Fulham. A charming show, with new costumes and burlesque songs that I always enjoy at this venue, although a new crudeness has, I feel, crept into the stage tableaux. Naked girls in neoclassical posings, impersonating 'Hylas and the Nymphs', offer an affecting sight to those who follow the charming tales from Homer, and who can, like I, look upon the pink areolae of the water babies without immoral yearnings. But I felt their sinuous writhings around the loins of a rather well-built Hylas went beyond the boundaries of strict classical authenticity. Delightful, nonetheless. Miss Ariadne Love (not, I suspect, her name at the baptismal font) was a dream in a lurid skirt of dangling bananas and cigars, singing 'Take Me Back to Old Havana, Where the Jasmine's Still in Bloom' most affectingly. Dear Joanna thrilled by it all and clapped her hands together spontaneously in glee. I hope her enthusiasm will direct her steps at the Kennington Dance Academy towards more, shall we say, *decorous* roles in the classical repertoire than those on show tonight.

I spotted Sir Tristram Pope in the crush, and saluted him with a cry of friendship, hoping to introduce him to my young companion, who enjoys meeting titled men who may help fund her balletic studies. To my surprise he hurried away, like the Fleeing Man in a German melodrama, but not before I spied his lady companion – none other than Eleanora Gilpin, late of the Pig & Whistle in Bow.

Well, well, how pleasant that she has found so eminent and moneyed a patron. And how splendid she appeared in her expensive broad-brimmed hat, though its elaborate finery, clamped to her shingled blonde mane with hair clips, is hardly the thing for an evening at the theatre. I must call on her, in her Bethnal Green apartment, to check on her progress, assuming she has not found herself in a more glamorous address!

London
10 September 1930

Paid a visit last night to my dear Rose Ellis in Camden. She is back with her parents for two years now, settled and comfortable, if a little frayed at the edges. Her father, retired at sixty from too many years' exposure to building-work dust, greeted me with his habitual Irish decency and pressed upon me the bottle of potato poteen he keeps in a kitchen cupboard. It is a reflex action to him, to offer this moon-shine concoction to every caller to his house. He should know my teetotal habit, he should remember the hundred times I have waved away his poisonous generosity when visiting Rose, yet still he persists. Poor man! His household is a dimly lit haven for Rose, after her many difficult years of confronting both the demon Alcohol and the sadness that periodically descends upon her beautiful violet eyes and pitches her beyond every stratagem of Christian reassurance.

Mr Ellis and I conversed desultorily for several minutes while waiting for Rose to appear. His talk is full of irritating Catholic asides: 'I've a few good years left in me, Father, DV,' he'll say, meaning *Deo volente*, 'God willing', an admirable ejaculation maybe, but not one that is found on the lips of any responsible Protestant believer, smacking as it does of a Muslim Arab punctuating his pronounce-ments with 'Insh' Allah' at every turn. And I am not 'Father' to him or anybody else except for my children. That tiny papist homage, that pregnant 'F' word, hangs between us with a small dusting of sarcasm, as if he regards me as a fake pastor, a second-best clergyman.

'Rose, well, she has her ups and downs,' he said, 'but on her bad days, there's no reasoning with her. A sponge of misery she is now,

Father, soaking up every small hardship like the parched earth soaks up rain. I pray to the Blessed Virgin to intercede with the man upstairs to put the light back in her eyes, but, sure, what can you do when she spends all her time broodin' and snifflin' and . . .'

After fifteen minutes I could stand his maudlin defeatism no more (or his dreadful Mariolatrous heresy, or his insulting demotic about the redeeming God as a kind of first-floor lodger) and asked, with an abruptness bordering on incivility, if Rose was at home. He left the room, and I cooled my heels and examined their dingy wallpaper and endured the smell of greens and bacon, until the door reopened to admit my dear Rose, steered into the room by her rebarbative parents who stood alongside her like sheepish gaolers.

Her golden hair was matted into slender ringlets, making her long, soulful face even longer – an El Greco saint, or martyr. She was clad in an old-fashioned Victorian white blouse with an amber bijou clamped at the neck, an unbecoming brown skirt in some fusty fabric, the whole ensemble enveloped in a housecoat of patterned wool that reached to the floor.

'Rose, my dear –' I clasped both her hands, as I surveyed her over-lagged frame – 'how good to see you! Forgive the lateness of this visit, but I was attending a homeless benefit in Euston, and my mind was filled with thoughts of you. It has been too long since our last meeting. I left you in June hoping that you might attend one of my Saturday soirées in Vauxhall. But seeing no trace of you, I reasoned that you had more pressing social engagements.'

I stopped. Released from the supporting hands of her parents, her body swayed back and forth like an aspen under the breath of a summer zephyr. Her eyes sought to focus on mine, and a sigh escaped her lips with a fugitive whiff of mint.

'Harold,' she said thickly. 'Harold, I –' As her thoughts struggled to form themselves into words, I realised she was the worse for drink. The aroma of toothpaste was overpowering.

'I been dreaming of horses,' she said, in a dull monotone, 'great white horses with streaming hair, galloping along the seashore. I thought I was riding one of them, only the horses in front kept charging off to the right, and the others that rode faster than me were galloping off to the left and all I was doing was running towards the sea, with no horse under me at all, and what good was that?'

She was sadly disturbed, my lovely Rose. Her father gazed at the floor neutrally, as if this were an occasion of blame and, wherever the blame could affix itself, it was certainly not to him. Her mother held my gaze as if asking how much of her daughter's current state was due to our friendship over the last ten years.

'Rose,' I said, 'I am shocked to see you like this. Sit down beside me here and tell me how you are, while your mother –' I waved an importuning hand, confident that no mother in England would refuse the classic clergyman's request – 'will bring us a cup of tea and leave us to discuss your troubles in private.'

Rose sank obediently down on the threadbare ottoman and, gathering her housecoat around her spindly shoulders, gave me her attention. Her parents slunk away. I had not criticised their obvious neglect of my old friend; and their relief was palpable.

'I've been very bad, Harold,' said Rose when her parents had departed to the dark regions of tea and kitchen smells. 'Sometimes I don't get up 'til three, when the light outside's changing to dusk, and the day is gone. I don't see no one for days. When there's visitors to the house, Dad'll say, "Put on some clothes and a bit of lipstick and come down to join the company for the love o' God, or they'll think we've murdered you and stuffed you in the attic." So I do what he says, and I try to talk, but I never know what to say to anyone no more, since I stopped hanging around with Violet and Ruth and the girls. I can't talk to people any more, that's the truth. I lost the art, if I ever had it.'

'Rose,' I said, 'you give up hope too easily. I had not thought domesticity would be such a trial. When you abandoned your old life, I thought steady work in the textile warehouse would give you a new community in which to thrive. When that failed, we tried the outdoors employment offered in the tulip beds at Kew Gardens, but you ran away from it –' I clamped my hand on her arm – 'you *ran away*, my dear, like a cat from a garden hose, saying it did not suit you. As if ministering to plants and flowers were not preferable to your ministering to strange men in Smithfield.'

'I know, Harold,' she said, shaking her sad ringlets. 'God knows I've tried. But the girls in the warehouse were horrible to me, they'd make out I was low and stupid and in the canteen they'd say to the skivvy, give her more potatoes, them Micks live on potatoes, until I'd cry. And the gardens at Kew were lovely in the summer with red camellias and the foam of apple blossom. But I couldn't stand the cold once October came, and the ground was hard and they made me poke the soil night and day. It was so hard, it was like poking sheets of iron with a thimble. And the gardening sergeant, he'd be nice one minute, and say, that's a fine bed there, the drills of seedlings in nice straight rows, marvellous, and before you knew it he was putting his big hands round my hips and saying, "Rhythm rhythm, you've got to *work* with the soil, shoving in the seeds this way and this" – and all the time, Harold, he'd be behind me pushing away while pretending to apprentice me, pushing so rudely until I could feel something that wasn't a dibber–stick at all.'

'Rose,' I said, 'I am so sorry. There is no reckoning the base appetites of men. But I gather, from your father and from your appearance, that your stay at home does not fulfil you either?'

'Bored, Harold,' she said. 'Bored bored bored. I'm so dull at home I could cry. And I do, every day.'

Her beautiful eyes were shining with liquid salt as she clutched my arm.

'We had such laughs together, going to the music halls in the old days, meeting them funny people you used to introduce me to. Them days, I felt I could do anything because you cared for me. When we went around together, I felt like a real person. I used to think, so bloody what if the showgirls look at me sideways and ask, "Who's she?" and "Who invited *her* backstage, into this bar or this hotel?" I could stand all their fish–eyed looks because I knew, well, at least the rector thinks I'm someone worth knowing. At least he talks to me like I got half a brain. I could endure anything because I knew you loved me.'

This was a little hard to take. Had I really told her such a thing, in those words? Of course I was fond of her and had taken her to shows, as I do so many of my young charges, to invigorate their sense of the wondrous drama that might one day fill their lives. But she has clearly been nursing a private delusion. I could not speak of love to her. I am a married man, the pastor to a village of dependants and a city of lost or about-to-be-lost souls. Love is an irrelevance in all this. Her solitude has invented a love between us.

'Rose,' I said, 'let us strike a deal. You must pull yourself together, read from the Book of Job in the Bible and stop abandoning yourself to misery. In turn I will promise to take you away from here and find some employment, no, some adventure, that will return a spring to your step.'

She looked at me sadly. 'I'd give anything to get away, Harold. But you won't send me back to the gardens, will you? I couldn't stand that.'

'My dear Rose,' I said, almost laughing, 'I will not *send* you anywhere. I am no evil slave-driver, like Mr Svengali in Du Maurier's book. *Together*, we shall find some employment that will fulfil and gratify you, until you are sufficiently invigorated to do something more cheerful with your appearance and dress. In three months, you shall be living in pleasant rented rooms in, I don't know, Pimlico or Bloomsbury, with fresh flowers in the hall and a white linen cloth on the table –'

'I'd love the white tablecloths,' she whispered.

'– and at the close of day, Rose, we shall meet as friends in the old delightful way, and visit the amusements of Shaftesbury Avenue and go on excursions to Tooting Common and Greenwich Park, and walk in the sunshine and watch the nannies and the bicyclists. You shall make new friends, and show off your finery on picnics. And you shall, perhaps, help me with my work sometimes when your own duties are not too arduous.'

'I *will*, Harold, you must count on it,' she said with new energy (my strategy was working better than I could have hoped). 'For there is no kinder, sweeter man than you, and I would like to help with the poor misfortunates.'

As I left, I reflected that nothing guaranteed her rehabilitation more than her blindness to her own status as the most dismal girl of my acquaintance. Once a fallen woman starts to feel sympathy for the wretchedness of others, she is on the path to recovery.

I did not seek out her parents. I left with a glow of satisfaction, that I could restore the meanest of God's creatures to life by a few simple promises.

Outside, I recalled that Barbara's address – 14 Queen Street, Camden – was only a few roads away, and I made the journey in short order. No traffic came or went (it was well after midnight). It was an ugly street of brick tenements. The moon hung above a shut-up public house, the Greyhound – and a single gas lamp at either end of the street illuminated the dismal flagstones and doorways. I found number 14, a common lodging house on three storeys, with an array of eight doorbells, beside each one a name on a dirty oblong of paper. The lowest one read simply, 'BARBARA'. Impetuously, I pressed the bell. A muffled jangle sounded inside the ground-floor window. Moments passed, a feeble light flicked on and was as quickly extinguished. Voices could be heard, one girlish and querulous, one male and indignant. I stood, inches from the window, uncertain as to how to proceed. When all had been quiet for minutes, I rapped softly on the window.

'Barbara?'

The reply was instant and unwelcoming. 'Just piss off, will you? It's one in the bloody morning.'

It was she. Miss Harris. I recalled her invitation to call 'any time', and was, frankly, disappointed. Seeing a crack in the curtains, I put my face to the glass, in the hope of perhaps alerting her to my presence.

Abruptly, the right-hand curtain twitched aside. A large black face looked out. The moonlight bounced off white teeth and the enormous whites of his eyes. Discretion was the better part of valour. I fled away.

London
12 September 1930

Visited Lady Fenella Royston-Smith. Her suite at Charing Cross Hotel is even more sumptuous than the one at the Ritz – which palatial address she has abandoned, *pro tempore*, after some altercation with the Food and Beverages staff over some detail of diet.

'Onions, Harold, they *would* serve onions in every dish that appeared before me. There was no escaping the pungent under-taste in every soup, every ragout and roast, every luncheon omelette and teatime savoury. I told them, time and again, "No onions, not in casserole nor mixed grill," but they would persist in their sickening, Frenchified obsession. I told Mr Ross, the general manager, onions *do not agree* with me, that my nervous metabolism cannot digest the damned things, that they bring up the colonic flux and leave me prostrate for hours on the chaise longue. Yet would they heed my simple requirements?'

'It must be very troublesome, Fenella,' I concurred.

'Troublesome! Nobody knows the torments I suffer. The other day, in St Bride's − a memorial service for Lady Henchard's late husband − I was so crippled with indigestion, I was forced to forsake the family pew and take a turn around the graveyard to regain my composure.'

Lady R−S is a handsome woman and a steady benefactor of my work, but she can sometimes offer too much insight for comfort into the workings of her intestines. She enjoys the aristocrat's conviction that every detail of her personal circumstances must be of interest to her confidants. I am glad to be one of this fortunate band, but sometimes the reports of her gastric eructations leave me at a loss, conversationally. (What am I to reply? 'A huge fart can be a marvellous liberation at such moments, Your Ladyship . . .' ?)

Since her husband, the brigadier, died face down in the mud along with a platoon of doomed infantry somewhere near the Belgian border in 1917, she has devoted herself to good works. A philanthropic soul, she has taken an interest in my Runaway Boys charity for many years. She has a wide social acquaintance with more liquefiable cash than they know what to do with. Without her, and their, monthly disbursements and ad hoc stipends, I could not continue my work among the Fallen. All she wants in return is some elevated literary conversation, and some shared outrage about public immorality.

'That madwoman Mrs Stopes has established yet another clinic in London where women of any class may procure contraceptive devices, and has now written a book flagrantly recommending the introduction of some form of' − she seemed to wince at the awful words – 'rubber tubing into the marriage bed. She encourages the benighted and the shamelessly perverse to take their sordid pleasures with no thought to consequences, to couple together like hares in a field – and I should add, Mr Davidson, she claims divine sanction for her folly.'

'No,' I said, heatedly. 'This is too bad. I have heard a great deal of Dr Stopes in the last few years, because my work leads me, as you know, into the realms of prostitution, where matters of sexual health are routinely discussed. But of her pretensions to religious endorsement, I was unaware.'

'Oh yes,' said Her Ladyship, vigorously nodding, 'I heard it from my maid. The dreadful woman said in court somewhere that her zealotry in this murky business springs from a divine visitation she had one afternoon, under a yew tree in her garden in Leatherhead.'

'My word,' I said, stifling a guffaw. 'A Home Counties Buddha – and a female to boot!'

'Her disgusting sexual fantasies are bad enough,' said Lady Fenella, 'in encouraging loose girls and factory women to fornicate with men, free from concerns of pregnancy, let alone morality. But to claim that Our Lord recommended such a course of action, as it were *privately*, in the ear of an hysterical Surrey quack is just too much.'

'I am almost accustomed to being shocked,' I said. 'Every day brings fresh news about the degradation of feeling and behaviour in modern life. That is why I wished to speak with you about –'

'Immorality is all around us, Harold,' said my old friend. 'Have you seen the dimensions of the skirts worn by young girls in Knightsbridge today?'

'I rarely venture to such select locations. My work keeps me confined to Piccadilly and Holborn. I rely on you, as in so many things, to keep me abreast of fashion.'

'I've seen young women walking into Harrods, Harold, in a skirt that reveals their calves, sometimes almost to the *knee*,' she said, her voice rising to a protesting squeak. 'The other day, I was popping in to buy a crystal vase for Lobelia Graham's wedding, and in front of me came this – this trollop in a long coat that opened to reveal a skirt so tight around the hips, it must have constricted her circulation. Were it not for a tiny flounce of fabric around the hem, it would have displayed the place where her hosiery ended! But I have shocked you, Harold, for your face has reddened alarmingly.'

'Not at all,' I said, applying a handkerchief to my brow. 'Do continue.'

'I thought she must be a tart, plying her trade in Brompton Road. But the doorman bowed with every sign of recognition, as if she were a regular customer.'

'I can only hope,' I said with feeling, 'that such fashions, if that is the word for such immodesty, do not spread as far as my dear girls in Norfolk.'

We stood together, shaking our heads in a chorus of disapproval.

'Fenella,' I said, 'my visit here today has a purpose beyond the delight of basking in your company.'

'Oh?' She rose from the sofa, smoothed her skirts and moved towards the window.

'Not, I hasten to say, money,' I reassured her, 'for you are more than generous already to my young charges. I wish to ask you the favour of an introduction.'

'Indeed. To whom?'

'You have been good enough to bring my work to the attention of dignitaries from many walks of life,' I said, 'and I have forged several relationship that have been invaluable to my work. Words cannot express my gratitude for so many favours done in the past. Without the patronage of your cousin, Lord Strathclyde, there would be no Runaway Boys' Retreat at Whitechapel. Without the intervention of your neighbour, Lady Kilfoyle, the Maidens in Distress Foundation at Bow would never have got off the ground. Had it not been for the generosity of Lord Staynes, and the Romany Rye Rehabilitation Unit, there would be a thousand homeless didicois on the streets of Sutton and Cheam. Were it not –'

'Too kind, Harold,' cut in Lady R–S, over her shoulder, as she peered through the glass to the view over the Strand. 'Awfully glad to have been of help. But what you're looking for now is . . .?'

I joined her at the window and, with slightly shocking directness, took her hand in mine. Did she flinch? Only for a second. Her long chilly fingers suffered the embrace of my insinuating touch (my hands are always warm) and seemed to thaw as I said, 'Fenella, no man could wish for a finer benefactor than you, but that is not the point. For no man could wish, either, for a more sympathetic friend to turn to in the dark reaches of the night, a more understanding ally to draw close when all seems lost, a warmer image to summon up before him when one is surrounded by the cold winds of despair. Fenella —'

With (I admit) shocking presumption, I encircled her considerable waist with my arm, and turned her away from the window so that I was looking up into her eyes. It was, may God forgive my lack of gallantry, like turning a dreadnought battleship 180 degrees to port in the Solent, but it was worth it.

'Fenella,' I said, softly.

'Yes, Harold?' she whispered. It was a romantic moment, or would have been had she not towered a good eight inches above me. Her prodigious bosom, wrapped in some cantilevered phenomenon of whalebone and rustling red silk, protruded before me like a vast cushion. I looked up, like a besieger looking over a wobbling battlement, to her handsome, troubled face.

'What you do, my dear Fenella, you do from many impulses — of *noblesse oblige*, of Samaritan generosity, of Christian decency. But I alone know that you do it from love.'

'Oh, Harold,' she breathed, 'what do I know of love any more? Since Augustus died, I have been a stranger to the tender emotions. While all around me have danced through their middle years, and some have found other partners, I have kept faith with Gussie. My sister took me to a ball at Nancy Cunard's, full of nigger minstrels and with a tiger from Sumatra and an ice statue of a swan whose beak some of the brazen flappers actually *licked*, and I was miserable throughout because there was no lovely Gus to lead me through the polka steps, and I went home early and cried into his dressing gown which stank of pipe tobacco, and I hugged it like a madwoman.'

'My poor Fenella,' I cooed into her bosom, startled to be allowed such intimacy. She laid her drooping head upon my neck and sobbed. Her cheek was hot against my skin.

We stood in an awkward embrace. I had, I confess, not the faintest idea what might happen next. I have known Fenella for years, ever since my work in London restarted after the war, and we have been through much together. Through night shelters in Pimlico and day-care homes in Stepney, I have introduced her to the needy and the profligate, to whom she has talked and proffered advice most helpfully over the years.

At first, the recipients of her advice did not find her engaging; she tended to address them like a duchess ticking off delinquent parlour-maids. She was always a little *too* intent on getting to the meat of their sufferings. Sometimes, it seemed she regarded them as turns in a burlesque show. 'Are you an Alcoholic?' she would ask. 'Are you a Prostitute? Did you become a Prostitute in order to Feed a Baby Born Out of Wedlock? To what level of indignity did your employer abuse you?' But I took her in hand, taught her to soften her voice, forsake her more intimidating hats, and learn to listen. It took a while.

Cynics might object to the enthusiasm with which she seeks out tales of sinfulness, and the relish with which she imparts the details of her findings to friends at lunch parties, but I know her impulses are pure. Disappointed by life, she has found a cause, as I have devoted my life to many causes, and she has stuck to it. Kindliness and sympathy have been her watchwords, and her transactions of money into my charitable funds have been the happy public outcome. Without her, I would eat bread and beef-dripping sandwiches every day, like the hapless masses in Lincoln's Inn Fields.

Was I wrong to embrace her thus, as she fretted over her dead husband? I am a tactile man. If it is a fault to translate emotional generosity into physical expression, then I own up to the fault unreservedly. The girls among whom I move in London are used to my gentle embraces, my occasional bestowings of chaste kisses. They know the innocent pressure of my arms around them, telling them not to fear. What harm can be done by offering the occasional close contact of the notional swain – the touch of love that we all secretly crave? And had our lips met yesterday, I would not have been surprised nor dismayed. There is a passion in the pursuit of virtue that must find an outlet sometimes, even in salivatory exchanges. I thought of my recent sermon: what would Jesus have done in similar circumstances? I have no doubt at all that he was a kisser. His relations with Mary Magdalene must have involved a degree of embrace and osculation, I am sure. His visits to the house of Martha and Mary would have ended in a flurry of fleshy connections in the doorway. I allow myself the thought that, while the one busied herself with household chores and the other was devoted to prayer and virtue, Our Lord might have stolen a kiss from the former, while the latter had her eyes shut in supplication. I can imagine him encircling Martha's aproned waist from behind, as her hands in the sudsy water paused in their cleansing digitations, and her lovely head (I see curly fair hair darkened by the sweat of her labours, white if irregular teeth, skin like a white Egyptian peach) turned round, her eyes half anxious, half incredulous that this could be happening, her Cupid's-bow lips parting, as he bent forward . . .

Lady Royston-Smith withdrew from my arms quite suddenly, with a forcefulness that suggested I had gone too far.

'You were, I believe, about to enlist my help in an introduction, Mr Davidson?' Suddenly, we were back on formal terms.

'I know, Fenella, that you are a friend of Sir Arthur and Lady Bassenthwaite,' I said, pulling my clerical jacket around me.

'Arthur and Frederica? Of course. They are old friends. Frederica's mother knew mine in Ashford. But I haven't seen them for years. I believe they live in Africa.'

'Indeed, they have spent the last three years in Kenya. But I notice from today's *Times* they are sailing for England, to resume residence in Eaton Square. I would not trouble you to bring my work to their attention, except that Lady Bassenthwaite has for years worked for a charity bringing comfort to distressed gentlefolk of the region. Now she is back in London, she may be looking for a fresh outlet for her kind work . . .'

'And you thought she might have some spare cash to steer towards your – ladies?' A steely note had entered her voice.

'All I ask, Fenella,' I said, 'is that I can meet them, with your help, and lay before them the size of the social problem that surrounds, for several miles, their comfortable Belgravia home.'

'Well –' she seemed fatigued by being asked for one more favour – 'I'll have to see. They'll be acclimatising to their new life, and I don't want to burden them with –'

'If I could guarantee a bishop would accompany me to the meeting?' I said. 'Might that smooth things?'

'Of course, Harold.' (Suddenly we were back to Harold and Fenella; how Lady R-S loves the purple.) 'You envisage a tea party? Here?'

'That would be ideal.'

'Perhaps. I'll have to speak to Frederica when she has docked. But apart from the expatriates and the bishop, is there anything else that might enliven the occasion?'

'I fancy,' I said, neutrally, 'I could bring a misfortunate girl – or two – to join our company, purely to demonstrate the scale of the problem.'

She pondered the arrangement: teatime at the Charing Cross Hotel with one peeress of the realm, one rector, one bishop and at least one prostitute, possibly two.

It was too good to turn down.

'Shall we say Friday fortnight?' And with that, she ushered me out the door, banished from the scene of our brief, romantic intermezzo. (Alas!)

CHAPTER 7

Journals of Harold Davidson
London
15 September 1930

Have finally made contact with Miss Harris! It has not been easy. The young lady, despite her iniquitous employment, seems to have a positive aversion to being At Home to callers. I have made the dismal trek to Queen Street, Camden, four times now, not counting the evening when I made the error of tapping on Barbara's window and finding an intimidating face looking out. From my knowledge of the Profession, I am aware that mornings are slow (the girls invariably sleep in), lunchtime finds some vigorous activity under way, listless afternoons speed up – like cricket matches! – after the tea interval, then die down from what we have learned to call 'the cocktail hour' at 6 p.m. until the pubs start to empty around ten, which is the signal for a great unloosening of sin all over the city.

I called three times in the early evening. Each visit was as fruitless at the last. I stood before the door of number 14, pressing the lowest bell, but heard only a distant inner jangling – like the twanging of my nerves as I awaited yet another hostile confrontation like the last. Resolving to give it up after this final attempt, I called yesterday in the mid-morning, pressed the bell, looked sadly at the drawn curtains and rapped my knuckles on the glass pane . . .

The door flew open. A small girl stood before me, clad in a garment made of towelling material, off-white or cream. Her feet were bare. With her right hand she agitated a hand towel through curly brown locks and looked at me with her head in one side. I did not recognise her.

'Yes?'

'Miss Barbara Harris?'

'Might be. Who're you? And what, more to the point, is your problem, banging on a girl's door at this hour of the morning?'

I examined my wristwatch. 'It is ten thirty, Miss Harris. The world has risen and been about its business for three hours at least. I am Mr Harold Davidson. We met at Marble Arch some weeks ago. We had lunch in a café and I expressed a desire to call upon you to discuss . . .' I faltered. What had we agreed to discuss? I blushed to recall our little colloquy.

'Oh, I remember *you*,' she said, 'the gent sweating to death in your long coat. You bought me lunch and come on all innocent about the pudding.' She laughed and towelled her curls. 'Well, hello again. So you thought you'd give it a go, did you? After all your high earnest chat, you've spent a few weeks tossing and turning in your bed every morning and thinking, "Oooh, shall I? Shan't I?" And here you are.'

Her face, suddenly revealed amid all the towelling, was not as I remembered it. In the morning light, she was a quite different proposition from the poised and *soignée* strumpet climbing aboard an omnibus. Before me stood a child, five feet nothing, in a childish towel gown.

'May I come in?'

'You're a bit eager, aren't you? I don't usually entertain gentlemen until after elevenses. Sorry, but I'm not in the mood. Can't you come back at lunchtime?'

It was not unlike calling upon one's dentist without an appointment.

'I have not called on you for – for that,' I said. 'I wish only to talk to you.'

'Talk to me? What about?' Under her curly brows, she was suspicious. 'You're not from some League of Decency?'

'I come to see you as a friend, nothing more. A friend who brings you only good news. If you'd let me cross your threshold. I have' – a brainwave struck me – 'two small gifts for you, and an urgent message that cannot be conveyed on the street. Where, I notice, we are already becoming the object of enquiring glances.'

Two doors away, a vacuum-cleaner truck had halted and its driver was speaking to a rough-skinned matron in a housecoat and fluffy mules at number 10. Both were watching us with interest.

'Don't mind that old sow. You better come in. And if all this stuff about presents and news and messages means that I'll be staring at some purple monstrosity two minutes from now, I swear to God I'll bash it with a teaspoon, all right?'

Dazed by this onslaught, I entered the house, through a hallway filled with bicycles – one parked, as it were, halfway up the wall, hanging from two rusting bolts – and was suddenly in her living quarters.

It was a room such as I'd rarely encountered, even among the habitats of the wretched sisterhood. In one corner was a basin surmounted by a tiny mirror hanging from a nail. In the other, a rudimentary cooking hob with two gas burners was all but concealed beneath a junk-yard of blackened saucepans. Nothing, it seemed, had been washed in weeks. Against the wall, a table, stool and triptych mirror were submerged beneath an accumulation of jars, potions and powder receptacles, dead flowers, tickets, theatrical handbills, scent bottles with rubbery squeeze mechanisms. Every square inch of space was tumbled with the debris of decadence. Torn squares of magazine pages, bearing the likeness of Ivor Novello, ragged pieces of muslin veil, random photographs, undergarments in vivid shades of crimson and aquamarine – and across the side wings of the mirror, a long lilac feather boa was draped like tinsel across a Christmas tree from Gamages store.

The word 'abandon' hardly did justice to this wasteland of human depravity. Its centrepiece was the bed that lay before the window through which the noonday sunlight weakly shone. It was *huge*. Most tarts of my acquaintance count themselves fortunate to possess a single bed with a soft mattress and pillow, rather than a hard divan and a bolster. Miss Harris could boast a king-size bed, opulently arrayed with cotton sheets, a satin counterpane, an over-blanket in green chenille, and half a dozen pillows that would not have disgraced a Byzantine seraglio.

'OK then,' she said, sitting in the edge of the bed. 'Where's these little presents?'

I dug through the inner folds of my coat. From the Gifts Pocket,

I located a small bar of Evening in Paris guest soap in a decorative box (special offer, 3/6, Boots pharmacy). In my Perishables Pocket, I found a bar of the new 'Crunchie' honeycomb-and-chocolate sweetmeat, and gave both to her with grave formality.

'I offer you these small tokens of my esteem, Miss Harris, to mark the beginning of what I hope will be a long and fruitful alliance, as together we walk the thorny path towards the light that forever gleams –'

'That it?' she said, gazing at her gifts with incredulity. 'Small is right. I never been given a *bar of chocolate* by a gentleman before, not since I was ten. As for the soap,' (she sniffed it suspiciously), 'you'd be better off cleaning drains with it rather'n giving it to a girl and saying it's a token of your blooming esteem.'

She looked boldly up at me, her brown curls bouncing on her brow like Medusan snakes. 'You're a beginner in this game, int'cha? D'you really think you can bribe people with chocolates and scent?'

I was hurt by her tone. All over London I am known for my generosity. In my missionary work, I have showered the Abigails and Idas, the Jennys and Pennys, with sweet-smelling concoctions and treats, until they welcome my arrival in their lives as children welcome Father Christmas. To call my little votive offering a bribe – it was an outrageous slur on my intentions.

'Oh, don't look so sorry for yourself,' said Barbara. 'I've had worse things given to me by gentlemen. And I do like a bit of chocolate round about now.' She broke off a piece of the orange-brown snack and popped it in her mouth. 'And I know you wasn't offering it to get a screw off me – you just wanna talk, right?'

I nodded.

'Well, if all you want's a little chat,' she concluded, 'you won't mind me going back to bed. On me own, I mean.' Upon which, still clad in her towelling robe, she slipped her legs under the sheets, lay back luxuriantly on the pillows and groaned. I feared that she might have suffered some injury, but it was a moan of sluggardly pleasure, as the chocolate melted on her tongue. Her face on the pillow split into a wide smile, like the Cheshire cat's. A beam of sunshine chose that moment to intrude through the dirty window and settle on her face in a long rectangle of saturated light, falling from brow to chin, bisecting the line of her mouth to make a perfect Christian crucifix.

She closed her huge brown eyes. 'Lovely sunny morning,' she observed. I stood by the bed, gazing in wonder, gripped by an epiphany such as I have seldom encountered. Lines from Keats's 'Eve of St Agnes' settled on my heart – that moment when Porphyro, hidden in his beloved's chamber, discovers her at her prayers:

> Full on this casement shone the wintry moon,
> And threw warm gules on Madeline's fair breast,
> As down she knelt for heaven's grace and boon;
> Rose-bloom fell on her hands, together pressed,
> And on her silver cross soft amethyst,
> And on her hair a glory, like a saint:
> She seemed a splendid angel, newly dressed,
> Save wings, for Heaven – Porphyro grew faint;
> She knelt, so pure a thing, so free from mortal taint.

Never was a romantic sentiment less appropriate to its context than Keats's words to this reeking boudoir, with its debris of flimsy undergarments by my feet, its indescribable cheap vests and grey bloomers half concealed by the huge bed. Yet I gazed at the girl as she lay silently basking on her kohl-stained pillow, illuminated by sunlight that seemed to conspire with the contours of her face and, like Porphyro, I too saw an angel there. No other word would do. Her caramel skin was flawless, her teeth, bared by a sensuous smile, were strong. Her hair, newly washed and dried, lay freed from the cloche-helmeted ropes I had encountered at Marble Arch. It curled in rich profusion around her ears and temples.

'Are you going to stand there staring at me like I'm an exhibit?' she asked, her eyes still shut. 'I'm not a piece of merchandise in a bleedin' shop, you know.' She laughed to herself, mirthlessly. 'Well, I mean, I *am* if that's what you're after. But I'm not here for winder-shopping, all right?'

'No, Miss Harris.' I recollected myself. 'I was merely speculating about how you live. I cannot reconcile the apparent squalor of your address with the richness of your sleeping arrangements.'

'You what?'

'This bed, for example. I am older than you, yet I can only dream that some day I might possess a bed of such magnificence.'

'Nice, isn't it?' She pulled herself upright, plumped the damask pillows into a fat double hillock and leaned back, like a plucky invalid – no, like a young duchess entertaining callers to hot chocolate and muffins at a breakfast levée in the days of Pope and Swift. 'When I got this room a year ago, courtesy of a gentleman friend, he said, "Here's a hundred quid, furnish it how you like," so I blued half of it on a proper big bed. I reckon it's where I 'ave the most fun by day as well as night, so I might as well get the best.' She yawned. 'You know they say people sleep for eight hours a night, so that's like a third of a whole day? That means you spend a third of your life in bed. With me, it's nearer half my life. So I like to be comfortable.'

'Marvellous,' I said, a little dazed. 'I had not done the mathematical calculation before.'

'What's *your* bed like then?' she asked. 'Since we're chattin'.'

I was nonplussed. 'My bed? Why it's, um, a solid cherrywood double divan for my wife and myself, with a large headboard. It cannot match this one for opulence, though it is very comfortable. The mattress is delightfully soft after a hard day's labour, and –'

'Hopeless,' she said, crushingly. 'Get rid of it.'

'I beg your pardon?'

'Soft mattresses. They're no good.'

'No good?'

'No good for screwing on. No good for the old fucky-doodah. You can't get any friction, or purchase, or whatever the word is. Soft bloody mattresses, they ride along under you, they go boing-boing-boing up an' down, but they're no use if you're into deep penetration, are they? I'm sure you knew that once, even if you managed to forget it down the centuries.'

I was unbothered by her rudeness. Few things are more delightful than provocative conversation with a young woman.

'Sit down here,' she said. 'See what I mean?'

I sat down, keeping my coat about me for fear of misunderstanding. The mattress was indeed a splendid combination of suppleness and give, like the sprung dance floor at the Strand Palace Hotel.

'Pass me the hairbrush,' she said, pointing to the floor. I found it between an ivory silk camisole and a single balled-up stocking. She tilted her head and began to brush her damp locks.

As she did so, the front of her towelling robe opened a good four inches. I looked away, discreetly. My gaze fell upon a plate of breakfast debris, easily a week old, wherein a curdled mess of scrambled egg had been impaled by a cigarette butt. Revolted, I turned back to my hostess. Her left breast lay revealed from the white robe. As she brushed her hair, stroke after languorous stroke, her head on one side, her eyes shut once more. Her left hand caressed her white bosom.

'I must go,' I said. 'I should not have intruded on your toilette. Forgive my impertinence.'

'There's no need to rush away, Henry,' she said. 'I still don't know what you're doin' here, but if you'd like to give me a bit of a fondle – well, I shouldn't mind. You're nice company in a funny sort of way.'

'Harold is my name,' I said sternly. 'And, as I have said, I have not sought your address in order to slake some carnal appetite. I am interested in you, Miss Harris, because you are a clever young woman doomed to a life of exploitation, the result of some wrong turning you have taken. I wish only to find out more about you, in order to rescue you from sliding further into moral disarray. I came here today to say that I am at your disposal, to guide, to advise, to befriend, to offer you a map out of the labyrinth of –'

'Yeah, yeah,' said the girl. 'I've heard it all before. Lot of my older clients say the same thing.' She adopted a music-hall voice of gruff, masculine gravitas. '"Let me take you away from all this, my dear. Let me find you a charming apartment just over a flower shop in Balham, where you won't be a common tart no more, you'll just be my personal private tart." But I never said yes. I prefer to have my own place and entertain whoever I like.'

'But, Barbara –'

'Yes, Harold, go on then, explain how, "Oh no, it's all different with me, I'm not like other men." I collect excuses from men all over the place.'

The time had come to lay my cards on the table.

'I am different, Miss Harris, because, you see –' I drew in my breath and exhaled, with a certain drama – 'I am a pastor, who wishes only to care for you and bring good things your way.'

'Pastor? What's that? Is that what they use to make milk taste better?'

'A cleric, my dear. A clergyman. A priest. I am the rector of a parish in Norfolk called Stiffkey. But I tend to spend my working days attending to the needs of girls – ladies – in troubled circumstances in London.'

'Oh, a sky pilot,' she said. 'Well, you didn't act like one when we met. Why didn't you tell me then? Where's your dog collar?'

'I tend not to wear one when going among the lower elements. Some of them find it . . . intimidating. A priest can be an alarming figure of authority, as well as an unwelcome reminder of the sanctity they have lost.'

'Right,' said Miss Harris. 'So when you meet young girls on the game, you don't tell them you're in the Church, and you don't tell 'em you're going to save their souls either. So who do they think you are, apart from a stranger who might or might not be a client?'

'A friend,' I said, as gently as I could. She had such need of a true friend, for all her brash ways.

'Oh yeah?' She sat up in the bed with a rivalrous glint in her eye. 'And in your friendly way, you take 'em for chops and mash in a café – and then what?'

'Sometimes I offer them sustenance, it is true,' I confessed, feeling a little defensive. 'Sometimes I take them to the theatre. Many of my young charges have a romantic passion for the stage.'

'Well, very nice of you, I'm sure. Young girl, in London, down on her luck, making a few bob off gentlemen callers, gets asked out to a West End play by charming gent in long coat, no strings attached, after which he'll buy 'er supper then he'll walk her 'ome, will he, and expect nothing in return?'

'Right so far,' I said shortly. I do not take kindly to being interrogated by children too young to vote.

'And that's it? Harry, I mean, who's kidding who 'ere?'

I smiled at her. St Augustine himself must have encountered just such blank hostility, when conducting his saving ministry.

'There is no question of "kidding", Miss Harris,' I said. 'My strategy is simply to befriend these unfortunate girls, to become their ally and intimate, to establish close relations with them –'

'I'll say you want close relations. Close enough to get into their knickers.'

'– in order to save them from a life on the streets, to find them work, to reunite them with their parents, to reveal the possibility of a better life. Perhaps a young girl such as you has never entertained the possibility that simple Christian altruism might govern human behaviour.'

'Al-what?'

'Altruism. It means doing good to others without thought of recompense.'

'And you get no reckon pence, do you, for all this work, and theatre dates and dishing out money for lamb chops?'

'None whatever.'

'So at the end of the evening, they never give you a little kiss?'

'I –' I was not sure where this line of enquiry would take us. 'I would not discourage any show of affectionate gratitude, within, of course, the bounds of decency.'

'But would you encourage it, when they say, "Oooh, Harold, you're so good to me,"' (she adopted a fey, mincing tone, as of a child who has been bought an ice cream in Hyde Park), '"here's a big kiss for all you've done for me, and there's plenty more where that came from if you was to take me to the Adelphi on Saturday night"?'

I rose from the bed, aware that my hand on the counterpane was in close proximity to her unshielded breast.

'I am a servant of Christ, Barbara. I am the rector of a flock who depend on me for guidance and enlightenment. It is no part of my morally directed strategy to solicit kisses from young women.'

'But you do, don't you?' Her beautiful brown eyes were suddenly narrowed to unappealing slits.

'I have a tactile nature. Many of these girls lack a father, or at least a father figure. I see no harm in enfolding them, occasionally, in the tender embrace of the Church, to reassure and soothe their flighty hearts, to offer them a solace that no other man of their rude acquaintance might bring.'

'Aha! I knew it!' she said. 'The old harmless squeeze. We all know where *that's* heading, don't we?'

'Not at all. My occasional embraces are paternal.'

'So you don't sleep with them?'

'Certainly not.'

'You just kiss them and hug them and leave it at that?'

A small tintinnabulation in my head told me it was time to move on from this potentially compromising discourse.

'I told you I had an urgent message to convey to you,' I said in a bustling tone. 'It is this. My friend Lady Fenella Royston-Smith, a long-standing benefactor and supporter of the charities I have set up to help fallen women and runaway boys in the metropolis, wishes to meet you. She has agreed to introduce me to a couple of noble philanthropists, but to convince them of the importance of my work they wish to meet an example of the, ah, ladies I seek to help.'

'Okey-dokey,' said Barbara. 'But I still don't see why she's invited me. I don't think I know anyone called Fenella.' She frowned. 'Plenty called Smith of course.'

'Do you not see, my dear Miss Harris?' I said, my voice dropping to a confiding whisper. 'This is your chance to move from your unfortunate occupation to a better life. To leave behind the sordid stews of prostitution, and find a position more worthy . . .'

Her eyes blazed. 'I think it's time you got one thing straight, Harold.' She swept back the counterpane and stood before me, five foot nothing of child-woman self-righteousness. 'I am *not* a bloody *prostitute*. Have you got that? Maybe I sleep with people, maybe I have sex with people I've just met, and maybe they might give me a little present now and again, to buy me a hat, but that's it. I have boyfriends, lots of them, and they can stay here sometimes because they're good to me and I like them. But I'm not flogging my body down alleys all night long, and I can't be had just for money. And if your Lady Fifi What's-'er-name wants to summon me round to some scabby hotel to show me off as a cheap tart, well, she can fuck right off, and so can you.'

Our conversation ended shortly afterwards. I will not inscribe in these pages the language used by Miss Harris to dismiss me from her premises. It was a fruitless encounter. I was unable to launch my usual campaign of prayers and spiritual exercises to cleanse her spirit. I could do nothing but try to defend my *modus vivendi* against this brazen, argumentative young wanton. I have never met a more obdurate sinner, so iron-clad against every prompting of moral decorum. Hopeless. I shall certainly not waste my time like this ever again.

London
17 September 1930

The papers are full once more of the exploits of Miss Amy Johnson who, after her remarkable circumnavigation of the globe in May, and her extended sojourn in Australia, has appeared back in London, to loud huzzahs. Frankly, I have been sceptical about the number of women who have taken to the skies in the last few years. Lady Heath, Lady Bailey, the elderly but intrepid Duchess of Bedford – their exploits in flying alone to far-flung bits of the empire, from Cape Town to Zanzibar, have become so commonplace, they seem merely a variant of the phenomenon of titled ladies racing sports cars at Brooklands, exchanging their Fortuny evening frocks for the problematic livery of mannish shirts, trousers and hideously unflattering goggles.

I have incorporated into my sermons the modern fascination of flight, and all the competitive, yearning spirit of women piloting their juddering crafts into hostile terrain, into Kalahari wastes and Nepalese foothills. I explained to the Stiffkey congregation on Sunday that all this aerial wanderlust is merely an emblem of mankind reaching for the heavens, trusting to the instruments on the dashboard, the ailerons and rudder, to steer them through the dangerous elements of wind, rain and gravity. Thus we all try to fly heavenwards on our journey of life, trusting to the guidance of Christ and the teaching of his apostles to carry us safely through the buffetings of corruption and sin. The less enlightened pilots may feel only a secular joy in flying above the territory of earth on which they once laboured, carried away by the exhilaration of freedom and amazed to feel they can land in Tartary or Samarkand in a matter of hours. But I know that their true impulse is not one of escape but of transcendence. They wish not to *depart* from their earthly chains, but to *aspire* to the upper atmosphere, the blue empyrean where Heaven resides. Watching one of these machines roaring overhead – I think it may have been the Duchess, en route to the East Anglian coast – I put myself in the pilot's position, and I know that passing every line of cloud must feel like stripping away the gauzy veils that mask the final mantle of Paradise.

That is a fine phrase. I shall certainly employ it again, when possible.

My disdain for the rich and titled lady pilots was brought up short by seeing a picture of Miss Johnson in the *Illustrated London News*. She is quite different. Indeed, she is a phenomenon of young British womanhood, and a splendid example to my London girls. Still in her early twenties, she is of working-class northern stock, toils by day as a solicitor's typist, and is full of simple common sense. Her aircraft is a second-hand Gipsy Moth, which used to be an air taxi! The lady herself is small, boyishly slender, with short hair and a delightfully healthy complexion, devoid of powder. She wears khaki shorts, a rough working shirt and a sheepskin jacket, and poses by her craft with spunky confidence, a large sun-helmet masking her doubtless sharp eyes. I imagine them blue, the blue of the Virgin's veil in the lady chapel of Westminster Cathedral.

How I would love to make her acquaintance. To introduce her to some of my girls and extend a hand saying, This, my dears, could be you, this *lady* could be you, shorn of make-up and marcelled curls, stripped to nothing more than enterprise and determination, the spirit that in ancient times moved Christians to sainthood! I would take her hand and thank her, humbly, for bringing such heroism to our lives. I would kiss the hand that steered the aeroplane as if it steered our dreams. I would perhaps encircle her waist in simple friendship and squeeze her to my side, drawing strength from her lithe young body and telling her . . .

Yes, well. I called upon Rose today, as promised. Took her to an art gallery to inspect some watercolours by Mrs Eugenie Prendergast, near Euston Station. It was not a success. She is listless, bored and frankly philistine in her appreciation of Mrs P's charming renderings of the northern Lakes. My little homilies on misfortune and hope fell on deaf ears.

'Can't we go somewhere else?' she kept asking, like a child. But I am loath to take her very far from home, into the reeking West End. It might remind her of her descent into vinous abandon.

I love Rose like any daughter in Christ, but, speaking purely socially, she can be a trial and, to deal plainly, a bit of a bore. No spark, that is her trouble.

Stiffkey
21 September 1930

A local girl, Minnie Bell, has fallen foul of a passing seducer from Norwich, a travelling salesman in women's gloves, shoes, hosiery, handbags and the like. Happening to call on her home in Church Street when the family were away – the senior Bells visiting relatives in Hunstanton, the juniors at school – and finding Miss Minnie in solitary study for her appointment as Sunday-school teacher, he inveigled his way into her parents' living room where he set out his wares with the oily plausibility of a gypsy pedlar. Momentarily entranced by the flashy accessories on display, the girl was urged to 'try on' all manner of meretricious habiliments, starting with the shoes and working up, as it were, to camisoles and fancy neckware. Heedless of the chasm of immorality that lay before her, she 'tried on' silken stockings under the man's impertinent gaze, revealing to him hidden areas of flesh that discretion might have judged private. The poor booby was taken in by his easy manner, as he remarked (her mother later told me) on the suppleness of her feet, the beauty of her skin and the 'caressing' quality of the underclothing. Within an hour he had persuaded her to disrobe in the parlour and return to him clad in vestments better suited to the Rue St-Denis in Paris.

I can imagine only too clearly his cries of rapture at her appearance in ever more abbreviated lingerie, his sweaty fingers as they adjusted her straps, his practised hand as it smoothed the hose over her legs, his breath in her hair as he turned her this way and that before the mirror, his hollow enquiries of 'Does that feel good?' and 'Does that not feel cool/warm/soft/agreeably tight on your skin?' et cetera.

Before she knew what she was about, he had forced himself upon her and departed, leaving her splayed upon the davenport settee. I am only relieved that she had not paid for any of the wispy items in which she stood, aghast and weeping, when her parents returned at teatime. The police were summoned. Charges may be pressed. The whole village is talking about it.

My sermon dwelt on the abuse of innocence, a theme naturally close to my heart. I addressed the young girls in the congregation who might find themselves in a similar quandary with a handsome young stranger, bearing fistfuls of cotton, silk and lace.

'Your body is a temple,' I said. 'How many times have you heard the phrase? Yet it is true. Pure, pristine and sacred, your body is, like a temple or cathedral, the work of human endeavour – the work of your parents – but blessed by the Lord, who has made it an edifice of unblemished perfection, by giving it a soul. Guard it well, dear sisters in Christ, for swinish forces are poised to attack it night and day.

'The nave is your spine, the side aisles your legs, the lady chapels your spread-out arms. The altar, with its spotless white cotton, represents the centre of your being and the location of the soul. Here, above all, are the areas you must guard against defilement. Here are found, to right and left, the candelabra of your flesh, the lambent flames symbolising the fiery perfection of your intimate regions. And at their heart is the tabernacle wherein lies the Godhead, revealed in the Holy Mass with the opening of the tiny door, the secret chamber wherein the white host and red wine are stored, immaculate, inviolable, to be received upon the tongues of the faithful, forever denied to the heathen. Keep them safe, little sisters in Christ, for they are your private, golden crucible of being, never to be invaded or manhandled by the unworthy.'

The pleasure I took in this extended metaphor was shaken by much impertinent giggling from the stupider young girls in the congregation, and the noise of slamming doors as some feeble-minded elder ladies chose to leave the service early, doubtless to

110

return home to the urgency of preparing lunch for their slug-a-bed husbands. I was momentarily put out by their departure, but felt my message had penetrated to the younger parishioners who, I feel sure, will have derived benefit from my words and resolved to feel differently about their firm, eager and easily betrayed young bodies.

London
22 September 1930

I am not well. A terrible ache in my spine has rendered me half crippled. I find it hard to walk more than a mile (Waterloo Bridge, Fleet Street, Ludgate Circus) without feeling enervated, and twinged with nausea. I am becoming, alas, an old man.

Dropped into Marina Carter's establishment in Drury Lane with a box of Levantine Silk beauty soap for Mrs Carter. It barely won a glance from its recipient before it was put aside like a cold potato from last night's supper. Marina was too preoccupied to chat. There is a problem with two of her girls and the place was all abustle with concern. One girl, Maureen I believe, has contracted gonorrhoea, despite Mrs Carter's strict examinations of all gentlemen clients and her insistence on her girls' regular douching before and after their evening's work. 'I have a nurse on standby, night and day, to take the men aside, skin 'em back and tell 'em, Look, sorry, but this is a clean house and it's the price you have to pay for your fun, we don't want no suppurating cocks in 'ere,' she told me when first I visited her house of ill repute. 'But what can you do, 'Arold, when they protest that they're clean-livin' chaps? If they're payin' good money for an hour with Maureen, you don't want to piss them off, do you?'

But poor Maureen is afflicted nonetheless. And the other girls – there are twelve bedrooms at the Carter brothel – are all atwitter because of what has befallen young Sarah McGivern. She was laid up with a grumbling abdominal pain. The girls had joked for an evening that 'It was all the fault of Mr Kellyn Jones, an' his enormous todger', and assumed she would be returned to health by the morning. By the time they realised her appendix was about to burst, it was too late. Sarah was taken, screaming blue murder, in a trade van owned by Marina's brother, and deposited at St Thomas's Hospital, where she lies still, stricken with peritonitis, but – God willing – will pull through. It has cast a damper on the household. It will be a long time before they trust again the judgement of Mrs Carter's 'house doctor', Mr Slattery, a man not qualified, as far as I can see, to diagnose fleas on a rat, let alone anything more complicated. He is a mountebank of the first order.

I have told Marina many times of Slattery's shortcomings, but what can be done? Our relationship is, of course, highly unorthodox. All my efforts are directed towards removing her girls from their base employment and relocating them in good jobs, decent company, God-fearing attitudes. Her efforts are directed towards keeping them at work, on their backs, bringing home the bacon, so to speak, at the rate of thirty shillings a day each. We should by rights be enemies. My every visit to her establishment is, theoretically, like the coming of a thief in the night, to steal the girls away. But Marina encourages my visits. Provided I do not attempt to convert the girls, *on the premises*, in front of the clientele, my presence is tolerated. Of course I have spoken, in the past, to Elsie Teenan, Nellie Churchill, Bridget and Lily and others, spoken urgently about the mortal danger to their souls, but I have had to temper the 'hellfire' strain in my homily for fear of making the girls cry (it is bad for business, apparently, unless Mr Isambard Merchant is in the building; he has a positive relish for weeping girls dressed up as urchins, complete with Alice Liddell rags and tear-streaked, muddied faces).

My visits therefore have become surreal variants on the ordinary pastoral calls I pursue in Stiffkey, upon Miss Maggs and Mr Colliston. To these blameless souls I enquire, respectively, how her home-made Seville marmalade has been affected by the frosts of January, and whether his pension allows him sufficient funds to visit his dead wife's family in Deal. To Bridget, Lily and the others I enquire whether their cold sores or groinal rashes have worsened. Different questions, vastly different modes of living, but approached in the same ameliorative pastoral spirit.

I tried once or twice more to speak to Mrs Carter, as she bustled here and there, bearing towels and cotton wool, offering excuses to gentlemen who called in search of Sarah or Maureen. I wished to ask her permission to borrow a couple of girls for an audience with Lady Fenella and her friends at the Charing Cross Hotel. Every time I went near, she became more preoccupied, until, exasperatedly, I said, 'Would it be possible for a humble servant of the Lord to crave an audience with you some time today?' She looked round and, with a curl of her lip, replied, 'Not now, Padre. I'm not in the mood for your old nonsense right now.' It was like a slap in the face. Two men were standing in the doorway of the drawing room, workmen fixing the lintel. They guffawed at my discomfiture.

My cold has worsened, and I have spent the afternoon at home in a slight depression. Perhaps it is the feeling that to be ignored, then dismissed, by a Drury Lane brothel madame represents a new low point in the narrative of my life.

Visited Rose later on. Took her to a music-hall show at the Alhambra near St Pancras. She barely cracked a smile, even during the mirthful drolleries of Walter 'Mr Comedy' Peasanhall. Neither of us is, I'm afraid, the other's dream companion any more. As we used to be, once.

London
23 September 1930

I am not giving in. Nothing could make me revisit that headstrong, ungrateful, heathen little trollop, Miss Harris. I was hurt by her remarks in a way I have seldom been hurt in my career. She wholly misunderstands the significance of my work, or maybe seeks to represent it in the worst possible light. Her tongue is like a scythe and her morals would degrade a cesspit. I dread to imagine in what stew of parental depravity she was reared.

Yet I have found myself thinking of her. Much as I disapprove of her employment, her refusal to admit her sin, her fathomless capacity for self-exculpation, there is no doubt that she is a remarkable person. In a way I admire her frankness – not, of course, in the arena of sexual invitation, but in her approach to the world, the way that she insists on doing everything her way, depending on nobody, feeling inferior to nobody. In another world than ours, she would be a young missionary in the deserts of Sudan, directing hordes of Dinka Hottentots to say their prayers and consume their free soup.

And there is something else. I am a practical man. I am not a dreamer, nor a prey to visions. Yet as I looked on her face last week, as that thin shaft of sunlight painted a glow — it seemed from Heaven — down her face and, bisected by her smile, became a crucifix, I saw, as clear as day, how an urchin strumpet in a towelling robe can be revealed as a saint. It was a sign, I think, meant for me alone. Miss Harris is to be my challenge. I am to reveal the perfect being within the off-white robes. She will be my personal crusade. I will seek her out, draw her close to me, keep her safe from harm and finally throw off her outward appurtenances to show what fundamental decency lies within. Then I can rest, my greatest work completed.

I was tremendously enthused by this . . . this *project* shall I call it? Mrs Parker upbraided me for whistling after dinner as she listened to the wireless.

Some of my old energy has come back. I shall seek out Miss Harris and start her transformation without delay.

CHAPTER 8

Journals of Harold Davidson
London
24 September 1930

Called on Miss Harris twice, both times mid-morning as before, but to no avail. Walked around Camden in hope of finding her taking a stroll with a gentleman friend, until I became all too familiar with the byways around Euston Station and Mornington Crescent, the grassy pocket handkerchief of St Pancras Gardens and the formal exclusivity of Regent's Park, until I felt I had traversed the whole of north London in my search for this headstrong girl.

Called on Rose, to break the tedium of my walks. Found her, as ever, sitting in the glum drawing room I have come to dread, wearing exceedingly hideous housecoat and mules, hair pinned up half-heartedly into 'bun' shape from which stray wisps occasionally droop. If only (I keep the thought to myself of course) she could apply a touch of rouge or lipstick, she might give more of the appearance of life. One thing, however, is different about her. She has, *mirabile dictu*, discovered modern magazines! I entered, to find her engrossed in *Lady's Realm*, a monthly journal printed on shiny paper and costing 6d. I feel almost like writing to the editors, to congratulate them on giving this chronically sad and silent woman things to think about and discuss, albeit subjects of a uniformly trivial bent, e.g. 'How to Fashion a Shawl from Lace Curtains', the 'Luckless Love of Princess Amelia' and similar prose excursions. She now prattles on charmingly about fabrics (the dear girl) and her eyes fill with tears about the romantic entanglements of long-dead royals. I have many reservations about ladies' magazines, and their capacity to fill the minds of dreamy spinsters with nonsense hardly a notch above mill-girl romances, but I now see how they can reconnect the depressed and despairing with a world outside their own bleak solipsism.

'I can see you were moved by the predicament of Princess Amelia,' I said, cautiously. 'It is a sign of your kindly nature that you should become emotional about a woman of privilege. You have always set much store by a title. Were you ever to meet high-born women, I'm sure you would find them very ordinary and down-to-earth people.'

'Course I'll never meet a real princess,' said Rose. 'How would I do that?'

'Would you care to meet a titled person on Friday?' I asked. 'I am paying a call on my friend and benefactor Lady Fenella Royston-Smith, and have asked if I may bring some of my young charges along. She has graciously said yes. Will you join me?'

'Oh, Harold —' her eyes were large and trusting — 'you wouldn't want me to meet a real lady. What would I wear? I'd let you down. I look a fright.'

'This morning, Rose, you have not yet had time, I see, to attend to your beauty preparations. But I'm sure that you will find something in your wardrobe suitable for a meeting with the aristocracy.'

'But should I wear something like I'm going out for the evening, or something simple like I'm staying in all day?' She glanced down at her housecoat. 'I got to find something nice.' Mentally, I pictured Rose typically dressed in her heyday of 'going out for the evening' — a riot of cleavage, bows, neck-ribbons and cheeky hat surmounting her marcelled waves. But then again (I reflected) why should she not dress as a prostitute since a prostitute was precisely what Fenella required?

'It will be an informal, or semi-formal tea visit in a hotel, Rose,' I said. 'I know I can rely on you to dress appropriately.'

Leaving her at 1 p.m., I recklessly decided to call once more on Miss Harris. I rapped softly on the front door.

'Who's there?' called a voice, in an indulgent giggle, as of one who had just come to the end of a bout of laughter.

'It is I, Barbara, your friend Harold, the vicar.' I could not believe that I was shouting my *bona fides* (and calling myself 'the vicar', the only name by which she might remember me) in the street.

After a silence, there came the sound of a bolt being unhoused. Miss Harris stood before me in bare feet and a white shift, her curly hair tumbled from (I assumed) sleep.

'Good God, it's you,' she said, laughing. There was no hostility in the sound, though perhaps a certain marvelling at my boldness. 'You do turn up out of the blue, Harold.' (It was the first time she had recalled my name accurately. A notable advance in our relationship.) 'Don't tell me, you were passing, on your way to some – what's the word you use? – *pasteurising* mission at Euston Station and thought you might drop in with a bar of chocolate and some soap and see if I might be grateful this time. Is that it?'

'I wondered if you had perhaps meditated on our last discussion,' I said. 'Do you remember? Lady Fenella is anxious to make your acquaintance as a modern girl, unencumbered by the dictates of social propriety –'

'As a cheap trollop she'd like to patronise.'

'As a shining example of the undeserving poor who struggles to maintain her independence in a world where waves of vice threaten to engulf her. If I could persuade her that, with my help –'

'Then she might give you a great big wodge of cash?' said the relentless Miss Harris. 'You're nothing but an old tart yourself, Harry, aren't you, for all your grand words? You'd do anything for, what? fifty quid, no matter how *degrading*?' She uttered the final word with delicious emphasis, as if using it for the first time. I suppose I was glad to think I had taught her something from the lexicon of responsibility.

'Once again, I see that I am wasting my time. I only hoped –'

'Oh, come in,' she said. 'Come and see how I live, for a moment, and spare me the preacher flannel.'

She disappeared. I followed her into her shameless boudoir.

There was a man in her bed.

He was young, swarthy, exotically foreign, naked under the damask sheets, his hair was oiled and gathered into a girl's ponytail, and he was reading the *Financial Times* with concentration.

'Kemal, this is Harold, a vicar friend of mine,' she said, like a dowager introducing hopelessly mismatched guests at Queen Charlotte's ball. 'Harold, this is Kemal. He's an Indian prince, you know.'

'How do you do?' he said, abstractedly, without looking up from the broadsheet pages. 'Delighted to meet you. I see that South African goldfields are down eight points. If this goes on, I shall be bankrupt by Christmas.'

I was at a loss. I have, in my work, had occasion to call on young women during their hour of repose, in the hope of making it, for them, a time of reflection on their Saviour and his infinite forgiveness. But this was the first time I had encountered a client, actually *in situ*, boldly reclined against the pillows.

'How do you do?' I said. 'I had no idea my friend Miss Harris was entertaining.'

'Would you care for a drink?' he said. 'We've been making Sidecars. Babs, darling, is there any more ice?' He relinquished his pink newspaper and reached down beside the bed where some orange-brown mixture was congealing in a jug.

'Thank you, no,' I said stiffly. 'My business with Miss Harris is strictly professional.'

'Professional business?' He condescended to look at me for the first time. He was indeed a handsome devil, his dark skin amazingly smooth, the colour of Mexican chocolate, his keen brown eyes hung in a huge oval whiteness. 'Whatever class of business can that be?'

'I have been educating Miss Harris in the ways of the Lord,' I said stiffly.

'Barbara,' he called out to our absent hostess, 'I am happy to think you have been educated by Mr Vicar here in the ways of enlightenment. I have suffered sleepless nights fearing for your immortal soul. But I now see there was no need.'

He poured himself a glass of the orange liquid. Did I detect a note of sarcasm in his question?

'I am not a vicar, but a rector,' I said coldly. 'But you are from foreign shores, I see, and would not perhaps recognise the distinction. I am here to provide solace to – to confused young women about the conduct of their lives. But you, sir,' (I wondered if soft soap might help this awkward scene), 'are, I take it, of the Hindoo faith?'

What a glance of contempt he turned upon me! I once saw a llama in Regent's Park, the sneeriest of God's creatures, which looked over a fence at me with less hauteur than my new acquaintance.

'I was indeed born a Hindoo,' he said, 'but you must not confuse me with some ignorant babu. My uncle is the Maharaja of Udaipur. I grew up with all the ceremony of a high-caste Indian, but my tutors were mostly Balliol men. And consequently' – he looked around the bed, located a box of tiny cigarettes, each wound round with a pink thread, lit one of them with a battered silver lighter and exhaled, luxuriantly, a cloud of halcyon fumes – 'my education tended more to the gods of Bloomsbury than of Ganesh and Shiva.'

'Balliol, eh? What did you study?' I asked with real interest.

'Politics and philosophy. At least that was my father's intention. I did not take in a great deal about either. Too keen on money, I fear. But they taught me some important things. The forward defensive stroke. The penetrating insights of Mr E. M. Forster, that clueless, spindly pervert. The *Enigma Variations* that make everyone in England, but nobody in India, weep. The iron law that teatime is at four thirty, not four o'clock, the –'

'I hate to break this up, boys,' said Barbara, appearing from nowhere in a diaphanous peignoir, 'but some of us have to get ready to go and do a day's work. Can we do this trip down memory lane some other time?'

'Kemal and I have been discussing Oxford tutors, my dear,' I said genially, 'unlikely though that may seem.'

He frowned. 'Unlikely why?'

'Why, because –'

'Please do not say, "Because this Indian fellow, though amusing, is black and I am a superior, high-caste person from the White religion",' said Kemal in a careless drawl. 'Spare me that.'

'What I meant, I assure you,' I said, 'was it might seem unlikely for us to discuss tutors because I am a generation older than you, sir. Do not dishonour me with imputations of bigotry where none exists.'

This awkward moment passed, and I repeated my invitation to Barbara, to accompany me to Fenella's tea party. Miss Harris made some pleasantry about becoming a public exhibit, a 'waxwork tart', as she put it, and how she should be mounted on a pedestal in Hyde Park, et cetera.

'It would make a nice change from being mounted on the park

bench,' observed Kemal. Hindoos evidently do not consider the feelings of ladies when exercising their sense of humour. But Miss Harris did not mind. Finally, my eloquence wore her down and she agreed to come on Friday. 'I'll come for the free grub, and to see inside the 'otel,' she said ungraciously, 'But I'm not doin' any prayin' nor telling anyone I'm sorry for myself, all right? You got that?'

'Crystal clear, Miss Harris.'

'Come on then,' she said, 'you'd better be off. Got work to do.'

She yawned. Kemal looked at his watch. I know little of these things but it was silver, inset with some sparkling items. It was evidently pricey. I assumed that Barbara's words applied to both of us. God help me, I really expected that he would rise from the bed, dress and leave the room with me, to continue our little talk in the street. Despite his absurdity, I could see he was pleased to bandy pleasantries with an educated man of the cloth.

I looked at Barbara, in her semi-transparent shift. She made no move, either of valediction or ejection. I looked from one to the other. The Indian displayed no impulse to rise and depart. He and Barbara looked back at me, as though curious to see what happened next.

The penny dropped. Her princeling was revealed as no more than a client of Miss Harris's, a prostitute's customer, waiting upon my departure through the door to resume the slaking of his lust. My Barbara (I had come to think of her as My) was likewise awaiting my exit, prior to her rejoining Mr Kemal beneath the covers.

I felt a wave of embarrassment. In my mind's eye I saw his hand upon her breast, her closed eyes, his large, hungry mouth upon hers, the languorous shifting of his beastly frame upon her schoolgirl body, her parting legs, his hands employed in shameless caresses above, between and below, his face buried in her breasts, her parted teeth, his flagrant buttocks, her sweaty loins heedless of restraint, the grunt of unity as he –

Could I not do something to stop it? I could not. Thirty years a clergyman, countless years of attempting to divert young girls from the immoral highway to Hades, and it came to this:

They were waiting for me to go.

There was nothing I could do.

Nothing to stop this

This

So I left.

But I will return. She needs me. She is a soul to be saved, more urgently than any other.

I *shall* return.

THINGS TO DO (URGENT):

1. *Imminent meeting with Lady Fenella. Lord and Lady Bassenthwaite.*
2. *Bishop not available. Monsignor George Coveney instead?*
3. *Find out info re Kenya, Africa. Population, staple diet, chief rivers, etc.*
4. *Haircut?*
5. *Leaflets for Whitechapel — 20 x 'More to Be Pitied'.*
6. *Savlon cream for Bridie.*
7. *Dr Legge's Throat Spray for Esther. Carr's All-Purpose Ointment for Lily's rash.*
8. *Tickets for* Private Lives *at Phoenix. Sandra? Matilda?*
9. *Sermon on Tolerance of Other Religons (Hindoos, etc.)?*
10. *Book for Barbara —* Damaged Goods?

London
25 September 1930

Called on George Coveney, my old friend and theology tutor from Oxford days. Now in his seventies, he is spry and clear in his thoughts, his memory miraculously unclouded by time. It is clearly a matter of astonishment to him to find his former student (and my tutorial partner) Cosmo Lang has become Archbishop of Canterbury.

'What can they have been thinking at the Bishops' Conference,' he asked with a rhetorical flourish, 'to choose for the highest position in the Church a man so cautious in his testimony, so tepid in his beliefs, so inimical to change and, if I may say so, my dear Harold, so very dull in company? I'm afraid it sends out only too clear a signal that the Church of England is now the natural home of compromise and reaction. Do you see anything of him now?'

'Our paths never cross, George, for he is embowered in the throne room of Lambeth Palace, while my work goes on where it always has, in the crucible of misery, want and sin that is the East End.'

'But you were friends, contemporaries at Exeter College. Surely you must meet at *Gaudeamus* reunions?'

'I haven't attended a Gaudy since the war. And if we met, I fear I would snub him for his behaviour towards me when I asked for his help and he, who could have made such a contribution, turned me down flat.'

'Remind me, my dear fellow. Was it about – forgive me – about money?'

'How delicately you bring up my state of penury in those days, George,' I said, laughing at his diplomatic way. 'No, it was the mission. You recall the Toynbee Hall Mission? The first charity with which I was ever involved, and my lifelong inspiration. The Barnett family, who set it up, wished to find idealistic students, children of privilege, who would work among the poor and homeless in Whitechapel and Limehouse and pay for the honour of doing so, before going out into the world of professional work with a fire inside them to change the conditions by which poverty is perpetuated. I asked Cosmo to join the mission, in whose future I so passionately believed. I urged him to channel his brilliance as a debater and firebrand into an area of real and visible want, and I failed. "It is too revolutionary for the time," he said, in his pompous way. "It combines the worst impulses of socialism and Catholic missionary nonsense. You cannot cure poverty by sending green young do-gooders from Trinity and Christchurch to walk among the wily card sharps and insolent strumpets of the East End, distributing their father's wealth and meddling in the everyday lives of the indigent. How will they be received? As languid fools on a holiday of conscience. The poor will take their money, bamboozle them with lies and rob them of their pocket watches, and they will return to the world where they truly belong with a lifelong hatred and suspicion for the great unwashed."

'I grew heated, George. I admit I may even have shouted, "So you would do nothing? You will not accept the possibility of change?

The rich man will remain at his castle, the poor man at his gate, and the two will never meet in a more equal society? Is that where your theological studies have brought you? To a recital of 'Onward, Christian Soldiers' and nothing more?" From that moment on, we were friends no more. Nor are we today.'

Thirty years after the event, I was still fuming! George chuckled at my liverish outburst. 'I see you remain, Harold, the young student of my recollections.'

He summoned a maid to bring us tea in his handsome drawing room at Bishop's House, and over our steaming cups and ginger biscuits we played chess.

George is a fine if old-fashioned player, a devotee of the Indian battery formation introduced to the chess world by, I am glad to recall, another clergyman, the Reverend H. A. Loveday in Bengal, India, before he succumbed to some malarial virus and was carried off at thirty-three. We fenced and fianchettoed in silence for an hour, I building an impregnable Sicilian defence behind two sturdily territorial knights and a blanket of pawns, he sending his queen and bishops hither and yon on wild diagonal sallies and potentially suicidal exchanges. Finally, I brought it up.

'George, I need your help. Tomorrow, I am to meet some women at a London hotel, to solicit their benevolence, and I hope you will accompany me.'

He made no answer for a moment, as he considered the capture of a stray pawn on the right flank of the board. 'Mmm?' Then, with a start he looked me full in the eye.

'You wish me to meet some women, Harold? In an hotel?'

'There is a financial transaction involved. It is a delicate business, and I know of no one I would more readily enlist as an ally.'

'A financial – Harold, what on earth are you suggesting?'

'They are aristocratic ladies of my acquaintance, whom I hope to impress with my credentials, not just as a cleric but as a man of action. Huge sums of money may be involved. Will you come with me and plead my case?'

My old tutor's face was all consternation. He looked at me with a shocked surmise, like a rural dean invited to burgle a poor box.

'You cannot seriously be suggesting that we – that you –'

'I know you are in retirement, my old friend,' I said, laughing, 'but I'm sure there is still a fire in your loins for performing a simple act that will bring the utmost pleasure, not just to you but to the ladies themselves. You will be doing me a favour. You will be doing them a favour. It could advance the cause of prostitution by leaps and bounds.'

'Harold —' he looked at me with an expression hard to fathom, somewhere between incredulity and yearning — 'I cannot quite believe what you are suggesting. Of course I am partial to the company of ladies, but since my dear wife died, I have given no thought to the delights of the flesh. I appreciate your kindness in suggesting this passionate liaison, but frankly, my dear fellow, I doubt that I . . .' He seemed to have difficulty forming his words. 'I mean, unless they were unusually patient and understanding young women —'

'George,' I said, a horrible suspicion dawning upon me.

'— and were prepared to devote a certain time and, ah, *energy* to the — mechanics of the operation.' A thought seemed to strike him. 'Would they object to a little corporal punishment? I used to find that to work in, ah, slow circumstances . . .'

'I am meeting Lady Fenella Royston-Smith and her friend Lady Bassenthwaite to try to persuade them to fund my charity for fallen women,' I said quickly, anxious to head off any further revelations about my friend's favoured paths to satisfaction. 'That is all. I wish only for you to speak on my behalf, as a distinguished Church elder, on the moral necessity of charitable giving.'

He came back to earth.

'Of course, of course. I was aware of your meaning.' He looked around him, covered in confusion. 'Is that the time? I really should be going.'

'This is your home, George.'

He blinked, like a man resurfacing from an overextended period under bathwater. '*Going*, I mean, to meet the parish council. We are drawing up a roster of pilgrimages for the spring.' His eye fell on the chessboard between us, with its unresolved stand-off of black pieces fruitlessly mustered around my impregnable royalty. 'I fear we must conclude this invigorating game at some other time.'

'But can I count on you, George, to come with me and support my solicitations? To make this meeting a success, I need you to summon apposite quotations from Leviticus or Samuel. I need you to be the image of the Church elder, the wise dispenser of plain common sense, backlit by the sanction of the Lord.'

He seemed relieved we were back on safe ground. 'I will come and walk with you in Galilee,' he said. 'And we shall persuade the moneylenders to be Good Samaritans all.' He smiled. 'Like this game, Harold, we shall be two bishops circling a nervous queen.'

What a good fellow he is. I left Bishop's House in high spirits, and not a little retrospective amusement.

'A little corporal punishment', eh? What on earth can he have had in mind?

London
26 September 1930

I telephoned Lady Fenella at 8 a.m. to ensure everything was ready for our meeting. She appeared a little grumpy and out of sorts, as though helping me find a new patron for the Virtue Reclamation League were a tedious chore; but I attribute this to the hour of my call. I had forgotten it is futile to call on anyone with a title before 10 a.m. But at length she revealed that she had made contact with Lady Bassenthwaite and had invited her to tea at four this afternoon. What a relief! I told her she was a true Samaritan et cetera, that I could never sufficiently thank her kindness et even more cetera, and explained that I would be accompanied by Monsignor Coveney.

'You promised me a bishop, Harold,' she said in a voice like a motor car being crushed in a scrapyard. I explained that the party would also be graced by two lady beneficiaries of the charity, two women who had, as I put it, 'seen better times'. She brightened audibly. I wished her *à bientôt* till four.

Arranged to meet Barbara, Rose and the monsignor at the Lyons Corner House in the Strand, a diagonal stone's throw from the hotel.

This was not, as it turned out, a good idea. My old stamping ground for years, the Strand, and the Lyons tea room has been the site of many fruitful encounters with young women on the edge.

But recently, I have felt a distinct *froideur* from the lady in charge, Jean or Jane something, a plain name for a plain and ignorant woman. Following my agreeable introductory meeting with Dolores Knight (then a waitress), my shepherding of Erica-from-Swansea (waitress ditto) into a more productive career in Mr Doughty's seamstress parlour, and my recent encounter with Sandra Hunt, I have been effectively 'banned' from the Corner House.

Jane or Jean bustled up as I took my seat, said, 'Oh no, sorry, not you again, we don't want any more unpleasantness,' and proceeded to recite some stuff about the management's right to bar anyone whose presence might cause a breach of the peace. Could I, a mild clergyman, be mistaken for a troublemaker?

Embarrassing minutes passed, as she raised her voice to a nagging pitch and the patrons at nearby tables (the place was packed at the end of summer, visitors from Yorkshire and Devon, bicyclists from Kent and Berkshire, young ladies in their candy-striped skirts a picture of seasonal health and activity) rudely eavesdropped. Thank God for the arrival of George, every inch of whose tall, imposing frame breathes dignity and lofty aspiration, like a church spire in a hat. Seeing his benign countenance, hearing his cooing reassurances, the harpy desisted and said, or hissed, 'Just this once, then!' at me and retired to the back room beyond the Toilets where she ekes out her days totting up bills for rock cakes and seeing evil where none exists.

I reminded George of the charities whose financial help we were soliciting and the good work in which I am ceaselessly involved. He appeared to take in the facts and statistics of the Saved, my long-practised recital of boys and girls rescued from penury and moral abandon, but seemed maddeningly distracted. Every few minutes, he would twist round in his chair, gaze into the faces of each arriving newcomer and ask, 'Will they be here soon?' like a child in a chara-banc to Margate.

'Rose and Barbara will join us here very shortly, George,' I said, slowly and clearly, 'and around 4 p.m. we shall make our way to the hotel. There shall meet Lady Royston-Smith and Lady Bassenthwaite with her husband, Sir Arthur. There will be tea and conversation, after which I shall make a short presentation about the good work of the League, the Retreat and so forth, and solicit the company's response. That is the point at which, I hope, you will feel able to make some pertinent points about the spiritual benefits of giving, and perhaps some edifying tales of parishioners whose lives have been changed by the timely interventions of charity.'

There was no reply.

'Do you follow me, George?'

Oblivious to my words, he was looking over my shoulder, his face a picture of wonder. I followed his gaze and discovered Miss Harris at the end of it.

She was sashaying through the crowded tables like a small bullock, her hips bumping into elbows and hats, upsetting canisters of sugar and making the milk in a dozen china jugs slosh and jiggle with her passing. The appalling confidence which I remarked upon at our first meeting was in full display. She seemed both to own the establishment through which she walked, and to find it hopelessly wanting in style and clientele. More immediately alarming, however, was her wardrobe. She had chosen, for the afternoon's crucial meeting with their ladyships, a lilac blouse of the dismayingly modern sort, without buttons but with a scooped-down frontage in which her striking bosom was not just apparent but luxuriously arrayed, like luscious fruit on a stall in Bermondsey Market. The hem of this straining garment barely skimmed the waist of her tight white cotton slacks, which stopped a good six inches above her ankles and clung around her calves like twin tourniquets. Her rich chestnut curls were freshly washed – indeed, her hair seemed still wet from the bath – and she wore no hat; the only covering on her face was a thick application of make-up that framed her huge eyes with spidery tendrils of mascara and carmined her extravagant lips as though she had lunched on cinnabar moths.

The whole tea room, that cramped and crowded bourgeois cell, was briefly silenced as she undulated to the table where George and I sat waiting.

'Hello, chaps,' said Miss Harris. 'Sorry I'm a bit late. Get us a cup of Rosie Lee, will you, I'm parched.'

I summoned a waitress, under a heavy enfilade of stares. It was, I admit, one of the most satisfying moments of my life.

'Miss Harris, this is Monsignor George Coveney, my old friend.

George, this is Miss Barbara Harris, a young protégée of mine from, ah, Camden.'

'How'd you do?' said Barbara. 'Aren't you a bit hot in that jacket?'

'I am a *little* warm,' said George with a flirtatious chuckle I have never heard him utter before, 'but I regret I have no light summer clothing. It is part of the burden of being a senior clergyman, Miss Harris, that one cannot adapt one's dress to the vicissitudes of the climate.'

'Tell you what,' she said, 'when nobody's looking, you could slip it off and 'ang it on the back of my chair. And your dog collar too, if you're feeling too, you know, choked up.'

'Barbara – Miss Harris,' I said, 'I'm glad you've agreed to accompany us today. It means a great deal to me, to be able to show my charitable benefactors how my work touches the lives of poor unfortunates who –'

'You don't 'appen to know, George,' said Barbara, cutting across me, 'who won the Gold Cup at Cheltenham? It was the two thirty, so the results 'ave been out for an hour already. I stuck ten bob on Butcher Boy to win.'

'I regret, my dear, I am not a devotee of the turf.' George seemed crestfallen that he was not a slave to gambling. 'But I could endeavour to find out for you, if you could wait a moment . . .'

The prospect of seeing a monsignor of the Church of England lurching into a bookie's shop in the Strand, demanding to know the outcome of a horse race on behalf of a teenage prostitute, was piquant indeed.

'Nah, don't bother,' she said, extracting an untipped Players from a shark-skin case and lighting it by striking a match on the underside of the table. 'I don't reely give a flyin' toss for the gee-gees myself. But my boyfriend Kemal, he's a demon for it. Oh, by the way, 'e liked *you*, Harold.' She nodded. ''E thought you were a right laugh.'

I was taken aback, not only by this revelation of my good standing in the eyes of a Hindoo whoremonger, but that she should pass on the information as though it should bring me delight.

'He seemed . . . interesting,' I said neutrally.

George looked at me.

'We talked about Oxford,' I assured him. 'Miss Harris has a wide and unusual social acquaintance.'

'Indeed,' said George. 'You have met many of her friends, have you?'

I did not care for his tone of voice.

'Only the Indian gentleman,' I said with emphasis. 'Miss Harris and I have met on just three occasions, in the course of my pastoral work.'

'Harold 'as been round a few times,' said the girl, matter-of-factly. 'He said he liked my bed. Enormous and bouncy were the words he used.'

'I assure you,' I said, attempting a laugh that came out in a strangled yelp, 'I was seeking to establish a rapport with this young woman, at her domestic quarters in the mid-morning, when it is her habit to rise and breakfast at a leisurely pace. Her bed, upon which I briefly sat, was decidedly —'

'No need to explain, my dear fellow,' said George equably. 'And tell me, Barbara — if I may — have you plans for the future with this gentleman, who is so keen on the sport of kings? Is he, to borrow the language of modern mothers, is he a prospect?'

'What, Kemal?' She lay back in her Lyons chair and laughed heartily. ''E's a *prince*, George. Chance would be a fine thing. What, is he likely to want to marry me? His mum's a *marrow-ranee*. She'd 'ave a fit if I turned up in the palace, blushin' and simperin' and hangin' on his arm in me fancy sateen frock. No, really.' She seemed mightily amused. George looked on, entranced. 'No, sorry to laugh, but that's not going to happen, more's the pity. 'E's a lovely boy, Kem, lovely smooth skin, but nah — when 'e's had enough of me, 'e'll just piss off back to Madras or wherever it is, and marry someone 'is mum would approve of.'

'Good heavens,' said the monsignor, 'you mean there is a rival for your affections back in India?'

'Lots of them, George,' said Barbara. 'Loads of 'em. Hundreds, maybe thousands. They're called virgins.'

It was perhaps the first time my old tutor had ever heard such a speech from such a brazen non-virgin.

It was then that Rose appeared. She might not have come near us at all, had I not spotted her skulking by the Ladies and beckoned her over with encouraging waves. She advanced towards the company crab-wise, in a sidelong, apologetic advance like someone convinced that the tables around her were wired for electric shocks. Her gait was a kind of ambulant cringe. I had perhaps spoken too firmly about the seriousness of our meeting, for she was dressed in a faded black net dress more suitable for her mother's generation, and a dismal black hat.

'My dear Rose,' I kissed her fondly on the cheek and squeezed her hand. Her veil stroked my skin like wire mesh. 'How lovely of you to come. Let me introduce Monsignor Coveney and Miss –'

'Barbara's the name,' said Barbara, rising to her feet. ''Ow you doing, darling? Just come from a funeral, 'ave you?'

'No – no,' said Rose, a little startled. 'I just come straight from home. My mum said to wear this, so I wouldn't look common.'

'Oh yeah?' said the unstoppable Barbara. 'She was dead right, wasn't she? No sense in looking common when you're bein' paraded round by His Lordship here as a tart down on her luck. Whoo, no. You need to get a bit dolled up when they're going to ask 'oo you been fucking lately.'

'Barbara! Miss Harris!' I was beside myself with embarrassment. (I did not dare to look at George, who had, quite possibly, never heard the word before.) 'There is no question of any such enquiry at our meeting. I would ask you both to curb your language and to try and enter into the spirit of the occasion.'

Barbara only tilted her head and raised both eyebrows with infuriating calm. But at least she held her tongue.

'You are not about to be paraded in front of my titled friends like cattle. Nor as sinners, nor as criminals, nor as examples of moral viciousness.' I spoke with as much eloquence as I could muster outside a pulpit, here in this noisy, crowded tea room. 'Your role, if I may call it that, is merely to be yourselves – intelligent, beautiful, sensitive, modern young women who may have strayed into the pathways of corruption, and who need enlightened assistance –'

'Money,' put in Barbara.

'– to begin a more fulfilling life elsewhere. That is all I ask. Be yourselves for a single hour in the company of my, ah, luckier and more fortunate –'

'Richer,' said Barbara, indefatigably.

'– and wholly well-disposed acquaintances, and let us see what benefits may accrue to yourselves and the beneficiaries of my charitable League.'

There was a silence.

'Hello,' said Rose to the shrunken figure on her right. 'My name's Rose. What's yours?'

'My *dear* young lady,' he said, rising to his feet. 'How are you? I am Monsignor George Coveney, a friend and former tutor of the rector here. May I get you some refreshment? Some tea perhaps?'

'I thought we was going for some tea at a hotel,' said Rose, with a pathetic pout. 'Harold said there'd be tea and fancy cakes and tiny little sangwidges. And these quality people.' She looked at me accusingly. 'Are they not coming?'

I saw in a flash what a fool I had been (in so many ways) in convening our little group at a Lyons, prior to our hotel visit – but where else could we have met? The station? The post office? Lyons Corner Houses are second nature to me as meeting places. I had not thought it out.

'I believe all these delights will be available to us very soon, my dear,' said George. 'This brief interval is merely for us to get acquainted before moving on.'

'Oh, that's nice,' said Rose. 'So what you do then?'

My old friend, in his clerical garb, seemed amused by the question. It had been some time since he had been asked the nature of his employment.

'I am involved in Church work at a high administrative level,' he said, without pomposity. 'Semi-retired of course, at my age, but I still attend meetings of senior clergy to determine policy and discuss various exegetical cruxes in the rubric.'

Rose looked baffled, as well she might.

'You ever go the theatre, George?' said Barbara. 'Harold 'ere is always taking girls to the theatre. D'you ever go?'

The drift of her words was all too clear to me, but I said nothing.

'Indeed I do, Miss Harris. Several times a month.'

'Oh, right then.' She brightened visibly at the prospect of a conversation about anything away from the subject of religion. 'I love plays. What you seen lately?'

'Oh – *Private Lives*. Mr Maugham's *The Breadwinner*. A drama called *Street Scene* by that American gentleman –'

'Elmer Rice. I read about him in *The Stage*. Is it any good?'

'The word "good" is not an adjective to be applied to any of these works,' said George in a steely tone. 'They are all, without exception, morally rebarbative. Other commentators than I will assess their merit as drama, in the modern heathen way, without addressing their immoral messages. But I visit the theatre in a different capacity, as one of the advisers to the Lord Chamberlain, and view them, I fear, in a very different light from yours.'

'I'd love to see *Private Lives*,' said Rose, dreamily. 'Gertrude Lawrence, she's gorgeous. I heard her saying some lines from it on the wireless, about India or something. She sounded really lovely. I can just see her in a long elegant frock, standing on a balcony by the seaside in France.'

'So that's what you do, is it, George?' said Barbara, with that silver dagger in her voice that I have come to dread. 'You go to plays to see what's wrong with 'em, and complain about the rude bits?'

The monsignor picked up the corner of his spectacles between finger and thumb and settled them more precisely on his nose, before regarding my teenage nemesis.

'The public have a right, Miss Harris, to be protected from material that may shock or provoke them into immoral ideas or impure thoughts. The Church cannot stand by and let depictions of adulterous liaisons and low-life violence go unquestioned and uncensored. The boundaries of taste must be carefully policed and properly controlled. Surely you must agree?'

'Harold, why didn't you take me to see *Private Lives*?' asked Rose, with a slight but perceptible whine. ''Stead of those blooming art shows and music things? You been a dozen times, you've taken Lily and Bridget and Sally, and you know *I* wanted to.'

'If you push me, George,' said Barbara, 'I'd say, what century you living in? The theatre ain't for old geezers now. Queen Victoria's dead. We don't 'ave time for your petty morality no more.'

George looked around, only mildly put out. He seemed under

the impression that he was dealing with an unruly child rather than a genuine troublemaker.

'Harold, you must help me here,' he said, laughing just a little. 'This young lady will confound our thoughts if we let her. Can it be that you expose your young charges to these plays, not once but several times over? To what spiritual end?'

'Good heavens, is that the time?' I said. 'It is well after 4 p.m. We must make our way with all speed.'

And we left.

We were late. Lady Fenella greeted us – not coldly exactly – but with reserve. Anything less than scrupulous punctuality can be turned, in her mind, to yet one more example of moral 'slide'. She glanced at Barbara's unfortunate get-up (shirt all bosom, slacks all calf) with distaste, and at Rose's funereal garb as though debating whether to offer sympathy. I introduced the monsignor, who twinkled and rhubarbed away ('Dear lady, how delightful, I think I once met your mother at Lambeth Palace,' et cetera) most efficiently.

Beyond us, sitting together on a heliotrope banquette, lay our prey, so to speak: Sir Arthur and Lady Bassenthwaite. He is a surprisingly short colonial grandee, sunburned as a Boer, whiskered as a walrus (a look that passed away from English aristocratic circles with the death of Queen Victoria), and carries himself like a man used to getting own way – ordering the natives around, throwing bridges across the Limpopo, drinking gin sundowners during torrential evening monsoons. His wife was a sweet-faced Hampshire rose of, I would guess, thirty-five, much his junior, her complexion deathly pale, the testimony of a decade spent under parasols, canopies, tents and African bearers with fronds. Excellent teeth.

'This, my dears, is Harold Davidson, my old and valued friend, the Rector of Stiffkey' – she called it Stewkey, as do many people not directly acquainted with the parish – 'and the terribly distinguished Bishop Coveney of Holborn –'

'You flatter me, ma'am,' said George, smiling, 'when the only title to which I can lay claim is Mon—'

'The *Bishop* of Holborn,' continued Fenella, with an emphasis that was not to be challenged, even by the holder of the spurious title, 'and these ladies are, ah, a pair of young London gels whose lives have benefited from our friends' charitable endeavours. Now we must have tea' – she clapped her hands together twice, like a sultan summoning a platoon of dancing houris, and two serving girls, hitherto hidden beside the curtains, moved in on the capacious Brown Betty pots and white milk jugs, the napkin-wrapped hot scones, the sliced ginger cake, et cetera, arrayed on a table – 'and then Harold will tell us of his work among the needy and misfortunate.'

It was the signal for general conversation. I enquired about the Bassenthwaites' home in Kenya and learned far more than I required to know as to the acreage, the lushness, the swooping landscape, the feral fauna, the indolence of the natives, the wiliness of the servants, the amusing evening games of the white 'neighbours' (who could, it seemed, live fifty miles away and still deserve the appellation), and the howling superiority of every facet of their lives in this far-off jungly paradise, to anything remotely 'bearable' in England.

Sir Arthur spoke in a kind of verbal telegrammese.

'Little trick we like to play on visitors. Green, you know. No clue about African ways. Come to stay, on third day usually he'll say, Safari, that's the ticket, when can we go? Good lady, equally green, clutches arm and says, Oh Gerald – not always Gerald obviously – Oh dear Gerald, is it dangerous, wild animals rushing from undergrowth, slavering fangs, how terrifying. I say, my dears, of *course* we could go this Friday, take Joseph and Umbeki, picnic on savannah, spot lions panthers kudu giraffes and so forth, but NO NEED.' He chuckled. 'They look puzzled. Not at all, I say, no need to make special trip, wild creatures so used to human presence, they come right up to the house. Stay up late enough, I tell 'em, you'll have panthers sidling up to porch lights looking for food. Usually' – he waved an index finger in the air – 'this is the best bit. Usually, I say, they head for side garden by east wing, where we leave some raw meat out for 'em. Always works. Visiting lady thinks for moment, you can hear gears grinding away in her poor head, and she says, But Gerald, that's just outside *our bedroom*!'

'Arthur,' put in his wife, 'will have his little joke. The poor wives always fall for it. I try to reassure them it's all nonsense and they will be perfectly safe, but that's when he takes it *all too far*.'

I looked from one face to the other. They were like the twin beams on a late-night taxi – mutually complicit, a self-delighting double act.

'What happens then?' I asked. 'This is tantalising beyond endurance.'

'Then,' said Arthur, 'I bring in the boys. Joseph and Umbeki and one of the maids, Florence I believe her name is, they pad around the east garden at two in the morning. Joseph has marvellous basso growl. Umbeki does wonderful thing with his mouth like this' – he threw his head back and ululated in a series of strangulated cries – 'and Florence, lovely girl, she can do this long mewing noise like, you know, like huge cat in pain. Doesn't take long before you hear screams from bedroom, frantic lighting of hurricane lamp, and they start peering out the window. But by then, servants are right up against wall where they can't be seen, still growling, barking, mewing and so forth, unseen, as if house now *invaded* by wildlife.'

He paused to shake his head, overcome by the humour of it all.

Lady B smacked him lovingly on the arm. 'Really, Arthur, you are *so bad!*'

'I generally meet them on the stair, as they're coming up in their nightgowns – and sometimes even less – crying, "The animals are coming in!" And I have to say, "Well, you're welcome to go outside and explore, but I need my beauty sleep so I fear I can't come with you." *Consternation* all round. It really is most *howlingly* funny.'

I have seldom met a colonial who was not a buffoon. Second sons of good families they are, usually, sent away from England where they'll be less trouble while their elder brother inherits the house and grounds. Sir Arthur seemed a particularly egregious example of the breed.

'How amusing,' I said. 'But I believe you both find time for less provocative excursions. Lady Fenella has been telling me that you are both involved in charity work in the Alatongwe district. I am most impressed that you should be such good Samaritans in such a rough and needy territory.'

Sir Arthur looked baffled, as if no Samaritan impulse had ever crossed his mind.

'Yes indeed,' said Lady B, clearly the trouser-wearer in this department. 'Arthur and I believe so much in the betterment and education of the Negro. Some of them come to us wholly unprepared for even the rudiments of service. They know nothing of cuisine beyond the application of water to mealie oats. They have never seen a mattress before, let alone know how to apply a cotton sheet and tuck in a hospital corner. They can understand English only if it is accompanied by an explanatory pictogram of, say, "cushion" or "fan". They bring drinks in the wrong glass, without so much as a tray or platter of nuts. So Arthur and I have endowed a small foundation for the education of Alatongwe boys and girls, where they spend three weeks at our expense, learning skills that would, in England, require the outlay of hundreds of pounds at a servants' academy in Bayswater.'

'How very good of you,' I said, with an attempt at approbation. 'I was not aware that servants generally enjoyed academic training. Even in Bayswater.'

She may have caught some flicker of asperity in my voice.

'I assure you such places exist. But I do not seek public approval for my – our – work. I – we – think it only a way of giving something back to the community in which we live. The better the servant in Africa, the better they will contribute to the local economy, as their offspring become estate managers, farming supervisors, plantation overseers and the like.'

'Some might argue, Lady Bassenthwaite, that teaching the black-skinned races to be better servants is merely a way of keeping them cowed, ignorant and disenfranchised, rather than making them independent members of society.'

She looked at me. Her eyes were dark and suspicious. It crossed my mind that nobody had ever confronted her before about the present condition, or the future aspirations, of the majority of her countrymen and women.

'Shall we have tea?' she asked, moving away.

I looked around the room. The monsignor was deep in conversation with Lady Fenella, perhaps seeking further details about her mother's social contacts. Barbara and Rose were talking together at the food table, glancing around as if waiting for a signal that they could begin wolfing down the buffet.

'Ladies,' I said, warmly, 'take a plate and make free with the food. And come and meet Sir Arthur Bassenthwaite, who is full of amusing stories about his travels in Africa. George – Bishop Coveney – will you take an iced bun?'

So I ploughed on, in this uncomfortably warm hotel room, full of ill-matched people.

George was enjoying himself. He had not for some years had the direct attention of so many ladies, neither *poules de luxe* nor the consorts of weighty colonial men. I was glad to see that he seemed at home with both.

Barbara seized a chocolate eclair in her right hand and crammed it into her cavernous mouth in a frankly lascivious fashion, plunging the long tube of pastry through her widened, pristine white teeth, planing off the chocolate icing, as half the bulk of the sweetmeat disappeared inside the lovely fleshy 'O' of her lips.

'Mmmmm,' she hummed. No organ could have produced a note more sweet, no basking, chops-licking lioness a sound more filled with animal satisfaction. In an instant I was back in her sunlit room watching her lying on the bed as her face was transformed by the rays of the Redeemer. Rose was also watching her. Her eyes went from the pastry to Barbara's mouth and back, entranced. 'Are we allowed to do that? Don't we have to eat the sangwidges first?'

Barbara laughed, a cruel, snarly little noise. 'No, you don't have to have the *sang*-widges before the cakes, you goose. You sound about ten years old, worried what your mum's going to say. Eat what you like. Lady Muck over there's paying for it.'

Gingerly, Rose accepted a Bakewell tart with a large maraschino cherry stuck into it. Barbara was right. Uncertain of herself at the best of times, Rose had temporarily regressed to childhood.

'My mother says I got to stop being bad-mannered,' she said to the company in general. 'She reckons I'm coarse and common and nobody thinks I'm fit to marry, or to talk to, or bother with at all because I say words all wrong and don't pass the butter sharpish when someone's asked for it.'

'She says that?' asked Barbara. 'You don't mean you still live with the old bag?'

Rose nodded, with an innocent smile on her face. 'I didn't used to, I used to share with another girl in Wapping, but Harold – Mr Davidson 'ere – he rescued me when I was a bit down and got me back to the family so they could look after me. Where d'*you* live then?' She suddenly wrested the initiative from the younger girl. 'You're hardly old enough to be out of school, are you?'

'I left school when I was thirteen,' said Barbara, 'been living on my wits ever since. Wits, men, bit of thieving, a lot of lying on my back. I tried going legit for a while, tried being a milliner's assistant in Burlington Street, making 'ats for a living. But it didn't take. I was bored out of me skull. And they sacked me for going off with the odd gentleman shopper around lunchtime, so I knew I wasn't cut out for it.'

'Go on,' said Rose, impressed by her headstrong new friend. 'You're a bit of a shocker, aren't you?'

'If you want my view,' said Sir Arthur, who had lingered on the periphery of the conversation like an old dog lurking near the family hearth, 'young women of any breeding shouldn't concern themselves with getting on. Jobs and so forth, management and shops and the like, are simply a distraction from their natural rhythm. They'd be far better off staying at home learning traditional, you know, skills.'

'Oh yeah?' said Barbara. 'Like what?'

'Oh —' Sir Arthur waved a vague hand. 'Breaking horses. Mixing cocktails. Scrutinising the dinner menu. Supervising the servants. Checking the security fence. That sort of thing.'

The noble knight had, of course, been back from Kenya only forty-eight hours or so, after a long absence. I warmed to his naivety about the ways of modern London women.

'I must try and do all them things,' said Barbara, witheringly. 'I'd love to be a traditional girl. I'll start first thing Monday morning with me servants and me fence. Won't be easy, though. There's not much call for breaking 'orses up Camden way.'

'I cannot imagine, Miss Harris,' said George, beaming like a village idiot, 'there is a horse in England which could not be mastered by having you ride upon its back for five minutes.'

She turned upon him a look of the utmost delight. For all her precocious self-possession, Barbara is a fool for flattery.

'You old saucebox. You're rather a dark 'orse yourself.'

Sir Arthur, standing like a bookend on the right of the ladies, addressed for the first time the clerical bookend on their left.

'How do you do, Padre? We haven't been introduced. Bassenthwaite's the name.'

'Monsignor Coveney,' said George coldly, not best pleased by the military nomenclature. 'I am here to assist my friend the rector in −'

'George has a funny job,' said Rose, in the first unprompted utterance I can remember her making. 'He goes to see plays to have them taken off. He was saying earlier, he only goes to the ones with dirty bits in.'

There was a silence.

'Indeed?' said Sir Arthur.

'No, no,' said George, laughing a shade nervously. 'I am on the board of the Lord Chamberlain's Public Decency Commission. As part of our mandate we exercise a power of veto over the language employed in modern dramas. But we are not, I assure you, philistines or prudes.' He laughed again, even more nervously.

'But how interesting,' said Lady Fenella, reappearing after a lengthy colloquy with Lady B beside the pastries. 'What kind of filthy utterance have you had cause to remove lately?' She can always be relied upon to ask for intimate details.

'Well now,' said George, 'this new play *Mercy Buckets*, for instance, just opened in the West End − a French farce, in translation − had to be cleansed of some regrettable references to foundation garments, and the liberal use of the words "Jesus Christ".'

'My mum used to come down on us real hard if we said that out loud when we were young,' said Rose gloomily, 'and then she'd say it herself, and if we said, Oi, how come it's all right for you to say Jesus Christ?, she'd make out she was only saying a prayer and not blaspheming at all.'

'Fascinating,' said George. 'Your mother is, of course, quite right. Ejaculations to the Most High are a form of prayer in trying circumstances.'

'Oh yeah?' said Barbara.

He regarded her with interest, trying to keep his gaze away from her scooped cotton front.

'And what is your favourite ejaculation, Miss Harris?'

'The kind that doesn't get in me hair,' said Barbara.

The monsignor blinked.

Lady Bassenthwaite let out a little shriek, instantly stifled.

Fenella looked at her as if afraid she had missed some modern allusion, understood by all the company except her. She turned the full beam of her condescension on Barbara.

'Mr Davidson tells me you are one of the needy girls to whom he has extended the hand of friendship?'

'Yeah,' said Barbara. 'He extends his 'ands to lots of girls, he does. Very nice of 'im, I'm sure.'

'And that he hopes to find you an interesting position before very long, is that not so?'

I could not bear to think what her answer might be. Years of experience have taught me to endure the base humour of street girls at any sign of a double entendre. I looked at the floor, waiting for some inexpressible vulgarity to fall from her lips.

'He's the only person I trust in this wicked town, Lady Royston-Smith,' I heard her say. 'Without 'im, I swear I'd be back on the game in no time. But for the rector, I'd still be in the clutches of foul and 'orrible men, who make you do things, Your Ladyship, that I wouldn't sully your noble ears by telling you about.'

I could not believe what I was hearing. Miss Harris, from being the most unhelpful exemplar of saved and grateful Unfortunates, had abruptly turned into their most shining paradigm. I looked up from the floor. Her eyes were fixed on me. Her mouth held a secret smile at one corner.

'Do not spare my feelings, Miss Harris,' breathed Fenella. 'It is important that you unburden yourself of your dreadful experiences. What did these horrible men make you . . . do?'

'I'm only a young girl, right?' said Barbara. 'And I bin in situations that brasses twice my age wouldn't 'ave 'ad to endure.' She glanced, a little unkindly I thought, at Rose, who was attending to her, open-mouthed.

'Gentlemen callers, sometimes six in an evening, sometimes twenty a day, bein' sent into my little room for their vulgar pleasures. I hardly 'ad time to put more lipstick on and wash meself down below before another one was on top of me. You know when you're below stairs an' at the sink —'

The noble ladies nodded – absurdly, given their probable unfamiliarity with such a circumstance.

'– and no sooner 'ave you washed up ten greasy plates and a dozen knives and glasses, and thought, Christ, thank Gawd *that*'s over, when another load of old greasy crap arrives an' you 'ave to deal with that pretty sharpish, because you can hear the waiters outside arranging for another load to arrive in twenty minutes' time? Well, that's what it's like. One more mad old fat stranger coming in, saying, 'Ello, how's things, lovely weather we're 'avin', and the next thing you know there's this fat nasty cock, all blue veins running down the side, that you got to put in your mouth and pretend you're reely keen about 'avin to suck it. It's real work, I tell you. Hot and slimy and exhausting and sometimes it seems bloody never-ending.'

She pushed back a strand of hair from her gleaming brow, as if sweaty from the memory of her exertions. 'I swear, sometimes you felt grateful for the funny ones who *didn't* want to stab you in the throat or hoick down your drawers the minute you met.'

The monsignor inserted his index finger inside his collar and ran it around the rim, as if the constriction pained him.

'Do go on,' said Lady Bassenthwaite, quietly. 'The funny ones?'

'Oh, I've 'ad them all. One old geezer didn't want a poke at all, 'e just wanted to crush some strawberries on me tits, and some cream on top, and lick them all off. And after that, just a lot o' chat about how well his granddaughter was doin' at school.'

'I had a client like that once,' said Rose, nodding eagerly. 'Back before I was saved. Fifty-ish, red-faced, hearty gentleman, very loud shouty voice. He used to bring a little kid's saddle along with him, and he'd want me naked on all fours with this thing strapped round me, and he'd chase me round the floor, shouting, "Boots, Saddles, to Horse and Away," trying to poke a riding crop into me private bits. I couldn't see what he got out of it. He was a bit touched if you ask me.'

Barbara nodded, like the chairwoman of a church committee, welcoming a sage intervention from a junior member.

'Ah yes,' said Sir Arthur. 'Pig-sticking. Went on a lot in Simla when I was a young subaltern. Not that I ever . . . you know . . .'

'And there's the spankers,' Barbara went on as he subsided in confusion, 'who'd put you over their knee and pull your skirt up and whack you on the arse a bit with their hand and tell you you're reely bad an' wrong. It took a while to realise they only got off if you struggled. If you just lay there thinking, "This carpet is a bloomin' disgrace, it needs a good clean," well, that was no good. You 'ad to wriggle and say, "No no, stop, I bin so bad, but I'll be a good girl in future, I promise," and you'd soon 'ear them gurglin' and groanin' and soon enough they were spent and out the door.'

I looked at George. His face betrayed nothing but the utmost concern.

'Shocking,' he said. 'How can such things go on in our city?'

'It goes on all over,' said Barbara. 'Every day, morning till night, all over town. I used to work down The Cut at Waterloo, till it got too crowded with brasses. There was fights all the time about who could 'ave which slot – by the Old Vic, by the chop'ouse, by the Ring pub. There'd be a dozen of us, shoutin', "Fuck off, bitch, this is my patch," and a minute later the gents'd come out of the play in their bow ties and we'd be all smiley and say, "'Allo, darlin', you need some company?" and when most of 'em had hurried off, we'd be clawin' bits out of each other's faces all over again.'

I marvelled at Miss Harris. I have seen many actresses in my time, but few so caught up in a role. Knowing that she had invented most of this vivid scenario entirely for the benefit of Fenella and Frederica only increased my admiration.

'But then I met Harold,' Miss Harris went on, 'round Marble Arch way, I think it was,' (I blushed to recall the occasion) 'and he bought me lunch and said how I was wasting my life. He never said I was bad or a sinner or any of that, he just told me that doing what I was doing was a waste of me talents and I should apply them elsewhere. That was what swung it. Not that I was bein' a sinner and all that, but that I was wasting my time, when I was a clever girl and should be makin' a better life somewhere. An' I'm all better now, in a lovely refuge in Camden, learnin' to play Mozart on the violin. So that's why you should support 'is charity and keep young girls like me from being shafted and pawed at and spanked and licked and choked with big willies all day long. You know what I mean?'

Her speech, though hardly edifying, was an extempore triumph of sordid detail. After it, I hardly needed to embark on my habitual sermon. She had done it all for me. The ladies, when they trusted themselves to speak after this vivid if perhaps overly frank tirade, murmured their commiserations to her, and congratulated me on my Samaritan energies. They seemed strangely thoughtful and chastened after her narrative. Sir Arthur busied himself with his pipe and asked the monsignor about the dismal record of the national Test match team in the English summer that had passed him by.

I talked for ten minutes about the Virtue Reclamation League, our work of rehabilitation and apprentice schemes, our record of success amid the currents of corruption that threatened the ever-deepening flood of young persons into the metropolis. I handed out mimeographed copies of the charity's accounts, explaining the dismal shortfall of cash that required much philanthropic giving before it could achieve financial equilibrium. My eloquence was received in a silence that was partly respectful and partly the echoing boom of boredom. They would, I fancied, have been happier with more of Barbara's and Rose's shocking revelations. I told them where the money would go, and George put in some helpful remarks about the interest taken by the Bishops' Conference in these local initiatives. 'I know how people such as yourselves value anonymity in your generous disbursements,' he said. 'But I assure you that, through the bishops that sit in the House of Lords, it comes to the ears of the highest in the land and is appreciated in ways at which I can only hint.'

George is a marvel at hesitant gravitas. He can summon up epic panoramas of regal benevolence and court intrigue, words muttered into the ears of kings and princes, nods of awesome private understanding, tiny gestures that beget huge consequences of land, wealth and public standing, all by a few choice remarks. By the time he had finished, Sir Arthur was picturing himself with the gift of Holyrood Castle, and already making arrangements for a zoo in the grounds.

'Harold, can we go soon?' said Rose, plucking my arm as George reached his peroration. 'I'd really like some fish and chips.'

'Very interesting meeting,' said Lady Fenella as she ushered us through the door. 'You must bring me to one of these refuges of yours, soon. I should love to hear more of the remarkable moral transformations you perform upon these poor wretches.'

Barbara extended her hand to Sir Arthur. For a mad moment, I wondered if he might kiss it, even after the many details of where it had been in recent months. Finally he shook it, but with enthusiasm.

'Marvellous,' he said. 'Admire your spirit. If you ever find yourself in Kenya, you must —'

'Goodbye,' said Lady Bassenthwaite firmly, flinching slightly as she edged past Barbara's thrusting front. 'I'm sure we shall hear more of your new life of virtue from Mr Davidson. Come, Arthur.'

In the Strand, I gathered my little group around me.

'That went well, I think,' I said, feeling a brief post-mortem was in order. 'I thought you ladies acquitted yourselves most admirably. A little, ah, salty, some of the language, but I felt the company benefited from the empirical testimony of those who have suffered the —'

'Harold,' said Barbara, 'you can stop now. You got what you wanted. You got what we came for.'

'But my dear —'

'I saw the young dame, the African one, writing a cheque. So you don't need to dish out no more speeches.'

'Did she?' asked Rose. 'Gosh, you see everything, don't you?' For the first time I registered that she was holding the younger woman by the hand.

'I wonder if I should have said something,' put in the monsignor, 'about the advantageous tax position that favours the charitable giver. Not of course that it compromises the virtuous impulse of the truly charitable.'

I looked at my troupe — for that is how I suddenly saw them; God forgive me, but I remember so well the camaraderie of actors — and a surge of love invaded my heart.

'There is a vespers service at St Bride's at 8 p.m.,' I said. 'Will you join me in celebrating the success of our outing?'

George nodded. For moment I wondered if it could be possible that the ladies might enter the church beside us, a perfect visual metaphor for all I sought to achieve.

'We're going for a drink at the Old Coal House, ain't we, Rose?' said Barbara. 'Toodle-oo. And, Harold?'

'Yes?'

'I think you know how much you owe me now. I expect to be repaid properly. I think you should take me somewhere nice.'

'My dear Miss Harris, I should be delighted,' I said, most sincerely. 'To the theatre? To the Opera House?'

'Nah,' she said, 'it's gone beyond that now. I was thinking more . . . Paris?'

I stood by the monsignor, as we goggled together at her presumption.

'See yer soon.' And with a toss of her wanton chestnut curls, she and Rose made their elegant way down the Strand, clasping their hands together in the air, like triumphant suffragettes on Derby Day.

CHAPTER 9

Letters from Mrs Moyra Davidson
Stiffkey Rectory
30 September 1930

My dear Oona,

It seems like an age since we were last in touch. How were the holidays, wasn't it Bundoran you were off to? How lovely, I remember it well from my own summer trips to the west when I was a girl, the beach was like a great wide sheet of glass you'd run across to get to the water miles out, like you were running across a big mirror and all the sunlight was blazing away underneath your feet as you ran to the sea. Did you take the children clambering among the rockpools and looking for little sand crabs? I cannot think of many happier ways of spending your time. Fat chance of me having a lovely seaside holiday. Harold is away all the time, at his ministry in London, chasing subventions for his charities, getting the money out of people before Christmas occupies their thoughts and they feel less disposed to dish out a few quid to the needy. He has to contact the harem of titled ladies he keeps all over London, and the senior clergy who have helped him out once or twice in the past from their discretionary funds and he has to beg from the businessmen who run the companies where some of his fallen women go to find employment. And have you seen the state of the unemployment figures? They were in the paper last night. Two and a half million souls in England out of work. No wonder the streets are full of people, walking up and down with this dead look in their eyes, like in some dreamland. I mean walking in the city of Norwich, of course, not Stiffkey, nothing ever happens around here, the main street gets hardly a whisper of traffic, except on Fair days, when the little vans come through the village with pigs and hens and grain, headed for the market in Wells-next-the-Sea.

You asked about H's mysterious absences in London. I liked your idea that I should put a tail on him or follow him to town and see what he gets up to. I can see myself skulking around Piccadilly and Oxford Street like a spy in a raincoat and a big hat, ducking behind pillar boxes and cab ranks when my husband stops in the street and looks round to see who's behind him. But, Oona, what if I were taken for one of the loose women he's trying to save, hanging about in the street without anything to do but follow a strange man wherever he goes?

I have no fears or doubts, dear, about Harold among the women. Of course I wish he was back here more, God knows there is enough for him to do in the village, with so many sick to visit, it's like an epidemic round here – Mrs Swarbrick riddled with cancer, Mr Teasdale crippled with his wasting spine, a wound from the war, and they both dote on Harold, he'd always visit them in the past and sit with them and talk nineteen to the dozen about political stuff in the papers and the new plays he'd seen in London. A lot of the time they wouldn't know what he'd be talking about, *Journey's End* and *Folly to be Wiser*, they're just random titles to the bedridden, but they like his enthusiasm.

Last Sunday he was in fine spirits after a successful meeting with some new rich ladies he's added to the harem. Some colonists out in Africa are putting up a thousand pounds for his Virtue Reclamation League, and another five hundred from his friend Lady Fenella Something, of whom I've heard much praise, Oh such benevolence, how she puts people at their ease, such conde-scension, etc., it gets on my nerves sometimes. But not as much as I've been hearing lately about some young one called Barbara. I mean really young, Oona, about sixteen or seventeen, and I can't establish from H whether she's a full-time, dyed-in-the-wool red-light pedestrian or just a Girl in Danger as he calls them – Harold has this sixth sense for girls who're about to fall. He says she's a brilliant little actress at playing the repentant Magdalene, and he calls her his secret weapon in extracting charitable donations from the reluctant.

I said, Oh really, she sounds nice, and he smote his brow and said, You must meet her, I shall bring her to the village, you shall see for yourself how delightful, how inspiring she is. I pointed out that the house is full to the brim right now, not only Colonel Du Dumaine and his sons, I've been renting a room to Mr and Mrs Quinn from Holt while they're having the central heating put in, PGs of course, because we're desperately short of money, it gives me some company in the evening when H isn't here and I'm tired of the colonel's moth-eaten gallantries and Nugent's globetrotting young bravoes and the girlish twittering from Sheilagh and Patricia. But that means all six bedrooms are crammed out and where's she going to sleep, standing up against the range? H said I shouldn't worry, Barbara's an adaptable girl, she can sleep in the servants' quarters.

Whether she's a strumpet or is just good at pretending to be, imagine the shocking things she must have experienced in her few tender years. And she's coming here for a weekend next month. It happens from time to time, a visit from one of H's unfortunates. Years ago, he brought a young one called Rose up for the weekend. A sweet-faced, rather weak-minded thing with Irish parents, charming and talkative but hopelessly disorganised. She was always losing everything, keys, handkerchiefs, make-up, umbrellas. If you sent her to the shop at the end of the street to get the messages, she'd lose her way home. She was always half an inch away from being in tears, do you know the kind of girl I mean, just too sensitive for this world, anything could start her off. I don't know how a girl like that gets to be a streetwalker, I'd have thought you need to be tough as nails. Anyway, the walks to Blakeney Point and Holkham Hall put a bit of a colour in her cheeks, sometimes she'd stay out all night long, after she'd found some new friend in a pub who'd lend her a mattress for the night.

Just getting out of London, these girls feel the benefit. We'll see if it will work with Miss Barbara, whom I cannot help but think of as the Infant Phenomenon in *Nicholas Nickleby*, prancing about and turning cartwheels for the edification of her smiling parents.

Write, darling, and tell me all about Bundoran and the rock crabs.

Your beloved Mimi

Stiffkey Rectory
4 October 1930

Dear Harold,

I fear things are coming to a head with Major Hammond. He is beginning to frighten me. I do not like the man and never have, but I don't see why I should be caught up as piggy in the middle in this vendetta between the pair of you.

Everybody thinks you did right to ban the old savage from reading the lesson in church when he's been drinking. And you showed me the letter, that incoherent rant about him banning *you* from his house and grounds. I know from Mrs Reynolds he's been uttering terrible calumnies about you around the village, stuff about the girls in London and your designs on them, such a cheap accusation, how crass to suggest that a man cannot be about the business of saving women without descending to depravity himself. I think you ought to know that the year's payment from the major should have been in just under a month ago, and you know what an important sum it represents – without it we may have to kiss goodbye to the church roof, not to mention the renovations to the south transept.

And now, Harold, something else has occurred. His wife died the other day, probably as much from neglect as from consumption, God knows I wouldn't have that drunken sot attending on *me* if I was ill. But the poor woman passed on, at the age of sixty-eight, and it's a fine and deserved rest she's gone to, away from his roaring and nagging.

Anyway, poor Mrs H was buried last Friday, Mr Reynolds got Roderick to dig the grave in the churchyard and the funeral was short and dignified. Obviously we could hardly ban the major from attending his own wife's funeral service, so he was allowed back in his family pew, the Rev. Blair officiated and gave a very nice sermon (St Luke – 'Thou fool, this night thy soul shall be required of thee') and it all passed very well. But after the burial, things started to go wrong. The major renewed his acquaintance with the hip flask before the procession to the grave and, by the time the poor woman's body was in the earth, he was grumbling and slurring his words and leaning against the wicket gate, saying 'Shedoesntbelonghere' and 'Shestoogoodforthelikesofyou' and similar uplifting sentiments. Eventually he was led away by Mr Grogan of the Legion, who can always be relied on to play the copper ('Now you come along with me, like a good gentleman'), while Roderick plied his shovel and the tiny group of mourners (few friends had she, poor Mrs H, but that's more the fault of the bad-tempered husband than the long-suffering wife) dispersed to their lunch. But wasn't the major back in the afternoon with a shovel of his own, and didn't he start digging up his wife's own grave? Would you credit it, Harold? Mrs Reynolds was nearby and asked what he thought he was about, but he ignored her. I telephoned the Rev. Blair and we bore down on the major, sweating away in his rolled-up shirtsleeves, sending claggy lumps of soil flying over the neighbouring graves, over the cards and wreaths and nosegays of violets.

'What are you doing, Major Hammond?' cried your locum. 'For pity's sake, man, this is consecrated ground. You cannot dig up your late wife. She has been laid to rest with the most sacramental dignity that the Church can offer.'

'She should not have been laid here,' said the major, never ceasing to delve with his spade, 'in this common grave, surrounded by whores and paupers. Whose decision was it to inter my beloved wife in this vulgar plot, in the most untended part of the cemetery, near a bank of nettles? It is just one more insult to me and my family by the rector, the most godless man to set foot in a church since Henry the Eighth.' His breath grew laboured as he plunged again and again into the mound before our horrified eyes. 'I shall. Remove her from. This place. Take her to. Garden of Morston Hall. Bury her among. The Gundogs . . .'

Reverend Blair put his hand on the major's arm. 'Please stop this now,' he said, as gently as anyone could under the circumstances. 'Cease this desecration of the village graveyard and go home, Major. You are distraught. You are overtired. As for the reinterment you propose, it is not possible. You cannot start burying people in their own back gardens, because it contravenes every rule about the disposal of the dead. Your wife's remains must stay here, sir, where they have been laid to rest with the most solemn exequies of the Church. Please allow this to be her final resting place, and let us both bow our heads and wish her *requiescat in pace*.'

Did the major humbly comply? Did he my foot. He looked with loathing at Rev. Blair, worked his mouth into a fury and spat voluminously in the poor man's face. Rev. Blair was stopped in his tracks. Grey saliva dripped in a pendulous glob off his chin, a spectacular insult to the cloth. The major was only dissuaded from further digging by Mr Reynolds, who led him away by the elbow.

Harold, come back and save us from further trouble. Think what that man might do to our family. He is opposed to all you stand for, he is devoted to devilment of every kind. If he can dig up his dead wife just to make a point against you, think of what worse abominations might follow. Take charge, Harold, I implore you, speak to him as the head of the local church, before this gets any worse.

With my love,
Mimi xx

‹

Letters from the Rector of Stiffkey
Stiffkey Rectory
5 October 1930

Dear Major Hammond,
It is with a heavy heart that I write to you in tones of reproof. I yield to nobody in my admiration for your war record, or the fine work you do as a local magistrate. But I must address you on the subject of appropriate behaviour in church.

My objections to your dishevelled appearance in St John's last month were prompted by more than a dislike of alcohol. I am as well disposed to conviviality as the next man, but when it leads to language more appropriate in the mess room or the squaddies' hut, I feel I must intervene. Likewise, much as I value your skill in reading the lesson at the Sunday service, I fear the effect is rendered much less impressive when drink has obviously been taken. For these reasons and others, I was obliged to speak to you and, as you know, I would rather you stay away from the church premises until your regrettable habit has been curtailed. You were good enough to inform me that I was likewise 'banned' from visiting your home. I took this as an exercise in humorous tit for tat, reasoning that no parishioner could wish to curtail his relationship with a man of God – the person who will officiate over the most important days of his life: his marriage day, the baptism of his children, and the applying of Extreme Unction in his final hours. I am not a connoisseur of army humour, but I must assume you were joking.

The latest development is no laughing matter. It was brought to my attention yesterday that the burial plot of your late wife in the graveyard of St John the Baptist has been vandalised. The freshly dug grave has been desecrated, and the earth flung aside. I was startled to learn that you, Major, were responsible for this shocking act. The reasons you advanced – some dissatisfaction with the 'vulgar' status of the burial plot – mystify me. We are a small village where everyone coexists without hierarchy of class, rank or status. Landlords, tenants, householders, shop owners, artisans, labourers in the field – all come to the same end, and are buried in the village graveyard with the same ceremony. I hope you will see that your wife's burial plot is no better or worse than any other, and its location does not proclaim or reflect its owner's status, save as a child of Christ and a loved friend and neighbour.

I hope, after reading this, you will feel no future impulse to interfere with the funeral arrangements of your charming wife.

Yours truly, my friend in the Lord,

Harold Francis Davidson

Stiffkey Rectory
10 October 1930

Dear Major Hammond,

I was disappointed not to receive any reply to my letter of 5 October, and even more disappointed to find it sent back, unopened.

My instinct, in a case such as this, would be to hasten to Morston Hall and have it out in a frank exchange until we both know where we stand and can resolve matters without sulks or threats. Since you have forbidden me from your house, this avenue is not open to me. It has been brought to my notice that you have returned to your wife's grave and once more attempted to dig her coffin from its resting place, until restrained by Mr Reynolds. I cannot allow this behaviour to continue. Please desist from any more of these scandalous and unchristian attacks on the consecrated ground where your wife's mortal remains should lie undisturbed.

Yours truly,

Harold Davidson, Rector

Stiffkey Rectory
12 October 1930

Dear Hammond,

So you have returned my second letter unopened. I thought you and I could deal with one another as gentlemen. Clearly, I was wrong. I am sending this letter by registered post, so that I will know for certain it has found its way into your hands, and that I may take a lack of reply to be a hostile act.

My wife tells me that, while I was away in London, busy at the pastoral work you disparage, you once again ignored my strictures and trespassed on the graveyard, once more intent on disturbing Mrs Hammond's grave. It is obvious that no appeal to Christian decency will stop your excursions into the grounds of St John the Baptist, so let me make the position clear. The church

here in Stiffkey, all its property and all its land, are my responsibility. I do not own it; the Church owns it; but I have local juris-
diction over it and nobody can dig it up without my permission.
Should you set foot on a single square inch henceforth without
a written invitation from me, I will not hesitate to contact the
Church authorities and the police, and prosecute you for aggravated trespass. Mark my words, Major, I will apply the letter of
the law, should you transgress further. The dead have a right to
lie undisturbed. The living have a right to bury their own without
fearing a madman will appear with a shovel and open up the
grave next door. We all have the right to be protected from the
rage of a vengeful drunkard.

I do not, of course, wish to stop you from paying your respects
to your late wife, so I propose a solution. I suggest you purchase
a family plot of land somewhere in the graveyard, and use it for
the burial of your wife, your children, yourself, any future Mrs
Hammonds, et cetera. Should you wish to propose a purchase,
feel free to apply to me in writing and I will see what can be
arranged. I expect you probably know the address by now.
Otherwise, stay away from here.

H. Davidson, Rector

Letter from Mrs Moyra Davidson
Stiffkey Rectory
20 October 1930

Dearest Oona,

My nerves are in shreds. The house has been full of the strangest
toings and froings, people arriving and departing all the time,
rows breaking out, doors slamming, Cook has resigned, Mrs
Henryson is all fired up to leave – and all because of Harold's
unfortunate women.

The young one I told you about, Barbara, she was supposed
to come up with H on Friday for the weekend. Well, of course,
he had better things to do than come near us on a Friday, and
he rang on Saturday morning to ask could somebody meet her

off the noon train to Wells. But she wasn't alone. She had that other one with her, Rose, the older girl who was here years ago, the one who loses everything and is always in tears. So we dispatched Mr Reynolds to the station and in an hour the visitors had arrived. It was comical to see the two of them together – one a schoolgirl of sixteen, not that you'd think it, what with her long cotton dress, a very nice pale blue thing with a belt and a V-neck, but you couldn't help thinking she must've raided her mother's trunk for it. The other is a woman ten years older but dowdy as a Dutch governess in her tweed jacket, her peasant skirt, her clumpy court shoes and her bun. Such a pair, Oona, it would have made you smile, the tarty school beauty and her plain governessy friend.

I tried making them feel at home, but my heart wasn't in it. There's too many people in the house for comfort. I don't mean the sleeping-quarters problem, I mean people wandering up and down all the time. Mrs Quinn has turned out to be a very demanding paying guest, she needs hot-water baths all hours of the day and night. Colonel Du Dumaine's elder son Gordon has conceived a passion for Enid the parlourmaid and pursues her like a mooncalf from room to room, trying to strike up conversations. But the main problem is the food. There isn't any. I've told Harold, God, *how* many hundred times, that his weekly food allowance just will not stretch to feed all the souls currently inhabiting the Rectory, that it hasn't changed since we came back to Stiffkey in 1920, when the children were small and we had just the housekeeper and no other help, and it was fine then, the few pounds a week, but now it borders on penury. He won't listen. He'll just pull open the larder door and his eye will fix on the bone-end of a gammon leg or a box of eggs and he'll say, '*Look* at all this provender. Here is God's plenty indeed. Good English ham and fresh farm eggs, a man could live like a king on this.' And I say, 'No, Harold, we're all starving, and the colonel doesn't get his morning porridge any more, we can't afford it, and we haven't had a decent roast since Easter Sunday,' and he'll say, 'Nonsense, my dear. The house is crammed with food, you are too accustomed to self-indulgence. Think of the poor girls with whom I deal every day – now *that* is poverty and want, in its starkest clothing,' and I say, 'Well, H, these girls you mention, at least they get a decent dinner in London, something I haven't had in years, but then it's being bought for them by my husband, while we're all sitting here at home starving and trying to make a potato omelette stretch across ten people.'

So imagine the frame of mind I was in when I met the girls in the hallway.

'I'm Barbara,' said the young minx, tilting her head so the big brim on her picture hat revealed her features in a discreet peek-aboo. She jerked her thumb sideways and said, 'This is Rose.'

'Pleased to meet you, I'm sure,' said Rose, essaying a curtsy, which came out more like a cringe.

'No bowing or scraping, girls,' said I firmly, 'that stuff went out at the end of the war.'

'Harold was going to travel up wiv us last night,' said Barbara, 'but 'e got tied up at a musical sworry.'

'How unfortunate,' I said. 'My husband is often –'

'Then he was going to come wiv us this mornin' but 'e got tied up in a benefactors' lunchen.' Her remarkably flat voice turned everything she said into outrage.

'I'm sure he'll be here by teatime, if he takes the two o'clock train. He tries to catch that one, some weekends.'

'Nice mirror,' said Barbara, admiring her headgear in the hall looking glass. 'Must've cost you a packet.'

I am not often required to call to mind the original sale price of the furniture in my home, Oona, so I ignored this.

'Rose,' I said, 'I was not aware that you were also coming to stay.'

'Oh,' said Rose, touching her hand to her mouth.

'Though, of course, you are as welcome as the flowers in the spring.'

'Oh.' She smiled helplessly.

'You've been here before, of course,' I continued brightly.

'What?' Her hand was suddenly back at her mouth. 'When?'

'Some years ago. Harold brought you up for the weekend. I thought you had a lovely time. I'm surprised you don't remember it.'

'What'd I do?' asked Rose, suspiciously.

'As I remember,' I said to her, nicely because she seemed decidedly jumpy, 'we sat up talking after dinner, and Sheilagh played some melodies on the piano and you sang some awful funny songs from the music hall.'

'Oh *no*,' said Rose in a mortified breath.

'That sounds nice,' said Barbara, nodding. 'I like a bit of action round the old joanna of an evening. I look forward to that tonight.'

I felt I had better wrest the initiative back from her. 'We are not planning a singing evening, Barbara. It is not something we pursue regularly at the Rectory. Discussions and exchanges of views are more our thing. You and Rose are welcome to try the Townshend Arms in the village, where Mr Cooper the patron's nephew, Giles, often regales the company with music.'

Barbara gave me a look not so much hostile, as exploratory. '*Oh* yeah?' it said. 'So we're being packed off down the pub . . .' But Rose seemed pleased. 'That would be lovely,' she breathed; whether because of the music or the prospect of drink, I couldn't tell at the time.

'I'm hellish sweaty,' said Barbara. 'I need a wash.'

I said, 'I'll show you your room,' and set off. The young one, Barbara, had a glamorous overnight vanity case, while Rose had nothing but the crocheted reticule that hung on her arm. I hoped for her sake it contained a toothbrush and a change of drawers. I led the way upstairs, up to the bedrooms, past the study and the bathroom, up to the second floor and the annexe. The girls followed until they reached the door of the room.

Barbara stopped on the threshold and looked in with disdain.

'Hang on,' she said. 'This is the servants' quarters, innit?'

'Well, yes, it's where Enid and Polly usually sleep,' I conceded. 'But we've put them next door with Mr and Mrs Reynolds for the weekend, so you'll be able to sleep in the house, as my husband's guests.'

'This where you usually put your guests?' demanded the little upstart. 'Your grand friends from Norwich and King's Lynn, you usually bunk 'em up in the cook's and the chambermaid's quarters, do you?' Rose, meanwhile, shifted uncomfortably from one clumpy black shoe to the other.

'My dear girl, the Rectory is full of people. Apart from my immediate family, there are some paying guests in other rooms and my husband's friend the colonel and his boys. There is no room to be had, unless somebody can be persuaded to sleep on the sofa. I don't know, Miss Harris, to what level of luxury you are accustomed,' (I allowed myself a tiny smile), 'but here we tend to mix in together without much ceremony. You must swallow your distaste and accept the only bed left in the house.' So she did. She and Rose sat on their two little beds, riding a little on the mattresses like a pair of Mayfair ladies inspecting the sleeping arrangements of a tribal hut on the Masai Mara.

Harold joined us in the afternoon, made a great fuss of his two charges, the way he puts his arms around their waists and draws them together to him reminds me of something; I think it's the music-hall posters of that eejit comedian in the tweeds, Farnon Percival, the one who's always saying, 'Come Now, Ladies!' and pulling faces. You mustn't ever tell Harold I said such a thing but he looks the dead spit, with his arms round the Ladies, like he's being photographed for *Reynolds News*.

'My dears,' he says, all genial, 'you are here to relax, to feel the cares of the city sloughed from your bodies and left behind, while the rejuvenating green blood of the Norfolk countryside infuses your spirits. You must walk energetically, breathe the good air, try the local produce, imbibe everything the village has to offer, talk to the local people and learn from their simple goodness of heart that there is more to human nature than the dregs of Whitechapel and Finsbury Park.'

Well, I've no idea whether they went about breathing and imbibing, for they disappeared around the house for the afternoon. There were comings and goings. The colonel and his boys went on a five-mile walk to Cley Head. The Quinns went shopping in Holt. Mrs Reynolds popped in with some fish, pulled lepping fresh out of the sea. Enid and Polly remade the beds. I gave Cook and Mrs Henryson emergency directions for feeding a multitude, and by teatime everyone was reassembled in the drawing room.

A cheery fire waved in the grate. Harold talked earnestly with Mr Q and Colonel DD about the news from Germany, where a gang called the National Socialists who don't like the Treaty of Versailles have won a hundred seats, and about the death of F. E. Smith the lawyer, a bit of a hero to H, he has many droll stories about him. Mrs Q and I were gassing away about the unfortunate pregnancy of Minnie Bell, the young one in the village who was attacked by an underwear salesman two months back. Enid and Polly handed round sandwiches and cake – the first time we've seen bloody cake in this house in half a year, and not because the bishop has dropped round, mark you, but because a couple of young tarts from London have paid a visit.

And just when everything was peacefully abuzz with conversation, the headstrong Miss B starts up.

'God, it's boring in 'ere,' she says to the two Du Dumaine sons, (fourteen and sixteen, and what you'd call sheltered types). 'Can one of you young fellers not give us a tune on the old piannaforty?'

Michael, the younger, blushes a deep crimson, even to be addressed by Her Majesty in her thin frock, but Gordon, his slightly more copped-on brother, says, 'Well, I, er, perhaps I could, er, if Mrs Davidson wouldn't, ah, but perhaps not, look, I mean . . .'

The poor kid was dying to impress this flirty girl with her big bosom, and he looks at me like a dying puppy, and 'Fire away,' I say, 'only not too loud now,' and he goes up to the piano and sits down all atremble like he's fronting the Norwich Philharmonic, and plays, of all things with which to serenade Barbara, 'Nearer My God to Thee'. Well, this *is* a house of the Lord, but even I could see it wasn't what was wanted by that particular company.

'Don't you know nothing a bit more lively?' says his tormentor, as the sonorous chords died away. 'Something with a bit of a swing?' She looks at me as if, once again, testing the potential opposition. 'If you got no objection, Mrs D. It's not like I'm going to start dancing or anythin'.'

So Gordon played one of Thomas Moore's *Irish Melodies* that we often sing in the duller evenings, I think it was 'The Harp That Once Thro Tara's Halls', and Barbara and Rose got off the sofa and went and stood on either side of the young lad, murmuring along with the notes like a music-hall double act, the Murmur Sisters, Rose bending down to see the music, like she could follow a musical score, until her face was practically touching Gordon's, and Barbara, sideways to the boy, with her long white hand resting on the piano top and her fingers slowly drumming to the music, lifting and resting like a seductive spider to distract his attention from the keys.

When he'd finished, the girls clapped prettily (glares from the men, deep in their serious conversation) and Gordon didn't know what to do with himself, so exciting was the chatter of female approval around him. Rose turned her face right into his and said, 'Marvellous, that was reely good, my, but you're the talented one in the family, ain't you?'

(I couldn't bear to look to see how poor Michael was taking this.)

Barbara just nodded and started in at something else. 'Look, Rose,' she said, pointing to the map of the Norfolk coast on the wall behind the piano. 'Here we are, look –' and she jabbed a finger at the word Stiffkey. 'Such a funny name, innit? Oh, but hang on, what's this? Look, the next village along is Cockthorpe,' said Barbara. 'That's a laugh. Be a bit embarrassing if a lonely traveller was asking for directions and got the names wrong.' She affected a highfalutin-traveller voice. 'May good man, Ay'm looking for Thorpekey. Whoops, sorry, no, I mean Stiffcock, no, dammit, I mean –'

A wild shriek signalled that Rose, at least, appreciated her friend's coarse humour.

'I expect there was somewhere called that once,' said Barbara. 'Before the villages got separated. Don't you think, Gordon?'

He looked up at her, wonderingly. I thought, this is how baby seals once looked up at Shackleton's men just before they had their heads bashed in to provide the explorers with their dinner.

'Think what?' asked Gordon, falteringly.

'Stiffcock. There must've been a Stiffcock round 'ere once.' A pause, a dreadful pause, in the awkward silence. 'You ever been to Stiffcock, Gordon?'

He was lost. 'Er, no, no, I –'

'Bet you'd like to, wouldn't you? With the right lady traveller?'

He searched her eyes, poor child, for some sign that she perhaps meant what she said and wasn't just having sport with him.

She returned his gaze. Her eyebrows lifted an inch in frank invitation. 'Mmmm?' she said.

'Oh look,' said Rose, mercifully. 'There's places here called the Snorings.' She let out a peal of laughter. 'They must be wild.'

Barbara consulted the map. 'Story of my life, innit? Heading south, you get a bit of Stiffkey, a lot of Cockthorpe, followed by a Great Snoring and then a Little Snoring, with some Fakenham at the end of it.' She pronounced it Faking 'Em. It was ingenious, but it had to be stopped.

'Girls,' I said, 'I've asked Mrs Henryson to show you round the kitchens and meet Cook and see how we organise things behind the scenes. I'm sure you won't mind helping out by chopping a few vegetables for dinner. As you can see, we're a little oversubscribed with guests tonight and —'

'What?' said Barbara, reluctantly turning from her cat-and-mouse game with the smitten Gordon. 'You want us to go and peel spuds?'

'I hope you will feel welcome in every part of the house. Since you are young and strong and not averse, or so Harold tells me, to honest labour, I hoped you might feel —'

'First we get jammed into the servants' quarters, in a bed no bigger than a mousetrap, and now you want us to be skivvies in the kitchen? Well, bugger *that* for a game of darts.' She seized her friend's hand. 'Come on, darling, we're leaving.'

'Miss Harris,' I said sharply, 'there's no cause to be obstreperous. I need some help in preparing dinner. You're a guest at that dinner, as you are my husband's guests for this weekend. But surely half an hour in the kitchen, when we are so understaffed, will not be a desperate burden for a girl such as yourself?'

Well, that did no good. The pair of them stormed out of the drawing room, saying 'See you later' in that annoyingly American style.

Cook and Mrs Henryson were livid, twice over, first when the help they were promised simply disappeared from the house, second when the meals that were prepared for them went to waste.

Where did they go? Don't press me for details, because it's still a delicate matter, widely debated all over the village. They went to the Townshend Arms, we know that much, because they went in at 6 p.m. and sat, flooring glasses of barley wine and cheeking the clientele, until ten.

After that? All I know for sure is the scene at one o'clock in the morning, when I was woken by a row in the annexe. I went up and – I don't want to assault your delicate nature, Oona – there was Barbara, with her blouse wide open, being pulled by the hair of her head by Enid, who'd got back in the house from next door, and the two of them were going at it hammer and tongs, Enid yelling, 'You f—ing bitch, I'll have your guts for breakfast,' and Barbara shouting, 'Take 'im and welcome, he's no good to woman or beast, little wretch, 'e's come all over me skirt while I was gettin' it off, stupid bloody kid,' and in case you're wondering, yes, it was poor Gordon, the awkward object of their attentions, peeping round the parlourmaid's door, looking desperately upset, as pink as a peeled prawn, doubtless telling himself never to go near a grown woman again as long as he lives.

I had to rouse Harold, for fear there might be loss of life. He spoke sharply to both women, and ordered Gordon to get back to his own bedroom. Enid was threatened with the sack for daring to attack a guest (this only redoubled her cries of 'Effing bitch', etc.) and Barbara was given a lecture on Occasions of Sin, though it was a bit late to instruct a connoisseur of a hundred such Occasions.

Where was Rose? Who knows? She appeared for breakfast without her bun, her hair tousled and matted, like she'd spent the night in a hedge. No explanation of her adventures, at the climax of their trip from the corrupt city to the simple purity of the Norfolk countryside.

I'm exhausted, just telling the story. Cook and Mrs Henryson have – no, sorry, told you that already. Poor Harold is upset that his experiment had such unsatisfactory consequences.

Come and stay with us soon, Oona, and bring a bit of sanity to this place.

Your dear friend,
Mimi

CHAPTER 10

Letter from Major Philip Hammond (retd)
Morston Hall, Norwich
20 October 1930

To the Very Reverend Bertram Pollock, Bishop of Norwich
My Lord,

I think it is high time somebody brought to your attention the behaviour of one of your clerical underlings.

He is a menace. He is a degenerate. He is a hypocrite. He is a damned bad hat all round.

I have been C of E all my life, never faltered, never flirted with any papist High Church wop nonsense. My only quarrel with the Church is this. No review structure. No monitoring of efficiency. No overseeing of where the weak links are to be found.

I'm an Army man. I came up through the ranks, got where I am through hard work and doing what was required without slacking or shirking. Why? Because I knew there was an Army Review Board at the end of every period of duty, waiting to rap a chap on the knuckles at the first sign of backsliding or lead-swinging.

I don't want to tell a bishop his business, but if the Church had an ARB of its own, it would soon weed out the rubbish. And the first bad apple it would discover in the pile would be this fellow Davidson, Harold Davidson.

He is the rector of our local parish of Stiffkey and Morston, has been since 1907. I moved to Stiffkey in 1912 but, except to say 'Good day', hardly encountered the man until 1920. The war, of course. I served in the trenches. He enlisted as naval chaplain, went to India and Middle East, well away from the real action. But that's not important. After the war, there was much talk about the Davidsons. I'm not one to pass on gossip, but Mrs D worked somewhere around Windsor as a nurse and got pregnant, and *not* by her husband. Some passing soldier on leave, I gather. Anyway, the family got very rocky, the Rectory lay empty for four years with the occasional locum vicar taking the odd service. (How did that make the locals feel, d'you suppose?)

They came back in 1920 and for the last ten years, My Lord, this so-called pillar of rectitude has spent more time in the capital than in his parish. He might as well be a scarecrow in the field, for all the good he is to his parishioners. He takes the last train from London to Wells on Saturday evening, and the first train back on Monday morning. This is a fact, I have spoken to the stationmaster. And what does he do in London? He spends his time in the company of whores and strumpets, pretending to convert them, but in fact clearly deriving every enjoyment from their blowsy company. I am told he misappropriates money raised through a network of false charities and uses it to wine and dine his dubious paramours, with heaven knows what to follow.

You think I exaggerate? My neighbours in Stiffkey are accustomed to seeing Davidson walking the lanes with some of his supposedly needy 'victims'. They are the dregs of humanity – raggedy street-boys who would steal the hands off a clock, and garish harlots who pursue their infamous calling in the quiet lanes of Stiffkey and Morston.

I would not have believed these stories, had I not experienced with my own eyes the depravity of Davidson's entourage.

Last Saturday night, I ventured from Morston Hall to Stiffkey, to speak with Dr Donald Runciman, a fellow magistrate, about a forthcoming court hearing and, our business concluded, I looked in at the Townshend Arms for a whisky and soda. I need the occasional 'wee dram' to curb the pain in my head from a wound sustained in the Boer campaign. I entered the public house at 1930 hours, to find, among the usual farmers and handymen, a brace of women on a low sofa by the fire. At first I took them for mother and daughter, so far apart did them seem in age, but as I examined 'em, it became clear that the older one was barely in her thirties, but so careworn and woebegone she looked twenty years older. Her friend, whom I'd initially taken for a dressed-up child, betrayed such confidence in her speech, it was clear she must be at least twenty-five.

I conversed with a couple of village pals, Geoffrey Talbot and Martin Saunders, both ex-Army, for a while, but our colloquy was distracted by much foolish yapping from the ladies. (I ventured to remark, not for the first time, that there should be a separate bar to house women at their infernal chatter.) The younger one had an extraordinarily carrying voice and, from what I could hear, the subject matter would have been better whispered. Phrases such as 'He wouldn't be the smallest I've had' and 'He seemed like a nice clean boy' rose above the saloon chatter and caused my companions to lift their eyebrows heavenwards. The dowdy one became more animated and playful, and laughed incontinently at her younger friend. She went to the toilet and when she came back, her death-pale lips were smeared with lipstick. More raucous remarks inspired another neighing fusillade.

By 2100 hours, things were quieter. I watched as the two women barged into a circle of young male drinkers – just stuck their conversational oar in and started holding court. The Devil's own cheek, but the young idiots played up to them. They seemed to be the rump of some sporting team, possibly football, and were flushed and swaggering, easy prey for these loose camp followers. After 2230, the noise level in the saloon had risen again, but things began to break up. The younger girl took herself off, though don't tell *me* she was looking for an early night. Four men remained around the lipsticked frump, bees round a honeypot. I said goodnight and set out for Morston, but realised I had left my copy of Tadcaster's *Tort and Common Practice* at my friend Runciman's. Needing to peruse it over the weekend, for a Monday hearing, I banged on his door. He invited me in for a nightcap and we discussed some minutiae of Wrongdoing With Intent for an hour. Venturing home once more, I stopped by the Church of St John the Baptist because I heard a noise beyond the gate, a muffled groaning as of a soldier in pain. I went through the gate and saw a fellow appear beside the church. He was doing up the buttons of his greatcoat. I tried to say, 'What the devil are you about at this hour?' but he was gone before I could confront him. I rounded the corner of the church – and what a scene met my eyes. The woman from the public house, the one with the dowdy clothing and the gash of lipstick, was being shafted against the wall, excuse me, My Lord, by a man whose breeches lay round his ankles. His hands clutched her shockingly white and parted thighs from underneath and carried the weight of her whole body. Her hands were joined around his neck. Her head was flung to one side, so that her face was towards me, though her eyes were shut. But the most infamous sight was of her peasant skirt, the hem of which she held in her clenched teeth. No more flagrant example of female abandon could be imagined.

The man leaned his head against the wall and widened the spread of her thighs as he battered himself against her, as though trying to finish off an enemy. Her teeth, with the skirt caught between them, were bared like a dog's. It was a scene of animal beastliness.

'Look here,' I said – to no avail. I stepped forward to remonstrate with the pair – and discovered, behind him, two other men, skulking, one smoking a cigarette, both clearly waiting their turn with this shameless slut.

Afraid I fled the scene. Should have demanded their names and had them arraigned in court. But didn't. Had to leave them to it. Just can't abide that sort of thing – demeaning to the village, degrading to the persons involved, and treacherous to the sleeping innocents in the modest little homes around here who do not know how their trust is being betrayed. Shocking, also, to think it was against the church wall that, you know . . .

You might say this is none of my business, that the private lives and consciences of other people are their own concern. But to have this kind of behaviour take place here in Stiffkey pains me as a landowner, a Christian, a Norfolk man, a magistrate and a churchwarden. You might say Davidson has done nothing wrong, that the only sin lies with the damned females he brings with him from the sink of corruption down south. But his behaviour towards me, of late, has not been that of a pastor and spiritual guide, but of a bully and a tyrant. 1) He refused to let me read the lesson at Holy Communion service on Sundays. Claimed my speaking voice was slurred or some damn-fool tommyrot. 2) He banished me from entering the church at all, after his mad Irish wife confronted me beside the font and accused me of drinking. I had had a bad cold for days and was in the habit of sucking eucalyptus comfits, which may account for her suspicions about my breath. 3) When Mrs Hammond died, she was buried in the graveyard of St John the Baptist, but in the lower levels of the field, where there is danger of flooding. I expressed my disapproval by digging up her coffin, but was stopped by Mr Reynolds, one of Davidson's henchmen. 4) Davidson sent a letter pretty well telling me I was not allowed to tend my wife's grave unless I bought from him the plot of land in which she lies!!! Can you credit it? I, the leading landowner and *de facto* governor of this village, told to buy his wife's grave from a toothy and opportunistic local cleric who wants only to line his pockets and cheek his superiors.

I tell you it won't do, Padre, it just damn well won't wash. Sorry, My Lord. But the man has been a thorn in my side for too long. I am sick of his capricious behaviour, tired of the unruliness he brings to the village, but hopeful that the senior echelons of the Church can root out this contagion before it gets worse. I leave it in your hands, confident that you will view the contents of this letter in a serious light and take immediate and radical steps.

I remain your respectful servant,

Major Philip Hammond (retd)

Journals of Harold Davidson
London
20 October 1930

Nothing has so gladdened my heart in months as the growing friendship between Barbara and Rose. How invigorating to see the working of divine grace, as it flows between two apparently lost and directionless sinners, making them draw comfort and strength from each other in confronting a world that seems to conspire against them.

I think their joint visit to Stiffkey for a weekend did them nothing but good. Of course there was some unpleasant shouting at night-time from the servants' quarters, because (as I understand it) young Gordon Du Dumaine took a fancy to Barbara and one of the maids, sweet on him herself, objected. But it blew over and we all had a most agreeable walk in the country. Rose made some new friends in the Townshend Arms and came home after I had retired for a second time. I am most encouraged to see her new confidence in striking up friendships with strangers. They were too weary to attend morning service, but I have high hopes for their next visit. The girls took it in turn riding pillion on my motor bicycle, as gleeful as children, each encouraging me to 'speed up' as I roared exhilaratingly around the country lanes. Fresh air, intelligent conversation and the comforts of a warm religious home have all had their effect.

Barbara now visits Rose every other day, and has made herself agreeable to Rose's suspicious parents. Rose, in turn, now bestirs herself to meet Barbara in the Café de Paris in Chalk Farm every Tuesday and Thursday. I have joined them, once or twice, to drink tea or cocoa at 11 a.m. and watch the girls consume custard tarts. Their conversation is mostly breathless nonsense of clothing styles and hair colouring, things seen in the street, things read in *Woman's World* magazine, 'The Magic of Pearls', 'The Secrets of Ouida', 'Beauty Methods of the Stars' – meretricious nonsense, but it fuels their discourse and enlivens their discussion. When I am included in this girlish colloquy, they ask politely after my health and seek bulletins as to the progress of my mission, for all the world like Lady Fenella and her friends, only more direct. They ask after the fortunes of Lily and Sally, Joanna and Bridget, Marina the madame and her former slaves, Madge and Sara, now safely rehabilitated. Some were well known to Rose years ago, when she was mired in corruption and Mrs Carter's academy of vice in Drury Lane was once a home from home to her.

I fear sometimes that the conversation of a valetudinarian such as myself may bore the girls, and try to adapt my subjects to their modern and sophisticated frame of reference. 'I was informed by Marina about a gentleman who wished to be attended by three ladies at the same time,' I explained to them as we enjoyed tea and a bun yesterday. 'Three! Such reckless depravity. I can hardly bring myself to imagine the scene. Surely when the vile bully had left off mauling one young lady, and proceeded to fumble in the under-clothing of a second, there must have been moments of awkward-ness as the third waited her turn, as though queuing for a number 15 'bus to the Haymarket?'

The girls looked at each other.

'*I* wouldn't want to be the one to go third,' said Rose. 'You'd feel such a fool, wouldn't you?'

'Apparently, the gentleman pays twice the usual rate for this service,' I remarked, 'rather than three times. It seems unfair, since he is employing the skill of a trio of unfortunates. Economically speaking – quite apart from the moral considerations – it seems illogical. But I understand it is a speciality of Mrs Carter's household, like those restaurants in the Strand which offer three courses for the price of two.'

In addressing such immoral matters, I affect a light tone of discus-sion, quite unlike my natural mode of clerical discourse. But a homily is never far away. 'There is a lesson here, girls,' I said. 'To see how, in the world of prostitution, one becomes no more than an economic unit, to be offered at a discount, or indeed a "bargain", should that be what the market demands. Is that how any woman of spirit could regard her sacred flesh? Is that how the core of your being should be splayed and fondled, as if you were no more important than a – than an *umbrella*, one of a hundred in Smiths' umbrella store, to be bought cheaply when the weather is fine, and at a premium in the showers of April and October?'

Rose nodded at my words. (I was pleased with my striking metaphor.) Barbara took a sip at her *café au lait*.

'I've never got it about foursomes,' she said. 'Threesomes are dead easy, as long as you like the other girl. One of you sitting on 'is cock, the other on 'is face, you're riding away, the pair of you, you can 'ave a little kiss and so on while he's spluttering and groanin'' underneath, but you don't have to move if you don't feel like it. But where's the third girl supposed to go, except to sit behind one of you, licking 'er ear?'

I busied myself with my Darjeeling, a little horrified by my protégée's disgusting worldliness. But she was unstoppable.

'Or else they want to poke you both, turn and turn about, so you 'ave to kneel there side by side with your arses in the air, while he pokes you for a bit, then your friend for a bit, and sometimes you catch 'er eye and you're both thinkin', What is this, some kind of competition, like 'e's judging a pair of prize marrows at a country fair? But I never 'eard of a bloke doin' that with three – what, like he's playing a drum kit or something?'

'Barbara,' I murmured. 'Too much detail perhaps.'

'Sorry,' said Miss Harris. 'Only, I can't work out where the third girl's supposed to go. Maybe she's, you know, like a decoration or something?'

Rose had remained silent during this dreadful outburst. So had I.

'I never had a threesome,' Rose confessed, quietly, like a flapper regretting she had never been to Paris.

London
21 October 1930

Excellent news. Vincent Doughty has agreed to take on both Sarah Blow (Vauxhall Tea Rooms) and Esther Vine (Chelsea Embankment) as seamstresses in his manufactory. Sarah was, I know, becoming restless waiting on tables and objected to the constant fug of tobacco smoke which aggravates her asthma, so I am happy to see her pass into Mr D's kindly hands, while to have finally persuaded Esther to forsake her Embankment 'patch' (as the working girls refer to the dismal rainy flagstones upon which they stand, hands on hips, from 11 p.m. every night) in search of genuine employment must count as a minor triumph.

Called on Barbara at nightfall. Distressed to find her still entertaining the smooth Hindoo prince, Kemal. It is distressing, on being admitted to her quarters at 11p.m. – a time when decent girls should be preparing for slumber, brushing their hair, removing their make-up, saying their prayers and reading Mr Shaw's *The Intelligent Woman's Guide to Socialism and Capitalism* – to find her sitting up in bed with this oily charmer. Lesser men might have made some excuse and quit this intimate scene, but my devotion to Miss Harris's salvation made me stay.

Kemal has temporarily ceased his lordly reminiscences about Oxford, his glamorous parents, his family's private temple, et cetera in favour of some racialist abuse about the prevalence of Chinamen in London's East End.

'Mark my words, Harree,' he addressed me, though I do not remember inviting him to use a diminutive, 'these Chinkies have penetrated the pool of London, arriving in scores at the West India Docks and spreading their coolie tentacles to Liverpool and Cardiff and the Clyde ports. They link up, on arriving, with their horrible kind, get jobs around the docklands and conspire to corrupt young girls, whom they buy and sell into slavery like vegetables. I have heard about it from my cousins in Whitechapel – the slanty-peepered brethren are the enemy we should most fear. If you are serious about saving young women from enslavement as skivvies and sex toys, Harree, you must start with the dread Chinaman.'

I have heard too much nonsense about the yellow peril, the sadistic Dr Fu Manchu, the opium dens of Wapping and the alleged network of Shanghai-style slave brothels across the eastern metropolis, to give much credence to such rantings, but I was intrigued to hear this charismatic foreigner voice them. Was he trying to distract attention from his own foreignness by stigmatising the Chinese so he might seem, by comparison, more respectable?

And then a seed of doubt was sown in my heart. Was Barbara's favourite 'boyfriend' all that he seemed to be?

When Mimi and I were temporarily estranged after the war – the baby, the soldier on leave, let me not dwell too closely on these sorry matters – I accepted a position as tutor to the son of the Maharaja of Jaipur. I never went – my leave of absence was cut back by the bishop to six months, when my contract stated twelve, and I was forced to withdraw – but I had familiarised myself about the wonders of Rajasthan.

'Tell me, Kemal,' I said, as nonchalantly as I could, as Miss Harris beside him pertly shielded her breasts by holding a small, pink, heart-shaped pillow over them, 'have you been to the spectacular lake palace at Jaipur? I stayed once, and do not know an experience to equal waking in the maharaja's bedroom, with the dawn light through the stained glass casting jewels over the white bedroom wall, a symphony of reds, oranges and blues –'

'Absolutely,' he cried, in an ecstasy of remembrance that would have been moving had there been a word of truth in it. 'I have stayed there many times when my parents were abroad on business. Is it not the most magical place? And the cry of the hoopoe birds over the lake, and the little boats coming home across the still water after a night of fishing those calm waters. Ah yes . . .' He gazed down at Barbara with liquefying but mendacious eyes. 'One day, my dear,' he breathed, 'when my business here is concluded, I will take you there.'

'But wait a bit,' I said. 'Surely I am wrong. Now I come to think of it, the lake palace was in Udaipur, not Jaipur at all. How memory plays tricks.'

There was an awkward silence. Barbara looked up at him, as if for confirmation as to which hoopoe-filled venue he had promised her.

'Was it?' said Kemal. 'No no, Harree, my memory of the place is so vivid, it was certainly Jaipur.'

'I'm afraid it's all coming back to me now, with redoubled clarity,' I said smoothly. 'It was certainly Udaipur. Which leads me to wonder why you should claim to have stayed at a palace that does not exist.'

Was I mistaken, or did his chocolate eyes flash with irritation?

'I know that age plays tricks with remembrance, Vicar, and since you are twice my age, I suggest that it's you are confused.'

'On the contrary. I have at home a volume of colour photographs entitled *The Glories of Rajasthan*, which would put the matter beyond dispute. The lake palace of Udaipur is on page 27, and is indeed a wondrous sight, which I would be happy to share with you. And with Barbara too, when you are planning your holiday there.'

Another mortified silence.

'Look, boys,' said Barbara, 'why're you arguing? Wherever this bloody palace is, I'd be happy to go there as long as I can wake up with them fancy sheets around me, and the colours all over the wall. It sounds lovely. I don't care if it's in bloody Bombay.'

'The point, Barbara, is not the palace,' I said, my voice taking on a steely determination. Were I not emotionally disinterested about Miss Harris, I might have seemed like a rival for her affections. But I simply did not wish for any more wool to be pulled over her eyes. 'It is the fact that your friend here is lying. He has clearly never been to either palace or, for that matter, either city. His knowledge of India is gleaned from books, as is his familiarity with Oxford. His supposed memories are the purest falsehood. His subcontinental genealogy is also, I fear, one hundred per cent moonshine. He is no more an Indian prince than Max Miller. I doubt that he has been any nearer India than the Taj Mahal restaurant in Bayswater.'

The figure in the bed began to laugh. 'Hah-*haaaah*. But this is priceless!' He turned to the girl beside him. 'Your friend the vicar has spent too much time among thieves and murderers in the East End, listening to their stories and cultivating a habit of disbelief. He now tries to discredit me, out of pure jealousy because he is old and impotent and without glamour, while I am everything he is not.' His smile of condescension would have justified murder in any court in the land.

'If you are not an Indian prince,' I continued, unruffled, 'who are you? Your name is Kemal. In all my dealings with Indians, I have never met the name. In my dealings with Asia Minor, however, the name has cropped up many times, from Mr Atatürk onwards.'

'I'm gettin' confused here,' said Barbara. 'Are you saying Kemal's some kind of Arab? Not that it matters or anything,' she reassured him with a smile. 'But an Arab, like a desert sheikh?' Bless the girl, for trying to find a romantic construction to put on things.

'If you enquire closely, Barbara,' I said, 'you'll find your friend is a penniless Turkish immigrant, more at home among the lascars of Tilbury docks than the court of St James's.'

It was pure guesswork on my part, but some word in this accusation galvanised the man into action. He flung aside the bedsheets, and came at me with a fury that suggested an imminent assault, a flurry of naked riot. I had but seconds in which to register a hideous woolly chest, thick burnt-umber thighs and a considerable girth of private parts, before I was bustled out of the room and deposited through the front door into the street. By the time I had drawn breath to retaliate, a rattling noise told me the bolt had been drawn across the front door of number 14 Queen Street, Camden, and that I was banished from the orbit of Miss Harris and her problematic amours.

London
22 October 1930

I spent an interesting morning on the phone to the Home Office and the Immigration Bureau. I have put a word out in constabulary circles. We shall see if Mr Kemal, the well-known Rajasthani prince, is all he seems when the Metropolitan Police shadow his footsteps for a day or two. Cheque duly arrived from Lady Fenella, hurrah, with charming note: '. . . impressed as always by your assiduous work in the lower depths . . . *delightful* to meet your friend George, though I remain stupidly hazy as to which episcopal see he represents . . . *very* impressed by the candour and simple gratitude of yr young charge Barbara, a girl of remarkable moral strength. Please accept enclosed + feel free to acquaint me with other poor unfortunates. I derive much spiritual nourishment from these meetings.' Signs off 'Your dear friend', promisingly.

Mrs Parker becoming increasingly difficult. Hardly speaks to me in the mornings now, without some complaint re lady callers. Cooked breakfasts a distant memory. How often must I stress that my door remains open night and day to sinners anxious for repentance, when their working hours – and the workings of their consciences – occupy the night rather than the daylight regimen of ordinary people? She remains obdurate. Lily Beane came to me at 2 a.m. on Tuesday in need of ressurance and I finally stilled her tears and tucked her into bed at four. By morning, she was refreshed and filled with positive new approach to employment, moral stance, Christian outlook, et cetera, but Mrs P decidedly frosty. Explained the chaste innocence of the encounter but her mind is black with suspicion.

Letters from the Right Reverend Bertram Pollock
Bishop's House, Norwich, Norfolk
22 October 1930

Dear Major Hammond,

I have before me your letter in which you lay out certain charges and accusations against Mr Harold Davidson, Rector of Stiffkey and Morston. The main thrust of your accusations is that you were the witness to an upsetting (and, if I may say so, gratuitously over-described) scene of debauchery that was not the result of any direct agency on his part. Your disapproval of Mr Davidson's eccentricities, and of the poor unfortunates to whom he offers both succour and hospitality, is clear to see; but I am afraid that neither disapproval nor personal distaste is strong enough grounds to warrant any punitive measures. As to the nature of his conduct in barring you from the church or its graveyard, whether on grounds of your alleged drunkenness or your admitted despoliation of graves, both are serious matters that would require a response from the custodian of the parish. I must trust to the discretion of my rector in doing what is right.

Mr Davidson is known as an unorthodox but devout clergyman. His career as Rector of Stiffkey since 1907 despite a period of absence when serving his country in the war – has been a record of good deeds, zealous work in schools and visiting the sick, and of heroic Samaritan efforts to rehabilitate the morally depraved. I feel he does not deserve your personal animosity, and I must dismiss your gossip-ridden accusations as mischief-making.

I am sorry I cannot be of more help.

Yours truly in Christ,

+ Bertram Pollock

Bishop's House, Norwich, Norfolk
22 October 1930

To Mr Henry Dashwood, Attorney at Law,
Dashwood, Ogilvy & Pearce,
Gray's Inn Road, London WC1

Dear Henry,

That bloody man Davidson is up to his old tricks again. I
enclose a copy of the letter I received a few days ago from Major
Hammond, the local landowner and churchwarden of Morston.
As you will see, he pulls no punches in complaining about the
rector. In fact, he has written letters of complaint about our friend
before, some to the Bishop of London, once to the Archbishop
of Canterbury (!), but this is the first time he has addressed me
directly. He is evidently not a man to be ignored when his blood
is up. All this military rodomontade about the 'weak links' and
'Army Review Boards' may strike you as the ravings of an Army
veteran with not enough to occupy himself. But I fear his rage,
unless mollified, will cause trouble.

You know of Davidson's peculiar record in busying himself
among the poor, the indigent and morally abandoned in London.
We know of the charities he has helped set up, the foundations
he has overseen, his enlisting the help of philanthropists to deal
with the needy, all without involving the Church at any point in
excessive expenditure. For this he is to be congratulated and
encouraged. However, you also know of my concern that he may
have 'gone off the rails' in the last few years, possibly due to
family circumstances, possibly from some overemotional attach-
ments formed amid the degenerates among whom he moves. I do
not enquire. I do not hold my downstream colleagues to account
for their pastoral strategies, any more than I follow my gardener
in his daily ministrations around the rose bushes.

Unless, of course, there is a concrete accusation. The major's
cavils seem to me a lot of liverish vituperation without much
substance, and I have written to him to dismiss them. But what,
Henry, shall I do if he returns to the attack? Where is the appro-

priate path of action if a) the rector is involved in ill-advised consorting with loose women in the Norfolk countryside, and b) if the major goes to the newspapers?

A scandal is the last thing we need. Canterbury would be outraged to find a minister of the Church of England dragged through the mire of exposure, and we ourselves should be arraigned as morally neglectful in turning a blind eye to a public sinner in the hierarchy.

I pray it will not come to this. But let there be one more transgression on the part of Mr Davidson, and something will have to be done. I await your advice in this matter, and send you my blessing.

Your friend in Christ,

+ Bertram

CHAPTER 11

Journals of Harold Davidson
London
24 October

Called on Miss Harris first thing and mildly put out to discover her in bed with a new man, of alarmingly robust appearance. Shoulders like ham flitches, completely bald head like flesh cannonball, comic moustache like the villain in a Chaplin two-reeler.

'I'll make some tea,' said Barbara, displaying the first housewifely impulse I have ever seen in her. 'This' – she waved a hand as though indicating the location of the bathroom – 'is Don. 'Is real name's Tony, but it's short for Don Stupendo.'

'Pleased to meet you,' I said. 'Any, ah, friend of Barbara's. May I ask the reason for your adoption of this alias?'

'How's the goin', like?' said the man, extending his hand as casually as one can when sitting up in bed, half naked. 'You're the parson Babs was telling me about. You can call me Tony. The Don bit worn't my idea. They said I needed to be called something that reflected me prowess, like.'

'Which is some expertise in, let me guess, the pugilistic arts?'

'What, boxing? Noa. That's a mug's game. I couldna stand bein' hit in the face alla time. No, I'm a strongman, me. In a circus, like.'

'But how absolutely delightful,' I said, sitting down on the bed beside him. 'I have always felt immensely drawn to the circus life. The lithe young women on the flying trapeze. The drollery of the clowns. The intrepidity of the lion-tamer. It is some time, alas, since I was inside a Big Top. They come so seldom to the coast of Norfolk.

But where is your circus? Tell me and I shall come to see it without delay.'

Barbara appeared with the tea, served not in cups and saucers but in highly painted jugs of some Continental provenance. 'Look at you, Harold,' she said benignly. 'You're all excited, like a little kid. "Ooh, ooh, can I go to the circus, Mum?" It's down Clapham way, on the Common. Me and Don met round there, in a boozer called the Windmill. 'E just come up to me and said, straight out, "Tell uz, pet, was it reet painful when you fell out of Heaven?"'

She beamed at him, girlishly. It was, in a way, charming to see how this hard-bitten, shrill and brassy young woman, the veteran of hundreds of sexual encounters with strangers, could melt like a snowflake in June on meeting a client who somehow passes himself off as a 'boyfriend'. I am surprised that more men do not aspire to this transformation, since one constituent of it is, presumably, that money no longer changes hands.

'And of what does your act consist, ah, Anthony? Do you lift enormous barbells? Do you conduct a tug of war with a baby elephant? Do you lift up a plank on which four ladies are sitting?'

'Four ladies on a plank?' His comical whiskers twitched upwards with curiosity. 'How would that work, like?'

'I remember seeing it at a circus I attended in Southampton when I was ten. A plank is rested between two sets of wooden steps arrayed in a ziggurat formation. Four chairs are placed thereon. Four ladies climb the stairs and sit modestly on the chairs, and the strongman appears under the plank and between the steps, taking all the weight of plank, chairs and ladies on his shoulders. It was a marvellous sight, especially the contrast between the exertion signalled on the man's face and the matter-of-fact way the ladies sat and chatted together as if they were in a tea room in Bath.'

'But that'ud be a *canny* stroke,' said my new friend with enthusiasm. 'I don't think that's been done in years, man. All I do is break things. Bricks, concrete flagstones, simple stuff. And pulling motor trucks on the end of a chain. And balance things on me yed.'

'Such as?'

'Manhole coovers. Seven or eight at a time. Once I did ten, but it gave me a blinding head for days.'

Barbara rubbed his bald cranium delightedly. 'Isn't he lovely? And you should see 'im do 'is little dance.'

'Indeed?' I said, genuinely intrigued. 'His little dance?'

'I canna do it here in the bed, like, Vicar,' said Don, or Tony, 'and I need me music. It's norra dance, though. Ah stand wi' me back to the audience, stripped to the waist, and the music cooms on – boomp, bah-boomp, bah-boomp-bap-*bah*-da-da-ba-da-boomp – and I strike a posture, like, and flex me muscles in time to the music. It starts wi' the biceps, and then the shoulder blades, that allus gets the ladies squawkin', and then I turn round and do me lateral ripples – ahh, I canna explain if you never seen a muscleman in action. You'll just havta coom to the show.'

'I shall look forward to seeing it. But I must make haste if I can to catch your performance, for surely it will be gone in a matter of days. Is that not the case? Here one day, gone the next, off to the next county, travelling the countryside, never staying long in one place, forever on the move, leaving London after only a regrettably short stay . . .'

They looked at me. (Had I given away my feelings?)

'Nah, it's all right,' said Barbara. 'They'll be in London for weeks. Clapham Common, then 'Ammersmith, then Kew, then Tootin' Common, then God knows where. They decided to stick around London for a while in the run-up to Christmas before heading back up north. So it means Don can be my lovely boyfriend and stay 'ere until he moves on.'

'I see,' I said, glacially. 'I'm sure, Barbara, you will benefit from the rent.'

'Oh, I can't charge my Donny anything,' she said with an artless wiggle of the shoulders. 'I'm sure 'e'll pay me in other ways, won'tcha?'

I was beginning to tire of their glutinous romance and I had registered gloomily that Barbara's acquisition of a new beau did not mean she would abandon her iniquitous profession. For she still needs money, and will be receiving no rent for her midnight activities. (I cannot believe that I sound for all the world like a prostitute's 'manager', or whatever the disgusting word for it may be.) As I said my goodbyes, and promised to meet them again, I silently vowed to renew my efforts to find her work, while extracting her from this ludicrous new acquaintance.

London
26 October 1930

Yesterday, had brainwave and called on Barbara, asking her to meet me later at the Old Coal House, perhaps with her musclebound beau; it will do no harm to establish friendly relations with this affable lummox, if only to show Barbara, by my example, that the world of intelligent men has more to offer than mere physical (or, indeed, animal) appeal.

She agreed to come. I had to wait only forty-five minutes, being barged by rowdy darts players and thuggish Maltese sailors on shore leave, before she arrived, with the enormous swain in attendance. The contrast in their respective height and build as they entered the bar caused a minor stir and some coarse whistling, which Barbara countered with a shrug and Don/Tony failed to notice (of course). I bought them drinks. Don/Tony has, it seems, accepted me without demur as a pal of his ladyfriend, despite the evident disparity in our ages and social standing. He talked amiably of the audience at his Clapham circus. He has tried, he said, to introduce my suggestion of carrying 'a plank o' ladies' on his shoulders into the act, but it had met with resistance. 'The manager, Mr Ackroyd, he wor all for it. But the ringmaster, 'e said it's hard enough persuading one lady from the audience to coom inside th'arena for the fire-eatin' act, and if we're lookin' for four of 'em, it would take all bloody night.'

'A crying shame,' I agreed. 'I would love to have seen you attempt it.' I found it hard to stifle laughter at the sobriety of our discussion, as if we were Church elders discussing a change in the Easter liturgy.

Just then, we were interrupted by a man. He pushed through the crush, hunkered down beside me with a show of easy familiarity, and said, 'So, Rector, how's things? I was wondering when I was going to run into you again. Aren't you going to introduce me to your friends?'

I looked him up and down. I have become used to the modern familiarity with which total strangers now address a clergyman (when wearing my dog collar), but this seemed excessive.

'I fear you have the advantage of me, Mr . . . ?'

'Charlie Norton,' he said, unabashed, '*Evening Standard*. We met in here back in July, I talked to you afterwards and wrote up our little chat in the feature pages. Did you never see it?'

'My dear fellow,' I said, rising awkwardly, 'I had forgotten your face. The befuddlement of age, I fear. Yes, yes, of course I recall the piece. Accurate and hearteningly well disposed. I am delighted to have a chance to thank you. Friends –'

I looked back to the table. Barbara was alone. She was gazing, with an unfriendly stare, at her fellow, Don the Strongman, who was at the bar talking to Bella, the rough-tongued serving wench, as she leaned across and tested the bulging convexity of his upper arm.

'Barbara,' I said, 'this is Mr Norton, a journalist who has been kind enough to write of my endeavours in the London newspaper. Mr Norton, this is Barbara Harris, a young protégée of mine.'

She surveyed him with suspicion. 'I read the *Standard*,' she said. 'I seen your name in there. You write about crime, don'cha?'

'Oh, this and that.' He waved an airy hand. 'Crime, politics, local news, human interest, anything in that line. I've done my stint in the law courts too, but there's always restrictions on what you can report.'

'Oh yes?' said Barbara. 'Must be a bit of a blow for you, not being able to tell the world all the sordid details.'

'Barbara,' I said, 'there is no need to take that tone. Mr Norton is a journalist of scrupulous fairness, and a friend to my – our – cause.'

'Yours maybe, Harold. I choose my mates from people who won't have an ear out, everywhere they go, for another bloody story.'

Mr Norton leaned towards me and said, 'I'd love to know about your young friends from that evening, Reverend. A very lively pair. Did you manage to find them work? That was the point of the evening, I believe. The one who you were trying to encourage to be a secretary? Dolores, was that her name? She was a piece of work, I thought.'

'Miss Knight still has ambitions to become an artist,' I told him. 'I entertain hopes that she will soon take up a foundation course at Camberwell Art College.'

He persisted, as does every reporter I have ever met. 'She was a bit peeved with you, I recall, because you'd set the cops on some boyfriend of hers, Max was it? Did it work out happily?'

'I –' I did not wish to discuss such a matter in front of Barbara. 'I do not remember. Oh look, Don is becoming quite a cynosure.'

Luckily, the strongman at the bar provided a distraction. He had somehow been persuaded to remove his jacket, revealing a black string vest through which his remarkable torso extruded like a Rodin statue. Around him, a contingent of silly young women had suddenly gathered, one of them summoning her idiot friends from a nearby table. They poked and prodded him with fingers at first shy then shamelessly emboldened. Instead of being shocked by the strangers, Don Stupendo came into his own.

'Turn up the wireless a bit, love,' he told Bella. A snatch of Strauss's 'Radetzky March' was playing. Don extended his brawny arms. The girls shrank back. As the music swelled, Don began to twitch his shoulder muscles in time to the music. Then, placing the knuckles of his hands on his waist, he caused his shoulder blades to rotate in time to the orchestra, as though in some gross accompaniment. The girls by the bar squealed. It was an exhibition of pure physicality such as I have seldom encountered. As Don turned round to rotate the sinews of his stomach region to the martial music, and the squeals redoubled, Barbara hissed in my ear:

'So you got rid of her boyfriend, did you? This Dolores, who was, let me guess, in some trouble you had to help her out of? Out the kindness of your heart, you decided to off the bloke she was having fun with? So is that what happened with Kemal, then?'

It was a most embarrassing moment. 'I assure you, Miss Harris, his imposture would have, sooner or later, caused you pain. I may have made enquiries on your behalf, which may have led to his unmasking. But Barbara –' I looked at her pleadingly – 'I could not stand for you to be taken in by this fake, this Turkish fakir.'

It was not the moment for a pun, however ingenious.

'Why? Because you wanted me for yourself?' Her tone was hard to judge. It was certainly not furious. It was frankly asking for information. As if asking if I were genuinely a suitor for her affections! I remonstrated, but was aware of the journalist by my elbow, pretending to take an interest in the (increasingly bizarre) cabaret turn at the bar.

'Barbara,' I said evenly, 'I want you to be freed from false company, to be happy, to be fulfilled, to become a young woman who is not seduced by plausible charmers, to achieve your potential, to discover the extent of your considerable intelligence –'

'Sorry, Harold, I gotta interrupt,' she said, rising from her stool and making straight for the bar, where her enormous beau was rippling muscular glissandi down his torso to the beaming girls around him.

There was little for me to do. I told Mr Norton that my work progressed satisfactorily, but that nothing could fathom the illogicality of the female heart. He looked at Barbara, as she wrenched the arm of an importunate young girl away from the territory of Don's corrugated abdomen, then looked back to me.

'Rector,' he said, in a voice of genuine bafflement, 'what are you doing? I mean, what are you doing with these people?'

London
28 October 1930

Things to do:

1. *Runaway Boys' Retreat is in disarray. Howard Shiner has left his post as manager without a word, a note, an explanation. I am cast down by this betrayal. He came to me as a newspaper boy of 17, red-faced, dirty-fingernailed, spindle-shanked, and I took him in, fed him, let him sleep on my floor on a shaggy rug, found him work as potboy at the Bell in Elephant & Castle. He was, beneath the dirt and adolescent surliness, a sweet-natured, intelligent boy, of a quiet competence and organised demeanour; at 19, I judged him ready to supervise physical jerks at the Retreat. With a class of 20*

*obstreperous runaways, he was impressively commanding. At 21,
I left him in charge of the whole Retreat, and of a monthly budget
(courtesy of Lady F's cousin Mary Cavendish's generous annual
endowment of £750). Now he is gone, 'runaway' himself from all
this rehabilitated responsibility. What to do? Retreat currently being
run by Peter the cook and Eddie Bones the janitor. Must move
fast.*

2. *Barbara Harris. Has expressed interest in being doctor's receptionist.
Call on surgery in Columbia Rd, and enquire?*

3. *Unpromising remake of* Man & Superman *at* Old Vic. *Will they
release a dozen free tickets to 'paper' theatre during matinées? But
could I endure 4 hours of GBS?*

4. *Don Stupendo, large well-meaning simpleton, needs more fulfilling
work. Can I help? Time for him to move on . . .*

Oh my goodness.
Have just had the most clever *idea.*

London
29 October 1930

Waited outside BH's house, discreetly, watching chess players in the
Morning Glory Café opposite, uttering helpful comments, from 11
a.m. until 1.15 p.m. At length Don Stupendo emerged, seen off in
doorway by Barbara with hugs and kisses while still (shockingly)
dressed in off-white nightie. The man is phenomenal. Six feet six or
seven, bald head disdaining the raindrops as if oblivious to the
elements (because an elemental spirit himself!), he strode off in direction of Mornington Crescent. I hurried after him, engineered meeting
on corner of Crowndale Road. Engaged him in conversation on
circus lore and persuaded him to take tea and lamb cutlets beside
station.

'You have a prodigious appetite, Anthony,' I remarked, as he
called for second helpings. 'Hardly surprising for a chap of your
physique.'

'Gotta keep yer strength oop, Harold,' he said, through a mouthful
of mashed potato, 'when you got three shows a day, lifting manhole

covers and barbells. Ye canna get slack or all yer moossels turnta fat, like.'

'Indeed. Do you find it congenial work, lifting weights for the edification of the curious?'

'Do ah find what?'

'Do you enjoy the circus life with its arduous regimen?'

'I dunno what you're on aboot sometimes, Rector, but if you mean, do I enjoy it, well, I got no idea. It's just what I do.'

Of course. I might as well have asked a drayhorse, its great face buried in a nosebag, if it appreciated its chosen career.

'There must be some hardships, I dare say.'

'Oh aye. When the days are colder, and you know there'll be frost on the grass as yer havin' a wash under the pump, it's all you can do to get up in the morning, wi' yer shoulders achin' and your hamstrings twanging like a fookin' harp. Excuse me, Rector.'

I waved away the obscenity.

'And as the winter announces its arrival' – I gestured at the grey rain falling on the Camden Palais, its gaudy turrets visible from our window table – 'it must be a bleak prospect sometimes . . .'

'You're telling me, Rector. Ah grew up in a Tyneside village, wi' a lovely couple of meadows to roam in. Ah don't like towns. If you never knew what "bleak" meant, try Clapham Common Old Town under the dirty clouds wi' the rain drippin' off the bus shelter.'

'It sounds as though you'd welcome an alternative form of employment. Or a change of scene.'

'That's very fine and easy to say,' he said, taking a swill of tepid tea, 'but who's gointa take on the likes of me? Jobs for strongmen dinna turn up every day.'

'You do not,' I pointed out, patiently, 'have to restrict your employment to the circus. I am sure many jobs exist for a physically robust chap such as yourself.'

'What you mean, working on a building site all day wi' a bunch of Paddies, like? No thank you.' The man was, it seems, just as prejudiced against other nationalities as my ex-friend Mr Kemal. 'Or pushing a lathe in a factory morning till night. I think I'll stick to the manhole covers.'

'Why this obsession with hours? Plenty of people work an eight-hour day, with only a break in the middle for luncheon.'

'I joost don't like rising early, Reverend,' he said, wiping his mouth. 'And I like a little snooze in the afternoons, like in Italy and Spain. They got the reet attitude to work on the Continent, if you ask me.'

If you asked me, Stupendo was revealing himself to be a remarkably idle and lazy person.

'If you're interested,' I said casually, 'there is currently a job vacancy at one of my charities. It is called the Runaway Boys' Retreat in Whitechapel, and it has urgent need of a supervisor.'

Don, who had visibly brightened at my first words, looked pained by the last one.

'Supervisor? Me? Ah couldna do that. I thought you wore gointa say janitor or handyman, but naah, I couldna be in charge of the place, like.'

'The wage is quite good,' I assured him, 'and paid weekly on Tuesdays. The duties are scarcely arduous for a man of your talents.'

'I'll have to say no, Rector,' he said obtusely.

'But why?'

'It joost — wouldna suit me, that's all.'

'Why not? You seem a capable chap, able to get on with all kinds of people.'

'It's not that. It's just, ah couldna be sure about the paperwork, like —'

'Why should that prove a burden?'

'Because I CANNA READ NOR WRITE,' he shouted, his gaze fixed on the table. 'Happy now?'

I had to think fast. I had become convinced he is what the Retreat needs in the absence of Howard Shiner. Mainly because of one thing: size. The boys who come to the Retreat are delinquents, some of them hardly more than savages, and to keep them out of trouble all day requires tact, imagination — and a certain brute force. Or at least the threat of force. They will listen in silence to a figure of authority, or join in history lessons which involve dressing up in tableaux of Drake and the Armada, they will exercise in the gymnasium without fighting — but they'll do these things only if they know that the supervising figure is capable of retaliation and chastisement. I do not know if Don Stupendo is capable of chastisement – he seems as gentle as a large pussycat – but he undoubtedly looks the part.

'I do not see that as a problem,' I said slowly, wishing to instil my plan into his head in one attempt. 'Most of the work requires no pens and paper. You will be more of a leader of games, sports and revels; your job would be to oversee their labours and discourage misbehaviour. Also to devise sporting schedules, gymnasial activities and long-distance running. We have at times tried to involve boxing in our little curriculum, but it can lead to trouble.'

'There'd be no trouble if ah was around,' said Don, darkly.

'I am delighted by your attitude. Also, while working as supervisor, you would be welcome to attend classes in learning to read and write.'

'You mean sit there in a class wi' a lot of kids? That'd be embarrassin', wouldn't it?'

'No. These boys are not middle class and therefore will not scorn people who never had an education. And your example would encourage any boys (there are always a few) who feel it is beneath them to become literate after they have reached double figures.'

'So I'd go to Whitechapel every day, tell these urchin kids what they're doing for the day, take 'em on runs, play-act bits of history and go to readin' and writin' classes myself?'

'Quite right, except for one detail. You wouldn't have to go to Whitechapel every day, because you'll be living there.'

'Living at the Retreat? How mooch's that going to cost then?'

'Your lodging is free. You will be expected to contribute to food supplies. The bills are paid by the Retreat. The wage is ten pounds a week, reviewed after six months.'

'It sounds too good to be true, man,' said Don, his forehead creased with thought. 'Can ah come and have a look at the place real soon?'

'Today, if you have a free afternoon.'

'I might be able – Oh, but wait.' He put a great paw up to his mouth. 'What about Barbara? She's been putting me oop and feeding me, and sayin' ah can stop wi' her a few weeks, and being really kind and generous.'

'I think, Don, that while it is delightful to accept Christian generosity, the day may come when you feel uncomfortable for having lived, for a time, on the immoral earnings of a young prostitute.'

To my alarm, he bunched a great fist and looked at me in fury.

'Nobody says things like that aboot my Barbara.'

'Do not misunderstand me. I am Miss Harris's devoted friend. But you are surely aware of her profession. And of the moral leap you would take in quitting Miss Harris's side to live and work at a charity devoted to the betterment of troubled children. Your reward in Heaven would of course be assured.'

'But I'd coom back and see Babs, wouldn't I?' he asked, pathetically. 'You're not sayin' I gotta stop seeing her.'

'Of course not. You must see her as often as you please. It will be good for her not to feel friendless after her recent unpleasantness.'

'Unpleasantness? What was that?'

'Oh,' I gestured as though it were no matter, 'a little scare, to do with, you know, infection.'

'What? What kind of infection?'

'I expect you can probably guess. It is something of an occupational hazard in her line of work, and when one or two gentlemen friends discovered – well, shall we just say evidence? – there was some trouble. Nothing renders a handmaid of darkness abruptly friendless as the rumour of venereal disease.'

Blood had drained substantially from the normally ruddy features of my lunch companion. 'When was this?'

'Oh – a couple of weeks ago. I'm sure Miss Harris indicated to me that the trouble was over. I'm sure there is no cause to worry. But she is understandably embarrassed and reluctant to discuss the matter, as doubtless you will be when next you see her.'

'Oh noah,' said Don very quietly.

'Would you,' I asked gently, 'like to see your new home this very day?' His great bald head gradually, slowly, turned itself up towards me, as if being turned on a spit. I could see there were tears in his eyes.

'Aw reet,' he said.

All week I have suffered from an ague that turns the muscles in my arms and legs to weary lead. My energy, the God-given fuse that daily powers my good deeds, has failed me. I took to my bed on Wednesday and lay sweating and melancholy in my chilly room, dozing but hardly sleeping. Some obsessional imp in my head has introduced random thoughts and phrases, even lines of popular songs, that go round and round my brain for hours like a torture. I have in the past recommended to my congregation that they would derive benefit from meditating on certain lines of Scripture, repeated over and over; but when you find nothing in your head for hours except Mr Astaire's 'Putting on the Ritz', the effect is wearisome.

I cannot afford to be ill. There is so much to be done, in the lead-up to the Armistice Day service at Stiffkey, in which I have a personal interest as an old Forces' man. For days I was unsure if I would be sufficiently compos to make the journey home for this crucial memorial. But by Friday I was, if not cured of the lead in my limbs, at least able to bestir myself enough to leave the house and sit shivering in the park in the dismal November gloom, ochre leaves wanly cascading around me.

I tried to make plans to visit my young flock – I must see how Lily is faring at Mr Doughty's factory, and Eleanora Gilpin at the Palais de Dance, while poor Sally Anstruther still languishes at her fishmonger's – but had not the heart to engage any of them in inspiring dialogue while I was feeling so wretched. At least in Stiffkey, the local parson is allowed to be moody and severe and thunderous of brow on occasion. In the metropolis, one is always acting a role. There are times, I confess, when one tires of this spiritual thespiana.

I had forgotten I was supposed to meet Barbara on Friday night. I had promised her a visit to the Windmill Theatre, where my former protégée Glenys Stack of Wapping now performs nightly under the *nom d'étage* of Gloria Starr. Miss Stack is one of my most notable rescue missions. Under my tutelage, she abandoned her dissolute life in the bars around Paddington Station, taking Swindon- and Bristol-bound businessmen to local hotels in the afternoon, and instead took to the boards as a singer and novelty dancer. Her gratitude for my help in supplying theatrical 'contacts' has been warm and heartfelt. I have been able to display her to many girls as a shining example of Virtue Regained, while simultaneously enjoying the talents she has so spectacularly evinced as a burlesque entertainer. I never see her perform her Banana Dance without experiencing a thrill of satisfaction.

Barbara came to see me on Saturday morning to complain at my failure to meet her. Her fury abated when she saw my sorry circumstances. The onset of illness had left me sunken-eyed and croak-voiced, and I greeted her in a fretful, shivery state.

'Bloody hell, Harold,' she said, looking round my room, taking in the mouldy bread and shrivelled ham, the crumpled sheets and discarded socks that testified to my reduced state, 'I didn't know you lived in such a tip. I thought vicars 'ad laundrymaids and 'ouse-keepers to look after them. I thought my gaff was bad, but this is – well, brutal, if you don't mind me saying so.'

'I have not had the opportunity to render my quarters spick and span for your inspection,' I said, crossly. 'I rarely entertain at home, since I enjoy a monastic regimen. But of course I value your opinion, coming from a young woman of such legendary domestic tidiness.'

'Oooh-er,' she said. 'Mr High Horse. Are you coming out for a walk with me, or are you going to stay in all day feelin' sorry for yourself?'

What could I do? We ventured out together. Her idea of a walk was a succession of omnibus rides to her various haunts of a Saturday morning. First to Bermondsey Market, where stallholders transform the unlovely wasteland off Tower Bridge Road to a bustling, chat-tery throng of bric-a-brac sales. Trestle tables proudly displayed a gallimaufry of gimcrack nonsense: brass door knockers, pieces of copper piping of no obvious utility, tin toys with bent flanges, Edwardian jigsaws of sentimental scenes involving babies and small dogs, battered pots and pans, towered pagodas of earthenware flow-erpots, booklets on personal hygiene and the care of pets, French postcards of anonymous strumpets displaying their grubby bloomers in saucy poses.

'Barbara,' I said at length, 'this is a fool's errand. There is nothing here that a sane person would wish to buy. The merchandise I see around us seems to have been purloined from below stairs at an unremarkable stately home, to be purchased by persons with very low taste.'

'Don't be stuffy, Harold,' she said, bending to examine a hideous phrenological bust, doubtless stolen from a chemist's shop. 'I love the market. I always come 'ome with something pretty, or shiny or a bit funny, to put on me dresser, and it never costs more than a bob or two. Oh, look –'

She clutched a child's doll, the old sort, with a visage of murderous blankness and a costume of yellowed lace.

'Look at 'er little face. She looks like she needs to go to a good 'ome. Don't you, darling?' she addressed the noisome figurine. 'You going to buy it for me, Harold?'

'No, Miss Harris, I am not,' I said firmly. 'Your days of playing with dolls are long gone. I would happily purchase some object that might be of use to you in furthering your career as a receptionist. A fountain pen, for example, or a dictionary. But I will not be drawn into a spending spree to crowd out your modest room with geegaws.'

'I don't need a bloody pen. I don't 'ave no use for a dictionary. I already know every word in the alphabet that I'm ever going to need. How about one of them hats?'

Regrettably I gave in, and we left with a ludicrous green object of basket-woven complexity clamped to Barbara's luxuriant curls.

'How you can imagine for a moment that this headgear will keep you safe from a shower of rain, I cannot conceive,' I said sternly.

'Oh, Harold,' she said, beginning to laugh. 'You are a silly old sod.'

She slipped her hand around my arm, above the elbow. I would have remonstrated about the insult, but her gesture was so sweetly unaffected, I had not the heart to upbraid her.

As we moved away from the crush of working people at a china stall, turning cheap, flowery-patterned dinner plates upside down as though to ascertain whether they were Spode or Royal Doulton, she spied someone she knew.

'Oh God, it's bloody Marshall,' she muttered. Marshall was a thin, whippet-faced individual in a glazed, coal-heaver's jacket, presiding over a stall of coloured rings and bracelets, too cheap to have been stolen.

'Ignore him,' I whispered, steering her away to the road. But it was too late.

''Ere, Barbara,' he shouted, 'how's business these cold mornings?' Her fingers tightened on my arm.

'I'm bloody freezing over 'ere,' he persisted. 'I need warming up. I'll bung you a quid for a quick one round the back of the Gallery.'

'Do not answer him,' I pressed her. 'Let us find our way to –'

She turned from my restraining fingers and let fly.

'I don't 'ave time, Marshall,' she cried across twenty yards of surprised shoppers. 'I couldn't even find your tiny dick on a morning like this, not if I was using both 'ands and a map.'

I cringed to hear such vulgarity on her lips. To my gratification, the object of her scorn was cringing too.

'Fucking cow,' he shouted. 'Go off and 'ave a good time with grandad then.'

On the bus, she was disposed to laugh it off. No, he was not a former client, she said, merely the envious associate of an old 'boyfriend', who had never persuaded her to look upon him with eyes of love.

'Just don't ask me questions, Harold, all right?' she said, in a tone that brooked no argument. I did not mind. Truth to tell, I was filled, despite my disabling cold, with an unusual happiness, to be about town with such a droll young companion.

The next stop was Spitalfields, where I admired the fine Hawksmoor Christchurch, but was soon pulled away to linger in another market, mostly clothing this time, of a markedly poor quality. This, clearly, was where Barbara acquired her wardrobe of scarves, camisoles, Great War jackets, theatrical feather boas and coloured stockings. Her abbreviated hat drew fawning cries of delight from women who transparently wished only to see her spend more money on their trumpery silks and satins. I extracted her from their evil patter and led her away.

As we left, she said, 'You got a camera, Harold? I want to be snapped under that sign.'

I looked around. Her finger pointed down a wretched side thoroughfare.

'Which sign, Miss Harris?' I looked around for some municipal signification such as 'No Entry'.

'Fashion Street, you goose. I want to 'ave a picture of me under it, like that's where I live. Fashion Street. Do you get it? That's my address, because I'm a London fashion girl.'

It took a while to fathom her meaning.

'Good heavens, Barbara. You are dealing in metaphor. It is the first time I have heard you speak in metaphorical terms.'

Her brow furrowed. 'I dunno about that. What's a mettafer? I just thought it would be a laugh, me posing like I'm real stylish, all right?'

My ague was lifting with every moment that passed.

We found ourselves, at noon, in a café on Moorgate. We sipped tea and ate iced buns, and talked about the attractive nature of Don Stupendo, and my heart pounded with sudden jealousy that she should invest so much emotional energy in her muscle-bound Geordie halfwit.

'I cannot fathom, my dear Barbara,' I said, 'how you live, pulled by your emotions from one unstable relationship to the next, taking men to your bed for money apparently without a care in the world, then becoming involved like a romantic schoolgirl with a fly-by-night muscleman.'

'They aren't fly-by-night, my boyfriends,' she responded with asperity. 'Some of 'em stay lots of nights. Right on into the weekend, and the next sometimes. And they're decent boys, they're nice to me.'

'Decent? My dear girl – one plausible but mendacious Turk conman, and one circus performer with the intellectual capacity of a – a fencepost?'

'Donny isn't stupid, Harold,' she said with admirable loyalty. 'He understands how to make a girl feel good. He's nice to me, he's funny, he puts me under his wing, and he's always got a lovely smile for me in the morning. I don't think it's nice of you to make him out to be bad sort when he's got a good heart and he makes me happy, all right?'

I smiled at her spirited defence of her temporary paramour.

'My objection to Mr Stupendo is not a moral issue, Barbara. I simply think he is not good enough for you. A doltish performer in a cheap carnival entertainment, whatever his doglike adoration, may amuse you for a while, but is not the man with whom you should be choosing to spend your life.'

'My life? Bleeding hell, Harold. I'm only sixteen. You think I should be married off to someone and 'aving babies?'

'By no means. I merely suggest you should be setting your sights a little higher. Perhaps towards someone with a little more sophistication, someone who has seen the world from a more advanced perspective and can engage you more fully in the pleasure of the examined life?'

'What, you, you mean?'

'Of course not,' I said, with horror. 'How could you imagine I was suggesting myself?'

'Well, you said –'

'I am a married man with a family,' I remonstrated. 'A vicar of the Church. I am not single, nor am I emotionally available, except to offer guidance where it is needed. I am shocked, Barbara, that you should misrepresent my intentions so cruelly.'

'Well, sorry, but you shouldn't be so bloody rude about my pals, calling them names an' that. All right, you're Mr Know-It-All and you can afford to look down on people who aren't educated like you, but sometimes, I swear to God, you sound just a bit like you're jealous of my young men.'

I should have laughed in her face to silence her foolish presumption.

'I may, Barbara, wish to see you parted from these men, not to save you for my own selfish ends, but to save you for yourself – for the other, different Barbara you could be. I have been many things in my life, and I know how I can change others – change the course of their lives for the better.'

'Go on then,' she said, 'give us an example.'

And so I told her about Cassie Shale. My first encounter with the plight of a young girl in trouble.

I was barely nineteen when it happened, and full of energy and spirit. I had yet to go up to Oxford. The theatre and the Church wrestled in my soul for the upper hand. I had loved the stage ever since I had performed my little monologues at school, at the end-of-term amusements. Few things so gratified my heart as the uproar of three hundred boys laughing at 'The Staff Room Polka', my lethal twenty-minute satire on the masters, adapted from the great Grossmith. In the autumn of '94, while others were attending to their studies, I was in a touring company playing the lead in *Charley's Aunt*. We appeared at Bristol, Cheltenham, Swindon, Richmond and as far north as Manchester, always to delighted audiences. Our last appearance was at Wilton's Music Hall, near Tower Bridge, and it was while venturing home on the penultimate night – my thoughts vainly filled with the success of the run, and regret that all our revels were soon to be ended – that I encountered Miss Shale.

The night was foggy and cold, and I wrapped my greatcoat around me as I crossed the noble structure at midnight, its great windowed pillars looming over my head. All at once I heard a noise, from the gangway that gives off the central section of the bridge, the place where foreign visitors daily gather to gawp at the view down the Thames.

I feared there might be footpads lurking in wait for an innocent walker, but no, it was a young girl, cursing under her breath at her own ineptness in climbing over the tall railing on to the extreme lip of the bridge. The wooden heels of her clogs clanged against the metal as she struggled to heave her small body over the safety hurdle.

I took her for a foolhardly reveller, perhaps seeking to impress some unseen male companion with her bravery. But something in her struggling brought me to realise the true nature of her communion with the Thames on this cold November night. She was bent on self-destruction, and her curses were directed at anything that obstructed her fell ambition.

'Miss! Miss!' I called out, coming nearer. 'Have a care, for Heaven's sake. What are you doing? You are in the utmost peril of your life if you perch there. I implore you to seek safety back here.'

'Go away,' she said in a small, weary voice. 'I know what I'm doing.'

She was so young, a dumpy little figure dressed in a simple jersey dress, with no coat against the night frost. Her movements were jerky, as though driven by some wildness in the brain, and one hand waved me away, the palm extended as though fending off an assailant.

'You must come down, or you will surely fall,' I cried. 'There can be no reason why you should fling your life away like this. Are you drunk?'

'I had some cider to stop me thinking what I had to do,' she conceded, 'but it didn't work. Please don't talk to me. This is none of your business. I just want it to be over, that's all.'

She stood on the ledge, one hand holding the railing – a single handgrip was the only thing between her and death in the glacial waters – and looked down into the foggy darkness, as though trying to identify the best place to land. The fastidiousness of her inspection touched my heart. She could have been my dear sister essaying her first dive in a swimming pool.

'My name's Harold,' I said, not knowing how to proceed, but reasoning that one might start with politeness. 'What's yours?'

'It doesn't matter,' she said with the same weary tone. 'He was called Harold, too, not that I want to be reminded, thanks.'

'He was called? Someone close to you has died? I am so sorry. But your bereavement cannot surely have led to your wishing for your own death?' A whisper of exasperation escaped her. 'Forgive me if I am enquiring too closely.'

Perhaps my stupidity encouraged her, but she began to talk.

'No, he's not dead. He's very much living, only not with me, not now and not ever. He made that real clear. He was real sorry to hear what had happened, but he couldn't get involved, he said. Like it was something he'd read about in the papers, and was sorry about, like some foreign war, then forgot it by the end of breakfast. But where do I go now? My mum'll kill me when she finds out.'

The penny dropped. 'You are in – a condition?'

She turned her face to mine for the first time.

'You know what I can't stand?' she asked, almost confidingly. 'It's that I absolutely love it, being pregnant. I mean, I hate it, but my body just loves it. You wouldn't understand, you're a man, but I knew it before I went to the doctor. Me ankles had swelled up, and my bosom, and my skin felt all different, and all over me I could feel everything changing and becoming softer and sort of – more spread out, d'you know what I mean, like all of me, I mean every cell in my body, was relaxing into it like it had always dreamed of this. And I knew that it was wrong to feel so satisfied and fulfilled when what I'd done was so bad and condemned. To feel so right and so bad at the same time, as if my head was fighting to the death with my feelings. That's what I can't stand. I can't go to my family when my love has deserted me. I can't be the cause of more shame.'

She looked at me, abruptly, as if for the first time. 'Will *you* tell them why it was?' she said.

I was utterly at a loss. 'I? I am in no position to –'

'I haven't left no note,' said the girl. 'I didn't think I'd go through with it until I got to the bridge. So I didn't leave a note. But when it's over, will you go and tell them everything, like I told you just now?'

I had no experience of the Church's policy with, or treatment of, the suicidal, but the poor girl's story touched my heart. She sought to make me her walking suicide note! What could I do but try to distract her from her awful course of action?

'How old are you?' I asked.

'Fifteen and a half.'

'What's your name?'

'What's it to you?' she replied. 'Doesn't matter any more.'

'I must know your name,' I reasoned, 'for without it, how am I to tell your grieving family that you threw yourself to your death because you loved being pregnant?'

'It's Cassie,' she said. 'Cassie Shale. But don't tell them about it like that, will you? It sounds like I'm a bit simple. It's the shame of it that's done me in, that and feeling nice about it at the same time.'

'Your mother,' I said, edging my way towards a solution, 'do you feel she would never understand what you are currently enduring? That she would be unsympathetic?'

She stared at me. 'You think she'd be overjoyed that her youngest daughter's up the duff?'

'I did not say happy. She will be most unhappy at your unfortunate condition. I asked if you thought she would not understand your feelings, and the conflict of emotions in your heart.'

'Well, 'course not. She's always been respectable. She's never gone through what I'm going through.'

'But, Cassie, do you not see, young as you are, that your mother, when she bore you, must have experienced precisely the same melting sensations, and can understand how helpless a body feels when it achieves the physical destiny for which it was made? How could she not?'

'Well, all right, but – whatd' you say your name was?'

'Harold. Harold Davidson.'

'All right then, but I just can't go and tell her. I just can't. It would be the worst thing in the world.'

'Would she turn you out of doors, to freeze on a park bench?'

'No,' said Cassie, grudgingly. (Did I see a tiny impulse of hope illumine her face?) 'She'd shout at me, over and over like she does, and bang doors, and say, "You stupid little bitch," and "Who's going to look after it?" and go on and on about the shame that'll come on the family, and my sisters would shun me. And then my dad would come home and – Oh, don't make me even think about that.'

'You have many sisters?'

'Three. And the eldest is getting married in June, and if this ever got out, and everyone knew about it in Poplar, they'll probably have to call off the wedding, and I'll have ruined Alice's life as well as mine and –' She buried her head, and sobbed into her cold-reddened fingers.

'Cassie,' I said, 'listen to me. The solution to this is not to hurl yourself into the freezing Thames. To destroy your life would cast more gloom on your family, and destroy its reputation more readily, than any number of babies. The solution is to tell your parents that you have been the victim of a cruel deception by a man you loved. You may say you have contemplated self-destruction, but that it was eclipsed in your mind by the certainty that your family may offer you support rather than condemnation. You must say you will bear the child, which is the issue of – as you fancied – true love, that you have money set aside for the trouble of its birth, and that you have consulted an adoption agency and will be prepared to give it up if that is what your parents deem an appropriate action. You must make them part of the decision. You must ask to be guided by them in all things, a line that cannot fail to strike home in the heart of any parent. And you must tell your sisters, with as airy a tone as you can muster, that they shall all be doting aunts slightly earlier than they may have anticipated. Only by insisting on facing this moral dilemma as a family will you be able to emerge as a heroine rather than a victim.'

She took her hand – at last! at last! – off the iron railing and studied the ground.

'Maybe – maybe I wouldn't be better off dead,' she said. 'Ta for that. And yeah, maybe they might be nice to me, once they'd stopped calling me names and saying "How could you? How could you?" over and over again. But how'm I to say I got money, when I never?'

I had made my decision midway through the tragic little speech about her mother calling her a b*tch. I dug my hand into my suit, extracted my pocketbook and drew out my personal takings from the final week of *Charley's Aunt*.

'There is thirty pounds here,' I said. 'In cash. Take it, go home to your mother and father and your problematic siblings, wake them up now and tell them of your brush with despair and the burgeoning secret of your spreading flesh, and your plans for dealing with this new phase in your life – in all *their* lives. I guarantee, Cassie, you will be put to bed with every sign of compassion and by the time you wake, your father will have grown sufficiently used to the idea, that he will not upbraid you. He may initiate a search for your lost gentleman friend, without much Christian generosity behind it; but he will privately plan to support you in this difficult new episode of your life.'

There were tears in her young eyes as she climbed back over the awful railings, gained the pavement of the bridge and looked around wildly, as if returned to life. When she spoke, it was like someone tunnelling their way out of a dream.

'I'll never remember to say all those things,' she said, 'but I'll remember some of them. But you can't give me thirty quid just like that. It would be like you were – you know – buying me or something.'

'Not at all. The money is a gift from the Lord. Just think of it: how else would I have arrived so fortuitously on Tower Bridge at this late hour, in these circumstances, except by some divine intervention? It was ordained that I should be here to protect you and offer you succour. Your immediate need is not to kill yourself, with which we have dealt now, I think. Your second is not to freeze, so you must take this greatcoat, heavy and awkward though it is – how you could have ventured forth without an outer-garment on this bitter night, I'm at a loss to understand.'

'I wasn't planning to be standing around shivering for long,' she said pointedly.

'And third, you must take the money, which I gladly give you because I am an eccentric fellow as well as a minister of the Church, or at least plan to be one day –'

'Wait a minute.' She took a step forward, to where the globe of gaslight was stronger. 'Let me look at you properly.'

It was an awkward moment. Released from her intense self-preoccupation, she scrutinised my face, even though I tried to shield it from the light.

'I thought so,' she said. 'My God, you're just a kid. I thought your voice was a bit young for all the advice. You're hardly older than I am, are you? "Eccentric gentleman" did you say? Strange boy is what you are. Where'd you get the money from?' Her face darkened. 'You didn't nick it, did you?'

'No I did not.' I was deeply hurt to be suddenly suspected of wrongdoing, merely because my (utterly irrelevant) age stood revealed. 'I am an actor. I am a member of an acting company performing *Charley's Aunt*. We have been touring the country and tonight was our last night, hence my pockets are full of wages. But I am scarcely "a kid" as you say. I am well on the way to becoming a vicar of the Church of England. Soon I shall begin my studies at Oxford University.'

'Ooooh,' she said, 'hark at you.' It was the first time I saw the suspicion of a smile brighten her sweet young face. 'Look, I dunno what you're doing here, giving me money and your good coat and everything, but I think I'm going to do as you say and go home and tell my mum everything. And she may scream and yell but she'll stop when she sees the money – Oh help!'

'What is it?'

'What if she thinks I got the money – you know, on the street? And that I got pregnant off a customer?'

'She will think no such thing, Miss Shale. You may say it is a charitable payment from –' I had no idea what to say. For the first time in my life, I invented a charity out of thin air '– from the Swaffham Hall Foundation for Modern Youth. They can be found at Monmouth Street, Covent Garden, as can I, should you wish to return my coat when you have no further use for it. And now I suggest you take the Underground from Tower Hill, on the first leg of your long journey home. The last train will be leaving shortly and you must hurry.'

She looked at the dimly lit sign above Tower Hill station. 'Monmouth Street,' she said, 'Covent Garden. I'll come back and find you there. Oh thank you. You really – you didn't need to do all this. I don't know what to say.'

'Will you for the love of Heaven make haste and get your train? Go now. You do not want to miss it.'

She stood, as awkward as a stork, not knowing how to conclude our first and only meeting, with its curious freight of importance: that without it she would have died, and because of it she still lived. 'Goodbye,' she said, 'and, oh –' Whereupon she seized me impetuously, laid her frozen cheek against mine and kissed it fervently. Then broke away, looked into my eyes as I smiled foolishly at her (she was no beauty, but her face shone in the cold moonlight and was flushed and full of suddenly returned life) and kissed me again, on the lips, lingering there for whole seconds. I closed my eyes and could feel her mouth contract slightly, a single slithery quarter-inch, but it sent a fire through to my loins such as few kisses had before or have since. By the time I stopped blinking, she was almost out of sight, my greatcoat flapping around her legs like the dark flames of Hades, from which I had recently delivered her.

I walked home to Aldgate almost penniless, entirely coatless, probably shivering, my breath clouding the air. But I felt nothing but elation, triumph, the warmth of divine benevolence, the knowledge that I had saved a human soul from destruction, from mortal sin, and from a long headlong descent into watery Pandaemonium. As I tramped through the streets, it seemed as if a divine breath from Heaven was breathing on me, warming my skin against the incursions of freezing night, as if the Lord Himself had become my protector, as I myself had become the protector of Youth and desecrated Innocence. I felt His kindly gaze upon me, as He enlisted me into His army of compassionate saviours; I felt – into what narcotic reverie had I fallen? – the touch of His lips on my forehead, as though in confirmation of my appointment, just as I had felt the girl's kiss upon my lips, in confirmation that I had done something right. By the time I gained my modest lodging house, I realised I was shaking with the fervour of this visitation. I slept for eleven hours, the last time in my life I ever slept so long, and woke a changed man, with a crusade, a mission and a point to my life, from which I have never diverged.

'Well, Harold, that was quite a story,' said Barbara. 'I'm sure it's all true –'

'Of course it's true. How could I possibly make up something so singular?'

'– but you do come out of it smelling like a saint in a rose bush. Did you ever 'ear from 'er again?'

'Sadly, no. Of course, the address I gave her was false. I made up the name of a charity in order for her not to be obliged to return the coat or the money. But I scanned the papers in the next few weeks and read nowhere of a young woman's body being found in the Thames, so I concluded she was safe from harm in the slightly nettled embrace of her family.'

'But what a big old softie you was, Harold, to give her all that cash. I couldn't see, in that story you just told, what she'd need it for.'

'She'd need it, my dear Barbara, for her mother. Better than any diploma, better than acquiring a Worker of the Week badge from Mr Doughty's factory, hard money is what would impress the likes of poor Cassie's parents and make them not think twice about taking her home.'

We had sat in our Moorgate café for two hours without noticing the time and without – as Miss Harris was quick to point out – my feeling a need to lecture her on any subject.

We moved on, up the City Road. I insisted on visiting the graves of John Bunyan and William Blake in Bunhill Fields, much to Barbara's scorn ('You really know how to show a girl a good time, don'cha?'), and we kicked through the leaves together as she talked about her own sad, chilly family.

Later, I bought us mutton chops and mashed potato, jelly and ice cream in the Old Street restaurant. She ate everything on her plate like a starving native, just as on our first meeting. I was shocked to see she has begun to smoke cigarettes, and did so openly, in the restaurant, calling for an ashtray like a working man.

'I mustn't overdo it, Harold,' she said, 'because I got to cook Donny's tea at seven. He's had to go off to Ealing for the day for some rehearsal with the circus.'

'Indeed,' I said neutrally.

'Some new routine or other. But 'e'll be back. Just can't keep away from my loving arms for long.'

'Are you planning to keep him as your gratis lodger indefinitely? It cannot be very remunerative for you while he stays in the premises.'

'Remunerative? It's all right. I get a few gentlemen callers when Donny's out, enough to pay the rent, and he doesn't mind, provided I got meself nice and clean for when he comes home. He's been very insistent on hygiene lately, got a real bee in his bonnet about disease, no matter how much I tell him not to worry. But why you asking me that?'

'I was merely seeking to establish –'

'No you bloody weren't. You were saying, Oi, you're not making any dosh while this boyfriend's around, this bloke who takes care of you and who you really like, you're not pulling in the cash. It's not right, my girl, that's what you're saying, Harold, you're saying, Get back out there on the street, with the twenty clients a night, and make some proper money.'

She subsided. Barbara is in many respects the sunlight of my days, but sometimes she can be a terrible shrew.

'Do you know what you sound like?'

'I'm afraid you misunder—'

'You sound like a pimp, Harold. Just like a pimp.'

Luckily, our growing fondness for one another survived this awkward moment. By the time we parted, it was four thirty. We had spent six hours in each other's company, constantly interested and amused. I may have persuaded myself that ours was a relationship between pastor and sinner; but yesterday I was trying to ignore the many signs that other, more potent, strands of feeling were in play.

I returned to Vauxhall, and set immediately to write my speech for the morrow. Armistice Day. A key date in the clerical calendar, especially for one such as I, who had seen action in uniform. I was keen to strike the appropriate note, asking 'What have we learned in the dozen years since the end of hostilities?' without giving the impression that we have learned only to mistrust the strategies of our seniors, the public-school code of duty to country and flag, and the complacent warmongering of politicians.

It should not have been an arduous task. I have made Armistice Day speeches all through the 1920s. But illness was stealing over me. The heaviness in my limbs became a dismal ache that no amount of stretching could settle. My throat itched and burned with inflammation, such that every attempt to swallow was like regurgitating a hot brick. I had written scarcely one paragraph when slumber descended. Suddenly, it was five minutes to 8 p.m. I jerked awake, threw some water on my face and went to the kitchen.

Mrs Parker looked at me with horror. 'What are you about, Mr Davidson? You look terrible. You look like death in a wheelbarrow.' I do not know where she finds these unhelpful similes.

'I am overtired, Mrs P,' I said. 'I have, perhaps ill-advisedly, been out of doors today with one of my ladies and have, I fear, caught a chill.'

'A chill, Rector? Your eyes are as red as radishes. Your face is — are you shivering?'

'Yes. No. I — I will be right as rain in no time. It is imperative that I stay awake to write my sermon for tomorrow. May I ask you to assist me with some coffee, quite strong?'

'What you need, Rector, is a good night's sleep. You can write your speech in the morning. You'd be better off with a hot toddy with plenty of honey in it.'

'Thank you, but I am a teetotaller. I thought you might know that after all these months.'

'It would do you more good than running around with them girls in the freezing cold, doing God knows what,' said Mrs Parker with a caustic note to her voice. 'Now look. I'm going out to see my friend at the Dog & Duck. I'll leave a plate of ham and tongue here for you, in case you're hungry. But I would say, Go to bed and stay there or you'll be half dead in the church.'

'I need to catch the 7.45 train from King's Cross as usual,' I said. 'So I must be up and about by 6.45 a.m. Kindly rouse me if I am not abroad by 6.50. Will you make sure of this?'

''Course I will, Rector,' she said.

The progress of the evening is blurred in my recollection. I sat at my desk, chewing my pen, wrestling with high concepts of the Just War, the ethics of Secular Martyrdom, and the role the Church should play in preparing a nation for war. Sometimes I dozed, sometimes I had moments of lucidity and wrote a page of rhetoric – then woke at 10 or 11 p.m., to find my handwriting had dwindled to a crablike, defeated scrawl. Around midnight, my willpower deserted me. I resolved to go to bed, and finish the sermon on the train in the morning, trusting to my powers of recovery. I thanked Heaven that I had never become the slave of the demon Alcohol, and that my mental faculties were undimmed.

In bed, I was poring over Pannenberg's *De Rerum Ecclesiasticum*, when I heard a strident knocking at the front door. Bang bang bang. A pause, in which I fancied I could hear breathing. Bang bang. Bangbangbangbangbang. The caller was clearly not going to be ignored. Mrs Parker was still out with her friend. Perhaps there was some emergency. I slipped my tartan dressing gown over my nightshirt, padded through the house in bare feet, and opened the door.

It was Barbara.

'Don't even think of sending me away,' she said, brushing past me. 'I've had quite enough rejection for one evening, thanks.'

'My dear Miss Harris – Barbara. The hour – do you know what time it is?'

'It's about one. What're you doin' in that get-up? I thought you never slept.'

'I rarely enjoy a full night's sleep, it is true,' I said (sleepily), 'usually I doze in a chair. But some fever has me in its clutches, and I have retired to bed. If there were any service I could offer you, I should be happy to offer it, but I am, as you see, hardly dressed to receive – my dear Barbara, what has happened to you?'

She had started to weep, silently, standing there in Mrs Parker's modest hallway, with the frosty moon shining through the fanlight. Barbara, the most resilient of girls, was upset to the point of tears. I had never seen the like.

'He's left me,' she said in hardly more than a whisper. 'Just upped and left, gone to live somewhere else and find a new life, he said. How could he? My Don, preferring some bloody night shelter to being with me. In our nice warm bed, where –'

'Barbara –'

'We practically *lived* in that bed,' she wailed, as if I had contradicted her, not a course of action I would pursue at any time. 'When we first met in October, we 'ardly left the room for a week. It wasn't just the sex, neither –'

'Miss Harris,' I murmured, 'spare me the –'

'– it was more the skin contact, you know? His 'ands were always warm. He wasn't like other blokes. He was gentle. We folded around each other, like a nest of kittens.' She wiped the sleeve of her long black coat across her nose, leaving a glistening residue.

'I am sure, Miss Harris,' I said, 'that the young man's departure does not reflect any dislike of you. It may be that he has become ashamed to find himself living off a – a young woman such as yourself, with no means of paying his way. It is no wonder to me that he has sought a different route.'

'You mean, he couldn't stand poncing off a tart? Whyn't you just say it out loud? He couldn't stand what people might think of 'im? That doesn't sound like my Donny. He didn't care a flyin' toss what people thought of 'im. He knew he was better than most of 'em.'

'No, Barbara,' I said. 'It was not the world's opinion he cared about. It was his opinion of himself.'

'Are we going to stand 'ere all night or are you going to invite me in?' said Barbara. 'I'm bloody freezing my fanny off in this 'allway.'

I stepped into the parlour, expecting her to follow but, when I turned, she had gone. Back in the hall I watched her long black coat trail like a cloak up the stairs. When I gained my bedroom, she had taken off her coat and was sitting in my armchair, looking about.

'That's better. Make us a cup of tea, Harold, there's a love. I promise I won't keep you long, but I had to talk to someone.'

'I am glad to think you would come to me first in a crisis.'

'I came to you because I knew you'd be kind to me. We had such a nice day, and I'd felt really warm and close by your side, and then' – she snuffled into a grubby handkerchief – 'that bloody man 'as to go and upset me. I read his note and I cried and cried, and the door went three or four times with boyfriend callers and I hadn't the heart to do it even though I need the money, and anyway me cheeks were all streaked with tears, and I 'ad a little drink and then I realised I was sitting there waiting for him to come back and he wouldn't ever. And then I pulled meself together, put on my hat and coat, went round to the Tube and headed for you. I knew *you'd* take me in, even if no one else wants to be with me.'

Down in the kitchen, pouring boiling water into the teapot, I felt touched by her words. 'I knew you'd take me in . . .' – how it took me back to my early days of dealing with the destitute. I learned to turn nobody from my door, however venal they might prove. Whose are those wonderful lines? 'So practise pity, lest you drive / An angel from your door.'

I came up the stairs with tea, milk et cetera on a tray. Imagine my surprise to find Miss Harris no longer hunched in the armchair, but now in my bed.

'I have your tea,' I said loudly, to alert her to my presence and give her time to recompose herself. There was no reply. I set down the tray, moved softly to the bed and leaned over. My breath faintly stirred a wisp of hair that curled beside her ear but she did not rouse. Looking round, I discovered her outer coat and a lilac cardigan discarded on the chair, while her shoes lay splayed at right angles nearby.

I drew back the counterpane, the blanket and sheet as gently as I could, not from prurient curiosity but to establish whether she might become uncomfortably hot in the night, if she were to stay, which of course would not be right. She was wearing the same grey cotton blouse and wool skirt she had worn earlier that day.

'Barbara,' I whispered, 'you cannot stay here. You must return to your home forthwith before Mrs Parker discovers your presence.'

She buried her face a little more emphatically in the pillow and made a small sound, thus: 'Mgngggnng.' She was, it seemed, profoundly asleep, tired out with play and sorrow. I set myself to sleep in the armchair, as so many times before. I dozed there, tried to read Pannenberg, failed again, dozed a little more, and woke to find the time was now 1.45 a.m.

It was hopeless. Slumbering in the chair was giving me a painful cramp in the neck that worsened every time I put my head on one side. I knew that I would never get to sleep, nor wake refreshed enough to give my sermon, unless I took to my own bed. So I did so. I removed my dressing gown, gingerly drew back the covers and introduced, first one leg, then a shoulder, then the other leg, at last my head. The pillow was freezing, but a considerable heat seemed to have built up on the left-hand side of the bed, where my unexpected guest lay in heavy dreamland. It was like a fire, towards which one might extend one's hands on a chilly night. I turned my face slowly, cheek to pillow. Before me, tickling my nose in the darkness, was a mass of brown curls. I brushed them gently away from my face and closed my eyes.

I guess half an hour must have elapsed when I woke with a start, to find Miss Harris upon me. Once again her hair was assailing my nose, but this time it was from below. She had turned quite round in the bed and now lay with her head athwart my chest, her brow towards my armpit. More alarmingly, her hand was brushing rhythmically along my nightshirt, over my right thigh.

'Erm . . .' I could barely speak. I hardly trusted myself to formulate a remark.

'Mmmnnggmm,' she mumbled. Was she fast asleep? I could not be sure. Her face twisted a little upon my shirted chest, as though her nose was itching. And then her head disappeared beneath the bedclothes. I could not see this – it was pitch black in the room – but I could feel everything. I could feel Miss Harris's left hand grow firmer and more insistent on my right leg, not merely stroking it now, but pushing at the cotton nightshirt until the material had ridden up so far, my naked thigh was under her commanding fingers. At the same time, her head was moving down my torso, burrowing and, it seemed to me in my delirium, nibbling or scoring her teeth along my side, inching down my night attire as though closely inspecting it in the darkness. So bizarre seemed her behaviour, both the teeth-play and the nightshirt-pulling (I would have called it a 'neurotic' behaviour pattern, had I been asked at that moment), so potentially mortifying for the poor girl, I was loath either to wake her or to dissuade her from either activity – for, as with somnambulists, it may be psychologically damaging to wake them into a knowledge or consciousness of their behaviour. Instead, I lay wide awake and most uncomfortable in feeling my body mauled and prodded in this unusual (and not-unembarrassing) way, but also feeling it respond to a foreign touch, like a warhorse raising its head to the sound of a distant bugle.

Then it happened. (I can hardly believe I am committing these words to a clergyman's journal.) The twin activities in which she was engaged came together. Her hand on my thigh pushed away the last remaining inches of cotton that clothed my dignity. Her hand was hot as the flames of Hades as it stole between my legs and closed around my organ of generation. Even as I instinctively jerked upright with shock, Miss Harris's slowly insistent head traversed the last few inches across my stomach. Her hand guided my straining flesh. Her mouth closed upon it. Her molten lips caressed it wetly. Her firm, slippery tongue traced a straight line along the underside.

I sat bolt upright in the bed, thunderstruck. No such thing had ever happened to me before. In my dealings with Mimi, we have always preserved a modicum of decency. We are not prudes; we allow what will happen to happen, without feeling any impulse to explore these territories closely with eyes or hands or mouths. Now here was I, allowing a young prostitute to perform a deed of the utmost perversity on my body, while still consumed by sleep. My eyes rolled wildly in my head. Her mouth seemed to gorge on its prey, to take me further and deeper inside its clammy chamber. Every instinct of decency rebelled in me against this wet, engorging, lustful O. Then all thought of morality, embarrassment or any other abstraction fled as the distant tremor of a seismic wave sounded in my body. Every scintilla of reason departed as the tremor came nearer and nearer, a rushing sensation such as I have hardly known before, a racing, all-embracing, torrential, chasmal, heart-surging, endlessly ramifying tidal whoosh of something beyond pleasure, closely bordering on agony.

Unbearable to have it stop. Unspeakable to let it go on, with its consequences in the mouth of the young woman who –

I seized Miss Harris by the hair and pulled her head away. Just then, as the eye of the great storm came overhead and silent peace momentarily reigned, I felt a stream of hot fluid gush from me, covering my thigh and some of the bedsheet with slippery glue.

'What you doing?' said the girl crossly. 'What the *fuck* you doing pulling my hair?'

'Dear lady,' (I was too startled to address her by name), 'I was overcome by sensation, and felt bound to move your position for fear that you might be . . . discommoded . . .' It was hopeless. I had no words. Even circumlocution failed me.

Barbara needed no explanation. She uttered one remark ('Oh really – look what you done to the sheets. *You* can have the bleeding wet spot'), then moved back to her original position. In barely two minutes, robust little snores came over her shoulder.

I lay in the dark, bled of my seed in the most shocking way imaginable, and racked with guilt. Had she been asleep at all? Had she thought she was with Don Stupendo? Had I encouraged her to pursue her wicked action by pretending to be her lost beau? Was I now condemned as a hypocrite, a snake in the grass, an immoralist, a libertine, an exploiter of women's affections – and a distressed and abandoned woman at that?! Oh God – of course I was the reason behind his abandoning her! Had I done it purely so that I could pursue her in his stead and brutalise her tender young flesh?

I knew that sleep's healing balm would never soothe me again. I told myself I would lie awake for the remainder of the night, trying to atone for my sin by prayer – then rise, finish my sermon, and depart in good time for the 7.45 a.m. train.

I closed my eyes. It had been a long day. An evening of delirium. A disturbed and disturbing night. I breathed in and breathed out. Soon I would be calm.

I woke to sounds of morning outside. Barbara was standing before the window, adjusting her hat. I looked at my watch. It was 9.13 a.m. I had missed the only train. I had missed the Armistice Day service.

Hell will follow.

CHAPTER 12

Letter from Mrs Moyra Davidson
Stiffkey Rectory
20 November 1930

My darling Oona,

You will never credit the to-do that's been going on here since Sunday last. Yes it's the bloody galloping major again, may he rot in a ditch. You remember I told you how he's had it in for poor Harold for years, brought to a pitch by the business of his wife's grave, the ludicrous little man? He's been vowing revenge ever since, and creeping round the village muttering away like the Ancient Mariner, to anyone who'll listen, about the shocking iniquities of poor H. Well now, there'll be wigs on the green and fire on the rocks, as the old Da used to say.

Harold didn't arrive home in time for the Armistice Day service. There – I've said it now, and isn't it an awful thing? You know my feelings about English military men who can't get over the war, of course the whole country's been knee-deep in mourning for the last dozen years, and quite right too, mourning the loss of everyone's father and son and brother killed for nothing at all in the trenches, but you and I and other outsiders could whisper that it's all a big welling-up of not just Sorrow but Guilt, since it was the British government and the Army high command who sent them off to their deaths and it's now the same people who're leading all the wailing about the Final Sacrifice and duty to their country, etc., when 'twas all their d—ded fault with their plan of attack, their stupid orders about walking the men into a hail of gunfire carrying a ton of equipment so they couldn't run away from the bullets.

I tend to take all the Army bellyaching with a pinch of salt, and I cannot believe them that say Armistice Sunday is the most important Sunday of the year – what, more than Easter Sunday or the last Sunday in Advent when we're all preparing for the birth of Christ Jesus? So I can't really agree with them that say Harold's done a terrible thing.

He was ill in bed all week with a feverish ague made worse by frustration, because he can never sit still when there's his saviour work to be done. He was all set to come to the service, he said, he'd his sermon written, his bag packed and he'd told Mrs Parker the landlady to call him nice and early. But the bloody woman didn't call him. It seems she reckoned it was the only time in a year when he'd slept all night long rather than coming home at all hours or prowling his room at 3 a.m., and she'd thought, Ah, let him sleep, the creature, 'twill do him good. So he woke to find the morning advanced, the train gone, there wouldn't be another till the afternoon and hadn't he gone and missed the big service for Armistice Day?

H was distraught. His voice on the telephone was frightful, I mean literally full of fear that he'd done something truly desperate. I tried to tell him, it was unfortunate but hardly his fault, people miss trains every day, but I couldn't console him. You'd think he'd committed a mortal sin. He gave instructions: I should tell Mr Reynolds to contact Rev. Blair and ask him to take the service, or find someone else if he was unavailable. I should tell everyone I met that he'd been ill, but had decided to go to the wreath-laying in London at the Cenotaph as a Private Act of Remembrance. He said I should pin up a bulletin in the church porch, saying the rector would hold a 6 p.m. prayer service to remember the war dead. He even gave the text he'd chosen for the eleven o'clock sermon (Isaiah, 2:4, 'They shall beat their swords into plowshares, and their spears into pruninghooks: nation shall not lift up sword against nation, neither shall they learn war any more') to help whatever substitute preacher could be found. And he sent a telegram to the church sacristan: 'DEEPLY REGRET UNABLE ATTEND

SERVICE STOP VERY ILL STOP CAN YOU GET REV BLAIR OR CANON BLAKISTON AT HOLT TO OFFICIATE ON MARK ARRIVING PM TRAIN STOP DAVIDSON ENDS.'

Can you guess what happened, Oona? The service went ahead. The front pews were stuffed with naval and military in their ribbons and medals. Reverend Blair was a trooper. Everything was proceeding in a dignified way until the final blessing, when – just the very *minute* when everyone in the church was crossing themselves – there came this desperate growling noise from the back of the church, like some grizzly bear was loose. The congregation paused in blessing themselves to look round for the source but I didn't need to look – it was Major Hammond, in uniform and campaign ribbons, standing by the porch door, red in the face and set on trouble, grinding away, making sounds rather than words until, having got the attention he wanted, he shouted out, 'Where is Davidson?'

It was a chilling moment. Mr Reynolds, ever my saviour at these times, made a move to stifle him, but before he could, the major was off again: 'Where is he? Away in London, I suppose, with his tarts and thieves! He should be here on this of all days! This is an insult to the glorious dead!'

The church was full of indignation. You could hear the congregation clamouring to make him stop – but clamouring in that discreet-in-all-things way the English have, as if they're doing no more than sucking their teeth and going, 'Tsk – *really*.' Rev. Blair went ahead and recited the blessing, making everyone turn to the front and bow their heads, while the major was shown the door by the Legion members. But the damage was done, and it was all I could do outside at the end, greeting the churchgoers in the unseasonal sunshine, to reassure them, as per H's instructions, that he'd been struck down with influenza etc., and nothing short of Death's Door could have kept him from an occasion of such vital significance.

Harold arrived at four thirty, gaunt, dark-eyed, remorseful, far from his usual energetic self. You'd think the hounds of Hell were after him, the way his eyes flickered around. The only good thing, Oona, was the unusually fond way he embraced me, stroking my cheek and asking if I was 'all right'. Why wouldn't I be all right just because he'd missed a train and upset his mad old enemy? But I was glad at the warmth of his greeting. We haven't for years been on a warm footing, let alone anywhere near the sunny meadows of the love we used to have for each other. To feel his arms about me again, holding me, even though awkwardly as if we were near-strangers embracing, was a welcome surprise.

I left it till after his tea to tell him of the major's outburst. He was oddly philosophical about it, just nodded and said, 'It was to be expected.' He seemed resigned to being abused by the choleric old fecker. Perhaps Harold is in a depression where he accepts any abuse as his due. He's so hard to read these days. Perhaps he had something else on his mind that he isn't telling me about.

The 6 p.m. prayer service was sparsely attended. Only nine people in the church, and the atmosphere glum and half-hearted. I expect people had had enough hand-wringing over the war for one day.

After dinner, I asked would we have an early night, since he looked so exhausted. Not at all, he said. He had to stay up late with church schedules, and asked Enid to air the sheets in the spare room for he would prefer to go there. So all the earlier fond embraces were forgotten, were they, and he couldn't bear to touch me after all? Sometimes men are beyond fathoming.

I'll get to the bottom of it one day. Missed trains, war medals, shouting majors, husbands blowing hot and cold – it's hard for a decent woman to keep on top of things in this aggravating masculine world.

Write soon.

Your ever-loving Mimi

Letter from Major Philip Hammond (retd)
Morston Hall, Norwich
20 November 1930

To the Very Reverend Bertram Pollock, Bishop of Norwich

My Lord,
I wrote to you barely a month ago, about the behaviour of

the local clergyman Harold Davidson, Rector of Stiffkey. I brought up the disgusting behaviour of his trollop pals in the village, and his high-handed behaviour towards me. You were good enough to reply saying my complaints were simply personal disapproval and that I was just making mischief. You recall these events so far? I laid out all his damnable faults for full inspection, and you elected to do nothing but say I was the guilty party because of some supposed 'animosity' on my part.

I can scarcely believe a bishop of the Church of England could so abdicate his moral responsibilities as to hear my reports of Davidson's grubby transgressions and call them anything other than sins. Yes, sins, sir, faults condemned by the Church of Almighty God. Mr Davidson is a sinner. He is not fit to hold office in a country parish such as ours, filled as it is with impressionable young folk and conservative-minded older people.

I have explained to you that he spends all his time away from Stiffkey, ignoring his parishioners (and neglecting his family, though that is, thank God, no concern of mine) and frequenting the bars and low music halls at which his scandalous consorts flag their wares. You evidently do not believe me. I could point out that he takes no interest in the sensitivities of parish feeling over such matters as the upkeep of the war memorial, the pollarding of the oaks in the graveyard and the discouraging of young reprobates from stealing apples in the Rectory orchard. You will say I am deluded and driven by dislike.

So, My Lord, consider this. Last Sunday was the Armistice Day service, a time of sombre commemoration nationwide; in north Norfolk, as you may *not* be aware, the British Legion is strongly represented and we take the anniversary of the armistice extremely seriously. A special service is held annually for the Legion of Blakeney, a service at which, any clergyman in Norfolk would tell you, it is a privilege to officiate. A different celebrant embraces the duty at a different church each year. What happened this year? Using your unrivalled shrewdness and judgement, plus the facts I have laid out above, take a wild guess.

The celebrant was Mr Harold Davidson. The service at Stiffkey Church was at 11 a.m. The date had been in everyone's diary for weeks, even months. But Davidson, our sainted vicar, did not come. Just couldn't be bothered. He sent some tommyrot telegram to the church, or so I was told, saying, 'Sorry but I've got a slight cold and better stay in London.' Later he changed his mind, probably when his conscience revealed the enormity of his crime, and arrived in the village at an hour when nobody could give two hoots about attending church. The result? One Armistice Day service at which the rector fails to appear. And one footling prayer service, a conscience-salving substitute, which nobody went near.

Do you think this is the way to tell our fallen colleagues – our fathers, brothers and sons who gave their lives for our sake – that their name liveth for ever more? Their name means nothing to your rector. He is a disgrace, My Lord, and if you do not deal with him in an urgent and condign manner, it will bring the name of the Church into a disrepute from which it will not quickly recover.

My previous correspondence was intended as a friendly warning about the potentially scandalous doings of someone employed by you, or if 'employed' is too secular a description, someone whose position in the Church is held under your juris-diction. I am no longer interested in giving friendly hints. I hereby accuse Mr Davidson, not just of negligence in attending cere-monies, but of gross and chronic immorality. I will send a copy of this letter to my lawyer in Wells, pending your official reply. Your reply, or lack of one, will determine whether I seek redress, with or without your permission, in the less discreet courts of the Fourth Estate. I trust I make myself clear. Please do not imagine I can be brushed aside by more assurances that the only fault is mine alone. I must tell you, Mr Pollock, that I possess an indomitable streak that may prove dismaying, should you risk making an enemy of,

Your servant in the Lord,

Major Philip Hammond (retd)

Remarkably chilly today. The sky is blue, no trace of frost upon the lawn, robins and blue tits flap and fluster in the bird bath and, looking through a window, you would think it a normal autumn day. But venturing out, one is assaulted by a chill and biting wind, that penetrates the warmest outer-garments and leaves one gasping for breath that is soon inscribed, in cloudy mists, upon the November air. I must take exercise and not fester at home all day; but these angry zephyrs will keep me penned up here.

Mimi has been kind. Most sympathetic to my sorry condition and reassuring as to my tardiness, et cetera. After the evening service (a wretched affair) I elected to stay up late, drawing lists of parish affairs followed by night in the spare room. She tried to pack me off early to bed in our room with hot lemonade and sugar, hot-water bottle, et cetera, but I insisted *parce que de mon pudeur*, and went to my chilly spare-room divan, where I climbed, teeth chattering, under the blankets, and derived some solace from *Five Red Herrings* by Miss D. L. Sayers until fell asleep. Troubled by dreams, shocking in their physicality. Remembered some details on waking and was alarmed lest some beastly occurrence might have taken place in the night; but inspected the sheets and all was well. Instead of returning to London on early train, rose at leisure, tried to make breakfast, but kitchen mysteriously denuded of food. Ate some stale bread and cheese I found in pantry.

Mimi had risen early, gone out on her Monday rounds and to look in at town hall, where she now gives talks on Home Management! (How odd she never consulted me on this important subject.) Spoke to Colonel Du Dumaine, coming up to fourth anniversary of his widowerhood. He is, regrettably, bored to death. Sons doing well at Morston School, but the days hang heavy on him. Living on Army pension a mixed blessing when he should be working. Chances of finding work very slim; I suggested some clerical work with British Legion, but of course his half-French blood will not let him consider anything remotely redolent of clerking. So he gets by, growing ever thinner, on his bread-and-water existence and does odd jobs around the home for Mimi.

The maid no longer sleeps here, but with her sister in the house five doors away. I asked her why and she said, bluntly, 'Mrs H says you can't afford to offer me full board and lodging no more, sir.'

Is this true? When she'd gone, I wished I had asked her to make up a fire. Went around garden collecting sticks of kindling and dry logs, but no coal in the yard. Has it run out and not been reordered? A foolish oversight. A house on the Norfolk coast without a coal fire in mid-November is a sorry place.

Mimi returned at lunchtime and made soup from a pot full of disintegrating root vegetables on the corner of the range. To my eyes the liquid resembles, not so much soup, as the water in which carrots, parsnips, potatoes and leeks have been boiled together until they have softened to a melting consistency. Delicious as a raw material for stock, of course, but it remains hot water sparsely flavoured with garden produce. We drank it with some broken biscuits she had procured at the baker's last week. I enquired why she had bought no bread for the family's repasts. 'It's not the day for bread,' she replied. 'Friday we get the bread, and make it stretch the whole weekend, though of course 'tis all gone by Monday, but for crumbs. But eat away there, Harold. I'll leave a bit of the soup for the children's tea, and go look in the orchard to see if anything's fallen down.'

By the end of lunch, an awful truth dawned on me, that my family – my wife, my children and our friendly lodgers – were living in abject poverty. When Arnold and Pamela were home from school (I was ashamed to think I had never seen Pamela in her uniform), they were given an apple each, cut into slices, and a mug of weak tea to fill them up. But they were cheery nonetheless, sweet children who did their homework in sober silence and did not indulge in horseplay. I remarked on it. 'Arnold,' I said, 'why do you and Pammy not run about and play as you once used to? Is there animosity between you?'

'No, sir,' replied the boy. 'But there's five years between us. And I'm sixteen and do not run about and play any longer. And neither does Pamela, because she is eleven. She has stopped being interested in dolls. She is learning to crochet and to play the tin whistle.'

Tears pricked my eyes at the dear boy's words. I looked at my youngest children again, like one who has slept for years oblivious to time – or like a man who has recently acquired spectacles, perched them on his nose and found the world and everybody in it unaccountably grown older. Of *course* they were sixteen and eleven, and no longer small children. I am sure I knew that. I had kept a tally of their young lives at the back of my head, but hearing their ages uttered out loud was startling. Arnold's curiously formal mode of speech, so strangely polite ('sir'?), half concealed the fact that his voice has broken. After a few seconds on an even keel, it goes into odd swoops and dives, abrupt changes of register and hairpin bends of timbre. When did this start happening? How had I missed it? I knew, of course, *why* it happened – the dear boy has been passing through the gates of Puberty. But how could I also have missed several of their birthdays, Arnold's first week in the school cricket team, Pamela's giving up dolls for the tin whistle?

I had not been there because I needs must be about My Father's business. I have grown used to balancing these hierarchies of responsibility. I am used to the sacrifices I make in my work, and would not wish it any other way. But seeing my children today, eating tiny portions of fruit with hungry concentration and talking to me (so glad they are to find me at home for more than a day) with a show of animation, a wave of love for them swept over me, and a concomitant wave of regret for all the flavours and textures of their lives that I have missed by being away, dealing in the salvation of Annie and Bridget and Elsie and someone called Jezebel.

Letter from the Right Reverend Bertram Pollock
Bishop's House, Norwich, Norfolk
21 November 1930

To Mr Henry Dashwood, Attorney at Law,
Dashwood, Ogilvy & Pearce,
Gray's Inn Road, London WC1

Dear Henry,
So it's taken just a month, and Davidson is in the soup again.
I enclose a copy of the letter I have received from Major Hammond. As you can see, it is a complaint about the rector's

non-attendance on Armistice Day, couched in the extreme language we have come to expect from this sad military boor. But at the end, he goes so far as to make an Accusation, and to utter explicit threats about going to the Press, though with what concrete evidence to back his accusation it is hard for me to judge.

I must ask you: how seriously should we take this? Is there a case to answer? How do we establish what that case is? As you know, I would not wish this matter to reach as far as any court of law, whether civil, Crown or any other, except perhaps behind the closed doors of a Church tribunal. What, then, should be our course of action?

I wish you to read the major's letter, and the exchange between us from a month ago, and let me have your reaction, as a matter of urgency, by return of post.

Yours sincerely in Christ,

+ Bertram

Journals of Harold Davidson
Stiffkey
21 November 1930

Ventured out today, for the first time since my awkward return on A——— Day. Five days of prowling through the rooms of my forgotten home, seized with vestigial cramps from the influenza, confined to bed in the afternoons due to the frightful chill in parlour and dining room, spending evenings of pleasant but desultory chatter with the children, and I am driven out of doors, to walk the pleasant lanes of Stiffkey once more.

What a revelation! I have been guilty, I see now, of a misjudgement. I had reckoned the everyday concerns of my parishioners to be of a lower order than the pressing needs of my young charges in the metropolis. So Mrs Hopkins is concerned that her girls may dress immodestly when attending a dance in Fakenham? It takes nothing but a word of reassurance and a suggestion that she recommend cashmere cardigans against the chill night. Mr Ebbs wishes to marry a Jewish lady from Norwich but his mother refuses to attend the ceremony? It is dealt with by a personal visit and a quiet word about Jesus at the Cana wedding feast. Pollie Dack, our organist, must attend to her sick father in Wells and cannot play next Sunday? We shall enlist her charming niece instead. The everyday concerns of the country parson are small indeed when set beside the charnel house of London, the disgusting apartments and style of living that brought young Emily Murray to her early decease, the ragged army of young girls milling around London looking for a life of money and contentment, fated to find only a life of sickness and brutality. But today, *mirabile dictu*, I found a mission just as worthwhile in my own backyard.

It is Mrs Miriam Oakes, who dwells in a cottage a mile outside the village, down the road that leads away from the Red Lion. I noticed she had not attended church in recent weeks but attributed this to her sad bereavement. Charlie Oakes was a splendid fellow, employed by the brewery in King's Lynn to deliver kegs of bitter and malt to alehouses all over the Norfolk coast. He smoked a churchwarden pipe, an odd affectation for such a working-class yeoman, and died of emphysema one night in late September while a tempest raged overhead.

We buried him beside the yew tree in the graveyard and all the village turned out to see him off – a well-liked, humorous fellow, his face bronzed as a horse chestnut, a man who whistled folk tunes as he humped the beer barrels down the cellar steps, gave the children rides on his dray and was gallant with elderly ladies. 'I'll have a pint with you later, lads,' he'd say to the men in the public bar after delivering his kegs in the Townshend Arms, 'but it's teatime, and all I crave is a slice of Mrs Ebbs's fruit cake,' and off he'd go to sit with the old lady next door for an hour, out of common kindness, and she'd hear next day what he'd said about her cake in the public bar, and her heart would swell with pride. That was the sort of man he was, simply decent and naturally kind. Anyway, Miriam, the widow, has taken his death to mean the end of her life too, and the doors of Willow Cottage are permanently shut against the world It took several notes through the letter box, handwritten pleas for admittance, to be given an audience with my old friend.

She was dressed in black, of course, but her bombazine skirts seemed to come from an earlier era of mourning, quite at odds with the spirited modern woman I used to know.

'Don't bother telling me, Rector, what a fright I look,' she said gloomily. 'These are my mother's widow weeds, and yes, they make me look like Queen Victoria, but the minute I put them on I felt they were the only thing I wished to wear, now all the light has left me. I just can't bear it without Charlie. I've nothing to make me smile now. He'd make me happy every evening I'd see him home from his rounds. He'd be talking nineteen to the dozen about who he'd seen, how Mr Samuel in Burnham Market had a new young barmaid with dimples and a stammer, who would say, "A p-p-pint of Ab-Ab-Abbot," and Mrs Baker at the Queen's in Sheringham had taken to throwing shoes at the customers if they lingered beyond 11 p.m., and so many times when we'd finished supper I would say, "Poor tired man, what about an early night?" – because I just adored the touch of his skin against mine and he was lovely to be in bed with, Harold, excuse me for saying so – but he'd say, "In a while, pet, first I have to feed the horse," and I'd lie there in the bed thinking of him in the stable, with the barn-yard smell about him, which he'd try to wash off when he finally came up to me, and I'd say, "You can do that in the morning," but he was so fastidious . . .'

So she mulled over her happy marriage, and I tried to make her see what unusual, what unique happiness had been hers. But it failed, I'm afraid, to appease her sorrow, and she remains a self-appointed recluse. From which sorry condition I must find a release. It will happen as long as there is breath in my body. It is my occupation. It is my point. It is what I am here for.

Letter from Mr Henry Dashwood of Dashwood, Ogilvy & Pearce
Gray's Inn Road, London WC1
27 November 1930

To the Very Reverend Bertram Pollock

Dear Bertram,
I have read the letters. My answer is brief and, I hope, clear: You have cause for concern.

Major Hammond has evidently received legal counsel. For, after months of complaining about the rector's absences, neglect of parishioners, dubious company, quarrelsome ways and so forth – which amount to very little in the eyes of the law – he has hit on, or been advised to concentrate on, something that the law takes very seriously. In the letter you kindly copied for me, he brings, not a complaint but a *very specific accusation of immorality* against Davidson. We cannot, I'm afraid, ignore it. Were it to come out that we received such a slur on a practising vicar and did nothing, we should seem culpable, if not downright corrupt, were it to come up in a court of law.

Nonetheless, time is on our side. There will be no question of this sorry business entering the public domain unless the major makes a fuss, or does something silly, such as brief the Press. I believe I can win him over with a double-pronged attack. I shall go up to Stiffkey in the next week or so, meet the Army man and make myself agreeable on your behalf, so that he will realise something is being done. I shall make enquiries around the parish as to the rector's behaviour and hope there will be enough outcry against him to get him ejected in a diocesan tribunal on grounds of neglect. The major will be happy, you will be happy, and there will be no need for further embarrassment at the hands of this 'turbulent priest'.

I will let you know my findings. Do not be concerned. I can deal with the major and rid us of Davidson, and hush it all up. It's what I do best, My Lord.

Courage,
Henry

Journals of Harold Davidson
Stiffkey
1 December 1930

An alarming day. Called a meeting of church domestics to arrange roster for cleaning, cut flowers, candles, et cetera. I wish the church to be spick and span for Christmas week. Cycled to Binham to enlist help of Gerald Morrell, the choirmaster, to come and drill our awkward songbirds for carols on Sunday before C. Day. Looked in on Canon Humphrey, and discussed the changing face of the Birth of Christ sermon, over frustratingly evasive game of chess. Never was there a player like Arnold for withdrawing his advanced pieces at the first onset of confrontation.

Called at Prince & Dunwoody art stores, to buy cartridge paper and poster paints for Mrs Oakes. I recall she was a keen landscape artist early in her marriage. Let us see if they will offer her inspiration and succour in her present sadness. I have also asked Ivy to visit the baker's, the grocery and flower shop with a modest list of fresh bread, fruit, vegetables and a small Christmas tree to be sent to Mrs O, with simple card saying, 'From your Stiffkey neighbours in your time of sadness.'

Lunch with Mr Reynolds in the Bell, and there I heard the first whisper of trouble. He voiced his concern about Major H and his decline into deranged paranoia.

'I really believe, Harold,' he said, 'that he hates you and wishes you ill.'

'There is surely nothing new about such a state of affairs,' I said lightly.

He furrowed his brow. 'No, I don't mean simply that he doesn't like you. Everyone knows he loathes and detests you, that he despises everything you're at and takes every chance to say –'

'Jack,' I raised my hand, 'I really would rather not know every detail of his incendiary dislike.'

'But when I say he wishes you ill, I mean it. He would have you put away. He's actually planning it as we speak.'

'Excellent news,' I said with sarcasm. 'It is always heartening for a clergyman to find that one of his parishioners is planning on murder.'

'Have you met his mother?' he asked. 'Queer old bird. In her eighties and a bit off her head, not surprising with a son like that. Gives orders like she's lady of the manor. I went round to help her unload some logs that the timber yard delivered to the big house, I sweated away for two hours turning the stack in her garden into a proper log pile you could eat your dinner off, and it was all "Do this!" and "Do that!" and "Come here, you!" and "Haven't you finished yet? I won't pay you extra." Oh, and she talked about you.'

'Indeed?'

'She wanted to know everything that'd been happening at the Rectory. I said, "When?" She said, "All the time." I said, "Could you be more specific?" She said, "The place is always filled with girls no better than they should be, doing each other's hair, wearing each other's clothes and pursuing frightful modern practices." I said, "Well, I been up there at the house hundreds of times and I never seen no funny business with girls doing their hair and so forth.'"

Bless him. He is a good, loyal man.

'But I asked her, "What are you doing spreading this calumny, Mrs Hammond? If ever there was an illustration of the words, 'Bear false witness against thy neighbour,' you've just supplied it." She told me I was naive and a simpleton, the old, 'scuse me, Rector, old boot, and said, Surely I must know the way her son had been treated by you, by which I mean you, Rector.'

He took a sip of home-made cider, and looked around the Bell. I could see there was more to come, and I waited for it with dread. Finally, it came.

'"There is a man coming," she said, "who will look into these sorry matters and pay the rector back for his misdeeds." "A man?" I said. "What kind of man?" She said nothing, just sat nodding in a meaningful way, her old face lined like a drawstring purse. "A policeman?" I said. "No," she said. "A magistrate?" I said. She shook her head. "What, a bailiff?" I said (I was getting to feel a little comical, Harold, what with all her veiled threats). At last she said, "You'll find out soon enough. And so will Mr Davidson." She puts the willies up me, I don't mind saying.'

I do not give in lightly to threats or intimidation. But I would not be human if I said I greeted this news with equanimity. All day, I have had flapping in my head a dread of repercussions about what happened in London just before I left. Nobody could have known the depths of degradation to which I fell. Can it have come out? For the last twenty-four hours, a nameless shadow, an avenging figure, shortly to arrive by the London train, has stalked my daytime thoughts and troubled my midnight repose.

Stiffkey
10 December 1930

CHRISTMAS GIFTS

M – *Pearl bijou from Plowrights, Queen St, Norwich*
Sheilagh – *Norvicland black kid shoes, Norwich*
Nugent – The Byzantine Achievement *by Robert Byron*
Patricia – *'Terence's Farewell to Kathleen' record by Count John*
    McCormack. Or some soap? (Evening in Paris?)
Arnold – *Safety penknife, Bushell & Co., Castle St, Norwich*
Pamela – *Doll's house furniture. Sewing machine, ironing board, etc.*

NB. Ask Mr R to chop C tree in meadow. Cannot afford expense of
    buying great 7ft monstrosity from Mr Cadogan. Also Yule log.
Look in Mrs Ebbs, Mr Daintry, the Wards, the Williamses, Mrs Sinclair
    and Mr Parson re winter fuel expectations and make sure all
    provided for.
Mrs Oakes – my art experiment a dismal failure. Not interested at all
    in poster paints, and the echo of happier days succeeded only in
    bringing tears to her eyes. Maybe recommend musical instrument.
    (Violin? Harmonica?)

Letter from M. Henry Dashwood of Dashwood, Ogilvy & Pearce
Stiffkey
10 December 1930

To the Very Reverend Bertram Pollock

Your Grace,
    As you can see from the postmark, I am here in Stiffkey pursuant
to our earlier correspondence. I have not been idle. Staying at
Victoria Inn, charming small hotel beside Holkham Hall, whence
I have set out daily to make enquiries. First port of call Morston
Hall, to hear complaints from Major Hammond.
    A stranger to restraint, the major. His handsome Jacobean pile

positively reeks of decay, wet dogs, navy-plug nicotine and an indefinable mustiness that put me in mind of Miss Havisham in *Gt Expectations*. He greeted me civilly enough, offered me a 'snifter' of gin (at 10.45 a.m.) and went straight on the attack.

'The fact that you're here means something's being done at last,' he said. 'It means they're running scared. Capital. I don't mind telling you, Hardcastle –'

'Dashwood,' I said.

'– Dashwood, that I was getting pretty cheesed off with the lack of response from the bishop. "Cast no clout", that was the gist of his response. "Our hands are tied, nothing can be done, I stand by my clergymen." Always the same bloody refrain, no matter how strong the evidence I laid before him. So now I've found his weak point, have I?'

Naturally, I remonstrated. 'Major, I speak on the bishop's behalf, and will not be enlisted by you or anyone else to speak against him. His Grace has apprised me of your correspondence regarding Mr Davidson, and I am here to see if there is a case to be made against him.'

'Speak on his behalf, do you?' the major sneered. 'So you're his mouthpiece, his parrot, his organ-grinder's monkey? Got no opinion of your own, have you?'

Really he is a most disagreeable person to deal with.

'Perhaps,' I said calmly, 'you could furnish me with the details of what you know to be true about the behaviour of the Rector of Stiffkey towards women, especially women known to be common prostitutes.'

'It's not just what *I* know to be true,' said the major, explosively, 'it's what the whole county knows. *And* every barman in London, *and* everyone who runs a shelter for women down-and-outs – they'll know what he's up to, morning, noon and night, always fingering and squeezing and rubbing 'em and pretending to be working for the Lord.'

'Where is your evidence?'

'Ask anyone who's ever worked at the Rectory, and seen the kind of female scum he invites there for weekends of debauchery. Ask anyone who worked in the church premises in the last ten years. They'll tell you what goes on when the rector's women pals arrive there. Hah! And what happens in the graveyard, if you take my meaning.'

'You have proof of the Rector's personal involvement in immorality?'

The major seemed close to losing his temper. 'Proof? Of course I haven't got proof, you imbecile. Parishioners seldom attend the Rectory with box cameras to take incriminating photographs. No, there was nobody to record the circumstances of the debauch. But it is common local knowledge, and that is good enough for me.'

'What is common knowledge? What exactly has he done?'

We fenced like this awhile, I pressing for details, he becoming more flushed and cerise-cheeked and bombastic.

After an hour of taking notes, I can offer the following:

1. The Rev. Davidson was once seen kissing a woman, apparently a former serving girl in his employ, in the porch of Stiffkey Church.
2. He was seen with his arms around two women of dubious reputation, in a milliner's shop in Norwich.
3. Ladies he has befriended in London can often be found visiting Stiffkey wearing 'immodest frocks' and causing scandal in local places of refreshment.
4. He is never 'at home' in the village. He is always away in London. The appeal of the metropolis is unfathomable to the major unless, as he puts it, 'there are women in the background'.
5. He has waged a personal vendetta against the major, banning him from the church and refusing to let him exhume and rebury his late wife.

These are not, on the face of it, mortal sins, or even ethical transgressions. I was about to write and advise you that we need fear no court action, if this is all Davidson is accused of. But that was before I encountered the formidable Mrs Marjorie Hammond.

A termagant of the old school, small, pinched, white-haired, ferocious as a terrier down a foxhole, she may be approaching her ninetieth year but is in possession of all her faculties, especially those of vindictiveness and palsied mother-love. Were Grendel's mother from the *Beowulf* saga to relocate to Norfolk and sit at home for a year nursing a grievance, she might eventually become the alarming Mrs H.

She has kept a file, or diary, of the rector's wrongdoings that stretches back to the early 1920s. Dates and times of the arrival and departure of Rev. D's ladyfriends from London, what they wore, where they went, their rude behaviour, and the smiling connivance of the rector – how he would go for walks holding their hands and chatting with them in the street. Also, some murky details of Rev. D's home life, gleaned from local gossip. Did you know the rector apparently fathered a baby in London in 1919, brought it to the village and passed it off as his own? Did you know that his wife, Moyra or Mimi, herself became pregnant while Rev. D was away at the war, and gave the child up for adoption? And that, according to rumour, the father was none other than Colonel Du Dumaine, who now lives at the Rectory with his children as paying guests, making up by his proximity for the scandal he precipitated in the years where the Davidsons were estranged? My head began to spin at the blizzard of tittle-tattle, the tales of want and woe, of child neglect and casual immorality, that fizz about the Rectory chimneys.

Let me make this plain, Bertram. If one-tenth of what the Hammonds allege about your rector should get into the papers, the Church would be in serious trouble. There is a case to be answered here, but not one that can be reduced to a single plain charge of immorality. Several individual matters may be laid at his door, but none that would survive for two minutes in a secular court of law. He is not a criminal. He is, or has been, a sinner, but no more a sinner than a million other men in the heat of wartime or the emotional wasteland of a failing marriage. But these stories would be meat and drink to the Press, and we must avoid that. It is in your best interests to rid yourself of this man as soon, and as finally, as possible, before the dismal record of his private life becomes a public embarrassment to you. There is a quasi-legal recourse in the tribunal system I myself initiated a few years ago – a religious tribunal in which his behaviour may be evaluated in suitably vague ecclesiastical terms, and he can be quietly removed from office without the pain and expense of a civic lawsuit. All we need is a suitably orchestrated babel of local voices, a harmony of parish disquietudes, if I may so express it, which will chorus his unsuitability to continue as a pastor.

I propose to go with Mrs Hammond to various local addresses in Stiffkey and extract from them enough material to furnish a charge sheet as long as the Bayeux Tapestry, to set in motion the wheels of a tribunal. By the time you next hear from me, I am confident that we will have enough to hang our miscreant rector, figuratively if no other way.

I am Your Grace's humble servant in all these matters and I take the opportunity to wish Your Grace a happy – and concern-free – Christmas.

Henry

Letter from Mrs Moyra Davidson
The Rectory, Stiffkey
15 December 1930

My dearest Oona,

Thank you for the lovely card and all your news. I'm so glad the scare over Eamonn's health turned out to be nothing. Thanks too for your kind words about Harold, though I fear I was a bit premature with talk about our new romantic entwinings. It hasn't been like that at all. Home now for a month, he is strangely distant with me, preoccupied with something beyond words, and is always dashing around the village like he hasn't done for years. Sometimes he'll talk in the evening, after our meagre dinner, always about money, how to pay off our debts, how to afford some new clothes for Sheilagh and Patricia, how to pay for Nugent's travels abroad, how to get some cash to afford a car (he's been motorbiking like a dervish around Stiffkey), how we will manage to afford this and that, and his obsession with Being A Family. He talks in a dreamy way sometimes about us all being embedded in a snug little cocoon like dormice, all warm and replete, and God knows what that's all about. Does it mean he forgives me for the terrible thing that happened in the war years and after? Is that what he's trying to signal to me behind this great blanket of words, night after night? Last evening, I went up to see him. I tapped on the spare-room door, sat down on the bed and came straight out with it. 'Harold, listen,' I said, 'I know things haven't been easy between us for a long time, and I've said to you often that we've become like strangers to each other. But it's been so nice having you home the last few weeks, and the children have been thriving and have some colour in their cheeks for once after running errands for you – and if you want to show that you love me and forgive me my trespasses as I forgive you yours, then let us start tonight by leaving off this solitary brooding in here and coming to the bedroom and lying with me for a while until we go to sleep in the warmth of each other and end the old estrangement.'

Did he spring from the bed and embrace me? No. His eyes seemed to glisten with tears. 'I can't,' he breathed, wretchedly. 'I can't explain.' And there we were, awkward as anything, me offering wifely perfumed embraces and him saying, No, sorry, I'd rather not. Eventually I fecked off to bed, because I can't bear it when someone won't tell me what's going on in their head, when it's written all over their face, I DO NOT WANT TO SLEEP WITH YOU AGAIN.

There are plenty of other things to worry us anyway. You should hear the row that broke out at Mr Reynolds's house. Who should appear at the Reynoldses' front door yesterday morning? Only the major's mother. A snappish, mithering old biddy of eighty-ish years, she's never happy but when she's got something to complain about. You know the old one in *David Copperfield*, Mrs Peggotty, who sits there going, 'I'm a lone, lorn creature and everything does go hard with me'? Imagine that, only cross along with it, cross as a bag of weasels. In she comes to the Reynoldses' house, a skinny nightmare in a big flowery hat with a curled-over brim, striding past dear Anne as if she was a servant. Trailing in her wake, like a little tugboat after the *Queen Mary*, was this short lawyer fellow, name of Dashwood, done up like some class of gangster in a long black overcoat and a trilby. They sailed off down the hallway, turned right and dropped anchor in the lounge. Anne came after them, and they looked at her as if she was impertinent even to glance their way.

'Can I help you?' Anne asked the apparition in the madwoman hat.

'Is your mistress at home?' said the old one. 'I should like to see her. My name is Hammond.'

'There are no servants in this house,' Anne declared, 'except for servants of the Lord. You can state your business with me.'

The old lady gazed around her in silence for a full minute, as if she wasn't used to being given backchat. Either that, or she was waiting for an invitation to be seated that never came. Anne knew this was no friendly dropping-by.

'This,' she said at length, 'is Mr Henry Dashwood, a legal gentleman. He is embarked on a quest for information at the behest of the Highest in the Land.'

'Good heavens,' said Anne, 'who can you mean? His Majesty King George? Whatever would the king like to know about us?'

'Do not prevaricate,' said Mrs H severely. 'I am not referring to the royal family, but to the highest powers of the Church of England. I am telling you this so you will know he is not to be trifled with, and nor am I.'

'And what is it you and the Church of England would like to know?'

'Mr Dashwood is seeking information about –' (The old lady stopped, as if reluctant to say the name aloud.) '– about Harold Davidson, your so-called rector, and the behaviour that has brought this parish into disrepute.'

Anne put on her politest frown. 'When you say "your so-called rector", do you mean Mr Davidson is some kind of impostor? Good heavens.'

'I –'

'Has he been only pretending to be a clergyman looking after the church and the parish and all our souls for the last twenty-three years?'

God, Oona, when Anne told me about it, I wished I'd been there to see the look on the old one's face. Nobody, I swear, had tried sarcasm on the old girl in her entire life.

'You are impertinent,' she hissed. 'You are aware, I have no doubt, of the shocking tales that surround his malignant name. I demand you to tell Mr Dashwood all you know about the dreadful goings-on at the Rectory.'

Anne looked at her like she was off her head. Did she really expect her to tell tales against her best friends?

'I'm afraid, Mrs Hammond,' she said, 'that if you're looking for scandal and gossip about my neighbours, you will not find it here. I recommend you try somewhere more naturally disposed towards tittle-tattle. Perhaps you and your friend might spend an evening at the King's Arms in Blakeney, where the locals sit around telling all manner of lies about us all, after they've had a few pints.'

'How dare you?' the old lady shouted. 'How dare you suggest I should set foot in a public house? I, who have been teetotal for –'

'Perhaps I should clarify our mission,' Dashwood interrupted smoothly, 'for I see that it may be open to misinterpretation.'

Anne went to the door of the lounge and shouted her husband's name. She knew that, once a lawyer got started, she might find herself being given Lord knows what kind of runaround.

Mr Reynolds came soon. He said the atmosphere in the room, you could've cut it with a butter knife. He offered them a seat, and tea and cake, and said, 'How d'you do?' to the lawyer, and said, 'Oh, but Mrs Hammond and I are old friends,' and greeted her with a show of kindness, 'I hope you're keeping warm on these cold evenings,' etc., then turned to Dashwood and promised that he'd be pleased to help any emissary from the bishop and told him to fire away.

So Dashwood resumed. His questions were careful, sneaky, full of false respect and *plaumas*, as my mam used to call any kind of buttering-up, but Anne said that nobody was fooled, it was like being in a court assizes.

'You are the warden of St John the Baptist Church?'

'I am, and have been for many years.'

'Your duties?'

'I look after the church land. I oversee the tending of the grave-yard, the digging of graves and the cutting of the grass. I super-vise the gardeners who work in the orchard and the surrounding fields, keep the pathways and local rides clear, discourage poachers and trespassers. I am responsible for the maintenance of the church, I make sure it is cleaned, lit, heated and in good repair all year round, and employ local folk to that end. I oversee the buying of church supplies, whether for flowers, candles, surplices or statue decorations on important saints' days. I also –'

'Very good, Mr Reynolds. Admirable, I am sure. You leave Mr Davidson free, in other words, to pursue his own interests?'

'The rector has no business ordering candles for Sunday Communion, Mr Dashwood. He is busy at other things. I have my work. He has his.'

'And how often do you see Mr Davidson, in the course of a working week?'

'I see him on Sunday mornings, 10 a.m., regular as clockwork, before the eleven o'clock service, to discuss any pressing matters of church and parish business.'

'And that strikes you as a sufficient amount of time to spend on the many issues at stake?'

'We're not a big parish. Stiffkey is a village. St John's is a church with a hundred people in the congregation. It's not like we're running Westminster Abbey. Half an hour is enough for a chat about clearing the snow away from the porch or finding someone to tune the organ.'

'Mr Davidson is away from the parish a lot, I believe?'

'I don't enquire about the rector's timetable. It's not my place to ask where he's been or where he's going.'

'It is "not your place"? If I may say so, Mr Reynolds, you speak more like a servant than a valued lieutenant.'

'I am neither. I am a warden. I look after things I'm employed to look after. None of them is how the rector chooses to spend his time.'

'I understand he chooses to spend a great deal of his time away from the parish. Does that not discommode you?'

'Mr Dashwood, I can be ordering logs in Binham one morning, finding a man to pollard the elms another morning, driving a

236

pregnant parishioner to the hospital in Holt that afternoon and mending the flintwork next morning. I don't need the rector to be there, any more than he needs me to write his sermons.'

'He spends the bulk of the week in London, I believe?'

'I wouldn't know about that.'

'Are you seriously telling me that, should some terrible emergency break out – should, for instance, the church catch fire one day – you would have no way of contacting the rector about it before your Sunday-morning conversation?'

'He would find out within a few hours.'

'But how?'

'By telephone, Mr Dashwood.'

'You would be able to telephone him? How interesting. I should like to hear the exact number, and the exchange.'

'I don't have a number. But he would telephone me.'

'Indeed? He would ring you up out of the blue, from London? On impulse, I suppose?'

'He rings me every day, sometimes twice.'

The bold lawyer was a bit stuck about this. But he rallied.

'Let me be quite clear about this. Your working weeks are so clearly delineated, you have no need to speak for more than half an hour on a Sunday morning. And yet Mr Davidson is so solicitous about parish affairs that he rings you from London every day?'

'We are old friends. We do not always speak about parish business. But he's always in touch with what's going on.'

'And presumably he tells you about his work in London?'

'Sometimes, if he has had a satisfactory outcome to his work among the poor.'

'He tells you about the rehabilitation of prostitutes?'

'He may say that, with God's help, his charitable work is progressing.'

'Does he discuss the fortunes of the ladies in whom he has taken such a striking interest?'

'He may say that he has managed to trace the parents of an unfortunate girl, and brought her safely home to the family bosom. Things like that.'

'Oh really? They tend to be young girls, I believe?'

'Young girls, ladies in distress, boys who are being exploited by their employers, homeless strays from the countryside. They are all taken in by the rector.'

'Indeed so, Mr Reynolds. In more ways than one, perhaps?'

'I'm sorry, I don't know what you mean.'

'Come now, man, you must be aware that he forms relationships with many of these women of – of loose morals, visits them, dines with them, and invites them on trips to the countryside?'

'I only know, Mr Dashwood, that Mr Davidson is kind to the poor unfortunates he meets in London and offers them a friendship they have never known before in their sorry lives. If he offers them a meal or a smoke, that is his business.'

'He offers them a deal more than that, Mr Reynolds,' continued the lawyer. 'You must have been here in Stiffkey when some of the London tarts under his care came to stay at the Rectory and conducted themselves with, I believe, shocking indecorum?'

Mr Reynolds suddenly grewn tired of the verbal fencing. He dropped his pose of polite co-operation.

'Mr Dashwood, I don't know what you're seeking to prove, but you'll not find ammunition in this house or in any house in Stiffkey. The rector is the most respected clergyman in north Norfolk, not for his sermons, nor his devoutness, not for what he does in London, nor for the way he walks or cycles or talks or conducts weddings or funerals. He is liked around here because he knows his parishioners and is good to them and cares about them. If he chooses to invite ladies or boys or gentlemen to stay at his home, it's because he is the Good Samaritan, pausing by the roadside to help people in trouble. Everyone around here knows his worth. Everyone in the village has personally felt his Christian decency, his help with rent, with advice, with neighbourliness. You evidently know nothing of this. But then, if you have heard nothing except the calumnies of Mrs Hammond and her son, I would expect no better. Now if there is nothing else you wish to know –'

'I salute your loyalty to your employer,' said Dashwood, rattled at last, 'but cannot believe your naivety in this matter. Have you not heard the rumours about some ladies in his care, whose stay in the village was marked by scenes of public outrage? I refer to the evening in which, at the Townshend Arms –'

God, Oona, I am so tired of the stories and half-truths about That Evening, you'd think it was the most important event in Norfolk in decades.

And then it happened.

Mr Reynolds rose to his feet, pointed to the lounge door and the street outside and said, 'Get out. I have heard enough. Mr Davidson is my friend and colleague, and I will hear no more.'

'There is no need to become roused,' said Dashwood. 'All I seek is the truth, in order to determine –'

'All you seek, mister,' said Mr R, 'is to poison the name of a decent man. You will leave my house this minute. And if I find that you have been spreading malicious gossip about my friend, Mr Dashwood, I will take steps of my own.'

'Do you presume to threaten a representative of the Archbishop of Canterbury?'

'Not at all. I have no quarrel with the archbishop, except in the people he chooses to speak on his behalf. But I threaten you as a man from whom I have heard too much evil nonsense. And if I hear from any source that you have been saying anything about Mr Davidson that strays from the truth, I will track you down and *presume* to beat you black and blue.'

Can you believe it, Oona? Fisticuffs in the village. Two minutes later, Mr Dashwood found himself standing outside Glebe Cottage, summarily ejected like a drunkard from a choir recital. Mrs H, the sour old thing, could hardly stay perched on the sofa, and followed her champion out the door.

Excuse me, Oona, for rattling on, but I thought you'd like to know all the developments. I must admit, it does me good to write it all down, sort of calming for me in the midst of trouble. The months of poverty, the toing and froing of all these people, the chill in the downstairs rooms, the price of food, Harold's mental disarray and his mutterings about the warmth of home – it's all too much to take in. I only hope the new year finds us happier and saner, and send you my fondest Christmas wishes,

Love,

Mimi

Letter from Mr Henry Dashwood of Dashwood, Ogilvy & Pearce
Gray's Inn Road, London WC1
20 December 1930

To the Very Reverend Bertram Pollock

My Lord,

This has been a most frustrating few days.

I set out for Stiffkey with the confident intention of gathering sufficient data on the Rev. Davidson, that would justify our proceeding to a church tribunal. I met the major, then met Mrs Hammond, learned her (extremely vocal) opinions and agreed that we should take the bull by the horns. She suggested that we start with Mr and Mrs Reynolds (churchwarden and wife) because, as she put it, 'they are church employees and their first loyalty is to the will of the archbishop'. The Reynoldses do not share this view. In a long and uncomfortable scene, Mr Reynolds resisted my questions, declared that he knew nothing of public wrongdoing by the rector or his associates, and all but ejected me from his front door. I am not used to being treated like this. Around the village, I found a similar response. 'Oh, we love the rector, don't we, so flamboyant, such a good talker, always has time for everyone.' 'The rector? Do you know he baptised Evie Stoddart in 1907 and only last year he baptised her daughter, Lily? Continuity, that's what he represents, he's a man as trustworthy as the seasons.' I have heard many variants on these sentimental bromides.

Here are the few slender stalks of usable material I could glean:

Davidson a molester of women. A Mrs Russ, widowed, says the rector surprised her by recommending she pursue the dictum 'What would Jesus do?' in certain disgusting circumstances. She claims HD more or less suggested she should sleep with strangers who come begging at her front door.

Mrs Moyra Davidson sexually entwined at the Rectory with Colonel Du Dumaine. This suggestion greeted with derision by two respondents beside war memorial ('It would take more than Mrs D to rouse that dried-up old stick!'), but the story about the baby born out of wedlock and given up for adoption is substantially true, and a source of pain for Mrs D ever since.

Two young prostitutes visited Stiffkey in September, stayed with the rector and family at the Rectory, became drunk in Townshend Arms, and at least one was seen performing intercourse with several men against the church wall. Most people know nothing about this. Frankly, 90 per cent of response was (pretended?) shock and amazement. Four men corroborated seeing the two girls in T Arms conversing to each other and to men at bar, but no information from any source re what happened after. 'Most unlikely,' they say, shaking heads. 'That would never happen around here.'

It will not be easy arraigning him for a tribunal unless something else comes up. For the moment, he seems unassailable. The villagers have mostly positive feelings about him. They bring up his record with the poor, his enlightened embrace (metaphorical) of sinners of every stripe, his war record, his enthusiasm, and many smaller matters, e.g. he has occasionally driven ladies to the train station in an emergency, riding pillion on his motor bicycle with their hands clasping his sides for safety. Very exciting, apparently. I am sorry to disappoint with this information and look forward to further instructions. We will get the Rev. Mr Davidson in the new year, by fair means or foul.

In the meantime, I wish Your Grace a discreetly Merry Christmas.

Henry

Journals of Harold Davidson
Stiffkey
26 December 1930

So Christmas, like Mr Dashwood, is over and gone. My nemesis has departed and I may breathe again. Mimi and Mrs Reynolds told me everything about his unpleasant enquiries, and the heroic way in which Mr R matched him blow for blow and finally sent him packing. For days I have felt in dreams the bony fingers of Mrs Hammond closing around my throat, and heard her son's accusations in the air, itemising my faults and seeking my downfall. They came to Stiffkey like thieves in the night to steal away my reputation – and failed. I am practically glowing with sinful Pride, which of course cometh before a Fall.

One thing alarms me. Can it be that this lawyer, Dashwood, is really working for Canterbury? Is he here because the archbishop knows or suspects or thinks I have done wrong? How can he possibly know what is on my conscience? I suspect there is a wider plot against me, and until I know what it is, my sleep will continue to be disturbed.

My conscience also. As Christmas stole over us, as Nugent helped Mr R cut down a tree, and Patricia and Pamela decorated it, as the family came together from all points of the compass and sat in the living room by the fire, reading the Dingly Dell chapters from *Pickwick,* we were briefly a picture of Dickensian family harmony. Mimi and I were linked together following the Armistice Day events, as we have not been in years, and we talked fondly and easily as we used to. Yet I could not accede to her wish that we share a marital bed as before – not with the knowledge of what occurred on my last night in London. I still shudder with shame, that I allowed myself to give in to such an Occasion of Sin. How can I approach my dear wife and offer her an intimacy fatally compromised by the memory of that night, and the hot, disgraceful cave where my swollen flesh briefly found a home? I cannot. And so she thinks me cold towards her. And I cannot explain. So I writhe in torment.

The new year draws near and with it a twin resolution: to redouble my efforts among the lost and benighted while there is breath in my ageing frame; to steer clear of Miss B— H— and her wiles, and to absolve myself with the words, 'Go thou and sin no more.' With the help of my Redeemer, I will succeed in both.

CHAPTER 13

Notebooks of Charlie Norton, *Evening Standard*
London
10 January 1931

I've been looking for the rector all over. Where the hell has he gone? Tried the Old Coal House in the Strand, where I first saw him with the two young brasses back in July. No joy. Bella, the fat barmaid, just shakes her head. 'Haven't seen him in months, darling, nor his dodgy pals. Can't say it's a blow, not having him in the snug all night. It's not like he boosted the profits, with his pints of squash.'

Reasoning that he might have moved his operational HQ a few yards down the road, I tried the Crown, the Grapes and the Running Footman, all popular dives off the Strand. The only sniff was the barman in the Grapes who said, 'If you see the padre, tell him there's a cheque of his for a tenner he cashed that's still bouncing between here and Lloyds Bank. Give him my compliments and say there's a bunch of fives waiting for him if he shows his face in here again.' Well, *that's* nice talk about a man of the cloth.

I've got to track him down. The editor's wife, Mrs Lees, read my little story about him all those months ago, and has been on to the boss ever since about the saintly tart-saver. Maybe she fancies herself as a lady of charity. More likely she's got a secret — some daughter or young sister that's gone off the rails, took up with a murky young cove, got dumped and swum into one of those distressed-girls retreats the rector told me about. Anyway, the word's gone out: find him, and run a catch-up story on whatever he's up to now. We had letters, back in July.

'Congratulations on some good news for a change,' one said, and

'Hurrah for a sighting of the Good Samaritan on the streets of London! Can we have more of this sort of inspiring material?' A right palaver about the little chancer.

If I can't find him, I need to find this Dolores, the unfriendly tart, and her giggly pal Jezzie. It'll take some research in the pubs of Fleet Street and the Strand, a terrible hardship that. If they're not in EC4 I'm prowling further afield, north into Clerkenwell and the edge of the City, east into Aldgate and Whitechapel stews, south into the pubs of Bermondsey. I'll find the girls, sooner or later, then find the reverend and learn what he's up to, for the edification of Mrs L and the reading public. It's my New Year resolution.

Journals of Harold Davidson
London
16 January 1931

My new home is 43a Macfarlane Road, Shepherd's Bush, W12, a snug little place on the first floor, with a separate front door in a side alley off the avenue. My landlady is a Mrs Osborne, who lives on the ground floor with her husband and daughter, a sweet child of twelve. I explained to Mrs O that I was in the habit of coming and going at odd hours, and that the pursuit of my charitable work sometimes required me to interview the needy at unsociable times of the evening. Also, that my strict diet did not necessitate morning or evening repasts, and that she should not trouble herself over them. 'As you please, Rector,' she said. 'You come and go just as you like. As long as my Bernard isn't made fretful by the rent, we shan't bother you. And if you run out of victuals while you're busy with − with the needy, why you just come and bang on the front door and ask, as long as it's before ten, all right?'

I was speechless with gratitude for her simple common sense. At last I am freed from the querulous cavils of Mrs Parker! I can make my own bed, wash my own cutlery, light my own gas heater and conduct myself as a free man. I can return home at any hour, safe from the tyranny of sarcastic notes on the kitchen table, and from the apparition of that Vestal virago (a happy phrase!) who used to wait and watch for my arrival. How did I endure it for so long?

Shepherd's Bush is not a handsome destination; it is a suburban nowhere on the western reaches of London. My new home is tucked between a noisy railway and an ugly generating station, but there is a pretty triangle of green at the head of the Uxbridge and Goldhawk Roads, and a lively street market on Wood Lane. St Gabriel's Church is but a stroll away. A lively-looking theatre, the Empire, commands the main square, and a new cinema is showing some frightening nonsense, from Hollywood by way of Romania, about a hideous, cloaked and staring-eyed villain called Dracula who preys on young girls. It is a far cry from my old stamping grounds of Vauxhall, Waterloo and the Strand hotels; but bearable, I think.

This flat was all I could find at short notice when forced to quit my old address, after my altercation with Mrs P. I should, perhaps, not have accused her with such vehemence of failing to rouse me for the Norfolk train that Sunday morning. But there was no call for her to respond with such verbal extravagance, about my visitor, nor her sleeping on the premises, nor the apparently 'ungodly' behaviour she infers to be my habit. She is a dim and doltish slattern, always has been. I am better off by myself.

Sometimes I lie, thought-intoxicated, beyond 9.30 a.m. and catch a glimpse of the life of sluggardly indolence that enfolds many of my charges and leads them into that dangerous lotus-land where they entertain fantasies of never rising at all, except to admit male clients to their cramped boudoirs and suffer their oafish advances, with the assurance that they can sleep again, just an hour later, the richer by ten or fifteen shillings. The life of, for example, Miss Harris whom I used to know but − I must not think of her. I must not yield to thoughts of her supposed charms, which were only a ruse to corrupt all about her. Yet she once held my interest − as a challenge, a test from on high. I thought I could bend her to my will. Instead, I found myself sucked into her shameless orbit. It shall never happen again. Help me, Lord Jesus, to find the path that leads to your shining dwelling, even in these groves of sin.

I shall begin afresh, looking out for potential sinners here in Shepherd's Bush, setting up a new network of kindly employers and understanding tradesmen to take them in. They will be like a new family to me. Now I really must shave and venture out. I have hardly stirred from this tiny room in two days, overwhelmed by unpacking my cases, my books and foodstuffs, my selection of cut-price toiletries. But to whom shall I give the latter, now I am so far away from my old life?

Oh, I shall find someone. The Lord will provide.

London
21 January 1931

In the Blue Bull public house in Goldhawk Road, I fell into conversation with two men of low morals and frankly alarming attitudes. Seeing my clerical collar (I thought it prudent to wear one, given the rough atmosphere in this seedy thoroughfare), they engaged me in conversation, initially of a jocular kind, as to my views on the local Jewish population. I told them my acquaintance with west London Jewry was as yet slight, but I had many friends of the old faith in east London. They pressed me to consider that the ancestors of such people were responsible for the death of Christ. I tried to explain that Christ was himself a devout Jew and his death a political not racial attack, but I was shouted down. Much nonsensical ranting followed, about an international Jewish conspiracy to control all British banks. When did this kind of thing start to exercise the minds of vulgar Londoners? Hitherto, their most strenuous intellectual exercise has been counting backwards to establish the score at darts. They had evidently come from a meeting of similarly minded ignorant firebrands. The name of some bigoted demagogue called 'Moseley' (?) came up once or twice. Who?

They were helpful, though. I told some white lies about looking for a young female cousin who might have strayed into bad company, and was answered with vulgar raillery. 'I don't want to upset you, Reverend,' said one, 'but I think I seen the girl you're talking about down the Calico Club.'

'And if not,' put in his friend, a halitotic rascal with a disgusting leer, 'you'll probably find her on the Pussycat Green on Friday night.'

There was much laughter, a horrendous noise. Further enquiries elicited that the former is a musical den in a cellar on Brackenbury Road; the latter a notorious patch of the greensward near my home, where prostitutes solicit at weekends. I said goodnight, and was rewarded with more drunken suggestiveness ('Give her one for me', et cetera). What a hellish part of town in which to establish my new domicile. But what a promising territory for the work of the Almighty!

Notebooks of Charlie Norton, *Evening Standard*
London
20 January 1931

Aha! Success of a kind. I was having a sharpener, Tuesday lunchtime, in the Prospect of Whitby down Wapping way, and Eric Danes from the *Tribune* was gassing on about some march or demonstration planned for next month.

'Mark my words,' he says, 'this fellow Mosley's going to shake things up a bit.' It was the first time I'd heard the blighter's name mentioned, and I was torn between a desire to hear more about the chap and a reluctance to let Eric gas on too much about his political views which are about as interesting as the Pope's views on jazz, when who should I see come in but that Barbara party, one of the rector's little girlies from back in October. I recognised the cheeky glowing little face, the huge brown eyes and chestnut curls. As soon as I could manage, I sidled over to where she was standing drinking gin with some tough-looking cove in a leather jacket. All buttoned up she was, fur-lined collar and brocade coat and a nice pair of boots, a very stylish young thing for a brass. She was looking very serious, and I was cautious of approaching her because I knew from before she had a tongue that could clip a hedge. But what the hell, time to take the bull by the horns.

'Miss Harris, isn't it? Hello there. Charlie Norton from the *Standard*. Nice to see you again.'

She looked blank.

'We met,' I said, 'a few weeks back, in the Strand. Lovely evening it was, you must remember. We had a few drinks and a chat. With your friend the rector –'

'Sorry,' she said coldly, 'you must be mistaken. I never met you any place. I don't know you. And I don't know no rector, either, so you got it wrong.'

I was a bit taken aback. 'Barbara,' I said, 'you can't have forgotten. The snug at the Old Coal House? Me and the rector and you had a nice chat and a few drinks, and we ribbed him about interfering with people's boyfriends. I was wondering . . .'

The leather jacket beside us was rustling. Its owner was a big bloke, shoulders out to here, and I found myself staring straight into a fancy (and very wide) waistcoat. His face wasn't at all friendly. I've seen lumps of granite more welcoming.

'The lady says you've made a mistake,' he breathed. 'You shouldn't pester her if you know what's good for you.'

'There's no need to take that tone. I was going anyway,' I said with immense dignity. 'Goodbye, Barbara.'

Back with Eric and his talk of anti-Jew movements, I watched and waited. Barbara had undone her coat, but showed no sign of stopping for a long session. Who was the bloke? He wasn't a client – their conversation was too serious for that. He might have been some kind of middleman or tart's fixer. I kept an eye out and in half an hour, he was backing away out the door, saying 'All I know is, 'e's left the circus. But I'll do what I can.' Then he was gone and she was by herself.

'Barbara,' I said, by her side once again, 'sorry, I know you're not keen to talk, but –'

'You still around? I thought you'd done enough poking and prying for one evening.'

I admired her directness. Suddenly there was none of the old who-are-you-I-don't-know-you routine. 'So you *do* remember me?'

'I remember enough to know not to get tangled up with the Press,' she said curtly. 'People round 'ere *don't like* bloody reporters waltzin' in and sayin', Tell me stuff, I just want to write down what you're sayin' and print it for everyone to read. They feel you're taking liberties. You want to watch you don't get yourself thumped one of these days.'

'Barbara,' I said, 'I don't want to write about you or your friend, whoever he is. I just want to find the rector. Do you know where he is?'

'Haven't seen him in two months,' she confessed sulkily. 'He's moved house. Doesn't get in touch. Doesn't go to the old dives. I'm not that bothered. Ridiculous old geezer, all his rushing around London, dustin' off the wallflowers.'

'You mean?'

'You know – he spends all his time visiting the girls he's saved or thinks he's saved, girls all over the place, Highgate, Holborn, Whitechapel, Vauxhall, you name it, night after night, checking up on 'em at home, work addresses, clubs. He'll go visiting to see they aren't backsliding into a spot of 'orizontal income-building. He calls on 'em in the middle of the night, to make sure they aren't goin' to start misbehaving.'

I caught something in her tone, some molecule of bitterness.

'You mean these visits of his aren't – quite kosher?'

'What's that?'

'Aren't what you might expect of a clergyman visiting his flock?'

'I don't know many clergymen. Don't run into them a lot when you're sixteen, and single, and not gettin' married or dyin'.'

A thought struck me. 'Did he ever try it on with you, Barbara?'

Her eyes came over all hooded with suspicion. 'Nobody takes advantage of me, mister. And I don't like all these questions. And I wanna go home now, so you can stop right there.'

She began doing up her buttons and looking round the pub, probably in search of some mug to give the eye to.

'Wait,' I said. 'I've got to find him. Hasn't he got a sister somewhere in London? What about his new lodgings? He must have left a forwarding address.'

'Well, you got your work cut out there, haven't you, Mister Journalist?' she said, snide as you like. 'See yer around.' Her witchy black mittens wiggled a contemptuous farewell.

It won't be easy finding the little padre, will it? Nor will writing about him as a modern saint, when I'm starting to wonder if he's a bit of an old Bluebeard, with his network of ladies. Top story, if true.

Journals of Harold Davidson
London
22 January 1931

Disastrous encounter on Shepherd's Bush Green. Briefed by my thuggish associates in the Blue Bull, I made my way to the greensward late on Friday evening.

The night was cold. I wore my greatcoat, its pockets replenished with medicaments, inspirational leaflets, playbills, perfumes, cigarettes, stationery, photographs of popular film stars, plus two tickets I had bought cheaply to the Glee Night at the Shepherd's Bush Empire in early February. Earlier, as I spread them across the work table in my living room, prior to arraying them about my person, I remarked on my resemblance to Santa Claus, piling his sleigh with toys and footling beguilements, in the hope of conveying a transcendent message, that behind all the flashy gewgaws lay the certainty of Salvation. Catching my reflection in a mirror, however, I could not help thinking of my other resemblance, to a pedlar of seductive wares, a Fagin festooned with stolen watches and handkerchiefs to entrance the innocent Master Twist into a life of crime.

A surprising number of folk were abroad on the Green at midnight (the bell tower of St Gabriel's chimed a dismal dozen), mostly men recently decamped from the Flask, the Queen's Head and the King of Denmark. They stood in listless camaraderie on the frosty grass, swigging bottles of ale from the 'Out-sales' counter, conversing in belligerent shouts. They looked at me coldly as I passed by, for I had relinquished my dog collar. I moved among them awkwardly, as though attending a party where one had no social acquaintance, and, at the apex of the greensward, between two public lavatories, I discovered that my friends in the pub had been accurate in their predictions.

A quintet of ladies stood gossiping between the privies, women in hats and fur-collared coats and cloaks who had no earthly business being out on such a chilly night, except for purposes of sordid connection. One of them detached herself from the group and approached me with the words, 'Got a ciggy, darling?'

I dug into my pockets and fished out a Woodbine. She took my hand in her lacy mitten as I lit it, and looked up into my eyes with a frank enquiry as she exhaled.

'Bloody freezing tonight, innit?'

'It is indeed.'

'Cold as a witch's tit.'

'Indeed so. Or a penguin's, ah, bottom.' (I could not bring myself to say 'arse' to a lady, though I had picked up the low phrase recently in a saloon bar.) 'It is a chilly night for a young woman to be strolling. And you would feel the cold night, less, my dear, if your frock were not so open to the elements.'

'Very sensible advice,' she said, 'but you wouldn't want me to cover up these, would you?' She indicated her surging bosom. Goose pimples were raised along her skin like a childhood rash. It was not a pretty sight.

'They would be better,' I said, 'covered by a modest shawl.'

'I thought real men liked looking at ladies' chests,' she said. 'I thought their perfect girlfriend would be that fat actress – what's her name, Mae West?'

'Miss West is thought by many men to be far too well uphol-stered to be appealing,' I assured her. 'We have only just emerged from the era of the flapper, where the bosom was taboo.'

'Why d'you talk funny?'

'I – I am not a native of Shepherd's Bush,' I said feebly, as if I had stumbled into Tanganyika, not west London, 'so I may speak with the accent of central London that may be unfamiliar to you.'

'You waiting for somebody?' she asked. 'Or you fancy some company? Cos if you do, we could both get out of this perishin' wind and go somewhere warm.'

Soon we were crossing the Green, walking briskly down Goldhawk Road, turning into Devonport Road and the woman was letting herself through a narrow door into a small, anonymous cottage.

Once inside, the electric light revealed a poky front room wretchedly furnished with three upright chairs and a threadbare divan. The woman removed her coat and draped it over a nail in the wall. Without her outer garments, she was a thirty-ish, matronly figure in a patterned frock of brushed cotton, hefty across the beam, but she was vestigially pretty: curly blonde hair, obviously dyed, blue eyes caked in mascara, a considerable chin, strong but protruding teeth. A seasoned trollop, but not unsusceptible to salvation.

In the grate, the remains of a meagre fire glowed under an ash blanket. My new friend threw on some sticks, knelt and blew some life into the little crucible of warmth.

'Had the fire on all afternoon and evening,' she said. 'I thought I'd bring you in 'ere while we get better acquainted, because it's a bit brass monkeys upstairs. Still, you won't mind that, willyer, in a while? You'll have other things on yer mind.' Her right hand caressed my cheek, smoothing some hairs at my temple. I decided to nip this in the bud.

'What is your name?'

'You can call me Laura,' she said, talking off her shawl and indicating that I should sit. 'Why'n't you relax a bit on the divan? Take your shoes off, the fire'll warm your feet up lovely. We can warm each other up. If I put my 'ead in your lap, you could give me a little stroke, starting with my 'air, couldn't you?'

'Wait a moment, Laura,' I said, seeing a moment of awkwardness coming near. 'I think you should know that I am not what I seem.'

'What?' she said unheedingly while her hands slipped off my brogues.

'I am not,' I said more firmly, 'an ordinary, ah, *punter*, as I believe your gentlemen clients are called. I should explain that –'

'Not your run-of-the-mill punter, eh? Well, aren't *you* the tiger in disguise?' Her sturdy, millgirl's hands began to trace hard, raking strokes along my right leg, from knee to thigh. 'So what is it you like then, Mr Out of the Ordinary? You want me to wear a mask? You want me to dress like an Injun squaw – I get a lot of that now, I dunno why – or like Marlene What's-'er-name? No, don't tell me, it's about you, isn't it? You want to dress up as that Tarzan geezer, or a baby, or a schoolboy.'

'Absolutely not. If I may –'

'No, wait, I got it. I know what you're after.'

I was taken aback. 'What?'

'You wanna be a clergyman,' said the woman with a horrible knowing sneer on her face. 'I know the type.' Her hand on my thigh increased its pressure. 'You wanna pretend to be a bishop or a vicar and bang on about virtue or some such, while I'm doin' the business down below. You want me to be some kind of urchin girl, am I right?'

'No,' I said. 'No, no, very much no. I think you should realise that I –'

'It's OK, cock, I've 'ad this before,' she continued. 'You'll be the saintly cleric in the dog collar, saying your prayers, all holy and not a thought about girls, then I come in, in this teeny ragged frock, dirty face, teary cheek, and I do a lot of sniffin' and sayin' how I'm miles from home and lost, then you sit me down against a wall or summing, with my knees bent up so you can see my little white drawers, and you start saying, "My dear, I feel you need some proper loving care as only I can provide," and I say, "Ooh, sir, I don't know where I am, I'm a stranger round here, and I'm ever so innocent," in a silly Somerset accent, and you unzip your trousers and say, "Have you seen one of these before, my dear?" and I get all wide-eyed and fearful and take your –'

'STOP!' I cried in terrible disarray, as this obnoxious scene was sketched before my eyes. 'Please go no further.'

'You what?' said she, irritated by the interruption.

'Madam, I *am* a clergyman,' I said with as much dignity as was available just then.

'Yeah?' She looked puzzled, as if I were in the grip of a tenacious fantasy. 'And?'

'I am a rector of the Church of England. I came to the Green tonight, not in pursuit of carnal activity, but to seek one such as yourself, dear Laura – named no doubt after St Laura of Padua, a handmaiden of the Lord, who helped St Jerome before he became a recluse. Interestingly –'

'Don't get carried away,' she said. 'It's not me real name anyway.'

'I came to the Green to seek you out and to help you abandon this life of shame,' I resumed. 'I have made it my business over the years to befriend ladies of your persuasion, in a way they have rarely encountered in male company for years –'

'Bragging a bit now, are we?' she said. 'I must say, you throw your-self into the part, don't yer?'

'I assure you,' I said, removing her questing hand, 'that I am a bone fide clergyman. Look, I have my clerical collar here.' Whereupon

I extracted the starched semicircle from my No. 3 pocket and held it against my neck.

'Oh, you've brought your own props along,' she said. 'Don't often see that. I got a whole cupboard of stuff upstairs – judge's wig, policeman's helmet, master's mortar board. I like a client who comes prepared.'

I stared at her in astonishment. Could it be that she did not believe me? That she genuinely took me for a person who acted the role of rector as part of a sordid game? Never in my long career have I been so flagrantly misunderstood.

'Tell you what, mate,' she said, rising heftily from the floor, 'since you're so keen right from the word go, we'll skip the preliminaries and I'll get into my raggedy urchin costume, and we'll just get on with it down 'ere, shall we?'

I sprang up from the divan. My heart was pounding.

'I'm sorry,' I said. 'I must go. This is – this is all wrong.'

'That's the spirit,' she said, relentlessly. 'Bad and wrong, and we must both be punished. You're a real actor, aren't yer? And –' her voice dropped to a conspiratorial whisper – 'we'll call it a fiver for the whole sesh, all right?'

I retrieved my coat and looked around wildly.

''Ere, where you going?'

When I left she was standing in the doorway, unsure of whether we were play-acting, still half convinced that I was not who I am. That I was what I most certainly am not.

It is now 3.30 a.m. My first foray into west London corruption has not been a success. Perhaps I should revisit the Green tomorrow night, in the hope of a more productive encounter.

Shepherd's Bush Hospital, Goldhawk Road, London W12
24 January 1931

Casualty Department Report
Re: Mr Harold Francis Davidson. Date of birth: 14 July 1875

This unfortunate gentleman admitted in the early hours of this morning, suffering cuts, bruises, mild concussion.

Following an altercation on SB Green, Mr Davidson was attacked by two men and a woman, evidently for non-payment of some fee. Police witness Miss Annie Vine reported much 'language and pushing', followed by a succession of blows to Mr Davidson's face and body, after which the men ran off, and Miss Vine escorted the victim to Outpatients Dept.

Initial examination, timed at 1.15am, revealed a 3-inch gash to patient's chin, extensive contusions to brow and temples, and bruising to 2 right-hand ribs. Suspicion of ruptured kidney, but further examination ruled this out. Evidence of mild concussion (patient gazing dully into space for several minutes, patient talking to self with religious invocations). No evidence of alcohol ingestion.

Treatment: 6 stitches to chin. Kept overnight for surveillance. Discharge tomorrow if condition not worsened.

NB: must warn people against straying on SB Green at weekends.

Letter from Mr Charlie Norton
Evening Standard, *Shoe Lane, London EC4*
1 February 1931

My Lord Bishop,

I am a news reporter on the *Evening Standard*, which, as you may know, is London's leading daily newspaper. Forgive my direct approach to your office, but I need some information concerning a clergyman whose living is part of the episcopal see of Norfolk.

I am trying to locate Harold Davidson, the Rector of Stiffkey on the north coast. You know the gentleman I mean? He has been creating quite a stir here in the Big Smoke, for his good works, and for his rehabilitation of homeless and otherwise unfortunate people. He was kind enough to give me an interview last July, which I wrote up as a piece in our Feature pages, and I enclose it for your interest.

For many reasons I won't go into, I am keen to trace Mr Davidson

and discover more about his charitable works. Some very important people are keen that I 'track him down'. But I can't seem to
find an address for him in London, my letters to his wife at Stiffkey
Rectory go unanswered and my leads and contacts in the hotels
and suchlike of London get nowhere.

Do you have a contact address for Mr Davidson, or know where
he could be found in the event of an emergency? I would be
grateful if you could reply by return.

I am Your Grace's humble servant,
Charlie Norton

Letter from the Right Reverend Bertram Pollock
Bishop's House, Norwich, Norfolk
3 February 1931

Dear Henry,

I don't like the look of this at all. Some reporter from London
is on Davidson's trail. He has written asking if I know the man's
whereabouts, and said he intends to write a newspaper article
about the rector at the specific request of 'some very important
people'.

Have you any idea what this can be about? If by 'important
people' this man means Major Hammond, I can imagine the
ensuing article will be very damning indeed.

Your investigations before Christmas temporarily put my mind
at rest, that there is at present no case to answer in a court. But
if Hammond has supporters in the London Press, and they are
unscrupulous enough to print his allegations of sexual misconduct, we shall be in the soup. We need to be prepared for such
an eventuality. Whatever our personal misgivings about Harold
Davidson, we need to mount a robust defence of the man.

I suggest we redouble our efforts to establish the exact nature
of his work among the indigent of London, and whether he is
exploiting his position in some morally rebarbative way. Not just
to enquire among his friends for anecdotal testimony, but to investigate his movements and his behaviour. The means I leave to

you, Henry. Follow Davidson from door to door if necessary, enlist the police force, bribe landladies, call in a firm of private detectives if you must, but find out the truth, if you please, and let us be reassured about this wretched matter and this accident-prone man.

Yours in Christ,
+ Bertram

Letter from Mr J. Fowler of Arrows Detective Agency
34 Flood Street, London SW3
6 February 1931

Dear Mr Dashwood,
Re: Possibility of putting Tail on Unnamed Suspect
Thank you for your enquiry of 5 February.

It is not easy to reply to your letter with a proper Prospectus of how we can assist you, because of a shortage of details, e.g. Who is this man you would like to find out about, Where is his dwelling, What is his mode of operation, What would you like to discover about him, What is it that he is supposed to have done, and so on.

We are always happy to help Clients establish certain Facts about people, but I am going to need much more information of the basic sort from you before we can proceed. All I can say at this juncture is that we are a reputable firm of Private Detectives, operating in all parts of Greater London but prepared to go as far afield as Kent, Surrey, Berkshire and Essex. We employ a number of ex-Metropolitan officers, physically robust crime fighters of various types, freelance gatherers of Information, even some former journalist reporters skilled in eliciting data where ordinary enquiries have failed.

We have a reputation as the 'Pinkertons of London'. We offer a full service under four headings, that is to say, Divorce, Crime (including Fenced Goods Retrieval, Debt Collection and Personal Protection), Total Surveillance and Pets. I am assuming it is total surveillance that you are after in this instance.

You ask in vague terms whether we could follow an unnamed man and see where he goes and find out who he meets in certain unidentified venues. Well, yes we could, we do it all the time, but what I need you to say is, is he a criminal hard case, a bloke who has jumped bail or escaped from prison or is he a bigamist or philanderer or runaway husband or what? And who is it that wants to find out and what is it to them?

You will understand I need to know these things before we can agree to take on your case or else the person, if innocent, may summon the Law and land us all in Queer Street. I am assuming the man you seek is in possession of a guilty secret or you would not be after him, but what? Please furnish me with more details, or feel free to drop into the Office at the address above for a proper consultation, and we can expedite your enquiry with all speed.

Yours truly,

J. Fowler

Proprietor, Arrows Detective Agency

Letter from Mr Henry Dashwood of Dashwood, Ogilvy & Pearce
Gray's Inn Road, London WC1
9 February 1931

Dear Mr Fowler,

Thank you for your letter of 6 February.

I have consulted with the power I represent, and we have agreed to employ your services. I am happy to brief you as follows.

His name is Harold Davidson. He is a clergyman, based at the Rectory, Stiffkey, nr Holt, north Norfolk, although he is often away in London. We have no clear address for him there – he appears to move house every so often, and my initial enquiries among former employees at his Norfolk home reveal that his wife has inscribed no London contact beside his name in the Rectory address book.

He is not, since you ask, a criminal, merely a man whose movements we seek to track as a matter of urgency. Forgive my apparent 'vagueness' as to his whereabouts and the events that have led to my approaching you. I can only say that important forces are interested in establishing where he goes in the metropolis and whom he sees. Mr Davidson may or may not be involved in sordid communion with people of loose morals. It is vital that we discover his exact movements, both in London and Norfolk, especially whether he consorts in public with Damaged Women and, most especially, whether he lingers overnight at their homes. I can say no more at this time, but will visit your offices next week to supply photographs of the subject, train timetables relevant to his weekly journeys, and other details that may be relevant.

Perhaps, in reply, you might indicate the names of the personnel who could assist us in this delicate matter, and the fee structure upon which we may proceed.

With professional good wishes,

Yours sincerely,

Henry Dashwood

Journals of Harold Davidson
London
10 February 1931

Took the Tube to Whitechapel and visited Runaway Boys' Retreat, to see how Don Stupendo is getting on. He is proving a great success in the gymnasium. 'They used to muck about something terrible at first, Harold,' he confided, 'and I had to slap a few heads when they tried to take the mick, but now they're as good as little lambs, and some of 'em, they're shaping up real well on the parallel bars.' He himself, as part of our arrangement, is learning to read and write and is up to Book 3 in the *Easy Pieces for First Readers* textbook series. Hearing him struggle, brow corrugated with concentration, through some rudimentary narratives about Ben and Lad (a youth and his mongrel pet) brought a catch to my breath, for I seemed to recall that Nugent wrestled with the exact same stories when he was five.

The Boys are mounting a small stage production called *Into the Woods*, a charming, sub-J. M. Barrie, Arcadian fantasy of children, wolves and robbers. I watched a rehearsal and itched to go onstage to direct the proceedings. A little echo of my former glories, to which I must not give in! But Don is now entranced by the stage, and shouts encouragement to the young actors in a way that must surely disturb their concentration. I extracted a promise from him that he will be more restrained, which he countered by asking that I take him to the 'proper theatre' one evening. It will not be difficult to arrange. There is a revival of Ben Travers's *Plunder* at the Aldwych which I am sure he would enjoy.

He enquired fondly after BH, for whom he still holds a candle. I said I had not seen her, and had no plans to visit in the future. I think he got the message.

In the new Chinese Dragon restaurant in Panton Street I encountered a young waitress of Scottish provenance, slender, charming and talkative, a virgin I am sure (something of a rarity in catering staff above the age of sixteen, sad to reflect), in whom the light of innocence shines like a star.

Shared many little jokes about 'Tam O'Shanter', haggis, et cetera, due to the recent Burns Night. She is somebody I long to protect, and will endeavour to befriend.

Took Lily Beane – at her suggestion – to this new film of *Dracula*, and very disturbed by it. I read Stoker's book when just down from Oxford, and thought it a devilish text, half in love with the evil it purports to condemn. The film is even worse, portraying an evil bloodsucking murderer as irresistible to women. And there is something wrong in its use of Christian paraphernalia – such as the crucifix – as weaponry, that is perilously close to sacrilege.

It is good to be back in my old neighbourhoods, after my few weeks away. How briefly it lasted, my new life among the fallen of Shepherd's Bush! I cannot get over the appalling Laura, who took me for a client pretending to be a vicar! When I left her side, outraged by her infamous assumptions, I heard her calling out, and assumed she was issuing more cooing seductions. In fact she was demanding money, and doing so with menaces. When I saw her next evening on the Green, with a little prepared homily that would explain my true intentions, she took up where she had left off, with a tirade of imprecations.

'Bilk!' she repeatedly shouted – not a word I had heard before – 'You f—ing bilk, I'll have you,' et cetera. I should have turned tail and run, but foolishly stood my ground and waited for her to cease, convinced that I could explain the error. Before this was possible, two men, possibly her professional protectors, came over and began pushing me in the chest.

'What's the big idea?' one said.

'I am a clergyman,' I said, 'and there has been a misunderstanding.'

'You're dead right there, mate,' said the second one with a horrible leer, 'and we must make sure you don't make no silly mistakes again, mustn't we?'

I do not know which of them commenced hitting me. It was extremely painful to receive a blow between mouth and nose that all but loosened three of my teeth and felt as though my cartilege was driven into the back of my head. As I fell, the men, encouraged by shrieks from Laura, kicked me again and again in the rib and stomach regions. With the last of my strength I kept my greatcoat wrapped around me and the boots of my assailants thudded against the contents of my several pockets. Biblical texts, playbills, packets of pills, gift bottles of perfume – all played their part in protecting me from disaster. My face was a red-and-blackened mess, a gash in my chin wept tears of blood and my vision was blurred and indistinct, but I was spared a worse fate.

A young woman, Annie I believe, pleasant face, lovely hair, excellent teeth, came to my aid and allowed me to lean on her as we sought the hospital. 'I won't even ask what you were doing out there in the middle of the night,' she said as we waited by the traffic lights. 'It's none of my business. But don't you think you're a wee bit old for this sort of thing?' I told her that I would not cease these activities while there was breath in my body, at which she pursed her lips.

Two weeks later, I am restored to health and energy. The scar on my chin is less livid and frightening, thanks to Mimi's kindly ministrations and Dr Warner's bandages. I find myself happy to be back among familiar sights. I took Madge and Sara to the music hall in Hoxton and went backstage for a word with Hettie Foster, whom I was able to help back in 1926 when the producer of *Stolen Kisses* was looking for an extra dancer. Hettie has done extraordinarily well, to progress from burlesque clubs to her present eminence. A delightful evening, though sadly the pressure to catch the last Tube to Shepherd's Bush precluded any chance to look in at Mrs Carter's establishment.

The girls pestered me earlier to take them to the Old Street restaurant. I declined. Too soon, I fear, after the memory of my last visit with BH. When I think of how happy it made me. And the lady with whom —

The feelings engendered there have not yet subsided as they should have. I hope they soon go away. I have no wish to entertain them.

Letter from Mr J. Fowler of Arrows Detective Agency
34 Flood Street, London SW3
12 February 1931

Dear Mr Dashwood

Very glad to get your letter. We are now fully briefed and able to proceed with surveillance as per your instructions.

I have selected two of our most able operatives, Mr Inglebert Thole and Mr Percy Butler. Both are reliable and discreet spiers, provenly astute at spotting things and noting down data, able to follow a mark all over London while blending into the background and remaining inconspicuous at all times. They will investigate singly and in pairs and establish the identity of the mark's contacts. They will follow him everywhere and never lose contact.

If he takes a train to Norfolk, do you want him followed up there? I ask because there is an extra Travel Fee involved when duty takes my men beyond the perimeters of London. Perhaps you will advise me as to how we should proceed.

In the meantime, our fee structure for this operation is as follows:

Total Surveillance:

Mr Thole (per diem) £15 + expenses (food, petrol, accommodation)

Mr Butler (per diem) £10 + expenses (food)

Week 1: 7 x £25 = £175 + expenses

I trust you will feel this fee realistic and await confirmation.

Yours very truly,

J. Fowler

Proprietor, Arrows Detective Agency

Report from Mr Inglebert Thole
To: Mr Jocelyn Fowler, Arrows Detective Agency
Re: Harold Francis Davidson
Date: 23 February 1931

Bit of a hard nut to crack, this one. He is everywhere, but nowhere. I checked his entry in *Crockford's Clerical Directory*. He has been Rector of Stiffkey since 1907. His official address is simply the Rectory of that village, 'nr Holt, Norfolk'. His salary is £800 per annum, fixed. Have attempted to telephone, purporting to be innocent salesman of Church supplies so as not to raise suspicions, but Rectory telephone line appears to be discontinued. They may have arranged privacy override mechanism or some such, or may not have paid bill.

Info from Mr Dashwood led me to check Official Record of Charitable Institutions (London). Found many such organisations in which subject named as founder or trustee: Toynbee Hall Mission, Newsboys Club, Docklands Homeless Association, Young Lads' Apprenticeship Fund, Actors' Church Union, Virtue Reclamation League, Runaway Boys' Retreat, the list goes on and on. Trouble is, many of the above are now apparently defunct, their HQ addresses yielding only silence.

Have investigated all over London, but no joy until Runaway Boys' Retreat. Discovered it to be modest-sized former school in run-down street in Whitechapel. Found 20/25 youths in large day room, occupied in gym activities, basket-weaving, elementary sums and playing cards. Was not allowed to inspect Dormitory arrangements. Short interview with Eddie Bones, overseer, small ex-boxer of Grade 3 Violence Potential, v. unforthcoming. My cover story, of seeking bolted second cousin, met with curt reply ('We ain't no hotel, mister'). Outside I met huge, bald, thickset individual coming from shops with groceries (I saw eggs, bacon, marmalade in brown paper bag) who seems to be employed as a kind of gymnasium trainer. Called Don something. V. talkative. Responded to 'Have you seen the rector? I have some money for him' with alacrity. Could not furnish address, but told me he and Davidson are attending play (?) together on Friday. Aldwych Theatre. I will be there, & will make first contact with mark.

One more thing. He said, 'You're not a friend of Barbara's, are you? I'd so love to see her again.' Barbara? Who she?

Journals of Harold Davidson
London
24 February 1931

Have I been weak? Or is this some divinely–ordained signpost towards redemption? She was sitting in a tea shop in Notting Hill, a flyblown district full of deracinated Europeans, Maltese mostly, with an admixture of swarthy Levantines. I had walked all the way from my lodging, buoyed up by the unusual sunshine, and was in need of a rest. For once I was not looking out for potential sinners. I was content to read the morning paper and reflect on my next meeting with Lady Fenella. (Funds are low. Her Ladyship's bounty has been distributed far and wide to keep the Virtue Reclamation League solvent, and her African friends have contributed a generous £500, but I fear by summer the whole enterprise will need some other tranche of capital from I know not what source.)

I was deep in the news about this man Mosley, an apparently charismatic politician who has broken away from the Labour ranks to form a 'New Party' devoted to the demonising of immigrants, especially those of the Jewish faith. I was silently contemplating the oddness of a Socialist ideologue denying the rights of one race of people to live in harmony with any other race of people – a philosophical absurdity – when I glanced up to find she had materialised in the chair diagonally opposite.

'Hello, Harold,' she said, a look of wry amusement on her painted face. 'So I didn't get a valentine card then?'

'Miss Harris,' I said, fumbling for words, 'how extraordinary to see you here. I have been reading about this man, Mosley, do you know who he is, a tremendously bad hat it seems, who wishes to send Jewish people "back where they came from" according to the report in *The Times*, as if the race had some country of their own to go to. Such ignorance. I am sure I once encountered his father when –'

'You're babbling, Harold,' she said. 'There's no need. Ain't you pleased to see me again?'

'I am pleased to see you looking so well,' I said neutrally. 'What brings you so far from Camden Town?'

'I come to see my sister. She lives round here, Ledbury Road, and we're having lunch and a chat and a bit of shopping. I was on my way when I spotted you through the window. 'Bit off the beaten track, aren't you? I doubt if there's a prozzie within two miles of here that's worth saving.'

'I live in Shepherd's Bush now,' I said, anxious not to reveal too much to this shameless manipulator. 'I was persuaded to move lodgings shortly after Christmas.'

'Got booted out, did you? Can't say I'm surprised, that old cow of a landlady you had.'

'Mrs Parker, if that is to whom you refer, looked after me very well for the several months I spent in her home. She was kind and generous, though sometimes perhaps not as understanding as she might have –'

'Understanding? She didn't understand much the morning I left your place. She called me names. I told her 'ow you were just being nice to me and she screamed in my earhole very understandingly, I must say.'

I could not believe how brazenly she brought up the (surely unmentionable) topic of our last meeting.

'I have no wish to be reminded of that infamous encounter. I would consider it a kindness if you never mention it again.'

'Oh come off it, Harold —'

'You made me miss my train to a vitally important Church occasion. You cannot conceive of the trouble it occasioned me in my home, my parish, and the faithful among which I live.'

'Well, sorry for that,' she said sleekly. 'I was upset, and you were being kind and let me in when I was desperate. It was the middle of the night. I just got a bit carried away. That's all that happened. Here —' she sat up in her chair, a frown threading her young brow with concern — 'you didn't lose your job because of it, did you?'

'I — I did not, as luck would have it, forfeit my employment.'

'You and your big words, Harold. Can't you say things straight?'

'I know you may find this hard to understand, Miss Harris, but it is not a matter of "losing a job" as one might be sacked from working a lathe —'

'What's a lathe?'

'— it is about losing one's standing in the community. Losing the respect of one's peers and parishioners. Losing, above all, one's self-respect.'

She sipped her tea. The fur stole around her shoulder slid towards the table like a feral creature searching for crumbs.

'Blimey, all that trouble because of a little bunk-up. At least you got a good night's sleep out of it, before it all went to hell. You who never, ever, got a proper sleep before, or so you told me.'

I permitted myself a bitter smile. 'What shall it profit a man, if he shall gain a whole night's sleep and lose his own soul?'

'You what?'

'You do not know the Gospel of St Mark? Of course not. How could you be expected to understand any impulse of spiritual longing?'

'Tell me something, Harold,' she said. 'Did you never cop a blow off anyone before? Was that it? Was that what did for you?'

I stared at her, unable to believe my ears.

'I must be going,' I said, rising to my feet. 'I have no wish to discuss these sordid matters further.'

'Don't go, Harold,' she said, putting her hand on my arm. 'We don't have to talk about anything you don't like. I don't want to make you uncomfortable.' She looked into my eyes. 'I miss you. I haven't seen you for months. I liked racketing around with you, and meeting the brasses and going to the plays and talking about savin' people. I really liked all that stuff.'

'I'm so glad,' I said stiffly. 'I'm sure you have many other acquaintances who can furnish you with tickets and dinner, and discourse upon topics of the day, without your having to endure lectures on purity and salvation by middle-aged clergymen.'

'Oh, I got *boyfriends*,' she said scornfully. 'I got a bloody great army of *them*. But you were different. We was a team, you and me. D'you remember the day we had tea with Lady Whatnot, and I made up a lot of stuff about gentlemen clients so they'd be shocked into handing over lots of cash for your charity thing?'

'Yes of course I remember,' I said. 'You were most helpful in persuading them. I was – I am – grateful. But that does not mean –'

'We could do it again, Harold,' she said, gripping my arm. 'We could milk people all over town. You got the contacts. I got the stories. We could make a fortune.' A pause. 'For your charities, I mean.'

Has there ever been a more disingenuous proposal?

'Barbara – Miss Harris – this is outrageous. I cannot be party to an attempt to defraud the charitably disposed by using you as some kind of – of degenerate trophy.'

'Yeah? You think you were doing something else at the Charing Cross Hotel?'

'I utterly reject the suggestion.'

'Then do it for *me*, Harold. Take me round town with you again. I loved all that. Not the nightclubs and the pubs, I can get that any time. I just liked the company. I think you're good for me. I liked reading them books you got me. I liked hearing stories about the people you've met. I never met nobody like you before. And – I can't believe I'm saying this – I feel a better person when I'm with you, even if we're arguing. It makes my brain go racing around, thinking of what to say next, and I really like it.'

Her grip tightened on my sleeve. Could she mean it? Was I being seduced all over again by this precocious strumpet? Or was I hearing nothing less than the awakening of a moral conscience?

267

'We must never allude to the – the night of the unfortunate incident.'

'Agreed. It'll never cross my lips ever again. Whoops.'

'I beg your pardon?'

'Nothing,' she said. ''Scuse my language.'

'You will come and go as I direct, and not cause me embarrassment?'

'Not if I can help it.'

'You will endeavour to learn, with my help, the workings of Jesus Christ in your soul, and strive for a better life?'

'I like the sound of a better life. I mean, who wouldn't?'

Was she truly my personal crusade, my burden, my gift from the Lord? I made my mind up.

'Very well, Miss Harris. I see no reason why we should not be friends again, if that is what you desire.'

The February sun came sliding, diagonal and ecstatically arrayed, through the window of this unprepossessing tea house.

'Oh, Harold,' she said, and flung her arms about my neck. I was bowled over by the warmth and feel of her body, encased in its solid wool coat, the fur of her shoulder-tippet nestling against my neck. She kissed me lightly on the cheek.

'So we'll be friends?'

'I see no reason why not. Perhaps all you need, Miss Harris, is a kindly friend, to deliver you from the dangers and temptations of modern London.' And we parted in that simple, virtuous, Christian understanding.

CHAPTER 14

Journals of Harold Davidson
London
27 February 1931

Took Don Stupendo to the Aldwych to see *Plunder*, his first ever visit to a West End production in all its glory. Had difficulty acquiring cheap seats, such is the public fondness for Mr Travers's works, but assured by the box office that some would be available thirty minutes before Curtain. Don and I were thus forced to join a queue. Tried to engage him in conversation about his studies of 'Ben and Lad', but he dismissed my enquiries.

'I'm past all that childish bollocks now, Harold,' he said. 'I canna be doing with all the stuff about See-how-Lad-runs-after-the-stick. It's just kiddie nonsense. I've moved on to the Intermediate.'

'But you are making excellent progress, Don,' I said. 'What are you reading now?'

'It's called *Jenny and Bob on the Farm*,' he said distantly, 'but it's a sight more difficult, man.'

He looked around at the glamorous sweep of the Aldwych crescent — the Waldorf Hotel with its liveried doorman, the lights outside the Tiger's Eye restaurant, the line of motor taxis in the middle of the road, the procession of minor swells, in black evening clothes, that glided past us in our huddled queue, insulated by wealth.

'It strikes me, Harold, that folks round here could do with a bit of entertainment, you know?' I looked blank. 'They're cold and bored just standing in the street, like. Someone putting on a bit of a show'd be right welcome just now.'

'What did you have in mind?' I asked. 'A cabaret turn? A serenade?'

Ignoring my question, he suddenly quit my side and strode round the corner to Wellington Street, to return, minutes later, bearing an iron railing with a spiked end, plucked from the front of a commercial property.

'Good evening, everyone,' he called out in a friendly fashion, sweeping off his cap. 'They call me the Mighty Stupendo, the Man of Iron. While we're waiting here, I think maybe we should have a little bet. I'll bet you – any of you gents – I can bend this 'ere iron rod into the first letter of your girlfriend's name. Coom on. Coom *on*. It'll only cost you a quid.'

He looked at the line of playgoers with amused eyes, confident in his animal energy. They looked back with (I surmised – for I was behind them) vacancy, shading into bemusement.

'Go on, pal,' said Don to a nervous-looking gentleman with a much younger lady companion. 'Will you give me a tanner if I can bend this iron bar for yer bird here?'

The man turned away, unused to being spoken to by riff-raff. His companion, however, did not.

'My name's Charlotte,' she said pertly to Don. 'Do me a C.'

My friend beamed, twirled the iron railing in his hands as if it were a wooden baton, brandished it in the air, hooked it behind his neck, bunching his giant meaty fists, and strained against the metal extremities. A thick vein stood out on his forehead as evidence of his efforts. The railing began to yield to the pressure of his mighty hands. A moment later, he handed a perfect metal C to the pert young madam with a grave bow.

'My hero,' said the girl. 'Give him a note, Gordon.'

'Good job she wasn't called Kate,' said a wag in the queue, to mocking laughter.

'Or Barbara,' said another.

'Or Winifred,' ventured a third.

I watched with fascination as he worked upon the crowd a form of childish magic. He spent twenty-five minutes of banter and show-manship, darting away to find more metal struts until I prayed no passing constable should take an interest in his casual appropriation of private property. By the time the commissionaire announced that the last seats in the house were on sale, the shivering theatregoers had become a smiling congregation, holding the initials of their lady companions fashioned in iron with no clue of how to explain them to the ushers, nor how to take them home.

When I had put Don into a motor taxi with a ten-shilling note, as a treat at the end of his exciting night, I pondered the events of the evening. How Don Stupendo had, through brute strength and carnival-barker patter, kept an audience of listless bystanders amused for a half-hour. There is a lesson here: that, in order to attract the attention of the greatest number, it is vital to adopt the most brutally obvious of means and turn the most meagre of props – iron railings, the pavement, impressionable women – to good use. How one might adapt one's Sunday homilies to become more popular entertainments by embracing this lesson, I do not quite know. But I have the germ of an idea.

London
10 March 1931

Miss Harris telephoned me at home this morning to say she was on her way to Shepherd's Bush, 'to view your new accommodation'! She complained that, after our rencontre, two weeks ago, she had heard nothing from me and wanted to ensure that I had not changed my mind. I could not run the risk of meeting her *chez moi*, for fear of – unforeseen outcomes. We arranged to meet for tea at the Strand Palace Hotel, after my meeting with the trustees of the Virtue Reclamation League. Fearing that we might fritter our time away in idle gossip, I urged her to read *Lives of the Saints* and ponder the significance of the life of St Ethelreda.

The VRL meeting was lively – no fewer than sixteen new girls admitted in last two months for consideration of funding, in order to track down parents, send letters to rehabilitation centres in Kent, Surrey, Berkshire, etc. Fund-raising initiatives included new scheme of Parish Rehousing, by which large disused properties in Home Counties may be designated Poorhouse Retreats in which several women cohabit in mutual support, rent-free, provided a benefactor guarantees maintenance of £10 per week. All that's needed is new benefactors. Have delegated large mailing to all philanthropic bodies, and confident of positive response. Meeting ended with smiles and enthusiasm, plus vote of thanks to Mrs J. Summerhayes for her clever suggestion.

Met Barbara at hotel. Tea, sandwiches, triple-decker cake stand, paid for by VRL but strictly for business, i.e. her insights into the mind of likely participants. Barbara demurely dressed for once, in long woollen skirt and jumper, small bijou at the neck, hair tidied away under soft cloche hat. I asked if she had tracked down the book.

'I asked the bloke in Smith's if he had the *Lives of the Saints*,' she said, cramming a fondant fancy into her mouth, 'and he was a bit saucy, he said, "What's a nice girl like you doing trying to be a saint?" I said, "None of your lip my lad, I got a special interest in thee-ology these days, so just hand it over." He come on a bit strong, said, "You fancy a drink? I get off at five, I could take you to a nice pub beside Southwark Cathedral, plenty of saints buried in there if you're looking for inspiration . . ."'

'Barbara,' I said, 'this is hardly the way –'

'No, Harold, listen. Of course I didn't go anywhere with him, I said I was interested in St Ethelreda, cos I was a serious student of faith and that. And he says, "Tell you what, You ought to read about the Forty Martyrs, much more interesting, some of the stories, they're dead gory. People being torn apart on racks, or having their stomachs ripped open, *and* it's about religion too, it's not some penny dreadful." So in the end, I got that instead. And you know, Harold? He was right. My eyes was out on stalks.'

I was shocked. 'Barbara – I cannot believe you have wasted your money on such a document. I asked you to consider the lives of virtuous men and women of the Established Church, and instead you choose to read this ghastly propaganda –'

'What? The ones I read about were as religious as anything. They all died for God when they didn't have to. What's the difference?'

'Barbara,' I said, irritably, 'that is a *Catholic* book. A papist text of dubious historical record, full of disgusting physical detail designed to appeal to the lowest, most sentimental appetites.'

'Oh bollocks, Harold. I'm not religious nor sentimental, but it was good, the stuff about dying for what you believe in, though I wouldn't fancy it myself. The best one was Margaret Clitherow, she was only young, married at eighteen, had three kids, all she done was take in a few priests and cook them 'am suppers, then they passed a law saying you couldn't look after priests no more, and some kid ratted on her, and she didn't want to cause no trouble so she ended up with a door on top of her, being squashed to death by bloody great stones.'

I held my head in my hands. 'God, give me strength,' I prayed, 'not to let this child fall into the clutches of papism through blind stupidity.'

'Who you calling stupid?' she said. 'What's wrong with feeling sorry for a woman who just wanted to help priests like you?'

'I am a rector of the Church of England, Barbara. I am not a Catholic priest, a perpetrator of heresy sanctioned by the Church of Rome. I would have had no need to call on Mrs Clitherow for sanctuary.'

'I bet you would've, if she'd been pretty.'

I said, evenly, 'I would have had no truck with Jesuits, nor do I welcome a discussion of their virtues, or their supporters in Tudor times.'

'When did vicars and priests start being different then?' She knitted her berry-brown forehead in real interest. When I elected to further her education in Christian morality, I did not foresee it taking such an argumentative turn.

'You know nothing of Church matters. The Reformation of the mid-sixteenth century is a closed book to you. Were you to study the theological ramifications of that event, I am sure –'

'The mid-sixteenth century. What's that, 1550? So before that it was all right to be a priest, and after that it was a crime? This Margaret was killed in 1580-something. That's, what, thirty years after it all changed?'

'She was an enemy of the Established Church, Barbara. I'm sorry, but these were years of shocking sectarian divisions. She was a traitor to Queen Elizabeth.'

'What, for cooking gammon stew for some French vicars, sorry, priests?'

'She was harbouring seditious elements,' I said, suddenly unhappy about religious events 350 years ago.

'Wait, Harold. Are you saying it was your lot did for her?'

'It was the newly established Church of England, of which the queen was defender of the faith, that sanctioned her – her removal.'

'Bloody hell.' She flung down her cake fork. 'So it was your lot who stuck her under a door and and dumped a ton of shit on her until she died?'

Some tea-sippers nearby turned their heads, as if unable to believe what they had just heard. 'Barbara . . .' I murmured.

'So that's what your religion does to people, is it?' she demanded. 'They get bloody men to dump rocks on you until your spine splits in half, because you believe now what it was all right to believe thirty years earlier?'

'Well, no – it was, I assure you, quite different then, when the laws of Church and State were more closely allied and –'

'Oh shut it, Harold,' she said rudely. 'Whatever you want me to sign up to, I don't want no part of it.'

I wish I could have explained better the working of Church politics. But Miss Harris is still only a young girl, with neither a proper education nor that intellectual perspective that makes all clear. For a while there was silence between us, as our neighbours in the tea room scrutinised our faces (hers angry, mine embarrassed) with interest. I turned the conversation, awkwardly, to her boyfriends (many) and her sightings of Rose Ellis (few) and we re-established a guarded amity.

Report from Mr Inglebert Thole
To: Mr Jocelyn Fowler, Arrows Detective Agency
Re: Harold Francis Davidson
Date: 17 March 1931

Have consulted with Mr Dashwood. Now possess photograph of Subject, home address in Stiffkey, Norfolk, list of registered Charities in London on whose documents he appears as trustee, and sod all else. Could not establish daily whereabouts, domicile, business address or place of worship. Enquired at Church House for list of visiting preachers at C of E churches, but no joy. Asked at offices of *Church Times*. In Archives, found 3 articles in local Press (July, Sept and Oct 1930) about Subject's activities with Poor & Homeless, praising work with down-and-outs and 'girls in Trouble'. Said he 'did not scruple to enter public houses and places of Vice' in search of young women 'in danger' (unspecified).

Switched my enquiries to pubs, cheap restaurants and down-and-out shelters in Whitechapel, Shoreditch, St Mary's, Shadwell, displaying photograph, but no joy. Evidently not a patron of E. End dives.

Moved investigation west to Aldgate, Liverpool Street, Blackfriars – and Fleet Street, where landlord in the Bell identified photograph. 'Was in here last month, but looking different, had huge bandage on head.' Could not establish if was with Loose Women or other persons of Vice. Bandage set me thinking. Telephoned Bart's Hospital, asked if had record of person called Davidson with head injuries, but no joy. Tried Guy's, Thomas's, Charing Cross, Chelsea, Fulham, Hammersmith.

Finally some progress – Shepherd's Bush Hospital has record of H. Davidson, brought in during early hours of 24 January with contusions to skull after affray on the Bush Green. They don't disclose addresses of outpatients, so trekked across London to W12 with fake Police identity documents, said imperative to locate Victim of Assault. Persuaded Receptionist to furnish details.

His address is 43a Macfarlane Avenue, W12. Will go find him tomorrow and follow him like barnacle clamped to side of battleship.

Journals of Harold Davidson
London
17 March 1931

Ran into Monsignor George outside Guy's Hospital. He had been to one of a series of lectures at the old Operating Theatre, on philosophical topics for the 'man in the street', whoever is meant by such an obnoxious phrase.

'The subject of the lecture, Harold, was "A Good Life?" I saw the talks advertised in Southwark Cathedral when I attended vespers on Friday night, and I went along to see what dilations on virtue were being offered to a secular audience. The sponsor is the "Society for the Promotion of Spiritual Health" but as to its members or its broad intentions, I am in the dark. The audience seemed composed of young men and women in their twenties – mostly single, I think, since they did not appear to sit in couples – and I feared that it might be a thinly disguised arena for seeking a mate, under the aegis of religious enlightenment. But after an hour, it was clear that no theological enquiry was to feature. Instead, the speaker, a Mr Jeremiah Hudson, harped upon the importance of healthy outdoor pursuits, such as physical exercise, walking, bicycle riding and something called "hiking" as a path to mental cleanliness. He was a robust young man, wearing rubber-soled shoes and sporting clothes, and he posed and agitated on the spot so fervently, it was hard to follow his train of thought.'

'*Mens sana in corpore sano*, eh?' I said. 'Is that cliché all that is now meant by the words "A Good Life"? He had nothing to say on matters of faith?'

'None, Harold. I believe it is part of a new trend to "rediscover" a connection with earthy energies, which has been lost by our immersion in daily routine and urban living. That is how the lecture concluded. The audience took it all in with enthusiasm.'

'It seems to equate virtue with nothing more than the gymnasium and the medicine ball,' I said. 'A dreadful heresy, surely?'

'Shocking. There was a fair bit about sex too.'

'Indeed?'

'Not explicitly, my dear fellow. Mr Hudson stopped short of recommending promiscuity as a cure for spiritual ills. But I fancied it was encoded in his constant mentions of "the breast" and "the bowels" and how they may be *energised*, or some such nonsense, by closer intimacy with grass and trees and streams, whether in the Forest of Dean or the Tyrolean Mountains.'

'Good God,' I said, with a start. 'I have heard this before. These ideas come from that blighter, D. H. Lawrence. I have read critiques of his work in the *Times Literary Supplement*, mocking his enthusiasm for intestinal rapture. And these notions are being advanced as a blueprint for daily behaviour!'

'Shocking,' said the monsignor, shaking his head as we wandered down Borough High Street. 'Most pernicious.'

'Have you heard about this last book of his?' I asked. '*Lady Somebody's Passion* it is called. It contains passages so vile that no British publisher could touch it. Yet they say that Continental houses, with fewer scruples than ours, have brought out editions in English which have somehow made their way across the Channel.'

'I have heard something of the sort,' murmured my old friend.

'I understand,' I went on, 'from liberal members of my flock that it is merely a succession of rutting encounters and Neanderthal dialogue unfit for human gaze.'

There was a silence. I thought I had shocked poor George with my description. But I was wrong.

'It's not *quite* like that, Harold,' he said blandly. 'You have to plough through a great deal of pontification and persiflage to encounter the most objectionable scenes.'

We walked on a few paces before the penny dropped.

'George, are you telling me you have read this book?'

'I was – introduced to a copy by a friend from Cambridge, who purchased it, while travelling in Florence, out of academic interest. He has followed the work of Mr Lawrence and pondered his intellectual development most seriously. He gave me the book to peruse one evening, and I skimmed through it, in search of depravity. The obscenities of speech are shocking, if only in seeing them in cold print; but the most rebarbative theme is the suggestion, advanced at length, that ladies of good breeding have physical needs that can be satisfied only by the attentions of a rough-mannered working man who lives in a hut, raises chickens and shoots rabbits.'

'George! May I remind you that you have been reading a book that is illegal in this country, a work smuggled in by criminals? I am shocked that you can admit to such a thing.'

We had come to a halt on the corner of Union Street. He plucked my arm.

'Let us go down here,' he said. 'There's something I must show you.'

We turned into Red Cross Way, a dark, bare alley with few lights and a lurking sense of danger. George led me along the pavement a hundred yards and stopped beside an enormous gate. Through the iron bars, I could see nothing but a concrete wasteland, with here and there some items of rubbish, ignorantly piled.

I shivered. The bleakest moorland, the most shell-damaged Belgian field after the war, would seem less bleak than this dismal spectacle.

'Well, George?'

'Do you not notice anything remarkable?'

I had no time for any Holmes-and-Watson joshing.

'What is remarkable about this ghastly place?'

'Look, Harold, at the bars of the gate.'

I looked again, and started. The gate – how had I not noticed? – was arrayed with upwards of two or three hundred grubby ribbons, votive offerings of flowers, brightly coloured dolls fashioned from some wool-coloured wire, pink and orange paper decorations. They festooned the whole thirty feet of the black iron gate, like baubles on a Christmas tree. Closer inspection revealed each ribbon and decoration to carry a name. All the names were female. Daisy Prince. Anna Markwell. Anita Summerley. May Blood.

'What on earth?'

'Extraordinary, is it not? This, Harold, is the Cross Bones. It is the site of London's largest prostitutes' graveyard. I discovered it a few years ago. It is a plot of unconsecrated ground that used to be the "Single Women's Churchyard", a euphemism for ladies of the night. According to an old survey of Bankside I found, these ladies were refused the rites of the Church while they continued their sinful careers. A customary threat was to deny them a Christian burial if they refused to give up their sordid work before they died.'

'But, George –' I was inexpressibly moved – 'there is nothing here. It is a lake of concrete.'

'I assure you, a hundred years ago, it was a seething Gehenna of dead unfortunates. They buried paupers here, too, when the area was known as the Mint. You've surely heard of the Mint? The most depraved slum in England, in those days. Policemen were afraid to walk through it unless in threes. But it was declared overfilled with the wretched dead and sealed up about the time I was born, and has remained frozen in concrete ever since.'

'And all these ribbons and wretched toys?'

'They carry the names of the dead *poules de luxe*. I find it a heartening spectacle, that, despite their lives of ignominy, these ladies still receive the equivalent of flowers on a Christian grave.'

Heartening? I could not agree. I went home in a state of profound gloom, and to bed with my head awash with images of a charnel house full of thousands of luckless women, whose final haven and resting place is a stark, featureless pit, sealed away from the ringing outside world as if they had never existed. As I closed my eyes, I recalled that – of course! – the place's name was not unknown to me. An old jingle, like a nursery rhyme, returned from my younger days. It was a variant on the old heartless lyric about the brevity of human life, 'Solomon Grundy, born on a Monday, christened on Tuesday', et cetera. It ran:

> Monday in the nursery ward,
> Tuesday in the schoolyard,
> Wednesday painting lipstick on,
> Thursday going with George and John,
> Friday at the Crown with Billy,
> Saturday weeping down the 'Dilly,
> Where will she rest from her tears and moans?
> Sunday at the Cross Bones.

It must have been recited, long ago, as a warning to girls who were overfamiliar, when young, with cosmetics and flirtation. I probably overheard it said by one of the old servants at my father's house in Scholing.

I never knew to what it referred until now. And the awful finality of the last line was made clear to me last night, as I looked through the iron bars at the utter nothingness of the girls' resting place, the wholesale abandonment it implied, the neutrality of that concrete seal upon their lives, as if they never existed as beings who could laugh and strut about town, and feel promptings of love and ambition and be delighted by a new frock, a sunny morning, a crusty gammon roll, a ride in a motor taxi; whose lives may have been full of wrongdoing but were also lives like everyone else's, full of thoughts and sensual everyday pleasures, sentimental imaginings, the conversation of their children, the remembered touch of a parental hand – and now they lie pestled together underground in a paste of disintegrated flesh, mud, bones and cement, remembered by no headstone but a few fluttering ribbons, and all their souls in Hell.

And all their souls in Hell.

Found myself unable to sleep, unaccustomed tears stabbing my eyes at 2 and 3 a.m. Is this why I have devoted my energies over the years to saving tragic young girls? Did some dim understanding of that foolish rhyme invade my young thoughts, so that I knew its meaning long before I stood before the gate of the Cross Bones? I would like to think so. I would like that very much.

Report from Mr Inglebert Thole
To: Mr Jocelyn Fowler, Arrows Detective Agency
Re: Harold Francis Davidson
Date: 19 March 1931

Watched over 43a Macfarlane Rd from the early hours, parked the Austin 7 nearby. Subject emerged 8.30 a.m. wearing long overcoat over dark suit (no dog collar). Was alone. Followed him to Isle of Capri Café on Uxbridge Road, where he breakfasted on bacon sandwich, iced bun, coffee, and engaged proprietor in banter. Elderly waitress present. No sign of molestation.

Subject took Underground train (Central Line), alighted at Holborn. Walked north, paused at Sicilian Avenue, where made purchases in 2nd-hand bookshop. Turned into Southampton Row, where visited Gerry's Fishmonger's. Subject addressed buxom young woman employee with whom obviously familiar. She and he went into back of shop, emerging after 8 mins. No sign of disarrayed clothing. When parting, he kissed her on (right) cheek and she stroked his face in intimate manner.

11 a.m., Subject retraced steps and went into Lincoln's Inn Fields. Sat on park bench, studying morning newspaper (*D. Telegraph*). Approached by 2 down-and-outs (one 20ish, one 40ish) looking for alms. Subject invited them to share bench with patting-hand gesture. The three conversed for 20 mins, as I watched from vantage point by tea stall. Subject extracted from greatcoat pockets some (?) photographs and/or (?) religious tracts, and talked uninterrupted for several moments with much gesturing of hands, after which new companions hurried away.

12 noon, Subject visited Courts of Justice (45 mins) but I could not follow inside; then went to Wig and Pen Club, emerging after 15 mins; proceeded down Fleet Street, called at offices of *Church Times* (already investigated by me), stayed half an hour, emerged looking out of sorts and brandished fist in theatrical manner at closing door.

1 p.m., Subject visited St Paul's Cathedral, knelt and prayed. No religious service going on. Sat in pew and brooded for 30 mins, spoke to senior clergyman (canon? bishop? – could not establish) beside baptismal font, donated silver coin and left.

Subject lunched at café in Watling Street. Through window, saw him engage waitress in chat for 5 mins. Disturbed by manager, girl sent back to work. Waitress brought plate of rissoles and more conversation ensued, plus he flourished photo (of who or what?) from coat pocket. Waitress laughing, sent about business by (now a bit angry) manager. Subject ate lunch, then went to Toilets. No sign for 5 mins, then emerged from kitchen area, being sent packing by (now irate) manager. Poss behind-scenes molestation going on? I watched through window long as poss but told to Keep Moving by constable, and when retraced steps, Subject was gone. Moves surprising fast for old geezer.

I have the distinct impression that I am being followed. I cannot be wrong about this. The same man keeps appearing on the periphery of my vision, and has done for three days. I can describe him only by the word 'nondescript', for he is a foggy monochrome unit of grey coat, black hat, grey face, black shoes, grey socks and tan brief-case from which, on the Tube, he extracts the *Reynolds News* and pretends to read while scrutinising my every move. I saw him in the bookshop in Sicilian Avenue, saw him again hovering by the tea stall in Lincoln's Inn Fields, and once more by the font in St Paul's, ludicrously pretending to study a cyclostyled leaflet about St Anthony of Padua. Later, I was aware of him lurking in Watling Street, pretending to wipe something off his shoe. Who is he? Why is he dogging my footsteps? He is not, I think, a police officer, but his constant presence is unsettling. I feel like the unnamed man in the book by the Czech writer Mr Kafka that came out last year, who, without having done anything wrong, is arrested and charged with unknown crimes. Can he be some emissary from the Church, sent to spy on me? Surely the holy fathers of the Norfolk see would not stoop so low? And what would they expect to find?

If he appears again, I shall be forced to confront him.

No sign of him (thank the Lord) when I rendezvoused with Barbara in town. We met at the Bell near Waterloo Station, where I conducted some business with Eddie Bones re leaking roof of Runaway Boys' Retreat. Barbara was late, *comme d'habitude*, but we greeted each other with the old fervour. I chose to remain silent on the fate of martyrs, saints, et cetera, and we conversed instead about friends: she has visited Rose Ellis ('Back with an attack of the glooms, Harold, so I took her to a tea dance with Lionel and Jeremy, old pals of mine, and she cheered up during the rumba') and has 'looked in' apparently at Marina Carter's bordello ('Only a social visit, mind, since I'm no prozzie') and she asked if I'd seen Don Stupendo, upon which – unable to lie – I said I had seen him performing to theatre-goers in the street.

'I dunno what went wrong between us, Harold,' she said. 'One minute we were going like the clappers, couldn't see enough of each other, he told me he loved me over and over. The next, he was gone, without a word of explaining. Even left a scarf behind, though it was freezing in November. You'd think I'd developed the plague or something.'

'You don't suppose, Barbara, that he might have – forgive me, my dear, but I must voice the suggestion – might have contracted some unfortunate infection that you perhaps knew nothing about?'

'Some infect—' Her eyes were suddenly hot with indignation. '*Naow*. I didn't give him a dose of the clap, if that's what you're suggesting. I get myself checked up regular. Believe me, I'd have known.'

'I was not asking as a prurient gossip, Barbara, nor as a father-confessor,' I said with dignity. 'Merely as a loving friend.'

'Oh, right.' She pondered this, then looked at me with a quizzical glance. 'So that's what we are now, is it? Loving friends, I mean?'

'Undoubtedly. I feel we have come to a mature understanding of our mutual worth and our capacity to help each other. I admit that, when we first knew one another, there were certain . . . ambiguities.'

'You reckon?' A smile lit up her cunning face. 'You mean, when you kept coming round trying to save me from men, you really wanted to have me for yourself, to –'

'Certainly not.' I spoke sharply. 'That is a monstrous slur.'

'What I was going to say was, you wanted me for yourself to parade around as a little slut you'd managed to save. Not a lot of friendship there, was there?'

'I befriended you because you were a charming companion, but also because you were a young girl whose immortal soul was in danger. There was never any suggestion that I exploited your good nature in any way.'

'No, Harold. You exploited my *bad* nature, when it suited you, in front of Lady Fifi, or whatever her name was.'

'Lady Fenella.'

'And I'm not blaming you, because I enjoyed all that, the play-acting stuff. But I couldn't work it out. Didn't you ever like me because you thought I was, you know, all right?'

'Barbara,' I said with feeling, 'I have known many thousands of women over the years, in my capacity as pastor and helpmeet, but I have seldom felt for them the – the simple, unforced affection that I feel for you in all circumstances.'

She took a swig of the Bell's cloudy beer. 'Really?' she said. 'Even when you think I'm a hopeless tart?'

'I have never thought such a thing.'

'Even when you was all bothered about the sex, that time I –'

'Barbara.' I held up my hand, to nip this area of discussion in the bud.

'OK then. And you still want to be my – what did you call it? My loving friend?'

'If you will have me so.'

She shot me a strange glance, in which native guile was mingled with a girlish enthusiasm.

'I never had one of them before.'

'Well, my dear, you certainly have one now.'

'And it's not because you want to save my soul, or parade me around, and it's not because you secretly fancy your chances?'

'None of these things. It is because I enjoy your company. I would, of course, like to see your way of life change for the better, but that does not influence the pleasure I derive from hearing your voice and sharing whichever evenings you might spare for me.'

'Oh, Harold.' She presented me at last with an artless smile. 'I'd be happy to.'

What I was offering her was, perhaps, the first decent, innocent relationship of her young life. I was elated within as I watched her accept it. 'So we're – what is it the Yanks say? – we're buddies?'

'Indubitably,' I said. 'Would you care for another beverage?'

Report from Mr Inglebert Thole
To: Mr Jocelyn Fowler, Arrows Detective Agency
Re: Harold Francis Davidson
Date: 1 April 1931

Things are starting to get a bit clearer. Subject arrives in London Mondays, gets to Shep Bush home around 10 a.m., with bulging leather case, spends first morning indoors, appears 12 noon regular as clockwork clad in long coat, otherwise dishevelled non-clergyman garb, calls in on Swan Café, Brahma Tea Rooms, Uxbridge Road Slipper Baths, Timothy Morgan Electrical Goods shop (why?), Fielding & Son Grocers & Dry Goods, Goldhawk Road Labour Exchange. All of 'em, over and over, in strict rotation, like factory manager checking assembly line. I was unable to explain such visits until Wednesday last.

I watched him leave Fielding the Grocer's (see above), then entered premises to purchase bananas (1/6). Had previously purchased small religious pamphlet – 'Seven Proofs of Heaven' – from St Olave's in Shep Bush, and now pretended to have found it on the floor.

'Oh look,' I said, while girl at counter twirled bananas into paper bag, 'someone has dropped a magazine. Can it have been the white-haired gent I saw coming out 5 minutes ago? Maybe I should run after him and –'

'No, give it here,' said the young woman. 'He'll be back tomorrow, I'll see he gets it.'

'Religious gent, is he?' I said, all innocent. 'He had that look about him.'

'He's a very nice man,' said the girl. 'Always looking to help out unfortunates.'

'Oh yes?' says I. 'I got no time for Bible-thumpers myself. Who's he been helping out round here then?'

'Shush, will you?' the girl said, indicating a poor, slatternly woman I had not seen before, weighing out flour into pound sacks in a corner of the shop. 'That's Molly, she was one of his ladies before he got her a job here, and he pops in, every so often, to see how she's doing.'

I looked. Molly about 24, big-boned, big bosom, considerable girth in her grey skirt, occupied in scooping and measuring, not the brightest pane in the window if you follow me.

'One of his ladies?' I said. 'What, you mean, like a girlfriend?'

'No-ah!' she giggled. 'Chance would be a fine thing. He

found her wandering around Brook Green one night, trying to find somewhere to stay after she was booted out by her folks for being in the family way, and he took her round the neighbourhood, asking about work, until he found her a job here.'

'Very nice of your boss to take her in,' I said. 'And her with a kid on the way.'

'He's very persuasive, Mr Davidson,' said a voice. It was the owner, a thickset geezer with long spiky sideburns. 'Very silver tongue. But he done right with Molly. He said, "She may seem a Desperate and Needy Wretch" – those were his words – "but all she needs is a job." And he was dead right. Good little worker, grafts away all hours, bless her.'

'Mr Fielding?' I says. 'I was telling this young lady, you're obviously a kindly bloke to look after them that's in trouble.'

His big forehead wrinkled, like he'd never considered it before. 'He told me she'd work hard for ten bob a week. And she does. I mean –'

We both looked at Molly, who was squinting in concentration at the weighing scales.

'So she's not on the game no more?' I asked. There was a curious silence.

'What you on about?' said the man. 'Molly was never – what you said.'

'The very idea,' said the girl. 'Well, really.'

'Sorry,' I said. 'I meant no disrespect. I just assumed the rector, when he found her wandering about, you know . . .'

'How'd you know he's a rector?' The Fielding bloke advanced towards me, a bit hostile. 'Who are you?'

Ignored him. Turned to girl at counter.

'So when's the baby due, then?'

She looked from me to the Fielding geezer. 'Couple of months, I s'pose.'

'Anything more you need to know?' said the bloke, nastily. 'Or were you on your way?'

Left premises. So Subject drops in on this Molly and lots of other of 'his ladies' most days, just to check progress. Or does he?

Easter Sunday, and the church full to bursting. Elected to try Saturday-night vigil service, 11 p.m. to after midnight, with candles and hymns – and sixty worshippers came! I expected mutterings re excessive High Church, neo-papist emotionalism, but fears unfounded.

Read from St Matthew Passion – could have heard pin drop. How can I be so moved at a passage I have read so often, i.e. chapter 26, verse 45, Christ in Garden of Gethsemane: 'Then cometh he to his disciples, and saith unto them, Sleep on now, and take your rest: behold, the hour is at hand, and the Son of man is betrayed into the hands of sinners'? Voice trembled, I confess. Much passion too in the congregation's singing. Many thoughtful and appreciative remarks in porch, as though of community united in devotion. Today, pews crammed with worshippers. Church lit with bright sunlight and sprays of wild daffodils in tubs. 'You've done us proud, Rector,' said normally censorious Mrs Russ. I have not enjoyed an Easter so much in years. Felt inappropriately as though pitched back to green room after successful night onstage in *Charley's Aunt*, circa mid-1890s, though obviously did not remark on this.

Worried about Mimi, though. She has become very silent and fretful because of awkward incident regarding unpaid bills for coal, fish, gas, telephone. It was latter which precipitated arrival of bailiff last Tuesday, a most unpleasant individual, according to Eileen, the new maid, a 'big bully' who stood immovably in doorway threatening to remove household items in lieu of payment! 'That a piano I seen in the front room?' he enquired. 'We'll start with that, shall we? And then that fancy rug . . .' This has never happened before. That the telephone company should send a professional intimidator to the door of the bishop's representative, demanding household fittings like a kind of licensed highwayman is intolerable. I shall write to the Exchange about it.

M took it badly. 'It's like being – invaded, in my own home,' she said over and over. She has taken to straying out of doors at unusual times, even in the small hours of the night (I heard her call for the maid, to let her in at 3 a.m. on Good Friday), apparently wandering in the orchard, the graveyard, even the fields towards Cockthorpe. Nugent and Patricia have both come to see me in my study to voice their concerns. I have promised to determine what is on her mind.

Must find £129 for outstanding bills. The indulgence of creditors, even for a clergyman's house with its multifarious outgoings, is no longer to be taken for granted in this hard modern world. I may soon have to consider breaking into Operational Cash Budget from Virtue Reclamation League, something I have never had to do before.

News of the bailiff's visit must have spread around the village, for we have become the recipients of charity! On Thursday (reports the maid, who is doubtless the spreader of our sorry news) a basket of eggs, sausages, cabbage and radishes (radishes?) along with a half-bottle of brandy (!) was left on our doorstep with no explanatory note. With a diplomacy that belies her youth, she said nothing of it to M, but dished up a nourishing supper that drew compliments from Colonel DD, who is still frustrated in finding employment. A dangerous precedent. I cannot have my parishioners labouring under the misapprehension that we are in some kind of financial trouble.

The strange paranoia that gripped me in London, about a man constantly shadowing my footsteps, seems to have accompanied me to Norfolk. I have been aware of a Presence – a gentleman in a hat, but a different one from the London grey man, this one is small and sturdy-looking, his collar generally turned up against the biting April wind – who appears when I am walking my rounds, always a hundred yards behind me. I fancied he was hanging around the lychgate of the church, I felt his presence outside the Rectory one night when I was searching for M in the garden, I am almost sure I spotted him looking out the window of the Townshend Arms as I passed by, whereupon I fled from him, like Mr Thompson's flight from the Hound of Heaven.

Perhaps I am going mad. But I think not.

Reports from Mr Percy Butler
To: Mr J. Fowler, Arrows Detective Agency
Re: Harold Francis Davidson
Date: 27 April 1931

Have been here in Holt, near Stiffkey, 5 days now. Funny place the Norfolk coast. The locals talk in harsh but grumbly voices, as though complaining and singing at same time. Have got used to being addressed as 'boy' despite my years.

Asked discreetly about rector in Holt, Holkham, Binham, Burnham Market and other villages. He's well known as local eccentric, but more for habit of travelling everywhere on bicycle and motorcycle than for corrupt practices. 'You can always see 'im passing the shop most days, flying along on 'is bike, calling out 'Allo as he whizzes by,' said friendly local clothing salesman called Inglewood or something. 'Nice chap but never 'as toime for a conversation, you know?'

I asked if Subject ever patronised his shop. 'Well, he moight do if we ever opened on Sundays,' said the man. 'But we don't.'

So: fact is, Subject only attends village on Sunday. Always elsewhere during week. Asked locals where they think he is rest of time, and got variety of opinions. 'He has a second parish in the Holloway Road,' said one, 'and runs a soup kitchen in some field in the legal district' – I took this to mean Subject's sojourns with derelicts in Lincoln's Inn Fields. ''E runs a church in Bayswater,' another confidently assured me, 'and 'e takes in deadbeats.' A third assured me, 'They say 'e visits royal folk to get money for gals in trouble.' Remarkable confusion about how Subject spends his time down south.

Rectory a handsome edifice shut off from road behind large wall. I hung around roadway with tripod device, pretending to be surveyor, Tues and Weds, to monitor comings & goings.

9 a.m. Deliveryman with groceries.
10 a.m. Two young men, student types, calling on? rector's son. Stayed indoors all day.

11 a.m. Wizened figure, military bearing, emerged, walked to postbox, posted letters, paused, tragic air, walked off moodily through fields.

12 noon. Van drew up, 'Whitaker's Bailiffs' on side, thickset individual called on house. Altercation with maid, raised voices. Hysterical keening from house. Bailiff withdrew (without household properties, i.e. must have been paid off).

1 p.m. Substantial matron called. Stayed for 2 hrs. Later identified as Mrs Reynolds. Wife of churchwarden, apparently, helpmeet and ally.

3 p.m. Young men reappeared with sturdy youth from house (Subject's son?), got into motor vehicle and exited west in direction of Holkham.

6 p.m. Small lady, green frock, battered hat, emerged and walked off through Rectory grounds. Strode through perimeter of woodland, talking to self.

I am not used to working in these conditions. I am a trained surveillance agent in urban contexts, I do houses and streets, hotel corridors and train stations, nobody can do a long-distance trail across e.g. Mayfair or Hyde Park like me, despite receiving (I am not fooled by assurances to the contrary) a lesser hourly rate than Mr Inglebert Thole, who is an uneducated, churly fellow, ill-suited to tasks requiring chat and reassurance. I do not do forest work, nor following odd people through fields, with obvious risk of exposure and confrontation.

To: Mr J. Fowler, Arrows Detective Agency
Re: Harold Francis Davidson
Date: 29 April 1931

Finally clapped eyes on Subject. Church service this morning at St John's, 11 a.m. Got there early, sat in empty pew at back, head in hands as though in private devotions. By 5 to 11, were 42 people in church, unenthusiastic congregation, I fancy, for mostly absentee vicar. By 11, had increased to 51. Mrs D took seat in front pew with 2 girls + 1 boy, Mrs D no longer looking barmy but serene in long blue coat.

By 11.05, still no sign of clergyman. Bespectacled matron in specs started organ. Mutterings, rustling of hymn books, muted noises of protest. By 11.12, open grumbling in church; sidesman kept rising and looking out church door. At 11.17, I rose, fanning face with hymn book as though needing air, and emerged into sunshine – and saw figure on bicycle, white head low over handlebars, long coat flying, come barrelling through lychgate.

He propped machine in porch, exchanged smiling confidences with sidesman, who was left in care of long coat, as rector shook himself like dog, extracted sheaf of papers from pannier and strode into church.

Service began with hymns ('Nearer My God to Thee'), a reading (from Exodus: 'I will not go up in the midst of thee; for thou art a stiffnecked people') and moved to a sermon delivered with great theatrical gusto, elaborating on Exodus text, saying the kind people of Stiffkey were not stiff-necked, and wouldn't condemn a Worker of the Lord just because he toiled in strange vineyards, and his labour seemed at times a bit peculiar, would they? I couldn't follow it. Seemed to be speaking in some kind of code, asking for permission.

'Sinners, in my view,' he said, 'are generally not devils, or hard and dangerous people. They are weak-willed, impressionable folk driven to sin by a desperate selfishness, which they later repent with wailing interior cries. Any man of virtue who courts their society does so, not as a Daniel in the lion's den, but as an appeaser, a philosopher, a cooing nursery presence to call home the lost children of Christ.'

I dunno what the last bit meant, but much nodding and smiling in the pews all round. All apparently v satisfied with Mr H's rectoring. Not surprised after sermon saying villains just big kids who want a good cry on your shoulder. Much hand-clasping as we filed out. Very tactile chap, i.e. clutched every hand and with left hand also clutched the clutchee's arm, elbow, even shoulder, in comradeship. You'd think everyone was his special best friend.

Before I left, turned to look for Mrs Rector. No longer in front pew, she'd gone up to altar and was leaning over rail trying to sniff big white trumpet-like flower. Her nose was so far up it, you'd think she was trying to disappear inside.

Reports from Mr Inglebert Thole
To: Mr Jocelyn Fowler, Arrows Detective Agency
Re: Harold Francis Davidson
Date: 5 May 1931

Have made contact with one of Subject's young women. A right piece of work, very thick with Subject. I spent all afternoon and evening last week tracking their progress across London. He and she met on 3 May at Spring Blossom Chinese restaurant in Russell Street, Bloomsbury. They were very heads-together throughout lunch, but seemed to have some kind of row, Miss H flouncing away, and Subject coming after her with outstretched hands and lot of embracing and hair-caressing. What that all about? Seems odd way for clergy-man to conduct self.

They took omnibus east to Providence Place (good name for man of cloth) between Commercial Road and Royal Mint. I followed in taxi (3/6). They called at No. 18, small private house, where stayed 2 hours, Subject emerging alone. Looked up address on electoral register and found is owned by Mr and Mrs Lake, respectable small hoteliers.

Followed Subject on lengthy walk through streets of Aldgate, him stopping five or six times to call on shops (2) and dwellings (4), all visited with noisy display on doorstep of utmost friendliness and expectation of welcome. Seems to know a lot of people and moves like royal progress through warren of backstreets.

4 p.m. he's still busily proceeding through Shoreditch,

ducking into Foster's tea room, then Clough's newsagent's, then common lodging house in Bishopsgate. Hard to keep up this knackering pursuit, while maintaining discreet distance.

Waited for him outside Slipper Baths by Broad St Station, and had brainwave. Took cab back to Providence Place, to see if could confront Mr & Mrs Lake to establish nature of young woman's relationship with Subject.

As reached destination, Subject's girl companion came out. Bold-faced young thing, hardly more than 20 if that, strode off down towards Cable St with determined gait. I caught up with her and said, "Scuse me, Miss, but I'm looking for the Royal Mint, can you help me?'

She looked at me coldly. Bit of a Total Surveillance operative herself, the way her stare took in my clothes, shoes, hat, eyes, the lot.

'What did you 'ave in mind?' she asked tartly. 'If you're plannin' a burglary, I hear security's quite tight down there. You'd be better off with a post office.'

'Ha ha,' I said. 'No, really, I am a tourist, looking out for the sights of London. Done St Paul's and the Tower and I wondered if perhaps you'd know —'

'Tourist, eh? Where you from then? Don't often get many cockney tourists round these parts,' she countered. 'Specially not tourists dressed like coppers' narks.'

'No need to be hostile, Miss,' I said, aggrieved. 'I only asked. Come in for a day trip from Essex, as it happens.'

'Yeah, I believe you. Well, no, I don't know were the Mint is, if that's what you're really after. Anything else on your mind?'

Could not establish if she was making some overture, but I pressed on.

'You're not from round these parts then? Only I saw you come out of that house, and thought you must be local.'

'Did you now? Well, I just moved in, if you must know. Just acquired a new apartment, and I'm off to buy some curtains and bedlinen, so excuse me if I don't stick around for a chat.'

I had to speed things up. I took a deep breath and said, 'If you needed some cash for some rugs and suchlike, I know how you could put a bit of money your way.'

She paused. 'Oh yes? I believe I've heard *that* before.' But I could tell she was interested, mercenary little tart.

'I've a few friends in the modelling business. Gamages store catalogues and the like. You ever tried that?'

'Let me guess. It wouldn't be the lingerie department by any chance?'

'Nothing dodgy, honest,' I was quite enjoying this. 'Let me take you to dinner, so we can talk it over.'

'Listen, mate, pull yourself back, will you? I wouldn't come across for you as long as there's dogs in the street, all right?' Her brown eyes flashed. She was a right little madam. But sexy with it.

To: Mr J. Fowler, Arrows Detective Agency
Re: Harold Francis Davidson
Date: 8 May 1931

Subject appears to be getting dangerously manic. Becoming difficult to follow. Takes taxi right across London from Notting Hill to Aldgate, switches to No. 78 bus, stops in Whitechapel, walks a mile, calls into scabby boozer at lunchtime, comes out 2.45 with young woman (barmaid going off duty?), takes her in another taxi to private dwelling in Old Kent Road, emerges this time with 2 women, one a car owner who drives them to Adelphi Theatre in Strand (matinée of *Sergeant Mills's Secret*), emerges 5.30, takes leave of ladies, drops into Charing Cross Hotel, orders tea and writes letters on hotel notepaper. Disappears upstairs (3rd floor according to lift, but could not follow him). Back downstairs 1 hr later, meets man of rough appearance in nearby pub (Gordon's Bar), earnest conversation, leaves 7 p.m., proceeds to Leicester Square, meets the curly-haired young woman with threatening manner in Godolphin restaurant, drinks tea, then accompanies her to Piccadilly Theatre to see something called *Folly to be Wiser*.

294

I'm just about to give up and go home after exhausting 6 hrs' pursuit, when a new thing happens.

Standing in theatre queue, Subject and surrounding theatre-goers were accosted by beggar with tin box looking for alms. Met with no success until Subject abruptly takes man's arm and addresses waiting people.

'My friends,' he says, 'this man is hungry and homeless, and is deserving of your charity. I know that you are kind people with many charitable impulses in your make-up, yet you will not give him money because you suspect he will spend it unwisely on drink. You wish to be assured of a moral *quid pro quo* before you will part with your small change. Let me offer you something else. You are gathered here this evening in search of dramatic entertainment, for which you will gladly part with cash. For this wretched man, who offers no entertainment, you will pay nothing. Very well. How would it be if I undertake to amuse you for five minutes on his behalf, after which you will pay him the modest fee I might solicit, were I in his shoes?'

The night owls greeted this suggestion with blank silence. Subject was kitted out in black suit and (for once) dog collar – odd spectacle of vicar offering to put on show for the sake of a down-and-out. Some gentlemen shook their heads and glanced at lady consorts, maybe thinking him deranged or drunk – but he had their attention. And there in Piccadilly, before 20 or 30 posh souls outside a theatre, he started in.

Performed a comic monologue called 'Father of the Bride', taking off a would-be toff making a wedding speech in which he reveals his dodgy background and shocking things about members of his family. On the repeated line, '. . . and Auntie Nellie's never been the same,' the crowd began to titter. The sight of a padre doing the hand gestures and the tipsy act, they'd never seen the like. He was a card, real professional, like he'd been doing it all his life. At the end, they all clapped. The beggar watched him through it all, pretty bemused, like he wasn't sure if it was a joke at his expense, but was laughing too, by the end.

'Thank you, thank you,' said Subject. 'Now perhaps you may express your appreciation by giving this man money. Nothing too generous, mind, for he can hardly stand, let alone drag himself around London, with his pockets full of change.'

One or two ladies burrowed in their handbags. Then a chap, probably not meaning it, called out 'Encore' and a few others did so too, and Subject looked around beaming and said, 'Very well!' Next thing, he'd spun on his heel, raised a hand for silence and said, 'I've just arrived in Paris from that sunny southern shore,' and he was off into 'The Man Who Broke the Bank at Monte Carlo' like he was on the Hippodrome stage – not singing exactly, more declaiming the words, but with such vigour and in his deep, carrying voice, well, it was like watching Jack Buchanan. Some people joined in the chorus: 'As – I – *walk* along the Bwadda Booloyne with an independent air . . .' A weird atmosphere, out there in the warm London night.

At the end of the encore, people pulled out purses and wallets, and handed over shillings and crowns and even the odd banknote to the beggar, whose greasy flat cap filled up with money. People were laughing, and one or two shouted 'Bravo!' and the Subject was smiling like anything. 'You should be on the stage,' said a woman in trousers. The tough-bitch girl was smiling too, her sulky little puss lit up, and it was really a scene to warm the old cockles. I won't forget the beggar geezer whose fortunes had changed that night, looking into his cap and counting the money all surreptitious, like he couldn't believe how much he'd made, and trying to thank the rector by saying, 'Look, I dunno –' over and over, as if he didn't have words to express it.

Then they went in to their play. I'd seen enough. I've followed him all over London for more than a month now, from supper to breakfast and back, and I got enough of a report now to fill a telephone book, but I can't see what they're going to pin on him except a lot of fannying around laying hands on people – on girls – in shops and pubs and cafés, and some disappearing acts in hotels. He never stops moving long enough to get up to any monkey business. He's an oddball, but a straight one. Know what I mean?

CHAPTER 15

Letter from Mrs Moyra Davidson
Stiffkey Rectory
10 May 1931

Dearest Oona,

I ventured out in the garden today for the first time in ages,
I've been so depressed with things, the silence from London, the
bailiffs, this bloody man asking questions all over the village, I
haven't had a minute to myself to go for a little wander in the
apple orchard, or trail around looking at how the lime trees are
thriving, the acers and the honeysuckle. I've always loved a bit of
a wander to see the magnolia buds bursting out of the branches
and the early roses starting to bloom, I don't know why, it just
sort of reconnects me to Nature. You never were fond of the old
gardening stuff yourself, were you, Oona, such an urban body
you are, but I've always felt able to inject something into the soil,
a fuse of love that made things grow out of the most unpromising
territory.

Anyway, after being a prisoner indoors for too long, prowling
through the rooms and having too many little naps, I steeled
myself today and went a-wandering outdoors. It started sunny,
then the grey clouds came muscling into the sky like a threat of
trouble, but I persevered. Found a cluster of violets beyond the
orchard, a little burst of colour beneath the climbing rose,
Albertine it's called, a lovely small white bloom at the end of a
shoal of sharky thorns. The combination of violets and roses
nagged at something inside my head and finally it came to me.

It's the bank where the wild thyme blows, isn't it? That bit of

A Midsummer Night's Dream, about the ox-lips and woodbine, musk-roses and eglantine, not that we've seen much of any of them in this part of Norfolk. Not much call for eglantine when you're surrounded by salt marshes. But it pitched me back, just thinking about it, to a happier time, when we put that very play on in the Rectory gardens to celebrate moving into the place.

It was back in September '07, post-honeymoon, we were about to start in earnest as the Rector and his lady wife running a proper parish. We got builders in to transform the Rectory while we stayed down the road with Mr and Mrs Reynolds, our new friends.

It was Harold who decided on the fancy opening. We'll have a charity launch, he said, it'll do no harm to have some people subscribe a few shillings to Dr Barnardo's in return for a ring-side seat at the big event. Harold still had contacts in the acting world. His friend from Whitgift school, Leon Quartermaine, with whom he used to act, had his own company of thespians, and his pal from Oxford days, Reginald Kennedy-Cox, who used to be the president of the Oxford Dramatic Society, they both chipped in to put on a garden production of the *Dream*. It was just wonderful to see a crew of real, professional actors arrive by the London train, chattering and twittering like a touring crowd of bohemians, and so confident in looking round the Rectory lawns and deciding, Oh, we'll do the scene with Bottom the Weaver here, and, Ah, here's the perfect tree under which Titania will have the love-juice put on her eyes. Of course, I was hardly a stranger to the acting scene myself, but I told Harold, I am *not* going to perform, thank you, this is my night to be a hostess and to enjoy the sights and sounds like a proper lady.

There was no stopping him, though, H, he had to be in it, playing Puck sitting in the branches of the wych elm, declaiming away

I knew we'd have a good crowd from Stiffkey and Morston, I knew the locals would come out in force, it isn't every day they have a big alfresco party right under their noses with the hog-roast and the free beer and cider, but I wasn't prepared for the crush of folk that descended on the village, a whole gang of vivid performers and hangers-on from London, people connected to the Actors' Church Union, protégés of Kennedy-Cox, blousy soubrettes who'd once acted with H in comic dramas, the thick and the flirty along with the grand and the stately, they all swanned about the Rectory, demanding tea and buns and somewhere to wash 'before showtime', can you believe the airs these people give themselves? But they had every right to be eager, because of who turned out to be in the audience that night.

Forgive me traipsing down Memory Lane, Oona, but I'm fairly drowned in reminiscence these days, Sheilagh says I'm running away from the present because I can't cope, and she's dead right, one more visit from the bailiffs and I swear I'll run away and live in the garden, in my own little Forest of Arden, where nobody will come and find me ever.

We'd got two hundred chairs from the town hall, the school and the British Legion, and all of them were needed, indeed twice as many wouldn't have been enough for the audience that came. People sat on the grass, and drank their free beer and cider out of paper cups, and Mr Angell, the butcher's son, sliced up the hog-roast and forked it into little paper plates so everyone had a bit, and Anne Reynolds and her husband hung lamps and lanterns from the trees so it was a real touch of fairyland as the lamplight took over from the declining light over the western hills, and the play began. Aunt Gertie played the piano entr'actes like she'd been doing it all her life, the old trouper, and she hissed to me that she flatly wasn't going to do the Wedding March unless I would sing, and I said no and no and no, because I had no costume and hadn't sung Mendelssohn in years, but she was adamant that didn't I go and find a frock that would suit, the midnight-blue velvet gown I bought with you in Brown Thomas's a century ago, and I was full of nerves but everybody was involved with this fantastic night, so why shouldn't I as well?

While I was changing, I heard a noise of clapping that confused me – we were only in the middle of Act One, there was no occasion for applause – and I ignored it and concentrated on my breathing warm-up. Kitted out in midnight blue – it was as tight as tuppence, for I'd put on a few pounds since the Dublin days – I walked across the darkening greensward and took my position by the piano, and asked Gertie what was all the clapping for? 'Nothing,' she said, 'the first appearance of Titania got them all excited,' but it was a lie. As I began to sing, I turned to the front row of seats with me mouth open and who should be sitting there, nodding and smiling in a flaming red silk gown that was streamed all over the grass, but Princess Mary of Teck.

Can you credit it? I'd sung in front of fancy audiences, Oona, I'd sung for rich men in the Antient Concert Rooms in Dublin, but I never expected to have the Princess of Wales in front of me, beaming away with her infinite condescension. I would have faltered at the shock, but something kept me going – and after it was over, I was introduced to the great lady in person.

'Charming,' she said, 'So very charming. Dr Ingram assured me I would be most beguiled by your little masque in the Norfolk forest, and he spoke the truth. I have never enjoyed Shakespeare more.'

I haven't thought about that night in 1907 half a dozen times since, and 'twas one of the most magical nights of my whole life. Isn't it awful, Oona, how the best and lightest memories get forced out by the sad and the black ones?

Your loving friend,
Mimi xxx

Journals of Harold Davidson
London
15 May 1931

I am still, I confess, rather startled by my own performance in the street outside the theatre the other night. Since I took Don Stupendo to see *Plunder* and witnessed his way of 'working a crowd' (as he calls it), some emulative virus has wormed its way past my better judgement and murmured, 'You could do it too,' in my ear.

I am not, of course, a beggar, since I solicit funds entirely for the benefit of the needy. Well, perhaps it could be said that I derive a small salary from charitable disbursements, but only enough to help me look out for the unfortunates that benefit from my assistance. But the money is never used in the pursuit of idle pleasures or low entertainments. Well, except the odd play or cinema visit, the occasional dinner or boat ride (there are pleasure boats on the Serpentine! I saw a handbill outside Hyde Park announcing it. How emblematic of everything that 'summer' means! How it would take me back to my punting days in Oxford!), the once-in-a-blue-moon visit to the music hall or concert, the rare trip to Blenheim or Windsor Castle. These are not self-indulgent excursions; they are way stations on the journey towards self-enlightenment and the growth of self-confidence.

Anyway, I am *not* a beggar, nor a performer who solicits money from the entertained, but something about the Don's familiar way with the crowd, his intuiting of what they were thinking and feeling and what they needed to happen – to see something amazing before their eyes – flashed something into my mind: that I have always been a performer; that the congregation at Stiffkey is but a symbol of the greater audience that exists to hear the truth, to heed my words, to be entertained, yes, entertained by my insights into the human soul.

I suspect that I possess some divine gift of connection with common popular audiences, about which I was not hitherto fully aware. I will strive to use it in the future to spread a message of hope.

Part of my delight at the reception of my little performance is occasioned by the response of Miss Harris. Since our discussion about martyrs and saints (and friendship) two months ago, she has been unaccustomedly thoughtful and quiet. As her seventeenth birthday approached, and our discussions grew more wide-ranging in subject matter (she seemed genuinely interested in everything I had to tell her, from the Peloponnesian War to the circulation of blood), I fancied a new maturity had broadened her mind. She seldom harped on about romance and boyfriends – once the only subjects of her limited conversational repertoire – but now asked, with a becoming seriousness, about housing.

After my lengthy dilation, the other night, on the nightmarish slums I encountered in Shoreditch and Southall, she asked, 'If them's the worst places in London to live, Harold, where's the best?'

'Anywhere is better than these regions of despair, Barbara. Anywhere that hope can flourish, or dreams take root, anywhere that children can grow up unburdened by –'

'Yeah, all right, Harold,' she interrupted. 'Spare me the politics. What I meant was, where's the best districts to live in? For people in houses?'

'The best districts?' I chuckled. 'I am not an estate agent. But I suppose the most luxurious places to live must be near patches of parkland, near an abundance of shops and near the West End. Mayfair and Park Lane are generally considered the *ne plus ultra* of glamorous living, I believe, although these are scarcely my normal habitats.'

'Yeah, but say you was a normal person, looking for a nice house with a husband and kids, and you always wanted a little garden to sit in and sniff the, you know, honeysuckle and that, well, whereabouts would you start looking for a place like that?'

Never had I dreamed that so infamous a public sinner could embrace respectability with such wholehearted conviction. A husband and children indeed! A garden with honeysuckle! I was not aware she could tell a garden plant from a pikestaff, let alone crave the simple pleasures of horticultural quietude. Has there ever been such an open expression of the desire for innocence and decency?

'Chelsea,' I said, neutrally, 'is often spoken of as the perfect combination of *rus in urbe*, of boskiness and brickwork. Clapham has some very grand houses overlooking the Common. But they are dwellings for the gentry, my dear Barbara, for salaried professional people such as surgeons and lawyers, for City merchants. The house you seek, with its garden and its nursery for Junior' – I mentally disposed inverted commas around the distant prospect of Miss Harris conceiving a child – 'could be available in some much less elevated district, with no loss of enjoyment of the pleasures you seek. All it would need, my dear Barbara, is the acquisition of a large cash sum, or the acquisition of a large, rich husband.'

Since that evening, she's returned to the subject again and again.

'How much would it cost to buy a real refrigerator, like they got in the States?' 'You know that actress Mary Astor? You told me about her lots of times. I read that she's got a walk-in wardrobe. How much would one of them cost?'

'Good heavens,' I said lightly. 'A walking wardrobe? However does she remove her frocks as it glides by?'

'No, you fool, a walk-in wardrobe, one so big it's like a room you can go inside and turn round while you're selecting what to wear. How much are they?'

'My knowledge of modern furniture for the young married woman is sadly incomplete.' It was good, however, to hear such queries about domestic matters on her lips. She has, as I say, grown fonder of me since the other night. After the Monte Carlo song outside the theatre, she came in front of me, while everyone's attention was on the tramp's cap, filling up with shillings and half-crowns, and she stood four-square in front of me, put her hands on the underside of both my forearms, so that my hands lay upon her arms. 'You're quite something aren'cha?' she said in a strange, distant voice, leaned into my face and kissed me, firmly on the cheek, just beside my mouth. I hoped nobody had seen, but my heart was flooding like a reservoir; a gush of divine benignity filled my heart. I was whisked back to the day when I saved a young life from extinction and received a similar benediction of a kiss, one that lit my steps home and filled the years to come with a vision, a point to life. She, the girl on Tower Bridge, was my first success. Will Barbara perhaps be my last?

Letter from Mrs Moyra Davidson
Stiffkey Rectory
20 May 1931

Dearest Oona,

Another of them awful men was back yesterday, bailiffs, they come every couple of days now, hanging round like wasps, buzzing and nosing around inspecting everything, the barrows in the yard, the farming implements, even the clothes on the line, as if wondering how much they would make for ready cash and preparing to take them all away.

'This paper here in my hand, madam,' one says with the utmost disrespect, 'is a bill for £93 pounds for fuel costs for the whole winter, that's electricity, gas, coal and logs, it's £93 pounds. It remains unpaid. What'll it be? Do I get paid, or do I look round the outhouses and take a few things away to the valuers?'

What could I do, Oona, but protest and make the same promises I made to the last lot of ugly men? The shame of having creditors coming to the door is bad enough, of course, but to have their rented thick-ear bullies coming to take your things away, it's insupportable so it is. But what could I do only stand and watch and cry my eyes out as they took first the harrow and the lawnmower and half a dozen bits of gardening equipment and loaded them up into a big lorry, and didn't your man, the lead bully, try to gain entrance into the house but I barred his way with my two arms spread out and said, 'You will not enter this house except by violence, my lad, and if you would lift a finger against the wife of the rector, you will soon find the entire village raised up against you, and your family as well, for we know exactly where you live and there will be a dozen local men happy to pay you a visit.' I could not believe I was capable of threats of this nature, Oona, it was like an echo of the old suffragist days. The man looked at the determination in my eye and something about it made him take off, saying to his henchmen, 'We'll be lucky to get thirty bob for all this farming tat. We'll be back in pursuance of this debt, and the next time we'll have a warrant to enter the house to distrain the chattels therein.' Distrain the chattels? I never heard the beat of it. It was like I was talking to the beadle from a Dickens novel. But once he'd gone, and I sat inside wondering if there was a ha'p'orth of bacon left on the gammon joint I boiled up last weekend that would do for the children's tea, I started weeping uncontrollably. Nugent came in to ask me something, took one look at my face and changed his mind. But before he left the room, he said a terrible thing. 'If you're going to be like this all the time, Ma,' he said, 'I won't be able to have my friends to stay. Perhaps you'd let me know when you intend to be more . . . normal.'

So I am an embarrassment to my children now, as well as a bad provider and a deserted wife.

Worse than that, I fear I may be heading round the twist, as they say in town. The other night, couple of weeks ago, I dreamed I was walking out of the house at night-time in autumn, heading into the forest at the back. I rested by a tree to get my bearings, and something made me reach down and pick up a handful of dead leaves and bring them to my face. And there, in a shaft of moonlight, I gazed at – what do you think? It was a handful of big banknotes, fives and tens of pounds, they were large and crinkly in my fist, and I looked at them with a flush of delight. Soon, I was hunkered down on the dark grass, scooping up more leaves, fistfuls, armfuls of the things, and then I was walking around the tree, and yes, all the leaves carpeting the greensward were banknotes. I flew hither and thither gathering as many as I could and piling them up, all this money, this fantastic wealth from nowhere. It was a very logical dream, in that I remember thinking, How the hell am I to get it all back to the house, should I run home for a wheelbarrow? Then it dawned on me – all over the forest, everywhere was a great sea of leaves that'd turned to money, and shouldn't I start collecting it all from beside the house? I wondered if I should wake Eileen or Mr Reynolds, and that was when the panic set in, for there was a light in the sky which said that dawn was coming soon, and other women and men would soon be astir and the secret of the leaves would be out, and all over the village and all over Norfolk, people would be busying themselves with the wheelbarrows. And I, whose need is greater than anybody's, would have to stand and watch all the wealth of the world be picked up by other people than me who was its discoverer. I started, in the dream, to cry at the unfairness of it all.

I've seldom had a dream that pitched me into such a state. Next day, after the meagre supper of cabbage soup with onions, I went walking in the wood and found a tree like the one in the dream. I rested my head, I even (am I going insane?) picked up a handful of leaves and pressed them against my face, but they refused to be anything but green ivy leaves that had been blown by the high winds, and not money at all.

And here's a thing. I felt sure someone was watching me from nearby – I even fancied I heard a twig cracking – someone who was on the lookout for a madwoman, and I hurried home before he or she or it could confront me like a bailiff of the mind.

I reached the house and found myself shaking. Luckily I remembered that, along with the fruit and the gammon some kind soul had left on our doorstep, they'd included a half-bottle of brandy, so I had a glass of that, drinking it down in one. I pulled myself together and had one more. Soon I was feeling right as rain, and the stupid dream stopped running through my head. I began to make plans for how we could get some money to pay off the next creditors, dressmaking perhaps, or I could ask the school to pay me for talks on Good Housekeeping. There didn't seem much left in the bottle so I finished it off and went to bed.

I haven't managed to set the new moneymaking schemes in place as yet, but will soon, I'm sure. If you have any bright ideas, darling, let me know. And don't worry about your loving M in her current troubles. I'll get through it all. I'll have a big talk with Harold and straighten it out. And in the meantime, the brandy is great stuff, isn't it? (Only codding!)

Your loving
Mimi xx

Journals of Harold Davidson
London
26 May 1931

How beautiful is London in the cheap finery of summer! I walked in St James's Park, taking the remains of last night's bread-and-butter pudding at the Stockpot to feed to the ducks. Without my collar, and hampered by my disintegrating boots, I blend in well with the undernourished wretches who lie beneath the oaks and cough and groan in the extremity of their maladies. Tulips and freesias line the water's edge in happy profusion. Splashes of colour in the summer dresses of office girls, eating their luncheon apples and 'Scotch' eggs in the sunshine. A bandstand orchestra played adroit snatches of *The Vagabond King*, to which I hummed along with eyes shut. Delightful. Truly, at such moments, all seems well with the world.

I am thinking of asking Miss Harris to stay with me. Her placement with Mr and Mrs Lake has not been a success. After only three weeks, she has been asked to leave for unspecified transgressions, and given a few days to find alternative accommodation. I thought when I first met Mr L that he was a man to be trusted not to take liberties with young girls in his care, but I fear I was wrong. Mrs L seemed to indicate to me that Barbara was somehow culpable in whatever event precipitated her departure. But I think I know Miss Harris well enough to discount such a suggestion. She is a changed woman. Her conversation has taken on a questioning, ruminative quality. Her fascination for saintlihood and martyrdom, though initially prompted by a fascination for its more grotesque aspects, bespeaks a classic case of the aspirational convert.

Apart from her unfortunate tussle with Mr Lake, she has, as far as I know, touched no gentleman in any physical sense for some weeks. And I think it my duty, now she is homeless, to offer the shelter of my home – an ark, as I see it, an *arca foederis* upon the tidal wave of modern filth. My new landlady, the bun-haired and (if I may be ungallant) bun-faced Mrs Osborne, has little to do with my comings and goings. There is only one bed, of course, but I am used to dozing in the chair. The benefit I will feel in having Miss Harris under my tutelage will outweigh the inconvenience of neck discomfort in the middle of the night. And when I have set her up, as I intend to do, at a new academy of design and modern fashion in Hammersmith, she will be able to pay me a modest rent from her seamstress activities in the evenings.

It is an admirable, missionary plan and I shall expedite it without delay.

From the Right Reverend Bertram Pollock
Bishop's House, Norwich
27 May 1931

Dear Henry,

I have studied the depositions of your private investigators with interest. While their dogged pursuit of our friend Mr Davidson seems admirably thorough, I confess myself disappointed that they have turned up so little of any consequence or value.

I'm sure you know what you are doing, Henry, employing these dogged men to traipse round London and Stiffkey 'looking for clues', as you express it, but the results of their labours are but meagre. To wit: one episode of kissing a young woman in a Chinese restaurant, apparently without much evidence of immoral passion. One or two visits to theatres in the company of young girls, safely delivered home thereafter. One ludicrous display of 'performing' in the street outside a theatre, ostensibly for a charitable purpose. One sighting, in the Stiffkey parish, of debt collectors at their work, and one pursuit of the hapless wife through a moonlit wood with no significant outcome. And far too many pointless wanderings, by taxi and omnibus, all over the metropolis in pursuit of a man who visits shops, cafés and public parks apparently at random and engages not just girls but hundreds of members of the public in conversation. It is a chronicle of time-wasting such as I have seldom encountered.

I began this enquiry in order to accumulate facts that would amount to a defence of Mr Davidson, in the event of his being accused of immorality. Now I am more disposed to go on the attack. Mr Davidson is not the sort of clergyman we want in the Church of England. His activities may not be actually sinful, but they smack of lewdness, antic misbehaviour, self-indulgence, wilful pleasure in fleshy regions. No other vicar of my acquaintance would consider his behaviour normal or appropriate. Rather than wait for Major Hammond or the London papers to lead the charge, we should arraign Davidson at a Church tribunal, confront him with his louche way of life and withdraw him from circulation. We can easily find a new rector for his tiny parish.

But first we need concrete evidence that he enjoyed some sexual relationship with a woman. Without that, we have nothing to put before a Church court but the threadbare diaries of Messrs Thole and Butler.

I know I can rely on you to turn up something suitably unpleasant ere long.

Your servant in Christ,

+ Bertram

Journals of Harold Davidson
London
1 June 1931

Miss Harris has set up house with me! What a very happy day. At 3 p.m. yesterday she telephoned me to say that any time that afternoon would be convenient. I treated myself to a taxicab, to fetch her to Shepherd's Bush in comfort, only to find a quantity of suitcases, hatboxes and files of fashion magazines and similar ephemera upon the pavement. It seems she had rescued all her belongings from the flat in Camden where I used to visit her, and tried to secrete them in her little room at the Lakes', whereupon Mrs L had decided that she'd had enough of Barbara and her paraphernalia. So – Barbara was, as the cockneys say, 'out on her ear' at 3 p.m., the time when she graciously informed me of her availability, like a duchess leaving an 'At Home' card.

Now she is installed, the place is a shocking morass of silk and cotton frou-frous, feathery boas and glittery bijoux, ludicrous costumes as though from some precocious children's party. I have told her to keep her belongings in her suitcase, since she will not be staying long. And her periodicals too. The shelves that used to bear my meagre library of inspirational works (*The Hero in Thy Soul, Norfolk Portraits, Our Exemplar, or What Would Jesus Do?, Wisdom of Juliana of Norwich, Collected Monologues of George Grossmith*, etc.) have been filled with pastel-shaded romances (*Sunset over Navarre, The Mystery of the Red Barn, A Factory-Girl's Story*) and umpteen postcard-sized images of actresses – Marlene Dietrich, Louise Brooks, Lilian Gish – propped up by their side.

As to the sleeping arrangements, I have conveyed to Miss Harris that during our temporary sojourn, she may avail herself of my bed between midnight and 8 a.m., when I am wont to sit in the chair dozing. She understands this as the offer of a kind benefactor, nothing more. What Mrs Osborne will make of it we must see, but I'm confident that a small addition to the rent, say ten shillings a week, will relieve her of the burdensome need to construct some landlady-ish response.

London
8 June 1931

Barbara has now been here a week. We sit together in the evenings, harmoniously, she perusing her magazines and her catalogues from Gamages, Marshall & Snelgrove and Harrods (if you please!), I reading in my prayer book (this evening's text: 'And the children of Israel gave to the Levites these cities with their suburbs . . . And they gave unto them, of the cities of refuge, Shechem in mount Ephraim with her suburbs; they gave also Gezer with her suburbs' – how alarmingly suburban, in many senses, is the Book of Chronicles), and sometimes we venture out to walk on the Green, and sometimes, when a sudden disbursal of funds has come from a philanthropic soul, we take the Underground to the Strand or to Drury Lane, or to Dolores Knight's charming new artistic 'cellar' in Frith Street, where the laughing convivium continues rather shockingly late.

I have urged Barbara to learn French, with a view to finding her a job in a luxury goods emporium. I have also urged her to call on Rose, with whom she was once so friendly. I would do so myself, but I have been busy of late. Barbara only pouts and complains like a ten-year-old. 'But, Harold,' she'll say, 'we got nothing in common no more, me and Rose. Poor old doll, she's been hitting the bottle again. I know you want your old girlfriends to get on with each other and be pals together –'

'Barbara,' I remonstrated, 'that is a shocking accusation.'

'Yeah, all right. But Rose, she's a bit of a gloom-bucket, isn't she? When she gets up in the morning, she never knows if she's gonna be ill or well for the day, d'you know what I mean? I know you're old friends, Harold, but sometimes she gets on my tits so much, I just want to wallop her.'

I told Barbara she was a needlessly superior and uncharitable girl. She poured herself a large gin and Italian vermouth and flicked over the pages of her magazine, murmuring, 'All right then, let's get dear Rosie-Posie out on the razz, one of these hot nights.' An undertaking to which I will hold her.

We have odd, dreamy interchanges at night-time, when she is almost asleep.

'Harold?'

'Yes, Barbara?'

'D'you get lonely sometimes? Flying around town on your own. Living on your own. Not having a real wife, I mean a wife by your side every day?'

'I have a wife at home, who is bringing up our children. Regrettably my work keeps me here a great deal. But sometimes, yes, I wish such a thing as you suggest were possible.'

'Me too, Harold. I get a bit lonely too. Be nice to be married, wouldn't it, Harold? With a proper kitchen and a garden and a chat in the morning, I mean, every morning.'

'I hope, my dear, that both our lives may find fulfilment some day.' There was a moody silence. 'Maybe with each other?'

'Maybe, Barbara,' I said sleepily. And maybe, I told myself, the Resurrection is at hand.

On the seventh or eighth night, as I sat in my chair, her voice issued from the bed.

'Harold?'

'Yes?'

'You know in French?'

'Yes.'

'How do you say, "I love the sun, the moon and the stars"?'

'But why, Barbara? What is the context?'

'Just say it for me, Harold.'

J'aime le soleil, la lune et les étoiles . . .'

'"But most of all, it's you I love."'

'Is this from some romantic tosh you have been reading?'

312

'Just say it, will you?'

'*Mais surtout, c'est toi que j'aime.*'

'How do you say, "You are the queen of my heart"?'

'Is this game going to continue all night?'

'Just do it, Harold.'

'*Tu es la reine de ma coeur.*'

'That's nice.'

Notebooks of Charlie Norton, *Evening Standard*
London
23 June 1931

Well, I'll be damned. It's the rector again. I didn't expect to cross his path any more, after my little altercation with that Harris bint. No one seemed to know where he was. Didn't visit his old haunts, never seen at meetings of his charities. My letters to his wife never answered. Thought he'd gone to ground and stopped all the malarkey with the brasses.

Now this cove gets in touch. Mr Inglebert Thole, if you please, *and* he's a detective. Not a copper. Works at some surveillance agency, like the ones in *Black Mask* magazine, and is hired to trail people through the streets and report on what they get up to.

He telephoned me at work and came round to the *Standard* offices. Funny-looking geezer, like a long grey ghost, with a black hat pulled down over his forehead. Conspicuously inconspicuous I'd say if I was Mr O. Wilde. 'This piece you wrote last year,' he said, 'the rector story. I want to know if you are aware of any, um, unfavourable stories that have been circulating about him. It's a legal matter, you see.'

'Legal, eh?' I said. 'Don't tell me they've got him at last for cashing dodgy cheques.'

'No, no, it's nothing criminal exactly,' said the man, his strangely grey face pursing in concentration, and making him look like he was lying through his teeth. 'More a personal matter for a client, that we hope will not turn into criminal proceedings.'

'And who's the client,' I asked, reasonably. 'Who's keen to find him?'

''Fraid I can't say, Mr Norton. But you're one of the few people who've 'ad his attention for a interview, and I'd be obliged if you could advise me of his standing in the community. Is he liked in London circles? Do people speak well of him? Are there any stories going round about him and the ladies he seems to hang around with?'

'You say you've read my piece in the paper?'

'Yes. That's why I come to see you.'

'That's all I know, Mr Thole. I met him twice. Once he had a pair of young girls with him, who seemed to be genuinely friends with him, or at least girls he'd taken an interest in. But I don't have any dirt on him, if that's what you're asking. I haven't seen him in months. I don't even know where he lives.'

'Oh, we know *that*. 43a Macfarlane Road, Shepherd's Bush.'

'Well, sorry to tell you your bizney, mate, but shouldn't you be calling on him yourself, or asking his neighbours about his comings and goings?'

'I done all that. But I can't go up and ask the gent himself if he's involved in anything funny. I thought a pressman like yourself . . .'

'Would have some dirt on him? Not me. But if there was something you turned up that resembled a real story, well, I might be able to help.'

He gave me another funny look. 'I don't think we're looking for coverage in the press, exactly. But I'd be happy to pay you for any light you could cast on his procedures with the women.'

'Oh yes? I dare say that might be arranged.'

Thole had a problem. He had to find out things, but he didn't want to find out enough to see it spread across pages of newsprint. The horns of a dilemma were goring his grey guts.

'I could fix up a meeting with him and maybe one of the brasses, where you could maybe sit in as a pal of mine. Would that be worth a small . . . reward?'

'Oh, indeed,' he said.

'I'm not promising I can get him for you, mind you. But I can try, if you give me a number where I can reach you.'

We parted with much handshaking, him looking down at the floor the minute he stood up, as though fearful of being watched, or looked at, or followed. Must be a curious life, following people for a living. Makes you paranoid. And that's a paradox, isn't it? Or am I sounding like Mr O. Wilde again?

Journals of Harold Davidson
London
24 June 1931

Alarming news from Barbara. She has seen fit to tell me that hardly had she moved into the Lakes' establishment than she was approached by some kind of investigator. My suspicions, it seems, were correct. I fear the same man may have been quizzing Mrs Lake about my role in finding lodgings for Barbara, a role that may be open to misinterpretation.

I have received a letter from Mr 'Charlie' Norton, the journalist whom I met with Dolores Knight and Jezebel last July, and with Barbara in that rather difficult evening in October. He says he wants to do a new piece about my work, because of the interest generated by the last. He suggests we meet in the Cheshire Cheese, his Fleet Steet 'local', and begs me to bring along 'that charming young woman, Barbara, and any other ladies who have benefited from your kind ministrations since we last spoke'. Of course I am wary of the Press, but it was a kindly disposed piece he wrote, and I feel it would do no harm to grant his request. I wrote to the newspaper, agreeing to the appointment. I could bring Barbara. Perhaps it would be an idea to include Rose. She needs to become familiar once again with the world outside her narrow ambit. But, at the risk of seeming uncharitable to the dear girl, we may have to smarten her up a little!

Notebooks of Charlie Norton, *Evening Standard*
London
26 June 1931

Well, *that* was one weird evening.

I was pleased as Punch to hear from the rector. Said he remembered me and the article, and how 'hearteningly well disposed' I'd been to him. So he agrees to the meeting in the Ch. Cheese, promises to bring a couple of the girls ('some of my more successful placements') along for a chinwag. I got in touch with Mr Thole, and told him it's all on, but that he's to leave me with the rector for an hour at least, before he sort of happens by. So I waited in the saloon bar of the Cheese, and they show up around 8.15, and it's obvious that something's gone wrong between them.

The reverend, he's the usual unsinkable charmer, rubbing his hands, saying, Splendid, splendid – but was there a touch of nerviness in his flickering gaze? Barbara, the little madam, has an angry colour in her cheek and she narrows her eyes at me until they were little slits. What the hell did I ever do to her? With them was a woman, a lot older than Barbara, who's in a right two-and-eight. I could tell she'd been crying, and from her attitude, you'd think she'd been dragged in here by force. She whoomphed down on the sofa cushion and started hissing something at Barbara. It sounded like a lover's quarrel. Barbara flapped her hand at her and said, 'Best behaviour, darling, Her Majesty's Press are here,' but it didn't help.

'Why can't I?' she kept demanding. 'So why the hell can't I?'

'Shoosh,' said Barbara as though soothing a small child.

'Nice to see you again, Reverend,' I began.

'Rector, if you don't mind. Could you perhaps advise us of the agenda this evening?'

'It's not a boardroom meeting,' I said, laughing. 'Just a little chat. Thing is, there's been a report from the Home Office that we're following up, about prostitution in London, which indicates there's more prostitutes working the metropolis than ever before. We got figures from the police, and penny-dreadful reports from houses of ill repute, and special columnists on the paper wringing their hands. But we haven't got a close-up piece from someone who sees this stuff all the time, who knows from day to day how bad it's got. Someone like you.'

'Is there a fee attached?' asked the rector.

'Well, no,' I said, 'we don't usually pay people from whom we gather information. Usually they're happy to see their views voiced in the newspapers.'

'I,' said the rector grandly, 'am in the nature of being an expert witness. I think you will find nobody with the breadth of experience that I can command in having private intercourse with ladies of the night in London.' He paused. 'Could you furnish these young women with drinks? I will have some barley water. The flavour is irrelevant.'

The rector made off to the Gents, and I tried the girls. Would they like a drop of gin? No thanks, they'd both like cider (at least they were cheap dates) and they went back to their talk, ignoring me. But as I squeezed by, I heard Barbara say, 'It's OK. You can come to the Whitehall with us next week. Don't take on so. It's nothing like what you think. He's dead fond of you, and he's only giving me a bed for the night while I get this place in New Cross, all right?' She paused, glancing up at me. 'You still here?' asked Barbara. 'Thought you was getting us cider.'

When we reconvened, the rector was voluble, entertaining, confiding, a bit actorish. 'The problem has worsened appreciably,' he said, shaking his silver-fox head. 'And the arms we must use to combat it are hard to find. I hope you will excuse the pun. Only by charitable *alms* can we fight the many-headed demon that is the slum, the brothel, the backstreet parlour, the burlesque revue – all places where the young girls flocking to London every day will find a warm welcome and a hearty handshake – a handshake that seals their fate no less completely than the kiss that Judas bestowed upon the face of Christ in Gethsemane.'

'I've sort of heard all this before, Rector,' I said. 'No offence, but I need to bring it up to date.'

'In what sense?'

'Well, don't get me wrong, but some new stories about, you know, degradation you have witnessed would be interesting to our readers, a sympathetic body of people, and you need not scant on the details on their account.'

He looked at me keenly. 'I know of shocking sights in public places that would bring a blush to any refined person's cheek.'

'Things in broad daylight?'

'Some things, yes.'

'What – down alleyways?'

'No!' He recollected himself. 'On the Green. In Shepherd's Bush. At night, mostly.'

'You've seen it yourself?'

'Indeed I have. To an extent, I have even . . . participated.'

I couldn't believe my ears. The venerable old rector, who'll never see fifty again, indulging in alfresco whoops-a-daisy? It took a while to straighten out that all he'd done was hang around a few brasses on the Green looking for trade, and bunked off home with one of them – for a chat he said – and she offered to dress up as an urchin kid for him. Or an Indian squaw (you what?) or a Boy Scout. Top details. I didn't ask him how long he stuck around in pursuit of his researches.

Anything else? I said. 'Yes there is,' he said. 'You ask if things have changed. I would say, only in this regard: a failure of sympathy seems to have stolen into the hearts of people who should know better. Many now look with suspicion upon the work of the charitable, as if their motives derive from something other than simple goodness.'

'Hang on, rector,' I said. 'You're saying people aren't giving as much to charity as they used to, because they don't think you care enough?'

'No, I mean there is a new moral disapproval in the air. I can feel the gaze of the uncharitable turned on our endeavours, in the street, in cafés and public houses. I feel eyes following me about, black with suspicion. You must explain to your readers that my activities in helping young girls may bring me into contact with women who are professionally concerned with sex, but that no hint of misbehaviour or wrongdoing on my part may be inferred. Can you help me in this?'

Christ, he was feeling got-at. Somebody'd obviously been telling him off. Was it the somebody who Mr Thole was working for? I said, 'Look, Reverend, I can't tell the *Standard* readers not to think of you as a chancer with the ladies, because nobody's suggested you're like that. You have to wait until an accusation's been made in order to defend it.' He seemed pleased with that.

Having got what I wanted, I went to the bar and signalled to Mr Thole to come and be acquainted with the rector. But stone me, there was a scene. As he came over, Barbara spotted him (she'd been ignoring me since I started talking to the rector, and had sunk down into the sofa, so the private eye probably hadn't seen her) and her face hardened into a look of fury. As he drew level, I started to say, 'Good heavens, look who I just met at the bar, my colleague Tim, who is a photog—' but his eyes were locked on to Barbara's.

'You!' she said (with the voice of someone whose next remark is going to be, 'You murdered my mum'), and she rose from the sofa and stuck one hand on to her hip, like a fishwife. 'I thought I told you what'd happen if you was to show your face round here again,' she informed Mr Thole. Then, turning to the rector, she said, 'This is the bloke who was snooping round outside the Lakes' house, asking questions about what I was doing there, and who you were, Harold, and whether I fancied a spot of cash doing God knows what.'

'Indeed?' said the rector. 'I believe he has also been making enquiries at the houses of friends of mine. And he is, you tell me, Mr Norton, a photographer on the *Evening Standard*?'

'Well —' I felt uncomfortable, being caught out in a lie by a sky pilot, but I braved it out. 'Among other things. He's what you call freelance. I don't know what else he might do. He just told me he wanted to meet you.'

Thole looked at me furiously, as if to say, Well, thanks a lot.

'I do not believe a word of it. I think this man is paid to follow innocent victims through the streets and gather information about them. But for whom? That is the question.' He brought his face up to Thole's, as tenacious as Edward G. Robinson in *Little Caesar*. 'For whom do you work, my dear Timothy?' For a short geezer, he could be a bit intimidating.

'Nobody,' bleated Mr Thole. 'I'm not following nobody. I just talked to this woman here because — because she reminds me of my late wife.'

The rector raised an eyebrow. So did I.

'No, really,' he went on. 'I been following this lovely girl because I wanted to make her acquaintance, she's so like my poor Mary, it's uncanny. I wasn't trying it on the other day, I swear, Miss, I just wanted to talk to you. And because I seen you going here and there with this gentleman, well, I took to following him as well, in and out of shops, in the hope of catching sight of you . . .' He came to a faltering stop.

'Don't stop now, mate,' said Barbara. 'We all love fairy tales, don't we? Whyn't you do the one about the cobbler and the elves?'

As I guffawed, Thole seized his opportunity. We watched his hurried departure, as we might have watched a drunkard being thrown out of the bar.

'Those people you were telling me about,' I said, 'the ones who keep an eye on what you're doing, and don't trust you. That chap wouldn't have been one, by any chance?'

'Exactly,' he said. 'He has, I now realise, been dogging my foot-steps for months, but not for the reasons he advances. I fear he is working on behalf of someone else to discredit me and my work.'

'Shocking,' I said.

'Evidently with the help of the newspapers.'

'The newspapers?' Damnation. That tore it.

'It is obvious that you and this gentleman are working together, in the hope of finding some scandalous material about me, to run in the paper along with the fruits of his peregrinations around town.'

'But, Rector, I had no idea —'

'Please do not lie to me. I have no wish to share your company a moment further. I am unable to assist you henceforth in any news-paper article about charity or the needy, now that I know the depths of treachery of which you are capable. Goodbye, Mr Norton. Come along, Barbara. Goodnight, Rose. I shall call on you next week.'

And he took off out the pub, the brassy Barbara steaming out with him in her green summer frock, giving me, en route, a look that would curdle mother's milk.

Fuck it. That was annoying. Did Thole not realise he'd been spotted, and that someone would recognise him? Had he hoped to witness the rector misbehaving with one of the girls? He must be very dim.

Speaking of girls, I realised that the older one, Rose, was still on the sofa beside me.

'You not going with Mr Davidson, love? You'll have to be quick to catch him up.'

Her tired blue eyes regarded the closed pub door. 'They didn't want me to come,' she said shortly. 'They said, "You can come to the pub, and meet the man from the papers, but not to the show. It's a special treat for Barbara."'

'Do you often go out in a threesome?'

'Oh yes, all the time,' she said. 'At least,' her face adopted a chin-on-chest sulk, 'we *used* to, when Barbara and I were first friends. Before she became the rector's favourite and moved in with him.'

'Really?' This was amazing. I'd just lost a story, and then stumbled on to a much better one. The rector's recent little speech about being 'misunderstood' came flying back to me. 'So are you a bit jealous of Barbara, then? Do you wish you were Mr Davidson's favourite?'

She looked up at me in a kind of puzzled fury. 'What you mean, do I *wish*? I *was* his bloody favourite for years. He loved me, he did. We went everywhere together. We had pet names for each other. And fake names for the trips abroad, of course.'

I could not, literally, believe my ears. This was fantastic.

'Rose,' I said, standing up, 'you fancy a bite to eat in a nice hotel? The Strand Palace does a very tasty steak dinner, if you're hungry, and you can tell me all about it.'

'Oh, OK,' said Rose, a bit dimly. (Bit of a faded Rose at thirty-five or so, if you ask me.) 'Could we have a little drinkie as well?'

'Rose, my darlin',' I said, my heart singing the hallelujah, 'you can have as many as you fancy.'

CHAPTER 16

Notebooks of Charlie Norton, *Evening Standard*
27 June 1931

It was quite a confession. Halfway through, I had to call for reinforcements.

She started off, this plain, bleary-eyed woman, complaining, like a little girl denied a teddy bear, that she hadn't been 'allowed' to go to the theatre with Harold and Barbara. Pathetic. But as we settled ourselves on the plush davenport of the Strand Palace Hotel, I realised she had a considerable story to tell.

I bought her a port and asked how they'd met. It was in 1920, she said, she was only nineteen and working in a haberdashery store in Charing Cross when he'd come in, bought two dozen ribbons in various colours.

What did you say to him?

'I said, "You must have a lot of daughters," and he laughed.'

Who were the ribbons for?

'Nobody special. He just kept them in his ribbons pocket, for when he might need them.'

His ribbons pocket?

'Yeah. He's got this greatcoat with a dozen pockets sewn into it, where he keeps all kinds of things that might come in handy when he's travelling around.'

Such as?

'Oh you know. Holy pictures. Perfume. Cigarettes. Bits of lace. Ointment for blisters. Spot cream. Photos of Clara Bow. Theatre handbills. Beauty soap. Song sheets. Prayer books. Contraception things. Bits of costume jewellery. Bus-route maps. Tube maps. Ribbons. Elastic –'

Yes, yes. Did you know he was a clergyman when you met him?

'No. I just thought he was a sweet gentleman. He had a lovely voice. All deep and chocolatey.'

Did he offer you inducements to sleep with him?

'Did he offer me what?'

Did he try to persuade you to have sex with him by giving you presents?

'No. He just wanted me to come along to the music theatre with him –' (darkly) – 'like he's doing with that bitch Barbara, right now.'

And after these pleasant excursions, what used to happen?

'He used to see me home and say, I trust you had a pleasant evening, and he'd hope that from now on I'd reflect on the importance of Living in the Light, as he called it. Or sometimes Living in God's Spotlight.'

And he would then leave you, until the next meeting?

'Sometimes he'd come in for a cup of tea and we'd chat about things.'

What kind of things?

'Stuff in the papers. He'd ask what I, as a young woman, made of all these flapper girls, and were they guilty of immoral behaviour?'

What did you reply?

'I said all they ever did was dance through the night and wear ropes of necklaces and drink red and blue cocktails, so they never seemed all that shocking. Except for Mrs Cunard, because she had the black jazz boyfriend.'

Fancy another port, Rose? Better make it a large one, they seem to go down so fast.

'Don't mind if I do.'

Did the rector ever put his arm around you?

'Ooh yes. He was very big on cuddling. But then he was like that with everyone.'

In public?

'In the street, in the shop, outside the theatre, in the park. In public. In private.'

He sounds a little indiscriminate.

'He'd do it with everyone.' She took a sip of port. 'Sometimes, you'd think, does that mean he doesn't care for me, and I'm not special to him at all? But it was just his affectionate nature.'

Did he ever try to kiss you?

'He was *always* kissing me. He'd kiss me when we met, and when we said cheerio. And lots of times in between.'

Where did he kiss you?

'In the Strand, in Oxford Street, in Knightsbridge, once on the Old Kent Road . . .'

I really meant, where on your person?

'On my forehead. On my cheek. Sometimes both my cheeks in that Frenchy way.'

On the lips?

'(Silence.)'

On the mouth?

'Only in secret, like.'

What do you mean, Rose?

'Only by mistake. Or accident. I don't know.'

How could he kiss you by accident?

'It would just happen. It wasn't arranged. It would just happen.'

When? Under what circumstances?

'At night.'

You mean, in bed?

'Yes.'

He was in bed with you?

'Yes.'

And kissed you in the darkness?

'Yes.'

And were you both in bed under the sheets?

'No. I was in my nightgown in the bed. He was in his clothes, lying on top of the counterpane.'

Did he often stay the night like that?

'He said he just wanted to watch over me as I slept. He'd do that sometimes, if I was feeling a bit lonesome and sad.'

And the kissing – did you implore him to desist?

'What?'

Did you ask him to stop?

'No, I didn't. It was . . . nice.'

And did further intimacies take place?

'Further . . . ? Oh, no. No!'

He did not attempt to have sexual intercourse with you?

'The rector? No. NO!'

Do not become upset, Rose. Have another port.

At the bar, I rang Thole's number. Astonishingly, he was at home, just back from his little dust-up with the rector.

'Nice to hear you're still in one piece, Mr T,' I said. 'If you turn right round and head back to the Strand Palace Hotel, one of the rector's little birds is here with me right now, singing like a canary.'

Thole was there within half an hour – an impressive burst of speed for the Man in Grey. By then, Rose had become a little bleary, and her head was nodding, so I had to take her for a little walk and suggest a trip to the Ladies, to splash some water on her face, before resuming.

Thole came back from his travels a bit of a bastard, I must say. He must've been fighting back at the rector in his head all the way home. Started right in on the poor girl from the off.

How'd you get mixed up with a bloke like that (he asked), a nice girl like you? I could see how things stood between you, just looking at you both in the pub.

'He's not a wrong 'un,' said Rose, with determined air. 'He was very good to me.'

Oh yes? said Mr Thole. Took you to nice places, did he? Paid for you? Showed you a good time, did he?

'He was very good to me. He treated me well.'

Is it the case that, when you met Mr Davidson, you were working as a prostitute?

'No. I never. The cops tried to – to stick it on me once or twice but they never proved anything, did they?'

Don't tell lies, Rose. Did you sometimes agree to have sex with men for money?

'They might leave me a little something when they'd had their fun, some of them. But that doesn't mean I'd do it with just anyone.'

Did Mr Davidson give you money? I mean, for anything, not just for sex?

'No he didn't. Well, in a way he did. He paid the rent on my flat in Chalk Farm.'

Ah-ha! On the expectation that you would agree to go to bed with him?

'No. He did it because he liked me.'

Mr Thole swivelled in his chair and arranged his features in an incredulous scowl, as if to enquire if I had ever met such a bird-brain. (And she did sound a mite simple, truth be told.)

And now, said Mr Thole, bringing in some things I'd told him about Rose's tearful outburst, and now, as we have seen, he likes another girl more than you. Does it make you feel bad, to be so cast aside, to be so cruelly abandoned?

'He hasn't abandoned me. He's still my special friend. He always comes to see me when I'm in trouble.'

Have another glass of port, my dear. I thought you told my friend Charlie here that he'd moved this other lady into his lodgings. Is that not true?

'She's staying there now, but it doesn't mean anything. Doesn't mean he loves her. He doesn't sleep there. He's always moving around. He likes dropping round to see his girls and stays the night sometimes.'

Excuse me, said Thole, if I jot down a few things in this little notebook. This is most interesting.

'He used to take me all over the place. It was lovely. He knows everyone in London, you know. Hello, Rector, they'd call out, how's all the girls? And then they'd look at me, like I was one of the girls he was saving, and he'd say, all defensive like, This is my secretary, Mrs Malone.'

He forced you to employ an alias in company?

'You what?'

He made you pretend to be someone else when you were out together?

'I didn't mind. I quite liked being Mrs Malone, and everyone thinking me a secretary. It made me feel, you know, organised.'

Did he ever take you to an hotel?

'Lots of times.'

For what purpose?

'He used to take me to the one in Basil Street for tea.'

Any other?

'And the Durrants one, we had a nice two-course lunch there once.'

Any other occasion you can recall? A time when, for example, you stayed the night?

'Oh, we never stayed the night in hotels, me and him.' She took a sip of her fifth glass of port. 'Only when we was on holiday abroad.'

Indeed? Mr Davidson used to take you on trips abroad?

'Oh yes. He took us to Paris. We stayed near the river, what's it called, the Seine, and we went shopping in the something Lafayette, and we walked across this lovely flat park, you could see the Eiffel Tower in the distance. And this friend of Harold's from his acting days, Marcel he was called, took us to an art gallery and afterwards we went to a fancy club, there were these black ladies onstage dancing around, they looked so funny.'

Did Mr Davidson try to convince you that visiting a Parisian burlesque club was good for your soul?

'No. We was just having a good time.'

And how do you feel about him now?

Long pause. 'I don't know why they have to go off and do things without me. We used to be friends. Me and him. Then me and her. Then all three of us. We used to have nice chats together, and have lunch, and it was like we were fast friends for ever, like in them children's books.'

But now he's given you up, hasn't he, Rose?

'(Silence.)'

He's dumped you and given you up as a lost soul, and he's taking another girl away on holiday. That Barbara. I heard them talking about it.

'No. NO. Don't say such a thing. Harold wouldn't do that.'

He's doing it, Rose. He's taking her to Lisbon, as soon as he can raise the wind. I heard him use exactly those words.

'No, no, no!'

A little hotel in Lisbon, a love nest just off the main square, and all the bars in the backstreets of the Bairro Alto, that's where they'll be, Rose, what a shame it's not you . . .

'(Weeps.) He's a fucking bastard. He never means what he says. He's just like all the rest, for all his bloody pious lecturing.'

I know you were fond of him, Rose.

'I loved him. And he said he loved me. He said it a couple of dozen times. He loved me for my simple goodness, which shines out of me like a ray from the clouds around Heaven. That's what he said. He admired me. If I hadn't known that or believed that, I couldn't have kept going. Oh God, I feel terrible now.'

Get another port, would you, Norton?

Did he tell you he loved you in the course of these holidays?

'Yes.'

While you were in bed?

'Sometimes.'

Would it be shortly after an act of carnality had taken place?

'What?'

Would he say it in bed, at night?

'Not just then. He'd say it over dinner in the evening. Or when we was walking by the Embankment with the children and the dogs everywhere, and the cathedral. Not that it meant a bloody word in the long run, did it? Ooh thanks, I can't believe I'm drinking so much port. You must think me a terrible sot. But it's good for you, isn't it, it warms up your circulation and keeps the blood rushing around your body, or so Reenie tells me. You know Reenie Callahan?'

I'm afraid not.

'You ought to. She knows ever such a lot about medical things.'

I think, Miss Ellis, it would be a good thing for you to sign a statement about the way the rector has treated you, so we can expose him as a trifler with young women's affections, an adulterer and a walking disgrace to the cloth which he stains and besmirches by wearing. Will you do this for us, so that we can ensure no other poor woman is made to suffer at the hands of this evil man?

'I dunno. I feel a bit sick. D'you know where the Ladies is?'

So we waited and waited. When she returned, she looked pretty green about the gills, and from my knowledge of ladies' behaviour in drink, I'd say some heroic scenes of vomiting and spewing had been going on. She said she wouldn't stick around for any more chat, thank you, and made to go. Well, we had to stop her, with her precious cargo of confessions, but what could we do to stop her, now that bribing her with drinks wasn't going to work any more? Mr Thole's ingenuity left me amazed.

'Yours is a sad story, Rose,' he said, 'and I'd love to hear the end of it. I don't know if we're going to try and prosecute Mr Davidson for the way he's treated innocent girls like you, but at this moment, I just want to hear what you have to say, all of it. In fact, I'll pay you, like as if I was Mr Norton the newspaperman, paying you for an article. So here's five shillings, and there'll be another five bob for you tomorrow, if you meet me back here in the hotel, four o'clock sharp. I know you're feeling tiddly, so I've written the details down on this bit of paper, all right? Till tomorrow then?'

He's a plausible cove, for a Man in Grey.

Journals of Harold Davidson
London
27 June 1931

A delightful evening. Took Barbara to the Apollo to see new Edgar Wallace, *The Squeaker*. B, though seldom roused to anything so demonstrative as applause, spontaneously clapped hands on seeing the set of the nightclub scene. Obviously her idea of Paradise. Must urge her to read *Vaults of Heaven*, fascinating anthology of inspiring essays on afterlife, eternity, the firmament, et cetera, far more edifying visions of our final resting place.

Greatly disturbed, however, by discovery that I am still being followed around London (and possibly at home in Norfolk too) by paid spies of the Church. This man Dashwood, whom I heard about from Mimi and Mr Reynolds, evidently an emissary of Bishop Bertram Pollock, came to Stiffkey asking questions, until Mr Reynolds threw him out. This man 'Timothy', with his pack of lies about Barbara and his shabby enquiries in shops. The appalling Major Hammond and his drunken rants about me to everyone in the parish. They are defilers of my cloth, thwarters of my mission, nay-sayers in the Lord's temple. They have been ranged about me like so many prowling lions, as I – an innocent Daniel – continue at my prayers and devotions, undistracted and unmarked by their spiteful claws.

The snooping man Timothy (O curséd name!) evidently wishes to make capital from my relationship with Miss Harris. He is a typical perpetrator of the eighth deadly sin – To See Evil Where None Exists. I shudder to think what fell inventions and barmaid tittle-tattle he will take back to his paymasters. He may even try to sell it to the newspapers through Mr Norton, my one-time devotee; perhaps I can rely on Norton's good sense and vestigial loyalty.

Then there is Rose. I thought it a kindness for us to remove Rose from her dismal incarceration in her parents' house, and take her under my and Barbara's wing for a day (I speak as if we were a married couple!). We enjoyed a pleasant picnic in Green Park, I took the ladies boating on the Serpentine (my constant recreation on these summer afternoons) and took them to St Leonard's Church at Lancaster Gate to pray for the soul of poor Nancy Thwaite, a former associate of Rose's in her Charing Cross days, who has died of an aggravated hernia.

Conversation was a little halting, once the girls had exhausted their fund of shared information about Libby and Dolores and Joanna and Sally, and exchanged tales of Nancy's tenure at Mrs Carter's establishment – but then Barbara indiscreetly mentioned that she had 'moved in' to my cramped quarters in Shepherd's Bush. Just as she was itemising the vulgar *objects d'art* with which she planned to decorate the shelves, a scarlet colour came to Rose's blanched cheeks, and an alarming hostility took control of her. From being, for hours, a happy member of our three-musketeer band, she spoke as a suspicious outsider, demanding, 'How long has this been going on?' and similar crass enquiries.

Barbara explained that she had nowhere to live after rejecting the sweaty advances of Mr Lake while I – though feeling no need to justify myself to a soul – murmured to Rose that of course any of my needy charges were always welcome to share my unprepossessing bolthole. She seemed mollified, we had tea and cakes at the Fuller's shop off Piccadilly, and I brought up the evening's entertainment, and the meeting with a newspaper journalist.

'You must not be concerned about him, Rose,' I reassured her.

'Some of these pressmen are good fellows and can write gratifying reports of our various enterprises. The thing is, not to be hostile with them. You should tell them, as straight as you can, all you know about whatever villainy you have witnessed lately – without, of course, involving my name or Miss Harris's or our friends.' I encouraged her to come to the meeting with Mr Norton, so she could hear my explanation of charitable assistance and the pursuit of virtue in an irreligious age so she could speak of it in a similar vein, should anyone ever ask her about it.

But alas! Along the way to the Cheshire Cheese, she learned that I had procured only a brace of tickets to the Wallace play and was unable to include her. At this news, she grew heated and complained of being 'left out' like a schoolchild denied a place on a Sunday-school treat. Her protestations continued inside the pub, and I was glad the pressman paid no attention to her.

Dear Rose – she was indeed very dear to me for years. Since the first day I met her, over ten years ago – she fainted, practically into my arms, in Leicester Square, partly from heat exhaustion and partly from alcoholic poisoning – I have looked after her, treated her like something between a daughter and a patient. I try to explain that her chronic bouts of nymphomania, which have involved her in performing sex with scores of strangers, naturally lessen her self-respect, her poise and grace. This always leads to weeping and remorse, so I mostly eschew the moral homily which the occasion deserves, and settle for calling her 'incorrigible'.

I will call on her, as arranged. I hope that she got home safely from the Cheshire Cheese.

Letter from Mr Inglebert Thole
London
29 June 1931

Dear Mr Dashwood,

Very frustrating, this last couple of weeks. I thought we had a result, only to see it slip through my fingers.

Alerted by Charles Norton of the *Evening Standard*, I interrogated

Miss Rose Ellis, of Camden, London NW1, long-term associate of Subject. She sang like a bird in the initial stages, and we have sworn testimony at last that:

1. Subject was in the habit of calling on young women late at night, sometimes sleeping all night with them, albeit on top of coverlet, apparently in his vicar gear.
2. Subject had serious sexual encounters (details unspecified) with Miss Ellis in course of trips to Paris, where considerable sums of money (embezzled from charities?) were spent in clothing and garment shops.
3. Subject gave Miss Ellis false name – 'Mrs Malone' – during walkabouts and vacations abroad, introducing her to strangers as his 'secretary' and leading them to assume innocent relationship when it damn well wasn't.
4. Miss Ellis now 'hates' Subject for abandoning her, like philandering husband or casual lover, and would agree to feature in any court appearance that sought to determine his strength of character, moral make-up, etc.
5. Subject announced he was prepared to give up wife, children, home and livelihood for love of Miss Ellis, later retracting this offer as romantic and unworkable. Possible Breach of Promise suit?

Trouble is, while we have sworn testimony, we also have her sworn retraction. She returned to the Strand Palace Hotel next day, four o'clock on the dot, claimed the residue of her ten shillings pay, read the sworn statement I'd had typed up and flatly refused to sign it. Said she'd been forced to invent a tissue of lies while under the influence of alcohol, and there was no truth in any of it.

Oh really, said I. No truth in the suggestion that Mr D often came to your bed, that he lay upon the coverlet quaking with lust and frustration, that on several occasions he shared your bed in a beneath-the-sheets way, and that he took you on holiday to European capitals.

'No, sir,' she said. 'I dunno why I said them things.'

Perhaps because you knew them to be true?

'But they're not true, sir. Mr Davidson was very good to me. He looked after me. For years and years he found me places to live. Him and Mrs Davidson, she used to order the maid to run a nice deep hot bath whenever I travelled up the Rectory, and she worried about me and saw that I ate tons of vegetables at supper.'

You are saying (I asked, a little put out by this revelation) that the rector's wife knew of your relationship with her husband?

'She knew I was one of his best girls. He told me I was a special case, sent by the Lord to try his superhuman powers of patience and moral strength.'

What do you think he meant by that?

'I think it was because I was always a bit confused. Some of his ladies, you see, were prozzies and they went on doing it in spite of everything he said, and some were prozzies and he stopped them doing it by finding them places to work, like a bakery or a clothes shop, and some of them were just poor girls who he thought might go on the game. But me, I was always confused because I'd be a good girl most of the time, and then suddenly I'd go a bit mad for a few days and I'd go with lots of men, like I couldn't control myself, and I never made much money out of it, so I'd come home a bit wretched and my mum would shout prayers over me and then throw me out, and I'd have to go to the rector and he'd take me in and stay up late talking to me about why I behaved like that, like it was a kind of madness.'

And he would encourage you to share his bed and perform upon your person unspeakable acts of darkness?

'No! He wouldn't! He wasn't like that!'

I'm sorry. You have already told us how things stood between you.

'But you're twisting it! The rector wasn't like my boyfriend. He was a pal. We liked hanging around together. He made me laugh. He took me places.'

You as good as told us that he had some form of sex with you, which you are now striving to deny.

'No I'm not. He just kissed me a lot because he was fond of me.'

We are wasting time. I need you to sign this statement, a faithful record of our conversation of last evening.

'But I didn't know I was saying all this. I mean, I was a bit upset. And him, the journalist, he kept buying me port until I didn't know what I was saying. I'm not signing nothing.'

I am sorry, Miss Ellis, but it is not possible to change your mind. The due process of law has already begun. Its awful gears and engines have started to grind. You cannot hope to influence or retard its movement by prevarication.

'I ain't signing anything. You can fuck off and take your sworn statement with you.'

Have you heard, Miss Ellis, of the words 'conspiracy to pervert the course of justice'?

'No. What's that?'

It means bending the truth until the truth can't be seen properly. It means withholding information that would help us get at the truth. And it means deliberately refusing to do your duty. If you are guilty of any of these things, you could be in serious trouble. It could mean going to jail.

'Jail? But I'm telling the truth!'

You have just informed me that your statements of last night were untrue.

'The statements – they weren't what I meant to say. About me and Harold and us being together in France.'

So you lied to me. This will not look good in court, Miss Ellis, not good at all.

'But I wasn't lying. It was true what I said, only I didn't mean to say it. And you've bent it all out of shape.' She began to cry, noisily. 'Look, take down this now, I'll give you a whole new statement, and that will do in court, won't it? Won't it? Oh please . . .'

I'm sorry, Miss Ellis. If you have admitted to lying in your statement last night, I have no reason to believe anything you wish to say today. I put it to you that you are incapable of distinguishing truth from fiction.

'(Loud weeping.) I wish I'd never got into this. I hate you. I hate it all, you and the bloody newspapers. It's all men, isn't it? All you bloody men, using girls, and poking and prodding them, and making them drunk, and calling them liars and making them sign things and trying to put them in jail.'

Just sign this simple statement of what you tell us is the truth and we'll be out of your hair for good.

And you know what? With a fresh little burst of weeping, she grabbed the pen, signed the bottom of the statement R. Ellis, flung down the pen so a long ink blot like an exclamation mark crashed on to the paper, and fled out the door.

Journals of Harold Davidson
London
29 June 1931

Lunch with Monsignor George in Holborn, round the corner from St Ethelreda's, and trip to Runaway Boys' Retreat (Don Stupendo in high spirits; his studies have moved on apace; is now attempting to read *Swallows and Amazons*, which will introduce him to a race of English people never before encountered, i.e. children of the *haute bourgeoisie* at their hearty play), tea in the Strand with Lady Fenella, who was not unfriendly, but *distraite* because of forthcoming trip to Florence, then I took myself to the Haymarket to view the screen production of *Dr Jekyll and Mr Hyde*.

I do not know how to account for the current filmic obsession with evil. It is everywhere. Films about men with guns and hats, films about organised crime in America – *Public Enemy*, *Little Caesar*, *I Am a Fugitive from a Chain Gang* – are mirrored by a curious macabre European fascination with inhuman horrors. The dark, menacing *Dracula* – about a Romanian count who metamorphoses into a bloodsucking vampire bat and preys upon young women in night attire – has been closely followed by the looming figure of *Frankenstein*, a man constructed from pieces of human body, into whom life is breathed by an electricity-harnessing scientist. What is there in these films to entertain an audience? Do lovers of theatrical spectacle, of music, wit and gaiety, submit themselves to being frightened, like small children in a nursery? I feel a homily on the subject would be important: how our secular world apparently needs to invent new devils, new Satans, to fear and against which to fight, as if they would rather not confront the true Satan who wreaks evil in the world and who is located in the hearts of men, installed therein by a loving God for us to encourage or to ignore as we choose. The Romanian bat and the German spare-parts creation are the stuff of children's picture books; persons of intelligence or sensibility should not be troubled by their foolish face-pulling.

Dr Jekyll is a different matter. Of course I know Stevenson's book, which was published when I was a boy, and I have often pondered its message, which flirts with Christian doctrine without ever becoming explicit. It confronts the presence of evil in every human being, without mentioning Original Sin; but Jekyll's desire to extract every evil instinct from one's moral make-up has echoes of the Catholic confession, where bad behaviour is, as it were, externalised from the sinner until he or she may leave the church feeling newborn, shriven, freshly laundered. In the story, of course, we're shown only the consequences of extracting badness from a human being, and watching as it wreaks havoc upon society. We are never shown the other side – the man who is all goodness. Perhaps it is just as well, for whom should he resemble but Jesus Christ our Saviour?

I had no lively hope of hearing a philosophical discussion about good and evil on the screen, but looked forward to seeing how they would portray the transformation into Hyde. It was disappointing – Fredric March, a handsome, lightweight matinée idol, played Jekyll as an unlikeably conceited, impetuous, finger-wagging, hectoring young man with an indecent determination to marry his fiancée sooner than her father wished. His desire for the lady was dressed up as an innocent impulse to enter the nuptial state sooner rather than later; but one look at March's burning eyes told you the nature of his true impatience. Mr Hyde, by contrast, made no bones about his desires: they were for drink (champagne, forsooth), music halls, women and violence. It was disheartening to find that the filmmakers, given the task of portraying the embodiment of pure evil on screen, could come up with nothing more alarming than a grinning, ape-like hooligan with a mouthful of sharp teeth and terrible table manners. This was not a portrayal of evil, but of Neanderthal primitivism, the primacy of raw feeling over moral self-restraint.

The scene that most disturbed me, however, was one in which Dr Jekyll rescues a prostitute called Ivy from an assailant, carries her up to her quarters and ministers to her. She is unhurt, but – discovering that a handsome, young, upper-class doctor is attending upon her – adopts a variety of seductive poses, apparently to lure the saintly quack into her bed. She was played by the lovely Miriam Hopkins, who enacted a scene of such wanton lubricity, I scarcely knew where to look. She sits on the bed, hitches up her skirts, removes shoes, stockings and garters, and flings them at Jekyll. When in bed – and *stark naked* – she kisses him impetuously as he stands near her. And as he leaves, the scene ends with Ivy sitting on the edge of the bed, swinging one gartered leg back and forth, softly cooing, 'Come back . . .'

I confess I was forced to apply a handkerchief to my perspiring brow. At first, I was shocked. But as I reflected, I saw how important it was to portray the moral quagmire that threatens people such as Jekyll – and even myself.

Ivy's swinging leg represents the temptation that often accompanies the giving of aid to young women in trouble. Their natural gratitude can tip over into something that counts, in their sordid world, as a gift – I have heard it referred to as 'a free tumble'. Naturally, one does not encourage such sordid overtures. That would be to confirm that the only currency or identity the ladies possess is a sexual one. Sometimes, however, to see on the faces of, say, poor Elsie or Bridget, their gratitude at the change in their circumstances, one would be churlish to refuse all offers of 'repayment', provided the quid pro quo they have in mind is no more than a kiss, a tender squeeze, a heartfelt hug. There is no harm in that. Sometimes it may extend into their requiring one to stay by their side as they sleep, as any benefactor would do, and I am happy to perform that kindly function.

The swinging leg that haunts Dr Jekyll's mind does not turn *all* decent men into Mr Hydes. We do not all behave like this. As the great Emerson has told us, the only reward for virtue is virtue.

Camden Hospital, Eversholt Road, London NW1
29 June 1931

CASUALTY DEPARTMENT REPORT
Re: Miss Rose Ellis. Date of birth: 21 February 1900

This unfortunate woman was admitted at 9.45pm, suffering from alcoholic poisoning and a borderline drug overdose.

She was discovered in a state of collapse in an alley near the George Tavern, Mornington Crescent, where, it was learned, she had spent the evening drinking gin and cider until ejected at 8.30pm. Witness who brought her to the hospital, Mr Geoffrey Ware, commercial traveller, said she had approached him and attempted 'to give him money', namely a ten-shilling note. Mr Ware recalls her speaking, apparently at random, 'about Judas'. As she became increasingly incoherent, he suspected that her mind might be befuddled with medicaments as well as drink, and brought her here.

Initial examination was hindered by patient's copious vomiting on the floor. Established that she had taken '10 or 12' sachets of codeine powder, procured from unknown source, but seemed confused as to her actual intentions. Kept repeating, 'What have I done?'

Applied stomach pump with reasonably productive results. Bed rest, sedative. Currently occupying bed 14, F Ward, under observation.

Present state: Stable, comfortable. Out of danger.

Letter from the Right Reverend Bertram Pollock
Bishop's House, Norwich, Norfolk
10 July 1931

My dear Henry,

Your letter brought excellent news. I had almost given up on the surveillance gentlemen, but they seem to have plucked some form of victory from the jaws of defeat.

For a proper case to be put at the consistory court, we need have only one charge to be answered – provided, of course, that it is unanswerable by the defendant. As you point out, the testimony of Miss Rose Ellis is damning and apparently conclusive, especially the confession that Davidson took her away for secret vacations in France under an assumed name. There is no gathering of twelve adult persons anywhere in the British Isles that would not infer some illicit sexual connection from this recital of circumstances.

But as you say, the witness – who appears to be a woman of remarkably weak moral courage – later tried to retract her confessions, and has tried to maintain that they were extracted under duress, under the influence of drink and with alternating threats and offers of payment. This combination of coercion and cajoling will not look good in court, should somebody try to bring it up for public scrutiny. It is vital, therefore, that we spread the risk of failure by multiplying the accusations we can bring to bear on Davidson.

Please try to think creatively about how we may present the worst possible case in court against this man. He has been a thorn in the flesh of the Church of England for long enough, and I wish him gone forthwith.

I know I can depend on you.

Yours in Christ,

+ Bertram

Journals of Harold Davidson
London
15 July 1931

Barbara and I have fallen into a settled routine. She rises at 8 a.m., and pursues her ablutions while I take possession of the bed for an hour or so, or she lies quietly by my side perusing *Reynolds News* and reading out any supposedly heartwarming items that catch her eye, even while I am drifting in and out of sleep.

Sometimes we both fall unconscious and wake, arms twined around each other, some time after 10 a.m. It is a sign of my new lightness of heart that I do not care, as I once cared so deeply, that I have wasted half the morning in idle slumber. Not when I awake to find Miss Harris's breath mingled with mine, and her warm forehead pressed so close to my raddled brow, as though we are thinking the same thoughts.

She is difficult in the mornings, a little grumpy and stamp-footed, but of course she has been accustomed to a life of wastrel self-indulgence. But I understand the need to be patient with her, and I am the soul of forbearance. The deep joy of having her share my modest living quarters, even for a few weeks, eclipses any other joy I have experienced in recent memory. The sight of Miss Harris wrapped in a bath towel, with one foot on the coal-scuttle beside the grate, snipping her toenails, as wholly absorbed as one of Degas's ballerinas at her toilette, is a weekly treat. So is her habit, of a Friday afternoon, of insisting we go 'window-shopping' in Shepherd's Bush, traversing the Uxbridge Road, finding two or three fashion emporia where Miss Harris tries on many skimpy frocks, all of them ludicrously outside her or my expenditure bracket, with an insistence that, 'Oh – my friend will pay for it.' 'My friend' indeed!

We have become close, to the extent that I now confide to her things I have told nobody else. She encourages me, for instance, to speak about Mimi – not a conversation topic I choose to air with brothers of the cloth, let alone with young streetwalkers of tender years.

'So, Harold,' she said the other evening, as we sat up late at home, listening to the wireless, 'what's the deal with your wife?'

'The *deal*? Barbara, I wish you would not speak in these frightful Americanisms. What do you wish to know?'

'I want to know when you stopped loving her. When you stopped caring for her, and when you decided hanging around with the likes of Rose and Lily and Sally and that bossy cow Marina was more your sort of thing than being married and being at home bringing up the kids.'

'I am afraid your extreme youth gives you away, Barbara. These are facile assumptions you make about extremely private matters. My wife and I may not be as closely allied in domestic union as we once were,' I told her, 'but this is hardly surprising after twenty-four years of marriage. I have my work in London, of which you, my dear, are both a beneficiary and a shining exemplar. She has our children to raise in Norfolk, and a hundred and one neighbourly actions to be performed every day by the pastor's wife, when he cannot himself be present.'

'Harold,' (her voice took on an unpleasant brassy timbre, like a dog handler addressing a disobedient pedigree chow at Cruft's),'when did you leave her?'

'I never left my wife,' I said fervently. 'Never! I am incapable of doing such a thing. To abandon the only things I love? Impossible! I may have many faults but inconstancy is not one of them. I am as constant as the Northern Star. Why do you think, every weekend, I desert my all-important mission, and my time here in London with you? It is for *her*, as much as for my church and my parishioners.'

'For saving yer face,' put in Barbara, coarsely.

I answered her in measured tones. 'My wife is very important to me. I go home to Stiffkey, to see her and be near her, to learn her news and her appraisal of the children's condition. We have genuine conversations, Miss Harris — nothing your febrile mind could easily comprehend.'

'Yeah, yeah, conversations,' said Barbara rudely. 'Don't tell me you really fret about her all the time, down here in London. "Is she happy?" you ask yourself. "Is she having it off with anyone I know?" Is that what you're thinking about her, when she's not around?'

'Such a question would, I am glad to admit, never enter my head.'

'No? Because it must have entered hers a million times in the last few years. "Harold," she must've thought, "who's he with tonight, eh? Who's he pitching salvation at tonight? Is it one of the girls he's brought to the house, or some other dimwit with big breasts who I haven't met yet?"'

'Such accusations could never be levelled by my wife. She knows that whatever I do is governed by a power outside myself.'

'Oh give over, Harold. Ring the other one for a change. All she knows is that you turned away from her, some time in the past, for reasons you won't tell about, and she's had this miserable life since then, up in bleeding Stiffkey, bringing up — how many children is it? — four? five? — on no money, and lots of debts, and mostly no husband by her side. All I'm asking, Harold, just out of interest, is why you turned your back on her —'

I turned and snapped at her: 'You absurd woman! Can you not get it into your head that at no time did I leave anybody? The plain fact is that she left me.'

There was an awkward silence in the room.

'Go on then,' said Barbara, all agog. 'What happened?'

So I told her about it. It was 1915. I had signed up to join the Navy as ship's chaplain, and I sailed away in May on Her Majesty's Ship *Excalibur*, a pleasingly legendary name for an epic enterprise, taking us down the long coast of Africa, through the Indian Ocean. She stood on the quay by my side at Tilbury, and we parted very lovingly. I remember bestowing a fond kiss upon her lips as she clung on to her gold hat in the spring sunshine. I promised to return in one piece, and she said, 'I'll be waiting' – a simple declaration, but one that was to fester in my heart for years to come afterwards.'

'But why're you telling me all this, Harold?' Barbara asked. 'I thought you just said, in big capital letters, it was about her leaving you.'

'I was away for eighteen months,' I explained. 'In Bombay, where I dined with maharajas and recited dramatic monologues for their families; then North Africa and the Arab tribes. I became part of an important initiative to unite the tribes and bind them to the cause of the Allies in the Great War. This was vital work to the outcome of the war, Barbara.'

'Yeah, I believe you. I'm still waiting for the point about how your wife left *you* while you were gallivanting with the Arabs. Were you even in touch with her while you were away at the war?'

'We corresponded as much as we were able, and as much as war security allowed. She sent me long letters, full of everyday dramas about Sheilagh and Nugent and the little ones, and their lives with my aunt Gertie, who had a house in Windsor.'

'It must've been a bit boring for her, cooped up there with the kids and a country aunt,' said Barbara. 'It'd drive me nuts.'

'Mimi evidently shared your point of view. She took up nursing – mostly from public-spirited motives, but perhaps also in order to be granted some hours' respite from demanding children.'

'Harold,' said my auditor. 'the point of all this . . . ?'

'And then, Miss Harris, since you are so keen to reach the denouement of this sorry tale, I came home to discover that my wife, my wild Irish swan, had in my absence forged an alliance with a stranger.'

'Bloody hellfire,' said Miss Harris. 'And you hadn't a clue about what she was up to?'

'I had no inkling,' I said with a touch of iciness. 'Being at the time in Alexandria, engaged in subtle negotiations about the course of the war, I was scarcely in a position to intuit my wife's drift towards infidelity.'

'Had she done anything like it before?' asked Barbara, the ridiculous child. I had no way of indicating, to a young mind coarsened by early exposure to careless sexual misbehaviour, the delight of spending eight years in the company of a woman you love – eight years of empathy and support, of midnight conversations in bed, about song lyrics we have enjoyed or the excitement of the coming Easter vigil; eight years of being allowed to watch her brush her hair before her vanity mirror, and climb into her blue gown for a concert where she would sing Puccini like a young girl; eight years of wearily consuming plates of cold roast lamb by her side at the end of an evening of parish revels; eight years of combustible arguments about the meaning of William Blake poems or the legacy of Cardinal Manning (whom I revered and she certainly did not). My wife was Irish, a suffragist and a reformist thinker, three differences between us that could have threatened our harmony. We used to celebrate our differences, but a gulf opened up between us that cancelled all the mutual understanding that had gone before. I knew that, although God could forgive her sin, I could not.

I told myself that our circumstances had drastically altered, that I had been away in North Africa, that she had been working at nursing tasks in Windsor, and that, in these altered circumstances, different behaviour patterns would become apparent. I told myself she was the mother of my four children, someone to whom I owed the utmost loyalty; then into my head would come the question of how much loyalty she had shown me when I was away fighting for my country in the Dardanelles and the sand dunes of the Devil's Anvil Desert on the outskirts of Akaba, and she was –

'Screwing some corner-boy, stay-at-home coward?' said Miss Harris vulgarly.

'He was, I believe, a soldier,' I replied. 'A patient with whose sufferings she sympathised beyond the limits of nursing propriety, and who then returned to the war.' By this stage, I had no more words of condemnation or explanation for my wife.

'And he told her what? That if only she'd wait for him, he'd be back after the war to claim her hand in marriage? She must've been daft.'

'Far from *daft*, Barbara,' I admonished her. 'When I saw her again, upon returning from duty, she was heartbroken.'

'Because the bastard hadn't been in touch, surprise, surprise?'

'Because he had been killed in action.'

'Oh. I see.'

'No, you do not see. It was an awkward and difficult time, where cheap accusations were bandied back and forth.'

'Accusations from who?'

'From the Church. They encouraged me to leave her. They said they would look kindly on a separation.'

'What business was it of theirs?'

'It is not something I wish to discuss, Barbara. I find it . . . hard to rake over the past like this, and I wish you would desist from these enquiries.'

'OK then. But you didn't leave her, your wife I mean, did you?'

'I planned to go away for a time, to India, taking the children but leaving my wife to consider her future. But it came to nothing, and we returned to Skiffkey two years later, bound together as a family, with all this sordid business behind us. So no, in the end, I did not leave her.'

'But you said she left you. So that ain't true either.'

'Only in a manner of speaking.'

'You're talking riddles, Harold. I'm going to bed.'

2.30 a.m. There has been silence in the flat for the past hour. I went out for a stroll on the Green while Miss Harris was at her toilette, and smoked a cigar and wrapped my greatcoat around me in the evening chill. Two or three strollers were abroad, one with a dog, but no sign of any immoral solicitation. My head ached with memories of long ago, and that awful time when I stood on the quay at Folkestone, grizzle-bearded and exhausted from my excursion to war, glad and wearily elated to be home at last, and found no one to meet me there but my cousin Mortimer, Aunt Gertie's son, who took my bags and said, 'Welcome home, Harold.' We got into his car in an awkward silence. He was never a man for small talk. He could hardly say, 'How was the war?' and I could not think of anything to say except, 'Where is my darling wife?' To which he replied, 'She's at my mum's. But she hasn't been well, Harold, and we thought it best not to disturb her with a long journey.'

I feared some illness had befallen her and pressed him for details. He would only say, 'She hasn't been herself,' and he drove in a doltish silence, my enquiries met with platitudes and 'You'd better ask her that yourself'. After two hours of frustration and gloom, we reached Windsor, and I found Mimi in bed, sedated by Aunt Gertie's family doctor. It was only next day that I found out the truth, as she struggled with the dementia that was beginning to engulf her.

How can I describe the condition wherein I found her? How to summon up the hunted look in her peerless green eyes, as I sought to find again the dear woman I had loved so truly, the gay, carefree songbird who had loved me so blithely, clung to me as a partner, abandoned a life on the stage to be a rector's wife? Even as she told me everything that had occurred, and clutched my hand and asked for forgiveness (which I readily bestowed), I looked in her face and knew that she had gone from me, left me for ever.

I flung the cigar away, its glowing tip arcing across the Green. I have now returned to my modest home, put on my dressing gown and been brooding here in my chair.

A moment ago Barbara awoke.

'Harold?' she said sleepily from the bed. 'Your wife and this soldier boy. Was there a baby? Is that what this is all about?'

'Go to sleep, Barbara,' I said.

CHAPTER 17

Letter from Mrs Moyra Davidson
Stiffkey Rectory
20 September 1931

Dear Oona,

Part of the ceiling came down in the guest bedroom, nearly braining the colonel who sleeps there with young Gordon, his eldest, in the bed beside him. The poor kid used to have his own room along the corridor, but since the debacle with Miss Harris and Enid the maid last year, Gordon's father felt it only right to keep an eye on his confused son during the hours of nightfall. Anyway it's been such an age since anyone looked at the roof, there must have been damp set in, for a nasty patch opened up where the ceiling meets the wall above the windows, but I ignored it and told the maid not to trouble about it. But then after the big thunderstorm of last Friday night, when I stood for a whole half-hour in front of the open kitchen door gazing out at the sheets of water cascading down, there was this awful crash and the colonel appears all disarrayed in his nightgown and says, Mrs D, this is the last straw, I was nearly killed by falling masonry, my son has sustained a wound in the leg and we must call an ambulance. But he couldn't use the telephone because it was cut off again this day fortnight ago, I told Harold on Sunday but he waved my entreaties away, so Nugent went next door for Mr Reynolds and he called for help and a white van arrived to transport the stricken boy away to Holt Infirmary, the colonel went with him saying he could not stay here a minute longer, he will pack his things and depart, and he made a bit of a speech about his sorrow that a hospitality he had taken for granted from the rector should be so woefully betrayed, something like that, I wasn't listening really for the deafness in my left ear has spread now to the right until I'm enclosed in a horrid box of silence and though God knows I am used to angry faces pushing into mine in the front door of my own house by strangers coming here at all hours, I'm glad in a way that I can hardly hear them any more and their demands for money, and if the colonel and his boys should depart in the morning bag and baggage, sure what harm in the long run, hasn't he been a damned great cuckoo in the nest for years and wouldn't we all be better off with a few less mouths to feed?

After he'd gone I couldn't sleep for fear that more ceilings might come down on my head, and before you start giving out to me, of *course* I worried about Arnold and Pammie, so I gave Nugent instructions to bring them down to the back parlour and make up a couple of beds for them before the fire, and he said, what fire, Ma, there hasn't been a fire in this house for months, and I said, don't give me cheek, go and find an electric fire and turn on both bars and look after them there's a good boy, your mother is tired. He said, do you not think it would help if you stopped drinking brandy and looked after them yourself, the cheeky little bollox, and I said, no, you do it, you've done little enough in this house for months, and there was a row and I said, DO NOT ARGUE WITH YOUR MOTHER, SHE NEEDS A LITTLE REST, and he stamped off in a rage but at least it was done, I think I heard the dragging of mattresses and so on, and crying, but I was too tired to go and investigate so I sat here and nodded off by the Rayburn.

He is a good boy, but fractious when he's hungry, and there hasn't been a sparrow's worth of supper in this house for weeks except for the bananas and biscuits that I bought in the village, the former a bit speckledy and the latter a bit broken, but that's why they were cheap, and Nugent does his best to bring home a few sausages and spuds at the weekend, only for H to drop by on Sunday on his flying visit and eat them all and say, Mmm but how deliciously tasty how can you say everyone is hungry when there is all this food, soon there will be Harvest Festival produce all over the church and we shall live on that . . . It takes me back, Oona, to the days when you and I were young and idealistic and ran a soup kitchen for the down-and-outs in Palmerston Park, and how glad the smelly old fellers were for bit of bread and dripping. Now, isn't it myself that'd be glad of a sup of bread and dripping if it was available anywhere in the village. But how would I explain myself?

I must busy myself, Oona, because today I remembered when thinking once more about the *Midsummer Night's Dream* evening and the Princess of Wales coming a-calling that it was 1907 when it happened, which means next year is the twenty-fifth anniversary of that glorious event and we must have a party to mark the occasion, with flowers and a band playing, and maybe theatricals in the trees and all the grand people from London must be invited, but how we are to pay for such a thing Christ only knows, may the Devil damn me black for blaspheming.

Your beloved,
Mimi

Journals of Harold Davidson
London
26 October 1931

I believe that I have been the victim of an attempted assassination. I cannot be mistaken in this.

I was walking down the Strand after visiting Lady Fenella at the hotel, where she received me most agreeably after her late sojourn in the Tuscan hills but could give few assurances of financial assistance until I can persuade her that the money is 'genuinely' finding its way to a charitable institution, rather than being directed 'into the purses of mere trollops'. I thought we understood each other better. (Has some emissary of this Dashwood man been calling and speaking against me?)

Anyway, I was walking past Coutts's Bank when I heard a commotion in the roadway. An omnibus had slewed across the far side and come to a diagonal stop, and a ferocious beeping noise was issuing from some automobile denied its urgent passage somewhere behind it. Beside the Adelphi Theatre I crossed the Strand, paused on the raised 'island' betwixt the lanes and stepped forward in front of the stranded bus. Out of nowhere, a long black car came howling around the side of the bus, its tyres buckling from the speed of its passage, and aimed itself at me! With an instinctive response, I leapt sideways back on to the safety of the concrete promontory and felt the curt blow of its wing mirror square on my elbow. The pain was excruciating. As I glanced up, I fancied I saw the face of the man called Timothy looking straight at me, his eyes narrowed. Then the long black car was gone, down towards Trafalgar Square. Two ladies, crossing the street at the same time, enquired if I was hurt. I so nearly cried out to them, 'It is nothing – only that the Bishop of Norwich is trying to kill me!'

What am I to do? It has taken weeks to recover my mental equilibrium after learning that his purple eminence has had me followed by private detectives, without a word of explanation as to why, or to what crime I have committed. But I will be hanged if I cannot venture through my familiar London walks without being mown down in the street.

I have much to do. Lily B needs a new place of employment. Dolores is back on the streets of Ealing. My network of rescued girls needs constant attention, for fear they will succumb to boredom and its attendant vices. Bridie Queenan needs some blister ointment after running away from home and sleeping rough in Hampstead Garden Suburb. One more push will rescue Blanche the octoroon from the clutches of Madame Carter. I will not be intimidated. I shall write to the bishop in person.

Letter from the Right Reverend Bertram Pollock
Bishop's House, Norwich, Norfolk
2 November 1931

My dear Henry,

I have received a letter from Davidson, addressing me in the most gallingly familiar terms ('Bertie' indeed) and laying out a litany of complaints against me – and you.

He has, it seems, encountered your Mr Thole once again. He writes to ask whether I know anything about 'this unwelcome surveillance' – which is bad enough – but he claims an attempt on his life was made last week, an encounter with a motor car in the Strand, with Mr Thole at the wheel. He does not suggest I was responsible for commissioning the assault, but asks my 'protection' against 'whatever forces are ranged against me'. The implication that I might know something of these 'forces' is infamous. I know nothing of the behaviour of the agents under your control, and do not wish to. But I *do* know that you, Henry, have set certain matters in train that now may be out of your, or my, control. Heaven forfend that any wayward behaviour, perhaps leading to the endangering of life, could be laid at my door. It is an alarming prospect. It threatens the moral credibility of my office and of the Church of England.

I shall reply to Davidson, distancing myself from any knowledge of Thole or motor cars or private detectives. But some direct action must now be taken. We have evidence against him, of a sketchy and incomplete sort. I wish you now, Henry, to approach him directly and confront him with his history of wrongdoing, in the hope that he will cave in and admit to his many crimes. He is, for all his bluster, a weak man who knows of my disapproval. I suspect he may be brought to heel and made to resign his office if you can sufficiently intimidate him with hints that All Is Known and that disgrace may follow his non-cooperation. Do it now, Henry. I wish to see a swift end to this chronicle of misbehaviour.

Your friend in Christ,

+ Bertram

Journals of Harold Davidson
London
7 November 1931

Three letters in one morning. Their content has given me much food for thought.

One from the bishop, replying to my plea for succour. 'Dear Reverend Davidson,' he begins with pompous formality – how long ago was it, when we were Bertie and Harold? – 'I was so sorry to hear of your unfortunate circumstances. You sound, if I may say so, like a man long deprived of sleep, of comfort and spiritual solace. From what I have gleaned of your activities in Norfolk and London, your schedule of activities would grind down many a man less energetic than yourself. Nobody yields to me in admiration for your unsleeping ministry among the homeless and desperate. Yet I wonder if your devotion to pastoral duty has been to blame for the parlous mental state you find yourself in. Nothing less than an upheaval in the brain – that most unknowable organ! – could lead you to such thoughts as you seem currently to entertain: of pursuit, of being watched and followed in the street, the recent conviction that someone tried to murder you in the Strand! Were you, my dear fellow, to enjoy a period of refreshing sleep, even perhaps spend a week or two in a retreat house well away from your "beat" in London, you would, I am sure, wake to realise that you are in the grip of a paranoia that has clouded your judgement.' Much episcopal chuntering follows this unhelpful advice, together with some addresses of sanatoria in High Wycombe and Tunbridge Wells, and he signs off, 'Your friend, Bertram'. To receive a communication of any sort from the Most High would, in former years, have delighted me. But this farrago of duplicity has only hardened my heart against the Established Church, until I feel ashamed to be its agent, its employee and apologist.

There. I have said it now. I have fallen out of love with my own masters. What now, without their benign wings above me, will drive my chariot in the future?

The second letter is from Dashwood. It is curt to the point of rudeness. 'Dear Davidson,' it runs. 'I wish to speak to you in person, on a matter of some gravity effecting your benefice. Please present yourself at my offices in Holborn as early as possible after the Christmas services. Yours truly, Henry Dashwood.'

I assume he means 'affecting'. But what subject can be so serious concerning the parish of Stiffkey and Morston that requires a summons to his sinister headquarters? I am in the dark. But I suspect mischief here. I must be on my guard.

The third letter is from Mrs Reynolds. It is about Mimi. 'I think you ought to know, Rector,' she writes with her habitual directness, 'that things are going bad up here. Colonel Du Dumaine has left, taking his boys because the roof has caved in. Nugent has found himself a ladyfriend down Holkham way and is not often here, only to buy some groceries, the young ones are freezing in their beds downstairs. And Mrs D is *not well*. I hate to advise you of this by letter, but she has taken to drink and spends the week indoors, writing letters, only going out at night to collect dead leaves and bring them home, never changing her clothes. You may not see this on weekends when you are occupied on church business, but the house is beginning to smell and there is no food. Please do something. It is with a heavy heart that I write to you like this. Your friend, Anne Reynolds.'

Drink? Mimi? Impossible. She has always been most abstemious, controlled in domestic management, emphatically clean in her habits. Is she unwell? I have noticed her deafness worsening in recent months, of course, but attributed it to her reluctance to talk with me about unsavoury matters such as creditors, money, the departure of servants, et cetera. If something is wrong with her, I must see to it very soon. Without the stability of her presence at the Rectory, I could not pursue my metropolitan initiatives with half the vigour I command. I shall look into it this very weekend.

Notebooks of Charlie Norton, *Evening Standard*
London
7 November 1931

Haven't heard a word from Mr Thole since our exciting evening at the pub with the rector, and our little chat afterwards with Rosie the down-and-out prozzie with the big mouth and the thirst for port. I was good enough to deal him in on my interview with the girl, only to see it aborted because of his insistent ways with her, and what's more he wouldn't let me come to his second chat with her in which she was going to reveal all about the trips abroad and the sex and everything. This is MY story he's interfered in. He owes me. But all he'll say on the phone is that neither of us can go ahead with it because she's only gone and denied everything she said on the first night!

Listen, mush, I said, it may be a problem for you getting a case all watertight for whoever it is you're working for. But I'm a reporter, and the little Rose party was singing away like a budgie for an hour, and I wouldn't have a qualm about carrying a story along the lines of CLERGYMAN MADE ME HIS MISTRESS CLAIMS WEEPING DRESSMAKER, it's a bit saucy for the *Standard* I know, but I could have run it if I'd had a bit more time with the girl, got some dates and times and places. But Mr Thole promises a lot. Says, with a tap on his long nose, that this will be a much bigger story if I wait. Says he and some other private dicks have been collecting evidence for ages against the horny padre, and they're working for some high-up churchman, give it a month and you'll be the first to know. I've heard this rigmarole before from people who just want stories hushed up, but Thole, I think he may be telling the truth.

And call me sentimental but I like the old rector. He's obviously as dodgy as a pink turnip what with all the brasses he hangs out with, and the iffy cheques he cashes in pubs (and where the hell *does* all the money come from?), but I'd feel bad to go landing him in the shite because of what one drunken woman says just because he went off to a play without her one night. So I'm hoping Thole will keep his word and I won't have to open the *Mirror* next week and see the whole drama splashed across a bloody double-page spread.

London
9 November 1931

Just after I wrote that last entry, on Saturday, I ran into Barbara in the Elephant & Castle. She was buying cushions in Cadwallader's, the cheap furnishings store, where I'd gone to get Ma's armchair upholstered.

'Hello,' I said. 'Nice cushions. What's that material?'

'It's proper velvet, this is,' she said, stroking the green surface like a cat in her arms. 'None of your old rubbish. What you doing in here? Bit off your usual beat, innit?' So I told her about my old mum's rocker, how it had seen better days and was threadbare, and she says, what about that tapestry stuff over there, only six-and-six a yard, very hard-wearing, the pattern doesn't come off after five minutes, and there we were discussing fabrics (not a word I use a lot) as friendly as a couple of old biddies at a Sale of Work. She didn't act like a brass at all. I was careful not to ask her anything about the prozzie world or the rector, in case she got the hump.

'Nice shade of green,' I said. 'You having the living room painted?' (The secret with talking to brasses is, treat them like they're ladies of the manor and they'll talk to you, rather than give you a smack in the mouth.)

'Just making things a bit more homely,' she says. 'I'm in this lovely place in Shepherd's Bush, you know. I've settled down a bit, actually.'

'Oh yes?' I picked my words as gingerly as a Flanders meadow pedestrian. 'Top place, the Bush. Very, er, leafy. I got friends moved in down Holland Park, they're pleased as anything with the place. Every Sunday they nip down to Hammersmith to go boating on the Thames.'

'I'm at a bit of a loose end on Sundays, so I go visiting my sister in Notting Hill,' said Barbara. 'Bit run-down of course, but there's nice pubs for a roast lunch.'

I could hardly recognise the bitchy little minx from our first encounter. She'd gone all mumsy and boring and sort of *satisfied with life*.

'You're a bit young to be settling down, ain't you?' I said, daringly. 'Got a rich fiancé lined up, have you?'

She turned her head to me, hugging her two cushions against her seventeen-year-old tits like someone hugging their dreams.

'I got this nice man to look after me, actually. He ain't rich but he treats me real well. We go everywhere together. We stay in sometimes in the evenings, having proper conversations. We're going to find a proper house too, very soon, where we can start a new life.' A tiny sigh escaped her lips. 'With a real garden and everything.'

'Make sure the bedroom walls are green, then, won't you?' I said cheekily. 'You don't want to waste good cushions, do you?'

And bloody hell, she *smiled* at me. I don't know how the rector's done it, but this one's saved all right. What's the word? Rehabilitated. How'd he pull it off? And who's the lucky man?

Journals of Harold Davidson
Stiffkey
14 November 1931

I took an earlier train than usual and arrived early afternoon, to find the house in shocking disarray. Enid and Jennifer, our most recent parlourmaid, have both given their notice and seek positions elsewhere. Patricia is away at art college, made possible by a local scholarship. Arnold and Pamela are looking dreadfully peaky, are grudging and sulky in conversation, poring over their homework in a listless silence in the chilly back parlour, their clothes stinking with mustiness and embrocation, their limbs vitiated and trembling with an ague that the twin-bar electric fire does little to improve.

The Du Dumaines have indeed departed, after many years of the colonel's stolid but reliable company. I tried many times to interest him in my work, but to no very productive end. (He once introduced a ten-shilling note into my hand one morning, as I was leaving the house to catch the London train, with a muttered, 'For the fallen, Harold . . .' as if I were planning to erect a war memorial in the streets of Limehouse.)

Mimi was in the garden, trailing about in *distraite* fashion, touching the ferny extremities of shrubs like a horticultural Lady Macbeth.

'Are there men at the front door, Harold?' she asked by way of greeting. 'If so, I'm not going in. They can stand as long as they like, with their bills of distrainment, or whatever they call them. I have nothing to say.'

'Mimi, there are no bailiffs here. I have borrowed some funds from a recent subvention to the Runaway Boys' Retreat, to pay some outstanding bills, and I promise you will no longer be confronted with, ah, demands.'

'I cannot stand it,' she said, turning dreadfully hurt eyes to mine, the gaze of a hunted animal. 'I explained about the piano, how it was a wedding present from your Aunt Gertie, brought from Harrods at great expense, and how they could certainly not take it away, and they wouldn't listen, and they tried to take it, Harold, but –'

'My dear,' I cried, 'how have you come to this? The servants are departed, the children are malnutritious, malodorous and unhappy, there is no food in the kitchen save some rotting fish and black bananas. How have our fortunes so declined?'

'I didn't use to notice so much, when you weren't here all week,' she said sadly. 'I mean, I got used to it of course, but it wasn't so obvious because there was always a crowd in the house, the colonel and his boys, and Aunt Gertie coming to stay, and all the children before they took off to college, and people dropping in at all hours, and there weren't enough hours in it for all the things that needed doing in the village, Mrs Russ and her seedlings, Mrs Telfer and her miseries, and if there was five minutes together, I'd look in on Anne next door, and it was a great life because it was passing by all the while and you'd never notice it. And then people started to leave, the children and the guests and the servants and there was more cleaning up to do and I wasn't able for it, and the grocer's boy and the butcher's boy they started appearing on the doorstep with their hands out for money, and as more people kept leaving me, more strangers started arriving, every day, until I was afraid to see what would be at the front door. So I stopped answering it and anyone calling would think the place was empty, so any friends stopped coming round. Only the bailiffs kept on and on.'

I stretched out my hand. 'This is a sorry chronicle . . .'

'So, you see, the house has become like a prison now, where I can't go out for fear of people in the village pointing and saying, "There she is, the madwoman from the Rectory," and I can't stay in the house because I'm scared to hear another ring at the door –'

'Mimi –'

'So I stay in the garden where they can't get at me. If anyone came out, I could pretend to be Titania and live in the trees.'

I moved over to her and took her hand. It was freezing. Her hair hung down over her shoulders in raggedy tails. Her feet were inadequately shod in some flat pumps, wet through. Her long cotton dress was stiff with cold in the November twilight. I was appalled to find her like this. Much has passed between us that was difficult, much that was unforgivable, but I could not leave her to fester in this distracted state one moment longer.

'Have no fear, Mimi,' I whispered urgently. 'I shall not abandon you.'

'Oh, Harold,' she said. 'It is too late. Didn't you abandon me years ago, and never give it a thought?'

'I had my work to do,' I said. 'The Lord's work. You know this.'

'*Me*,' she said, 'Me, me, *me*. You should have looked after me. And kept the children fed and the debtors from the front door. You should have taken better care of the village, and not have people like the major up in arms against you, and everybody talking.'

I was silent for a moment. Then I said, 'I might have taken better care of you if you had not betrayed me a second time.'

'I was not well. A kind of madness came upon me.'

'A kind of madness, my dear, that seems to recur whenever you wish to have sexual intercourse with a stranger.'

She shook her head. 'I was mad with loneliness. You were cold and distant with me. You told me the Church wished us to part. I was overwhelmed with sadness, Harold, as I am now. Will you condemn me all over again?'

I shook my head. 'Let us go indoors, Mimi. I will speak to Mr Reynolds about the heating and put you in a hot bath, and I shall call Mrs McDonald from the village to come and wash all your clothing and the children's too. I shall ask Nugent to bring his car and we shall buy vegetables and fruit and some meat from the market at Holt, for it will still be open. And if you can remember how to cook lamb, we shall dine together like in the old days.'

'It's too late, Harold. I have fallen out of the habit of eating. The children will not speak to me. Some person leaves bottles of liquor on the dining-room table and I take a small sip in the evening, just to stop the feelings of damp creeping up my legs, and the next morning find the bottle empty, and I am confused. I wish only to sleep but I cannot, for fear that another ceiling will come down. But I have written to Oona, my schoolfriend, telling her about my distress. Perhaps she will come and visit me and make it all right.'

My poor wild Irish rose, so confused and woebegone. I folded my arms around her and walked her indoors.

Nugent came at once after my telephone call from the Reynoldses, he is a good boy, and we bought provisions for the house, a quantity of cabbages and runner beans and great floury potatoes, plus enough chump chops to feed an army, and I summoned Mr Evershot from the village to fix the boiler and by 9 p.m. a hint of warmth was creeping into the atmosphere like a thin bedspread pulled over our desolation. We ate together, the five of us, for the first time in an age and although Mimi was mostly silent, the children revived sufficiently to tell small tales of adventures that have lately befallen some village playmates. Told them to Nugent, of course, rather than to me. You would imagine I was a stranger, just walked in off the street.

I cannot believe I have not noticed how, in the space of a few weeks, my home had decayed like some neglected vegetable. The upstairs guest bedroom is like a battle zone, rubble and white dust everywhere. The downstairs back room, where Arnold and Pammie sleep, is a morass of dirty clothing and empty tin cans of beans. The parlour is a sorry sight – every inch of the table crammed with letters, some folded and stuffed into envelopes and addressed to someone called Oona in Dalkey, Co. Dublin, though obviously never sent. Nor is there a sign of any answering letters from this lady, whoever she may be. Around the table lies a sorry platoon of empty brandy bottles, a cheap Spanish variety, bought clandestinely, I have no doubt, with money I left for the children's daily teatime.

The strangest sight, however, is Mimi's bedroom, where the curtains are not just gathered together in the middle but nailed there. At the end of her bed, by the wardrobe, a thousand oak and ivy leaves have been piled up in a dry, sinister mound, clearly brought into the house in armfuls by Mimi herself, in the grip of some pitiful delusion. But what? The children claim not to know. She has now retired to bed, having accepted a hot bath and reviving dinner without protest, and will not tell me. But I must entertain the possibility that my wife, my former beloved, has been for some time gathering together the paraphernalia with which to kill herself by self-immolation.

London
16 November 1931

THINGS TO DO:

1. *Visit Don Stupendo at RBR.*
2. *Call on Sandra, Nellie, Elsie, Blanche, Millie and Eve.*
3. *Appointment with Lady Fenella? (Last 2 cancelled . . .)*
4. *Acquire fresh supplies Elastoplast, mouthwash, bunion cream, lip salve, gingivitis balm, eye drops.*
5. *Stock up with 'How Do You Know Jesus Loves You?' leaflets.*
6. *Theatre tkts for* Autumn Crocus *at* Old Vic *and* The Sunshine of the World *at Ambassadors?*
7. *Get mind-doctor for M? Psychiatrist?*

London
17 November 1931

'So, Harold, about this baby then?' said Miss Harris as we prepared to visit Marina Carter's house of ill repute.

'Please, not again, Barbara.'

'Your wife and the soldier. They were . . . together while you were away in the war, then you came back, saw her again, discovered she'd been playing across the street, you get cross, then the Church finds out and tells you to break up with her, when it's none of their business. I was thinking about it. It only makes sense if she had a baby. You'd come home while she was pregnant, and she wouldn't get rid of it because that'd be a sin, because I know she's Irish and Catholic, or else she had the baby and it was there for you to see when you got home, knowing it couldn't be yours because you were away fighting in the Navy with the Arabs.'

'Barbara, I have no wish to discuss that unhappy period of my life. Please do not torment me with demands for details.'

'But, Harold, I'm interested in it all because I'm interested in you. Because I think I understand something about how your mind works.'

'I should be fascinated to hear your insights into human psychology, my dear,' I said, patting her hand. She snatched it away. She can still resemble a spoilt child whose whims must be indulged. I am frankly dreading the moment when I have to explain that she must vacate the room in Macfarlane Road when Mimi comes to visit.

It was an inspired suggestion. After my discovery of the empty brandy bottles, the unsent letters, the dead leaves in a pile, I felt uncomfortable at leaving my poor wife to mull over her 'imprisoned' state. I talked with Nugent, who promised to 'drop by' the house more often as she recuperates from her current attack. I spoke to Arnold and Pamela about their mother's sorry state and – such good, cooperative children – they undertook to be quiet and obedient and eat up their evening meals, henceforth to be prepared by Mrs Bolt from the village stores. I have taken a small disbursal from the Virtue Reclamation League to repair the ceiling in the guest bedroom and take away the rubble. I have directed Arnold to remove the dead leaves etc. from his mother's boudoir. And as I sat with Mimi on Sunday afternoon, chatting to her – as though we were, for a short while, *not* a hunted criminal under investigation by the Church authorities and his deranged and suicidal wife, she said, apropos of nothing, 'I should like to hear some music.'

'I cannot switch on the wireless, dear, for the bailiffs have taken it.'

'I didn't mean the wireless, Harold. I should like to hear some proper music, played by an orchestra, with beautiful singers in long evening gowns and men in dinner suits singing in chorus.' She looked up at the kitchen window. 'Take me to a concert, Harold.'

At first I thought, Oh dear, she is off on one of her turns, imagining she is on the concert-hall platform as she was when I first met her. But she was serious. I hadn't been to a musical concert (several hundred musicals, however) for years. How would I accede to her request?

'Very well. We shall look up in the *Eastern Daily Press* and see when next there's a church concert in Sheringham or Holkham, and I shall be happy to accompany you.'

'I don't mean a church one. I mean a big one, in a huge concert hall with a high roof and a real orchestra and the singing so glorious, it'd be like angels, and afterwards you'd hardly be able to speak but we could have a nice dinner and talk about it all.'

I suddenly recalled I had read in *The Times* that Mr William Walton's new work, *Belshazzar's Feast*, an ambitious chorale, is being sung at the Albert Hall. It is the kind of evening M would love. It would give her new heart and purpose. It would give her a sense of the might of the Lord, directing her steps and watching over her. It might, in short, cheer her up a bit. But how shall I engineer it? She has no social acquaintance in London. I cannot afford a hotel room. So where . . . ?

'I can stay at your little room in west London,' she said, momentarily restored. 'I've heard you say often enough how delightfully snug it is. We can go to the concert, hear the lovely music, eat something simple in town, take an Underground train home and get a good night's sleep, the two of us.' She clutched my arm, like a small daughter. 'Oh do let's.'

What could I do?

I had to say yes.

Letter from the Right Reverend Bertram Pollock
Bishop's House, Norwich, Norfolk
18 November 1931

Dear Henry,

Interesting to hear of your developments. I am impressed with your hard work securing the depositions of landladies who have witnessed Davidson visiting girls at 2 a.m. I'm not sure they add up to more than a picture of a man who likes to see young women in their night attire – an unedifying picture, but not enough to secure a conviction of immorality. On the other hand, there are *so many* landladies, and *so many* girls involved, could any court not presume his guilt by sheer weight of probability?

Davidson has replied to my last letter. He flatly contradicts my assurances and says, 'You evidently have never experienced the feeling that there is a man, the emissary of some minatory power, pursuing you in the street, ducking into shops and public facilities when you turn to see him; never been surrounded by investigators who seem to know all about you but who lie and prevaricate when asked about the nature of their enquiries; never been run down by a car driven by the agent of some enemy. Perhaps, My Lord, you have never felt you had an enemy? Well, I have. In fact, I feel I have many – snoopers and investigators, and the people for whom they work, and over them all the figure of some super-enemy whose identity remains a mystery to me. He is the employer of a man called Dashwood. Do *you* know this man Dashwood, My Lord?'

There is more in this vein. Davidson's paranoia leads him to jump to conclusions which are, unfortunately, accurate. You must confront him as soon as possible, Henry, and persuade him to resign. And if, beyond your sterling work among the landladies, there is anything more you can do to discredit him, I should be most appreciative.

Yours etc. in Christ,

+ Bertram

Journals of Harold Davidson
London
19 November 1931

I have had a most peculiar encounter, which has left me bewildered and concerned as to what my enemies have in store for me now.

Two days ago, I received a call from Estelle Douglas, a child of fifteen, known to me only through her brother, Arthur, one of the boys who has flourished under the kind ministrations of Don Stupendo at the Retreat; she came to visit him three months ago when I was present, with news from his home in Brighton, where his father had thrown him out for being insolent to the father's new ladyfriend. Naturally I quizzed Estelle as to her own circumstances and learned that she too had run away, to find comfort with her aunt in Dulwich. I asked the child her ambitions, and learned that she hoped to run a stall selling jewellery of her own design. She showed me some examples: hopeless, unfortunately. She has obviously no talent for that. She was a pretty young thing, with a precociously developed figure and a tiny waist. In the course of a brief interview, I learned that she was a keen swimmer on Brighton beach and, in a moment of inspiration, I pulled a copy of *Health & Efficiency* magazine from my Publications Pocket. I jabbed a finger at a New Fashions feature. 'There, Estelle,' I said, 'is where your future lies. You see these young ladies in their aquatic swimwear, posing for the camera? Note their smiles and sunny demeanour, their well-tended appearance. There is nothing to stop you joining their ranks and becoming a sought-after model. The pay is, I understand, remarkably generous. The work is less burdensome than spending afternoons in Greenwich or Bermondsey Market, trying to drum up custom in the rain for your charming though, if I may say so, primitive bijoux. I could make some enquiries among my wide acquaintance in the modelling world.'

I gave her my telephone number but heard nothing in the intervening three months. Nothing, that is, until two days ago, when I received a call from Estelle, asking if I would meet her in an address in Victoria, to discuss 'a matter of business, like that modelling thing you was talking about before'. Naturally I was pleased, and telephoned Margot Binns, whom I was able to assist in finding a position in 1928 in the Swanky Modes model agency. She assured me they would be happy to meet a young girl such as Estelle, with good face and figure, and would see what could be done. Scarcely had I replaced the receiver when the telephone rang again. A gruff male voice was on the line. His message, delivered in a muffled voice as if through a muslin cloth, was:

'I'm just telling you, don't go to Victoria tomorrow. That's all. If you know what's good for you, give it a miss.'

'I'm sorry,' I said, 'who is speaking?'

'Never mind that,' said the voice. 'Just steer clear of Victoria. They're out to get you. Just a friendly warning.' The telephone went dead.

I confess, I have become so used to being watched, followed, scrutinised and threatened, I am almost oblivious to danger. Somebody (a relative? a putative swain? a slave trader?) wishes me to stop helping this vulnerable young woman achieve her true potential. Well, let them try. I would not desert poor Miss Douglas.

Unabashed, I set out for Victoria at the arranged time, found the place – a respectable apartment building off Horseferry Road – and climbed the stairs. At the door marked '23' I knocked.

Estelle answered the door. She was not as I remembered her. Her hair was newly bobbed in the style of Miss Louise Brooks, she was clad only in a cream towel, and she seemed alarmed, and wary in her speech.

'Hello, my dear,' I said. 'Have I arrived too early? I have interrupted your ablutions. I will retire until you have made yourself decent.'

'Come in,' she said, pulling me into the room. 'There's someone here who wants to meet you.'

As I looked around, she raised her arms to let the towel fall to the carpet, revealing her young torso in its freshly bathed loveliness. Instantly, a man appeared from around the door with a large camera, the hefty kind you see at official church functions. Miss Douglas stepped forward to me. I seized the towel from the floor to shield her modesty, but the flash of a photograph caught us in a moment of seemingly lubricious – though wholly fictional – communion, her naked porcelain skin and my vicar's garb and reaching hands telling some sordid tale.

After the camera flash, an awkward silence filled the room. I thought of the anonymous telephone call. It had been, it seemed, not a warning to leave Miss Douglas alone. It had been a warning of a trap.

'Estelle,' I said. 'I have secured you an interview, as I promised, with the Swanky Modes model agency. That is the happy news I brought for you today. What is it that you have brought me?'

She stood wretchedly before me, pulling the towel around her nakedness, and burst into tears. The man with the camera, his employment at an end, fiddled sheepishly with his equipment and would not meet my eye.

On my way downstairs, I realised the identity of the muffled voice on the telephone. It had been that of Arthur, her brother, from the Runaway Boys' Retreat, regretting that he had agreed to help Mr Dashwood with his enquiries.

London
20 November 1931

I arrived home exhausted at 8 p.m. to find a remarkable change in the place. Barbara, evidently at a loose end, has been exercising her skill as a homemaker. The whole room was swept, dusted, tidied and perfumed with some domestic eau de cologne. My books had been gathered up and arranged on the windowsill. A new rug, regrettably a brown shagpile, lay under my desk. The grey settee was camouflaged underneath a large piece of Indian bedroom material. Two green velvet cushions were plumped at either end. The naked light bulb had been shrouded in a dark blue lampshade. The cooking hob had been cleaned for the first time since my arrival, and a saucepan of tinned tomato soup was coming to the boil. On the wall, two carnival masks of menacing rather than comic appearance hung by strings attached to a nail. Most extraordinary of all, Ravel's 'Pavane for a Dead Infanta' was issuing from a new wireless in the corner.

'Barbara, how delightful,' I cried. 'You have transformed my humble quarters into a palace of luxury. This rug! These cushions! Those shuddersome masks! And a new wireless. I have not enjoyed the pleasure of music in the home for many years.'

She stood on tiptoes to look into the saucepan. In her bare feet, she seemed a tiny woodland sprite kitted out as a cook's maid.

'Nice, isn't it, Harold? I went shopping down at the Elephant, and got a bit carried away. Do you like the rug? There was a sale on and – oh, but you don't mind, do you? I mean, I shoulda asked you first, but I wanted it to be a little surprise. But maybe you don't like the colours.'

Her face was a picture of girlish concern. It was remarkable to hear the combative Miss Harris asking anybody's permission about anything.

'It is all perfectly splendid. If I seem startled, it's only because I am not used to the presence of beautiful things. I do not deserve to live in such splendour. I am, as you know, a man of frugal tastes and requirements. I know nothing of exotic furnishings.'

'I don't know,' said Barbara, 'you seen the inside of a few tarts' bedrooms, 'aven't you? Mine included, though of course I'm not a tart.'

I ignored her. 'And the reason for this transformation?'

'I thought you needed cheering up after that business with your wife going nuts. You seemed a bit down when you told me.'

'It was a shock. Not just Mrs Davidson's condition, but the state of the rooms and the silent children. It was neglect, Barbara, of which I must hold myself responsible.'

'Come and sit over here,' she said, turning off the gas under the soup and leading me to the settee. 'I wanna know something.'

I sat obediently down beside her, leaning against the soft verdant cushions. 'What would you like to know?'

'I want to know about your wife. About what happened to you two. The time you nearly split up, that you won't tell me about.'

'What of it?'

'I want to know: did she have a baby with this character, this dead soldier?'

There was a silence as I wrestled with my better instincts.

'Yes. Your suspicions were correct.'

'And did she keep it?'

'She wished to. I would not allow it. I persuaded her to put it up for adoption. After a few days of agonising, she did.'

'A few days? She was looking after it for a few days, knowing you wanted to send it away?'

'I made my view perfectly clear.'

'You're cruel, you know, Harold, making a woman go through that. Parting a woman from her kid like that.'

'Cruel? Have you no interest in *my* feelings? And how it felt to be betrayed by my true love with another man when I was away in the war fighting for her safety.'

'All right, I admit the timing was crap, but she fell in love with someone, didn't she? Probably needed a bit of fun to keep going. Lots of people had it off with complete strangers in the war. If she'd got herself kitted out with some skins like a modern girl, you'd never have known about the boyfriend, and there wouldn't be no baby to upset you, would there?'

'I was not "upset", Barbara,' I said icily. 'One becomes "upset" about breaking a china ornament or losing at cards. I was shattered. This, you must recall, was the woman I chose out of all others as my helpmeet, my adviser, my shining exemplar of Christian decency. She was all goodness when I met her. Her beauty was eclipsed only by her virtue. I knew she could never be guilty of duplicity. I saw in her shining face that she could never be unfaithful. I was wrong.' I shook my head. 'Very wrong.'

'Where'd she meet him?' asked Barbara, irrelevantly.

'In Windsor. I told you. He was a patient in a hospital where she worked as a nurse.'

'What was she doing when she first met you?'

'She was an actress. And a singer.'

'On the stage?'

'Yes.'

A silence fell. Barbara rose from the settee and walked across the room to reheat the soup. Her next words came from over her shoulder.

'It that what all this has been about, Harold? Is that why you've spent all these years since then, saving girls?'

'What do you mean?'

'I told you I had a theory about you, didn't I? It's dead simple. You been looking for little copies of your wife all over London, you have, week after week, year after year. You been trying to find girls just like her – young and silly and flirty but innocent about men and sex – and warn them off going to the bad. "Don't hang around in coffee shops taking up with wicked boys who might shag you or put you on the street," that's what you tell 'em. "You go onstage instead and become a famous actress and star . . ."'

'I do not see the application –'

'. . . just like your wife would've become if she hadn't gone and married *you*!' Barbara almost shouted the word in my face. 'Can't you see? All the little trips to the theatre, the teas and lunches and little visits at night, the closeness and advice, the dishing out medicine, the . . . foot salve – it's like you're pretending to be married to half the girls in London. They think you're their friend, some of 'em, the ones who don't think you're a slimy old git always getting his arm round their waist. It'd be funny if I told them you thought they was all your wife – or at least the way you want your wife to be in your memory, before she went to the bad.'

Her words were nonsense, of course, a shallow and impertinent interpretation of a career devoted to social improvement. But I sat for a time in a puzzled silence, as she stirred the soup, and a shadow came between us as I wondered whether I had devoted my prime years to protecting an image of purity that was mostly in my head. I thought of Rose and Elsie and Belle and many other salvaged young women in the past. Not one bore the slightest resemblance to Mimi. One or two, now I thought about it, had a passing resemblance to Sheilagh, my firstborn – but let me not think down those murky alleyways!

No, she, Miss Harris, is quite wrong. I know the point and value of my work, that it is done from love of God and love of my fellow man, whom I wish to protect from spiritual destruction. I suddenly resented her interference. How dare she – a girl abandoned to wrongdoing – speak of my wife 'going to the bad'? I became agitated with irritation. My eye fell upon the frog-hued cushions beside me.

'Barbara? How did you afford all these pricey furnishings?'

She turned to me. 'Same way as I always paid for doing up my rooms. Couple of afternoons, couple of boyfriends, whoomph. Bob's your uncle. You're not going to start objecting, are you? I'm not in the mood for lectures.'

I could not believe my ears. 'Can you be serious, Miss Harris?'

'I love the way you change it back and forth all the time. "Barbara" when I'm a good girl, "Miss Harris" when I'm bad. My teachers used to do it too.'

'Silence!' I cried. 'Can it be true that, after all these months spent together, this campaign of instruction, these fulfilling conversations, you can think nothing of lapsing into prostitution, as casually as one might give up or resume smoking cigarettes? And in order to pay for some cheap masks and pillows and gewgaws and frippery, to turn a perfectly good bed-sitting room into an approximation of a French bordello?'

'Wait a minute, Harold. I don't care what you think of the stuff – old geezer like you wouldn't have much of a clue about fashion anyway – but just remember this: I did it for you, because I was sorry for you, because your home's such a mess and it's shabby and falling down, you said, and so's your wife, and I wanted you to feel better because this is sort of your new home. With me.'

I stared at her. 'Are you off your head? We have not *set up home* together. I have allowed you temporary accommodation out of simple goodness, while you have nowhere to stay, and because I thought it important to keep you close, while putting you through a period of – of spiritual recuperation. I thought you were responding well. I thought I marked a change in you, into a decent, thoughtful, charitable young woman. Now I find that you can revert in an instant, and sell your body in an afternoon like the whore of Babylon.'

'I told you I did this for *you*, so we could live better.'

I laughed. 'I am a servant of God. It is not part of my make-up, my inclinations or my job description to live off the earnings of a young prostitute.'

She stepped back a pace as if I had threatened to strike her. 'I thought you liked me.'

'I like you immensely. I have indeed felt prompted at times to say, in the language employed by pilgrims, 'I love thee.' But it does not mean –'

'I thought I was special to you. You said I was special. You said I was chosen, or at least you'd chosen me, and you wanted to take care of me and be with me all the time –'

'In a spiritual sense, Miss Harris, I meant us to be loving friends. I believe I said as much, many moons ago. You can't have thought I was planning any more than that.'

'So all the evenings together,' she began to snuffle noisily, 'all the talk about perfect houses and honeysuckle gardens, that was all bollocks?'

'It was entirely in the realm of the theoretical, Miss Harris. I am sorry if you were misled.'

'You called me the queen of your heart.'

'I seem to remember the endearment was invented by you, for me to translate into French and speak aloud.'

She burst into tears, a loud wailing noise, awful to hear.

'I bought so many things to make everything nice for us,' she cried. 'And now you've gone and ruined it.'

'Not as much as you have ruined your own soul, Miss Harris, on an immoral caprice.'

'Oh fuck off,' she wailed. 'You fucking little lying fucking bastard.'

'All these things you bought with your tainted money will have to go anyway,' I said, heedless of the consequences, 'for my wife is coming down to London on the train on Tuesday night for a concert, and I need to remove all trace of you and your various *objets d'art*.'

'Your wife is coming here? But you said she'd gone mad. You said she was a physical and spiritual wreck. You said she was trying to kill herself. And you gaily invite her to stay at our flat where I bin living like your –'

'Like my wife? I don't think so. Mimi is recovering from her bout of depression, and I judged it wise to offer her a change of scenery, and show her some of the sights of London.'

'Including me? Or did that not figure in your plans?'

'I was going to tell you about it this evening. I was going to ask for your understanding, and invite you to stay elsewhere.'

'And remove any traces of me from the bed and the bathroom in case the little wife finds out?'

'There will be no need now, Barbara. You have slid back into the ways of dereliction despite my strenuous efforts and I will have nothing more to do with you. Please gather your belongings and go.'

And she left. Simply walked out into the night – presumably, once her tears had dried, to seek some low companion upon whom to slake both her lust and her fury.

Was I wrong? I could not condone or excuse her behaviour. But having pondered it for three hours together, I think something good may have come out of this experience. I feel that I may have brought her closer to the experience of genuine love than anybody else. Unfortunately, I may have performed the same kind office to myself.

London
21 November 1931

Wretched, wretched. Such an *ordeal* of a day.

Enjoyed the rare treat of having a bed to call my own for the first time in months. And of sleeping for approximately nine hours, waking with a start at 2.10 a.m., 3.25 a.m. and 5.01 a.m., and calling, 'Barbara?' as I was sometimes wont to do when we shared this accommodation, and night terrors assailed me.

This room is full of the sense-data of Miss Harris – her primary-colour clothing, the reek of her Woolworths scent and the slightly gamy odour of her skin upon towels and bedlinen, the rasp of her cushions and tapestries as I strove to remove them from settee and wall and secrete them downstairs. Hoping that Barbara would welcome the opportunity to retrieve some of her belongings while I was out, I spent the day visiting my old haunts and old friends – Bridget in Highgate, Joanna in her Whitehall public house, Sally at the fish-monger's in Holborn, Elsie (regrettably back at Waterloo Station), Madge and Sandra in the Vauxhall tea rooms, Esther and Matilda now happily waitressing in Chelsea, Lily Beane tearing tickets at the Apollo in Shaftesbury Avenue (it is, I remind her, *a start*) and Dolores who is now working as telephonist for the Pitman's centre in Piccadilly. Many have been approached, I am shocked to learn, by Mr Dashwood and served with subpoenas – but none wants to be dragged into any legal jiggery-pokery and they have mostly discarded them.

I managed a brief meeting with Vincent Doughty of the clothing manufactory that I have never, to my regret, had time to visit. He was in melancholic mood.

'The supply's dried up, Harold,' he said, gazing sadly into his lunchtime pitcher of Bass. 'What's happened to all the girls you used to send me?'

'I was rather hoping you'd be able to tell me,' I replied. 'How, for instance, is Miss Jezebel Torrington getting along?'

'Jezebel? Blimey, there's a name from the past. Hardly lasted two weeks. Very enthusiastic at the start. Took to the work well, nice attitude, sweet nature if a bit scatty. Wouldn't buckle down to the steam ironing in mid-afternoon. Said it was ruining her complexion. Not that her complexion was all peaches and cream, ever. The boys used to rib her a bit. Used to suggest some remedies of things she might rub into her skin to make it better, if you follow me. She used to fight back at them all right, at the ones with terrible acne anyway, but it got a bit serious. Things turned a bit sour and not funny any more, so I had to move her.'

'Move her? To where?'

'To the dyeing room. It's a bit smelly in there, with the veggie dyes and the dunking vats, not to mention Big Albert who's always stripped to the waist when he's dunking.' He laughed. 'He's a sight is Big Albert, I tell yer, frightening really, well, he's twenty-four stone, but I thought he'd be company for young Jezebel after the little baskets in the main factory taking the mick out of her name and her spots. But I thought she'd last a bit longer than nine days and not run off like that with her clothes all torn.' He stopped for a reviving swig.

'Why did you not tell me of this before?'

'Didn't think you'd want to know, Harold, until we heard word of her. You're a busy man. Didn't want to worry you.'

'Mr Doughty. I entrust these young girls to your care, as well as to your employ. If they disappear, in unusual circumstances, it is vital that you let me know. I am, in a sense, *in loco parentis*.'

'Don't be so hard on yourself, Reverend. I never thought you were barmy.'

'I did not mean that. I mean, I am partially responsible for them, having placed them in your care. And if they leave you —'

'If they leave, it's their lookout. They had the chance of a nice steady job, with a few perks on the side, and if they bugger off one day, I got to find someone to cover their shift, and I don't feel too happy about that.'

'Would it not occur to you to telephone me about a girl's disappearance?'

'Only if there was money involved. Like if she'd had 'er hand in the till.'

'I assume Jezebel did not stoop to theft?'

'Oh no. Matter of fact, she left without drawing her pay. We only start paying 'em after a couple of weeks, you see.'

'You mean, she received no payment for her time in your sweatshop?'

'Well, no. But don't you go calling it no sweatshop.'

'Mr Doughty.' A dreadful suspicion began to beat at the back of my mind. 'Exactly how many girls have I brought to your factory over the last six or seven years?'

'I dunno, Harold. There's been so few of 'em lately. About a hundred I suppose.'

'And how many remained in your employment above a month or so?'

'A few must've done, the real grafters I mean. The ones who could see what might be gained by grasping the opportunities . . .'

'You mean, the money they could make by whoring on the side when the work was done?'

'There's no need for that kind of talk, Reverend. I run a classy business. If these girls want to make some private arrangements, it's their affair.'

'Vincent!' I sprang to my feet. 'I have not been guiding these poor, misguided girls into your care for years, only for them to be coerced into some private brothel at the hands of your jeering, priapic bullies!'

'Leave it out, Harold. You know what kind of girls we're dealing with here. If they want to work, they work, and I pay them. If they want to maximise their assets, and supply a demand right there on the premises, that's up to them.'

'What?' I jumped up and dashed the tankard of beer out of his bovine hands. 'You ignorant swine. You degenerate pagan. You mean for years . . . I cannot believe I have sent a hundred young women into your clutches, and listened to your assurances, and bought you luncheons, and trusted you with a duty of care of my girls.'

His ham-sized paw clutched the front of my clerical jacket. 'You better watch your tongue, little padre, or you'll wake up with seven types of shit kicked out of you. I've had it with you and your little lectures. And the funny thing is, you're no better'n me. You use tarts as currency, to get your own way. I've heard enough about your charities to know where all the money really goes. So piss off and don't bother me with any more silly bitches who don't know where their bread's really buttered.' He let go of my lapels. His red, broken-veined skin moved out of my face. We parted company for, I sincerely hope, ever.

I was very shaken. First Barbara, now this. I needed some strong coffee in the Haymarket to pull myself together. I had no time to digest the significance of his confession. I needed to return home to survey the damage left by Miss Harris.

When I arrived, the house was still. It was not (as I feared) a smoking ruin. No fugitive scent of Jungle Rapture, her jasmine-based favourite, hung around the entrance. Inside, all was as I had left it that morning − regrettably. That left me one whole evening to divest the room of every trace of Barbara's uniquely pungent presence, a fug of corruption made the more redolent by her absence. I divested the room of armfuls of silk blouses, chiffon scarves, cotton brassieres, lacy underthings, feather boas, a collection of green cloche hats like exotic turtles, a grazing herd of footwear in a dozen styles from ballet pumps to diamanté-heeled slingbacks. I staggered under the weight of wall hangings, tapestries, Indian bedspreads, collections of *Vogue* and *Modern Woman* magazine, wirelesses, fluffy towels, emetic paintings of kittens, *Picture Post* studies of Mr Novello and Miss Dietrich. I gathered whole boxfuls of powder compacts, cheap razors, elderly scent bottles with tasselled rubber pumps, hairbrushes (2), toothbrushes (3!) and certain creamy unguents of inscrutable purpose. I had to make five journeys downstairs to where Mrs Osborne, with increasing disbelief, supervised their storage in her spare bedroom and (when that was exhausted) airing cupboard.

'Just a few days, Rector, is that right?' she asked. 'You did say a few days, didn't you?'

I reassured her, and borrowed some cleaning agents to, as it were, un-Barbara the room just as I had, apparently, in a sudden convulsion, un-Barbara-ed my life. After ninety minutes of scrubbing with Jeyes Fluid and Coal Tar soap, I had returned my tiny living quarters to the semblance of a monastic cell. I retrieved the old horse-hair blanket from where my quondam tenant had flung it dismissively

('I'm not sleeping under that,' she said, on moving in, 'I'd sooner sleep under a Greek sailor, and *that's* saying a lot'). By midnight, I was exhausted, but it was done. A transformation, from sweetly pungent, talcum-and-jasmine, bosomy-lacy girlish excess to a savoury, ascetic, cigar-smelling, gentleman's lamplit retreat. I could, at last, entertain my wife and try to embrace, if not Mimi herself, at least some kind of normality.

CHAPTER 18

Journals of Harold Davidson
London
2 January 1932

A deeply horrible encounter with a truly horrible man.

Mr Dashwood wrote to me in November, asking, or rather demanding my presence in his offices to discuss 'a matter effecting your benefice'. My benefice? I thought of every parish concern in which I have acted lately, from the timing of the Harvest Festival to the prosecution of Lionel Grubb for attempting to steal the lead flashings from the porch roof, and I have found nothing that would occasion my being summoned to his office. My thoughts turned to Morston. I have seldom set foot in the church in the last few months. Then I recalled that the side door of the church is so rusted about the hinges, it is falling off the lintel, and the surrounding brick-work so decayed it offers no purchase for screws or nails. I recalled with a start that I had received in the post a 'dilapidation order', demanding urgent renovations. They were never carried out. I simply did not have the funds. Maybe this is the matter effecting my benefice.

At least, I thought as I set off to Gray's Inn Road, by the end of today I shall know the nature of the accusations against me. I will have the enemy in plain sight at last.

Unfortunately, I was caught in a shower of rain and, having no umbrella, was forced to shelter under an awning. In consequence, I was fifteen minutes late to see Dashwood. He is an irritable young fellow, black-haired and brisk in manner, without a trace of respect for my seniority or my role as God's anointed.

'Here you are at last, I see,' he began coldly.

'I was delayed by the weather,' I said. 'I am sorry. Sorry too about the repairs to Morston Church, about which I fear I have been dilatory. If you will give me a week to arrange the necessary funding, it will be addressed forthwith. The door is a security hazard, it is true, for any passing —'

'You are not here, Mr Davidson, because of Morston Church, or its doors or any issue of parish finances,' he said, cutting across me. 'You are here on a matter of the utmost gravity, and I urge you to treat it seriously.'

His manner was sinister. He was the image of the cruel-eyed vizier, the pitiless adjutant, employed to carry out his master's dread wishes, after toying with the victim like a cat with a bird.

I felt my legs giving way and clutched the chair beside me.

'Sit down, Davidson, before you faint.'

'What — what is the matter of gravity?'

'No, I have a better idea. Do not sit down. Better you should fall to your knees and beg forgiveness for your sins.'

'My sins?' What could he mean? 'I would gladly ask forgiveness, Mr Dashwood. But to which sins do you refer?'

'I cannot name them aloud. You know yourself what you have done and the enormity of your crimes against the Commandments, the Church and your cloth.'

'Be so good,' I said with remarkable coolness, 'as to name them for me. We are both, I think, men of the world.'

'It is not fastidiousness that prevents me,' he said. 'They are far too serious to reveal without the consent of the bishop.'

'Will the Bishop of Norwich tell me what they are, if you will not? Perhaps I should go and see *him*.'

'No,' said Dashwood with a kind of thin ferocity, 'His Grace has no wish to see you. He has asked me to deal with you directly, and left the conduct of the affair in my hands.'

'Perhaps you could begin this admirably direct dealing by explaining the crime I am guilty of?'

'In a word, Mr Davidson — immorality.'

'Immorality? How? Where? With whom?'

'Do not prevaricate. You know exactly what I am talking about.

I suggest you go away and think about the implications of your conduct and you will see that no other course is open to you but resignation.'

'What?' I cried.

'You are not fit to preside over the parish of Stiffkey and Morston any longer. I suggest you sign a confession of immorality and resign from your rectorate forthwith. I can offer assistance in this. You may use a lawyer friend of mine, who has seen cases like this before. He could perhaps also help transfer you to another diocese.'

I stood in amazement before this cold-eyed jackanapes, as he casually informed me how he chose to deprive me of the parish where I have lived and guided my faithful flock for twenty-five years. I had a strong impulse to box his ears. Then the significance of his last remark struck me.

'One moment, Mr Dashwood. I'm not sure I understand your words. Are you offering to assist me in finding a new diocese away from Stiffkey?'

'That is what I said. But only if you agree to certain terms and sign a confession prepared by me.'

'There lies the root of my confusion. If I am accused of immorality, how can I be allowed to pursue a ministry in any parish in the land?'

'I did not quite mean that. I meant –'

'Either, Dashwood, I am a sinner or I am not. You can have no feelings for the parishioners of any diocese to which I am sent, if you allow them to be cared for by a clergyman as immoral as you say I am.'

'This is all irrelevant.'

'It is perfectly relevant. It is also relevant that I do not know you, Mr Dashwood, and I fail to see how a pipsqueak lawyer such as yourself can be given the power to prepare confessions, solicit resignations or make offers about alternative employment in the Church of England.'

'Nonetheless, I have that power. I enjoy the confidence of the bishop.'

'Is the bishop actually still in charge of Church business in the Norfolk region? Or is he now delegating it to junior laymen with instructions to hire and fire, to harry and insult, whomsoever they please?'

'Nothing will be gained by insults, Mr Davidson. What's done is done, and you must take the consequence. I wish to have your resignation, together with a signed confession of immorality – you need not go into details, we shall spare you that – in my hands by the 15th of this month.'

'And if I refuse?'

'Then the weight of the Church will be ranged against you in a public trial. It will destroy your reputation. You will be finished in England as a clergyman, or anything else.'

He said these words quietly, as unemotional as a viper.

'Dashwood,' I said, quietly in my turn, from the depths of my chair, 'why am I to be persecuted in this way?'

'There have been complaints,' he said, looking away through the window to the grey beyond. 'Complaints, allegations, private reports, gossip. It is unwelcome. It brings the Established Church, which we both serve, into disrepute.'

'But who has been doing the complaining? Am I to resign because someone – a stranger – informs the bishop that I am in the wrong?'

'Mr Davidson –' To my surprise, his voice took on a softer, more conciliatory tone. 'I do not wish you to resign from any personal animus. I have nothing against you. But I have been asked to expedite this sorry business in the shortest time and with the minimum of fuss. I am anxious to bring the least pain to you and your family. Believe me' – and with this, he laid his hand on my arm, with the gesture of a true friend – 'I understand what you must be going through.'

'I can assure you, Mr Dashwood, you can have no possible conception –'

'And then there is the problem of your youngest child . . .'

I stopped dead. A chill flowed like mercury through my blood.

'What about my youngest child? What do you know? What can this possibly have to do with the case?' I would have said more, but the only sound in my head was a repeated, 'No no no no no no no . . .'

'It is my business to know things, Mr Davidson. Let us say that

I am aware of the illegitimacy of your youngest child, and must repeat that it would be a shame if, should this come to court, the circumstances of her birth were to emerge and upset both her and you, and Mrs Davidson.'

'Are you trying to blackmail me?'

'Only to convince you to see reason. Resignation is the only way.'

I turned and strode out. It was galling to let the – forgive me, Lord – sewer rat have the last word but I was beside myself with fury. Not only at him, but at Bertie Pollock – how shocking, for a bishop to hide behind the legal arras of such a man and have him do his dirty work. I should confront Bertie and demand an explanation.

Letter from the Right Reverend Bertram Pollock
Bishop's House, Norwich, Norfolk
6 January 1932

Dear Dashwood,

Thank you for your report on the meeting with Davidson. It sounded a painful encounter, which you appear to have conducted with your habitual diplomacy and resolve. I of course regret that you did not secure a clean resignation from him. But despite his bravado, our man is clearly rattled. The 'deadline' you have given him is enough to give him sleepless nights and force him to a moral decision. Your invocation of the trouble that publicity would bring to his ailing wife, and their problematic youngest child, was a master stroke. He now knows that unstoppable forces are ranged against him. He will, I feel sure, crumble if we maintain the attack.

I remain, as you know, unconvinced that the evidence gathered thus far constitutes a prima facie case for prosecution. The charges you have drawn up – e.g. the kiss in the Chinese restaurant – hardly count as sins, let alone criminal activities when considered separately; but if there are enough of them, and he can be proved guilty of each one, they would appear to a jury as a blizzard of wrongdoing.

I do not, of course, want a jury to try this case. In a consistory court, the verdict is usually left to the discretion of the chancellor of the diocese. The chancellor here is Mr F. Keppel-North. He is a good man. He will know what must be done.

Please join me in prayer that, by the 15th, Mr Davidson will choose to (in Army phraseology) 'do the decent thing' and apply the equivalent of a service revolver to his ancient and troublesome head.

Your friend in Christ,

Bertram + Norwich

Letter from Mr Harold Davidson
Shepherd's Bush, London W12
11 January 1932

Dear Dashwood,

I have been considering your proposition.

I have consulted friends and colleagues in the cloth, and they say they have never heard the like. To ask a vicar of the Lord to confess to sins (or crimes) that remain unnamed . . . no, let me start again – To find a *secular official* of the Church of England instructing a vicar of the Lord to confess to unnamed sins is simply bizarre. To a man, my friends' counsel is: do nothing of the sort. This has remained my view since our meeting.

But because of your warnings about the odious publicity that may attend on me, should this matter come to trial – warnings that may be kindly concern on your part, but which I suspect to be veiled threats – and because of my reluctance to see my family dragged into the mire of gossip and innuendo, I am prepared to offer the following.

You say my sins concern 'immorality'. I take this to be a reference to my activities among the wretched and/or fallen women of London. I know just how innocent I have been in my conduct. But I am prepared to give up my ministry in the metropolis, to confine my activities henceforth to the parishes of Stiffkey and Morston, and to supervise my charitable work from the rectory. Will this satisfy your employer?

I have, let me remind you, done the Church some service. I

have been Rector of Stiffkey for twenty-five years, in which time I have buried the dead and christened the newborn of the parish, dried the tears of the desperate, helped with the finances of the destitute, taught drama, lectured in theology, organised singing clubs, opened fêtes, closed down gambling dens in public houses, and conducted at least 1,250 services. I have tried to serve the Church of England according to my lights. If at times I have seemed neglectful of my duties, it is because a more pressing duty called me away to London. But I always came back. And I will not have all this commitment to my village flock thrown away because some fancied transgression has displeased the bishop and his jack-in-office.

Perhaps you could let me know if this will bring an end to the investigations that have been mounted against me these last few months.

Yours truly,

Harold F. Davidson

Rector of Stiffkey

Letter from Mr Henry Dashwood of Dashwood, Ogilvy & Pearce
Gray's Inn Road, London WCI
12 January 1932

Dear Davidson,

Thank you for your letter.

I have presented to My Lord the Bishop your petition re your confining your activities to Stiffkey and relinquishing all further work in London.

The answer is No. Your behaviour has been infamous. It requires a confession, an apology and a humble resignation from all services and activities connected with the Church of England. Merely distancing yourself from the stews of iniquity that have become your second home will not be sufficient. It will not change your inclinations or your capacity to embarrass your superiors, wherever you go.

You have three days left. You must either sign a confession, as drawn up by me, in my presence; or you must face Trial. I recommend you go home to your much-neglected family and ask their opinion as to how you should proceed. They will be your wisest counsel. Otherwise, to speak plainly, you will shortly be thrown to the wolves, and you will not survive the experience.

Wishing you a happy new year.

Yours sincerely,

Henry Dashwood

Journals of Harold Davidson
Stiffkey
13 January 1932

I have had a raging toothache for a week. Visited Dr Opie-Smith in Wood Lane yesterday, and have derived some relief from his explorations. Through 'excessively grinding your back sevens', I am faced with the prospect of root-canal work in two molars – a long and painful procedure, in order to correct a fault brought on by fury, frustration and *ngngngngngng* – I am so enraged by my meeting with Dashwood, I can scarcely construct a sentence.

I am shocked by his, and the bishop's, reply. But I am buoyed up by a remarkable rapprochement, since arriving in Stiffkey this morning. This is the first time I have seen my family together under the same roof in five years! A most moving experience. I telephoned Nugent at his rooms above the solicitors' office in Norwich, and asked for his help. Once a studious, rather dreamy boy with a tendency to pretension, he has matured into a sober, judicious man of twenty-two, who rang Sheilagh at her nurses' home in King's Lynn and alerted her, tactfully, to my parlous circumstances. He sent a message to find Patricia, at her art college, and, with barely a day's notice, they all presented themselves at the Rectory, avid for news but also gratifyingly wholehearted in their filial support. Arnold and Pamela, perhaps buoyed up by the signs of improvement at home (the plasterers, the decorators), seem more sunny-tempered than I have seen them in a while. At seventeen, Arnold communicates in some odd, fantastical slang decipherable only by his schoolmates.

Pammie, at twelve, has become very masculine in her trousery, short-haired way, but her dark lustrous eyes hold a promise of great beauty to come.

And then there is Mimi.

I wish I could say there was a transformation in my former beloved since I came to rescue her in Stiffkey after the summons from Mrs Reynolds. But I regret to say, the demons of depression, of deafness and melancholia that inhabit her are not easily defeated. Even after *Belshazzar's Feast* at the Albert Hall and a large, self-indulgent dinner, it was clear she was far from cured. My attempts at conversation were shot down like so many clay pigeons. My attempts to humour her love for Shakespeare's comic romances, and her passion for living in the past, were likewise rebuffed. She spoke about the concert, the music, the spectacle as though talking to herself, luxuriating in her temporary membership of the concert-going classes. When describing what she has seen, she becomes animated — but it is a performance, unconnected to real life.

So there we were, assembled in the living room, like suspects at the conclusion of a Lord Peter Wimsey mystery.

'You all know, I believe, why you are here,' I said. 'The Church authorities have taken against me and my work in London. They believe they have found some evidence that points to sordid behaviour on my part. I want to assure my family, before all others, I am innocent of immorality, and ask you for your support and assistance.'

'But, Pa,' said Nugent, 'what are the charges? What do they say you've done?'

'There you have it, my boy. They will not tell me. They wish me to sign a confession, resign from the parish, give up the rectorship, give up this parish to another incumbent, quit this house and try to find some alternative career.'

'Give up the house!' cried Patricia. 'But I spent my whole life here! We all did. And you can't give up being rector. The parish wouldn't survive without you.'

'I have no desire to abandon the parish any more than I could abandon you, my dears,' I said with feeling.

'I don't want to seem contrary, Pa,' said Nugent, 'but you haven't exactly been ever-present at the heart of this family. Not for years. You haven't been here in the parish most of the time.'

I looked sorrowfully at my older son.

'I am afraid what you say is true. I have been neglectful, I know. But if you knew of the vital work that kept me in London so long, you would not, I'm sure, condemn your father.'

'Nugent wasn't condemning you, Pa,' said Sheilagh. 'He's just stating the facts. But you need to tell us: what have you done that's made them suspicious, or given them reason to charge you with immorality? You should tell us. Well, not Arnold and Pamela perhaps.'

'I can think of nothing,' I said, with a tremor in my voice. 'I am guilty of no sin of commission. But many of my associates in London are, or have been, involved in prostitution and, as far as the Church is concerned, some kind of pollen of sordidness may have rubbed off.'

'Ridiculous,' said Patricia. 'They can't try and fling you out of the parish because you became friends with tarts. You were probably just what they needed between their labours, like a nice sit-down and a cup of tea.'

Mimi had said nothing. The youngest children gazed at her face, which was as closed as the door of a safe. Could she hear what was being said?

'My concern is this,' I said to them all. 'If the case goes to trial, this family – all of you – will become public property. They may pry into my work, into your short lives, into your mother's health. Your names may be mentioned in the paper as connected to scandal. Terrible accusations may be thrown at your father, and the taint of accusation will outlive my being vindicated. You will feel intruded upon, fingered, inspected, made subject to gross and ugly rumours. It is too much of a burden to place upon my family. The only way to prevent it happening is for me to sign a confession of guilt. It is an action I abhor, but on which I am prepared to embark if you wish it. Tell me what I should do. I am entirely in your hands.'

There was silence for twenty seconds, before Mimi exploded.

'Don't be ridiculous, Harold. How could you have any doubt about what to do? Will you cop on to yourself? Are you going to go out there and disgrace your family?'

Strangely, despite the passion of her outburst, I had no idea what she was telling me to do.

'So you think I should . . . ?'

'Fight them. For feck's sake. Take them on. How can anyone make you sign a confession without saying what you're accused of? No one can ask you to do that, not even the bishop.'

'Evidently, my dear, he can. And as his humble servant, I should do what my master tells me. That is the point of a Church hierarchy.'

'So you're going to give up without a fight? Let them accuse you of anything they like?'

'I thought I might negotiate directly with the bishop and see what –'

'The bishop! He's behind all this. That Bertram Pollock, the weaselly little troublemaker. Wasn't he once your friend? Well, he's showing his true colours now. The bastard.'

'Mimi, there is no call to be excited. This can all be discussed with –'

'Don't be such a bloody milksop, Harold,' she shouted. 'Stand up for yourself. Write to Pollock and say you want nothing more to do with him. And if he says another word, tell him you'll take it to the *Daily Mirror*, how you were pressured to resign for nothing. But for Christ's sake, *do* something.'

She stormed out. I had never seen my wife so incensed. Warily, I followed her into the back parlour.

'Moyra,' I said, 'how would Pamela feel, if it all came out? She is twelve, and should not discover the truth of her conception by reading about it in the papers.'

My wife's eyes were reddened with crying. 'It was years ago, Harold,' she said between tears. 'It has not been spoken of in that time. She is our child. You love her and I love her. Nothing will change that, no matter what capital they seek to make of it.'

'They will say terrible things from which we will never recover.'

'There's nothing worse than to resign for no reason.'

'What if I agreed to resign, provided there's an investigation by the Church into this whole business?'

'You still might lose in the end. But at least you'd know what it is you've done.'

So we did just that. I wrote to Dashwood that afternoon, saying I was prepared to accept the findings of the Church, and offered my resignation conditional on there being a proper examination of the bishop's actions against me. Dashwood replied, turning my offer down flat. He had no wish for an investigation, only for my signature. If none was forthcoming, there must be a trial. If I disliked the outcome, I could appeal.

So it is war. I have bent over backwards to accommodate the Church, and they have pursued their obstinate course. Very well. They will see that I am a worthy adversary. But for the present, I am an adversary who suffers from night sweating and morning tremors – not from drink of course, but because I have no clue with what dreadful ammunition they plan to attack me. Can it be about sexual intercourse? (What else does 'immorality' signify?) What do they know?

London
20 January 1932

Good heavens. So *this* is what I have been worrying about for so long. I was summoned to Dashwood's office this morning 'to face charges' as if I were being invited before a firing squad.

The meeting was brief. Dashwood said, 'I have this for you' and handed me a paper.

On it were four lines of typewritten condemnation.

You are charged with immoral conduct since 1921 with Rose
    Ellis;
With immoral conduct towards a woman in a café in Walbrook;
With immoral conduct in embracing a girl in a Chinese restaurant in Bloomsbury;
With the immoral habit of associating with ladies of loose character.

I read the lines, and read them again, this time saying the words on my breath. I could not believe my eyes. I looked up at

Dashwood's furrowed and fake-serious countenance and said, 'Is that all?'

He looked back at me. 'What were you expecting?'

I very nearly laughed in his face.

News report, *Eastern Daily Press*
2 February 1932

COMPLAINTS AGAINST THE RECTOR OF STIFFKEY
MAY COME BEFORE CONSISTORY COURT

It is understood that complaints concerning the moral conduct of the Reverend Harold F. Davidson, MA, Rector of Stiffkey, Norfolk, have been lodged, and unless withdrawn in the meantime they are to be investigated at a consistory court. A denial of the allegations contained in the complaints has been entered on behalf of the rector. No date has yet been fixed for the consistory court, but it will probably be some time next month. The Rev. Davidson has been Rector of Stiffkey since 1906. He was formerly a curate at Holy Trinity, Windsor, and St Martin-in-the-Fields, Westminster. During the war he was a chaplain in the Royal Navy.

News report, *Daily Herald*
6 February 1932

CLERGYMAN ON TRIAL FOR IMMORAL CONDUCT
Several charges of misbehaviour for Stiffkey parson

Long-serving rural rector and social missionary Harold Francis Davidson, 56, is to stand trial next month after official 'complaints' about his 'moral conduct' were made by the Diocese of Norwich.

Mr Davidson is charged with no crime and the hearing will not take place in a criminal court. His past behaviour will be investigated in a religious 'consistory' court, with a judge but no jury. The Rev. Davidson is a well-known figure in London's East and West End, for his tireless work among homeless young people and professional streetwalkers. Precise details of the

complaints against him have yet to emerge, but may concern the moral basis of his friendships with young women over a period of years. Mr Davidson was not available for comment.

Journals of Harold Davidson
London
27 March 1932

The trial begins in two days' time. Mimi and I have secured lodgings in Pimlico, usefully close to the Church House, where the trial will be heard, and for Victoria Station, whence we may escape to, say, Brighton if we feel the need to 'take a break'. It is only a two-room flat in Hugh Street, and the parlour is weep-makingly gloomy, but it could be rendered cheerful by lighting a fire in the evenings, were Mimi so disposed. I trust we shall not spend our evenings in fretful anticipation. Nugent and Sheilagh have friends in Kennington with whom they can stay; they promise not to 'let me out of their sight'. Since I told them of my strange evening with young Estelle Douglas, and the appearance of a photographer in her room, they have warned me against being ambushed by hostile people, whether detectives or strange women.

I do not wish to concern them and so have not mentioned the approach from some gentlemen from, I think, the *Daily Express*. They were imprecise about the publication, but wanted me to appear in 'a photographic story', posing with a young lady on my knee; I assumed they meant her to be fully clad, but they said she would be half undraped. 'It's only a bit of fun, Rector,' they said again and again, 'a bit of fun because of this Church trial. Everyone knows you're innocent, and this would show the world you are.'

'Your suggestion is appalling. A young girl, undraped, on my knee? The idea is both obscene and preposterous.'

'We could offer you a nice fee for the pictures, Rector,' said the lead tempter's voice, attacking my weak point. 'Fifty quid, maybe, if you play ball.'

'I have no intention of "playing ball". The issue at stake is moral, not financial. Good day.'

'You don't want to reconsider?'

'One moment,' I said. 'I am puzzled. How do you imagine it would help my case and assert my innocence to the world, by showing myself in an immoral situation?'

'Oh, that's easy. There's you, charming old vicar, young girl on your lap, and you're looking at the camera and saying, "Chuh, hark at muggins 'ere, the ladies' man," like you're poking fun at the idea of you being this depraved character, when everyone knows you just want to help people. The readers'd take one look and say, "That rector bloke, 'e's a game old bird, isn't he, look at him with the girls, you can see there's no harm in him, bless him." It would do your case no end of good.'

I sent him away with a flea in his ear. I abhor cheap publicity.

London
29 March 1932

First day of the trial.

Owing to some confusion over the whereabouts of Mimi's hat and veil, we arrived at Church House, Westminster, after the event had begun. I sat behind Mr Levy, my stalwart counsel, while Mimi went downstairs to the witnesses' room. She would sit with me, she said, but cannot endure the stares from all around. I am reserving judgement as to my response. Amazing to think that this noble hall, where the archbishop annually presides over the Church Assembly, is to be the setting for these grubby, trumped-up insinuations. Mr Keppel-North, the bishop's lackey, sits in high style in his chancellor's robes, a Bible and prayer book on the table before him. He will have need of both, in attempting to indict an innocent man.

I arrived in time to hear Mr Oliver, the chief prosecutor, seek to add a further charge to the ones against me. I am now also charged with 'the immoral habit of accosting and molesting and importuning young women for immoral purposes'. He says he had a list of such ladies and a list of places where I supposedly molested them. The purest fabrication, of course. Mr Levy has added my new 'habit' to the other charges – namely, that I was guilty of immoral conduct with a woman (Rose) since 1921, that I made improper suggestions to a woman in a café in Walbrook, that I embraced a girl in a Chinese restaurant in Bloomsbury, and that I 'habitually' associated with ladies of loose character in order, it is to be inferred, to perform sex with them at some fortuitous moment when their guard was down.

Can these idiotic charges be made to stick for two minutes? A false confession from Rose, obtained by deception, a word out of place in Walbrook, a kiss in Bloomsbury and a lot of women friends, made and nurtured over the years – this is the whole case against me!

Mr Oliver spoke for an hour about my 'systematically misbehaving' with girls – was I associating with them innocently, he rhetorically enquired, or for my own 'purposes'? What 'purposes' could I have with upwards of two or three thousand young women? Does this odious man think I wished to make them all my mistresses? And if not, what could my purpose have been with the ones who escaped my 'immoral habit'? Mr Oliver remained silent on this conundrum. And pooh-poohed the idea of my rescue work.

Another call from Mr B at the *Daily Express*, re the photograph, followed by Mr C from the same organ increasing the fee to £100 and asserting that I need to 'win the public vote'. This is nonsense. No public intervention will have any effect on the chancellor's mind, or the outcome of these hearings, more's the pity.

London
30 March 1932

The unspeakable Oliver spoke for two hours without ceasing. My jaw was on the floor of the consistory court for most of that time. The tissue of lies, no the web, no the cat's cradle of falsehoods that has twined around my feet has been enough to make a lesser man despair.

Take what they say about Miss Harris. That, for instance, she did not know I was a clergyman for months, until she discovered it 'by accident' upon seeing letters in my room addressed to me thus. What rodent cunning! Oliver said I had 'claimed' to be her uncle, and embarked on a course of seduction. In this he is deluded, as he is in affirming I was sixty years old when I met her – an ancient, desiccated lecher. I was fifty-five at the time, and hardly doddering. What else? Oliver told the court that Barbara came to my house in Shepherd's Bush, but claimed such visits dated from two years ago! And that B's affair with the egregiously fake Indian 'prince' was conducted at his home when he was visiting London as a distinguished policeman (!) attending a conference. Now that he has disappeared back to whichever Turkish hovel he sprang from, his provenance (conveniently) cannot be traced. And that B slept at my room many times, but that no sexual misconduct took place – at last, a modicum of the truth emerges. Let us see how the prosecution gets round this testament to my sexual continence.

I cannot believe they could bring up my supposed 'proposal' of marriage to Miss Harris. I merely expressed once a hope for the future, that our two lonely lives might find some fulfilment one day, perhaps even with each other. That was all.

Rose Ellis's name came next – how I used to embrace her in front of Barbara, as though that were of any consequence. They have homed in on the occasion of my taking the girls to Stiffkey for a holiday, and turned it into a tale of woe, of domestic slavery. How the poor innocent creatures were pressed into service as cleaners, how they were destitute and starving, how they fled from me and were forced to walk all the way to London, sleeping in the fields and ditches. Such infamous inventions! And all to display me in the worst possible light, as a neglectful employer as well as a seducer and sexual bully – I, who spent ten years drying Rose's gin-scented tears, and holding her head as she vomited into the gutter outside her Camden home after being thrown once again on to the streets by her exasperated and unchristian parents.

My defence is always the same – I was involved in rescue work, to stop innocent women from falling into immoral habits or succumbing to the blandishments of young predators in London seeking female prey. Yet they now belittle me in court, saying that many such women were 'perfectly respectable' and had no need of rescue. I fear for the future of the British Bar. Have they never heard of preventative medicine? Can they conceive of the importance of protecting the young against the assaults of the ungodly? Fifty times or more they describe me as taking a waitress by the hand, showing her photographs, offering her seats at the theatre – as if these were heinous crimes! They cite with distaste my kindly suggestions, such as: 'Ring me if you ever feel lonely' or 'Come out and we will go and have a good time.' How could such sentiments be construed as intimidating to any woman?

Pestering, pestering, pestering. I have grown heartily sick of hearing that infamous word. I pester, thou pester, he she or it pestereth. In every case, I was *befriending*. They call it 'handling' and 'pawing' when I laid a comforting, fatherly hand upon an arm, or encircled a young waist with purely jovial intent.

Rose, now they come back to Rose, my poor faded friend, my wilted bloom whose vulnerability they have exploited and whose credulity they have abused. But there is something odd about their approach to Miss Ellis. They say that they will not call her to give witness, because 'it would be idle to attach the slightest reliance upon her word'. But they ask the court anyway 'to infer that the charge was true without her evidence'. What does this mean? That she might give evidence in my favour, and therefore should not be heard? That no one should rely on the truth of her words, but that her story of suffering at my hands can be relied on as the truth?

Then Barbara took the witness stand. All in black save for a striking green hat I bought her in Bermondsey Market, clamped to the side of her brown curls, she was a picture. Her vividness of personality was on display, but only intermittently – she mostly affected a pretence of demureness, lowering her voice to a whisper. I was, I confess, proud of her, even as she reduced our delightful and inspirational relationship to a travesty, in which I emerged like a creature in a fairy tale – a strange, unwanted visitor who came upon a belea-guered maiden in a dark tower and pressed his unsought and otiose attentions upon her. 'He asked me to give myself body and soul to him, just once,' she declared, failing to recall that I expressed this sentiment as a sorrowful recognition that this was precisely some-thing I could not ask her to do. As for my climbing into bed beside her, it is the purest fabrication. Except, of course, for the infamous night before Armistice Sunday, when events befell of which I cannot speak. (B told them I missed the Sunday service because I had been kissing her at the time. Perhaps it is as well that the actual facts were not aired in court.)

There was a moment of grotesque misunderstanding. Miss Harris was asked if I ever spoke of my wife. In her vulgar, reductive way she replied that I'd said I seldom saw M, did not like her and was not liked by her, that M was jealous of the women in London, and that I wished to get a divorce and marry her (BH) instead. The rank unfairness of this foolish litany fell on my ear like pain. To hear the complexity of my feelings for M reduced to this threadbare outline, as though describing the relations of children in a playground, and the stupidity of the girl in thinking I could contemplate marrying anyone so emotionally stunted – I fear my face fell into a hopeless grin, and something between a sob and a guffaw escaped my lips. Instant censure followed, as the appalling Oliver sought to make capital out of it. But I had not laughed, as he maintained. I had been close to tears.

Later that afternoon, in my lodgings near the station, I received a telephone call. Mr B from the *Express* had secured the services of a young woman to be photographed, with her mother's permission, in a humorous pose beside me. The newspaper folk were all supporters of mine, he said. 'We want you to show the world that they shouldn't take the case too seriously.' The fee now stood at £120, and this was the final offer.

What could I do? Had Mimi been there to advise me, I might not have gone. But I was weak. I thought of Estelle Douglas, and the damning picture that was taken. Surely a properly posed photograph – of clearly inoffensive and humorous intent – would mitigate the harm the other image might cause?

London
31 March 1932

Unfortunately delayed once again. Poor M showing signs of chronic depression. Tell her to buck up her ideas but she returns only a hard stare. At 6 a.m. I found her, in her nightdress, curled up in the stairs outside our rooms, resisting all attempts to return her to the twin bed where she had passed the most restless and fretful night. I quietened her with sympathetic words and, at 8 a.m., persuaded her to dress for breakfast. Soon after, she had another attack. I had merely ventured down the street from our lodgings, but she evidently suspected me of visiting an inappropriate person. I regret to say that, on my return, she attacked me with her fists and, in the mêlée, my lower lip was split. Applications of hot water and salve took an unconscionable time, and I arrived in court twenty minutes late. Black looks all round.

Barbara, back in the witness box, gave evidence that seemed to last all day. Five hours of calumnies and half-truths.

My counsel, Mr Levy, did well, I thought, to mock the idea that I'd tried to become intimate with Miss Harris while knowing she was suffering from a social disease. A shame, though, that he left the suspicion hanging in the air that, had the girl not been apparently thus stricken, I would have solicited intimacies with her, morning, noon and night. This is how things go, when one seeks the truth by question and answer: embedded in every simple question are a dozen other, unasked questions that surface in the minds of the hearers.

I could only hang my head as the full scale of her betrayal was revealed. Levy disastrously overplayed his hand by suggesting that she had attempted to seduce me with lascivious kisses, whereupon Miss Harris let fly: how, on the contrary, she had instinctively fled, repulsed, from me and tried to hide from me as from the Hound of Heaven (though I fear the allusion would be lost on her), returning home or getting back in touch only in order that I might find her employment. All the intensity of our friendship, empathy, learning and mutual kindness reduced to an economic dependency! I feel a hole like an ulcer in my heart to think how our innocent connection was vandalised in the witness box. 'You would bear his attentions, much as you disliked them,' asked Levy, 'in order to get his money?' 'Yes,' said Barbara, 'for him to set me up in business.' Business indeed!

There was a moment of fine theatre when Mr Levy, having established that I had never resented Barbara's sexual involvement with her fake Indian, confronted her with the simple truth: 'I am suggesting throughout that he [that is, I] had no desire to be intimate with you at all.' I looked at Miss Harris with interest. Faced with the simple truth, what could she reply? Instead of denying it, Miss Harris changed tack. In a tiny voice, reminiscent of Binnie Hale in one of her charged emotional 'moments', she said, 'He had plenty of other girls.'

Levy rightly upbraided her for such an infamous suggestion, asking, 'You do not mind what scandalous things you say about him, do you?' To which she replied, 'No, and he doesn't mind what scandalous things he says about *me*.' The childish nature of the response merely confirmed the untruth of the statement – that she speaks out of revenge for what I was unable to do for her. What a state of affairs. During our period of association, it seems that our intentions were completely at odds. I wished – Pygmalion to her Galatea – to mould her into a proper young woman, intellectually alive, well read, thoughtful, modest in behaviour, decent in impulses. She wished only for material success, to be set up 'in business' – she to whom 'business sense' meant ensuring her gentlemen callers did not disturb her slumbers until midday.

I suppose I must sustain myself with the few crumbs of generosity that fell from her lips. She admitted that I attempted to reconcile her to her family. And that I tried to find her places to live. What more could a man do to start off a poor unfortunate on the road to decency? But despite it all, it's clear she has no love for me now. In fact, she hates me. It emerged during the questioning. When Mr Levy asked about my giving her job references, he suggested to her: 'The only reason you wrote to Mr Davidson was because he was kind to you and useful to you and you had no sort of resentment against him whatsoever.' 'He was kind and useful,' Barbara said.

'And,' Mr Levy pressed her, 'you had no sort of resentment against him?'

'Yes I had,' Barbara said.

The question of the exact nature of this resentment hung in the air, but Chancellor Keppel-North intervened to make some footling general point about girls-of-this-sort, and the moment was lost.

What can it be, this resentment Barbara feels so strongly? Why should she have turned on me like this? Because I failed to find her employment? She was wholly unsuited to any office or dentist's surgery. Because I was responsible for Don Stupendo leaving her? She never knew. Because I could not help fulfil her dream of domesticity, her wish for a house with a garden? Or was it that I constantly reflected back to her the kind of person she had early become – a brassy young termagant, morally lost, emotionally cauterised, hardly capable of a single generous or disinterested action towards another human being?

On my way out of Church House, the porter handed me a bulky envelope with the words, 'All yours, Padre.' At the lodgings, I discovered no fewer than seventy-one letters from members of the public, the addresses mostly handwritten, though some were sternly and precisely typed. 'Dear Rector,' read the first, 'I saw that thing in the papers about what you did bringing young tarts together with their families after years of estrangement. I know what it is like to be cold-shouldered by your family for doing NOTHING WRONG and I think it was lovely of you. If only more people would give their family members a CHANCE the world would be a happier place. Good luck with your work, Mrs Ada Lumley.' Dazed, I picked up a second.

'Rector,' it began, curtly, 'I understand from the *Eastern Daily Press* that you served as an RN chaplain, Middle Eastern region, in the last hoo-ha. I don't suppose it was HMS *Fox* was it? I was chief petty officer, and am sure you were the chap, though our paths didn't cross much, me not having much time for sky pilotry, pardon me saying so. Think I remember you were bit of a chess player? Anyway, sorry if this is wrong end of stick. If you fancy getting in touch, contact me at address above and we'll go for a noggin. I see you're a bit in the soup at present. Chin up. Henry Ballhatchet.'

I sat for a full hour and a half, as envelopes piled up around my feet, and I read on, entranced. Most of the letters were supportive of my case, a handful were not, while some did not mention the trial at all. They contented themselves with cheery familiarity, greeting me as like an old friend, passing on compliments from family members wholly unknown to me ('Gerry and Julia send their love, and of course Mrs Gardiner from the Social').

Of the hostile missives, they tended to emanate from the lower end of the educational scale (e.g. 'Yore a flippin disgrace gong round London kissin them sluts and tryig to get yore endaway. I'm glad yore not marryin my Susan next week, Yores truly Mrs Ann Pond') and included a few sordid fantasies about what the correspondent would have done, were he alone with Miss Harris for five minutes ('Did you like banging it into her? Did you shove it up her arse? Did you make her bleed? Did you fuck her with a crucifix? What I'd like to do to one of them slappers, right, I'd . . .').

By the end, I was completely stunned. I had never received such a vivid correspondence before – so animated, so confiding, so frank at times, so ethically and intellectually challenging. I had never received letters on such varied subject matter (HMS *Fox*; kissing sluts; crucifixes) and such a wide scope of sympathy.

'I felt I must write,' read one letter, 'to say it seems wrong to put a man on trial for trying to be kind and understanding to the down-and-out, the damaged and disreputable. These stories of you putting your arms round them, and kissing them, sound like the Archangel of Love folding poor sinners under his vast and cooling wings.' What an extraordinary thing to say. I wonder if I could perhaps adapt it for my defence.

I spent all evening considering this great public – what? – outspilling of emotion, aimed at me and my tribulations. I am accustomed to receiving occasional letters at the Rectory. If they are from parishioners, they are invariably direct. They seek my help, make demands on my time, money or influence and sign off with a 'Yours sincerely'. They do not generally adopt a confiding tone, nor engage in chit-chat, nor ask advice about family troubles. I have never encountered the like in twenty-five years of pastoral care. It is like discovering a land that I never knew existed.

London
1 April 1932

For once, was on time for court, with M beside me in black hat with veil and Sheilagh very kind and supportive clad in her fine blue mackintosh. Mr and Mrs Reynolds also down from Norfolk to lend welcome support. I am no expert in these matters but it seems to me an atmosphere of lively, rather *too* lively, interest has begun to supervene in court. The place is full of pressmen. The public galleries are full of busybodies and gawkers in nondescript hats, their pockets apparently full of sweets. They sit there reading the *Daily Mirror* in between the sessions of advocacy, for all the world like tourists at Cheddar Gorge. If one were to pull out a Thermos flask and a picnic lunch with hard-boiled eggs and salad cream, I should not be surprised.

One journalist, from the *Eastern Daily Press*, remarked on what he discerned as my unusual serenity, even while damning testimony against me was being read out by the egregious Mr Oliver – namely Barbara's letter to the Bishop dated 9 February, scarcely two months ago. It was put forward by the prosecution as a damning document – but it says nothing! Nothing directly accusatory, at any rate. It merely drops murky hints that, e.g., I attempt to save young girls from immorality but not young boys (show me, someone, which boys are in danger of being raped by immoral ladies, or forced to embrace a life of prostitution!). The silly goose claims that I charged her to 'speak well of me' in the event of any policeman or detective asking questions (who would *not* wish for such a happy response to a police enquiry?) and concluded with the suggestion that people who speak well of me must be motivated by fear! It is too priceless. 'I think it will be found out in the end,' she wrote to Pollock, 'that half the people who are going to praise him are frightened of him.' Frightened of me? What a novel idea! A harmless, ageing, white-haired clergyman and social helper, with no money and no bad intentions to a soul? Preposterous! It will not help the prosecution's case to have such half-accusations advanced as testimony. As for her breezy invention that I once offered to settle £500 a year on her, all I can say is, I wish I had half a prospect of earning a quarter of such a sum in the next calendar year.

The appalling Major Hammond, my sworn enemy and quite possibly (I suspect) the original begetter of my present misfortunes, appeared in the witness box but was allowed only minutes of 'stage time' in which to unleash all his loathing for me. All he could say was that I had failed to preside over a church service for Armistice Day. Hah! Perhaps these proceedings will not be as alarming as I thought.

A dull day in this increasingly farcical legal pantomime. They brought two waitresses to testify against me. One was Violet from the Spring Blossom in Bloomsbury, a place I have patronised many times. Violet identified me and Barbara, and said she had seen us arguing, then kissing and making up. What could be more natural between loving friends, locked in a struggle for her immortal soul? As B came to realise the depths of her degragation, of course she often became upset, of course there were tears. But like a child chastened by its loving parent, she came to me in tears of relief and acceptance. And this is what young Violet saw. It is not my fault if she is both a cluster-fisted waitress and a birdbrain when it comes to human sympathy.

The other girl was Dorothy from the Lyons Corner House in Walbrook, whom I stand accused of 'molesting'. A grumpy blonde woman, pretty but with an unyielding quality about the mouth, she complained about my friendly attempts at conversation, which she rudely construed as 'pestering'. 'He did not belong to my tables but wanted me to serve him' – can one believe that the Upper Seraphim of the Church of England have to listen to such stuff? I remember her. I remember telling her she was too clever and too pretty to last in such employment without becoming bored, a prey to wickedness and immoral beguilements. And she found better employment elsewhere. She is now the manageress of a corset shop. I was right! But instead of showing gratitude, she told the court that she did not like me or my 'advances'. My invitations to her, to spend a relaxing weekend at Stiffkey, were presented as a subject for humour, as when she replied that she 'did not like to chance it'.

One curious detail. I did not realise that, in the Lyons Corner House, St James's, I am apparently known by the soubriquet of 'The Mormon'. Why? All I know of this sect is that they hail from Salt Lake City in the United States and their male adherents are allowed to have several wives. But how their religious beliefs or observances match or mirror my own, I am completely in the dark.

The unspeakable Dashwood took the stand – 'Mr Henry Thomas

Alexander Dashwood' if you please – to tell the court about our conversation in January. It was clear that Mr Levy saw through him straight away, had him down as a sneaking, oily, corrupt, manipulative spymaster, and humiliated him by asking whether he had set special detectives to follow the defendant through the streets of London. The awful man spoke of my being 'shadowed' as though it were the most natural thing in the world for a servant of the Church to organise, as if subterfuge and espionage were time-honoured features of a bishop's ministry.

There he stood, this Iago, this smiling villain (Mr Levy ticked him off like a schoolboy for smiling at inappropriate moments), this creepy, oleaginous impresario of other people's misfortunes, this orchestrator of duplicity, this serpent of chaos, blithely discussing his hiring of special enquiry agents. That the Church should stoop to such methods, that the modus operandi of Chicago gangsters should be employed by the Bishop of Norwich, is nothing short of disgusting. My devotion to Mother Church was dealt a blow today, in the person of this dreadful man, their devoted and slimy servant, from which it will not quickly recover.

Levy brought up my first encounter with Dashwood, when he would not tell me of my wrongs, only giving me a form of resignation to sign. Mr Levy taxed him that this was 'a grossly oppressive and unfair proceeding'. Dashwood said, 'Not in this case,' and told the court that, when I was advised of the complaints against me, I said, 'Is that all?' They seek to make capital out of this innocent enquiry, as though my surprise hinted at some dreadful secrets yet to be brought into the light; when all it meant to say was: 'After all your dark and dreadful hints about the sins with which I am charged, is *this* all they amount to – a kiss, a conversation, a social acquaintance?'

Stiffkey
3 April 1932

I am euphoric and bewildered after the day's events. I scarcely know how to account for them, nor even describe them accurately.

I travelled up last night on the last train, arriving in Norwich at 2 a.m., where I slept awkwardly in the station waiting room – solitary and cheerless, though thank God a fire had been lit therein – while waiting for a motor taxi. At 4.30 a.m. I was awakened by noise of a revving engine. It was not my taxi, which had evidently abandoned me along with so many other false friends lately, but a motor bicycle, ridden by a snarly young villain called Clive. His mission at the station so late at night was inscrutable (I fancied he was hoping to burgle the ticket office) but I persuaded him to give me a lift to his home near Sheringham. Riding on the passenger seat was at first terrifying, then elating as we sped through the lanes and backwoods with the dawn breaking ahead and the dew burning off the sea lavender, bringing a sharp tang to the nostrils. At Sheringham, I thanked him, he roared off and I banged on the door of the Crown Inn, seeking shelter like a wandering pilgrim, until a Mrs Marion Todd in a floral housecoat admitted me grudgingly and allowed me to sit in the warmth of her parlour before retracing her slatternly steps to bed. I dozed for an hour, indescribably happy to be away from London and the dismal, mendacious courtroom and the imbecilic nagging voice of Mr Oliver, until I was wakened by the clashing of cutlery as the maids prepared the breakfast tables.

In the gentlemen's lavabo, as I sloughed off my clerical jacket, my collar and shirt and performed rudimentary ablutions, I realised I was starving. I had not eaten anything more than biscuits for two days, nor slept more than an hour or two in forty-eight. Weakness, dizziness and bad humour brought on by malnutrition had turned me into the rheumy-eyed, unshaven, ill-tempered monster – Mr Hyde in person! – that stared back from the looking glass.

Mrs Todd regarded me coldly as I approached the empty dining room.

'My good woman,' I said, 'I am so hungry. I would dearly love to try some of your excellent breakfast, but I am embarrassed by a current financial dearth, so grave that I can hardly afford a cup of tea. If you would allow me to send you a cheque the moment I reach my home, I –'

'Sorry, mister,' she said, turning her substantial bulk four-square before me, like a destroyer turning athwart the English Channel to repel invaders, 'but we don't give credit at the Crown. You've had your little snooze, now I'll thank you to be on your way.'

I let out a sigh of disappointment. 'In that case, perhaps you would be good enough to telephone a taxi. I must be in Stiffkey Church by 10 a.m. to take a service, and hired vehicles can be scarce on the Sabbath.' I turned to leave.

'Hang on a minute,' she said. 'You're not that bloke in the papers, are you? The Rector of Stiffkey? The one with all the girls in London, and the little tarts giving out about you in the witness box?'

Was she about to abuse me? I'd had enough abuse. I was so tired.

'I *am* the rector in question, but I shall not sully your establishment any longer. If you would just make this telephone call –'

'Phone call, my foot. You come in here this minute, sit at that table by the window with the view of the garden, and I'll bring you a menu directly. Poor man, you must be starved, travelling all this way.'

'I confess I am a little weakened. But as I say, my financial –'

'It's on the house. Eat whatever you like. You want sausages? We got some lovely Cumberland sausages, made here in the kitchen with lots of black pepper. Scrambled eggs? You can have two if you like, on some buttered toast, with some plum jam, made by my sister in Lowestoft, and I expect you'd like some grapefruit juice, freshly squeezed, to wake you up a bit? You look a bit rough. Here, I'll go and do it myself.'

'My dear woman, you are . . .' I could not continue. Tears, foolish tears, were prickling into my eyes. I had not received such impulsive kindness from anyone in years.

'Oh stop it. Go and sit down and Cecily will be in to take your order. I got to wake up George. He'll be tickled pink to find he's got the famous Rector of Stiffkey right here under his roof.'

I do not know when I enjoyed a meal as much – the procession of savoury treats, the smokiness of the bacon rashers, the exploding spiciness of the sausages, the infinitely soft, buttery mounds of egg on their Medusan raft of toasted bread. As I wiped the last jammy crumbs from my mouth, the proprietor appeared, a gruff individual clearly unused to rising before noon on a Sunday. He welcomed me and asked a series of frankly impertinent questions regarding 'them girls in London – I expect you've seen some sights in your time, among the, you know, night walkers . . .'

I would not indulge him, notwithstanding his wife's generosity. 'It is a most uncomfortable experience,' I said, 'to finish such a delightful breakfast and find oneself being grilled. Is my taxi here?'

Miraculously, it was. Once Mrs Todd had apprised the local car people about their passenger, there had been no problem. As we drove away, the proprietors of the Crown Inn stood in front of their modest front door, waving me goodbye.

Mimi and the children were in London so the Rectory was deserted. I was alone in the house for the first time I can ever remember. The silence, as I walked through kitchen, drawing room and bedroom, was the silence of a tomb – advance warning, perhaps, of what was to come for the family.

Time was short, so I put on my robes in haste, not daring to lie down for even a moment's rest. I was aware of the reception that might greet me at the church, should the major and certain enemies of mine try to make capital out of the court proceedings. There was no time to repine: I would have to brave it out, no matter how uncomfortable the event might prove. A combative djinn entered my head, an impulse to fight and not flee, and I extracted my old war medals and pinned them, in a tiny trinity of glory, on my soutane before venturing forth.

Outside the Rectory some people were waiting. They greeted me with shy smiles and little waves, keeping their distance as though uncertain of how to approach a pastor suddenly thrown into the public eye. A photographer from some local newspaper bade me remove my hat to be 'snapped' and I obliged. As I gained the church lane, I found larger numbers – at least fifty souls – awaiting my arrival, also a little shy and awkward. Without a thought, I swept off my hat and inclined my head to them all, a theatrical gesture that drew a ragged cheer. You would think I was onstage, acknowledging (or anticipating) some earned applause!

I moved into the half-empty church, which was quickly filled by the throng outside, and I announced that, as it was the first Sunday in the month, there would be a shortened morning service. I had decided, on the train, which text to address. Nothing would be gained by modesty, or pretence that I lived in anything but extra-ordinary times. I chose the Third Psalm:

'*Lord, how are they increased that trouble me! Many are they that rise up against me. Many there be which say of my soul, There is no help for him in God. But thou, O Lord, art a shield for me; my glory, and the lifter up of mine head. I cried unto the Lord with my voice, and he heard me out of his holy hill . . . I will not be afraid of ten thousands of people, that have set themselves against me round about. Arise, O Lord, save me, O my God: for thou hast smitten all mine enemies upon the cheek bone; thou hast broken the teeth of the ungodly.*'

A murmur of approval greeted these words, a muted, then strengthening hum from the souls of the faithful. I felt buoyed up, not by the Lord, but by the convocation of village souls. They appeared to be on my side. Poor Pollie Dack being indisposed, there was no organ recital, but the congregation sang 'O God Our Help in Ages Past' with heart and spirit, and a conviction I have seldom heard in our little church.

I asked for prayers on behalf of everyone interested in or affected by the court case, both those giving evidence and those affected by it. And, taking the bull by the horns, I announced that most of the revenue from the collection would go to some of the poor girls in London whom I have been unable to help while burdened by legal procedure. I held my breath – but was rewarded by a chinking of coinage and rustling of purses and wallets, as though their owners were happy to embrace the cause to which I have devoted my recent life.

As I began my sermon, a photographer tried to take my picture as I stood in the pulpit. Had he no shame, to bring his equipment into a house of God? I upbraided him from my higher vantage point, saying, 'I'm sorry, I cannot consent to this. I will give you anything you like outside the church but not in here,' and he subsided in embarrassment.

My sermon argued that it is in the moral choices we make every day that character is established. 'As far as we choose, by individual acts in daily life, we build up our character, either on a good basis or a bad.' I hoped that the subtext was suitably apparent to all – that I, as their moral exemplar, am confronted by moral choices every day in an atmosphere of rampant immorality, and have come through it unscathed, weathered like oak, tempered like steel, while the bishop and his evil associates seek to damn me *for the very atmosphere in which I work*, as though it must contaminate my soul.

Outside, they crowded around me. The women of the parish – like so many Veronicas around the suffering Christ on his way to Calvary! – shook my hand, congratulating me on the texts, the choice of hymns, the sermon. They patted my sleeve. Men made so bold as to slap me on the back, in some confused attempt at camaraderie. In Morston, this afternoon, the pattern was repeated – a crowded church, an influx of strangers, a deal of handshaking, shoulder-patting, flushed faces wishing me good luck ('Luck, my dear woman, has nothing to do with it,' I said, a hundred times) and boldly alluding to aspects of the trial which they had all followed in *The Times* and the *Eastern Daily Press*. There was hardly time to close my eyes for twenty minutes at the Rectory, or discuss the case with Mr Reynolds, before I took the evening service in Stiffkey.

What a sight greeted my eyes – upwards of two hundred people turned out to see me, to cram the greensward from the lychgate of St John's as far as the roadway. Motor cars of all sizes were parked higgledy-piggledy on the slender lanes, until two policemen arrived to regularise the traffic flow. A coach party from Norwich arrived, like a charabanc of trippers to the Bangor fair. Once more we sang 'O God Our Help', followed by 'Abide With Me' and 'Rock of Ages'. The soaring voices in the church, harmonising with the muted roar outside, were simply amazing. I have never heard the like – not just in my church, but in any house of God short of Westminster Abbey. Preaching my sermon to such a crowd (half of them unseen but a palpable presence nonetheless), I was strengthened – glorified – emboldened to quote from Kipling's 'If . . .' about keeping your head when all men doubt you.

I left Stiffkey with cheers and huzzahs ringing in my ears, took a taxi to Norwich and then the train to London, on which I am writing these words. Never have I experienced such a ringing affirmation of my labours. Never have I felt so close to the community of believers whose souls it has been my mission and destiny to save.

The journey passed in a glow of benevolent thoughts, an image-cluster of delight. I return to the ghastly fray a transformed soul, hardly beatified perhaps, but sanctified certainly, washed in the divine waters of popular approval, baptised anew in the affirmation of the people!

London
4 April 1932

After my elation in Stiffkey, the warmth of my parishioners' greeting, the crowds of well-wishers that stretched across the church approach and spread out on to the road in both directions – after this glowing affirmation, I returned to the trial buoyed up in spirit but emotionally frustrated. Suddenly the proceedings seem tiresomely trivial, a fatuous recital of dates and times, waitresses and rooms, a chronicle of suspicion and prurient suggestion that amounts to nothing.

Today, it was an anonymous boyfriend of Rose's, someone who met her last August in a pub. His testimony? That I had called to see her once or twice in the evenings and asked her what she had said about me to a detective. Fascinating, I'm sure.

Then came Ada Woodford, the charming landlady of some flats in Old Compton Street where Rose lodged for a time. All this was a decade ago, and I remember the details dimly – why we decided to call Rose 'Mrs Malone', and to say she was my secretary. (Because she had no wish to be introduced as a rehabilitated harlot. It is not a complicated explanation.) It all seems so long ago. Lastly there was Kathy Grant, a lovely vision in a long black coat with fur trim, speaking about her time as a waitress at Maison Lyons, recalling how I used to engage her in conversation. Since her mother lived in Stiffkey, this was hardly surprising. Much was made of my having called to see her at midnight, with a message from her mother; but at least she admitted I never made an improper suggestion. One wonders how exactly the bishop feels about how his case is progressing. Many more witnesses like today's, and I shall become a candidate for sainthood rather than obloquy.

There was, however, a remarkable close to the day's proceedings. The court rose at lunchtime and went off in motor cars to Camden Town, to hear the testimony of Mrs Bright, Barbara's former landlady at Queen Street. She is ill and temporarily bedridden, and was obliged to give her witness replies from a horizontal position. How oddly playful it was, to have Keppel-North, Mr Levy, the awful Mr Oliver, their helpers and advisers and the court clerks and functionaries, all setting off – as though on a charabanc ride! – to invade the seedy purlieus of Queen Street, with all their clever argumentation and logic.

Somehow, word had got out about the planned visit, and the streets were crammed with people, hundreds of them. So many that the cars could not enter, so that the police had to be called and were obliged to clear a path to the Brights' front door. When the crowd realised which house was the court's destination, they rushed to anticipate the cars' arrival; again the police fought them back, with every exertion, as though quelling an angry mob in Amritsar or Khartoum rather than a gang of excitable Londoners.

I was detained on the journey north, owing to a sudden decision to look in on Elsie Teenan while I was passing – and what with my prayers and her tears, I was fifteen minutes late. I do not think anyone noticed. The crowd had no idea who I was, and I made my way unmolested through the crush of bodies. It was a different story when we left after an hour of rambling and inconsequential landlady tales. As I emerged from the house, a shout of 'It's the rector!' went up, the crowd pressed forward and I was directed to stand still and pose for photographs, along with Elsie and her friend Kath who had come along for the ride. I am becoming quite taken with – and quite used to – this unlooked-for and unanticipated new role of 'semi-celebrity'!

London
5 April 1932

Time, time, time. Why is everyone obsessed with time? Are we not regulated enough in our everyday lives – the office life that demands (not me obviously, but the majority of working people) we arrive at 9 a.m. and labour until 5 p.m., the teashops which cease to allow one to consume gateaux at 6 p.m. sharp, the restaurants whose kitchens close at 9.30 p.m., the public houses which send drunkards into the streets at 11 p.m. – that we must mind our manners in timing our calls upon our fellow beings?

It has been my way, for ten years, to fill my days with activity. So many visits, so many souls to call on, so many new friends to make, so many lives whose course must be altered. Should they fall outside the hours considered decent by Mayfair rules, or by the proprieties of social visits in the novels of Miss Austen, it is because a new urgency is abroad in 1930s England. London is full to bursting with itinerant young people occupying squalid bed-sitting rooms in faceless properties, from Tooting Bec to Turnham Green, a benighted herd ambling to work each morning, wheezing home each night on tram, bus or 'Underground', their lives circumscribed by routine, deadened by habit, enlivened only by the promise of weekend trips to cinema or seaside, by bicycling aimlessly around Richmond Park or pursuing hobbies, constructing balsa-wood aeroplanes or racing tiny boats around the park ponds. What a life for the four or six millions who inhabit London! But if, in my ministry, I choose to call on the many young ladies in whose lives I have intervened, to bring spiritual succour and material help (prayer, mostly, at their bedsides – but also conversation, theatrical gossip, some perfumed soap, sweetmeats, inspirational leaflets and, very occasionally, money), what in the Lord's name does it matter at what hour I attend them? Yet I have had to listen, hour after hour, to the rancorous suspicions of landladies (that lard-faced, intractable breed of petrified femininity) about my supposed behaviour when closeted with my young charges in their lonesome, chilly rooms.

Mrs Bright's testimony, concerning the times when I called on Miss Harris in her rooms in Camden, although I never recall any sign of a landlady there, was read out today. Mrs Jordan of Euston Street complained about my giving succour to two young women whom I allowed to sleep in my room when they were homeless (I prowled the streets of Peckham while they slumbered, and wakened them with tinned pineapple slices and fresh rolls from the bakery in Walworth Road). Mrs Flora Winter produced a pack of lies about my tenancy in her wretched home, including a farcical, wholly fictional scene in which I apparently tried to take a bath at midnight and she came in through the bathroom window to remonstrate with me. Through all her testimony breathes the fetid air of a woman long resigned to frustration, disappointed in her husband, haunted by bad luck and poor judgement, driven to invent lurid fantasies about wicked women and predatory men. But there was one interchange which will, I feel, lodge itself in the heart of this pointless inquiry:

Mr Levy: 'A point I want to make is that Mr Davidson is the sort of gentleman who is always helping or trying to help people, and sometimes makes a perfect nuisance of himself.'

Mrs Osborne: 'Quite right.'

Mr Levy: 'He is always getting his finger into the pie.'

Mrs Osborne: 'Yes, but he would pester you to death. Three pennyworth of good, and shilling's worth of harm.'

Harm? I do greatly hope that this does not serve as my epitaph.

As I was leaving, the door clerk beckoned me towards him.

'Getting a cab are we, Rector?' he asked.

'No, my good fellow, I will walk as usual,' I said. 'But when I win this case, you can order me a Rolls-Royce to bear me home in triumph.'

'No, Rector, I ask because you're goingta need a cab. Look here.'

He went behind the door of his office and returned with two jute sacks, the kind in which coal might be delivered.

'Letters to Church House. All addressed to you. You got to take them because they're silting up the doorway and I can't hardly get in.'

I tried to pick up the sacks, but they were too heavy. Only with the aid of a brawny visiting plumber and a fresh-faced seminarian did I manoeuvre them into the back of a taxicab. At Hugh Street, the cabman and I staggered through the gate and I gave him sixpence to deposit them in my bedroom – where I spent the next three hours pulling out random envelopes and disgesting their contents. I counted up to 320 before suffering a kind of correspondence fatigue. The sentiments uttered were much the same as the first batch, in their congratulation and disfavour, their ad hoc advice, impertinent enquiries about what I 'really got up to', gossipy disburdenings of family information as if I knew or cared about any of the members, plus a handful of communications so utterly bizarre and surreal, I knew not what to do with myself. One lady, from an address in Portland, Dorset, enquired if I were married and said she would 'seriously consider me as a husband' if the 'timing' was right and 'nobody'd get hurt'. I am beginning to wake up to the fact that there is a vast audience out there that nobody – not just I, hitherto – knows anything about. Where have they come from? What do they want?

London
6 April 1932

It seems that several people have protested about the reports of the trial that have appeared in the newspapers. They say it is wrong to have it thrashed out in public, and that the case should be heard in camera. The chancellor, Mr Keppel-North, made a pretty speech about the Press, and said how much he believes in publicity. 'Serious as the mischief may be of publishing nasty details, it is not nearly so serious as the mischief of secret trials might be.' I know nothing of secret trials, but I am, of late, all in favour of publicity. When I left the court today, after hearing yet more landladies (Mrs Alice Ernst complained that she did not think it was quite the thing for a gentleman in my position to be in a bedroom in the dark with a girl. The girl was Nellie Churchill. We were sitting talking about the fate of poor Emily Murray. There was no need to light candles. I could easily imagine her face), there was a crowd waiting for me outside. No more than forty-five people in fact, hardly a multitude, but I was surprised to find them surrounding me, as if hoping to touch my clothing, and as I smiled to acknowledge their kindness, they broke out into cheering! I am standing trial for being (the word keeps coming up, over and over again) a 'nuisance' to young women all over the metropolis, I am accused of lingering in darkened bed-sitting rooms with weeping prostitutes in the hope of having my evil way with them, and still the people cheer me. What is all this about?

Disaster strikes. I have run out of money.

The trial is lasting much longer than I imagined it would. My defence has cost somewhere in the region of £700, and the trust I set up is almost empty. Even though I have been trying to supplement it with articles in the *Daily Express*, even though a few pounds have been forthcoming from well-wishers in Stiffkey and the trustees of the Actors' Union Charity, I do not see how sufficient cash can be raised to keep the 'show' afloat. We need approximately £1,500 to be able to proceed. Where will that come from? Shall God provide?

My financial problems were brought up in court, and there was an audible groan of disappointment when Mr Levy explained that soon I would not be able to afford representation by my legal advisers. I think members of the public in the gallery (which has become very crowded of late) took it to mean that the case would cease if I ran out of money, and were expressing their sorrow that this popular entertainment – this stage show of my humiliation – might come to an end, like *The Desert Song* finally closing on Broadway after years. In fact, when the prosecution has subsided in its tirade of half-allegations and prurient nosings, there will be an adjournment, in order for me to look for more funds. The chancellor adumbrated this course of action, very slowly and clearly, five or six times until everyone virtually had it by heart. But how and where to raise £1,500 remains an insuperable problem.

Perhaps I can appeal to the public? I understand from Mr Levy, my legal wizard, that the case is being avidly followed in the daily papers by the general public, in a way no court case in history ever was. If every reader were to part with five shillings, to be put towards my defence fund . . . It is a nice thought. What splendid entertainment they could buy with their money: such as Mr Kingsley of the ABC café chain assuring the court that he never received a single letter of complaint about me. Mrs Ernst explaining that Nellie Churchill was a modest, decent girl whom I introduced to film and stage managers (oh, *that* Nellie Churchill). Mr Thole, one of the odious 'private eyes' who followed me all over London, lying through his teeth about the statement he extracted from Rose after plying her with most of a bottle of port.

Just after lunch, startling news came – the prosecution has offered to put £250 at my disposal for the conduct of the defence, and when the money is exhausted, to offer further advances as necessary.

Very generous I am sure. But 'advances' is just the word, is it not? I am being offered seductive inducements by the office of the bishop, in order that the trial shall go grinding on with twenty or thirty more witnesses, whose chatty and inconclusive testimony will coil around me like an anaconda until I am strangled and speechless.

Mid-afternoon, they returned to Mr Thole. It is interesting that the prosecution has no idea how to deal with Miss Ellis. She was persuaded to tell lies against me. She tried to retract them next day, but signed the confession, regretted it instantly and tried to kill herself. Now they would like to put her in the witness box, but only if she gives the testimony that she so passionately tried to rescind.

Mr Thole was asked by the defence if it was true that, out of all the statements and enquiries, there was only one woman with whom I allegedly committed 'misconduct', namely Miss Ellis.

Thole nodded, and said, 'Yes.'

'And Miss Ellis is not giving evidence in support of that allegation?' asked Levy.

'That I know nothing about,' said the hapless Thole. How, realistically, are they to proceed with their star witness, when she will never testify against me?

Thole was a model of the modern surveillance man, offering a recital of every hour of every day that he followed me. How he saw me leave Macfarlane Road with Barbara and Rose, go shopping with them, travel by bus and train, visit 'various places', go to the theatre and a Soho restaurant. It was, in a way, exquisite – an accurate recital of blamelessly innocent days, just as deadly dull as ordinary, innocent life will always sound, without drama, violence, sin or blame. Poor Mr Thole. How they mocked him. What sport they had.

'Did you notice whether he smoked cigars?' asked Mr Monckton, acting for the bishop.

'Continuously,' said Mr Thole.

'What has that got to do with it?' asked Keppel-North, the chancellor.

'It has some purpose,' said Mr Monckton (sulkily).

Mr Levy cut in. 'I thought it was evidence of immoral intent.' (At which there was laughter in the courtroom.)

'And did you,' persisted Mr Levy, 'see him walking about with a cigar that was out between his fingers?'

'I could not say,' Mr Thole replied.

'I suggest,' said the admirable Levy, 'that this great "extravagance" mostly consisted of holding a cigar which was not alight. You also omitted to tell us how many times he sneezed that day. Did you notice that?'

The stolid birdbrain Thole furrowed his brow. 'Sneeze?' he said. 'No.'

Sometimes, even in my despair for justice, the conduct of this court makes me smile. What evidence has he gathered against me? He had seen me speaking to young ladies on a Tube train and giving them my card. He had seen me quarrelling, then making up, with Barbara at Euston Station. He'd seen me go to the Piccadilly Theatre. I am struggling to imagine how any of this can be interpreted as having some venal undertow. Mr Thole even reported on the day I intro-duced Barbara to Sheilagh. How immoral can one be, to introduce one's mistress to one's daughter? No, I cannot see any harm being caused by the detective's indefatigable researches. The only harm came in one reported exchange: Mr Thole recalls hearing the landlord of the Marquis of Cornwallis address me with the words, 'Hullo, you old thief. Still getting cash? How are all the girls?' The people in the public gallery laughed it off. I hope that others will too.

London
8 April 1932

I announced my decision this morning – I refuse to take any charity from the Bishop of Norwich, or to be under any obligation to him, and that consequently I decline his offer to pay part of the defence's expenses. Furthermore, I said, if my defence counsel will not be available in future, I will conduct my own defence.

There was an agreeable susurration of shock at this news. I have become used to gasps of amazement in this trial. I was less amused to hear Mr Oliver announce that the offer of money did not come from the bishop but was made in 'what was conceived to be the interests of British justice'. Such casuistry. He went so far as to say that, while the case continues into the summer, I should be debarred from exercising any sacred functions in the church.

Debarred from holding church services! Just as I am gaining my largest audiences – I mean, congregations! 'Unless Mr Davidson ceases dissembling propaganda, he will have to be inhibited, or else I must ask you not to grant this adjournment,' said Oliver. As though I were a spy for a foreign power, spreading pernicious messages to the faithful. But while I am reluctant to do anything suggested by Mr Oliver and his like, I must say I would rather enjoy being relieved of my clerical duties for a few weeks. The size of the faithful notwithstanding, it is becoming hard to conduct prayer readings and communion services without aching to comment on the trial, or to refer in acidic terms to the conduct of the Church of England. So I shall stand down, temporarily, and ask the Reverend Blair to stand in for me. Leaving me free, as the prosecution case comes to its bitter end, to construct a magnificent defence and to arraign all my tormentors, in and out of the Church, as the low, venomous, treacherous beasts they are!

News report, *Eastern Daily Press*
9 April 1932

RECTOR OF STIFFKEY'S DEFENCE FUND
Appeal for Public Subscriptions

Following the statement made at Church House, Westminster, to the effect that the Rev. Harold Davidson, Rector of Stiffkey, would no longer be able to be represented by his legal advisers,

Mr Davidson is appealing to the public for the necessary funds to carry on his defence, as all his personal resources, including his July tithes, have been more than exhausted. He has requested that any subscriptions should be sent direct to his solicitors, Messrs Glynn Barton & Co., of 36 Red Lion Square, London WC1.

CHAPTER 19

Journals of Harold Davidson
London
20 May 1932

The trial resumed today. Mr Levy, my counsel and dear friend, spoke for five hours! When I got to the chamber, he was dealing with some risible, but apparently crucial, details of my behaviour with waitresses. The evidence of Dorothy Burn, the Lyons Nippy, and Violet Lowe from the Chinese restaurant, was examined and found to be without any trace of improper behaviour on my part.

Shrewdly, Mr Levy elected to call me insulting names as part of his strategy, to abuse me for a minor transgression in order to absolve me from a major: 'That he annoyed this girl, and many others, there can be no possible doubt. He will insist upon talking to people, asking them about themselves, and he will insist upon telling them everything about himself. He is, and I say it in his presence, a troublesome busybody. But that is not the charge. He annoyed Miss Burn, says the charge, and that is true. He made improper suggestions, according to the charge, and that is lamentably and obviously false.'

I was not gravely insulted. I rose above it with an indulgent smile (noticed by the newspapers).

He then proceeded to denounce Mr Dashwood for legal misbehaviour.

'An atmosphere was present in this case even before it was launched. Long before the charges were drawn up, and when the evidence collected by the detectives was being considered, Mr Dashwood issued a perfect wave of subpoenas right and left upon everybody connected or concerned with the case, whether they were going to be called or whether they were not, on behalf of the prosecution, and having done that, said to the defence, "You must not interview any of these witnesses. We have subpoenaed every single person who can give evidence bearing upon this matter, and having done that, you are barred, until this case actually comes into court, from approaching any of them or from getting any statement which you may use for the purpose of preparing your defence." This matter was conceived in obstinate ignorance, launched in venom, and carried on to the very end in spite and in persecution.'

Did I know about any of this? I looked at Dashwood. Not a line of concern troubled his sleek brow. He sat in a bored attitude, folded sideways on a bench in the gallery as though riding side-saddle. A fastidious sneer distended his left nostril. He seemed to me not a real person at all, but a fictional figure, both oleaginous and sinister – James Carker, the treacherous secretary in *Dombey and Son*, say, or Mr Obadiah Slope, the oily chaplain in *Barchester Towers*.

Mr Levy's speech then explained my normal behaviour with ladies. 'Mr Davidson may be a very unusual and unconventional person,' he said. 'It is not unusual for him to kiss women. His kisses have been paraded before you as signs of guilt, but you will hear from many that he is quite accustomed to kissing women. You will find he kisses his landlady, his landlady's daughters, his maids, not in a sensual or sexual way – it is a kiss on the cheek or forehead – but it may lead to all sorts of suspicion on the part of evil-minded people . . .' Why should he make such a song and dance about it? On our journey through life, should we not greet all fellow pilgrims with a fond pilgrim's kiss?

I was a little surprised to hear Mr Levy say he would call Mrs Osborne, my landlady at Macfarlane Road, to testify that Barbara never slept in my room night after night, but slept downstairs in her daughter's bed. I wonder how he prevailed upon Mrs O to oblige with such evidence. But these things matter little at present for I am all primed and ready for the morrow. At last I shall testify. I shall defend myself to the death against the bishop, against Dashwood, against Barbara, and against the might of the traitorous Church of England.

Letter from Mrs Moyra Davidson
Church House, Westminster, London
21 May 1932

My dear Oona,

Do you see the address I'm writing to you from? Only the most important room in the whole Church of England, the great hall of Church House, where the Archbishop of Canterbury addresses the Protestant nobs in their great mitres and croziers every year. For the first few days, Harold sent me off down below to the witnesses' room, so I wouldn't start to cry or make a scene, like I do at the drop of hat these days. But I couldn't stick it, sitting there with these brassy young women and these saggy old landlady types, all looking sideways at me as if wondering which class I fitted into. So now I'm in the main section of the court, watching everyone come and go, and very interesting it is. It's a hushed and sacramental kind of place, not a room for dancing in, but not really like a church, it's a big serious room in a big serious place, like the House of Lords, all wood panelling and people shushing you. There's an upper gallery with seats for about ninety or a hundred people. It's packed out today, but I can't believe it's with the families of witnesses. Who are these people that've come along? They cannot be strangers, just off the street, can they? As if this was some kind of a theatre?

Anyway, Harold's name was called in a loud ringing voice and he bustled across to the dock, looking a little hunched and scuttly, like Mr Mole in *Wind in the Willows*. He's in a serious black jacket, dog collar, grey trousers, black shoes and looks every inch the decent (and harmless) clergyman. A fellow called Ryder Richardson, one of the team defending him against the bishop, asked him right out: 'Have you ever been guilty of immorality?' H said NO! in a very determined voice. 'Have you lived in adultery with any woman?' he was asked. No! again. 'Have you ever importuned a woman with immoral intent?' the man enquired, and with a heartfelt catch in his voice, H said, 'Never. In. My. Life.'

After that, it was a straight run through his life. Family (the

revelation of his twenty-seven churchmen relatives got a laugh),
school, acting, Oxford, his first curacy, first charities, the Band of
Hope, the Actors' Union, the curacy at Stiffkey, our marriage, his
founding the Three Arts Club providing safe lodgings for young
girls studying art, music or drama. Then the Newsboys' Club, the
Lads' Apprentice Fund, the Docklands Settlements – the list went
on and on. I believe there were a few charities in there even *I'd*
never heard of.

There was a pause, and they completely changed topic and
started talking about Rose Ellis – remember her, Oona? She's the
not-so-young tart who came to the house, caused trouble and was
always weeping – how H took her to Stiffkey, gave her a job as a
gardener and became her guardian, paid for her shorthand and
typing lessons and even (I didn't know about this, and am in two
minds about it) took her to Paris looking for work for her in
domestic service. They asked about the rooms in Euston Street,
which H rented for years, and where Rose went to live. But I
remember being shown the place and meeting her there. The
only exchange I remember between them was that Harold asked
Rose to dress the boils on the back of his neck, like a nurse. Not
much likelihood of romance there! It's surprising how rude to
Harold the chancellor is. He's called Keppel-North, and runs the
diocese of Norwich, but I've never heard of him. Very direct and
personal he is. When Harold was talking about how little rest he
needed at night, he demonstrated how his father used to sleep
in a chair, huddling down with his head on his hand. He looked
so small and cuddlesome, dear H, but Mr Keppel-North said,
'Thank you, I do not wish for a demonstration.' When H resumed
the dock after lunch, Mr Keppel-North said, 'You must not fidget.
You must sit upright at all times, keeping your hands out of your
pockets.' What a way to address a man of H's distinction. What
is he, some class of nursery nanny? But there was laughing in the
public gallery, as if H was a figure of fun. For the first time, I
suddenly saw him, Oona, as he might appear in the world's eyes,
a slightly ludicrous, furtive, fiddling, hands-in-pockets person.

And this Ryder Richardson, who's supposed to be on H's side,
he asks impertinent questions too. Had H ever been punctual in

his life? And, 'If everyone paid as much attention to waitresses as you do, nobody would ever get served.' There was a very silly exchange when Richardson asked, 'Are you nervous in the use of your hands, and do you touch people?' Harold replied, 'Yes, I often emphasise things. I had to restrain myself a moment ago from touching the chancellor,' to which the chancellor said, 'You'd better not.' Like schoolboys in the playground accusing each other of being, you know, a bit funny.

They asked H why he invited young girls to Stiffkey Rectory. H told them: 'It is a very beautiful place where they could get a change. It would give me an opportunity to chat with them and find out if they were better suited to some other occupation than the one they held.'

They asked about him going backstage during theatre performances, when actresses are getting changed, and he explained about his roots in the theatre and his unshockable nature. Mr Richardson asked him directly: 'In asking girls to go out with you, have you ever done it for the purpose of seducing them?' 'Never,' said Harold. 'Never in my life.' He said it so heartfelt, Oona, in hardly a whisper, that I practically wept for him, standing there so small and besieged. Because I believe him. I always have. He isn't like that. He likes girls, no, he *loves* girls, but he's not someone who fits snugly in the seducer category.

After that, the day ground along with talk of many things I knew nothing of. It was dull, and the courtroom was warm, and I snoozed a little, waking to hear odd snatches of evidence about Barbara and how he once kissed her in a Chinese restaurant (I'm pretty sure it was she kissed him, that little saucebox was always making eyes at every man), about a waitress called Violet, about H's nightwear. I felt that, for a trial conducted in high seriousness in the most solemn religious court in the land, this hit a low point.

Then I snapped awake, to hear some terrible things. My hand is shaking as I write them down. The man Richardson, out of the blue, said that Barbara had told the court that Harold had asked her to marry him – and had told her that he didn't love me because of what happened with Pamela.

'No,' Harold said, looking very shaken, 'that is totally and absolutely untrue.' He seemed sincere, but how could the girl have known anything about it, if Harold hadn't told her? I am sick inside, Oona, to hear the awful secret we've kept for years come out into the open, just as H warned me that it might. Illegitimacy is a terrible thing. Infidelity likewise. I still cannot account for the madness that gripped me just after the war when H and I were estranged, and I fell for a young actor, he's pretty famous now, very handsome, an electrifying voice. And when I got pregnant by him, he couldn't look after me because of being betrothed to someone else, so I was on my own, but I decided to have the baby and keep it this time, after what happened with the last one, my poor child that went for adoption. My mind was made up, Harold could see that, and stood by me, God bless him for that, and we came home to Stiffkey at last, as a family, only harbouring a secret the size of a policeman. And now it's mentioned in court, for the world to know about. I'm too upset to continue, dear. I'll finish this another time.

Journals of Harold Davidson
London
22 May 1932

I cannot believe that snake Dashwood could do such a thing. Barbara knew nothing about Pamela being illegitimate. But Dashwood knew, because the bishop *told* him. And when Dashwood and I spoke in January, part of his tactics in telling me to resign was to insist on the undesirability of publicity, especially for my youngest child. I am so shocked. I begged him, should the matter come up in court, he should keep poor Pammie out of it. Dashwood actually *put his hand on mine* and swore that it would never be brought up in public. Then, heedless of my entreaties and his promises, he told Barbara, who now tells the court that my youngest child, my darling Pamela, was born in 1919, illegitimately, from another man, and that my wife shamed and betrayed me a second time. I told the court, 'This is the only bitter feeling I have in this case, that this poor child should have to read about it in the newspaper.'

At this there was a commotion in the public gallery, some applause and a strange noise. The chancellor ordered that a woman be removed. I craned through the crush of heads to see who she was, and fancied for a moment that it was Mimi. I thought she was in the witnesses' room downstairs.

London
25 May 1932

Mr Ryder Richardson came to pick me up at the flat at 9 a.m. I had been up since 6 a.m. hunting for documents that might sound well in court, so I was pleased by his solicitude. I fear that, without him, I might have been late.

Perhaps light-headed from lack of sleep, I took a combative stance to Mr Oliver's questioning. When I suggested that Barbara Harris must have had help in writing her letter to the Bishop of Norwich, Oliver said, 'Are you not prepared to suggest anything, whether it is the truth or not?' And I replied, 'I am prepared to suggest any kind of dirty trick possibly imaginable to this prosecution.' More laughter in court. More banging on the table by the pompous chancellor. I was aware of some late-spring sunshine peeping in the windows of this murky court, a promise and harbinger of summer, making me inappropriately elated. When more accusations were thrown at me of improperly touching servant girls of whom I've never heard (Lottie Green? Who is, or was, Lottie Green?), I blew my top, as the Americans say. 'I have been accused of misconduct with everyone I have been associated with for years. I have been misunderstood. I have been gossiped about by evil-minded people in connection with every young girl I have helped. I have been accused of being a white-slave traffic agent, that I have taken girls to my room and then sold them to the Argentine . . .' But I was advised that I was not helping my case, and therefore susbsided.

I was, however, able to give my considered view about the import-ance of taking young girls at the right age and moulding their intellect and sensibility. Oliver said that I seemed particularly anxious to meet girls between the ages of sixteen and twenty. I said: 'No I like to get them from fourteen to twenty-one. Those are the most impressionable ages of young girls who are going to be the mothers of the future generation, and that is why I have always striven to get the highest principles inculcated into girls between those ages. In that way we are living in the future.'

I must say, giving these miniature homilies is so much more congenial to me than answering foolish questions from prurient heathens. They asked about Rose's drinking, about my letter to the bishop, about my trips to France, even about the boil on my neck. It all whirls around my head now in a clanging charivari. But I am losing interest in the legal process, in the system, even (can I believe I am saying this?) in the outcome.

London
26 May 1932

Rather a shock to discover the ill feelings harboured against me by the Bishop of London. I had thought our relations perfectly cordial. But in a letter written to my defence counsel he writes: 'I do not wish Mr Davidson any harm. I wish him to have a perfectly fair trial. Therefore I do not wish, unless I am obliged, to say how constantly he has pestered me for the last twenty years with begging appeals to myself and my friends. He has used my photograph, which I gave him, for a purpose of which I should not approve. It would be far wiser from your own standpoint not to bring me into the case at all.'

Humph. This from the man who, when I apprised him of the Bishop of Norwich's sign-or-be-tried ultimatum, urged me to fight and suggested several names I should call in sympathy. I see now that he was only 'passing on the buck'.

I was asked to explain why I had so many photographs taken of Rose and myself in 1928. (I explained it was in order to help aspirant actresses in the registering of certain expressions onstage – suspicion, relief, cruelty et cetera; I should have thought that was obvious.)

As I was considering the art of role-playing, it occurred to me that this whole ordeal has been a performance. The stage in this draughty building is tiny, the audience minute – but the wider congregation, out there where they read the newspapers and recite my words to each other over provincial breakfast tables from Sunderland to Sheerness, is my audience too. Almost by accident, certainly not by design, I have become a big stage success, even while my career and livelihood as a serious reformer is under threat. I have played an eccentric clergyman, a character part of which English audiences have always been particularly fond. I have been involved in small adventures which, though I was as innocent as a lamb, occurred in suggestive circumstances. I have drawn around me, again by no design, a colourful supporting cast of landladies, tea-room supervisors, bishops, circus strongmen, Indian fakirs, detectives, majors, prostitutes, mad people and actresses. It is scarcely to be wondered at that I have become the 'hottest ticket' in Victoria, if not the West End too!

Oliver questioned me closely about Barbara. I have not been looking forward to this moment. Ever since our emotional break-up before Christmas, when I upbraided her for returning to a life of prostitution in order to pay for curtains, we have not spoken. I had wondered if my emotions would be stirred by seeing her again – but then I *did* see her (angry, self-deluding) face, and heard her treacherous words and learned of her supposed letter to the bishop, outlining my allegedly seductive ways. It was a calculated slur, designed to blacken my reputation in this courtroom and the country. So when Oliver asked me about her, I tried to be kind. He asked if I thought her pretty. 'Yes, for those who admire that type,' I said. 'She is very attractive when she smiles. Her face at rest, I think, is rather ugly and repulsive.' I wondered if she was in court. I rather hoped she was.

'She must have been an abandoned little creature,' ventured Mr Oliver.

'Abandoned morally,' I conceded, 'but she had some very remark-able qualities of character. In our personal relations I could trust her, and she had a very, very keen sense of duty. I could not say, though, that she ever had a pleasant manner. She could be exceedingly nice if she liked, but she very seldom troubled herself to be so.'

Why, Oliver wanted to know, had I taken such a personal interest in Barbara? I decided not to mention the shaft of sunlight through the window, the illuminated face, the angelic radiance, the tiny whisper in my head from God that He had sent her to me as a special mission. I said, simply, 'I felt so awfully sorry for her, being so young and her life smashed at sixteen.'

Then the business with the photographs started up. It was d——ed uncomfortable. They held up a picture of young what's-her-name, Delia or Della, a very young thing provided for the photographic event by the *Daily Express*. She was snapped wearing a shawl and nothing else. I was in the picture, posing with the young woman who sat on my knee, unfortunately shedding most of her single garment.

I was obliged to prevaricate a little about the photographs and found myself becoming entangled. First I maintained that I knew nothing about it at all. Mr Oliver pointed out that, since I was *in* the photograph, this could not be true. I suggested it had been part of an advertisement for swimwear, but had trouble explaining the young lady's lack of a bathing costume. I tried to maintain that it had been Mr Thole's idea and the picture was to be sold by him for £150, but this did not wash. I embarked on a long elaboration of why, in the picture, my hands are touching the girl – i.e. because the piece of gauze I was holding slipped out of my hand at the last minute.

Mr Oliver said, 'I suggest they are Press photographs taken in the presence of newsmen for the purpose of publication,' and naturally I denied this. But I was so rattled, I cast about for an alternative story.

Remembering the evening when I called upon Estelle Douglas and was photographed in a compromising tableau, I explained that I had been telephoned on the day before the trial and told that a trap had been laid for me, but I didn't believe it; that I would be phoned by a lady of title and asked to her home, that when I got there, she would suddenly remove her dress and stand before me naked, while two detectives jumped out. It is not, perhaps, a wholly watertight story, but I think my version of events prevailed, and the cross-examination moved on.

I passed a rough night. Mimi, Nugent and Sheilagh were mostly silent after yesterday's photographic revelations and seem not to listen to my pleas for understanding. I could not sleep for fear that I had said too many conflicting things about the damning photographs. It is a terrible thing, to be disbelieved.

My worries were justified. The moment Mr Keppel-North resumed his seat, he demanded to see the photographs. Eventually, I was obliged to confess that some members of the Press had approached me and offered me a large sum to pose with an undraped young woman. I said that, though I was almost starving at the time, I considered their suggestion repugnant and improper. But they persuaded me that my character was considered so pure, no one in the world would think badly of it; that it would be a picture of me, posed against an artistic setting. I pointed out that the girl's mother had agreed to have her daughter pictured in a draped tableau, but had not been there for the shoot because she had gone to the theatre.

Finally Mr Oliver referred to an article about the trial that appeared in the *Evening News*, hinting that it amounted to contempt of court. I mentioned that I thought it probably came from the prosecution, and that the newsman had been briefed by the Arrows Detective Agency. Mr Oliver as good as suggested that I was lying. I told him that every newspaper had approached me to ask that I give them all the papers connected to the case, and that I had been asked to write my life story but I had refused. The fee mentioned was £750.

Bathetically, Mr Oliver's last questions were about some other photographs, showing me posing in naval uniform and upon a camel. I said I had given the newspapers some pictures of me and saw nothing wrong with doing so. And with that, my stint in the dock was over. Mr Oliver's cross-examination had lasted fifteen and a half hours and I trust he was mortally exhausted, while I emerged refreshed and triumphant.

As though in celebration, a great multitude could be heard outside attempting to rush the doors of Church House. Some were admitted. Among the remainder, several robust fellows formed a human battering ram and forced the doors open. There was a struggle, in which several young girls fainted. The police were called, and after a period the mêlée subsided, with hundreds of people locked outside.

This had been the watershed in my life. My sympathies are no longer with the Church of England, as represented by the loathsome Dashwood and the bishop, or the procedures of impious and carping legalism. They are with the wider congregation of souls – the thousands of my new supporters and believers beyond the locked doors of Church House.

London
29 May 1932

We're now at the tail end of the trial, no new revelations forthcoming. Just more landladies protesting their respectability, and wan young girls struggling to remember if they might or might not have met me in Victoria Station and had to endure my conversation for three minutes.

Far more interesting to me, every day, is the post that continues to flood in. This morning's brought a sturdy white box, inside which was a rose or shrub. It is called the Rambling Rector and, according to my correspondent, Mrs Margaret Hart, 'has a tendency to climb all over the wall in an undisciplined manner, putting out secondary shoots apparently at random. Given careful tending, it will bring forth tiny white flowers.' Mrs Hart is on the committee of the gardening society in Over Wallop, and has been empowered to ask if I would open their garden fête on 20 June? Delightful, but however can I agree? The lady evidently has not been following the scandalous coverage in the papers, and has surely heard of me only as somebody 'in the news'. Were I to come to Hampshire, no doubt the local vicar would have something to say about having a noted enemy of the Church of England on his 'patch'.

Letters came in the afternoon from two publishers, Duckworth and the Bodley Head, asking if I would consider writing my memoirs for them. I have replied that no fewer than five newspapers have already contacted me to ask the same thing, albeit in a smaller form.

The top bid, by the *Daily Express*, was £750. I mention this only as a guide to these courtly gentlemen, when deciding what the advance for a full-length book might be.

Notebooks of Charlie Norton, *Evening Standard*
London
1 June 1932

Well, well, well. The rector. Hasn't he come far? It's nearly two years since I first set eyes on old Harold – and I look at him now and I think, Charlie Boy, you always had a nose for a story. When you saw him in the Coal House, you knew there was something going on. 'Course, I wasn't to know how weird it would get, or how many people it would involve. Or that it would involve bishops, and photos of naked kids, and Indian men, and pyjamas.

I never knew it would catch the public's attention like this. Everybody's talking about it. Every instalment in the papers – *The Times*, the *Standard*, the *Express, Reynolds News* – puts on about another ten or fifteen thousand copies. I hear people gassing on about the case on the top deck of buses, in cafés, in shops; I've heard workmen digging holes in the road voicing their opinion, saying that girl Barbara, isn't she a one, only seventeen and such a performer, cheeking the defence briefs. I saw my bank manager yesterday, to ask about the remortgage, and at the end he says, 'You're a pressman, Charles. What's the news on the rector and the girl in the photo? They got him bang to rights if you ask me.'

They're probably reading about the trial in the Commons lobby and the Lords tea room. It's just so hellishly absorbing because of all the little details. I must have read twenty or thirty divorce hearings, but I never knew a trial where we were allowed to report everything without restriction. Mind you, most trials, it wouldn't be at all interesting to report every word, would it? Dead boring, most trials. But this one – it's got the lot. Sex, religion, morals, good girls, bad girls, foreign johnnies, foreign travel, theatre, circus strongmen, landladies, grand ladies, tea shops, films, Chinese restaurants, evangelists, palm reading, you name it. The rector doesn't know it, but he's perfect for the newspapers. Perfect. As I knew instinctively, the minute I saw him.

At work they discuss the trial all day, at conference, on the news desk, in the Gents, and in the Crown and Two Keys after the edition's gone to bed. Some women like the idea of the rector popping round trying to save them from disaster in the middle of the night. They think it's sweet. Some others reckon he's just a pervy old git. But if you've just met a new girl, say, you can break the ice by talking about the trial. Everybody's following it, and everybody's got an opinion. It's like some national hobby. The rector may be the gassiest man I ever met, never lets you get a word in sideways. But he's got the country talking now, hasn't he? And to think that I got him going first.

Journals of Harold Davidson
London
3 June 1932

The photograph of me with the fifteen-year-old girl has caused me to forfeit some public sympathy judging by the one of some recent letters ('I can see why a man such as yourself, engaged in rescuing vice girls, might feel the temptations of the flesh from time to time; but posing with a naked girl who's no more than a child, that's disgusting. I thought you were nice for a while, but actually you're a bit sick, aren't you?'). Luckily, my friends in the newspaper have come through. 'Miss D' as they call her (she is now just sixteen), or Delia to me, explained about being called for a bathing-costume advertisement, about being told to remove her clothes and pose in a shawl, and about me trying to help her by holding the shawl against her naked body. It still sounds a little unconvincing, and the chancellor has asked for evidence to prove it is not a fake. But I think we got away with that too.

Headlines have appeared in the newspapers, saying 'Stiffkey Rector: Hearing Coming to an End' – as if warning readers that their daily dose of scandal and calumny may shortly dry up. But things continue well. A cook who used to work in Maddox Street testified that Nellie

Churchill was 'a very peculiar girl' and 'tried to talk with an Oxford accent' but that she never saw anything untoward between Nellie and me. The Bishop of London was called. An imposing vision in his episcopal purple and gold cross, he conceded that I was 'a very great nuisance' but said he had never heard a word to suggest that my reputation for morality was other than spotless. He said I had approached him many times over the years, always looking for money, and that I had used a signed photograph of him to convince the gullible that we were intimate friends. Such disobliging stories from my mentor and the man who married me and Mimi! He *could* have been more helpful.

Sir Reginald Kennedy-Cox, from my early acting days, was called – this is like having my whole life flashing slowly past my eyes – to offer a backhanded compliment: 'I regard him as a moral man, but I also regard him as an exceedingly tiresome, unconventional man, who might be misunderstood, and I think injudicious.'

My darling Patricia stood in the witness box – a lovely-looking, sensible girl of twenty-one in a leather coat, beret and horn-rimmed spectacles – and talked about Rose's and Barbara's visits to Stiffkey. I had no idea she disliked the latter so much. I was much impressed by the way she spoke about my manner with people, treating the rich and the destitute just the same. She mentioned the times we both stayed up in an all-night café, as I wrote letters and talked to the bad girls. She has a very observant eye and I am proud of her.

Letter from Mrs Moyra Davidson
Church House, Westminster, London
4 June 1932

My dear Oona,

Sorry, I broke off a few days back and never finished this letter. I was upset that they brought up the Pamela business in court. But nobody's mentioned the matter since, so the newspapers may not go to town on it, thank God. I've been torn this way and that in watching Harold on trial. Lord knows I love and trust Harold, but he gets himself into desperate scrapes. There's been a scandal about a picture of H beside a young girl in a photograph, with nothing on! Of course he's not doing anything in the picture, but she's a child, Oona, and when H tries to explain how he came to be in the photo, he gets into unmerciful tangles. But then I hear the testimony of his former friends, saying he's a pest and a nuisance, and I feel a flood of sympathy for him.

Today's a good day to finish this letter, it's the final summing-up by Mr Levy, Harold's main defence person. He is a brilliant man, very rude in that breezy way you want lawyers to be. He said the prosecution hasn't proved anything. 'There has been a certain amount of evidence put forward by the prosecution,' he said, 'evidence which consists, in the main, of suggestion. The charges have been placed before you and the attitude adopted in this court has been: now, there are the charges, there are the suggestions and the suspicions, now disprove your guilt, now prove that you are innocent.' He spoke at length about H's character. I thought he might call him names like the others, but his assessment was kindly: 'You have seen that he is a man completely and utterly indifferent to the way other people judge his behaviour. He has been engaged on work upon which he has set his heart, involving conduct in which most people would not be involved, and he does not realise that his conduct has left him open to misunderstanding and misrepresentation on the part of those people he meets.'

To my relief, he said anyone could tell that the photograph showing the half-naked girl was an accident and that it shows no more than could be seen on the cover of an art magazine or when women are dancing at an hotel. Then he went to town on Barbara Harris, and her life of vice – her rising at 1 p.m., going to cafés in the evening, sleeping with men all night. The people who contradicted her story, he called them respectable and hard-working people who should be believed. But you'll never believe what he said about her motivation for testifying against H. He said Barbara was probably driven by her dislike of being put to work at the Rectory, or because Harold refused to fulfil her physical cravings! I let out a yelp at that, I couldn't help myself, it was such a bizarre thought. I was afraid one of the policemen might throw me out. My mind's still not right, Oona, and I have some terrible mornings of intense sadness, and then the clouds lift and I feel chirpy again, light-headed, like I've been taking brandy, only I don't drink any more. And I get strange sudden cravings for food like I was pregnant, but no danger of that, it's only because we had no food at all for so long.

Sometimes H and I will talk in the evenings, and I feel excited because I'm connected to his world again, and to the great world outside (do you realise we've been in all the papers for months now, photographs of the family and everything?), but sometimes I feel the weight of it all, and the prospect of H losing his job, house and reputation, and all for some silly girls who wouldn't give him the time of day, and I cannot speak to him at all. But I must send this letter off at last and say, pray for us, Oona, that the verdict will go our way.

My love to you,
Mimi xx

Journals of Harold Davidson
London
8 June 1932

The hateful Mr Oliver rose to close proceedings by summing up for the prosecution. It was a dismal performance. He whiningly justified all the ugly means by which the prosecution collected their evidence. How private detectives were thought 'necessary' to follow me around. How they plied Rose Ellis with drink purely to get at the truth, not to ask her to lie. He mentioned the girl in the photograph and said it had obviously been taken to be sold abroad for money. Wholly untrue. (There was no question of 'abroad'.) He insisted on the truthfulness of Miss Harris, brought up my impoverished state and claimed, without the slightest shred of proof, that 'for a long period, the rector was living on charity, not for his girls but for himself'. He also called me a liar, my lengthy testimony 'a labyrinth of lies' and said, condescendingly, 'We must not find him guilty solely because he is such an awful liar.' I am sure this is action-able. I shall look into it.

His speech went on for hours in the same vein, pointing to moments of confusion in my testimony. Oliver claimed there were thirty-nine separate moments in which I contradicted my own evidence. I do not have the time or the energy to dispute them in this journal – but has the man nothing else to do other than pick tiny holes in the extemporised stumblings of a man on trial for his professional life? He said he found it odd that we did not summon Rose Ellis to give evidence – doubtless because we were afraid she would testify against me. He even started to complain about the non-availability of poor Mimi, saying if ever there were a relevant witness in this case, it is she. He seemed to laugh at my explanations about her deafness, her fainting fits, her frailty, the heartless brute. The remainder of his time he devoted to an emetic rapture about Miss Harris, especially the details of her sad and abandoned early life, as if that had turned her into a better or more reliable witness. He went to town on a line in her letter, 'It is hard to be good, when you have been bad,' as if it were the profound conclusion of a moral philosopher. Really, the man was idiotic. My Mr Levy had concluded by saying that a verdict against me would reflect discredit upon the name of British justice. Oliver said this had been 'an invitation to the public to think that the case has never been properly proved, or has not acted fairly on the evidence. It is for that reason that I have laboured to bring all the evidence before the world and to show what is the true evidence.' He said the trial could have only one outcome. He is, if I may descend to a common vulgarity, a complete bastard.

London
9 June 1932

So the trial is over at last, and I must wait a whole month to learn my fate or my triumphant return. If it goes in my favour, I go back to my old life, my charitable ministrations, as though nothing has happened, but with no word of sympathy or apology from the tormenting Church. If it goes against me I am finished, degraded in every sense, removed from office. (How did Levy put it? 'This man shall be damned and ruined, and his family shall never again look people in the face.') And all because of an unknown malevolence against me in the heart of the Bishop of Norwich and Mr Dashwood!

Yet how could I return to my old life? My face is now known throughout the kingdom. I will be recognised on every street corner, in every café, every theatre, every refuge. The chances of going quietly about my old work are, frankly, nil. Would I be able to pursue the life of a rural priest as before, when every service I conduct could be interrupted by the sniggers of brutish attention-seekers and corner boys? (I have heard their vulgarities close up; outside Church House last week, two youths passed me by. 'Stone me, there's that rector,' said one. The other looked. 'E-rector more like,' he observed, to laughter.)

My friends have begin to fall away. Rose, after her suicide attempt, is in a sanatorium for the terminally alcoholic. Barbara would not look at me in the courtroom, and is presumably lost to me for ever. Monsignor Coveney responded to my request for a character witness by saying he wished me well but could not be 'compromised' or have his retirement jeopardised by 'joining in such a circus'. Lady Fenella was at home only once when I telephoned to discuss the trial; my friendly overtures were rewarded only with the click of the receiver being hung up. Kennedy-Cox and Bishop Ingram, my twin mentors, have proved in the witness box their true opinion of me. Thank God for Mimi and the children, whose support is unswerving and true as steel – although of course M is little more than an invalid now, spending her evening listening to Mendelssohn's *Midsummer Night's Dream* (with that awful hackneyed Wedding March) on the gramophone, played at punishing volume because of her deafness.

Family apart, my only solace now is the postbag, which continues to cheer and delight with messages of support, baffling inanities from lonely persons who seem to regard me as their friend, and curious offers. I have received at least a hundred invitations to speak at social events, dinners, 'club evenings' (the Durham Miners' Guild? the Muswell Hill Conversazione Society? What could they possibly want with me?).

Newspaper reporters have courted me from day three of the trial. Formal letters from 'managing editors' initially asked for my reflections on prostitution, justice, poverty, child-rearing and the like. Now they flagrantly want 'the inside story' of my ten years' work in London, 'told in your own inimitable style', as though I were some famous comedian or vaudeville 'turn'. Interestingly, they now always end with the rubric, 'There will, of course, be a fee attached.'

Stiffkey
14 June 1932

There seems to be some continuing confusion about the suitability of my conducting services at St John's. I thought I had made it perfectly clear that I would cease to officiate in church for the duration of the trial, in order not to spread what the prosecution like to call 'propaganda'. Now the trial is over. The verdict is not yet given, but the trial itself is done, and no amount of propaganda from myself or anyone else can affect its outcome. Therefore I have decided to resume services at my parish.

Unfortunately, not everyone seems to have understood my intentions. On Saturday I sent a telegram to the Archdeacon, explaining that I was going to resume my duties. I later discovered that he sent me a telegram early on Sunday morning, telling me not to take service, but I was not at home to receive it (I was travelling up from London with Bridie Connolly, whom I have taken under my wing once again). But after everything I have endured, I feel I could not allow any archdeacon to dictate to me how my parish should be run. They may have found substitute pastors in the weeks of the trial; but enough is enough. We got to Stiffkey just before 11 a.m. Bridie drove (I thought a day in the country would do her good) and as we pulled into the church grounds, I heard an alarming piece of news: that another clergyman, William Harcourt, the Vicar of Wighton, was in the vestry waiting to preach.

As though anticipating trouble, a young reporter from the Press asked if I planned to take the service. 'Yes,' I said firmly. 'And if I cannot do so in church, I shall invite the congregation to the Rectory and we shall have it there.' I put on my robes for the first time in weeks and strode to the church. A few dozen visitors formed a natural path to watch my progress. At the church, an officious person in a black suit raised his hand to bar my way, saying, 'The archdeacon has made other arrangements.' I ignored him, ducked under his outstretched arm and entered the church. I made straight for the vestry where I discovered Harcourt, the blandest divine in Christendom, cowering in his robes. 'They told me to come,' he squeaked. 'They said you couldn't perform any more services, and that I should stand in.'

'Harcourt,' I said, 'this is my church. Get back to Wighton and look after your own flock. You are not wanted here.'

'Don't you speak to me like that,' he whimpered. 'I shall report your words to the bishop.'

'Report them and be damned,' I cried. 'Do you think, you fool, I am afraid of the *bishop*?'

He opened the vestry door, fled down the chancel, out to the porch and was gone. I calmly began the service, taking as my text, 'The wages of sin is death, but the gift of God is eternal life.' At the end, the whole congregation shook my hand.

So that little confrontation passed painlessly, but worse was to follow. In the afternoon I went to Morston Church to preach. From what I gleaned from my auditors, word had spread all over the region that I was back in my old church, despite the trial, and that some trouble was anticipated. One woman was the wife of a policeman. She told me that the force had been alerted and that officers were watching the church for signs of 'activity'. I returned to Stiffkey to take the evening service. A crazy spectacle met my eyes. Across the greensward, upwards of two hundred cars were parked. The path from Rectory to church was lined with hundreds of men, women and youths (and a delightfully large contingent of pretty girls). They were all waiting for me.

Unfortunately, so was Mr R. H. Cattell, the Vicar of Warham, two miles from Stiffkey. He must have known I was coming, to claim what was rightfully mine, for he got there early, vested promptly and began the service sharp at 6.30 p.m.

I arrived a few minutes late, leapt from the car and was told by my old friend Mrs Russ, 'You're too late. There's another parson in there, and he's already preaching.' I walked to the vestry door and found it locked against me. Against *me*! I summoned Mr Pells, the clerk, and demanded he open it immediately, which he did. Inside, I sent Mr Pells to speak to Cattell and tell him, 'The Rector of Stiffkey is in his church. Please leave now.' He could not perform this simple duty in front of the congregation. I knelt by the altar rails but the bullish vicar would still not take the hint. I walked over and stood by the choir stalls but the wretched man refused to budge.

I found an old charity envelope in a pew, wrote on it in big letters 'GET OUT OF MY CHURCH' and passed it to Mr Cattell. He was still leading Psalm 27. As soon as it was finished he picked up the Bible from the lectern, with a proprietorial gesture. I could not allow that. It is my Bible. I walked on to the altar and seized it from him. He snatched it back and for a full minute, we wrestled for control of the Holy Word. Being more determined, I won the day and read the second lesson, while Mr Cattell stood foolishly by, wiping his brow. Seized with inspiration, he called to Mr Groom, a sidesman, 'Fetch the police! Fetch the police!' Groom left the church only to return moments later, indicating to Mr Cattell with a shrugging gesture that the police had no wish to be involved. Just as I thought he would go and sit down, or just go, Cattell turned and addressed the congregation.

'I am extremely sorry this has happened.' he said. 'It reduces the service to a farce. I received orders from the bishop to take this service, but as nothing short of force will prevent Mr Davidson taking part, I can see nothing left to do but withdraw. I cannot take part in a service in association with him.'

This was the signal for mayhem. Twenty people applauded Mr Cattell's stand, a dozen got up and walked out in protest, some women raised shrill cries of lament at the Lord knows what. I tried to calm everything down by crying, 'Remember you are in the house of God,' but the uproar persisted for minutes.

You see what the bishop and his man Dashwood have brought upon us? I said I was sorry for the shocking events that had befallen our Sunday worship. At the end, I made haste to shake hands with all my congregation; but some cold-shouldered me and walked past with their disapproving heads in the air. So I won the day. I wrested back my kingdom from the intruders. But at what cost?

Stiffkey
27 June 1932

I have received some intriguing invitations from all over the country. One comes from a Birmingham skating rink, a venue that takes up to 6,000 persons. The managers wish me to come and give a talk about 'whatever I please' for a fee of £18 plus free dinner and travel expenses. I do not know whether to accept or not. Is an ice rink demeaning? Would I be able to hold such a large audience by a lecture on any subject? Another kind offer in the post yesterday: a playwright has sent me a copy of his new work, in whose dramatis personae there is 'a sophisticated clergyman'. He thinks I would be 'wizard' in the role, which I take to be a compliment.

Hmmm. To tread the boards once more. How thrilling, yet how alarming. I know how desperately we need money, but – can I go back to the stage?

London
9 July 1932

Today was my Day of Judgement. Mr Keppel-North gave his summing-up of the case and his verdict. Frankly, I could have seen it coming a mile away.

Unfortunately, I was obliged to set out for the grocery shops this morning because of an urgent whim of Mimi's to have apricot jam. Being anxious to keep her sane and equilibrial, I tried four establishments before discovering the preserve in question. In consequence, I missed the first quarter-hour of the chancellor's findings. Luckily the clerk of the court, with whom I have forged an acquaintance over the months, was able to enlighten me for the sake of this journal.

Mr Keppel-North began by talking about Rose. He has decided that I am guilty of sexual intercourse with Rose for ten or eleven years. I, with Rose! It is simply amazing. He believes the stories of the landladies, and – he put it with dismaying bluntness – he just does not believe me. In fact, if I can decipher the scrawl before me, he said:

'Mr Davidson has given evidence denying his guilt. I watched him anxiously in the dock for something like four days. I do not believe him. His evidence in chief was a tissue of falsehoods and, as Mr Oliver has demonstrated, reckless and even deliberate falsehoods. He went down as an absolutely discredited witness on whose oath no reliance can be placed.'

It is terrible to be called names like this. Both Keppel-North and Oliver called me a liar in open court. But what seems to have clinched my guilt in what passes for his mind is that I failed to put various people in the witness box – especially my wife and Rose herself. But my poor wife is not well. She is scarcely able to tell the days of the week apart, let alone answer a cross-examination. And Rose's reputation for telling the truth was so discredited by the prosecution that nobody would have a believed a word she said. This is typical of the chancellor, to condemn me for a sin of omission rather than of commission.

The remainder of his pronouncements followed the same path. Did I molest a waitress by inviting her for tea, offering her my card and recommending a weekend in Stiffkey? Yes, apparently, if my little invitations were 'coupled with the rest of his behaviour – telling her she was lovely, and that he was a friend of a number of actresses and their confessor [I am sure I have never said that – far too Church of Rome for me], talking to a young girl about marriage, pursuing her to the waitresses' private room and trying to be alone with her – it does amount to improper suggestions'.

How? In what law book? It does *nothing of the sort.*

The third charge, about embracing a young woman in a Chinese restaurant (i.e. Barbara) – I rather gave that away by admitting it. But putting an arm around a lady's waist is hardly an expression of grotesque intimacy – or has society changed since I was a young man?

The fourth charge. Have I been guilty of an Immoral Habit of associating with women of loose character? On this, Keppel-North confined himself to considering Miss Harris, and asked himself simply: Did he believe Miss Harris, when she said she slept in a bed with me for several nights? Or believe the occupants of the house who testified that she did not?

'I believe Barbara,' he told the court.'In my judgement it is important to observe that though she frankly admitted the bestowal of her favours on a number of men of all sorts, her story is that the defendant, although he provided her with money and clothes, gave her a gold watch and got her places from time to time, never succeeded in repeated attempts to enjoy those favours.'

Well, well. This is priceless. In answer to the charge that I have a habit of keeping company with fallen women for immoral purposes, the chancellor says that I gave my main accuser many things but never actually 'enjoyed' her 'favours'. So how was I guilty of immoral acts, if I committed none?

The last scene in this painful farrago was the fifth charge, namely that I importuned three young waitresses and Miss Nellie Churchill 'with immoral intent'. The flimisiness of the evidence was once more apparent. All he found worthy of mention was a small detail about a young lady whose fine teeth and hair I praised – how I said, one should take a girl and pull open her mouth and examine her teeth, as one might a horse. Apparently this was going too far! He quoted the opinion of some foolish minx:'Another girl thought he was mad. I agree with her. I think he was mad – about women certainly.'

Once again, he exceeds his brief (his opinion of my sanity is neither here nor there) and, through false logic and legal chicanery, delivers a verdict as unfair as it is squalid.

I am guilty on all five counts.

Realising that my defence counsel had departed, I snatched up my tall hat and ran down the aisle of the great hall. Mr Levy was all charm and commiseration, I told him he had done his best, and we shook hands warmly. A group of well-wishers came to pay their respects. They were men and women, young and old, from all walks of life, who had followed the trial minutely in the Press. One young lady in a green summer frock impetuously kissed me on the cheek. 'Was that wise?' I asked smoothly. 'That kind of behaviour could land us in trouble.' We laughed. I signed my name on newspapers, pocketbooks and (what were they doing here?) hymn sheets.

A reporter asked me what the future held. 'I have made no arrangements just yet, my dear fellow,' I said. 'I must consult my solicitors about an appeal. But' – a moment of madness struck me and I said, with a theatrical flourish, 'they have not heard the last of the rector.'

Stiffkey
15 July 1932

Mimi and I quit our lodgings at Hugh Street, packed two suitcases with the help of Nugent and Sheilagh, made our farewells to our friends in London, took the train to Holt and returned home in a taxicab, holding hands for much of the way. We did not speak of the chancellor's judgement, but kept up our spirits by talking of what might be done to make enough money to survive our departure from the Rectory, as we go – where? To disappear, I suppose, into oblivion.

I am ruined. My career is over. My life as a minister of Christ has ceased to have any meaning – or will cease when they pass sentence. Yet all around me, there seems to be a potential for making money such as I have seldom encountered. Even as Mimi prattled on about making ten shillings here and there, giving talks to local societies on Home Management, I reviewed the possibilities.

How much did the *Daily Express* promise for my own report of the trial? Was it £750? And the *Daily Herald*? And *Reynolds News*? Trouble is, I cannot recall to which paper I finally promised my memoir. They cannot all have them, for I believe one will pay more than the rest for an 'exclusive' treatment. But which one?

What I need at present is some disinterested person – some secretary or 'agent' similar to a theatrical agent – who could speak to all the newspapers and determine which would pay most. A kind of 'auction' with only a single 'lot', which is my life story. What a droll thought. Yet where could I find such a person? Perhaps my solicitor, Mr Glynn, could be asked to negotiate. But is he worldly enough to deal with the slippery wiles of newspaper men?

Then there are the publishers. One of the two, I cannot recall which, wrote to offer somewhere in the region of £1,500 for a book on my life, taking in my childhood, acting career and everyday work in London, as well as my revelations of Mr Dashwood, the bishop and the trial. That is the equivalent of two whole years' parish stipend! I had no idea that publishers will pay 'up front' for one's words. I thought it depended on the number of books one sold in shops. I know so little of these matters. Hmmm. £750 plus £1,500 is £2,250. But my debts are enormous. And if we lose the house, which is Church property, we must find another dwelling soon, which will devour all this sudden capital. There must be other ways of supplementing my new double windfall as a writer.

'Mimi,' I said, 'what would you say if I were to go before the public, not as a clergyman or sermoniser, but as an actor? Would it be too demeaning? Would you think badly of me?'

'Oh, Harold,' she said, 'it's a lovely idea. You could dust off your comic monologues that used to have people in fits before the war. Sure comedy is comedy, and it never goes out of fashion.'

'But what if I fail to draw an audience? I am not a young man. Some of these routines are a little old-fashioned. "Father of the Bride" will remain timeless, of course, but some of the more Edwardian skits – you know? There are so few plays with butlers in any more. One needs to find more topical material.'

She laughed – the first unprompted laugh I have heard escape her lips in an age.

'Harold, you eejit. Sure what could be more topical than yourself? Aren't you in all the papers? Can you not adapt some comic monologues to bring in a bishop, and some girls, and some snooping detectives, and –'

I was almost speechless. 'Mimi, I am shocked. Can you seriously suggest I turn these dismal events into a farce?'

'Only if you know you'll have the audience on your side.'

I said nothing more until we reached the Rectory. What a sight met our eyes! Across the wall by the entrance gate, a Babylonian garden of flowers had been hung to welcome us, pinks and purples, blues and reds, orange trumpets edged with cream. On the pathway, bouquets of wild flowers had been strewn as though to welcome a bride – or to launch the dead into the afterlife.

Mr and Mrs Reynolds were out in the roadway to shake our hands. I was disappointed not to find a crush of friends, as I have grown used to finding outside the trial building in Westminster. But Mr Reynolds had advised the congregation to leave us in peace after the outcome of our two months of trial. Gathering as many of the bouquets as we could carry, Mimi and I stepped up the drive to our silent house, into a future that will take us God knows where.

It will not, I feel, be a quiet time.

Harrogate
20 July 1932

Have been looking at properties in this handsome town, home of Mimi's uncle and the favoured retreat of the family in many summers past. Now staying at cousin Felicity's agreeable home.

No word yet from the Church, but the awful pronouncement of my dismissal from its damnable folds cannot be far off.

I have made enquiries, discreetly, at the Gaumont Theatre, to see if there might be room, one evening, between performances of *Private Lives* by the amateur society, to try my hand onstage. Encouraged by Mimi, I have taken a sketch by George Grossmith – 'Human Oddities', one of his first attempts – and adapted it a little, to incorporate an encounter between a bishop and an actress, in which I play both parts (without of course stooping to appear *en travestie*.) The bishop's pompous condemnations of the lady's profession are countered – amusingly, I hope – by her stout defence of 'dressing up and pretending to be someone else' as she wickedly discerns the bishop's function to be, just as much as it is hers.

It is a satire on hypocrisy, that most abhorrent of vices, but with comic moments built in: a little rough at present, but can be polished. My experience of playing Charley's Aunt when young will be useful when impersonating the lady; to play the bishop in all his life-denying pomposity, I need only think of Bertie Pollock.

The theatre person was dubious about finding a 'slot' for a personal performance by an unknown; it was, he said, without precedent. He seemed to think I would pay for the event, and supply my own audience. I assured him of my bona fides as an actor, however rusty, and said I would be glad to audition with the theatre management, if he would only pass on my details. He took my name and Felicity's telephone number and promised to reply in a day or so.

Perhaps I have been overconfident in hoping to return to the stage.

Harrogate
21 July 1932

The telephone rang as I was breakfasting. A voice said, 'Can I speak to Mr Davidson?'

'I am he.'

'Is that Mr *Harold* Davidson?'

'Certainly. Whom am I addressing?'

'James Topham, theatre manager at the Gaumont. Look, sorry, but you aren't the *Reverend* Davidson, are you.'

'Indeed I am. Though sadly,' I permitted myself a weary smile, 'not for much longer.'

'You mean the Rector of Stiffkey?'

'Yes, yes. I rang yesterday to enquire if perhaps, one evening, I might be allowed to perform a one-man show, such as I used to mount in younger days. I realise this is unorthodox, but if perhaps I could meet you for an hour and explain what I have in mind –'

'Bloody hellfire,' said the man. 'You want to do a show at the Gaumont? *You?*'

I was unhappy about his tone. It smacked of condescension.

'I was merely enquiring as to the possibility, Mr Topham. You are quite at liberty to reject my performance instantly.'

But he had gone. I heard only a muffled sound, the kind occasioned by placing a hand over the receiver. Then he came back on the line.

'How soon can you get here?'

'Any time today. My diary is a little sparse at present.'

'Come and see me at noon, Reverend. And don't tell anyone about your plans, all right?'

'Very well. And I think you should know I am unable to pay for this event I am planning. The gentleman to whom I spoke yesterday seemed to think it was what I believe is called a vanity project?'

'He's a fool. I'll sack him. Come and have some lunch, Harold, and let's talk. See you at noon.'

I noticed how his tone veered between the respectful ('Reverend') and the familiar ('Harold' indeed). But I was flattered by his response.

At noon I went to the Gaumont, dressed (rather daringly) in an open-necked shirt and cheap 'slacks', in a shameless attempt to look younger than my fifty-seven years. Topham was the image of a modern actor-manager, effortfully busy, cravatted, noisily fulsome, fussily effeminate. He made me as welcome as if I were Jack Buchanan and John Gielgud rolled together. 'Marvellous, just marvellous,' he began, 'to meet the most famous man in the kingdom.'

'I feel the word "notorious" lurks behind your kind words,' I said. 'I must say, at the outset, that I do not solicit your stage as a disgraced clergyman, but as a former actor with, I hope, some talent for humour that will draw an audience.'

'You leave the marketing to us, Harold,' (I flinched at his repeated familiarity), 'and tell me what you plan to do in front of the good people of Harrogate.'

I outlined my plan: an evening show, no more than two hours long, with my adapted Grossmith sketch, bishop, actress, et cetera, followed by a recital of 'The Silver Wedding', provided a piano could be procured ('No problem,' said Mr Topham, in a reassuring ejaculation I had not previously encountered) so that I could essay the spoken-singing number, 'I Am So Volatile', that used to bring the house down in my Oxford days.

'And that's it?' asked Mr Topham, pausing in the midst of his gala pie. 'Nothing about the trial? Or the girls? Or your actual life?'

'I was hoping to put the whole episode behind me,' I said. 'I plan to move on from these melancholy events and find a new role in an old passion, namely the comic theatre.'

'Okey-dokey,' said Topham. 'Let's see what you're about then.'

'I beg your pardon?'

'If you're a performer, go perform. Finish your lunch and let's get cracking. The stage awaits you.'

I was struck by a wholly uncharacteristic bout of shyness, that I soon recognised as stage fright. I had not performed for twenty years before an audience larger than my immediate family and some uncritical friends in the parish. As Topham gathered some motley staffers from the Gaumont bar – the waiter, the barmaid, a brace of surly stagehands and a chain-smoking lighting man – with the words, 'All hands on deck for the audition!', I found myself conflicted between an impulse to flee and an urgent desire to visit the lavatory.

Ten minutes later, purged, soothed with a mental snatch of 'O God Our Help in Ages Past' and calmed with draughts of water and a consultation of my script, I found myself on a stage for the first time since 1907, when I played Puck in the Rectory gardens. In the stalls, Topham and his entourage sprawled like aesthetes.

'Begin!' he called.

I began. Haltingly, creakingly, I embarked on 'Human Oddities' and realised, after five minutes, that I had completely forgotten how to move onstage. I stayed rooted to the spot, saying the words, concentrating on simply getting the lines out. The silence from the stalls told its eloquent tale. Then I summoned, from some thespian Limbo, the moment when I had to turn and address the audience with an admonitory forefinger. Turn again, and do the comical walk of the aged professor. Spin around and adopt the mincing gait of the dancing master. And gradually, like an old dinosaur bizarrely restored to the kingdom of animals, I was restored to the company of actors. My voice soared to unexpected heights as the duchess, and burrowed deep into the earth to play the country squire. I could hear a stirring in the stalls that I recognised; an audience leaning forward in their seats.

When it came to the new material – the bishop, the actress, et cetera – a visceral loathing leapt from my heart and hit the stage like a splash of colour. I found I could evoke the arrogance of clerical office with every muscle of my body; could embody the soul of innocence with a turn of the head. I was on fire. Afterwards, Mr Topham clapped me on the back.

'You'll do,' he said. 'A couple of hundredweight of prize gammon in parts, Harold, but you'll do very nicely.'

'Why,' I enquired, 'is the barmaid weeping? Why is that gentleman beside her stuffing a handkerchief into his mouth? Are they unwell?'

'Don't you mind them, Harold,' he said. 'She's having one of her turns, and Walter there, well, you know what kids are, always taking the mick.'

'Did they not enjoy the performance?' I was annoyed to find a strange wheedling tone had entered my voice.

'Harold, old son, you were marvellous. When can you start? I need a few days' notice, so I can get the handbills out, call the papers, arrange a few interviews, all that.'

I was pleased as Punch. It was, I suppose, my first critical notice in a quarter-century.

'Do you really think it might work?'

'Harold,' said Mr Topham, 'it'll be a panic. You'll see.'

And thus, I begin my new life as a public performer!

Stiffkey
9 August 1932

I returned from Harrogate, where Mimi is now ensconced with Nugent and his fiancée Lorraine, to pick up some important documents. Important, I suppose I should say, only to me: a bushel or two of handwritten sermons, books, biblical exegeses, correspondence with the bishop, the archbishop and my friend the monsignor (the seraphim of a Church from which I am shortly to be excluded), together with some droll paintings by my children, executed when they were innocent of the hardness of this unjust world. The house is appallingly silent. Coarse seagrass has invaded the front garden; soon it will resemble the wild terrain abutting the salt flats on the coast, and all Mimi's dutiful coaxing of lawn and flower beds will be obliterated. Wordsworth's poignant poem 'Michael' comes to mind, with the old father's sheepfold that is never completed, once he learns of his son's disgrace, and gradually yields to the encroachments of nature.

I arranged for a taxicab to meet me at the church, where I went to pay a sorrowful visit.

Imagine my surprise. On the door of the church I found this document, affixed there like Martin Luther's declaration of the articles of Reformation pinned on to the doors of Wittenberg Cathedral:

BERTRAM by Divine Permission BISHOP OF NORWICH To the Reverend HAROLD FRANCIS DAVIDSON, Rector of Stiffkey with Morston within Our said Diocese of Norwich WHEREAS you have been charged under the Clergy Discipline Act 1892 with certain immoral acts immoral conduct and immoral habits specified in a Complaint dated the eighth day of January One thousand nine hundred and thirty-two and a Notice dated the twenty-sixth day of February One thousand nine hundred and thirty-two AND WHEREAS you have in pursuance of the said Act been prosecuted and tried for the said offences in the Consistory Court of our said Diocese and have by the Judgement of the Worshipful Frederick Keppel-North Chancellor of our said Diocese delivered on the ninth day of July One thousand nine hundred and thirty-two been found guilty of the said offence AND WHEREAS in pursuance of the Rules made under the said Act Our said Chancellor has adjourned the said Court to a time and place to be notified for the passing of sentence upon you and has made certain recommendations to us concerning such sentence AND WHEREAS in consequence of the Appeals hereinafter mentioned We have not thought fit to pass such sentence so long as any such appeal should be pending AND WHEREAS you have presented a petition for leave to appeal to His Majesty the King in Council against the said Judgement in respect of the facts but your said petition was on the thirtieth day of July One thousand nine hundred and thirty-two dismissed AND WHEREAS you have now (as we are informed) appealed to His Majesty the King in Council against the said Judgement in respect of some matter or matters of law AND WHEREAS your said appeal cannot in the ordinary course be heard and determined before the twelfth day of October One thousand nine hundred and thirty-two AND WHEREAS from the nature of the offences charged against you as aforesaid it appears to us that great scandal is likely to arise from your continuing to perform the services of the Church while such charges or any of them are or is under investigation and that your ministration will be useless while such charges or any of them are or is pending NOW in exercise of the power in this behalf vested in Us by the said Act we do hereby inhibit you the said Harold Francis Davidson from performing any service of the Church within Our said Diocese of Norwich from and after the expiration of fourteen days from the service of this Notice and until sentence shall have been given in the said Cause And thereof We do hereby give notice accordingly to you and to the Church wardens of Stiffkey and Morston aforesaid and to all other Our officers throughout our said Diocese.

GIVEN under our hand and seal at Norwich this ninth day of August in the year of Our Lord One thousand nine hundred and thirty-two and of our Consecration the twenty-third.

B. NORWICH

I have never read a piece of prose so deadening, so blankly, dispiritingly, coldly dismissive, so bereft of any trace of Christian understanding. So I am to be forcibly 'inhibited', I whose life has been devoted to the inhibiting of human misery and want?

It is also the longest sentence I have ever read. A sentence of dismissal. Good heavens. In the midst of my gloom, I have made a rather good pun.

CHAPTER 20

Journals of Harold Davidson
Harrogate
12 August 1932

As I was unpacking a suitcase of bits and pieces hastily thrown together at the end of the trial – some trousers, slippers, a box of cigars, some papers, bars of fragrant soap I had purchased as gifts for young women I might meet – I made a startling discovery: what must have been Barbara's copy of *Forty Martyrs of England and Wales*. It dates from the time I was attempting to convert her to some form of structured belief. She was, I recall, distracted by this book and used its harrowing details to argue with me against the justice and mercy of the Established Church.

I picked it up – a light book, scarcely more than a pamphlet – and glanced at its pages. The forty essays were brief lives indeed, two or three pages apiece, bulked out with portraits of the faithful departed. I read about the 'seminary priests' who went to Catholic temples of learning in Rome, Douai, Lisbon and Valladolid and trained to be proselytisers of papism, returning to England like spies, administering the sacraments to other traitors in hiding. I noted how every essay ended the same way – not merely with the death (obviously) of the martyr, but with a lengthy description of his or her final agonies, as drawn out as the victims' intestines. No detail was spared of the butchery visited on the hapless victims: the torture, the racking, the hanging, the disembowelling, the executioner's seizing of the heart and tearing it out, the burning of bowels before their owner's eyes, the impaling of human heads on spikes. It was disgusting. Yet I read on, appalled by the small trajectory of these careers, of men who might easily have been me (one of them, Ralph Sherwin, born a Protestant, went to Exeter College, my Oxford alma mater) if only their lives had not taken a bad turning.

Something about the booklet tugged at my heart, and finally I realised what it was. For of course, *my* life, like theirs, took a bad turning somewhere, though I cannot say with clarity when or where. And when it went wrong, there was the unsmiling face of the Church of England, willing my downfall. In these pages, the Church becomes a horrible, looming presence, an institution without mercy. Time after time, the priests are told to swear allegiance to Queen Mary or Elizabeth as head of the Church, or face a hideous, barbaric demise. The book tells of one martyr, Edmund Arrowsmith, who, in 1628, while being dragged to the gibbet to have his guts incinerated, met a Protestant minister called Leigh who called out, 'Pray, sir, accept the king's mercy. Take the oath of allegiance and your life will be granted. Here is a man come straight from the Judge to offer you mercy. You may live if you conform to the Protestant religion.' The voice of a typical craven bureaucrat. Arrowsmith replied, 'Oh, sir, how far am I from that! Tempt me no more, for I am a dying man. I will do it in no case, on no condition.'

How his admirable stance reminds me of my own confrontation with the Church, when they demanded from me a confession without limits, when they demanded I kneel and beg forgiveness! But I stood up to them. And for it I am burned and publicly disembowelled too, by the same Church of England. After fighting the doctrines of the Roman persuasion for years, I have, it seems, joined the ranks of their Blessed!

Leicester
15 August 1932

I have had to make some changes to my act. Some of the more elderly monologues – particularly 'Beauties on the Beach' – are considered a little too old-fashioned to find the funny bone of the modern audience. It seems that the generalisations we could once confidently make about the fair sex are no longer common currency. It its place,

I have adapted an hilarious piece of stage business entitled 'The Drama on Crutches', in which famous scenes from Shakespeare (Juliet's balcony, Desdemona's strangling, the murder of Duncan) are reimagined as performed by the temporarily disabled. This kind of physical comedy is best suited to the young and vital of limb, as they fling themselves about the stage while declaiming 'heroic' lines, to near-hysterical audiences; but I am willing to give it a try.

After the difficult first night on the Harrogate stage, I feel much more confident. Having not faced an audience for many years, I felt unequipped both for their approval and their dislike. As I faltered through the opening pages of 'Human Oddities', as stiff as a girder, someone shouted, 'Can you save a couple of girls for me, Reverend?' and the audience guffawed. Instead of working it into the act, I pressed on with playing the crusty country squire (an impersonation that was moth-eaten when first performed in 1870). I can now offer advice to aspiring young comedians: It is unwise to ignore hecklers and stick to the script; the audience will be waiting for another freelance humorist to put you off your stride. I passed a *mauvais quart d'heure* as one laughter opportunity after another died on my lips, and the audience's only interest lay in making oafish pleasantries about my public shaming. 'You plucked any good Roses lately, Reverend?' someone called out. 'You dirty old plucker,' called another, to mocking raillery.

Eventually, stung by their lack of interest in classic humour, I decided to play to my strengths, and bring up the consistory court. As their restless murmuring turned to jeering and slow handclaps, I put together in my head a little satire of recent events; then raised a hand, demanding silence; then began:

'I've just arrived in Harrogate from the heart of London Town,
I to the assizes went,
Just to prove that I'm not bent,
For the bishops they don't like me and they carp, complain
    and frown.
They say I'm too familiar with the dames;
They shout at me and call me dreadful names . . .'

I paused. There was a genuine *atmosphere* out there. It was unmistakable. You never lose this facility – no actor does – of knowing when you've gauged the house's mood aright. I looked down at the stalls. The faces were turned up to mine – flushed, suddenly excited, anticipating a real show. Hardly knowing where the next line was coming from, I sang:

'As I walk along High Holborn with a twinkle in my eye,
You can hear the girls all sigh:
It's the Rector – I shall die!
For *he*'s got the solution to our chronic prostitution;
And his manly arms will save us,
And he never will deprave us,
For he'll take us all to Heaven in his bulging fly!'

I realised that the innuendo in the last line – culled from God knows what low vaudeville act in my past – was revolting and disgusting, and I wondered if I should apologise to the congregation, or rather crowd. But the first five rows were laughing heartily, so I felt no need.

Next day, I burnished the little song, and it has gone into the act and always elicits a glowing response. Audiences are beginning to sing along. In the meantime, I am looking into suggestions as to how to 'beef up' my act for more public acceptance. *Tableaux vivants* are apparently quite the thing now. I am currently exploring a humorous skit involving a Hindoo fakir explaining to me – in my rector persona – how spiritual bliss is best achieved by lying on a bed of sharp nails wearing only a loincloth. After much hilarious cross-talk and mutual misunderstandings, I strip down to the simple garment, lie upon the (thankfully rubber) device of torture and cry out, 'My word, you're right! I can see, shining before me, the face of . . . the face of God!' (Pause.) 'Oh no! It is only the face of the Bishop of Norwich!!' The baser elements will not understand the references to Nirvana, but will find the Babu accent hilarious. And the final line will bring the house down, mark my words.

Yesterday was one of the saddest days of my life, and today one of the happiest. I came to the village yesterday morning after driving through the night from Nelson, Lancashire. I sat in the sidecar while Ted Cowin, my new friend, the music-hall performer with whom I have lately shared the stage in Rochdale, Wigan and Oldham, drove the motor bicycle.

Unseasonal rain poured down on us, lashed at poor Cowin's goggles and saturated my clothing. We stopped in Leicester for tea and a hot pasty at 7 a.m., and arrived in Stiffkey just in time to take the morning service – the last I shall ever take. The condemnation of the bishop was posted on the church door on the 9th of this month; my 'inhibition' or debarring from performing any church service came in effect yesterday (the 23rd).

My dear sister Alice, my niece and the loyal Mrs Reynolds met us at the Rectory. The ladies clucked and fussed about my wet clothing, but I had no time to spare, and robed myself for the service. I looked into the church to speak to Mr Gray-Fisk, the organist. The pews were almost full – about seventy souls, all local – but I felt a disappointment that more people had not attended. Perhaps it was as well. I was tired and wet, my limbs were a-tremble and I felt unspeakably miserable. When I read the lesson, it was an effort to stop myself weeping. Then I heard a noise, as of someone coughing far away, and realised there were people outside the church. When the congregation said 'Amen', the 'Amen' was taken up and echoed by a large chorus of voices outside. During the hymn, I went out, to find a great crowd standing in the porch and churchyard. 'Good people,' I cried. 'Do not stand out here, but join the faithful in the chancel.' The first thirty or so found seats, thirty more stood by the wall; the others could not enter the glutted environs.

My sermon was meant to be a soaring farewell to the parish I have served for so long. I wanted to regale the crowd with stories of droll encounters with local 'characters', lost chapel keys, amusing children, farcical misunderstandings and the like, but they failed to materialise in my head. I, who can turn any everyday event into a hilarious 'routine' when faced with an audience of strangers at the Rochdale Hippodrome, was tongue-tied when trying to entertain my own flock. Instead, I mumbled some words of regret for the darkness into which we all must pass, and the hope of resurrection, that we may all meet again one day in Paradise. Thus I signalled my intention not to die or fade away, even when I am officially 'degraded', but to go, reborn, to a better life. I blessed them all, parishioners and strangers, and saw some ladies weeping into their handkerchiefs.

Because of the crowd at the back of the church, I left by the vestry door, and found, to my amazement, about a thousand persons standing outside the church and down the lane – more than any gathering that has attended my recent appearances.

I tried to shake a few hands, and was sucked into the mêlée, which opened and closed around me like a giant sea creature, until I was enveloped in its folds. My back was slapped until it became sore, as though flayed like poor Marsyas. I tried to escape but my limbs were impeded in the crush, tried again with an arms-outstretched swimming motion, and reached the Rectory with the great sea creature still clutching the hem of my jacket. A strange, chaotic sign-off! I invited fifty members of the congregation to come to the Rectory, to pray with me and help themselves to what remains of my meagre wine cellar. (Since I do not drink, some bottles have been lying here for twenty-five years.) They did so, some staying until 2.15 a.m., commiserating and, eventually, singing comic songs from *Iolanthe* and *The Yeomen of the Guard*.

This morning, I rose late and alone in the empty Rectory, still a priest of the Church, but no longer allowed to take part in any liturgical rite. I can read no lesson, collect no tithes, preach no sermons, baptise no children, marry no sweethearts and bury no dead. Am I, technically, allowed to speak to parishioners in the street, to offer them advice and counsel? I expect not. I am deprived of the point of my life. I am a sultan become a eunuch, an oyster without its pearl. The Church has thrown me out of its respectable club like a drunken roughneck ejected from the Athenaeum. I am an evil man. Everybody knows me to be an evil man. But I am not an evil man. I must start to believe in myself.

That was my dark mood this morning. With the congregation, the well-wishing strangers and the late-night carousers all gone, with everyone gone from me and everything taken from me, I was in danger of falling into despair. Yet I would not submit. Some impulse of preservation made me eat some breakfast, go downstairs, extract my old bicycle from the outhouse, and go for a ride.

I must have cycled miles this morning, pedalling with manic determination all the way to Blakeney, cutting south homeward through the little lanes, cherishing the myriad sights and smells I would soon be leaving for good. The smell of burnt cherrywood in Langham, the white hips of wild rose in the hedges near Saxlingham, the eighteenth-century cottages studded with flinty stones, the meadows populated with stooks of corn like Red Indian wigwams, the orange barley waving in the summer breeze, the red poppies dotting the green fields. And here and there I received a whiff from the sea in my nostrils, and saw the marram grasses by the edge of the road, leaning forward, as though they were all pointing a thousand fingers and saying 'Go!'

By the time I reached Binham, I was weary and out of breath, so I paused to look inside the priory. And there, I made an extraordinary discovery.

It is a magnificent old Norman edifice, with graceful stone arches on both sides of the nave, original ancient timbers vaulting up to the roof, a marvellously calm and airy atmosphere, like a breeze from Heaven upon the soul. I stood for a time by the baptismal font, brooding on my fate and the events that have brought perdition upon me, until I was obliged by the stares of the curious (for now I am recognised, wherever I go) to find the haven of a pew. There I sat lost in thought about the trial, Mr Levy, Mr Keppel-North, Barbara in the witness box, the awful voice at the end pronouncing anathemas on my endeavours . . . I might have succumbed to melancholy, had I not been moved to look at the rood screen. Newly reframed, and as long as a church door, it rested against the pew furthest back from the altar. On my way in, I had given only a cursory glance at this wooden display cabinet. Now I found myself examining it, as a distraction from thinking about the only thing I could think about − my imminent defrocking.

I gazed at the inscription on the first of the four sections – a familiar text I have preached many times, from I Timothy, chapter 6, verses 10–12:

> For the love of money is the root of all evil; which while some coveted after, they have erred from the faith, and pierced themselves through with many sorrows. But thou, O man of God, flee these things; and follow after righteousness, godliness, faith, love, patience, meekness. Fight the good fight of faith, lay hold on eternal life, whereunto thou art also called, and hast professed a good profession before many witnesses.

Seeing these words now, under the glass, under my hands, seeing this singing, divine endorsement of my long career in pursuit of righteousness, godliness, et cetera, made plain before me in this beautiful old church, was profoundly sad.

Then my eyes fell upon the painting that illustrated the text in the pages of an old Bible. It was the figure of Christ, but as Christ is seldom seen – as the Man of Sorrows, his face melancholy, his eyes wide and staring, the crown of thorns lacerating his scalp, and – most unusually in the iconography of the sixteenth century – his bearded cheeks and chin hanging down in terrible disappointment. Artists of the Renaissance were discouraged from representing the Son of God as a sorrowing figure. He is shown as calm and resigned when dying on the cross; as manly and heroic when throwing the usurers out of the temple; never as giving way to grief. What I held before me in Binham Priory was a rare portrait of a depressed Jesus. It is evidently a Tudor painting obliterated to make room for the inscription from I Timothy, and over the years had gradually showed through the page like a guilty secret.

I gazed at Christ, at the great hurt in his saucer-like eyes, the bedraggled, dog's-mane quality of his matted cheeks, the rosebud sulk of his red lips, and I felt, for once, not prostration before my Redeemer, but an equality of suffering that bound us together.

In my heart, pride and noble resistance flashed a sudden light. I was glad I had come to this lovely priory.

I moved on, to the inscription in the third panel of the rood screen. A creeping sensation on my arms brought me the strange conviction that my visit to this church was preordained, my steps driven by Providence to this cool and airy Norman nave to find out some great secret.

I leaned over the glass and read the following:

> Be ready allwayes to geue an answer to euery man that asketh you a reason of the hope that is in you, and that with meekness and feare: hauynge a good conscience that whereas they back-byte you as euyll doers they may be ashamed, that falsely accuse your good conuercation in Christ. For it is better (yf the will of God be so) that ye suffer for well doynge than for euyll doing.

I rubbed my eyes.

Of all the verses, in all the books of the New Testament that I might have found, I had found this one. May God forgive such a foolish thought, but I knew, with a thrill, that this reading was meant for my eyes alone.

'Having a good conscience' – yes, yes – 'that whereas they back-bite you as evil doers they may be ashamed, that falsely accuse your good conversation in Christ.' What has this whole trial been, but a procession of backbiters and backbiting, and misrepresentations of my work for the Lord, the false tittle-tattle of small men and ignorant women, compared to my intense conversation with Christ?

My enemies are not, of course, ashamed. They are triumphant. They have turned me into a figure of fun, condemned me as a felon and lecher, unfit to hold ecclesiastical office. But what was the burden of the Lord's message? That it is better I suffer for well-doing than for evil-doing? How had I not called this text to mind before?

Back at Stiffkey Church, I looked up the reference: I Peter, chapter 3, verses 15–17. There it was: 'Having a good conscience; that, whereas they speak evil of you, as of evildoers, they may be ashamed that falsely accuse your good conversation in Christ.' But my Bible is the King James Version. The words in Binham Priory were from Cranmer's Bible, where 'they backbyte you' becomes, in the modern version, 'they speak evil of you'. The difference is crucial. The trial was a tirade, not of merely speaking against me, but of backbiting, suggestion, innuendo, gossip.

I am greatly elated. I have suffered for well-doing, in the name of Christ, and now I am free of the backbiting Church! I can go where I want, and do as I please, with this certainty of the continuance of our divine conversation to buoy me up. Hurrah!

Harrogate
30 August 1932

THINGS TO DO:

1. *Write back to Mr Summerscale, of Norwich Football Club, re his kind suggestion that I become interim manager of said club. Can he be serious? 'While we're looking for a replacement for Alfred Manley,' he writes, 'we need someone to bring the crowds in. I don't know about your football experience, but you're obviously a dab hand at publicity and making people do what you want. Why not come to see us, now you've a bit of time on your hands?' I am not at all sure how to take this bizarre proposal.*
2. *Mrs Eunice Jones from Whitby, Yorkshire, writes to say she is founding a club of nature-worshippers on a private beach, and wishes to enlist me as a patron. 'There is no immediate need, Mr Davidson, for you to embrace the delights of naturism, unless you feel so inclined. But to add your name to the list of well-disposed public figures behind our enterprise would be a boon. There would be a small honorarium in payment, in return for your addressing the new society (fully clothed of course!) one Friday in October.'*
3. *Respond to several cinemas which have invited me to talk, one evening before the main feature, on 'Girls, Guilt and God' (or variants on these three subjects). Must reply to the Rialto in Worthing, the Hippodrome in Deal, the Ritz in Cardiff, et cetera.*
4. *Must arrange weekly grocery delivery in Harrogate, while Mimi strives to conquer her shopping agoraphobia.*
5. *Do I want to pose on Hampstead Heath for photographs with a dead whale, brought to London by refrigerated lorry from its sad final resting*

place in Folkstone? I am at a loss to decide. If I could determine some
symbolic property that would connect the poor mammal to my sacerdotal
life (Jonah in the whale's belly?), I can think of no obvious objection.

Playhouse Theatre, Birmingham
3 September 1932

An excellent evening. House almost two-thirds full. I performed two monologues, three musical skits with Miss Florence Welch, a comely young chanteuse and comedienne, and climaxed the show with a fantastical tableau in which, to thunderous musical backing, I appeared in a glass vitrine, clad in a white surplice, clinging to a long metal rod that was turned by a villainous Gothick slave in a studded leather costume, to suggest that I was being spit-roasted in Hell, all the time being prodded by three young ladies in tight, red, elastic 'Devil' costumes. The audience were most enthusiastic. I received £12 and signed many autographs at the stage door.

This morning, I received a letter from a Mr Luke Gannon, the proprietor of an 'entertainment circus' in Blackpool. He wishes me to appear for ten days as 'the star attraction' of his show on the beach, which regularly brings audiences of five or six hundred per diem. There is no stage. Instead, he offers to exhibit me in 'a barrel-like structure', where I can sit in comfort from 10 a.m. to 10 p.m. and greet members of the public, putting my views of the trial and the iniquities of the modern Church 'and anything else you care to chat about'. For this, he offers me £20 a day, plus 'a good fish lunch and a superior tea', and promises to find me accommodation at a guest house, 'if you haven't had a surfeit of landladies in your life already!'

I have not consulted Mimi about this. It would take too long to make her understand how one can transcend the baseness of such a public stage for the greater good of bringing the Truth to a thousand strangers. I am not sure that a circus is a legitimate arena for my talents, but £200 is £200 – it used to represent all the capital to which I had access for a whole year!

So I shall go. I shall send Mr Gannon a telegram this afternoon.

A visit to Blackpool would lift my spirits. I can assess what Mr Gannon has in store, and can always contrive some white 'porky pie' (as my publican friends in Whitechapel used to term a falsehood) to make good my escape home, should it seem too demeaning.

Central Beach, Blackpool
6 September 1932

An embarrassing kerfuffle has occurred. On arriving at Blackpool, I was approached by a member of the *Lancashire Evening Post*, who asked if it was true that I had undertaken to fast in a barrel for a week. Naturally I denied it. (I never said anything about fasting.) When pressed by the irritating scribe, I answered that some wretched hoaxer must have impersonated me on the telephone, used my name for his own advancement and promised to take part in this foolish display. The journalist pointed to a sign that read: 'The Rev. Mr Davidson, Rector of Stiffkey, will watch over Barbara Cockayne [a 'bearded lady'] for £200 for ten days and nights.' Having gone so far (I could never govern my tongue!), I renewed my denials. Unfortunately, the newsman contacted Mr Gannon for a comment. He telephoned me at my guest house to enquire about my commitment, citing the telegram he had received from Birmingham, saying 'Will certainly be in Blackpool on Sunday; into barrel Monday morning' and signed in my name.

I was obliged to repeat that it was a hoax, and recommended that the miscreant be brought to justice since (I ingeniously suggested) he must be in the vicinity, dressed as a clergyman. Gannon threatened to call the police to investigate the matter.

Reluctant to deal with the law at this difficult time, I said it was my duty to help him by going into the barrel, and thus I find myself, on this overcast morning, with the noise of the broken pipe organ driving my ears to a frenzy of irritation.

The crowd is prodigious. They spill out all over the footpath, the carriage drive and the roadway, easily a thousand ignorant souls, chewing sweets, smoking pipes, shouting nonsensical pleasantries at each other, blocking the traffic with their bovine curiosity.

Any minute now, I have no doubt, the police will arrive to regularise the pedestrian flow and remove my barrel to a safer location. They may even pitch it into the sea. And should I mind so greatly, if my life ended now, at the height of my fame, when everybody knows me, everybody wants to touch my garments, everyone wishes to engage me in conversation, if only for five minutes or fifty seconds, so that they can say, 'I met that chap, the Rector of Stiffkey, in Blackpool, *you* know, the one in the trial that was written up in all the papers, the vicar with the harem of prostitutes and the saucy photographs,' and all their friends will say, 'Oooh, what was he like?' and they will reply, 'I don't know, I only met him for a minute, but he spoke to me and he has a deep voice and lovely white hair and a sweet manner, you wouldn't think an old gent like that could get up to such things'?

There will be my fame, my reputation, the point of my life, reduced to the memory of a few seconds of contact, a trivial encounter replicated ten thousand times on the lips of simple, sensation-seeking folk like the brief memory of a day trip to Southend, or the fugitive strains of a Cole Porter song, popular last year, now half forgotten.

Mr Gannon has kindly brought me some tea and a digestive biscuit. He looks at me coldly, however, as though he suspects I may have lied to him about the hoaxer story. It occurs to me, with a shock, that I may have been guilty of lying for years without realising I was doing so.

So much of the trial passed in an agony of memory, as I strove to recall what I had said earlier about this girl, or that photograph, or those sleeping arrangements. 'It is hard,' Barbara wrote to the bishop, 'being good when you have been bad.' I would abbreviate that sentiment. It is hard being good. So much is at stake in the pursuit of virtue, it is not surprising that one must cut some corners – a small financial transaction here, a small strategic fiction there. So many subtle adjustments must be made in the business of saving souls – the clanking, outmoded machinery of virtue – that some will not withstand close scrutiny. Without editing the truth, young girls will not come to you and listen to your wise counsel. Claim acquaintance with Mr Jack Buchanan, and their aspiring souls will be more readily drawn to you. Offer them a close friendship, such as they have never known, and they may themselves seek out similar friendships, rather than the superficial, fleshy attractions that will lead them astray. Yes, I may have played some sport with the truth; but it was always in the service of a higher truth, the certainty of spiritual fulfilment.

Some policemen are walking towards me. Day trippers are being ushered off the congested road, back on to the overcrowded path. I fear that an ugly scene may soon develop. They will blame Mr Gannon, I hope. They cannot – surely? – blame me. All I ever wanted was to save young women from becoming lost. As Mimi was lost to me. She was my Irish singing rose, tight-budded, full-throated, a perfect hymn made human. I do not think Barbara was right to imagine my ten-year sojourn in London was a constant search for Mimi-as-she-might-have-been, because of her pregnancy with the soldier while I was away at the war.

No, it was because of her later forgetfulness, when she fell in love with a Shakespearean actor and had a second child by another man, the little girl we called Pamela. She was born in 1919. Her father's name I shall never divulge. But once we returned to Stiffkey, to restart our life, we brought Pamela with us. Is it so strange that I could not bear to stop at home, watching the child that bears my wife's lover's face grow more like him every day? Can anyone condemn me for sending myself to London, to escape this daily reminder of my wife's double treachery? And to find there, every week, girls in similar trouble – girls unsuitably allied to strange men, girls with their moral compass all awry, girls opening their precious temples to infidels and raiders because they were too poor to find an alternative – and seek to make them whole? Was that wrong?

And after all this labour in the vineyards of the Lord, my reward is not to sit at His right hand, exulting in bliss, but to sit in this wooden throne explaining to mad strangers that, no, I am no whoremaster, no abuser of young girls' trust, only a friend in need, a lover of women in the simplest, kindest way, loving their innocent warmth, their intimate conversation, their vulnerable flesh, their blue-eyed resilience.

Ah well. It is the burden of the do-gooding divine to strive after the happiness of the afflicted, and to be misunderstood.

The police are milling through the crowd more forcibly now, with frankly bullying intent. Soon I will be ejected from this throne. But I shall not complain. For here comes a young mother, twenty-two at most, chestnut-eyed, curly-haired, cotton-shirted, dragging her small, sweet, tiny daughters in their stained blue smocks, eager to pass whatever few seconds may remain to us both in conducting a tiny conversation with the smallest god on earth.

AFTERWORD

The rector remained in the barrel at Blackpool for only a day and a half. Inspector Scott, Inspector Pye and a constable from the Blackpool police closed down the show and dispersed the crowd, fearful that 'this awesome exhibition' would result in ugly scenes and afraid that the barrel might be 'seized and pitched into the sea'. Mr Luke Gannon, the amusement caterer, was summonsed to the Blackpool court for 'causing a public nuisance by exhibiting a certain person, Harold Davidson, in a barrel whereby crowds of people were attracted, thereby causing an obstruction on the footpaths'. The now-former rector was summonsed for aiding and abetting this felony. Mr Gannon addressed the bench and said there had never been a more flimsy case in the annals of law, but that he would abandon the exhibition of the rector, 'for safety's sake'. The bench agreed to withdraw the summons.

The Rector of Stiffkey was officially defrocked in Norwich Cathedral in October 1932. Thereafter, for five years, as plain Mr Harold Davidson, he pursued his lonely crusade to clear his name. He embarked on increasingly bizarre public stunts, until he was banned from stage appearances, and was obliged to find work where he could. For a while he worked as a porter at St Pancras Station, helping people with their luggage. Despite his defrocking, he regularly wore a dog collar in public, but now attended Catholic Mass services.

His final appearance was in a Skegness amusement park. Through an agent, he agreed to appear during one July weekend of 1937, beside and then inside a lion's cage, denouncing the Church of England and presenting himself as 'Daniel in the Lion's Den'. The lion into whose home he strayed was an alpha male called Freddie and was, the circus authorities assured their new star, old, toothless and sedated.

The Rector's first appearance in the cage drew an appreciative crowd and was considered a great success. Then, for reasons that remain opaque, a lioness was introduced into the cage. On the second day, as Mr Davidson finished speaking, he stepped back and trod accidentally on the lioness's tail. Her roars brought Freddie, her new mate, from his sedated slumbers and he seized Davidson's head and neck in his huge jaws. The gaping audience were unsure whether or not it was part of the act. The attendant lion-tamer, an intrepid girl of sixteen called Irene – a girl whose company Mr Davidson would unquestionably have sought in earlier years – leapt into the cage, freed the rector and pulled him to safety. But he had been fatally mauled and was rushed to hospital. The doctors, under the impression that he suffered from diabetes, administered a dose of the new drug insulin, which induced a coma from which he died the next day, 30 July 1937.

His funeral was attended by three thousand people. The coffin was carried through the streets between Stiffkey and Morston, followed by his family and the British Legion Band from Blakeney. He was buried in the graveyard of Stiffkey Church. Scores of mourners struggled to acquire handfuls of the earth that was piled on his coffin. So many of them pushed and shoved against each other in the crush to acquire a souvenir, that many swooned and collapsed right there on the immemorial greensward, where the Reverend Davidson had buried so many of his parish faithful.

ACKNOWLEDGEMENTS

I first encountered the story of the Rector of Stiffkey thirty years ago, in *The Age of Illusion* (Penguin, 1960), Ronald Blythe's delightful social history of England between the wars. The book has been in and out of print for decades, and is warmly recommended for its uniquely breezy style as much as for the fascination of its contents. A biography of the Reverend Davidson by Tom Cullen, *The Prostitutes' Padre: the story of the notorious Rector of Stiffkey*, was published in 1975, but is now impossible to find.

I am indebted to the *Eastern Daily Press*, the Norwich newspaper, for their archival record of the rector's trial, an exhaustive piece of reportage that runs to approximately a million words, from which I have drawn certain salient facts and legal disputes that seem to have a bearing on my main character's complex motivations. I have no doubt that the trial will, one day, energise a splendid, if rather surreal, movie.

My thanks are due to Victoria Barnsley of HarperCollins for giving this project the green light on a handshake, in the heat of a charity quiz at the Café Royal in 2004. And to Clare Reihill of Fourth Estate for her cheery encouragement as deadlines came and went, winter and summer, and her calm stoicism in the face of the 894-page manuscript that resulted. I'm very grateful for the forensic editorial skill of Katherine Fry, who clarified a chaotic manuscript with cool efficiency; it's a chastening experience to discover that your copy-editor knows more about your book than you do yourself.

My greatest debt, however, is to Karilyn Collier, the rector's granddaughter, whose privately printed *Harold Francis Davidson: A Biography of his Life and Trial* (Zevrika Publications) is full of fascinating details and vivid family recollections.

I should make it clear that Ms Collier has not endorsed, or encouraged, or in any way given her blessing to this work of fiction. She has striven for years to clear her ancestor's name and overturn the judgement of the trial, and is frankly hostile to any fictional interventions (no matter how well-intentioned) that might muddy the waters. I can only say, in my defence, that nobody knows for certain the workings of the rector's mind as he went about his work of salvation. Was he a social worker, *avant la lettre*? Was he a parasite on helpless young women? Was he a sexual opportunist? This novel offers an imaginative solution to questions that have seethed about his nimble shade for seventy years.

It was prompted by a detail in Ms Collier's brief life of her grandfather. After Harold Davidson died, in 1937, a bogus biographer called on the family and took away all the rector's diaries, letters and private documents, promising to turn them into a sympathetic biography. They never heard from him again, but later suspected that the caller was an emissary from the Bishop of Norwich, the rector's nemesis, the man who did for him in the end.

What would they have revealed about his life? In the absence of the real thing, I decided, with terrible arrogance, to write his journals on his behalf. I hope Ms Collier will forgive me. It is, as they say, only a novel.

P.S.

Ideas,
interviews
& features . . .

About the author

2 A Sixteen-Pocket Skirt-Chaser: John
Walsh talks to Travis Elborough

3 Life at a Glance

5 Ten Favourite Prostitutes in Literature

7 Have You Read?

10 A Writer's Life

About the book

13 The 1,001 Nights of Little Jimmy by John
Walsh

A Sixteen-Pocket Skirt-Chaser

John Walsh talks to Travis Elborough

I WONDERED IF WE **might start by talking a little bit about how the novel came about. In your acknowledgements, you mention first encountering the rector's story in Ronald Blythe's** *The Age of Illusion* **over thirty years ago. What was it about Blythe's book and the Reverend Davidson that left such a lasting impression on you?**

It's just such a fantastic read. Blythe is a very good writer; he dramatises things so well. And what he was dramatising in the chapter on Davidson was a particular kind of sneaky English sex scandal, one involving your classic furtive, hand-rubbing greasy vicar.

Blythe had a very firm idea of what Davidson must have been like. He was astonishingly unfair about Davidson. At the time, though, just after Oxford, I found it just an extraordinarily interesting story. It has a terrific cast of characters, a carnival of grotesques and circus people. The girl, Barbara, appeared terribly worldly in Blythe. She stuck in my mind as this brilliant sixteen-year-old tough bunny. She was the Mandy Rice-Davies of her day, and, for God's sake, it's 1932. She's an incredibly sassy young bint who confounded the judge.

And Davidson?

I couldn't help admiring Davidson. Whatever Davidson was doing – and we really don't know the details to this day – the powers that be were trying to bang him up, and succeeded, which seemed unjust to me. I admired his energy. I admired the way he stood up to the bishop. And I admired the way he bounced back after the scandal. We have to remember, he did this sixty years, at least, before Neil Hamilton or Jeffrey Archer or Jonathan Aitken, all of those people. Because in the old days, if you were disgraced or struck off, court-martialled or cashiered, you were expected to do the decent thing. You took a service revolver and a bottle of whisky and you shot yourself. What you didn't do was turn round and become a celebrity, on the grounds that the public should be able to judge you for themselves. I was intrigued by all of that and intrigued by his toughness.

I have to say, though, there was also that curious . . . *chuckling* . . . quality about him. For some reason I *do* absolutely love a particular strain of cowardly lecher. By which I mean people like Leslie Phillips. I would put Davidson in this curiously English mould. I'd written a book, *Are You Talking to Me?*, which is all about movies and their potential to affect real life. One of the chapters was about love and trying to find a romantic leading man to identify with. For me, it was never going to be James Bond, because no one could speak to women like that. But the hopelessness of rather ridiculous seducers like Bob Hope, I absolutely identify with. That notion of being basically hopeless but frightfully keen on girls – that was the rector!▶

LIFE
at a Glance

BORN:

24 October 1953 in Wimbledon, London

EDUCATED:

Wimbledon College

Exeter College, Oxford

University College, Dublin

CAREER:

I started off on *The Tablet*, the Catholic intellectual weekly, selling advertising space, often to convents in lean times for vocations. After a year in publishing, at Victor Gollancz, I began my journalistic career as associate editor of *The Director*, the house magazine of the Institute of Directors. I left to go freelance for three years, then joined the *Evening Standard* as literary editor. I've been literary editor of three newspapers – the

Standard, the *Sunday Times* and the *Independent*. I was also editor of the *Independent Magazine*, and am now the newspaper's assistant editor, columnist, feature writer, interviewer, restaurant critic, travel writer and a few other things.

I was director of the Cheltenham Festival for three years, 1997–9, and both judge and chairman, in successive years, of the Forward Prize for Poetry.

FAMILY:

I live in Dulwich, south London, with the journalist Carolyn Hart and our three children, Sophie, Max and Clementine.

A Sixteen-Pocket Shirt-Chaser *(continued)*

◄ **You're an editor, critic, journalist and memoirist. What made you finally decide to turn the events of his life into a novel?**
Well, years and years later, I read William Donaldson's amazing *Brewer's Rogues, Villains and Eccentrics* and there's a brilliant entry on Davidson in it, which rekindled my interest in the rector. I discovered he'd gone to the same Oxford College as me and that when he'd first approached Barbara on a London street, he'd told her she looked like the actress Mary Brian. It started to make me wonder. If he's innocent, what the hell is he playing at, using this classic chat-up patter?

I'd spoken to a friend of mine, D. J. Taylor, the novelist and critic who lives in Norfolk, about all of this. And he suddenly sent me a pamphlet published by the rector's granddaughter. It was a modest, self-published thing, forty pages or so that she'd put out to exonerate her grandfather. It cast him as a rather godlike figure: he was a social worker, he never laid a finger on any women at all, the trial was full of complete lies, the photograph of him with the young woman was obviously spliced, it was all a bit like that. But it was full of fantastic details – one in particular just hit me. She wrote that he was a very eccentric fellow, and that he had a coat with sixteen pockets specially sewn into it. Sixteen pockets? What the fuck? What did he need a coat with sixteen pockets sewn into it for? And suddenly after all these years of not writing fiction an extraordinary creative thing started to kick in my head. You start to work out what on earth these pockets could be for. Suddenly, this coat wasn't just a piece of clothing, it was like a basket or filing-cabinet. And the novel all built from there.

And then there was the matter of the missing diaries that some supposedly reputable biographer had spirited away from a cupboard under the stairs. When I read about that, I thought: What could be in them? Would they be full of self-exculpation? Would they be full of euphemisms, or could they be in code or stuff like that?

Initially I felt I had to decide, was Davidson innocent? Was he guilty? Was he a nice person? And that's when it dawned on me that rather than just deciding like Blythe that he was simply a bad guy, the most appalling skirt-chaser who tried it on with every young girl he met, or like his granddaughter that he was a saint . . . I thought, isn't it possible he was just an ordinary flawed man? Both of these possibilities were inherent and so he was both of these things.

What makes the novel so impressive is that you succeed in rendering Davidson a largely sympathetic figure but still leave the reader to draw their own conclusions about his possible guilt . . .
You are supposed to be able to read between the lines. He is always justifying himself in a way, saying, 'I think I am going to put my arm around this young girl's waist, just to show solidarity,' when he's secretly attracted to them. He'd tell himself that he'd never had an impure thought in his life. He's too much of a ninny to see he tries it on with too many girls.

The novel is about lots of things, hypocrisy, celebrity – and the cheapness of ▶

TEN
Favourite Prostitutes in Literature

Corinna in *Dialogues of the Courtesans* by Lucian (second century AD)

Moll Flanders in *The Fortunes and Misfortunes of the Famous Moll Flanders* by Daniel Defoe (1722)

Fanny Hill in *Memoirs of a Woman of Pleasure* by John Cleland (1748–9)

Bell Calvert in *The Private Memoirs and Confessions of a Justified Sinner* by James Hogg (1824)

Nana in *Nana* by Émile Zola (1880)

Mrs Warren in *Mrs Warren's Profession* by George Bernard Shaw (1898)

Sadie Thompson in *Rain* by W. Somerset Maugham (1921)

Bella Cohen in *Ulysses* by James Joyce (1922)

Jenny Maple in *Twenty Thousand Streets Under the Sky* by Patrick Hamilton (1930–34)

Tralala in *Last Exit to Brooklyn* by Hubert Selby Jnr (1968)∎

◀celebrity – but what it also looks at is idealism and how our purest intentions are invariably compromised by our baser instincts. I provided Harold Davidson with a reason for why he did what he did – all made up. To begin with he was supposed to be a bit like Pooter, a figure of fun who was terribly concerned about doing the right thing but was often confounded by the world's intransigence. He was naïve beyond belief. But as the thing went on I did come to like him.

There's the scene in the novel that was mentioned in Willie Donaldson's book, about him rescuing a girl from the Thames. It took me a long night to write that part. I wanted to capture the idea that he would be that impulsive and altruistic – that he would feel this *amore* thing about being kissed by the Lord. I found it rather affecting. And once it had been written I liked him more. I came to believe he'd been driven by pure motives all his life.

I was also intrigued by his wife; she comes across as a rather pathetic figure in the memoir. But she had these terrible family secrets that offered a reason why the rector had spent twelve years in London. Maybe the motivation lay in that: Davidson was attempting through these girls to reclaim the innocence of his own wife before she went off the rails. Once you give him this hinterland, he becomes a much more comprehensible figure.

Did you find making the transition to fiction difficult?
God, the nerves . . . I had to keep asking myself: Can I do this? Suddenly I was living

❛ The novel is about lots of things, hypocrisy, celebrity – and the cheapness of celebrity – but what it also looks at is idealism and how our purest intentions are invariably compromised by our baser instincts. ❜

with this fifty-five-year-old rector, who thinks that everything he does is absolutely fine and everyone will be his friend. Rather than write as the Rector, I wrote lots of stuff about the journalist in a bar watching him and thinking, who is this funny old bloke having an orange squash? And then finally it clicked; I got the voice. I have been trying to write fiction since I was twenty-one. I am in my fifties now, it is ridiculous to be writing my first novel now, but I couldn't really find the voice before.

What I didn't want to do was write about myself, in some kind of supercharged sub-Martin Amis style. We all revered Martin so much. But trying to find a style of one's own is hard. Journalism teaches you to have style, which is like your own voice but only tweaked up.

I interviewed Martin Amis once and asked him about style or how he writes. He said it's the voice inside you that you work up into prose. And he's exactly right.

If you become a columnist you become aware that some weeks you have no opinions. You are strangely opinion-free. There you are gazing at the world or looking at a DVD or eating some Japanese food and suddenly out of nowhere you can construct a voice which is full of attitude. It gives you a kind of confidence about writing.

So when you come to write about your Irish family or about what the movies in your life mean to you, you take on this swishy actorish voice. Otherwise it won't really be worth reading about.

Blake Morrison showed us all how to ▶

A Sixteen-Pocket Shirt-Chaser *(continued)*

◄write a family memoir even if your family isn't famous, simply by going really close up, right inside it, telling it as truthfully as you can and as passionately as you can. That was a fantastic liberation. But finding a voice for fiction was my problem. And after years and years of trying, I discovered that being able to write in the voice of chronic hypocrisy and sexual opportunism came as naturally to me as anything. That's really alarming, don't you think? Whatever happened to the voice of blinding virtue and loveliness, eh?

You mention the influence of Amis and Blake Morrison; which other writers inspired you? And, also, given the period setting, did you go back and read writers like Patrick Hamilton whose novels in the 1930s were peopled by similar waifs and strays?
Yes, Patrick Hamilton was useful. Without Hamilton I wouldn't know how much it cost to hire a prostitute. I wouldn't know what girls on the streets said. I mean, 'Do you want me?' It's extraordinary, isn't it? Like you wanted food, like you wanted bangers and mash.

I really decided I wanted to be a writer when I was about ten after I read James Clavell's *King Rat*. It's macho war nonsense but it made me determined to get some words down about the war. I was born only eight years after the war, which seems like nothing now. Eight years, it's amazing.

After university, I can remember being knocked out by Al Clark and Mark Williams, these rock-and-roll reviewers for *Time Out*, who wrote hyper-expressive, brilliant, clever

⸂ after years and years of trying, I discovered that being able to write in the voice of chronic hypocrisy and sexual opportunism came as naturally to me as anything. ⸃

8

prose. And then Martin Amis came along with *The Rachel Papers*. He set the bar so high.

The three writers who inspired me in those days were ABC: Amis, Burgess and Carter. Angela Carter had such style. I met her during my job as an assistant at Victor Gollancz. My God, being in her presence . . . She was like a great cat. She had an incredible feral quality. I can remember talking to Beryl Bainbridge who was asking about Simon Raven – and I told her he was a raffish, broken-veined English novelist who liked public school, cricket, buggery and vampires. And Carter chipped in and said, 'Yes but . . . he's also reputed to have eaten human flesh . . .' The idea was so delicious to her.

Will there be more fiction from John Walsh?
Yes, I am being pulled in two different directions at the moment. I've been exploring a very colourful character from the Edwardian period and also toying with the idea of a novel about the state of modern marriage. It is absolute bliss though to be writing fiction at last. I am able to say, 'John, you're a novelist'; I've finally fulfilled that ambition, after years and years. I told my children when we were on holiday in the Côte d'Azur, if they saw me getting into trouble on the beach they were to call out: 'Help! Our father, *the novelist*, is drowning'. ∎

❛I told my children when we were on holiday . . . if they saw me getting into trouble on the beach they were to call out: 'Help! Our father, *the novelist*, is drowning ❜

A Writer's Life

When do you write?
Between the hours of 10 p.m. and 2 a.m.

Where do you write?
In the shed at the end of my garden in
Dulwich. It's 120 feet from the house, and
backs on to a railway line, so it's very
secluded. There are always scratchings and
scrabblings on the roof from squirrels,
and yelps of pain from shagging wildlife,
and the occasional fox strays across the
garden, trips the security light, and turns
upon me a look of the utmost contempt, as if
to say, 'Who the *fuck* are you?' I've written
three books in this shed and I absolutely love
it, sad though that may sound.

Why do you write?
Oh God, I don't know. To recreate the past and
make it understandable, if only by me. To show
off my, you know, jewelled and glittery prose
style. To make up characters who sometimes
surprise their creator by their behaviour. To
indulge a lifelong fantasy that I might one day
make readers laugh, or weep, or (best-case
scenario) both at the same time.

Pen or computer?
Are you kidding? Computer. An Apple Mac
Power Book. I've had four of them nicked so
far by burglars . . .

Silence or music?
Music generally, quite softly. Old favourites,
so I already know their cadences and
trajectory: Pink Floyd, Mark Knopfler, Ella
Fitzgerald, Nina Simone, Paul Simon. When

I'm editing, I prefer something more rocky:
Springsteen, say, or Alabama 3.

What started you writing?
Being a journalist, and finding a certain confident
fluency that feels cheated at never being allowed
more than 2,000 words to say anything.

How do you start a book?
I woke up one morning, shortly after my mother
died, with the first sentence of *The Falling Angels*
in my head ('Beside a bus stop on the road to
Galway Hospital, the devil is advertising
margarine') and realised I was bursting to write
a memoir about my Irish family. With *Sunday at
the Cross Bones*, I was so nervous about getting
the voice of the rector right, I started with a
scene in a pub, told by a journalist – I started, in
other words, cautiously, on home territory.

And finish?
Something towards the end – it's always about 3
a.m. – gives you a succession of metaphors to try
out, and one of them will seem sufficiently
resonant to let you type 'The End' just after it,
upon which you howl like an elated banshee, pour
yourself a slug of Scotch, walk about the moonlit
garden in triumph and eventually go to bed, dizzy
with achievement. Of course you invariably
change it the next day for something better.

**Do you have any writing rituals or
superstitions?**
I have a reward system: I won't allow myself
another glass of wine or a fag until I've cracked
a scene, or hit 500 words, then 1,000, then
1,500 . . . ►

❝ If it had to be a
not-writing-at-all
job, I hope I'd be
a faded rock
singer, a seedy
second-hand-
book dealer, or
the piano player
in a house of ill
repute in New
Orleans. ❞

A Writer's Life *(continued)*

◄**Which living writer do you most admire?**
William Trevor, I think, for his delicate,
understated delineation of extreme states of
mind; and for his refusal to interpose any
authorial presence between the characters
and the reader, so that we're reduced to the
condition of children at a Punch and Judy
show, shouting, 'Don't do that!' and 'Don't go
near that awful person!' and 'For God's sake,
do not have another drink!'

What or who inspires you?
My children inspire me all the time, by the
way they see the world afresh. I read *Enemies
of Promise* by Cyril Connolly every year, for its
amazing analysis of writing styles, and what
exactly it might take to write a masterpiece
one day (yeah, right).

**If you weren't a writer, what job would
you do?**
Well, I'm a journalist so I write every day
anyway. But if it had to be a not-writing-at-all
job, I hope I'd be a faded rock singer, a seedy
second-hand-book dealer, or the piano player
in a house of ill repute in New Orleans.

**What's your guilty reading pleasure or
favourite trashy read?**
Being a father of teenage children, I'm
empowered to read the irresistibly delicious,
snogtastic fictional journals of Georgia
Nicolson by Louise Rennison. When I'm
prostrate with male flu, I read old *Just William*
books by Richmal Crompton. My favourite
trashy books, if we must call them that, are
Jilly Cooper's *Riders* and *Rivals*.■

The 1,001 Nights of Little Jimmy

by John Walsh

THE REAL-LIFE HAROLD DAVIDSON, in whose head I dwelt, creatively speaking, for a year and nine months, led for years a perfectly decent, God-fearing, uncontroversial family life. Seven years, to be precise, from 1907 to the outbreak of the First World War. In that time he devoted himself to tending to his flock in Stiffkey on the north Norfolk coast, writing his sermons and conjuring ways to improve the lot of the homeless and destitute. But even before his life began to fall apart, he was a character of vivid oddity.

He stood five foot three, his parishioners nicknamed him 'Little Jimmy' and in 1932 he became the most famous clergyman in the nation. A. J. P. Taylor called his trial 'the most sensational of the decade' and said he deserved a more significant place in the history books than the Archbishop of Canterbury. He has become a byword for the cheapness of fame. But nobody in history embraced renown with such enthusiasm as the rector of Stiffkey.

Then again, nobody embraced so many *people* as the rector. In the twelve years in which he patrolled the streets, cafés and bedsits of London while pursuing his work of saving young women from perdition, he encircled the waists, patted the knees and kissed the cheeks of hundreds, maybe thousands, of girls. He was crackers about girls. He loved their shining eyes, their marcelled hair, their strong teeth, their healthiness. But not everyone looked upon his fascination with girls as expressive of mere innocent Christian concern.

He was born in 1875 in Hampshire to a▶

13

The 1,001 Nights of Little Jimmy
(continued)

◀family awash with clerics. While still a teenager, he showed natural gifts as a fundraiser, public speaker and setter-up of charities for the poor, homeless and exploited. He was also dashingly theatrical, paying his way through university by touring the provinces delivering humorous monologues. After Oxford, he took holy orders, became a curate in London and married an Irish singer and suffragist called Moyra (Mimi) Saurin. In 1906, when he was given the joint parishes of Stiffkey and Morston, he and Mimi married, moved north and started a life of snug domesticity, keeping open house for beggars and homeless people, and raising a family of four.

Things started to go wrong during the war, when Harold went to serve as a naval chaplain in the Middle East. Mimi became a nurse, fell pregnant by a soldier on leave, and gave the baby up for adoption. Harold lost whatever money he possessed to a corrupt financier. Estranged from Mimi, Harold arranged to go away to India as a tutor to a maharajah, but the deal fell through. His wife became deaf and slightly mad, and became pregnant again by another man. This time, they decided to keep the child and, after years away, the Davidson family returned to Stiffkey.

That much we know. From 1920, we don't know precisely what he got up to, but we do know this: for twelve years, every week he rose early on Monday morning, took the first train from Holt to Piccadilly, and spent every waking hour (he seldom slept) walking the streets looking out for 'fallen women' or girls between the ages of sixteen and twenty-four who seemed likely to fall unless he intervened. On Saturday night, he'd take the last possible train home to deliver his Sunday morning sermon and see to parish matters, before plunging back into the flood tide of girlish sinfulness the following morning.

As the trial revealed, he was especially keen on meeting waitresses, in particular the girls – known as 'Nippies'– who worked in Lyons Corner Houses. He would invite them out to dinner or the theatre, counsel them and dry their tears. Often he would visit them at night, calling on them at 1 a.m. or 2 a.m. to see if they'd remembered to say their prayers. Sometimes, when visiting less morally rigorous girls, he would find them in bed with clients and hang around for a little chat.

He came unstuck when he failed to return from London in November 1930 to attend an Armistice Day service. A local major complained to the Bishop of Norwich, and accused the rector of 'immorality' with some of the London girls he'd brought to Stiffkey on remedial holidays. Because the Church couldn't ignore an immorality charge, the bishop sent detectives after Harold Davidson. After months of getting nowhere, they found one of his former charges, Rose Ellis, and wrung a testimony from her while plying her with port. After much toing and froing and attempts to make the rector resign, he was accused on four counts of immorality and tried at Church House, Westminster, in a consistory court – tried, in other words, for a sin rather than a crime.

As the witness box was filled, every day, with a colourful throng of brasses, madams, titled▶

⸺ On Saturday night, he'd take the last possible train home to deliver his Sunday morning sermon ... before plunging back into the flood tide of girlish sinfulness the following morning. ⸺

The 1,001 Nights of Little Jimmy
(continued)

◀ladies, charity workers, circus strongmen,
Indian princelings and hostile clergymen, the
trial reports in the provincial press were spotted
by the nationals. *The Times* took to reporting
the trial evidence every day, and the public
lapped it up. When the rector's defence funds
dried up, it felt as though a huge public
entertainment had been inexplicably
derailed, and it was soon ushered back on
track.

Huge crowds of rubbernecking rector fans
crammed the lanes and fields around Stiffkey.
Hundreds more tried to force their way into
the trial building in London. He became the
world's first-ever media-generated public
celebrity – or anti-hero, depending on your
point of view. His embrace of celebrity (or
notoriety) was heartfelt but ambiguous. He
knew how much he'd lost in swapping a
congregation for a nationwide audience.

He remains a potent symbol of idealism
fatally corrupted by compromise. And an
emblem of celebrity at all costs, the kind that
bounces back in triumph from public
disapproval. Whatever we may think of the
modern tendency of disgraced public figures
to cling to the limelight – Jeffrey Archer,
Jonathan Aitken, Neil and Christine
Hamilton, Major Charles Ingram – we know
that the rector of Stiffkey got there first. ■